P9-DNA-603

NO LONGER PROPERTY OF
KING COUNTY LIBRARY SYSTEM

JUL   2018

BIBLIOMYSTERIES

VOLUME TWO

STORIES OF CRIME IN THE WORLD
OF BOOKS AND BOOKSTORES

EDITED BY
OTTO PENZLER

PEGASUS BOOKS
NEW YORK LONDON

BIBLIOMYSTERIES

Pegasus Books Ltd.
148 W 37th Street, 13th Floor
New York, NY 10018

Compilation and introduction copyright © 2018 by Otto Penzler

Remaindered copyright © 2014 Peter Lovesey
The Compendium of Srem copyright © 2014 F. Paul Wilson
The Gospel of Sheba copyright © 2014 Lyndsay Faye
The Nature of My Inheritance copyright © 2014 Bradford Morrow
The Sequel copyright © 2014 R.L. Stine
Mystery, Inc. copyright © 2014 Joyce Carol Oates
The Book of the Lion copyright © 2014 Thomas Perry
The Mysterious Disappearance of the Reluctant Book Fairy
copyright © 2014 Elizabeth George
From the Queen copyright © 2015 Carolyn Hart
The Little Men copyright © 2015 Megan Abbott
Citadel copyright © 2015 Stephen Hunter
Every Seven Years copyright © 2015 Denise Mina
Condor in the Stacks copyright © 2015 James Grady
The Travelling Companion copyright © 2015 Ian Rankin
The Haze copyright © 2016 James W. Hall

First Pegasus Books cloth edition August 2018

Interior design by Maria Fernandez

All rights reserved. No part of this book may be reproduced in whole or in part without written permission from the publisher, except by reviewers who may quote brief excerpts in connection with a review in a newspaper, magazine, or electronic publication; nor may any part of this book be reproduced, stored in a retrieval system, or transmitted in any form or by any means electronic, mechanical, photocopying, recording, or other, without written permission from the publisher.

Library of Congress Cataloging-in-Publication Data is available.

ISBN: 978-1-68177-784-9

10 9 8 7 6 5 4 3 2 1

Printed in the United States of America
Distributed by W. W. Norton & Company

To Rob W. Hart

My friend and invaluable colleague as
Publisher of MysteriousPress.com
and the outrageously talented author of six novels,
including *The Warehouse*,
which will be the hottest book of 2019

Contents

Introduction
Otto Penzler

~∽

I f you like mysteries, and if you like books, what could be better than mysteries featuring the world of books? These wonderful tales have come to be called bibliomysteries. If you go to the dictionary (as a traditionalist) or hit your computer's spellcheck, you will discover that there is no listing for this word, and if you type it onto a Word document it will appear with a squiggly red line underneath it, indicating that you have misspelled or entered a non-existent word.

Nonetheless, bibliophiles who also are mystery fiction aficionados certainly know what the word means, however abstruse or esoteric it may seem to those poor, deprived souls who do not share those pleasures.

As a "book person" my entire life, and a mystery fan for the past half-century, I've had a special warm spot in my heart for books about books ever since I read Christopher Morley's *The Haunted Bookshop* when I was a teenager.

A few years ago, when the Mysterious Bookshop was having severe financial difficulties (it always has had financial difficulties, but in 2010–12 it was dire), I thought we might make a little money to keep the creditors at bay if we published some things that could only be bought in our store. My deep affection for stories involving books and for mysteries combined and I asked several authors who were friends to write an original biblio-mystery for the book store. I mostly had to define what I meant but, once they understood it, most of them found enough time in their schedule to write a story and produced amazingly creative variations on the theme.

We published them as paperbacks, and even produced a small number (100) of each title in hardcover, numbered and signed, for collectors. The stories subsequently have been published as e-books and many have been translated in a dozen countries, essentially preventing the death of the bookshop.

The first fifteen stories in that series were published under the creative title *Bibliomysteries* and now here are the next fifteen in this massive collection with the equally ingenious title *Bibliomysteries Volume 2*. The series of individual stories continues to be published in the Mysterious Bookshop and we all hope a third volume will appear in due course. In the meantime, I hope you enjoy the wide range of stories in this handsome book.

Ian Rankin sets his tale of the lost original manuscript of *Dr. Jekyll and Mr. Hyde* in the legendary Paris bookshop Shakespeare & Co., while F. Paul Wilson offers a book with magical powers. Joyce Carol Oates portrays an overly ambitious dealer in mystery fiction, while James Grady puts the "Condor" in the Library of Congress. Stephen Hunter tells a previously unknown story of Alan Turing during World War I about a book that could change the history of the world, while Megan Abbott and Denise Mina add their Edgar-nominated stories to the collection.

Whether your taste is for the traditional mystery, something a little more hard-boiled, or the bizarre and humorous, you will find exactly your cup of tea in this outstanding collection of fifteen stories by some of the most distinguished mystery writers working today.

Remaindered

Peter Lovesey

⁓〜

Peter Lovesey, born in 1936 in Whitton, Middlesex, is a highly celebrated author of historical and contemporary crime novels. He is best
known for the Victorian-era Sergeant Cribb series and the Peter Diamond series set in modern-day Bath. In 1944, Lovesey's childhood
home was destroyed by an F1 flying bomb, forcing him and his family
to evacuate to the West Country. This episode would be the basis for
his critically acclaimed novel *Rough Cider*, published in 1987.

While teaching at Thurrock Technical College and then Ham-
mersmith College, Lovesey penned his first novel, *The Kings of
Distance*, a sports novel named Sports Book of the Year by *World
Sports*. He quit teaching to write full time after the completion of his
seventh Victorian crime novel in 1975. The last of the Sergent Cribbs
books, *Waxwork*, won the Silver Dagger in 1978, and in 1982 *The
False Inspector Dew* won the Gold. In the States, he was awarded the
Anthony Award for *The Last Detective,* a Peter Diamond book. He
was presented with the Cartier Gold Dagger for his prolific career
in crime writing in 2000. Many of his works, including *Goldengirl*,
Waxwork, Abracadaver, and *Wobble to Death* have been adapted
for television and the silver screen. Peter Lovesey now lives in West
Sussex, England.

A gatha Christie did it. The evidence was plain to see, but no one *did* see for more than a day. Robert Ripple's corpse was cold on the bookshop floor. It must have been there right through Monday, the day Precious Finds was always closed. Poor guy, he was discovered early Tuesday in the section he called his office, in a position no bookseller would choose for his last transaction, face down, feet down and butt up, jack-knifed over a carton of books. The side of the carton had burst and some of the books had slipped out and fanned across the carpet, everyone a Christie.

Late Sunday Robert had taken delivery of the Christie novels. They came from a house on Park Avenue, one of the best streets in Poketown, Pennsylvania, and they had a curious history. They were brought over from England before World War II by an immigrant whose first job had been as a London publisher's rep. He'd kept the books as a souvenir of those tough times trying to interest bookshop owners in whodunits when the only novels most British people wanted to read were by Jeffrey Farnol and Ethel M. Dell. After his arrival in America, he'd switched to selling Model T Fords instead and made a sizeable fortune. The Christies had been forgotten about, stored in the attic of the fine old weatherboard house he'd bought after making his first million. And now his playboy grandson planned to demolish the building and replace it with a space-age dwelling of glass and concrete. He'd cleared the attic and wanted to dispose of the books. Robert had taken one look and offered five hundred dollars for the lot. The grandson had pocketed the check and gone away pleased with the deal.

Hardly believing his luck, Robert must have waited until the shop closed and then stooped to lift the carton onto his desk and check the contents more carefully. Mistake.

Hardcover books are heavy. He had spent years humping books around, but he was sixty-eight, with a heart condition, and this was one box too many.

Against all the odds, Robert had stayed in business for twenty-six years, dealing in used books of all kinds. But Precious Finds had become more than a bookshop. It was a haven of civilized life in Poketown, a center for all manner of small town activities—readers' groups, a writers' circle, coffee mornings and musical evenings. Some of the locals came and went without even glancing at the bookshelves. A few bought books or donated them out of loyalty, but it was difficult to understand how Robert had kept going so long. It was said he did most of his business at the beginning through postal sales and later on the internet.

Robert's sudden death created problems all round. Tanya Tripp, the bookshop assistant, who had been in the job only a few months, had the nasty shock of discovering the body, and found herself burdened with dealing with the emergency, first calling a doctor, then an undertaker and then attempting to contact Robert's family. Without success. Not a Ripple remained. He had never married. It became obvious that his loyal customers would have to arrange the funeral. Someone had to take charge, and this was Tanya. Fortunately she was a capable young woman, as sturdy in character as she was in figure. She didn't complain about the extra workload, even to herself.

Although all agreed that the effort of lifting the Agatha Christies had been the cause of death, an autopsy was inescapable. The medical examiner found severe bruising to the head and this was attributed to the fall. A coronary had killed Robert.

Simple.

The complications came after. Tanya was unable to find a will. She searched the office where Robert had died, as well as his apartment upstairs, where she had never ventured before. Being the first to enter a dead man's rooms would have spooked the average person. Tanya was above average in confidence and determination. She wasn't spooked. She found Robert's passport, birth certificate and tax returns, but nothing resembling a will. She checked with his bank and they didn't have it.

Meanwhile one of the richest customers offered to pay for the funeral and the regulars clubbed together to arrange a wake at Precious Finds. The feeling was that Robert would have wished for a spirited send-off.

The back room had long been the venue for meetings. The books in there were not considered valuable. Every second-hand bookshop has to cope with items that are never likely to sell: thrillers that no longer thrill, sci-fi that has been overtaken by real science and romance too coy for modern tastes. The obvious solution is to refuse such books, but sometimes they come in a job lot with things of more potential such as nineteenth century magazines containing engravings that can be cut out, mounted and sold as prints. Robert's remedy had been to keep the dross in the back room. The heaviest volumes were at floor level, outdated encyclopedias, dictionaries and art books. Higher up were the condensed novels and book club editions of long-forgotten authors. Above them, privately published fiction and poetry. On the top, fat paperbacks turning brown and curling at the edges, whole sets of Michener, Hailey, and Clavell.

The saving grace of the back room was that the shelves in the center were mounted on wheels and could be rolled aside to create a useful space for meetings. A stack of chairs stood in one corner. Robert made no charge, pleased to have people coming right through the shop and possibly pausing to look at the desirable items shelved in the front rooms. So on Tuesdays the bookshop hosted the Poketown history society, Wednesdays the art club, Thursdays, the chess players. Something each afternoon and every night except Sundays and Mondays.

And now the back room was to be used for the wake.

The music appreciation group knew of an Irish fiddler who brought along four friends, and they set about restoring everyone's spirits after the funeral. The place was crowded out. The event spilled over into the other parts of the shop.

It was a bittersweet occasion. The music was lively and there was plenty of cheap wine, but there was still anxiety about what would happen after. For the time being the shop had stayed open under Tanya's management. There was no confidence that this could continue.

"It has to be sold," Tanya said in a break between jigs. "There's no heir."

"Who's going to buy a bookstore in these difficult times?" George Digby-Smith asked. He was one of the Friends of England, who met here on occasional Friday nights, allegedly to talk about cricket and cream teas and other English indulgences. Actually, George was more than just a friend of England. He'd been born there sixty years ago. "Someone will want to throw out all the books and turn the building into apartments."

"Over my dead body," Myrtle Rafferty, another of the Friends of England, piped up.

"We don't need another fatality, thank you," George said.

"We can't sit back and do nothing. We all depend on this place."

"Get real, people," one of the Wednesday morning coffee group said. "None of us could take the business on, even if we had the funds."

"Tanya knows about books," George said at once. "She'll be out of a job if the store closes. What do you say, Tanya?"

The young woman looked startled. It was only a few months since she had walked in one morning and asked if Robert would take her on as his assistant. In truth, he'd badly needed some help and she'd earned every cent he paid. Softly spoken, almost certainly under thirty, she had been a quiet presence in the shop, putting more order into the displays, but leaving Robert to deal with the customers.

"I couldn't possibly buy it."

"I'm not suggesting you do. But you could manage it. In fact, you'd do a far better job than old Robert ever did."

"That's unkind," Myrtle said.

George turned redder than usual. "Yes, it was."

"We are all in debt to Robert," Myrtle said.

"Rest his soul," George agreed, raising his glass. "To Robert, a bookman to the end, gone, but not forgotten. In the best sense of the word, remaindered."

"What's that meant to mean?"

"Passed on, but still out there somewhere."

"More like boxed and posted," the man from the coffee club murmured. "Or pulped."

Myrtle hadn't heard. She was thinking positively. "Tanya didn't altogether turn down George's suggestion. She'd want to continue, given the opportunity."

Tanya was silent.

"When someone dies without leaving a will, what happens?" George asked.

Ivor Ciplinsky, who knew a bit about law and led the history society, said, "An administrator will have to be appointed and they'll make extensive efforts to trace a relative, however distant."

"I already tried," Tanya said. "There isn't anyone."

"Cousins, second cousins, second cousins once removed."

"Nobody."

Myrtle asked Ivor, "And if no relative is found?"

"Then the property escheats to the state's coffers."

"It *what?*"

"Escheats. A legal term, meaning it reverts to the state by default."

"What a ghastly-sounding word," George said.

"Ghastly to think about," Myrtle said. "Our beloved bookshop grabbed by the bureaucrats."

"It goes back to feudal law," Ivor said. "It should have stayed there," Myrtle said. "Escheating. Cheating comes into it, for sure. Cheating decent people out of their innocent pleasures. We can't allow that. Precious Finds is the focus of our community."

"If you're about to suggest we club together and buy it, don't," Ivor said. "Paying for a wake is one thing. You won't get a bunch of customers, however friendly, taking on a business as precarious as this. You can count me out straight away."

"So speaks the history society," Myrtle said with a sniff. "Caving in before the battle even begins. Well, the Friends of England are made of sterner stuff. The English stood firm at Agincourt, a famous battle six hundred years ago, in case you haven't covered it on Tuesday evenings, Ivor. Remember who faced off the Spanish Armada."

"Not to mention Wellington at Waterloo and Nelson at Trafalgar," George added.

"Michael Caine," Edward said. He was the third member of the Friends of England.

There were some puzzled frowns. Then George said, "*Zulu*—the movie. You're thinking of the battle of 'Rorke's Drift.'"

"The Battle of Britain," Myrtle finished on a high, triumphant note.

"Who *are* these people?" the coffee club man asked.

It was a good question. Myrtle, George and Edward had been meeting in the back room on occasional Friday nights for longer than anyone could recall. They must have approached Robert at some point and asked if they could have their meetings there. An Anglophile himself, at least as far as books were concerned, Robert wouldn't have turned them away. But nobody else had ever joined the three in their little club. This was because they didn't announce their meetings in advance. If you weren't told which Fridays they met, you couldn't be there, even if you adored England, drank warm beer and ate nothing but roast beef and Yorkshire pudding.

George was the only one of the three with a genuine English connection. You wouldn't have known it from his appearance. He'd come over as a youth in the late sixties, a hippie with flowers in his hair and weed in his backpack, living proof of that song about San Francisco. In middle age he'd given up the flowers, but not the weed. However, he still had the long hair, now silver and worn in a ponytail, and his faded T-shirts and torn jeans remained faintly psychedelic.

Edward, by contrast, dressed the part of the English gent, in blue blazer, white shirt and cravat and nicely ironed trousers. He had a David Niven pencil mustache and dark-tinted crinkly hair with a parting. Only when he spoke would you have guessed he'd been born and raised in the Bronx.

Myrtle, too, was New York born and bred. She colored her hair and it was currently orange and a mass of loose curls. She had a face and figure she was proud of. Back in the nineties, her good looks had reeled in her second husband, Butch Rafferty, a one-time gangster, who had treated her to diamond necklaces and dinners at the best New York restaurants. Tragically, Butch had been gunned down in 2003 by Gritty Bologna, a rival hood he had made the mistake of linking up with. The widowed Myrtle had quit gangland and moved out here to Pennsylvania. She wasn't destitute. She still lived in some style in a large colonial house at the better end of town. No one could fathom her affiliation to the old country except there was not much doubt that she slept (separately) with George and Edward. She had travelled to England a number of times with each of them. Either they were not jealous of each other or she controlled the relationship with amazing skill.

Little was known of what went on at the Friends of England meetings in the bookshop. Comfortable and cozy as the back room was, it was not furnished for middle-aged sex. Tanya, understandably curious, had questioned Robert closely about how the Friends passed their evenings. He'd said he assumed they spent their time looking at travel brochures and planning their next trip. The meetings did seem to be followed quite soon after by visits to England, always involving Myrtle, usually in combination with one or other of her fellow Friends.

The three were now in a huddle at the far end of the back room, where they always gathered for their meetings and where—appropriately—three out-of-date sets of the *Encyclopedia Britannica* took up the entire bottom shelf.

"If the shop is . . . what was that word?" Edward said when the music once more calmed down enough for conversation.

"Escheated."

"If that happens, they'll want a quick sale and we're in deep shit."

"But there's a precious window of opportunity before it gets to that stage," George said. "They have to make completely sure no one has a claim on the estate and that can't be done overnight. We need to get organized. Myrtle was talking about a trip to the Cotswolds before the end of the month. Sorry, my friends, but I think we must cancel."

"Shucks," Myrtle said. "I was counting the days to that trip. You figure we should stay here and do something?"

"We can't do nothing."

"Do what?" Edward said, and it was clear from his disenchanted tone that it had been his turn to partner Myrtle to England. George glanced right and left and then lowered his voice. "I have an idea, a rather bold idea, but this is not the time or the place."

"Shall we call a meeting?" Myrtle said, eager to hear more. "How about this Friday? We don't need Robert's permission anymore."

"In courtesy, we ought to mention it to Tanya," George said.

"Tell her your idea?"

"Heavens, no. Just say we need a meeting, so she can book us in."

On Friday they had the back room to themselves. Tanya was in the office at the front end of the shop and there were no browsers. The footfall in Precious Finds had decreased markedly after Robert's death had been written up in the *Poketown Observer*.

Even Edward, still sore that his trip to the Cotswolds with Myrtle had been cancelled, had to agree that George's plan was smart.

"It's not just smart, it's genius," Myrtle said. "We can save the shop and carry on as before." She leaned back in her chair and caressed the spines of the *Encyclopedia Britannica*. "The Friends of England can go on indefinitely."

"For as long as the funds hold up, at any rate," George said. "We've been sensible up to now. Let's keep it like that."

George had to be respected. His wise, restraining advice had allowed the three of them to enjoy a comfortable retirement that might yet continue. If the truth were told, the Friends of England Society was a mutual benefit club. George and Edward had once been members of Butch Rafferty's gang and they were still living off the spoils of a security van heist.

"My dear old Butch would love this plan," Myrtle said with a faraway look. "I can hear him saying, 'Simple ain't always obvious.'"

"If Butch hadn't messed up, we wouldn't be here," Edward said, still moody. "We'd be back in New York City, living in style."

"Don't kid yourself," Myrtle said. "You'd have gambled away your share inside six months. New York, maybe—but by now you'd be sleeping rough in Central Park. I know you better than you know yourself, Edward."

"There are worse places than Central Park," he said. "I've had it up to here with Poketown, Pennsylvania. We should have got outta here years ago."

"Oh, come on."

"It's only because we live in Pennsylvania that my plan will work," George said.

Edward's lip curled. "It had better work."

"And I'm thinking we should bring Tanya in at an early stage," George said.

"No way," Edward said. "What is it with Tanya? You got something going with her?"

"How ridiculous. You're the one who can't keep his eyes off her."

Myrtle said, "Leave it, George. Act your age, both of you. I'm with Edward here. Keep it to ourselves."

Edward almost purred. "Something else Butch once said: 'The more snouts in the trough, the less you get.'"

"As you wish," George said. "We won't say anything to Tanya. She'll get a beautiful surprise."

"So how do we divide the work?" Myrtle said.

"Unless you think otherwise, I volunteer to do the paperwork," George said. "I'm comfortable with the English language."

"Keep it short and simple. Nothing fancy."

"Is that agreed, then?" Edward agreed with a shrug.

"But we should all join in," Myrtle said. "Another thing Butch said, 'Everyone must get their hands dirty.'"

"Suits me—but what else is there to do?" Edward said.

"I need one of Robert's credit cards," George said.

Edward shook his head. "The hell you do. We're not going down that route. That's a sure way to get found out."

George took a sharp, impatient breath. "We won't be using it to buy stuff."

"So what do we want it for?" Edward said, and immediately knew the answer. "The signature on the back."

"Right," Myrtle said. "Can you take care of that?"

"Tricky," Edward said.

"Not at all. Robert must have used plastic. Everyone does."

"How do we get hold of one?"

"How do *you* get hold of one," Myrtle said. "That's how you get your hands dirty. My guess is they're still lying around the office somewhere."

"Tanya's always in there."

Myrtle rolled her eyes. "God help us, Edward, if you can't find a way to do this simple thing you don't deserve to be one of us."

George, becoming the diplomat, said, "Come on, old friend, it's no hardship chatting up Tanya. You can't keep your eyes off her ample backside."

Myrtle said at once. "Cut that out, George." She turned to Edward. "Get her out of the office on some pretext and have a nose around."

"It's not as if you're robbing the Bank of England," George said.

"Okay, I'll see what I can do," Edward said without much grace, and then turned to Myrtle. "And how will you get *your* hands dirty?"

"Me? I'm going to choose the perfect place to plant the thing."

Almost overnight, Tanya had been transformed from bookshop assistant to manager of Robert's estate as well as his shop. It wasn't her choice, but there was no one else to step into the breach. At least she continued to be employed. She decided she would carry on until someone in authority instructed her to stop. She would allow the shop to remain open and operate on a cash only basis, buying no new stock and keeping accurate accounts. She couldn't touch the bank account, but there was money left in the till and there were occasional sales.

Meanwhile she did her best to get some order out of the chaos that had been Robert's office. He had given up on the filing system years ago. She spent days sorting through papers, getting up to date with correspondence and informing clients what had happened. Someone at some point would have to make an inventory of the stock. What a task *that* would be. Nothing was on computer, not even the accounts. He had still been using tear-out receipt books with carbon sheets.

She glanced across the room at the carton of Agatha Christies that had been the death of poor Robert. After his body had been taken away she had repaired the carton with sticky tape, replaced the loose books and slid the heavy load alongside the filing cabinet. She really ought to shelve them in the mystery section in the next room. But then she wasn't certain how to price them. Robert had paid five hundred for them, so they weren't cheap editions. The copy of the invoice was in one of the boxes. The titles weren't listed there. It simply read: *Agatha Christie novels as agreed.*

She went over and picked up *The Mysterious Affair at Styles*, the author's first novel, obviously in good condition and still in its dust jacket. A first edition would be worth a lot, but she told herself this must be a second printing or a facsimile. It was easy to be fooled into thinking you'd found a gem. According to the spine the publisher was the Bodley Head, so this copy had been published in England. Yet when she looked inside at the publication details and the 1921 date, she couldn't see any evidence that the book was anything except a genuine first edition. It had the smell of an old book, yet it was as clean as if it had not been handled much.

Was it possible?

She was still learning the business, but her heart beat a little faster. Robert himself had once told her that early Agatha Christies in jackets were notoriously rare because booksellers in the past were in the habit of stripping the books of their paper coverings at the point of sale to display the cloth bindings.

Among the reference works lining the office back wall were some that listed auction prices. She took one down, thumbed through to the right page, and saw that a 1921 Bodley Head first edition *without* its original dust jacket had sold last year for just over ten thousand dollars. No one seemed to have auctioned a copy in its jacket in the past fifty years.

She handled the book with more respect and looked again at the page with the date. This had to be a genuine first edition.

"Oh my God!" she said aloud.

No wonder Robert had snapped up the collection. This volume alone was worth many times the price he had paid for them all. He was sharp enough to spot a bargain, which was why the Christie collection had so excited him. It was easy to imagine his emotional state here in the office that Sunday evening. His unhealthy heart must have been under intolerable strain.

The find of a lifetime had triggered the end of a lifetime.

And now Tanya wondered about her own heart. She had a rock band playing in her chest.

If a copy without its jacket fetched ten grand, how much was this little beauty worth? Surely enough to cover her every need for months, if not years, to come.

So tempting.

Robert had never trusted the computer. He'd used it as a glorified typewriter and little else. His contact details for his main customers were kept in a card index that Tanya now flicked through, looking for wealthy people interested in what Robert had called "British Golden Age mysteries." She picked out five names. On each card were noted the deals he had done and the prices paid for early editions of Agatha Christie, Dorothy L. Sayers and Anthony Berkeley. They weren't five figure sums, but the books almost certainly hadn't been such fine copies as these.

It wouldn't hurt to phone some of these customers and ask if they would be interested in making an offer for a 1921 Bodley Head first edition of *The Mysterious Affair at Styles*—with a dust jacket.

"I'd need to see it," the first voice said, plainly trying to sound laid back. Then gave himself away by adding, "You haven't even told me who you are. Where are you calling from? I don't mind getting on a plane."

Tanya was cautious. "In fairness, I need to speak to some other potential buyers."

"How much do you have in mind?" he said. "I can arrange a transfer into any account you care to name and no questions asked. Tell me the price you want."

Collecting can be addictive.

"It's not decided yet," she said. "This is just an enquiry to find out who is interested. As I said, I have other calls to make."

"Are you planning to auction it, or what?"

"I'm not going through an auctioneer. It would be a private sale, but at some point I may ask for your best offer."

"You say it has the original jacket? Is it complete? Sometimes they come with a panel detached or missing."

"Believe me, it's complete."

There was a pause at the end of the line. Then: "I'd be willing to offer a six figure sum. If I can examine it for staining and so on and you tell me the provenance, I could run to more than that."

A six figure sum? Did he really mean that?

"Thank you," Tanya succeeded in saying in a small, shocked voice. "I must make some more calls now."

"Screw it, a hundred and twenty grand."

She swallowed hard. "I'm not yet accepting offers, but I may come back to you."

"One forty." He was terrified to put the phone down.

"I'll bear that in mind," Tanya said, and closed the call.

She tried a second collector of Golden Age mysteries and this one wasn't interested in staining or provenance. He couldn't contain his excitement. "Lady, name your price," he said. "I'd kill for that book." Without any prompting, he offered a hundred and fifty thousand, "In used banknotes, if you want."

She didn't bother to call the others. She needed to collect her thoughts. Robert's sudden death had come as such a shock that no one else had given a thought to the value of the Agatha Christies. She was the only person in Poketown with the faintest idea and she could scarcely believe what she'd been offered. Could the existence of a dust jacket—a sheet of paper printed on one side—really mean a mark-up of more than a hundred grand?

She lifted more books out, first editions all. *The Murder on the Links,* *The Secret of Chimneys* and *The Murder of Roger Ackroyd*. The beauty of this was that there was no written evidence of how many were in the carton. The invoice had lumped them all together. *Agatha Christie novels as agreed*. She could take a dozen home and no one would be any the wiser. But she would be richer. Unbelievably richer.

Her time as stand-in manager would soon end. There was already talk of an administrator being appointed.

The phone on the desk buzzed. She jerked in surprise. Guiltily, as if someone was in the room with her, she turned the books face down and covered them with her arm.

"Miss Tripp?"

"Speaking."

"Al Johnson here, from the bank, about the late Mr. Ripple's estate."

She repeated automatically, "Mr. Ripple's estate."

"You were planning a further search for his will when we last spoke. I guess you'd have called me if you'd been successful."

"I guess."

"Are you okay, Miss Tripp? You sound a little distracted."

"There's a lot going on," she said. "Sorry. You asked about the will. It didn't turn up. I looked everywhere I could think of."

"How long has it been now—five weeks? I think we're fast approaching the point of assuming he died intestate."

"I'm afraid so."

"Neglecting to provide for one's death is not as unusual as you might suppose, even among the elderly. The law is quite straightforward here in Pennsylvania. We get an administrator appointed and he or she will calculate the total assets and make a search for relatives who may inherit."

She made a huge effort not to think about the Agatha Christies. "I tried to contact the family before the funeral, but there doesn't seem to be anyone left. He was unmarried, as you know, and had no brothers or sisters. I couldn't even trace any cousins."

"If that's really so, then the Commonwealth of Pennsylvania will collect. Robert's main asset was the bookshop and his apartment upstairs, of course. Do you have other plans yet?"

"Plans?" Sure, she had plans, but this wasn't the moment to speak about them.

"To move on, get another job."

"Not really. How long have I got?"

"In the shop? About a week, I'd say. It's up to me to ask for the administrator to take over and there's usually no delay over that. Everything is then put on hold."

"We have to close?"

"Between you and me, you should have closed already, but I turned a blind eye, knowing what a blow this will be for our community."

After the call, Tanya reached for a Precious Finds tote-bag and filled it with Agatha Christie firsts. She couldn't help the community, but she'd be crazy if she didn't help herself.

Edward, the David Niven look-alike from the Friends of England, was waiting outside the office door, immaculate as always, a carnation in his lapel, when Tanya unlocked next morning. He held a coffee cup in each hand.

"How ya doin?" The charm suffered when he opened his mouth.

"Pretty good," she said, and meant it. "But it's looking bad for the shop. I think we'll be in administration by the end of the week." She was trying to sound concerned.

"Soon as that? Too bad." Strangely, Edward didn't sound over-worried either. "I picked up a coffee for you, Tanya. Skinny latte without syrup, in a tall cup, right?" He handed it over.

"How did you know?"

"I was behind you in Starbucks the other morning."

"And you remembered? What a kind man you are. Why don't you come in?" She could offer no less.

He looked around for a chair but there wasn't a spare one, so he stood his coffee on the filing cabinet Tanya had been trying to get back into some kind of order. He appeared to stand it there. In fact the cup tipped over, the lid shot off and his black Americano streamed down the side of the metal cabinet.

Tanya screamed, "Ferchrissake!" She grabbed some Kleenex from the box on her desk and moved fast.

"No sweat," Edward said after rapidly checking his clothes. "Missed me."

She was on her knees, dragging the remaining Agatha Christies away from the still dripping coffee, her voice shrill in panic. "It's all over the books."

He stepped around the cabinet for a closer look. "Aw, shit." He pulled the pristine white handkerchief from his top pocket and sacrificed it to mop the surface of the filing cabinet. Then, seeing Tanya's frantic efforts to dry the books in the box, he stooped and began dabbing at them.

"Don't—you'll make it worse," she said.

"Are they special?"

"*Special?*" She felt like strangling him, the idiot. Words poured from her before she realized how much she was giving away. "They're first edition Agatha Christies, worth a fucking fortune. Help me lift them out. The coffee has ruined most of them."

He started picking out soggy books and carrying them to her desk. "Agatha Christies, huh? And you say they're valuable?"

"They were until you—" She stopped in mid-sentence, realizing she'd said too much. She tried to roll back some of what she had revealed. "Okay, it was an accident, I know, but Robert paid five hundred dollars for these."

He whistled. "Five hundred bucks for used books? I thought people gave them away."

"Not these. Most of them are more than seventy years old and with hardly a stain on them . . . until now."

"You can still read them when they're dry."

Tanya sighed. The blundering fool didn't get it. He had no conception of the damage he'd done—but maybe this was a good thing. After the initial shock she was trying to calm down. They had finished emptying the carton. She told herself this could have been a far worse disaster. Fortunately the real plums of the collection were safe in her apartment. The ones she'd left were there for show, in case anyone asked about Robert's last book deal.

Edward gave another rub to the filing cabinet, as if *that* was the problem. "You tidied this place good."

"Sorting it out," she said, still shaking. "Robert wasn't the best organized person in the world."

"And you never found the will?"

"The will?" She forced herself to think about it. "Let's face it. There isn't one—which is why we don't have any future."

"Where did he keep his personal stuff?"

"All over. Birth certificate upstairs. Tax forms and credit card statements down here in the desk drawers. His bank documents were at the back of the filing cabinet."

"Driving license?"

"In the car outside on the street. I even looked there for the will."

"Credit cards?"

"A bunch of them were in a card case in his back pocket. They came back from the morgue last week. I shredded them after making a note of the numbers."

"Good thinking," Edward said, but his facial muscles went into spasm.

"So it's the end of an era here in Poketown," Tanya said and she was beginning to get a grip on herself. "What will happen to your Friends of England group? Will you be able to go somewhere else?"

Edward shook his head. "Wouldn't be the same."

"The end of the line for you, then?"

"Seems so." But he still didn't appear depressed at the prospect. He glanced at the line of sad, damp books. "I wanna find some way of saying sorry. How about lunch?"

"It's not necessary."

"After what I just did, it's the least I can do. Someone I knew used to say, 'You shoot yourself in the foot, you gotta learn to hop.'"

She managed a smile. "Okay. What time?"

They lunched at Jimmy's, the best restaurant on Main Street. By then Tanya had recovered most of her poise. After all, she had enough undamaged Agatha Christies at home to make her rich. And this tête-à-tête with Edward was as good a chance as she would get to discover the main thing she had come to Poketown to find out.

She waited until she had finished her angel-hair pasta with Thai spiced prawns—by which time Edward had gone through three glasses of Chablis.

"Now that Precious Finds is coming to an end, do you mind if I ask something?"

"Sure. Go ahead."

"What exactly went on at the meetings?"

"Meetings?" he said as if he didn't understand the word. She hoped he hadn't drunk too much to make sense.

"Of the Friends. I asked Robert once, but I don't think he knew. He was pretty vague about it, in that way he had of telling you nothing."

Edward gave a guarded answer. "We don't do much except talk."

"In that case, you could talk in some other place. It's not a total disaster if the shop closes, as it will."

He seemed to be avoiding eye contact. "It's not so simple. We can't just shift camp."

"I don't understand why not."

"You don't need to."

She should have waited for him to sink a fourth glass of the wine. "But you can tell me how you three got together."

"We know each other from way back, when we all lived in New York City."

"And Myrtle was married to that man who was murdered?"

He nodded. "Butch Rafferty."

"Mr. Rafferty had a hard reputation as a gang leader, didn't he? I can understand a woman being attracted to that kind of guy." She noted his eyes widen and his chest fill out. "Did you know him?"

"Did I know Butch!" Out to impress, he jutted his jaw a fraction higher.

"Closely, then?"

Edward put down his glass, made a link with his pinkies and pulled them until they turned red. "We were like that."

"Wow! They must have been dangerous times for any friend of Butch Rafferty. Is that why you moved away?"

"We didn't run," he said.

"When you say 'we', do you mean yourself, Myrtle and George? You knew each other in New York?"

"Sure. It suited us to come here."

"I heard there was a big robbery of a security van that in some way caused the falling-out between Butch and Gritty Bologna."

His mouth tightened. "You seem to know a lot about it."

She felt herself color a little. "It was in the papers at the time. I looked it up later after I heard who Myrtle's husband had been. I was curious."

"Curiosity killed the cat," Edward said and ended that line of conversation. It wasn't one of Butch's sayings.

"Well, thanks for the meal. I really enjoyed it," Tanya said a few minutes later.

"Let's do it again tomorrow," Edward said, and it was music to her ears.

"Why not? And I'll pay." She could afford to, now that she was dealing in first edition Agatha Christies. She'd get him talking again after a few drinks, no problem.

Her mention of the robbery hadn't put him off entirely, she was pleased to discover. And now Edward played the assertive male. "This afternoon I'm gonna check the filing cabinet."

"There's no need. It was locked," she said.

"Some of my coffee could have seeped inside. I'll take a look."

"What in the name of sanity is Edward up to?" George asked Myrtle later that week. "I saw them leaving Jimmy's at lunch today. It's become a regular date."

"He's keeping her sweet, I figure," Myrtle said. "We encouraged him, if you remember."

"That was when we needed the credit card with Robert's signature. He found an old receipt book full of Robert's signatures in the filing cabinet, but that was three days ago. He handed it to me and it's all I want. His work is done. He has no reason to be lunching with Tanya every day."

"Silly old fool," Myrtle said. "He stands no chance with her. Smart clothes can only do so much for a guy. God help him when he takes them off."

"Is that one of Butch's sayings?"

"No. I said it."

"I'm worried, Myrtle." George showed the stress he was under by pulling the end of his silver ponytail across his throat. "We don't want him telling her anything."

"About this?"

"No—about the heist of the van."

"She isn't interested in that. She has too much on her mind, and soon she'll have a whole lot more. How's the project going?"

"My part is complete," George said, reaching into his pocket. "It's over to you now."

"Fine," Myrtle said. "I'll plant the little beauty tomorrow lunchtime, while Edward is working his charm on her in Jimmy's."

"I was thinking," Tanya said, at the next lunch date.

"Yeah?" Edward had already finished the bottle of Chablis and was on Bourbon. His glazed eyes looked ready for a cataract operation.

"About Robert," she went on, "and how you three linked up with him. Was he ever in New York?"

"Sure," he said, with a flap of the hand, "but way back, when we were all much younger."

"In Butch Rafferty's gang?"

"I wouldn't say Robert was in the gang," he said, starting to slur the words, "but we all knew him. He was a bartender then, some place in the Bowery where we used to meet."

"Someone you trusted?"

"Right on. Like one of the family."

"Butch's family?"

"Yeah. Butch liked the guy and so did the rest of us. Robert knew how to keep his mouth shut. Jobs were discussed. It didn't matter."

"A bartender in New York? That's a far cry from owning a bookshop."

"He had a dream to get out of town and open a bookstore and that's what he did when he had the money."

"Just from his work in the bar?" she said, disbelieving.

"Butch helped him. Butch was like that. And it wasn't wasted. Butch knew if he ever needed a bolt-hole he could lay up for a while here in Poketown, Pennsylvania." He shook his head slowly. "Too bad he was shot before he had the chance."

Tanya knew all this, but there was more she didn't know. "So after Butch was killed, some of you left town and came here?"

He nodded. "Myrtle's idea. She knew where Robert had set up shop."

"Was she an active member of the gang?"

"She didn't go on jobs, but she has a good brain and she's cool. She helped Butch with the planning." He blinked and looked sober for a second. "You're not an undercover cop, by any chance?"

She laughed. "No way. I'm starstruck by how you guys operate."

Reassured, he reached for the Bourbon and topped up his glass. "Sexy, huh?"

"It's a turn-on. I'll say that."

"You're a turn-on without saying a word."

"Flatterer." She was still on her first glass of wine, picking her questions judiciously. The process required care, even with a halfcut would-be seducer like this one. The query about the undercover cop was a warning. Edward couldn't have been more wrong, but it would be a mistake to underestimate him. "What is it with the Friends of England? Is that the only way you can meet in private?"

"We could meet anywhere. It's a free country."

"Be mysterious, then," she said, smiling.

He grinned back. "You bet I will. There's gotta be mystery in a relationship."

"Who said anything about . . ." She didn't get any further. His hand was on her thigh.

She'd got him just as she wanted.

He needed support as he tottered back to Precious Finds and Tanya supplied it, allowing him to put his arm around her shoulder.

"Why don't we close the shop for the afternoon?" he said.

"What a good idea," she said. "I was thinking the same thing." She'd already closed for lunch and didn't have to reopen. She let them inside, fastened the bolts and left the *closed* notice hanging on the door.

Inside, she said, "After all that wine, some coffee might be a good plan."

"I can think of a better one," Edward said, reaching for her breasts.

She swayed out of range. "Coffee first. I only have instant, but I'm not sending you to Starbucks again. Tell you what. I'll make it here and we'll carry it through to the back room, so we can both have a chair."

"And if I spill it, I can't do so much damage," he said with a grin.

She carried both mugs through the shop after the coffee was made, insisting he went ahead. She didn't want him behind her.

Edward managed to lift two chairs from the stack in the back room and sank into one of them. "Never thought I'd get to be alone with you."

And so drunk you can't do anything about it, Tanya thought, but she said, "Yes, it's great to relax. And in the company of a famous New York mobster."

He looked stupidly flattered.

"I'd love to hear about the last big job you did—the security van," she said. "I thought they were so well protected no robber would even think about a hold-up."

"Takes brains," he said.

"Was it your idea, then?"

"The part that worked, yeah." He ogled her. "You wanna hear about it? I'll tell you. In a job like this you go for the weak spot. You know what that is?"

"The tires?"

"The people. You surprise the guard in his own home, before he reports for work. You tell him his mother has been kidnapped and he has to cooperate. You tape dummy explosives to his chest and tell him you can detonate them by remote whenever you want."

"Brilliant," Tanya said. "Was that you, doing all that?"

"Most of it. From there on, he's so scared he'll do anything. He drives you to where the vans are kept. You're wearing a uniform just like his. He drives the security van to the depot where the bank stores the money. He does the talking and you help load the van."

"How much? Squillions?" She was wide-eyed, playing the innocent.

"They don't deal in peanuts," Edward said. "And when you're outta there and on the street, your buddies follow in the transit van."

"George?"

"He was one of the bunch, yeah. Some were Butch's people and some worked for Gritty Bologna. Gritty had a line into the security outfit, which was how we got the uniform and the guard's address. You drive to the warehouse where you transfer the loot and that's it."

"What about the guard?"

"Tied up and locked in his van. No violence."

"How much did you get?"

"Just under a million pounds."

"*Pounds?*"

Edward looked sheepish. "Yeah. We screwed up. We thought this van was delivering to the major banks like all the others. Too bad we picked the one supplying British money to currency exchanges at all the major airports in New York."

"You had a vanload of useless money."

"Uh huh. Crisp, new banknotes for tourists to take on their vacations."

"What a letdown."

"Tell me about it. Gritty went bananas. He blamed Butch. There was a shootout and Butch was the loser. Some of us figured Gritty wouldn't stop at one killing, so we left town."

"You and George and Myrtle?" She'd been incredibly patient waiting for the payoff.

"Myrtle remembered Robert here in Poketown, and this is where we came."

"With the pounds?"

"With the pounds. I figured we might think of a way to use them. It took a while, but with Robert's help we worked it."

"All those trips to England? That's neat."

"Twenty, thirty grand at a time. Some notes we exchange and bring dollars back. Some we spent over there. It's small scale. Has to be, with new, numbered banknotes."

"And this is why you call it the Friends of England? I love it!" She clapped her hands. "Edward, you're a genius. Is there any left, or is it all spent?"

"More than half is left."

"Who's got it?"

"It's right here in the safe. That's why we can't let the place close."

He was losing her now.

"I haven't found the safe," she said as casually as if she was talking about the one copy of Jane Austen the shop didn't stock. "I don't know what you're talking about."

He just smiled.

"When you say 'right here' do you mean the back room?"

He wagged his finger like a parent with a fractious infant. "Secret."

Infuriating. To her best knowledge there wasn't a safe on the premises. Robert had always left the takings in the till. There wasn't enough to justify using a safe. She gathered herself and gave Edward a smoldering look. "If that's how you want to play this, I won't be showing you my secret either."

"Whassat?" he asked, gripping the chair-arms.

"Wouldn't you like to know, naughty boy."

She watched the struggle taking place in front of her, rampant desire taking over from reality. "You gotta do better than that," he said.

"Okay. To show you my secret we have to go upstairs, to the bedroom."

"Hell," he said, shifting in the chair as if he was suddenly uncomfortable. "Is that an offer?"

She hesitated, then gave a nod.

He groomed his moustache with finger and thumb and took a deep, tremulous breath. "The safe is right where you are. You could touch it with your knee."

She looked down. "Get away."

"The Encyclopedia Brit . . . Brit . . ." He couldn't complete the word.

"Britannica?"

"Middle five volumes. False front."

She stooped and studied the spines of the large books that took up the whole of the bottom shelf. With their faded lettering and scuffed cloth bindings they looked no different from the others.

"1911 edition," Edward said. "Green. Press that showy gold bit on volume twelve and see what happens."

She pressed her thumb against the royal coat of arms and felt it respond. Just as Edward had said, the five spines were only a façade attached to a small, hinged door that sprang open and revealed the gray metal front of a safe with a circular combination lock.

Eureka.

"That's amazing."

"If I could see straight, I'd open it for you," he said, "but there's only stacks of notes in there."

"You have to know the combination."

"Zero-four-two-three-one-nine-six-four, but I didn't tell you that, okay?"

"Smart. How do you remember?"

"It's Myrtle's birthday. April twenty-three, sixty-four. Shut it now and we'll go upstairs."

In his inebriated state, he couldn't have stopped her if she'd walked out and left him there. But, hell, she wanted the satisfaction of showing him her secret, as she'd put it.

"Will you make it?"

He chuckled. "You bet I will, baby." And he did, even though he took the last few stairs on all fours. "So which one is the bedroom?" he asked between deep breaths.

"That's another adventure, loverboy. Next floor."

"Stuff that. There must be a sofa right here."

Tanya shook her head and pointed her finger at the ceiling.

After some hesitation Edward seemed to accept that this had to be on Tanya's terms. "Which way, then?"

"The spiral staircase at the end of the corridor."

Gamely, he stepped towards it and hauled himself to the top. "Makes you kind of dizzy."

"That's not the fault of the staircase." She pushed open a door. "In here, buster."

Robert's bedroom matched the size of the back room downstairs. It overlooked the yard at the rear of the property so it was built over the same foundations. The king-size bed was constructed of oak, with headboard and footboard graciously curved and upholstered in a French empire style. All the furniture matched and there was plenty of it, dressing table, wardrobes, chests of drawers and easy chairs, but no sense of crowding. More books lined the facing wall and there was a fifty-inch plasma TV as well as a sound system with chest-high speakers. There was an open door to an *en suite* shower room. A second door connected to a fire escape.

"This'll do," Edward said, stepping towards Tanya.

She moved aside. "Not so fast."

"C'mon, I showed you *my* secret." He patted the bed.

"Fair enough. Here's mine." She crossed to the dressing-table, swung the mirror right over and revealed a manila envelope fastened to the back. "It's ridiculous. I checked the mirror a week ago, and nothing was there. This morning I found this. Robert's will."

"Yeah?" he said, his thoughts elsewhere.

"You'd better listen up, because it names you." She slipped the document from the envelope and started to read. "'This is the last will and testament of Robert Ripple, of Precious Finds Bookshop, Main Street, Poketown, Pennsylvania, being of sound mind and revoking all other wills and codicils. I wish to appoint as co-executors my good friends George Digby-Smith

26

and Edward Myers.' That's you. Unfortunately as an executor you're not allowed to profit from the estate."

"No problem," Edward said. "Now why don't you put that down so we can give this bed a workout?"

"Listen to this part: 'I leave my house and shop in trust to become the sole property of my devoted assistant manager, Tanya Tripp, on condition that she continues to trade as a bookseller on the premises for ten years from the date of my decease.' Nice try."

"Don't ya like it?" Edward said, frowning.

"It stinks. This wasn't drafted by Robert. It's a fake. I know why you wanted his credit cards the other day and why in the end you walked off with that old receipt book. So you could fake his signature. Well, it's a passable signature, I'll give you that, but you forgot something. A will needs to be witnessed. There are no witnesses here."

"No witnesses, huh?" He raised his right hand in a semi-official pose and intoned in a more-or-less coherent manner, "The state of Pennsylvania doesn't require witnesses to a will. You're in the clear, sweetheart. It's all yours, the house and the shop. Just be grateful someone thought of you."

"Thought of *me*? You were only thinking of yourselves, keeping up the old arrangement, taking your stolen pounds from the safe and spending them in England. I'm supposed to give up ten years of my life to keep this smelly old heap of wood and plaster going just to make life dandy for you guys. Well, forget it. I don't buy it." She held the will high and ripped it apart.

The force of the action somehow penetrated the alcohol in Edward's brain. Suddenly he seemed to realize that there was much more at stake than getting this young woman into bed. "I've got your number. You figure you can do better for yourself with those Agatha Christies you have in the office. Worth a fucking fortune, you said. Few spots of coffee didn't harm them much. You're aiming to take them with you when the shop closes down and cash in big time."

Tanya felt the blood drain from her face. She'd been hoping her agitated words the other day had passed unnoticed. This was dangerous, desperately dangerous. It wasn't quite true because the best books weren't stained. They were safe in her apartment. Even so, this stupid, drink-crazed man could put a stop to everything.

She still had ammunition and her reaction was to use it. "You don't know who I am. I can bring down you and your thieving friends. I'm Gritty Bologna's daughter, Teresa. That money in the safe isn't yours to spend. We spent years tracking you to this place. I took the job with Robert to find out where the banknotes are and now I know."

"You're Teresa Bologna?" he said in amazement. "You were in school at the time of the heist."

"I'm family, and family doesn't give up." He moved fast for a drunk. Fear and rage mingled in his face. He came at her like a bull.

He was blocking her route to the door and the *en suite* would be a trap. Her only option was to use the fire escape. She turned and hit the panic bar and the door swung open. She grabbed the rail and swung left just as Edward charged through.

No one's movements are reliable after heavy drinking. Edward pitched forward, failed to stop, hit the rail hard with his hips and couldn't stop his torso from tipping him over. He may have screamed. Tanya (or Teresa) didn't remember. But the sickening thud of the body hitting the concrete forty feet below would stay in her memory forever.

The autopsy revealed substantial alcohol in Edward's blood. No one could say what he had been doing above the bookshop in the dead owner's bedroom. Those who might have thrown some light had all left Poketown overnight and were not heard of again. So an open verdict was returned at the inquest.

In the absence of a will from Robert Ripple, Precious Finds was duly put under the control of an administrator and escheated to the state of Pennsylvania. It ceased trading as a bookshop and was converted into apartments.

About a year later, a married couple set up home on a remote Scottish island. He was thought to be an ex-hippy, she an American. They called themselves Mr. and Mrs. English and they helped the home tourist industry by forever taking holidays in different towns.

Copies of several rare Agatha Christie first editions in dust jackets enlivened the book market in the years that followed, changing hands for huge sums. Their provenance was described as uncertain, but they were certainly genuine.

The Compendium of Srem
F. Paul Wilson

F. Paul Wilson is the author of more than forty novels, ranging from science fiction to horror thrillers, most famously about his long-running series character, Repairman Jack, and has contributed to a number of collaborations. He has also written for the stage, the screen, and interactive media.

His books have appeared on the *New York Times* bestsellers list, won numerous awards, including the Prometheus Hall of Fame Award and the Bram Stoker Award for Lifetime Achievement, and made the recommended readings lists of the American Library Association and the New York Public Library, among others. He was recently awarded the prestigious Inkpot Award from the San Diego Comic-Con and the Pioneer Award from the RT Booklovers Convention.

His novel *The Keep* was made into a movie by Paramount in 1983 and his novel *The Tomb* is currently in development as *Repairman Jack* by Beacon Films.

1

Tomás de Torquemada opened his eyes in the dark.

Was that . . . ?

Yes. Someone knocking on his door.

"Who is it?"

"Brother Adelard, good Prior. I must speak to you." Even if he had not said his name, Tomás would have recognized the French accent. He glanced up at his open window. Stars filled the sky with no hint of dawn.

"It is late. Can it not wait until morning?"

"I fear not."

"Come then."

With great effort, Tomás struggled to bring his eighty-year-old body to a sitting position as Brother Adelard entered the tiny room. He carried a candle and a cloth-wrapped bundle. He set both next to the Vulgate Bible on the rickety desk in the corner.

"May I be seated, Prior?"

Tomás gestured to the room's single straight-back chair. Adelard dropped into it, then bounded up again.

"No. I cannot sit."

"What prompts you to disturb my slumber?"

Adelard was half his age and full of righteous energy—one of the inquisitors the pope had assigned to Tomás four years ago. He seemed unable to contain that energy now. The candlelight reflected in his bright blue eyes as he paced Tomás's room.

"I know you are not feeling well, Prior, but I thought it best to bring this to you in the dark hours."

"Bring what?"

He fairly leaped to the table where he pulled the cloth from the rectangular bundle, revealing a book. Even from across the room, even with his failing eyesight, Tomás knew this was like no book he had ever seen.

"This," he said, lifting the candle and bringing both closer. He held the book before Tomás, displaying the cover. "Have you ever seen anything like it?"

Tomás shook his head. No, he hadn't.

The covers and spine seemed to be made of stamped metal. He squinted at the strange marks embossed on the cover. They made no sense at first, then seemed to swim into focus. Words . . . in Spanish . . . at least one was in Spanish.

Compendio ran across the upper half in large, ornate letters; and below that, half size: *Srem*.

"What do you see?" Adelard said. The candle flame wavered as his hand began to shake.

"The title, I should think."

"The words, Prior. Please tell me the words you see."

"My eyes are bad but I am not blind: *Compendio* and *Srem*."

The candle flame wavered more violently.

"When I look at it, Prior, I too see Srem, but to my eyes the first word is not *Compendio* but *Compendium*."

Tomás bent closer. No, his eyes had not fooled him.

"It is as plain as day: *Compendio*. It ends in i-o."

"You were raised speaking Spanish, were you not, Prior?"

"As a boy of Valladolid, I should say so."

"As you know, I was raised in Lyon and spent most of my life speaking French before the pope assigned me to assist you."

To rein me in, you mean, Tomás thought, but said nothing.

The current Pope, Alexander VI, thought him too . . . what word had he had used? *Fervent*. Yes, that was it. How could one be too fervent in safeguarding the Faith? And hadn't he previously narrowed procedures, limiting torture only to those accused by at least two citizens of good standing? Before that, any wild accusation could send someone to the rack.

"Yes-yes. What of it?"

"When . . ." He swallowed. "When *you* look at the cover, you see *Compendio*, a Spanish word. When *I* look at the cover I see a French word: *Compendium*."

Tomás pushed the book away and struggled to his feet.

"Have you gone mad?"

Adelard staggered back, trembling. "I feared I was, I was sure I was, but you see it too."

"I see what is stamped in the metal, nothing more!"

"But this afternoon, when Amaury was sweeping my room, he spied the cover and asked where I had learned to read Berber. I asked him what he meant. He grinned and pointed to the cover, saying 'Berber! Berber!'"

Tomás felt himself going cold.

"Berber?"

"Yes. He was born in Almeria where they speak Berber, and to his eyes the two words on the cover were written in Berber script. He can read only a little of the writing, but he saw enough of it growing up. I opened the book for him and he kept nodding and grinning, saying 'Berber' over and over."

Tomás knew Amaury, as did everyone else in the monastery—a simple-minded Morisco who performed menial tasks for the monks, like sweeping and serving at table. He was incapable of duplicity.

"After that, I gave Brother Ramiro a quick look at the cover, and he saw *Compendio*, just as you do." Adelard looked as if he were in physical pain. "It appears to me, good Prior, that whoever looks at this book sees the words in their native tongue. But how can that be? How can that *be*?"

Tomás's knees felt weak. He pulled the chair to his side and lowered himself onto it.

"What sort of deviltry have you brought into our house?"

"I had no idea it was any sort of deviltry when I bought it. I spied it in the marketplace. A Moor had laid it out on a blanket with other trinkets and carvings. I thought it so unusual I bought it for Brother Ramiro—you know how he loves books. I thought he could add it to our library. Not till Amaury made his comment did I realize that it was more than simply a book with an odd cover. It . . ." He shook his head. "I don't know what it is, Prior, but it has certainly been touched by deviltry. That is why I've brought it to you."

To me, Tomás thought. Well, it would have to be me, wouldn't it.

Yet in all his fifteen years as Grand Inquisitor he had never had to deal with sorcery or witchcraft. Truth be told, he could give no credence to that sort of nonsense. Peon superstitions.

Until now.

"That is not all, Prior. Look at the pattern around the words. What do you see?"

Tomás leaned closer. "I see crosshatching."

"So do I. Now, close your eyes for a count of three."

He did so, then reopened them. The pattern had changed to semicircles, each row facing the opposite way of the row above and below it.

His heart gave a painful squeeze in his chest.

"What do you see?"

"A . . . a wavy pattern."

"I kept my eyes open and I still see the cross hatching."

Tomás said nothing as he tried to comprehend what was happening here. Finally . . .

"There is surely deviltry on the covers. What lies between?"

Adelard's expression was bleak. "Heresy, Prior . . . the most profound heresy I have ever seen or heard."

"That is an extreme judgment, Brother Adelard. It also means you have read it."

"Not all. Not nearly all. I spent the rest of the afternoon and all night reading it until just before I came to your door. And even so, I have only begun. It is evil, Prior. Unspeakably evil."

He did not recall Adelard being prone to exaggeration, but this last had to be an overstatement.

"Show me."

Adelard placed the tome on the table and opened it. Tomás noticed that the metal cover was attached to the spine by odd interlacing hinges of a kind he had never seen before. The pages looked equally odd. Moving his chair closer, he reached out and ran his fingers over the paper—if it was paper at all—and it felt thinner than the skin of an onion, yet completely opaque. He would have expected such delicate material to be marred by wrinkles and tears, but each page was perfect.

As was the writing that graced those pages—perfect Spanish. It had the appearance of an ornate handwritten script, yet each letter was perfect, and identical to every other of its kind. Every "a" looked like every other "a," every "m" like every other "m." Tomás had seen one of the Holy Bibles printed by that German, Gutenberg, where each letter had been exactly like all its brothers. The Gutenberg book had been printed in two columns per page, however, whereas the script in this compendium flowed from margin to margin.

"Show me heresy," Tomás said.

"Let me show you deviltry first, Prior," said the monk as he began to turn the pages at blinding speed.

"You go too fast. How will you know when to stop?"

"I will know, Prior. I will know."

Tomás saw numerous illustrations fly by, many in color.

"Here!" Adelard said, stopping and jabbing his finger at a page. "Here is deviltry most infernal!"

Tomás felt his saliva dry as he faced a page with an illustration that moved . . . a globe spinning in a rectangular black void. Lines crisscrossed the globe, connecting glowing dots on its surface.

"Heavenly Lord! It . . ." He licked his lips. "It moves."

He reached out, but hesitated. It looked as if his hand might pass into the void depicted on the page.

"Go ahead, Prior. I have touched it."

He ran his fingers over the spinning globe. It felt as flat and smooth as the rest of the page—no motion against his fingertips, and yet the globe continued to turn beneath them.

"What sorcery is this?"

"I was praying you could tell me. Do you think that sphere is supposed to represent the world?"

"I do not know. Perhaps. The Queen has just sent that Genoan, Colón, on his third voyage to the New World. He has proven that the world is round . . . a sphere."

Adelard shrugged. "He has proven only what sailors have been saying for decades."

Ah, yes. Brother Adelard fancied himself a philosopher.

Tomás stared at the spinning globe. Although some members of the Church hierarchy argued against it, most now accepted that the world God had created for Mankind was indeed round; but if this apparition was supposed to be that world, then the perspective was from that of the Lord Himself.

Why now? Why, with his health slipping away like sand—he doubted he would survive the year—did a tome that could only be described as sorcerous find its way to his quarters? In his younger days he would have relished hunting down the perpetrators of this deviltry. But now . . . now he barely had the strength to drag himself through the day.

He sighed. "Light my candle and leave this abomination to me. I would read it."

"I know you must, dear Prior, but prepare yourself. The heresies are so profound they will . . . they will steal your sleep."

"I doubt that, Brother Adelard." In his years as Grand Inquisitor he had heard every conceivable heresy. "I doubt that very much."

But no matter what its contents, this tome had already stolen his sleep.

After Adelard departed, he looked around at his spare quarters. Four familiar whitewashed walls, bare except for the crucifix over his bed. A white ceiling and a sepia tiled floor. A cot, a desk, a chair, a small chest of drawers, and a Holy Bible comprised the furnishings. As prior, as Grand Inquisitor, as the queen's confessor, no one would have raised an eyebrow had he requisitioned more comfortable quarters. But earthly trappings led to distractions, and he would not be swayed from his Holy Course.

Before opening the *Compendium*, he took his bible, kissed its cover, and laid it in his lap . . .

2

Tomás read through the night. His candle burned out just as dawn began to light the sky, so he read on, foregoing breakfast. Finally he forced himself to close both the abominable book and his eyes.

As he slumped in his chair he heard the sounds of hammers and saws and axes and the calls of the workmen wafting through his window. Every day was the same—except Sunday, of course. Main construction on the monastery—*Monasterio de Santo Tomás*—had been officially completed four years ago, but always there seemed more to do: a patio here, a garden there. It seemed it would never be finished.

The monastery had become the centerpiece of Ávila. And that it should not be. It had grown too big, too ornate. He thought of the elegant studded pillars ringing the second-floor gallery overlooking the enormous courtyard, beautiful works of art in themselves, but inappropriate for a mendicant order that required a vow of poverty.

It housed three cloisters—one for novitiates, one for silence, and one for the royal family. Since the king and queen had funded the monastery, and used it as their summer residence, he supposed such excess was unavoidable. The queen was why he had moved here from Seville—he had been her confessor for many years.

He opened his eyes and stared at the cover of the *Compendium of Srem*. He wasn't sure if Srem was the name of a town or the fictional civilization it described or the person who had compiled it. But the title mattered not. The content . . . the content was soul rattling in its heresy, and utterly demonic in the subtle seductiveness of its tone.

The book never denounced the Church, never blasphemed God the Father, Jesus the Son, or the Holy Ghost. Oh, no. That would have been too obvious. That would have set up a barrier between the reader and the unholiness within. Tomás would have found shrill, wild-eyed blasphemy easier to deal with than the alternative presented here: God and His Church were not presented as enemies—in fact, they were never presented at all! *Not one mention.* Impossible as it was, the author pretended to be completely unaware of their existence.

That was bad enough. But the tone . . . the tone . . .

The *Compendium* presented itself as a collection of brief essays describing every facet of an imaginary civilization. Where that civilization might exist—or when—was never addressed. Perhaps it purported to describe the legendary Island of Atlas mentioned by Plato in his *Timaeus*, supposedly sunk beneath the waves millennia ago. But no one took those stories seriously. It portrayed a civilization that harnessed the lightning and commanded the weather, defying God's very Creation by fashioning new creatures from the humors of others.

But the tone . . . it presented these hellish wonders in a perfectly matter-of-fact manner, as if everyone was familiar with them, as if these were mere quotidian truths that the author was simply cataloguing for the record. Usually when imaginary wonders were described—the Greek legends of their gods and goddesses, came to mind—the teller of the tall tale related them in breathless prose and a marveling tone. Not so the *Compendium*. The descriptions were flat and straightforward, almost casual. And the way they interconnected and referred back and forth to each other indicated that a great deal of thought had been invested in these fictions.

Which was what made it all so seductive.

Many times during the night and through the morning Tomás had to force himself to lean back and press the Holy Bible against his fevered brow so as to counteract the spell the *Compendium* was attempting to weave around him.

By the time he closed the covers, he had dipped barely a fingertip into the foul well of its waters, but he had read enough to know that this so-called *Compendium of Srem* was in truth the *Compendium of Satan*, a library of falsehoods fashioned by the Father of Lies himself.

And the most profound lies concerned gods, although he didn't know if "god" was the proper word for the entities described. No, "described" was not the word. The author referred to two vaporous entities at war in the aether. The people of this fictional civilization did not worship these entities. Rather they contended with them, some currying favor with one so as to help defeat the other, and vice versa. They had not bothered to name their gods, and had no images of them. Their gods simply . . . *were*.

But reading the *Compendium* was not necessary to appreciate its hellish origin. Simply leafing through the pages was all it took. For the book had no end! It numbered one hundred sheets—Tomás had counted them—but when he'd leafed to the last page, he'd found there was no last page. Every time he turned what appeared to be the last page, another lay waiting. And yet the sheet count never varied from one hundred, because a page at the front was disappearing every time a new one appeared at the rear. Yet whenever he closed and reopened the book, it began again with the title page.

Sorcery . . . sorcery was the only explanation.

3

Brother Adelard and Brother Ramiro arrived together.

Tomás had rewrapped the *Compendium* in Adelard's blanket and carried it to the tribunal room. He had been shocked at the thick tome's almost negligible weight. Once there, he summoned them and waited in his seat at the center of the long refectory table. The room was similar to the tribunal room at the monastery in Segovia where he had spent most of his term as Grand Inquisitor: the long table, the high-backed leather-upholstered chairs—the highest back reserved for him—facing the door; stained-glass windows to either side, and a near life-size crucifix on the wall above the fireplace behind him. The crucifix was positioned so as to force the accused to look upon the face of their crucified Lord as they stood before the inquisitors and responded to the accusations made against then. They were not allowed to know the names of their accusers, merely the charges against them.

"Good Prior," Adelard said as he entered. "I see in your eyes that you have read it."

Tomás nodded. "Not all of it, of course, but enough to know what we must do." He shifted his gaze to Ramiro. "And you, Brother . . . have you read it?"

Ramiro was about Adelard's age, but there the resemblance ceased. Ramiro was portly where Adelard was lean, brown-eyed instead of blue, swarthy instead of fair. Those dark eyes were wide now and fixed on the *Compendium*, which Tomás had unwrapped.

"No, Prior. I have seen only the cover, and that is enough."

"You have no desire to peruse its contents?"

He gave his head a violent shake. "Brother Adelard has told me—"

Tomás gave Adelard a sharp look. "Told? Who else have you told?"

"No one, Prior. Since Ramiro had already seen the book, I thought—"

"See that it stops here. Tell no one what you have read. Tell no one that this abomination exists. Knowledge of the book does not spread beyond this room. Understood?"

"Yes, Prior," they said in unison.

He turned to Ramiro. "You have no desire for first-hand knowledge of these heresies?"

Another violent shake of the head. "From what little I have heard from Brother Adelard, they must be contained. Heresies spread with every new set of eyes that behold them. I do not want to add mine."

Tomás was impressed. "You are wise beyond your years, Ramiro." He motioned him closer. "But it is your knowledge of book craft that we need today."

Ramiro was in charge of the monastery's library. He had overseen its construction in the monk's cloister—was still attending to refinements, in fact—and was in charge of acquiring texts to line the shelves.

Ramiro approached the *Compendium* as if it were a coiled viper. He touched it as if it might sear his flesh. Adelard came up behind him to watch over his shoulder.

"I do not know what kind of metal this is," Ramiro said. "It looks like polished steel, but the highlights in the surface are most unusual."

Tomás had wondered at the pearly highlights himself.

"It is not steel," Adelard said.

Tomás raised his eyebrows. "Oh? And you are a metallurgist as well as a philosopher?"

"I seek to learn as much about God's Creation as I can, Prior. But I think it is obvious that the covers are not steel. If they were, the book would weigh much more than it does."

Ramiro gripped the *Compendium* and hefted it. "As light as air."

"Note the hinges that connect the covers to the spine," Tomás said. "Have you ever seen anything like that?" As Ramiro raised it for a closer look, Tomás added, "I ask because we must determine where this was fashioned."

Adelard was nodding his understanding. "Yes, of course. To help us hunt down the heretic who made it."

Ramiro was shaking his head. "I have never seen anything like this. I cannot fathom how it was put together."

"Through sorcery," Tomás said.

Ramiro looked at him, eyes bright. "Yes, that is the only explanation."

He hid his disappointment. If Ramiro had recognized the workmanship, they would have brought them that much closer to naming the heretic.

"This Moor who sold it to you," Tomás said, turning to Adelard. "He was in the marketplace?"

"Yes, Prior."

"Could this be his work?"

"I doubt it. He was poor and ragged with crippled fingers. I cannot see how that would be possible."

"But he may know who did make it."

"Yes, he certainly may." Adelard slapped his palm on the table. "If only we had jurisdiction over Moors!"

Ferdinand and Isabella's edict limited the inquisition's reach to anyone who professed to be Christian, but its focus had always been the *conversos*—the Jews to whom the Alhambra Decree had given the ultimatum of either converting to Christianity or leaving the country.

"We have jurisdiction over the purity of the Faith," Tomás said, pointing to the *Compendium*. "That includes heresy from any source, and this is heresy most foul. Have him brought here."

4

The Moor stood before them, quaking in fear.

Because of the sorcerous nature of the *Compendium* and his determination to keep its very existence secret, Tomás had decided to forego a full tribunal inquiry and limit the proceedings to himself and the two others who already knew of it.

After Adelard identified the Moor, soldiers assigned to the Inquisition had rounded him up and delivered him to the tribunal room.

Tomás studied this poor excuse for a human being. The name he had given upon his arrival was mostly Berber gibberish. Tomás had heard "Abdel" in the mix and decided to call him that. Abdel wore a dirty cloth cap and a ratty beard, both signs of continued adherence to the ways of Mohammed. His left eye was milky white, in stark contrast to the mass of dark wrinkles that made up his face. He had few teeth and his hands were twisted and gnarled. Tomás agreed with Adelard: This man did not craft the *Compendium*.

"Abdel, have you accepted Jesus Christ as your savior?" Adelard said.

The old man bowed. "Yes, sir. Years ago."

"So, you are a Morisco then?"

"Yes, sir."

"And yet you still wear your beard in the style required by the religion you claimed to have given up."

Tomás knew what Adelard was doing: striking fear into the Morisco's heart.

The old Moor's good eye flashed. "I wear it in the style of Jesus as I have seen him portrayed in church."

Tomás rubbed his mouth to hide a smile. Adelard had been outflanked.

"We are not here to question your manner of dress, Abdel," Tomás said, wishing to turn the inquest to the matter that most concerned him. "No accusations have been made."

He saw sudden relief in the Moor's eyes. "Then may I ask why—?"

Tomás lifted the *Compendium* so that the Moor could see the cover. "We *are* here to question why you are selling heresy."

His shock looked genuine. "I did not know! It is just a book I found!"

"Found?" Adelard said. "Found where?"

"In a trunk," he said, head down, voice barely audible.

"And where is this trunk?"

The Moor's voice sank even lower. "I do not know."

Adelard's voice rose. "Do you mean to tell us you have forgotten? Perhaps some time on the rack will improve your memory!"

Tomás raised a hand. He thought he knew the problem.

"You stole it, didn't you, Abdel?"

The Moor's head snapped up, then looked down again without replying.

"Understand, Abdel," Tomás went on, "that we have no jurisdiction against civil crimes. We are concerned by the immorality of your action, yes, and trust that you will confess your sin to your priest, but we can take no action against you for the theft itself." He paused to let this sink in, then added, "Who did you steal it from?"

When the Moor still did not reply, Tomás kept his voice low despite his growing anger. "We cannot punish you for stealing, but we can use every means at our disposal to wring a confession from you as to the source of your heresy." He released his fury and began pounding on the table. "And I will personally see to it that you suffer the tortures of the damned if you do not—"

"Asher ben Samuel!" the Moor cried. "I stole it from Asher ben Samuel!"

Silence in the tribunal room. Ramiro, who had sat silent during the interrogation, finally spoke.

"Asher ben Samuel . . . at last!"

Samuel was a prominent Jewish importer who converted to Christianity rather than leave the country after the Alhambra Decree, but no one on the inquisition tribunal believed his conversion had been true. They had dispatched townsfolk to spy on him and catch him engaging in Judaist practices. They watched for lack of smoke from his chimney on Saturdays, which would indicate observance of the Jewish Sabbath. They would offer him leavened bread during Passover—if he refused, his true faith would be revealed. But he always ate it without hesitation.

Still, the tribunal had not been convinced.

But now . . . now they had him.

Or did they?

After Abdel was removed, to be freed again to the streets, Tomás said, "What accusation can be leveled against Asher ben Samuel?"

"Heresy, of course!" Ramiro said.

"Who will accuse him?"

Adelard said, "We will."

"On the word of a disreputable Morisco street merchant who will have to admit to thievery to make the accusation?"

They fell silent at that.

"I have an idea," Ramiro said. "In which are we more interested: exposing a crypto Jew, or learning the origin of this hellish tome?"

Tomás knew the answer immediately. "I think we can all agree that the *Compendium* presents a far greater threat to the Faith than a single *converso*."

"It surely does," Ramiro said. "Although in my heart I believe that Asher ben Samuel is guilty of many heresies, we have not caught him at a single one. But in the course of our attempts to catch him over the years, we have kept too close a watch on him to allow him the opportunity of fashioning this book without our knowing."

Tomás reluctantly agreed. "You are saying that if the book did not originate with him, he must have bought it from someone else."

"Exactly, good Prior. Each owner and subsequent owner is a stepping stone across a stream. Each one brings us closer to shore: the heretic who fashioned it. And so I propose that Brother Adelard and I confront Asher ben Samuel in his home with the book and learn where he obtained it."

"That is most irregular," Tomás said.

"I realize that, Prior," Ramiro said. "But if we wish to limit knowledge of the book's existence, we cannot keep bringing suspect after suspect to the monastery. Who knows how many we will have to interrogate before we find the fashioner? Eventually the other members of the tribunal will begin to ask questions we wish not to answer. And by our own rules of procedure, each accused is allowed thirty days of grace to confess and repent. If the trail is long, the fashioner will have months and months of warning during which he can flee."

All excellent points. He was proud of Brother Ramiro.

"But how will you induce him to speak in his home? The instruments of truth lie two floors below us."

Ramiro shrugged. "I will tell him the truth: that we are more interested in finding the heretic behind the *Compendium* than in punishing those through whose hands it happened to pass. Asher ben Samuel is a wealthy man. He has more to lose than his life. He knows that if brought before the tribunal he will be found guilty, and then not only will he face the cleansing flame at the stake, but all his property will be seized and his wife and daughters cast into the streets." Ramiro smiled. "He will tell us. And then we will move on to the next stepping stone."

Tomás nodded slowly. The plan had merit.

"Do it, then. Begin today." He tapped the *Compendium*'s strange metal cover. "I want this heretic found. The sooner we have him, the sooner his soul can be cleansed by an *auto da fé*.

5

From within the sheltering cowl of his black robe, Adelard regarded the twilit streets of Ávila. He was glad to be out in the air. He left the monastery so seldom these days. Spring had taken control, as evidenced by the bustling townspeople. When summer arrived, the heat would slow all movement until well into the dark hours.

Brother Ramiro carried the carefully wrapped *Compendium* between his chest and his folded arms as they crossed the town square. Adelard glanced at the trio of scorched stakes where heretics were unburdened of their sins by the cleansing flame. He had witnessed many an *auto da fé* here since his arrival from France.

"Note how passersby avert their eyes and give us a wide berth," Ramiro said.

Adelard had indeed noticed that. "I don't know why. They can't know that I am a member of the tribunal."

"They don't. They see the black robes and know us as Dominicans, members of the order that runs the Inquisition, and that is enough. This saddens me."

"Why?"

"You are an inquisitor, I am a simple mendicant. You would not know."

"I was not always an inquisitor, Ramiro."

"But you did not know Ávila before the Inquisition arrived. We were greeted with smiles and welcomed everywhere. Now no one looks me in the eye. What do you think their averted gazes mean? That they have heresies to hide?"

"Perhaps."

"Then you are wrong. It means that the robes of our order have become associated with the public burnings of heretics to the exclusion of all else."

Adelard had never heard his friend talk like this.

"What are you saying, Ramiro?"

"I am saying that we are not an order that stays behind its walls. We have always gone out among the people, helping the sick, feeding the poor, easing pain and sorrow. But the order's involvement in guarding the Faith seems to have erased all memory of our centuries of good works."

"Be careful what you say, Ramiro. You are flirting with heresy."

"Are you going to accuse me?"

"No. You are my friend. I know that you speak from a good, faithful heart, but others might not appreciate that. So please watch your tongue."

Adelard was surprised at Ramiro's familiarity with the people of Ávila. He had imagined him spending all his time in the library or tilling the monastery's fields. He changed the subject.

"I've known you for a number of years now, Ramiro, but I don't know where you are from."

"Toro. A province north of here."

"Do you still have family there?"

"No. My family was wiped out in the Battle of Toro. I was just a boy and barely managed to survive."

Adelard had heard of that—one of the battles in the war for the crown of Castile.

"How did you come to the order?"

"After the horrors I'd seen, I wanted a life of peace and contemplation and good works. And that is what I had until the Inquisition changed everything."

Adelard had come to the Dominicans for very different reasons. The order provided him a place to pursue the philosophy of nature and to write papers explaining God's Creation and how what he had learned bolstered the doctrines of the Church. Sometimes he had to stretch the truth to avoid censure, but in general his papers were well received and seen as a cogent defense of doctrine. As a result, when the pope decided that the Spanish Inquisition needed outside influence, he assigned Adelard to be one of the new inquisitors.

But concerns about doctrine faded as the *Compendium* took command of his thoughts, much as it had since he'd opened it yesterday and begun reading. The ability of its text to appear written in the reader's native tongue certainly seemed sorcerous, and yet . . . and yet it seemed so congruent with the civilization described within.

Since his youth, Adelard had been fascinated with the philosophy of nature. When his father would bring home small game from the hunt, he would insist on gutting them, but doing so in his own way—methodically, systematically, so that he might understand the inner workings of the creatures. And even now he had reserved a room in the monastery where he could mix various elements and record their interactions.

He wondered if there might be a natural explanation for the marvels described within the *Compendium* and for the wonder of the tome itself—something that would not violate Church orthodoxy.

He would have to ponder this alone. He could not discuss it with Ramiro, who had not read it, and he might be risking his position, perhaps even his life, if he broached the subject with the Grand Inquisitor.

They reached the large plot of land on the edge of town where Asher ben Samuel lived, and started down the long path that led to his house.

"Does it seem right that a Jew should have such fortune?" Adelard said as they passed through a grove of olive trees.

"He is a *converso*—no longer a Jew."

Even though they professed to be Christian, *conversos* were mistrusted and even held in contempt. Especially someone with the financial influence of Samuel. Was his "conversion" simply economic pragmatism, or had he truly rejected his old beliefs? Adelard suspected—nay, was convinced—of the latter. The problem was proving it.

"You are so naïve, Ramiro. Once a Jew, always a Jew."

"I have Jewish blood. And so, no doubt, do you."

"You lie!"

"There's hardly an educated person in Castile who does not carry Jewish blood."

"I was raised in France."

"Probably the same there. Even our own prior—were you aware that a grandfather in the Torquemada line was a Jew?"

Tomás de Torquemada, the Hammer of Heretics, the Queen's confessor . . . had Jewish blood? How was this possible?

"That can't be true!"

"It is. He makes no secret of it. He has said that the purpose of the Holy Inquisition is not to stamp out Jewish blood, but to stamp out Jewish practices."

"All right, then, if the Prior says it is true, I accept it as true. But even so, his Jewish blood and yours are different from Asher ben Samuel's."

"How?"

"The prior and you were raised in the Faith. *Conversos* like him were not."

At the end of the path they found the high-walled home of Asher ben Samuel.

Ramiro said, "It reminds me of a fortress."

They stopped before the wrought iron gate and pulled the bell cord. An elderly footman exited the house and limped across the gap between.

"Yes?" he said, his eyes full of fear.

"We have come to see your master," Ramiro said.

"On a matter of faith," Adelard added.

The old man turned away. "I must go ask—"

"Open immediately!" Ramiro said. "Members of the Tribunal of the Holy Office of the Inquisition do not wait outside like beggars!"

With trembling hands, the old man unlocked the gate and pulled it open. He led them through a heavy oak door into a large, tiled gallery that opened onto a courtyard. And there sat Asher ben Samuel, reading under a broad chandelier.

A squat man of perhaps fifty years, he rose and came forward as they entered. "Friars! To what do I owe this honor?"

Adelard wondered why he didn't seem surprised or upset. Had he seen them coming?

"We will speak to you in private," he said.

"Of course. Diego, go to your quarters. But first—can I have him bring you some wine?"

Adelard would have loved some good wine, but he would accept no hospitality from this Jew.

"This is not a social call," he said.

Still apparently unperturbed, Samuel waved Diego off and then faced them. "How may I be of service?"

Ramiro pointed to the large illuminated manuscript that lay open on the table behind Samuel. "You can first tell us what you are reading."

Samuel smiled. "The Gospel of Matthew. It is my favorite."

Liar, Adelard thought. He *had* seen them coming.

Ramiro unwrapped the *Compendium* and placed it on the table. "We thought this would have been more to your liking."

Finally Samuel's composure cracked, but only a little.

"How—?"

"How it came to us is not the question. How did it come to you?"

He backed a step and sat heavily in a chair. "I collect books. This was offered to me. Since it was of such unusual construction and written in Hebrew, I snatched it up."

"Written in He—?" Ramiro began, then frowned. "Oh, of course."

"When I began to read it I realized it was a very dangerous book to have in one's possession."

"Why did you not bring it to the tribunal?" Adelard said.

Samuel gave them a withering look. "Really, good friars. For years you have been trying to find a reason to drag me before you. I should provide you with such a reason myself?"

"You know as well as we that many *conversos* pay only lip service to the Church's teachings and hold to their Jewish ways once their doors are closed. One cannot shed one's lifelong faith like an old coat."

"Ah, but you forget that I am a Castilian as well. If my queen and her king want to rule a Christian land, then I become Christian. It is not as if I am forsaking the Jewish God for a pagan idol. As I am sure you know, Jesus was born a Jew. The Old Testament of the Jews leads to the New Testament of Jesus. We worship the same God."

He possessed a persuasive tongue, this Jew; Adelard would give him that.

Ramiro said, "So, instead of bringing this book to the tribunal, you packed it in a trunk. For what purpose?"

"You seem to know so much . . . "

"Answer the question!"

"I intended to throw it in the river. I did not want such a dangerous text in my library, nor in anyone else's." He spread his hands. "But when I reached the river, I could not find it. It was gone, as if by magic."

Not magic, Adelard thought. A thieving Morisco.

"Who sold it to you?"

Samuel said nothing for a moment, then took a deep breath. "I hesitate to condemn another man to the rack. Do you understand that?"

"We understand," Adelard said. "We wish to find the author of this heresy as soon as possible. If you assist us in locating him, I have the authority to overlook the time the book was in your possession."

Asher ben Samuel tapped his fingers on the arm of his chair as he pondered this. He knew the enormous cost to him and his family to withhold the name.

Finally he looked up and said, "You will make the same offer to the man I name?"

"We offer you absolution and you dare to bargain with us?"

"I merely asked a question."

Adelard hated conceding to the Jew, but they had to stay focused on their ultimate goal.

"As long as he is not the fashioner. If the book merely passed through his hands, he will not be punished. But the fashioner . . . the fashioner has committed heresy most foul and will pay a severe penalty."

Samuel smiled. "No possibility of the man in question being your fashioner. He is a simple carpenter. I doubt he can read a dozen words, let alone concoct such a fiction as you have in this book."

"He stole it then?" Ramiro said.

Samuel shrugged. "He told me the book had been freely given to him, but who is to know? He has done work for me, building shelves for my library. He knows of my love of learning and so he came to me to sell it."

Adelard raised his voice. "The name! We want his name, not your empty excuses!"

"The only name I have for him is Pedro the carpenter."

Ramiro was nodding. "I know him. He built shelves for the monastery's library as well. He does excellent work." He looked at Adelard. "But I agree: It is inconceivable that he wrote the *Compendium*."

"Perhaps. But he will be able to tell us how it came to him. And then we will be—as you like to say, Brother Ramiro—one stepping stone closer to the source."

6

Eventually, after asking questions at a number of intersections, they came to a meager shack down near the east bank of the Rio Adaja. The river ran sluggishly here, and stank from the waste thrown in the waters upstream.

Faint light flickered through the gaps in the hut's weathered boards. Certainly no more than a single candle burned within.

Adelard stopped in the darkness and stared at the hovel. Ramiro drew close to his side.

"Does it seem fair to you, Ramiro, that a skilled craftsman should live in such poverty while a man who simply buys and sells lives in luxury?"

"We are not to expect fairness in this world, brother, only in the next."

"True, true, but still it rankles."

"Pedro is a simple man. I fear the two of us appearing at his door will terrify him. He might flee and hide. But he knows me. Let me go in and speak to him alone, assure him that he has nothing to fear if he tells us the truth."

"Very well, but be quick about it."

Adelard was exhausted. He had not slept last night. How could he, knowing his aging, ailing prior was up alone reading that hellish tome? All he wanted now was to complete this step in the investigation and return to his cot.

He watched Brother Ramiro approach the door with the *Compendium* under his arm, hesitate, then enter without knocking.

Immediately a cry rose from within, a hoarse voice shouting, "No! No, I'm sorry! I did not know!"

And then a scream of pain.

Adelard rushed forward, almost colliding with Ramiro as he stumbled from within.

"What happened?"

Ramiro was shaking. "When he saw me, he grabbed a knife. I feared he was going to attack me, but he thrust it into his own heart!"

Adelard pushed past him and looked inside. A thin man with graying hair lay on the floor with a knife handle jutting from his chest. His unseeing eyes gazed heavenward.

"Do you see?" Ramiro cried. "See what you and your Inquisition have done! This is what I said before: The very sight of this robe terrifies people! Pedro did not see me, he saw torture and burning flesh!"

7

"Do we have no other path to follow?" Tomás said to the two monks standing before him.

He had napped this evening while they were out, but then had waited up for their return. The news they brought was not at all what he had hoped for.

Adelard shook his head. "I fear not, Prior. The carpenter's death cuts off all further avenues of inquiry."

"How did this come to pass?"

Brother Ramiro spread his hands. "As soon as I stepped inside, he began to cry out in fear. Before I had a chance to say a single word, he snatched a knife up from his table and thrust it into his heart."

"He must have thought Brother Ramiro was there to drag him before the tribunal," Adelard said. "He knew he had transgressed and feared the stake."

Tomás shook his head. After all these years of the Holy Inquisition, the common folk remained ignorant of the process. They saw someone taken in for questioning and later saw that same person tied to a stake and screaming as the flames consumed them. They assumed the *auto da fé* was the outcome of every arrest, but nothing could be further from the truth. They forgot that the vast majority of those detained were eventually freed after confessing their guilt and doing penance. The instruments of truth were used only on those who refused to confess. Those consumed at the stake were usually *relapsos*—sinners who returned to their heretical ways after having been released by the tribunal.

"So unnecessary," Ramiro said, shaking his head. "And so frustrating. He lived alone, so we will never know where he obtained the book."

Tomás pounded his fist on the *Compendium*. "We must find this heretic!"

"How?" Adelard said. "Tell us how and we shall do it."

Tomás had no answer for him.

He sighed. "I see only one course now." He gestured to the fireplace behind him. "Consign it to the flames."

The fire had burned low by now. He watched as Adelard and Ramiro added wood and fanned it to a roaring blaze. When the heat had risen to an uncomfortable level, Tomás handed the *Compendium* to Adelard who opened it at the middle and dropped it upon the flames.

Tomás waited for the cover to scorch and then melt, for the pages to smoke and blacken and curl. But the *Compendium* ignored the flames. It lay there unperturbed as the fire burned down to faintly glowing embers around it.

"This cannot be," Tomás muttered.

Ramiro grabbed the tongs and pulled the book from the ashes. As it lay unmarred on the hearth, he held his open palm over it.

"It doesn't seem . . ." He touched it, then looked up in wonder. "It is not even warm!"

Tomás felt his gut crawl. A heretical text that would not burn . . . this went beyond his worst nightmare.

"Brother Ramiro . . ." His voice sounded hoarse. "Bring the heads-man's ax."

As Ramiro hurried off, Adelard stepped closer to Tomás.

"I am glad that Ramiro is gone," he said in a low voice. "He has not read the *Compendium* and you and I have. His absence offers us an opportunity to discuss its contents."

"What is there to discuss about heresy?"

"What if . . . " Adelard seemed hesitant.

"Go on."

"What if this *Compendium* speaks the truth?"

Tomás could not believe his ears. "Have you gone mad?"

"This is just supposition, Prior. We have this strange, strange book before us. I ask you: Is it heresy to theorize about its origins? If you say it is, I shall speak no further."

Tomás considered this. Heresy involved presenting falsehoods about the Faith or the Church as truth. Merely theorizing rather than proselytizing . . .

"Go ahead. I shall warn you when you begin to venture into heresy."

"Thank you, Prior." He stepped away and began pacing the tribunal chamber. "I have been thinking. The *Book of Genesis* tells about the Flood: How the evil of Mankind prompted God to bring the Deluge to cleanse the world and start afresh. What if the *Compendium* tells of an evil, godless civilization that existed before the Deluge? What if the *Compendium* is all that is left of that civilization?"

Adelard . . . ever the philosopher. However . . .

"The Holy Bible makes no mention of such a civilization."

"Neither does it give specifics about the 'evils of mankind' that triggered God's wrath. The *Compendium*'s civilization could have been the very reason for the Deluge."

Tomás found himself nodding. Adelard's theory would explain why neither the Church nor Jesus were ever mentioned in the book, for neither would have existed when it was supposedly written. His idea was certainly unorthodox, but did not contradict Church doctrine in any way Tomás could see.

"An interesting theory, Brother Adelard."

Adelard stopped his pacing. "If it is true, Prior"—he waved his hands— "no, I mean if we *suppose* it is true, then this tome is an archeological artifact, an important piece of pre-Deluge history—perhaps the last existing piece of the pre-Deluge world. Do we then have a right to destroy it?"

Tomás did not like where this was leading.

"Right? It is not a matter of our *right* to destroy it, we have a sacred *duty* to destroy it."

"But perhaps it should be preserved as a piece of history."

"You tread dangerous ground here, Brother Adelard. Let us suppose that the *Compendium* does predate the Deluge and that the heretical civilization described therein did exist in those ancient days. If the book is preserved and its contents become widely known, then people will begin to ask why it was never mentioned in the *Book of Genesis*. And if *Genesis* makes no mention of that, then it is logical to ask what else *Genesis* fails to mention. And right then and there you have planted a seed of doubt. And from the tiniest seed of doubt can grow vast heresies."

Adelard backed away, nodding. "Yes, I see. I see. Indeed, we must destroy it."

He didn't have to explain to Adelard that questions had no place where faith was concerned. All the answers were there, waiting, no questions necessary. Questions, however, though a necessary part of philosophy and the pursuit of knowledge, were toxic to faith. If one feels the need to question the Faith, then one has already fallen from grace and entered the realm of doubt.

Tomás was well aware that every thinking man contended with doubts about some aspect of the Faith from time to time. He had experienced one or two himself during his middle years, but he overcame them long before he was appointed Grand Inquisitor. As long as a man confined his doubts to his inner struggle, they did not fall under the authority of the Holy Inquisition. But should that man communicate those qualms to others for the purpose of infecting them with his uncertainty, *then* the tribunal stepped in.

"You have an inquiring mind, Brother Adelard. Be careful that it does not lead you astray. And see to it that our discussion here goes no further than this room."

"For certain, Prior."

Ramiro returned then, puffing from the exertion of hurrying his portly frame to the basement two floors below and back up again with the burden of the heavy, longhandled ax.

Not all recalcitrant heretics were allowed the cleansing flame of the *auto da fé*. Some were simply beheaded like common criminals. The ax was stored below and its wide cutting edge kept finely honed.

"Shall I, Prior?" he said, approaching the *Compendium* where it lay open on the hearth.

Tomás nodded. "Split it in two, Ramiro. Then reduce it to tiny scraps that we may scatter to the wind."

Ramiro lifted the ax high above his head. With a snarl and a cry, he swung it down with all his strength and struck the *Compendium* a blow such as would have severed any head from its body, no matter how sturdy the neck that supported it. Yet, to Tomás's wonder and dismay, the blade bounced off the exposed pages without so much as creasing them.

"This cannot be!" Ramiro cried.

He swung again and again, raining blow after blow upon the *Compendium*, but for all the effect he had he might as well have been caressing it with a feather.

Finally, red faced, sweating, panting, Ramiro stopped and faced them.

"Surely this is a thing from hell!"

Tomás would not argue that.

"What do we do?" Ramiro said, still panting. "Asher ben Samuel said he was going to throw it in the river. Perhaps that is the only course that remains to us."

Tomás shook his head. "No. Not a river. Too easy for a fisherman's net to retrieve it from the bottom. The deep ocean would be better. Perhaps we can send one of you on a voyage far out to sea where you can drop it over the side."

Ever the philosopher, Adelard said, "First we must make certain it will sink. But even if it does sink, it will still be intact. It will still exist. And even confined to a briny abyss, there will always remain the possibility that it will resurface. We must find a way to *destroy* it."

"How?" Ramiro said. "It will not burn, it will not be cut."

Adelard said, "Perhaps I can concoct a mixture of elements and humors that will overcome its defenses."

Elements! An idea struck Tomás just then—why hadn't he thought of it before? He pointed to a small table in the corner.

"Adelard, bring the holy water here."

The younger man's eyes lit as he hurried across the room and returned with a flagon of clear liquid. Tomás rose slowly from his chair and approached the book where it lay on the hearth. When Adelard handed him the unstoppered flagon, he blessed it, then poured some of its contents onto the *Compendium* . . .

. . . to no effect.

Angered, Tomás began splashing the holy water in the shape of a cross as he intoned, "*In Nomine Patri et Fili et Spiritus Sancti!*"

Then he waited, praying for the holy water to eat away at the pages. But again . . . nothing.

A pall settled over him. Had they no recourse against this hellish creation?

"Good Prior," Adelard said after a moment, "if I could take the tome and experiment on it, I might be able to discover a vulnerability."

Tomás fought a burst of anger. "You seek to succeed where water blessed in God's name has failed?"

Adelard pointed to the *Compendium*. "That thing was fashioned from the elements of God's earth. I know in my heart that it can be undone by the same."

Could philosophy succeed where faith had failed?

"For the sake of the Faith, let us pray you are right."

8

Tomás did pray—all that night. And in the morning, when he stepped into the hall outside his room, an acrid odor assailed his nostrils. It seemed to issue from Adelard's workroom at the end of the hall. He approached the closed door as quickly as his painful hips would allow and pulled it open without knocking.

Inside he found Adelard holding a pair of steel tongs. The gripping end of the tongs suspended a glass flask of fuming red-orange liquid over the *Compendium*.

The *Compendium* itself rested on the tile floor.

Adelard smiled at him. "You are just in time, Prior."

Tomás covered his mouth and nose and pointed to the flask. "What is that?"

"*Aqua regia*. I just now mixed it. The solution will dissolve gold, silver, platinum, almost any metal you care to name."

"Yet the simple glass of its container appears impervious."

"Glass is not metal. But the *Compendium* is."

Tomás felt his hackles rise. "This smacks of alchemy, Brother Adelard."

"Not in the least, Prior. Aqua regia was first compounded over one hundred years ago. It is simply the combination of certain of God's elements in a given ratio. No spells or incantations are required. Anyone with the recipe can do it. I will show you later, if you wish."

"That will not be necessary. What I want to know is, will it work?"

"If gold cannot stand against aqua regia, how can the *Compendium*?"

Tomás remembered having similar confidence about holy water last night.

"Please stand back, Prior. I am going to try a small amount first."

Tomás held his ground. "Start your trial."

He watched as Adelard tilted the flask and allowed a single drop of the smoking liquid to fall onto the cover. It stopped fuming on contact.

It neither bubbled nor corroded nor marred the patterned surface in any way. Frowning, Adelard slowly poured a little more over a wider area with similar result. A container of spring water would have had the same effect.

Adelard used his sandaled foot to flip the cover open, revealing a random page onto which he emptied the flask. The corrosive had no more effect there than on the cover.

Adelard's shoulders slumped, and Tomás imagined his own did as well.

"I see no recourse but a deep-sea burial," Tomás said.

Adelard lifted his head. "Not yet, good Prior. I am not yet ready to surrender. Give me three days before I must admit defeat."

Tomás considered this. Yes, they could spare three days.

"Very well. Three days, Brother Adelard, but no more. And may God speed."

9

Tomás spent those three days in prayer, often with Brother Ramiro at his side. Tribunal matters were postponed, meetings were canceled for the time being. Two *relapsos* awaited their *auto da fé* but Tomás delayed the sentence until this more pressing matter was resolved.

They did not know what Brother Adelard was up to, but Tomás was aware of the monk making many trips to and from his workroom carrying mysterious bundles of materials. Questions were raised by other members of the order, inquiring as to the cries of anger and anguish, the cacophony of hammering and sawing and smashing glass issuing from behind the closed door. Tomás was able to put them off with the simple truth: Brother Adelard was engaged in the Lord's work.

Toward the end of the third day with no results, Tomás called Ramiro to the tribunal room. He squinted at the stains and sawdust on the monk's black robe. Ramiro must have noticed the scrutiny.

"I have been making some changes in the library, Prior—doing the work myself since I no longer have a carpenter to call on."

Tomás wasn't sure if he detected a barb in that last remark. Never mind . . .

"While Brother Adelard's efforts have been heroic, every time I pass him in the hallway he reports no progress. I have given up hope of success by philosophical means. I see the ocean bottom as the only remaining option."

Ramiro nodded. "Yes, Prior. I am afraid I agree. I will be happy to make the voyage."

Tomás smiled. "How well you anticipate my thoughts. I was just about to tell you that I was assigning you the task. I do not think Brother Adelard has slept at all these past three days and he will be in no condition to make the journey."

"It is the least I can do after all his efforts."

Just then they heard a voice calling in the hallway.

"Prior Tomás! Prior Tomás! I have done it!"

Praying that Adelard was not mistaken, Tomás allowed Ramiro to help him down the hall to the workroom.

"I have been trying one combination of elements after another," Adelard said, leading the way. His eyes looked wild and his robe was pocked with countless holes burned by splashes of the corrosive compounds he had been handling. "Finally I found the one that works—quite possibly the only combination in all Creation that works!"

He reached the door and held it open for them. The workroom was full of fumes, which billowed out and ran along both the floor and ceiling of the hallway.

Ramiro waved his free arm ahead of them, parting the fumes as they reached the threshold. Tomás squinted through haze to see an odd structure sitting in the middle of the floor. It appeared to be a wooden cabinet but a deep glass bowl took up most of its upper surface. Through the smoke rising from the bowl Tomás spied what appeared to be a rectangular block of metal, immersed in a bubbling, fuming orange solution.

"What is happening here?" Tomás said.

"The *Compendium*! It is dissolving!"

Tomás prayed he wasn't dreaming. The letters and designs had been eaten off the cover, and the whole book appeared to be melting.

"But how—?"

"Through trial and error, Prior! I kept adding different compounds and solutions to the aqua regia until . . . until *this*! Isn't it wonderful?"

Yes. It was indeed wonderful.

"Praise God. He has worked a miracle." Tomás looked at Ramiro. "Don't you agree?"

Ramiro's expression was troubled, then it cleared and he offered a weak smile. "Yes, Prior. A miracle."

Tomás wondered what was distressing him. Jealous of Adelard's success? Or disappointed that he would not be going on the ocean voyage?

They watched for nearly an hour, with Adelard periodically adding fresh solution, until the *Compendium* was reduced to a mass of semi-molten metal. Adelard used tongs to remove it from the solution and lay it on the floor.

"As you can see," he said, his voice full of pride, "the *Compendium* of *Srem* is no more. The solution has fused it into a solid mass. It is not even recognizable as a book."

"I'll dispose of the remains," Ramiro said.

Adelard stepped forward. "Not necessary, Brother Ramiro. I—"

"You've done quite enough, Brother Adelard," Tomás said. "Go rest. You have earned it."

"But Prior—"

Tomás lifted his hand, halting discussion.

He did not understand Adelard's uneasy expression.

10

Tomás awoke to soft knocking on his door. It reminded him of that night not too long ago when Adelard had shown up with that accursed tome.

"Yes?"

"It is Brother Ramiro, Prior. I must speak to you on an urgent matter."

"Come, then."

He remained supine in his bed as Ramiro entered with a candle. "Good Prior, I must show you something."

"What is it?"

"It would be better to see with your own eyes."

Tomás looked up at him. "Tell me."

Ramiro took a deep breath and let out a sigh. "I wish to show you the *Compendium*."

"It was not destroyed?" Tomás closed his eyes and groaned. "How is this possible? I thought you buried what was left of it."

"I regret to inform you that what you saw dissolving was not the *Compendium*, Prior. That was a sheaf of tin sheets."

"But—"

"In addition to gold and silver and platinum, aqua regia dissolves tin."

The meaning was suddenly all too clear.

"You are accusing Brother Adelard of deceiving us!"

"Yes, Prior. Much as it pains me to say it, I fear it is so."

"This is a terribly serious charge."

Ramiro bowed his head. "That was why I wanted to show you."

"Show me what?"

"Where he has hidden the *Compendium*."

Tomás realized he would have to see for himself.

"Light my candle and wait for me in the hall."

Ramiro pressed the flame of his candle against the cold wick of the one on the desk and left. Tomás struggled from his cot and slipped on his black robe. He grabbed his cane and joined Ramiro in the hallway, then followed him to Adelard's workroom.

"I found it here," Ramiro said, opening the door.

He stepped to the acid-scarred cabinet in the center of the floor. The glass bowl in the top still contained residue from the dissolution they had witnessed yesterday. He knelt and removed a panel from the side of the cabinet. Then he removed a board from the base of the inner compartment.

"A false floor," Ramiro said.

From within the hidden compartment he removed a blanket-wrapped parcel. He placed it atop the cabinet and unfolded the wrapping, revealing . . .

The *Compendium*.

For a moment Tomás did not know what to think. Was this a trick? Was Ramiro so jealous of his fellow monk that he would—?

Just then Adelard rushed in, gasping. "Oh, no! Prior, I can explain!"

No denial on the young monk's part, only the offer of an excuse. Tomás felt crushed by this betrayal.

"Oh, Adelard, Adelard," he said, his voice barely audible. "Preserving heresy."

"It is not heresy if it is true!"

"It goes against Church doctrine, and it will raise dangerous questions. We have discussed this."

"But Prior, it won't burn, it won't be cut, it laughs at the most corrosive compounds we have. It is ancient and it is a wonder—truly a wonder. The Colossus of Rhodes, the Hanging Gardens of Babylon, the Lighthouse at Alexandria—six of the Seven Wonders of the Ancient World are gone. Only the Pyramids at Giza remain. Yet we hold the Eighth Wonder here in our hands. We have no right to keep it from the world!"

Tomás had heard enough—more than enough. Adelard was condemning himself with every word.

"Brother Adelard, you will confine yourself to your quarters until members of the Inquisition Guard bring you before the tribunal."

His eyes widened further. "The tribunal? But I am a member!"

"I am well aware of that. No more discussion. You will await judgment in your quarters."

As the crestfallen Adelard shuffled away toward his room, Tomás had no worries that he might run off. Adelard knew there was no escape from the Holy Inquisition.

What concerned Tomás was bringing a member of the tribunal before the tribunal itself to be judged. It was unprecedented. He would have to give this much thought. In the meantime . . .

"Brother Ramiro, wrap up that infernal tome and make certain that no one else sees it. Prepare to take it to sea on the earliest possible voyage."

"Yes, Prior."

He watched him fold the blanket around it, then carry it off toward his quarters. Tomás made his way to his own room and was just about to remove his cowled robe when he heard a knock on the door.

Was he never to have another full night's rest?

Ramiro's hushed voice came through the door. "I am so sorry, Prior, but I must speak with you again."

Tomás opened the door and found the portly friar standing on the threshold with a stricken expression. He held the wrapped *Compendium* against his chest. The blanket looked damp.

"It floats," he said.

"What do you mean?"

"I dropped it into a tub of water in the kitchen. It will not sink."

Tomás was not surprised. Why should it sink? That would make it too easy to dispose of.

"We will place it in trunk weighted with lead and wrapped with iron chains and—"

"Trunks rot in salt water, as do chains. Sooner or later it will surface again."

Tomás could not argue with that.

"What do we do, Brother Ramiro?"

"I have an idea . . . "

11

Tomás stood to the side while the two *relapsos* dug a deep hole at the rear of the Royal Cloister.

King Ferdinand and Queen Isabella would be arriving in a week or two to spend the summer, and the cloister would be empty until then. The queen had wanted a patio on the north side that would be shaded in the afternoon. Since the royal treasury was funding the monastery, her every whim was a command. The area had been cleared and leveled, and was now half paved with interlocking granite blocks. The remainder was bare earth. That was where the *relapsos* labored. Lanterns placed around the hole illuminated their efforts.

"Here, Prior," said Ramiro from behind him. "I brought you a chair."

He set the leather upholstered chair on the pavers and Tomás gladly made use of it. He had been holding the wrapped *Compendium* against his chest. Standing for so long had started an ache in his low back.

"This is a brilliant plan, Ramiro," he whispered.

"I live to serve the Faith. I would like to think that the Lord inspired me."

His plan was simple and yet perfect: Bury the *Compendium* in a section of the grounds that was scheduled to be paved over with heavy blocks. The *Monasterio de Santo Tomás* would stand for centuries, perhaps a thousand years or more. The *Compendium* would never be found. And if it ever were, perhaps the monks of that future time would know then how to destroy it.

But that day might never come. There would be no record anywhere of the existence of the *Compendium of Srem*, let alone where it was hidden. The two *relapsos* had no idea why they were digging the hole, and would not know what went into it. And even if they learned, what matter? Each had been sentenced to an *auto da fé*. Tomás would see to it that they had their time at the stakes early tomorrow.

Only Tomás and Ramiro would know its final resting place. The secret would die with them.

Together they watched the progress of the hole. The *relapsos* took turns in the pit: one would climb down the ladder with a shovel and fill a bucket with earth; the one topside would pull the bucket up on a rope, empty it, and send it back down. This went on until the top of the ten-foot ladder sank to a point where it was level with the surface.

"That is deep enough, I think," Tomás said.

Ramiro ordered the *relapso* down below to come up and pull the ladder from the pit. He tied their hands behind their backs. After blindfolding them, he made them kneel, facing away.

He held out his hands to Tomás. "May I, Prior?"

Tomás handed him the *Compendium* and watched as he unwrapped it. The flickering lantern light revealed the strange cover. The background pattern was crosshatching now. He closed his eyes for a few heartbeats, and when he reopened them it had changed to asymmetrical swirls.

"This is the last time anyone will ever see this book from hell," Ramiro said. He handed Tomás two cords. "I believe you deserve the honor of tying the covering around it."

Tomás tied one cord vertically and one horizontally, forming a cross, then handed it to Ramiro.

"Do you not wish to consign it to the pit?"

Tomás shook his head. His legs were tired and his back pained him. "You do it, Brother Ramiro."

"As you—?" His head shot up. "I believe I just saw a falling star."

"Where?" Tomás searched the cloudless heavens.

"It is gone. A streaking flash that lasted less than the blink of an eye. Do you think that has meaning, seeing one fall at this moment? Is it the Lord blessing our work?"

"Some say they are damned souls being cast into hell, others say they are signs of good luck. And still others say that falling stars are just that: stars that have slipped free from the dome of heaven and are falling to earth."

Ramiro was nodding. "Perhaps it is just as well not to read too much into these things." He held up the tied bundle. "I would carry it myself to the bottom but I fear my girth will not allow it."

He lifted one of the lamps as he approached the pit and held it high over the opening. Tomás watched the *Compendium* drop into the depths. Then Ramiro began shoveling dirt atop it. After half a dozen shovelfuls, he untied the *relapsos* and had them finish the job.

When they were done and the earth had been tamped flat over the hole, he bound them again, but this time he gagged them before leading them back to their cells.

Tomás remained seated, gazing at the bare earth. He would keep close watch on this patio until it was completed. Once the pavers were in place, the *Compendium* would be hidden from Mankind . . . forever.

12

The *relapsos* finally stopped screaming within their pillars of flame.

Ramiro lurched away from the town square and stumbled back toward the monastery. He had always avoided the square during an *auto da fé* but today he felt obliged to brave the dawn's chill and bear witness. Those two had repeatedly preached against the Church's practice of selling indulgences. In his heart Ramiro agreed with them, but would never be foolish enough to profess that aloud.

He had imagined the horror of seeing someone burned alive, but the reality proved worse than he had ever dreamed. Those *relapsos*, however, were gone for good. They would preach heresy no more, but more important, the location of the hole they had dug last night had been consumed with them.

As he walked along, the people who passed him averted their gaze—as usual.

He hated the Inquisition and what it had done to the Spains. He found it logical that the Church should want to safeguard the doctrines that empowered it, but at what cost? Thousands upon thousands had been tortured, hundreds upon hundreds had died in agony, tens of thousands had been banished from the land. A whole society had been upended.

But preserving the Faith was only part of it. The war for the crown of Castile, in which his family had been slaughtered, plus the war in Grenada—the whole *Reconquista*, in fact—had bankrupted the monarchy. Banishing the Jews and Moors did more than make the Spains a Christian realm. It left the abandoned properties to be looted by the Church and the royal treasury—an equal share between them. The same with heretics: the Church and the treasury divided their property and money down the middle.

Wealth and power—the two Holy Grails of church and state.

When he reached the monastery he ventured around the Royal Cloister to monitor the progress on the patio. The masons were hard at work, fitting the paving blocks snugly together, chipping away at the edges to assure a tighter fit. By tonight, or mid-tomorrow at the latest, the patio would be fully paved.

Satisfied, Ramiro moved on, entering the cloister that housed his quarters. His fellow monks spent spring mornings tilling the monastery's fields for planting. Soon he would join them, but first . . .

He descended to the basement that housed the heretics and what Torquemada liked to call the "instruments of truth"—the rack, the wheel, the thumbscrews, the boots. Adelard had been locked in one of the basement's windowless cells. No guards were needed because the doors were thick and the locks sturdy.

He approached the only locked cell and looked through the small iron-barred opening.

"Brother Adelard?" he whispered.

Adelard's face appeared. "Ramiro! Have you news? Have they decided what?"

"I am sorry. I have heard nothing. I feel terrible for betraying you."

"I know. But you had no choice. I might have done the same. I don't . . . I don't know what came over me. Almost as if that book had put a spell on me. Against all reason, I had to have it, I had to save it."

Ramiro nodded. He knew the feeling well.

He reached through a slit in his robe into a pouch strapped to his ample abdomen. From it he withdrew a small wineskin.

"Here," he said, pushing it between the bars. "For strength. For courage."

Adelard pulled off the stopper and drank greedily.

"They don't feed me and give me very little water."

How does it feel? Ramiro thought. How many have you treated the same to make them weak and more easily persuaded by your tortures?

When Adelard finished the wine he pushed the empty skin back through the opening.

"Thank you. I had no hope of any kindness here."

"I will save you some bread from the midday meal and return with it."

Adelard sobbed. "Bless you, Ramiro. Bless you!"

"I must go. I have no business here and do not wish to be caught."

"Yes. Go. I anxiously await your return."

"Good-bye, brother."

As Ramiro climbed the steps to the ground floor, he knew he would have no reason to return. The poison in the wine would kill Adelard within the hour.

He sighed with relief when he reached the library on the second floor. As usual, he had the library to himself at his time of day.

At the rear of the room he lifted one of the larger tiles and gazed at the *Compendium of Srem* where it rested in the space he had hollowed out for it. He ran his fingers over the cover.

The crimes I have committed for you . . .

The *Compendium* had been under his family's care seemingly forever, handed down from father to first-born son for more generations than he could count. But no generation had taken credit for fashioning it. The book simply *was*.

Ramiro had not been his family's first son, but after the Battle of Toro he was the only son left. He had guarded the *Compendium* then, from the

Inquisition and from others who had been searching for it down the ages. But as the Inquisition progressed, strengthening its hold on the populace and penetrating deeper and deeper into the lives of all within reach, he realized that possessing such a magical tome endangered his life. His anxiety grew to the point where he knew he had to change his ways: either flee to a different land, or hide in the belly of the beast.

He chose the latter and joined the Dominicans. He brought the *Compendium* with him, thinking the last place anyone would look for a heretical book would be in a monastery inhabited by the very order running the Inquisition. His family had never followed any religion, merely pretending to be Christians to fit in. After joining, Ramiro had found it easy to pretend, and came to enjoy the serene life of a monk.

But still his anxiety grew. He kept the *Compendium* hidden in a false bottom of his tiny bureau of drawers, but if someone found it, he would end up on the rack. He decided that he wanted to be done with guarding the *Compendium*. That had been his family's tradition, but he could no longer honor the commitment. He had to rid himself of the book, hide it for some future generation to find. But he could not allow himself to know where it was hidden, for he did not think he could resist digging it up and paging through it one more time. And one more time after that. And again after that . . .

So he had wrapped it and tied it and given it to Pedro the carpenter. He trusted the simple man to follow his instructions: Do not disturb the wrapping and bury it somewhere safe of his own choosing; he was to tell no one the location, not even Ramiro. Pedro had agreed and hurried off into the night.

Days later, Ramiro had almost swooned with shock when Adelard had invited him into his room to see the wondrous new book he had bought in the marketplace.

Pedro had betrayed him.

Right then and there Ramiro had known he wanted it back. The *Compendium* had to be his again.

He pretended to be ignorant of the book and followed along with Adelard until the trail led them to Pedro. When he'd entered the carpenter's hovel alone, he drew a knife from the sleeve of his robe and stabbed him in the heart. He had felt no remorse then and felt none now. He had trusted Pedro with a task and the man had betrayed him in a way most foul, a way that could have cost him his own life.

Ramiro knew from his family tradition across the generations that the *Compendium* had survived flood and blade and fire. That was why he had attacked it so enthusiastically with the headsman's axe: He had known the book would be impervious.

And then Adelard's pathetic attempt to fool them into thinking he had found a solvent to destroy the *Compendium*. Torquemada's eyes were poor, but Ramiro knew the book too well and had recognized the decoy for what it was. After that it was a simple matter of finding where Adelard had hidden the original.

Regaining possession had been the easiest. After making sure Torquemada had tied up the *Compendium* himself, Ramiro pretended to see a falling star. While the old man was searching the sky, Ramiro reached through the slit in his robe into the same pouch where he had hidden Adelard's wine this morning. He removed Adelard's tin fake, wrapped identically as the original. The true *Compendium* took its place in the pouch and Adelard's fake went into the earth.

Ramiro shook his head. He had lied for the *Compendium*, killed for it, betrayed and killed a friend for it, then stolen it back from the Grand Inquisitor himself.

Perhaps you are from hell, he thought, touching the raised lettering. Look what you've made me do.

But no, the *Compendium* was not from hell. Adelard had been right: It came from the past, from before the Deluge. Indeed, it *was* the Eighth Wonder of the Ancient World. But it must remain hidden from the modern world. Not for Torquemada's reason of a threat to the Faith—Ramiro cared not for any faith—but because the world did not need it yet.

He replaced the tile and headed for the fields.

Pedro and Adelard and the two *relapsos* were dead. One look at Torquemada and anyone could tell that the Grand Inquisitor would soon be joining them. The Morisco from the marketplace was practically illiterate and had no idea what treasure he had held. Only Asher ben Samuel remained, and as a *converso* targeted by the tribunal, he would never talk about it.

The *Compendium* seemed safe . . . at least for the moment.

Ramiro's family tradition said the *Compendium* was a thing of destiny, with an important role to play in the future. Ramiro had rededicated himself to preserving it for that future. It would be safer hidden under the library floor than in the chest of drawers in his room or buried in a field. Someday it would find its place in the future and fulfill its destiny.

One day he would leave the order and find a wife. He would have a son and start a new tradition of protecting the *Compendium*.

But until then it would belong to him and him alone. No one else could touch it or read of the marvels described and pictured within. Only him.

Ramiro liked it that way.

The Gospel of Sheba

Lyndsay Faye

A soprano with a high pop belt, Lyndsay Faye holds a dual degree in English and Performance from Notre Dame de Namur University and worked as a professional actress throughout the Bay Area for several years.

Faye's first novel, *Dust and Shadow: an Account of the Ripper Killings by Dr. John H Watson*, is a tribute to the aloof genius and his good-hearted friend whose exploits she has loved since childhood. Her second and third novels, *The Gods of Gotham* and its sequel, *Seven for a Secret*, follow ex-bartender-turned-policeman Timothy Wilde as he navigates the rapids of violently turbulent nineteenth century New York City.

Faye and her husband live just north of Harlem with their cats, Grendel and Prufrock. During the few hours a day she isn't writing or editing, she is most often cooking or sampling microbrew. Faye is a proud member of Actor's Equity Association, the Adventuresses of Sherlock Holmes, the Baker Street Babes, the Baker Street Irregulars, Mystery Writers of America, and Girls Write Now.

Letter sent from Mrs. Colette Lomax to Mr. A. Davenport Lomax,
September 3rd, 1902.

My only darling,

You cannot possibly comprehend the level of incompetence to which I was subjected today.

You know full well I *never* demand a private dressing room when stationary, as the very notion implies a callous disrespect for the sensitivities of other artists. However, it cannot pass my notice when I am engaged in a *second class* chamber en route from Reims to Strasbourg. The porter assured me that private cars were simply not available on so small a railway line as our company was forced to book—and yet, I feel justified in suspecting the managers have hoaxed their "rising star" once again. The reek of soup from the dining car's proximity alone would depress my spirits, even were my ankles not confined one atop the other in a padlock-like fashion.

I do so loathe *krautsuppe*. Hell, I assure you, my love, simmers with the aroma of softening cabbage.

The little towns with their sloping roofs and single church spires whir past whilst I write to you as if they were so many picture postcards. It's dreadfully tedious. Loss of privacy for my vocal exercises notwithstanding, my usual transitory repose is impaired by the snores of a typist en route to a new position as well as a mother whose infant does us the discourtesy of weeping infinitely. Bless fair fortune that our Grace has already grown to be guiltless of such alarming impositions—though as you often remind me, I am not present at our home often enough to state so with scientific certitude. The fact you are right pains me more than I can express. Please pull our daughter close, and know in the meanwhile that I have never been more revoltingly ungrateful to be engaged in an operatic tour.

How have your colleagues responded to your request for a more appropriate wage as sublibrarian? The Librarian in particular? I cannot imagine a more worthy candidate than you for promotion, and thus live in hope that you have been celebrating so ardently that you simply neglected to inform your wife of the good news.

All my love, infinitely,

Mrs. Colette Lomax

Note pasted in the commonplace book of Mr. A. Davenport Lomax, September 3rd, 1902.

Papa,

This morning after chasing butterflys in the back area with the net you gav me I was asked by Miss Church if I wanted to go inside and record the shapes of their wings as I remembered them, I wanted to but more than that thought if there are butterflys why not faeries? You've allways said they don't exist apart from our imaginashuns but I know we must use the sientific method to find out for certain and maybe they are real after all. I tried to find proof they *weren't* real and didn't manage it.

Love, Grace

Excerpt from the private journal of Mr. A. Davenport Lomax, September 3rd, 1902.

I have been pondering imponderables of late.

How comes it, for instance, that within mortal viruses like anthrax and rabies, potions can be extracted from poisons, and a doctor the caliber of Pasteur can create a vaccine from the disease itself? How comes it that my wife, Lettie, who apparently loves me "infinitely," accepts operatic contracts removing her from my presence for the foreseeable future? How comes it that a sublibrarian constantly assured of the value of his scholarship cannot so much as afford to keep his own carriage, let alone an automobile, and more often than not travels via the Underground?

I've always adored paradox but, admittedly, some are far more tedious than others.

Take this contradiction, for example: compliments, at least insofar as my position at the London Library is concerned, have become a decided blight. The moment I accept a semi-public compliment from the Librarian—a press of his withered hand to my shoulder as we pass amidst the stacks, a wet and fibrous cough of approval when he is within earshot of my advice to our members—I am automatically consulted upon countless further topics. Last week it was rare species of maidenhair ferns, this week the principles of bridge engineering. Next week, I brace myself to field queries upon monophonic chants or perhaps the dietary habits of the domestic black pig.

The life of a sublibrarian surely wasn't intended to be quite this difficult? Walking through St. James's Square towards the queerly narrow building, the fog's perennial grime painting a thin veneer upon the Portland stone and the many windowpanes distorting movements of blurred, faceless strangers within, I feel worn after merely setting boot upon the Library's foyer rug. By the time I've hung my overcoat in the cloakroom, I've practically exhausted myself. I adore learning of all types, but one cannot imagine that Sisyphean labour was countenanced in Carlyle's day.

Or perhaps it was, and the sublibrarians present wisely elected not to record their woes.

To boot, Lettie's travels leave me the indisputable guardian of little Grace's heart and mind. I find myself fretting over this critical task more often than is remotely necessary, given that 1) I am a scholar of some note, and an intellectual omnivore, and thus should act with confidence 2) Grace is a singularly apt and gentle child, and 3) Lettie has not been at home for longer than a fortnight in six months' time, so I ought to be accustomed to this by now.

Her absence is far more wearing than her presence is costly. Mind, I knew when we wed that her tastes ran more to champagne and cracked oysters than beer and peanut shells. But Lettie is brilliant in her own whimsical fashion, and back when I rhapsodized more over lights flickering across her hair arrangements than what was beneath the tiara, we hadn't a daughter demanding to know whether moonbeams possess the quality of weight. Lacking Lettie, who would have delivered a wonderfully silly answer, I found myself at an absurd crossroads this morning between wanting to assure Grace that one could feel the weight of a moonbeam if sensitive enough and to tell her that, according to recent postulations, velocity is much more relevant to the subject than density.

Well, never mind Lettie. I ever want to think of her as happy, and I've told her so numberless times, and she is happiest when singing. Therefore the rest of us will toddle along on our own and no one the worse for it. I shall think of Lettie with her golden hair piled atop her head, smiling in a sly, knowing fashion over the footlights, and be content.

After all, I find myself effortlessly contented when with Grace. And she with me, shockingly. All is watercolours and learning to whistle and nothing extraneous to distract us from the immediate bright sun of the rear yard or the cheerful green ivy paper of the nursery walls. Arrogantly, I suspect spending more time with Grace will prove a benefit to her. I trust that Miss Church does her best, but she is neither a close reasoner nor an artist, and thus as a governess cannot be expected to shape a child into anything other than a prosaic mouse.

Earlier today, speaking of mice, I enjoyed a bizarre appointment with one at the London Library. Mr. Theodore Grange entered my little office with the stated purpose of consulting me upon the subject of ceremonial magic, but he could as easily have wondered where the best cheese rinds were to be found (either way, I am armed with sufficient books to oblige him). His thin lips twitched following every pronouncement, his eyes were dull and brown, his hair without shine, his blinks frequent, the skin beneath his eyes too loose, his aspect altogether melancholy.

"I was sent to you upon the very *best* recommendation, Mr. Lomax," he squeaked, mopping the sweat from his upper lip though it is quite frigid in the library for September, and the light through the windows tinged coolly blue. "It's imperative you tell me everything you know about black magic—and at once."

"In that case, I shall," I answered hesitantly, this request being without precedent. "Mr. . . . ?"

"Grange, sir, Mr. Theodore Grange. Thank heaven," he exhaled. "I feared lest you hadn't the time. I have it from the head Librarian himself that you are positively encyclopedic in your studies, sir!"

"Do you," I sighed.

"Indeed so! You are my last and best hope—the Brotherhood of Solomon may not exist in a year, sir, without your expert support. We are tearing apart as a society! Ripping at the very seams, and even as its newest member, my heart breaks at the prospect."

"Then we cannot allow such a thing to happen," I said dubiously, leading him through tall byways of polished wood shelves and worn leather binding to the appropriate stacks.

Whilst eager folk demanding I tell them definitively whether faeries or dragons or succubus exist are often fanciful simpletons (leaving aside little Grace, who ought to be asking such things), I found myself feeling strangely sympathetic towards Mr. Grange. The man seems fragile as antique paper, and I lent him a friendly ear as we went, our boots singing softly against the wrought iron stairs. Specifically, Mr. Grange is interested in grimoires and their efficacy. I felt nearly as delicate in telling him their efficacy was negligible as I would discrediting Father Christmas to Grace, so determined not to press the issue. We've several occult texts within the collection, which ought to suit him admirably well.

"With your expert help, I can now prove or disprove the validity of *The Gospel of Sheba* once and for all!" he proclaimed, shaking my hand.

"I should like nothing better," I assured him, as in the dark as previous and increasingly amused by the fact.

Mr. Theodore Grange lingers in my memory still, brandy in hand and feet stretched towards the hearth as Grace flips through my astronomical charts. I admit my preoccupation strange, for I cannot know whether I shall exchange words with him again at all; I lent him our most reliable books upon the dubious topic of dark magic, and I may not be present when he returns them to the collection. My curiosity over the man is likely to go unslaked. In any case, I must assist Grace in constructing a mobile of the solar system at her request and then pen a reply to Lettie. Mr. Grange's intentions are by no means the business of a sublibrarian after his duty has been executed.

Unsettling, the way a man's mind can wander from subject to subject. I sit here adoring every aspect of Grace which makes her unmistakably Lettie's this evening—pale skin pearlescent in the firelight, the nearly stubborn pout of her lip, the green-tinged blue of her eye—while simultaneously experiencing a joy akin to relief that she owns copious soft brown curls like mine, that her hands are steady and deft as mine are, and that her chin is square and without cleft.

What an altogether unworthy observation, though I suppose a predictably paternal one. Who the devil else should Grace look like? I shall make every effort never to repeat such a brutish study and consider the subject well closed.

Letter sent from Mrs. Colette Lomax to Mr. A. Davenport Lomax, September 8th, 1902.

My only darling,

Have just attempted to rectify a ghastly nightmare in which my production company saw fit to house me in a dwelling which could rock the scientific community were mould studies a lucrative exploit. (Are they, love? Hasten to me and capitalize upon a fresh source of riches!) In lieu of longer explanation, I shall state that the colour of the bedclothes were not typical and leave the remainder to your fertile imagination.

How is Grace faring? The picture she sent of the star system you were studying through your telescope was such a comfort to me. Shortly before I come down with fatal pneumonia—as seems inevitable when I allow myself to study the state of this place in any detail—I'll mark down the constellations I can see from my thin little window and request you quiz her on the subject.

Performing Massenet's *Sapho* in a European pretension of a city is not the activity I wish to be engaged in during my final days, alas. Think of me fondly, and know that I suffered for my art.

All my love,
Mrs. Colette Lomax

Excerpt from the private journal of Mr. A. Davenport Lomax, September 9th, 1902.

"It's absolutely no good, Mr. Lomax!" Mr. Theodore Grange piped shrilly this morning, reappearing after an absence of six days and dropping the magical texts I'd recommended upon a table from emphatic height. "This grimoire of Mr. Sebastian Scovil's is the genuine article. I have researched extensively along the lines which you suggested and am forced to conclude that a hitherto undiscovered demonic text of great power and possibly greater malevolence has been unearthed!"

Looking up while removing my set of half-spectacles, I took a moment to goggle at the poor fellow. He'd discovered me in the reading and periodicals room. I'd tucked myself out of immediate sight under one of the tall white pillars in a commodious leather armchair, subtly hiding from the Librarian as I studied ancient Celtic coins on behalf of a member. Mr. Grange landed in the chair opposite, the hearth's glow illuminating the unhealthy sweat upon his brow.

"Your friend Mr. Scovil is likewise interested in occult studies?" I hazarded, glad to see him again in spite of my preoccupation.

He waved an unsteady hand before his face. "All of us are, to a man—the Brotherhood of Solomon exists to study the supernatural. I am its newest member, as I told you, and thus less tutored than my fellows in what ignorant folk term the dark arts. The club is a small one, and consists of influential men of business, you understand. My firm invests in a wide variety of securities, and thus cultivating acquaintances with such people is essential to me—and really, what is the difference between forming friendships over whiskey and cigars at a horse race versus whiskey and cigars hunched over magical manuscripts?"

There seemed to me to be quite a bit of difference, but I neglected to point this out.

"I was a skeptic, I'll admit as much," Mr. Grange said hoarsely, shuddering. "A grimoire which poisons all who dare to study it, save for those with the purest of intentions and keenest skills? Preposterous. And yet, I am convinced. *The Gospel of Sheba* is a text of extraordinary power, and a power Mr. Scovil alone can wield."

Tapping my spectacles against my lip, I pondered. Grimoires are paradoxes after my own heart. They tend to contain explicit instructions as to the rituals necessary to summon demons and, having summoned them, bind them to the magician's will. Ceremonial magic to an enormous extent, however, is said to depend upon the virtue of the sorcerer—his altruism in calling upon angels or their fallen brethren to do his bidding—and by definition, to my mind, a chap whistling for Beelzebub is likely to be up to no good.

"A book which poisons those who study it?" I repeated, fascinated. "Surely that is impossible."

Mr. Grange shook his head, pulling a small square of silk from his pocket and mopping the back of his neck. His appearance was, if anything, more unhealthy than the man I'd met six days previous. An ashen quality dulled the limp folds of his throat, and his eyes reflected steady pain.

"I am myself suffering from the effects of reading *The Gospel of Sheba*," he assured me. "After reaching the conclusion, thanks to the volumes you lent me, that its provenance is undoubtedly genuine, I lost no time in returning the wretched thing to Mr. Scovil. He is a great scholar of the esoteric, the discoverer of the gospel, and the one man who suffers no ill effects from it."

A numismatist, perhaps, would have absorbed this madness with aplomb and returned to the study of the lyrical golden images stamped upon the coinage of the Parisii. I am not a numismatist, however, and thus closed the volume on Celtic coinage and begged Mr. Grange to tell me more. The poor man seemed eager to unburden himself. He shifted in his chair, darting glances along the sparsely populated reading room as if he feared being overheard.

"It's been two months since I joined the Brotherhood of Solomon," he murmured. "An acquaintance of mine, a Mr. Cornelius Pyatt, recommended it to me as a worthy hobby—one followed by men of intellect and character and means. I attended a meeting and found the company and the wine cellar both to my liking, and the subject to be of considerable interest. Are you familiar with the types of ceremonial magic? I confess I was not, and have since grown quite obsessed, sir."

"Somewhat familiar," I owned, wiping my half-spectacles upon my sleeve. "Spellcasting is divided in the broadest sense into white magic and black magic, which differ less in execution than in intention. White magic attempts to summon good spirits, and to a good purpose—black magic evil spirits, and to a wicked purpose. Other categorical distinctions are regional, of course. One would find different instructions in a text of Parisian diabolism than in the Hebrew Kabalah, but all are paths to mastery of the spirit realm. Or so they claim."

"Just so!" he approved. "Just so, sir, and the Brotherhood of Solomon's express purpose is explore the sacred mysteries recorded by the legendarily wise Biblical King Solomon."

A less than comfortable thrill wormed its way through my belly. "You study S. Liddell Mathers' eighteen eighty-eight English translation of *The Key of Solomon the King*, in that case. I read it with interest when I was at university."

"Did you indeed? Wonderful! What drew you to it?"

"I felt I needed to see for myself what the fuss was about, probably because all types of knowledge interest me and that one seemed marvelously forbidden. I'm sorry to tell you I didn't find much sense in it."

The Key of Solomon the King is the monarch of all the grimoires, the eldest surviving copies dating from the Italian Renaissance, though its purported author was the great Hebrew ruler himself. The Latin codex translated by Mathers resides at the British Museum. It's full of orations, conjurations, invocations, and recitations, some of them for the purpose of summoning spirits and others for tricking one's enemies or for finding lost objects. I never went so far as to write anything out in bat's blood, but I do recall, as a more than half-humourous experiment, searching for a lost penknife by means of reciting:

O Almighty Father and Lord, Who regardest the Heavens, the Earth, and the Abyss, mercifully grant unto me by Thy Holy Name written with four letters, YOD, HE, VAU, HE, that by this exor-

cism I may obtain virtue, Thou Who art IAH, IAH, IAH, grant
that by Thy power these Spirits may discover that which we require
and which we hope to find, and may they show and declare unto
us the persons who have committed the theft, and where they are to
be found.

The penknife never turned up, but I felt suitably irreligious
afterward that despite owning no very strong godly passions,
I plunged myself into a study of the early Christian martyrs
until I felt that some balance had been restored to my soul.
And Lettie, upon being told the tale when we were courting,
had a heartily fond laugh over my foolishness.

"The Brotherhood of Solomon revere his teachings above all
others." Mr. Grange loosened his necktie. He seemed feverish,
a bright red flush adorning his cheeks. "We've all been thrown
into *such* disarray since Mr. Scovil found the Sheba text. Our
meetings generally consist of debate over particular ceremonies
found in *The Key of Solomon the King*—whether incenses and
perfumes are of any tangible efficacy when enacting spells,
study of the Order of the Pentacles, the proper preparation of
virgin parchment and whether blood sacrifice is truly evil if
enacted for a noble purpose, that sort of thing."

Fighting not to laugh, I gestured with the spectacles in my
hand to continue.

"But then Mr. Scovil announced that a secret library had
been found within his very own townhouse in Pall Mall, and
that it was full of magical texts, and that one of them—*The
Gospel of Sheba*—was an unprecedented find. Mr. Sebastian
Scovil is from a very long line of esoteric scholars, Mr. Lomax,
so we greeted his discovery with ardent interest. But the book
itself is cursed, I assure you, sir! There is no other explanation."

"A little slower," I requested. "As a bibliophile, not to mention a lover of conundrums, your story is terribly interesting.
Let me be certain I understand you?"

"By all means, Mr. Lomax."

"First, speaking historically, King Solomon was renowned for his great wisdom, and for his closeness to God, and the hopes of those studying grimoires ascribed to him are that his words remain largely intact. The Queen of Sheba was the monarch of a lost African kingdom who appears in the Koran as well as the Bible and traveled to meet with King Solomon after tales of his great wealth and wisdom reached her people. Have I got the proper context?"

"As concise as any encyclopedia and as accurate, sir! The gospel purports to be written in her hand, revealing ceremonial rites more powerful than any King Solomon developed before meeting her. Apparently the King and the Queen were lovers, Mr. Lomax, and brought the study of ceremonial magic to new heights."

"The text is in Hebrew?"

"The text is in Latin, sir, transcribed by a sixteenth century monk, we believe."

"And you claim it has made you physically *ill*?" I demanded, awed.

Mr. Theodore Grange did, to give him credit, look very ill indeed. Even were his colour not similar to candle wax and his limbs all a-quiver, he seemed to have shrunk somehow in the six days since I'd seen him, his skin shrugged on as if a child were wrapped in its father's coat. His navy blue suit was likewise too large, twiglike wrists obscenely thrusting out from gaping cuffs.

"Not just me!" he protested. "First my friend Cornelius Pyatt took the volume home to study, and he fell ill almost instantly. Then Huggins had a crack at it, and we're all three in the same sad straits. No, I tell you, that gospel is the genuine article and Mr. Sebastian Scovil is the single man worthy of its powers."

"Oh, there you are, Mr. Lomax, at last I've found you."

The gentle, rasping tones of the Librarian startled me out of my rapt attention. My head shifted upward to take in his bowed back, the genial tufts of hair about his ears, the air of absentminded benevolence that wafts about with him like the aroma of his sweet pipe smoke, and prayed that I would not be complimented.

"Apologies, sir, did you want me?" I asked.

"Oh, no, no, my boy, you appear engaged. But Mr. Sullivan, I should tell you, was *most* pleased by your assistance with his geological studies. He claimed that you identified a book which shed all manner of light upon his research into sedimentary facies. You are to be congratulated again, Mr. Lomax."

There is a many-paned window at the end of the periodicals room, and reflected in its glass I could see Mr. Grange and the Librarian, my own slender seated figure with its mop of wildly curling brown hair, and the six or seven members who had perked up and were now eyeing me with interest, wondering what arcane knowledge I could gift them before tea time.

"Thank you, sir," I said, rubbing at my eyes. "I did my best."

"Quite right, quite right. Carry on, then! You do us credit, Mr. Lomax, and I don't care who knows it."

Chuckling in resignation, my eyes drifted back to the volume I'd abandoned when Mr. Grange arrived. It was nearly lunch hour and time for a hastily procured sandwich or at least the apple in my greatcoat pocket, I didn't know nearly enough about Celtic coinage to assist Mr. McGraw yet, and he was due at the Library at one o'clock sharp. Outside, a thin patter of rain had commenced, darkening the paving stones of St. James's Square and quickening the steps of the shivering pedestrians below.

"Mr. Grange, I should love to hear more about *The Gospel of Sheba*, truly, but my mind is spoken for at the moment." Rising, I gathered the magical volumes he'd returned, meaning to check them in. "When is the next meeting of the Brotherhood of Solomon? Might a stray bibliophile be welcome in your company?"

"Oh, undoubtedly, Mr. Lomax!" Mr. Theodore Grange cried, mirroring me. Grasping my hand in his palsied one, he shook it. "I was about to propose the very thing. Tuesday next is our regular gathering. We dine at the Savile Club in Picadilly. The works of scholarship you were kind enough to lend me introduced no doubts in my mind as to the authenticity of *The Gospel of Sheba*, but I would greatly value a fresh pair of eyes. We have been at each other's throats over this discovery, and two chaps have quit the club entirely, claiming outright Satanic influence at work regarding our sudden poor health. I shall look forward to seeing you at eight o'clock sharp, Mr. Lomax, and in the meanwhile wish you a very good week."

Frowning as I watched Mr. Grange depart, I went to check in his returns, placing them upon a cart to be shelved. A book possessed of such occult power that it worked upon the reader like a disease? Impossible.

And yet, I had witnessed the decline of Mr. Grange myself. The man appeared to be shriveling before my very eyes into a grey husk.

Could poison be at work here? Something more pedestrian but no less sinister than demonic influence?

The very question is unnerving. I am not callow enough to suppose that books are not powerful—on the contrary, a book is the most delicious of paradoxes, an inert collection of symbols which are capable of changing the universe when once the cover is opened. Imagine what the world would look like had the Book of John never been written, or *On the Revolutions of Celestial Spheres*, or *Romeo and Juliet*? One day I attended the opera and was captivated by a beautiful blonde soprano with a mocking blue eye and a milk-white neck with the loveliest smooth hollows, but I fell in love with Colette when she admitted to me that she couldn't read Petrarch's poems to Laura without weeping and had never bothered over being ashamed of the fact.

I look forward to Tuesday with the greatest interest. Meanwhile, Celtic currency calls to me and I've a new set of picture-books to bring home to Grace this evening.

Excerpt from the private journal of Mr. A. Davenport Lomax,
September 15th, 1902.

What a ghastly day this was.

My friend Dr. John Watson stopped by the London Library in need of my assistance late in the evening, looking battlefield-grim. All the newspapers have been screaming that his friend Mr. Sherlock Holmes was attacked by men armed with sticks outside the Café Royal a week ago today and is languishing at the door of death. Whatever they were investigating, they still seem to be in the thick of it. I berated myself at once for not having wired asking after Watson's well-being. He little considers the topic himself.

"My God, Watson, how are you?" I whipped my half-spectacles off when the doctor came into sight cresting a spiraling staircase. Lost in thought in a peculiarly narrow Library byway, I stood seeking out a book on native Esquimaux art for a member. "More to the point, how is Mr. Holmes?"

Watson smiled, a sincerely meant expression that nevertheless failed to meet his eyes. As a collector of dichotomies, I am rather fascinated by Watson. I met him four years ago, before being hired at the London Library, when I used to frequent his club prior to my marriage to Lettie. We share an interest in cricket, and I think the kaleidoscopic quality of my studies amuses him. Watson is a doctor and a soldier, about two decades my senior but no less hearty for that, and the man is so utterly decent that he ought to be the most appalling bore in Christendom. The fact that he is just the opposite is therefore rather baffling. He is well-built and sturdy, a bit shorter than I am, with a neatly groomed brown moustache and an air of rapt attention when he is listening to you. But this evening he looked exhausted, a solid line etched between his brows and his hat clutched a bit too hard in his fingers.

"Between the two of us, Lomax, Holmes is better than can be expected, which . . . frankly is still not well at all," he sighed, shaking my hand. "I'm to lay it on thick for the papers, but I trust in your discretion. He'll make a full recovery, thank God."

I have never been introduced to Sherlock Holmes, but like the rest of London and possibly the world am deeply intrigued by Watson's accounts of his exploits. "His attackers are known to you?"

Watson's determined jaw tightened as he nodded once. "The case is a complex one, with the safety of a lady at stake, or I should have horsewhipped them by this time."

"Naturally. Can I do anything?"

"As a matter of fact, you can. I'm to spend the next twenty-four hours in an intensive study of Chinese pottery."

"To what purpose?"

The smallest hint of mystified good humour entered his blue eyes. "Surely you know better than to ask. I haven't the smallest notion."

Laughing, I waved the doctor further into the labyrinthine stacks. He left with a mighty book under his arm, making promises of an evening of billiards. Watson has a brisk military stride, and I could not help but compliment myself that it appeared more buoyant as he exited than when he'd first appeared.

I saw the two of them once, outside of a tobacconist's in Regent Street. I'd have known Mr. Holmes from his likeness in the newspapers, not to mention the *Strand Magazine*, but when Watson appeared in his wake, I was sure of myself. Sherlock Holmes and John Watson were exiting with replenished cigarette cases, Dr. Watson casting about for a cab, and they were so complete together. Wanting no other company save themselves. Watson, just as their hansom slowed, stopped to flip a coin to a crippled veteran by the side of the road—and Mr. Holmes, who cannot be a patient man at the best of times, rather than pull a face, simply called out to the driver to ensure they kept their cab. They reminded me of my wife alongside her cohorts at the end of a lengthy curtain call, air reeking of hothouse roses and the heat sending trickles of sweat down the faces of worshipful spectators—and all the while, the performers in perfect, casual tune.

They are just as Grace and I are together, I've decided. The harmony. The friendship, the complete ease. Mr. Holmes's genius seems the icy sort, all edges and angles, but despite his legendary prickliness, he is most certainly held in the highest esteem. I don't like to think of how Watson looked this afternoon.

I must turn the lamp down and retire shortly. What odd connections we make as we pass through life—old friends, new ones, perhaps if we're lucky even ones we've brought into being. But why do I remain so pensive over such a happy topic? I must confess, though camaraderie of the highest level is deeply satisfying and fatherhood still more so, I miss Lettie terribly. The romance which so bafflingly visiting a bookish scholar's life has departed, leaving bare halls with traces of magic swept away under carpeting. It has been so long since the early days of our marriage, when we lay entwined with the windows open, breakfasting upon stale bread and returning hastily to mussed bedclothes, hours lost in poetry and skin.

It has been so very long since Lettie chose to *stay*.

Tomorrow at least I shall have the distraction of the Brotherhood of Solomon. What on earth can the matter be with these people and their accursed new acquisition? I've been dying to discover the truth, and I don't mind admitting it. One hopes that the morrow will reveal all.

*Letter sent from Mrs. Colette Lomax to Mr. A. Davenport Lomax,
September 16th, 1902.*

Dearest,

I fear that I write with as much speed as affection today. The sudden epidemic of stupidity which appears to have beset our company managers has led to our being double-booked: both at the theatre where we are paid to sing, and at the country home of a Bavarian duke's who has decided that I am a better English interpreter of Germanic music than many of my predecessors, where we *are not paid to sing*.

You can imagine I am both flattered and furious. But the Duke himself is charming enough despite being pasty and made all appropriate apologies for my being forced to attend a champagne fete when in a state of such exhaustion, so I suppose complaints are unworthy of me. The repast was admittedly beyond reproach—I haven't tasted caviar this fine in a twelvemonth or more.

More anon, love, and kiss Grace for me,

Mrs. Colette Lomax

Excerpt from the private journal of Mr. A. Davenport Lomax, September 16th, 1902.

I've emerged victorious, with a terribly queer book upon my desk. But I shall tell it in order, I suppose, or never recall it correctly.

Not having been there previous, I noted that the Savile Club is done in the traditional style, its walls teeming with textural flourishes and a quiet pomp in the mouldings accenting its ivory ceilings. Art abounds, as does crystal, as does the sort of furniture inviting terribly expensive trousers to be seated. There was quite a grand fire in the dining room we occupied, and the requisite set of picture-windows—all the details one expects when one comes from old money, not actually possessing any. But that is the lot of having a great many brothers, I suppose, and when one is younger, and a natural scientist, one is trusted to do well on one's own. I arrived at ten minutes to eight, rather at a loss over introductions after handing away my coat. But I was prevented any awkwardness by Mr. Grange, who charged (well, made weak haste, anyhow) towards me within seconds.

"Mr. Lomax!" he cried. His complexion, previously grey, had gained a slight touch of pink in the week we were apart, though his appetite clearly had not returned and his upper lip twitched tremulously. "Just the man we wanted—here, may I present my friend Mr. Cornelius Pyatt, another investor like myself and the one who introduced me to the Brotherhood of Solomon."

As I entered the dining room fully, I shook hands with a sallow man of perhaps forty years with a calculating expression and a crow's sable hair. Mr. Pyatt, according to Mr. Grange, likewise suffered the ghastly effects of *The Book of Sheba*, but he seems to have made a full recovery if so. His handshake was certainly firm enough, and his aspect one of clear, cutting focus.

"Delighted to meet you, Mr. Lomax," he professed. "I hear you've consented to get to the bottom of this business. And high time, too, though I am by now convinced we are dealing with mighty supernatural forces. I was quite prostrate with the effects of studying this volume some weeks ago."

"So I have heard. I'm happy to see you are well again," I answered. Another man stepped forward from the depths of the carpeted dining room, and I stepped aside to include him. "But I cannot understand how such a thing could be possible outside the realm of ghost stories. The best sort of ghost stories, of course."

"I thought precisely as you did, Mr. Lomax," admitted the newcomer. "Especially since I failed to suffer the symptoms associated with exposure to the book myself. It all seemed the merest coincidence, or else an especially grim fairy tale. But as the evidence mounts, I grow ever more convinced that my find was a monumental one. Mr. Sebastian Scovil, at your service, and eager to hear your conclusions."

If I come from old money which leaked away from the Lomax family in small but steady trickles, surely Mr. Scovil's funding commenced with the Pharaohs and built its way upward from there. He was a small man, very quietly dressed in grey, with every seam and tuck so perfectly tailored in the finest traditional taste that you could have made a model of the chap based solely upon his clothing and not the other way round. His brown eyes twinkled, his apple cheeks shone with cheer, and the pocket watch he consulted after shaking my hand cost a hundred quid if it cost a shilling. Which it probably hadn't, since the initials etched upon it ended duly in *S*. An inheritance, no doubt, to the diminutive yet decisive heir apparent. Mr. Sebastian Scovil was so very small, as a matter of fact, and so very wealthy in appearance, that he brought to mind a Lilliputian dignitary.

"I am eager to see it, as I've dedicated my life to books of all sorts," I owned, my pulse quickening.

"Come, come sir!" Mr. Grange exclaimed. "I told Mr. Scovil as much, and you shall examine it at once! Right this way."

We passed further into the dining area, towards a table where several well-to-do fellows stood muttering—some angrily, some raptly—over a cloth-veiled object. They were successful businessmen on the clubbable model, warm when it came to handshakes and ruthless when it came to figures. The fact they didn't suppose consorting with the devil to be any particular blemish so long as the chequebook balanced at the end of the day failed to shock me; the acquisition of money is a high virtue indeed in some circles.

I was such a man myself once, at university. For a month after I was given to understand there would be a small allowance but no inheritance from the Lomax estate, I studied with the deliberate intent of becoming a tycoon. Then a fellow cricketer left a book upon Persian stonemasonry lying about and I was lost to the world for days save for the classes I could not miss. After coming out of my trance by means of finishing the final page, I realized that I didn't actually desire the rare objects money could procure me—I only wanted to know all about them. I told Lettie that tale, on one of her tours when I scandalously joined her in Paris before we were wed, and she smirked and reached in all her bare glory for her wine glass and said it was all right, we could have the smallest house in the West End.

"But *in the West End*, mind," she'd added mock-sternly, pulling her fingertips down the planes of my chest.

"Mr. Lomax is here as an impartial expert!" Mr. Grange squeaked. "Please, gentlemen, step aside and allow him to view *The Gospel of Sheba* uninhibited. Your questions and comments will be answered in due course."

"It's not much to look at," Mr. Scovil said ruefully as the Brotherhood parted and he flipped aside the black velvet wrapping. A pair of white cotton gloves rested next to the shabby volume he uncovered, and I donned them after sliding my half-spectacles up my nose. "Which to my way of thinking—as a connoisseur and never a professional, mind—stands in its favour. I've a wretchedly old townhouse the family expects me to care for, eighteenth century you know, impossible to heat, and I discovered this in a secret room behind a sliding panel along with many other books of esoteric medicine and alchemy. Here is *The Gospel of Sheba*, Mr. Lomax, make what you will of it. Apparently I'm the only chap it's taken a liking to thus far."

Leaning down with pale gloves hovering, I eased back the cover. The Brotherhood of Solomon behind me engaged in muttered speculations—questions as to my presence, accusations of the book's fraudulence, warnings over the dangers in dabbling with ancient vice.

The Gospel of Sheba certainly looked like a sixteenth century document to me. It still does, here upon my desk, while Grace slumbers down the hall with her stuffed rabbit clutched to her neck. It was re-bound around two hundred years ago, I believe, with crackling blue animal hide stamped in black, but the paper seemed very old indeed and the penmanship typically cramped and mesmerizing. Books can own a curiously hypnotic draw, and this is one of them, whatsoever its occult capacities may be.

Conscious of many eyes boring into me, I moved with care through the pages, noting esoteric symbols paired with line drawings of recognizably African beasts, and recalled that the Queen of Sheba was the all-powerful ruler of her Ethiope empire. There was something electrifying about thinking it possible—that here were her occult studies, combined with King Solomon's over the sort of giddy intimacy Lettie and I used to share, preserved by an obscure Christian monk without a name or a legacy many centuries later. I said as much.

"Yes, precisely!" cried one of the Brotherhood. "It's the most important discovery since *The Key of Solomon the King* itself."

"It's a bloody hoax," sighed a bearded banker.

"It's evil made manifest, Mr. Jenkins, and you ought *not* to be playing with such fire," whimpered a third man, who kept himself well away from proceedings and had poured himself a very large glass of claret. "We are scholars, mystics, men who seek the ancient insights of a Biblical king—we are not *sorcerers*, scheming to unleash the furies of hell upon our enemies."

"I can think of one or two enemies I'd not mind lending that book to, as a matter of fact, if it weren't a fraud," quipped the banker called Jenkins, and several chuckled.

"Stop *touching* it, I tell you. No purity of soul could withstand the summoning of the creatures listed in that blasphemous thing."

"It's a little thick, don't you think, Huggins, whinging over blasphemy at this point?" drawled a City type with a waxed moustache. "By Jove, next he'll be trying to wring spells out of the Sermon on the Mount. I say let a scientist study it rather than we financial types—it isn't as if we have any clue what we're talking about in the forensical sense."

To tell the truth, neither do I. I am a student of all disciplines, a kite upon the wind of the rare and the beautiful. I only know that something in me loved this book from the beginning, wanted to peel back its feather-soft pages and lose myself in the gentle curlicues of its embellished borders. I confess I am doing so now between jotting down these notes, my amber lamplight lost eternally the instant it hits the void-like black of *The Gospel of Sheba's* ink. The Latin is lyrical enough never to be tedious, and I just translated:

> *Come further into the night, O spirit longing to serve me, O Many-Eyed, Hairy Tongued Beast of Burden. Come further. Come into me with your seven furred tongues and your single hand beckoning, place your hand in my darkest place and be made flesh among the living, as you were living, as you are dead, as you were gone, as you are returned, as you are summoned, as you are MINE TO COMMAND.*

It isn't Shakespeare exactly, but it gets the point across.

At the Savile Club earlier, after I'd completed a cursory examination, I closed the book and glanced over my shoulder. Hunger must have burned in my gaze, for Mr. Scovil behind me winked a single genteel eye and gestured at the book, tilting a shoulder in question to Mr. Pyatt. Mr. Pyatt, his black head cocked at me like a magpie's, grinned suddenly and called out to the small assembly.

"Mr. Huggins, it seems your fears will soon be tested against the facts," he announced, proffering Mr. Scovil a flute from a waiter's champagne tray and taking another for himself. "Our visiting scholar is having a turn with the blasted thing. You'll see for yourself, as I promised you, Mr. Jenkins—there is an otherworldly presence in this book, and Mr. Lomax will prove it to you. Is not electricity a real, if unseen, force? Is not magnetism, is not gravity? Does not the earth travel round the sun despite our inability to sense the fact, and are these not universally acknowledged to be ancient and wholesome laws of nature?"

"I think Galileo would have words with you on that subject, were he here," I observed, earning a few appreciative grunts.

"Just so!" Mr. Pyatt nodded sagely, his inky hair gleaming. "We men of mettle cannot allow ourselves to be hampered by outdated morals and petty superstitions. It seems this book has chosen a master for itself, and if that is the case, well, we must have Mr. Scovil upon our side in the future. That's all I can say upon the subject. In fact, let none of us argue any further and come to regret it before our impartial judge has returned with an assessment."

Understanding I was definitely allowed to take *The Gospel of Sheba* home for study, I wrapped the gloves within the covering and placed all in a leather satchel I'd carried thither in hopes of just such an event. Mr. Grange hobbled on unsteady legs towards me, breathing heavily.

"I am most grateful," he whispered as the others turned to more usual talk of business and of ritual. "You'll save us yet, sir, deliver us the hard *facts*, and we'll make a judgment accordingly. All this political bickering will be a thing of the past."

"Bickering can be ruinous to any club, I quite under—wait, did you say *political*?" I questioned, a bit bemused. But Mr. Grange had already teetered off to herald the cold pheasant's arrival.

"Bickering aplenty. He means the role of the book and its potential spiritual dangers, obviously, but he also refers to my possible election as president of the club." Mr. Scovil appeared at my elbow, passing me a frothing glass of champagne. "There are whispers. We've never had one previous, you see. I don't want any such thing, I'll tell them no outright if they force me, but it would be rather piggish of me to decline a position I haven't been offered yet."

Taking the drink, I nodded. I don't have to employ many words for men of his type to peg me. *Old money, bit of a poet, younger son, has to make his own way.* They can read it all in my manner and clothing, likely spy reflections of silver spoons in my disordered hair follicles even as my mended kerchief screams penury.

"Frankly, it's a rotten situation to be placed in." He took a discreet pull of sparkling liquid, his eyes dancing—an aristocrat, yes, but one who exuded affability. "I can't explain why the book doesn't hurt me, no more than I can explain why Mr. Grange has been so pallid since he studied it. Nor why Mr. Huggins developed severe heart palpitations, nor why Mr. Pyatt fell so dreadfully ill. It wasn't even *my* idea to lend the book out after I'd presented it to the company. Oh, you'll take every care with it, won't you? If nothing else, it's an antique curiosity as well as an esoteric wonder. I'm pleased to have found the thing no matter what sort of trouble it causes. I'm mad for such treasures. Isn't it beautiful, in a simple way?"

"Yes," I said, thinking of calmly drawn letters in perfect horizontal lines, the hours spent making words appear by hand and will. "Yes, I agree with you. I'll use the gloves, as a matter of course."

"Obliged," he said, raising his glass.

Prior to dinner, I inquired as to the health problems suffered by each of *The Gospel of Sheba's* borrowers chronologically—Mr. Pyatt first, then Mr. Huggins, and finally Mr. Grange. Each reported identical symptoms: freakish numbness, chest pains, the virulent inability to digest foodstuffs. But I am no doctor, so such details meant little to me. After dinner and talk of stocks, banks, acquisitions, and rites enacted within sacred circles chalked by holy madmen, I made my goodbyes. As I departed, I passed Mr. Scovil and paused to ask him the question which had been nagging me.

"Why this hobby, Mr. Scovil?" I inquired. "You've the means to explore any field you desire, and then add more—form Arctic expeditions, excavate tombs. Why dark magic?"

He shrugged in the fashion very rich people do, when the slight flex of a muscle is pleasing to their own bodies.

"It's in the family, as it were. Anyway, why art?" he replied, smiling. "Why hospitals? Why battle and conquest? Why patronage or charity? A man has to have something to work for, doesn't he, besides money?"

I thought so, too. I think so now. And yet . . .

I want to know whether or not Lettie believed me when I told her we would never be well off all those years ago. Is it reasonable to wonder if perhaps she imagined me overly modest, or afraid of designing females, or simply a liar? She may have thought me the branch of a great tree which would flower in its due course, showering her with perfumed blossoms that glimmered in the sun.

When in fact, as is becoming heartrendingly clear, I am only a sublibrarian.

Note pasted in the commonplace book of Mr. A. Davenport Lomax, September 17th, 1902.

Papa,

I wonder if you could say when mother is coming home I only ask becaz Miss church wants me to pick new clothes for spring and when mother is heer it's a lark. If you tell me, Ill paste it in my small calendur she sent from Florents.

Love, Grace

Excerpt from the private journal of Mr. A. Davenport Lomax, September 18th, 1902.

My life has taken a stark turn towards madness.

The Librarian approached me in the stacks today, exuding pipe smoke and benevolence, and I seized my opportunity.

My wife is beautiful, and she is kind, and she is witty. She deserves better than cold meat picnics in Regent's Park. So does Grace, for that matter, even if she is quite content when in the company of bread and ducks. Is it humiliating for a man of my breeding to *ask* for money? Exceedingly. But I cannot always be sending Lettie accounts of new research projects and old books, not when she is art to be held up and wondered over and praised by dukes and even kings—sometimes, I must write to her of victories. Even of *salary increases.*

The Librarian opened his mouth to compliment me, and I mine to request a larger wage, one Lettie might consider livable and may even bring her home, when suddenly he stopped.

"Are you all right, Mr. Lomax?" he asked. "You seem very pale, my dear boy, and your expression . . . I've never seen it before. Are you resting quite enough?"

Standing there, dumb, I found he was correct. I was wearing a look painted by an unknown artist—and I found it singularly difficult to adjust my features into my usual warm if somewhat harried expression. My heart was racing for no earthly reason, and my fingertips had gone decidedly numb.

The Librarian clucked sympathetically. "I fear my great enthusiasm for my most admirable sublibrarian has led to overwork on your part. Go home, Mr. Lomax, and leave a list of your appointments upon my desk. I shall see to everything."

I obeyed him and, after returning home and resting for an hour, drew out *The Gospel of Sheba* and returned to studying it, translating the Latin as I went into a separate notebook:

> *When summoning the Nameless Crone who Birthed the Five Pale Ones, suffer a virgin lamb to be drugged but not killed. And after calling unto the Crone, take up the iron needle you have forged, and sew into the live lamb's flesh the words . . .*

To my shock, I grew dizzy midway through my third paragraph. I tore my half-spectacles off my face, panting. My heart leapt like a fish on a glad summer's day. The nausea I have been feeling and ascribed to purposely cheap meals and poor cuts of meat increased.

Is an ancient tome to cause my demise? Can such an object actually send evil through its ink into my person? It would prove ironic, I grant, for a lover of books to be murdered by one—and yet, stranger things have happened. I study paradoxes, after all.

Abandoning the project, gasping for air, I threw open a window in my study and hid *The Gospel of Sheba* in its dark cloth. There must be a scientific explanation for this phenomenon. There simply must, for the two remaining options are quite untenable: either I am a lunatic, or the world's delicate mechanism has smashed to pieces before my eyes.

Meanwhile, the relations between the Brotherhood of Solomon were rather peculiar, I think. Their conversation nags at me just before sleeping, when usually I am dreaming of Lettie's rare guileless smile or of Grace's belly-shaking laugh. The pressure in my chest, a sensation I'd attributed to the sudden steep fall in London temperatures, tightened to a bone-crushing ache just now, as if an iron crowbar had struck my heart.

Perhaps I ought to seek a doctor after all. Or barring that, some sort of priest.

Letter sent from Mrs. Colette Lomax to Mr. A. Davenport Lomax, September 19th, 1902.

Darling,

It is horrible, it is unfair to you, but I cannot write at any length just now. Forgive me. There are no canals in Strasbourg, and you know how the sight of water always calms me when I am distressed, and I am engaged yet again to be paraded like a show pony before the Duke. I long so for home, and a good pint of bitters though you know I cannot palate beer generally, and for a little stillness.

Love,

Mrs. Colette Lomax

Excerpt from the private journal of Mr. A. Davenport Lomax, September 19th, 1902.

The numbness in my hands is increasing. Every time I pick up *The Gospel of Sheba*, it sinks into my veins and spreads outward like bad liquor in the gut.

I cannot bring myself to care. There, I have set it down at last, hours after I should have done. The post arrived this morning as usual, I sorted my correspondence, we sat down to dinner, I read *One Thousand and One Nights* to Grace, I worked at the translation, and finally I have opened my journal and hereby admit that I cannot *care* whether or not I am being poisoned by a blighted book of spells. I want to fight, desperately. It shames me, this lack of will, this *sorrow*. Grace is beginning to notice, and Grace deserves none of this. Who is meant to shield her from such things if not her father?

I hope most ardently that Grace will never be exposed to a document as wicked as *The Gospel of Sheba*. Nor learn after I have read her mother's latest letter to us aloud that there are in fact plentiful canals in Strasbourg.

Where in the world has my wife taken herself?

Excerpt from the private journal of Mr. A. Davenport Lomax, September 20th, 1902.

A light glimmers, though a dim one, and one which gives no appreciable warmth. Casting my mind back throughout the day, I recalled every nuance of conversation I could glean from the gathering of the Brotherhood of Solomon, and I believe an answer may be close to hand. The Librarian commented again upon my haggard looks, but I blamed it on the dagger-like turn in the weather and my wife's extended absence.

The latter cause of my symptoms, I will confess here if only here, is not far from the honest truth.

Excerpt from the private journal of Mr. A. Davenport Lomax,
September 21st, 1902.

Casual herbalism and knowledge of where to find the best books on the subject within my intellectual anthill of a workplace has never served me so well as today, which already makes this date worthy of note. And this evening for the first time—which must be of some significance, if only to me personally—I consulted the celebrated Mr. Sherlock Holmes of 221B Baker Street.

To my great happiness, after ringing the bell and being shown upstairs by a porcelain figure of a snowy-haired old woman, I found Watson occupying the rooms he once called his own. Indeed, it was he who opened the door to the first floor flat, just as Mr. Holmes was chuckling, "No, it's a positive crime you weren't there, I tell you that Lestrade couldn't breathe for laughter and Hopkins will never look at a pennywhistle the same way again in his life."

Into this easy merriment I intruded, just as Watson was laughing his fullest. Despite my devastating circumstances, I could not help but smile at him in return as I clasped his hand.

"You've solved it, then?" I said to the doctor. "The . . . Chinese pottery matter?"

"Lomax! I'd meant to wire you on the subject—we have indeed, and no small thanks to you, my good man. Am I already delinquent in returning your book? Well, well, that's all right, then, I didn't suppose you lot made house calls. Come in at once, it's ghastly out there. Take the chair nearer the fire," Watson greeted me, shutting the sitting room door.

"Thank you."

"Did you see the results of the Kent match last night?"

"I've been terribly occupied, I'm afraid," I admitted, entering the room in a sort of numb daze.

Their hearth was roaring like a chained beast, and the gleefully untidy parlour smelled of tobacco and the remnants of a curry supper. Mr. Holmes was stretched full out upon the settee, his head thickly bandaged, only trousers with white shirtsleeves and a dressing gown covering his gaunt frame. If Mr. Holmes is a bit of a scarecrow, I grant he is an impressive one—a wiry, hawk-nosed giant with a queerly abrupt grace in his movements. Seeing me, his smile dimmed but failed to disappear.

"Mr. Arthur Davenport Lomax of the London Library," he drawled, taking a pull from the cigarette in his hand. Closing his eyes, he settled further back into the furnishings, careful of the cloth bound over his brow. "Watson's friend the sublibrarian. Cambridge, I think, cricketer, economical, genteel, bearing an object of some import—probably a book—and suffering from hyperopia, of all the vexing ailments for a bibliophile. Do sit down."

Watson, moustache twitching in amusement, took my coat. Then his face adopted a darker cast. "By George, Lomax, have you fallen ill?"

"I think not," I said carefully, "but that is for Mr. Holmes to determine."

My friend took no offense, for I meant none. "I am at your service should you want me. You truly don't need a doctor?"

"I need a detective. More specifically, a detective who is also a chemist."

Mr. Holmes half-opened one eye as I sat across from him in an armchair. I learned then that it is a quirk of his to feign boredom, for that is the best way to draw some subjects out. I had the man's full attention—from the slight quirk of his pale brow to his naked toes.

"Cambridge, cricketer, economical, bearing an important object, and hyperopia I can work out myself based on the way Watson just greeted me and the physical clues I present," I remarked. "I read the *Strand*, everyone does. The last is the most venturesome, and even when I'm not wearing my spectacles, their imprint is probably on my nose. Why genteel? We've never had a conversation."

Whatever else I expected the great detective to do, I did not expect him to dissolve into helpless laughter, wincing at his injured ribs. Somehow managing to bow to me from a fully supine position using only the stub of a cigarette, he cast a glance at Watson as the doctor passed me a generous spill of brandy. Sherlock Holmes would have been famous, or perhaps infamous, in any field he chose, I think. His eyes are positive razors.

"My dear fellow, what *have* you brought into our establishment?" he asked without desiring an answer. His gaze returned to me. "Of course you're genteel, Watson thoroughly enjoys your company. Out with it, then. You are being poisoned. How and by whom?"

Watson's jaw dropped in dismay as he settled into his chair with his own glass, having refilled the sleuth's en route. "Good heavens. Is this true, Lomax? What on earth can have happened?"

I told them. Watson sat, eyes bright, nodding at my every pause, mouth twisting in muted but obvious sympathy at twists in the plot. Mr. Holmes reclined, motionless, carved into his own ivory statue, his fingertips steepled before his closed eyes and his bare ankles demurely crossed at the other end of the sofa. When I reached the end, he placed one arm under his head and rolled to face the room.

"I am at your service, Mr. Lomax, but you must tell me," he said in a slightly theatrical whisper, "what you would have me do to bring about resolution? Take this to the Yard? Decide my own penances? Watch those involved for greater misdeeds and take no action yet, only to pounce at a later date? Justice lies in your hands, you know."

"Holmes," Watson chided, shifting in his chair as if it were a very old argument.

"Watson," the detective returned, eyebrow quirked.

"It's a serious matter."

"I am treating it seriously."

"No, you are playing at judge, jury, and executioner, and it's not even October yet. He gets this way in winter, especially close to Christmas, but not usually so early," Watson added to me, shifting a rueful hand across his moustache. "He just ruined a wedding by breaking and entering followed by theft, and I confess I'd hoped it might hold him for a week."

"You were every particle as dead set against that wedding as I was, and a fully apprised participant in the charade!" Mr. Holmes exclaimed in an affronted tenor.

"Chinese pottery," Watson explained to me on a sigh. "Fully apprised, Holmes? No, that is not quite right, something sounds amiss about your phrasing . . . ah, yes, the word *fully*. And also the word *apprised*."

"You have never previously shrunk from such tactics. Why grow squeamish over feigning an expertise in Chinese pottery of all things?"

"Because, Holmes, such enterprises on our part do not usually dissolve into utter chaos. Usually, when I am assisting you at housebreaking, you are not badly injured and subsequently questioned by the police on the topic, having allowed the man of the house to discover you in the act of stealing his lust diary. And let me remind you that the only reason Baron Gruner failed to shoot us both is that he was the *victim of a vitriol throwing enacted by your accomplice Miss Winter*. No! No, not a single word from you about my lack of aptitude when impersonating a lover of Oriental antiquities, I haven't the stomach at present."

Mr. Holmes had the grace to look, if not chastened, then magnanimously sympathetic regarding his friend's chaotic whims. Frowning, he splayed his fingers across his breast in an unconvincing but nevertheless droll protestation of innocence. "I am not playing at judge, jury, and executioner. I am asking your friend Mr. Lomax to do so—he solved the crime, he knows best what's to be done about it."

"No, he doesn't!" Watson exclaimed, waving his brandy glass. "No offense, Lomax, there's a good fellow."

"None taken."

"You aren't following me. If he's right about this crime, which he is, which I shall determine once and for all tonight, I presume, or else why would he be here, none of it can be proven in court," Mr. Holmes protested, a scowl distorting his lean features.

Watson sat forward, moustache bristling. "Why the devil can't it be? Attempted murder I should think would do nicely. Any one of these four men—Pyatt, Huggins, Grange, and now Lomax—could easily have been killed over this dirty business."

"Not Pyatt," I suggested, sipping at the brandy. Its pleasant burn distracted me from other, deeper aches.

"No, I rather think not," Mr. Holmes agreed, his thin mouth quirking.

"Why . . ." Watson began, and then his eyes lost themselves in the crackling flames. "Oh!" he said softly, glancing back at Mr. Holmes. "The swiftness of Pyatt's recovery. The dismissive attitude Scovil evinced towards presidency of the Brotherhood of Solomon. Yes, I see."

"Do you really, or shall your sublibrarian friend explain it?" Mr. Holmes asked pettishly. "Go on, Mr. Lomax, I believe your reasoning is quite sound. Put it in order, and tell me whether you think a jury would swallow it."

Hesitating, I turned to Watson, who sat with his head angled in expectation. If he was piqued by the detective's remark, he failed to show it.

"Scovil really did discover a centuries-old grimoire hidden in a secret room in his family manse and saw a rare opportunity," I said slowly. "The book itself is genuine. I honestly don't think he believes in ritual magic himself—it's a pastime, not an art. If he could introduce his grimoire to the Brotherhood and then insinuate that he was the only mage righteous and disciplined enough to wield it, however, they'd naturally desire him for their leader. So he picked the right toxin and sent the book off with his comrades one by one, poisoning them. But lest he be suspected of a power grab, and lest he create an obvious motive for himself which would be noticed should a death occur, he brought Pyatt into his scheme. Scovil would shun the presidency as a true holy priest might—but Pyatt, who had believed in him, would be chosen in his stead. Pyatt claimed to have suffered the same symptoms when he studied *The Gospel of Sheba*, but he was probably shamming all along, spreading rumours so the club would be primed when Huggins fell ill. Pyatt and Scovil meant to rule that club with an iron fist."

"To what specific object, I wonder, though I doubt not you are right," Mr. Holmes mused, tapping his index fingers together.

"Would you like my friend the sublibrarian to explain it to you?" Watson asked in a tone dryer than their fireplace.

Mr. Holmes's head drew back fractionally. "Yes, do go on, Mr. Lomax," he suggested, and I knew it a peace offering, for all that the entire exchange had been encoded. Watson smiled briefly before returning his attention back to me.

"Money," I said. I twisted my shoulders in apology for my class. "There are some for whom it is a religion. More money, always more. Scovil was of the type who hide the avocation well—outwardly open, inwardly grasping. He loved treasures, he told me, and such objects have their price. Pyatt was more obviously greedy, but no matter; Scovil's mask was complete enough that they could milk the Brotherhood for all they liked. It was always more of a businessmen's club than an occult academy. As for potential challengers, well, send *The Gospel of Sheba* home with any upstarts and they would at once fall ill and surrender. Frankly, though, Mr. Holmes, I agree with Watson—I don't see why they shouldn't be prosecuted for poisoning their supposed friends."

The sleuth waved his hand in the air bonelessly. "Watson does, though, now you've stated the case so clear. Explain the legal difficulties to your friend the sublibrarian, there's a good fellow."

Watson's face gave the oddest twitch imaginable as he stifled a laugh while half-rolling his eyes. "I am afraid," he confessed when the fond exasperation had passed, "that no one can say when or where the poison itself was introduced. The book was discovered, the book was presented to the group, and later the book was lent out. Therefore, among the Brotherhood—"

"Everyone touched it, thus everyone is a suspect," I realized, wincing. "After all, they are convinced Pyatt likewise was sickened by the text. And Scovil professed to abhor the notion of presidency to me, but later, he could simply claim he failed to study his find altogether due to business obligations or some such, and thus escaped unscathed. Nothing ties him to the poison directly."

"When did you suspect him first?" Mr. Holmes inquired, head listing towards me as he pulled a cigarette case from behind a settee cushion. "You've a keen eye and a wit to match, but you're no detective. As a fellow man of science, I can understand your hesitancy to believe a supernatural agency at work, but what led you to decide Scovil was the mastermind?"

"He warned me to handle the book with care explicitly when he lent it to me," I recalled. "I found it . . . superfluous. I'm a bibliophile and a sublibrarian. It was a nonsensical thing to say."

Nodding, Mr. Holmes pulled matches from the pocket of his dressing gown and lit a fresh cigarette, watching the smoke spiral upwards. Watson crossed his legs, cogitating. We were quiet briefly.

"There's something else troubling you, Mr. Lomax," Mr. Holmes said after several long seconds. "Can I help?"

"Not unless you can remove all the canals from Strasbourg."

"Pardon?"

"No," I said hoarsely. "You can't."

A quicksilver flash was all it was, without any movement of his pale profile, but the famous detective glanced at me. There was a great deal in that peripheral stare—catlike curiosity, intellectual interest—but also sincere goodwill, which confirmed what I had long suspected as a reader. Dr. Watson tolerates the company of Mr. Holmes not because they are very different and thus complimentary, but because they are at heart very similar.

A disquieting thought occurred. I would have to like Mr. Holmes, in that case, I realized. I'd have to like him despite his theatrics, his glib remarks, and his almost childlike demand that all attention be riveted upon him perennially, achieved alternately by fluid, frenetic movement and by absolute still-ness. I'll confess the prospect was a little daunting.

"Never mind, then," Mr. Holmes said, half-stifling a yawn with the back of his hand, and once again it was a cryptic message. He did not mean he was disinterested; he meant that I need not speak of what pained me. Almost at once, I relaxed my brittle bearing.

"Friend Watson, are you yet convinced we are clearly the law of the land in this matter?" the detective continued in a more grave tone. "I ask for efficiency's sake as much as anything. Do we pass judgment ourselves, or do we tie up the courts with aristocrats who'll be declared innocent after all of three minutes of jury deliberation? I leave the matter to you and the sublibrarian."

The appellation "the sublibrarian" was ostensibly dismissive, of course. But it was not an empty compliment, as I have so often experienced. It was instead a tribute disguised as a dismissal. Despite myself, I laughed. Neither noticed me. Mr. Holmes resumed contemplating the ceiling as he smoked while Watson rubbed at his brow with his knuckles.

"All right," Watson said, finishing the last of his brandy. "Holmes, you'll test Lomax's assertions tonight?"

"Oh, supposing he wants me to," Mr. Holmes said airily.

"Supposing he wants you to, and supposing he is right, might I suggest the following courses of action?"

"By all means," I prodded.

"You know I follow you in these matters as much as the converse is true," the sleuth said nearly under his breath.

"First," Watson declaimed, holding up a finger, "we inform Mycroft Holmes—my friend here's brother, who moves in very high circles indeed—to keep an eye on Mr. Sebastian Scovil and to hamper him whensoever he sees fit."

A tiny grin flashed to life on the detective's face, which, at lightning speed, returned to composed neutrality.

"Second," Watson continued, adding another digit, "while we cannot see Pyatt gets quite what he deserves, perhaps an inspector might visit the next meeting of the Brotherhood of Solomon following an anonymous complaint? This inspector would know all the true facts of the case and be instructed to make a very public show of believing Pyatt poisoned his comrades. Dark hints would surface, apt accusations. If nothing else, it would be humiliating. There would be a . . . lessening of trust among the brothers towards Pyatt, and in business, trust is everything. I say make a deal of noise at the Savile Club, maybe even clap a pair of derbies on the scoundrel, and thoroughly trounce his reputation. Might even scare a confession out of him, but it doesn't matter if we don't. The horse will already have fled the barn."

"Bravo!" Mr. Holmes exclaimed, a wide smile crinkling his eyes as he raised himself upon one elbow. "I hadn't thought of that, but it would prove a most effective stopgap measure."

"Well, one can't think of *everything*," Watson returned.

Standing, I approached the settee with the object in question. I passed it to Mr. Holmes, who covered his bare hand with the kerchief stuffed in his dressing gown pocket before accepting my evidence. He consigned it to the side table behind him. When he turned back to me, his grey eyes were pinched worriedly at the corners. I knew what he was about to ask, and dreaded it.

"You want me to test this for poison tonight?" he asked softly. I nodded. "The symptoms you recorded and, I fear, suffer from, speak clearly enough—you want me to confirm aconitine?"

"I consulted a book upon herbaceous poisons this afternoon so as not to waste your time, and yes, that was my amateur conclusion, Mr. Holmes," I agreed.

"Aconitine!" Watson said, gasping. "Lomax"

"I was . . . not very long exposed," I half-lied.

"But my dear chap—"

"He's young and vigourous and sturdy of constitution, Watson," the detective pronounced as if blessed with the authority to decide such things. "Why, he must be twenty years our junior. How old are you, Mr. Lomax?"

"Twenty-nine," I allowed.

"Ha! You see?" Mr. Holmes demanded, as if a point had been scored. He jerked his thumb at Watson. "The doctor here was twenty-nine when we met, and after a bullet on the battlefield didn't manage to kill him, enteric fever couldn't finish the rogue off either. I've every expectation of your full recovery, Mr. Lomax. When you are twenty-nine, you are invincible."

"A fact I have multiple times stressed when making a different point entirely," Watson muttered with a harried glance at the detective's bandaging.

Laughing, I gave them a small wave. "I appreciate the vote of confidence, gentlemen. As well as the assistance."

"Won't you stay for another brandy?" Watson asked in a measured tone as I donned my coat.

He wanted only to cheer and reassure me, but I didn't find myself in a very expansive humour any longer despite his gracious intentions. For of course, there is no cure whatsoever for aconitine poisoning. There is only rest, and will, and perhaps fate.

"I must be getting home—my daughter will be worried," I said.

"It was a pleasure," said Mr. Holmes. Strangely enough, he sounded sincere. "Get some rest, my good man, and I shall see to the remainder."

I took my leave of the pair, and—living in the West End a very short distance from Baker Street indeed—chose to walk home. As I strolled, I thought of the architects who had built the houses I passed. The impressive stone facades, the careful masonry, the uniformity of the scarlet bricks. Did those paying to erect the grand townhouses, I wondered, spare any thought towards the actual makers? The men with rock-steady grips and calloused fingers? Did capitalists of Scovil's sort see beauty in work and skill, or was everything denuded into pounds and pence? If the latter, how could they live that way?

Not that I'd any sound advice to offer regarding how to live life, apparently.

Constructing a house is a craft, I concluded as I walked, one boot before the other, in a sort of trace. Constructing a life, meanwhile, is an art, and one I'd apparently lost the knack of. And could I countenance shaping a *human*—a living, breathing human called Grace, who'd survived an acute bout of croup at age two thanks only to her mother's ferocity and my mute, terrified assistance—alongside someone who clearly didn't love me and had perhaps never intended to do so?

The biting wind filled my nostrils with an ephemeral bitterness, and the occasional harmless raindrop all but lashed against my skin. I was in a vicious mood, I recognize now, and a dangerous one.

For the first time in my life, I wanted to hurt somebody.

So, as any sublibrarian would do, I categorized the sensation.

What sort of hurt was I after, exactly? A senseless public house brawl soon forgotten? A rash act harming my own person? A delicious personal revenge?

Then the word *divorce* hit me like a physical slap.

An ugly event, divorce—a rare one, and still uglier for being so rare. Were more people officially divided, one might not be so very shamed by it. I could never put Lettie through such a trial, I comprehended in that moment. I was still in love with her, after all. Her sideways smile understood my jokes too well, and her top notes were too pure for me to throw her out upon the unpoetic streets.

No, I realized. That premise was grossly incomplete. I would never put *Grace* through such a thing. No matter who her mother was, or where for that matter.

An arrangement will have to be made.

I've just arrived home, and all the house is asleep. For some reason, I've pulled *The Gospel of Sheba* out of its covering and brought it with me as I retire to bed. The spells are absurd, the propositions either dreadful or ridiculous despite the elegance of the Latin used, and ceremonial magic is all comprehensive nonsense anyhow.

Nevertheless. The book is a marvel. It is a very old copy of very old spells made by a long-dead scholar, even if the Queen of Sheba had nothing to do with its provenance.

But what if she had? What if an African queen, arrayed in scarlet and purple and orange silks, skin oiled until it shone brighter than the gold dripping from her every appendage, heard a rumour of another monarch far away who loved knowledge the way other men loved gemstones? What if she scryed him in a polished quartz and saw in him her double, though they ruled two distant lands, and knew she had to meet with him or regret his absence forever? And what if, when she came before Solomon's throne, divinity crackled like thunder in the air between them, and they set about recording their sinister secrets?

The Gospel of Sheba resides upon Lettie's pillow now, but I shall find a safer resting place for it on the morrow. I hate to think of returning it.

Exhaustion claims me even as I pen this, and my body revolts against the poison saturating it. Whether I will awaken after sleep takes me tonight is by no means a certainty. If I do, I must live better henceforth, of that much I am certain. I have caught glimpses of true happiness—in Lettie, who expanded my dreams; in Grace, for whom I can live to see hers be realized if I am lucky. But just now my heart dully throbs, pumping naught but cinders and grief, and I must consign myself to oblivion hoping I land in the proper sphere.

If I fail to wake on Earth, pray God Lettie never sees this. I did so desire ever to see her happy, and always told her so from the beginning.

Telegram from BAKER STREET to LISSON GROVE, September 22nd, 1902, marked URGENT.

EXAMINED WHITE PROTECTIVE GLOVES FOUND HIGH CONCENTRATION OF MONKSHOOD THEREIN STOP ACONITINE NEED NOT BE INGESTED, ABSORBED THROUGH TOUCH PARTICULARLY HANDS THUS ALL YOUR THEORIES CONFIRMED STOP INSIDIOUS BUT YOU MUST ADMIT VERY CLEVER STOP HAS YOUR CONDITION IMPROVED? STOP GLOVES WILL RETURN TO YOU BY AFTERNOON POST, ADVISE WHEN YOU MEAN TO RETURN ALL TO BROTHERHOOD AND I SHALL HAVE AN INSPECTOR AT THE READY PER WATSON'S PLAN—SH

Telegram from STRASBOURG, GERMANY to LISSON GROVE, September 22nd, 1902, marked URGENT.

SIR WE REGRET TO INFORM YOU OF SERIOUS EMERGENCY OVERSIGHT STOP YOUR WIFE MRS. COLETTE LOMAX HAS BEEN FOR NEARLY TWO WEEKS LYING ILL WITH PNEUMONIA IN STRASBOURG STOP SHE ASSURED US THE ISSUE WAS FATIGUE AND VOCAL OVERWORK STOP PLEASE PROCEED WITH HASTE TO THE HOTEL JOSPEHINE, AS SHE IS UNABLE TO TRAVEL ALONE, OR WIRE FUNDS FOR AN ESCORT—MDW, ESQ, COMPANY MANAGER

Letter sent from Mrs. Colette Lomax to Mr. A. Davenport Lomax, September 22nd, 1902.

Oh my Arthur,

I've lied to you, which is absolutely horrid, and forces me to see myself as I am—a woman who would rather invent a duke than admit to sleeping in mould. By this time even lifting a pen is a challenge, so I must confess quickly: I am really sincerely unwell, to my honest dismay. I haven't so much as set foot in Strasbourg proper yet, only hidden in this rathole of a hotel they booked for me, but I hope so that you will take me to see the sights when you come. If you do come.

Forgive me, I beg you. You said you only wanted me to be happy, you see, and I turned it into something false and dreadful, imaging you wanted a meadowlark in a cage and not a free songbird. At any rate, I've invented an entire duke at this point to stop you from fretting and I cannot continue in this vein any longer. A bit of pride was at work as well. I know you didn't wish for me to accept this tour, but I so wanted to feel valued in my profession, and I couldn't admit that you were right, and a better-organized engagement would have come along sooner or later. Even if you are angry, which you've every right to be, please take me away from this small corner of hell.

Always,

Mrs. Colette Lomax

Excerpt from the private journal of Mr. A. Davenport Lomax, September 22nd, 1902.

I fairly ran through the tiny spaces between the stacks today, breathless and dizzy, having been told by a new hire that my governess wanted to see me urgently in the foyer (Miss Church not being a member). Subtle iron finials were subjected to brutal treatment upon my part as I raced to what was certainly—I imagined—more unhappy news, this time involving my little girl.

Seeing Grace safe and quiet and clutching her doll next to Miss Church, my heart commenced beating in the usual manner again. Well, not quite usual, yet suffering from aconitine poisoning absorbed through monkshood-laced gloves and all. Still, closer to hale than its condition the night before. While weak and willowy, I find myself harder to kill than I'd imagined, if not nearly so hard to kill as Watson.

"What the devil has happened?" I exclaimed, advancing towards Miss Church's ruddy, slightly obstinate countenance.

"You can read, I think, or do y'want the likes of me to open your mail?" she desired to know. It was a fair answer to a stupid question. "These said *urgent*. What's happened, then? Where's the missus?"

I read my correspondence, hardly daring to breathe.

I gasped aloud.

After making arrangements with Miss Church to tend Grace for the next few days without me, and kissing my darling girl goodbye, I rushed for the exit. I was stopped by an elderly gentleman returning from lunch with several equally grey peers. The Librarian's hair curled invitingly, his merry brown eyes sparked, and he held out a hand as if preparing to compliment me before his cronies.

I was having none of it. There are more important things in this world—though not very many—than a position at the London Library. I surged ahead. But the Librarian was surrounded by men I now recognized as donors, and the group blocked my path.

"Are you all right, Mr. Lomax?" the Librarian questioned.

Laughing, I nodded. "Yes, everything's marvelous! My wife is very ill, you see. I'm to fetch her home from Strasbourg."

"Ah," he answered, eyes wide. "I am sorry to hear it."

"Don't be sorry, I'm alive this afternoon to go to her, and she has been bedridden for a week, so things really couldn't be going any better," I assured him. "I'll be back in three or four days, sir. Farewell!"

"But I mean to speak with you!" the Librarian called after me as I edged past baffled patrons.

"No time!"

"But I mean to increase your wage, given your unprecedented work ethic, Mr. Lomax! Allow me to make you an offer at least."

"I accept!" I cried happily as I reached the door, throwing my arms wide.

"Marvelous!" exclaimed the Librarian. We were really making far too much noise for the foyer of the London Library, for arriving members were turning to stare in dismay alongside the shocked donors. "Magnificent! I shall adjust your figures accordingly and enter them in the books. Strasbourg, you say? Godspeed, Mr. Lomax!"

I write this from a second class train, retracing Lettie's path. My fingertips are still numb, and thus clumsy, but I have never cared less for penmanship. The little towns with their church spires do resemble picture postcards, just as my wife said, and upon viewing them I know they bored her dreadfully. How tedious her travels must have been, and still worse her confinement to unhygienic chambers. If Lettie insists upon one thing, it is absolute cleanliness.

Details continue to flood back to me as I draw closer to her—the tiny gap in my wife's front teeth, the faint spice to her skin, the fact that if she wishes to raise a single eyebrow, it will assuredly be the left one. So many of her aspects are unusual. She is as vain as any artist, and yet ferociously protective of her fellow singers, and refuses to put on any airs they are not likewise entitled to. She is gleefully dismissive of works others deem important and she thinks trite. She is nearly always ruminating over food and drink and luxurious surroundings, and she reads Shakespeare when in the dumps. She doesn't want more children and asked me, "But darling, how much toll to you expect my body to *take*?" but would tear apart a wolf with her bare hands if it threatened Grace. She is absent, but she loves me.

I honestly cannot conceive how I could have forgotten: when it comes to studying complex subjects, Colette has always been the most satisfying paradox of them all.

The Nature of My Inheritance
Bradford Morrow

Bradford Morrow grew up in Colorado. In his mid-teens he traveled to rural Honduras as a member of the Amigos de las Americas program. Morrow received his undergraduate degree from the University of Colorado, then went on to do graduate work on a Danforth Fellowship at Yale University. After graduate school, he moved to Santa Barbara, California, and worked as a bookseller. In 1981, Morrow moved to New York City, where he began editing the literary journal *Conjunctions* and started his career as an author. His first five novels (*Come Sunday*, *The Almanac Branch*, *Trinity Fields*, *Giovanni's Gift*, and *Ariel's Crossing*) are all available as e-books through Open Road Media. Morrow has been a collaborator, contributor, and editor of many anthologies and journals.

For over thirty years, Morrow has lived in New York City and rural upstate New York. He is currently a Bard Center Fellow and professor of literature at Bard College. He is the recipient of the Academy Award in Literature from the American Academy of Arts and Letters, a Guggenheim Fellowship, O. Henry and Pushcart Prizes, and the PEN/Nora Magid Award.

For Peter Straub

He that with headlong path This certain order leaves,
An hapless end receives.
　　　　　　　—Boethius, *The Consolation of Philosophy*

I n the wake of my father's death, my inheritance of over half a hundred
Bibles offered me no solace whatsoever, but instead served to remind
me what a godless son I was and had always been. Like the contrarian
children of police officers who are sometimes driven to a life of crime, and
professors' kids who become carefree dropouts, my father's devotion to his
ministry might well have been the impetus behind my early secret embrace
of atheism. In church, listening to his Sunday sermons, as I sat in a pew
with my mother near the back of the sanctuary, I nodded approvingly along
with the rest of the congregation when he hit upon this particularly poi-
gnant scriptural point or that. But in all honesty, my mind was a thousand
light years away, wallowing, at least usually, in smutty thoughts. His last
day in the pulpit, his last day on earth, was no different. I cannot recall
with precision what lewd scenario I was playing out in my head, but no
doubt my juvenile pornography, the witless daydream of a virgin, did not
make a pretty counterpoint with my father's homily.

Why he bequeathed all these holy books to me wouldn't take a logician
to reckon. My mother spelled it out in plain English when we were in
the station wagon, along with my little brother, Andrew, heading home
after the funeral, and she broke me the news about my odd inheritance.
"He worried about you day and night, you know. He thought you should

have them so you might start reading and find your path to the good Lord."

I didn't want to sound like the ingrate I was, so suppressed my thought that a single Bible would have been more than sufficient.

"Take care of them, Liam," she continued. "Do his memory proud."

"I'll try my best," I said, trying to sound earnest.

"And never forget how much he loved you," she finished, her eyes watering.

"I won't, ever," I said, in fact earnest, praying she wasn't about to crash our car into a curbside tree.

My mom was a good soul and her intentions were every bit as virtuous as my father's. Both of them were delusional, though, to think I was going to sit in my attic room, put away my comics, set aside my Xbox, turn off my television, and switch over to Genesis. I was fourteen back then, though I looked older, was recalcitrant as a wild goat, locked in a losing battle with raging hormones I didn't understand, and while I was capable of barricading myself behind a bolted door to read every banned book I could lay my hands on, I wasn't about to launch into the Scriptures. To please my poor distraught mother, I did make the gesture of moving the unwanted trove of Bibles up to my room, where I double-shelved them alongside *Catcher in the Rye*, *Candy*, *Lady Chatterley's Lover*, and the rest of my more profane paperbacks.

To my eye, the Holy Books were ugly monstrosities, all sixty-three of them, bound variously in worn black leather with yapped edges, frayed buckram in a spectrum of serious colors, tacky over-ornamented embossed leatherette. Most of them were bulky, bigger than my own neglected, pocket-sized copy, and as intimidating in their girth as they were in their content, tonnages of rules and regulations from on high, miles of begets and begats. I was fascinated that a dozen of them were bound in hard boards fastened shut with brass or silver clasps that needed a key to open. I would have to look for the keys sometime, I supposed, but since I had no intention of reading them, there was no rush to go hunting around the house. The whole passel of stodgy books contained the same basic words, the same crazy fairy tales, anyway, so what did I care?

It needs to be said at the outset that my father, the Reverend James Everett, minister at the First Methodist Church of—, did not die from natural causes. He was as hale as he was oldschool handsome, with cleft chin, distinguished wavy hair, and the coral-cheeked glow of an adolescent rather than a man well into his forties, the result of clean living and a lineage of parents, grandparents, and great-grandparents, all of whose middle names were Longevity. He never smoked, not even a pensive evening pipe. He drank exactly one glass of rum-spiked eggnog every year before Christmas dinner, which brightened his cheeks all the more, but other than that and maybe a taste of communion wine, he was as abstinent as Mary Baker Eddy. In winter he shoveled our walk and our next door neighbors' in his oversize shearling coat, and in summer mowed our lawn—me, I was relegated to weeding my mother's flower garden—wearing a white short-sleeve shirt, clipon bowtie, and straw boater hat. He was an exercise nut who did a hundred sit-ups every morning and a hundred push-ups before bed. Above all, my father loved walking. He walked here and walked there, and for longer distances, much to my embarrassment, rather than drive the family station wagon, a relic that dated back to the Triassic, he rode a bicycle, his back as straight as Elmira Gulch's in *The Wizard of Oz*—except with a faint smile on his face rather than her witch's frown. He was slim as a reed and wiry as beef jerky. Some of my friends thought he was a bit of a dork, and while I didn't argue, I knew that if he and any of their dads stripped down to the waist and squared off, my father would pummel them to pulp.

He seemed to have no enemies, my pop. It was safe to say, or so all of us thought, that he was one of the most liked and respected people in the whole town. All who knew him, whether they were members of his congregation or not, from councilmen who sought his support during elections to pimply grocery boys who happily sacked his free-range steaks and organic greens, agreed that my father was never meant to die. My flaxen-haired and walnut-eyed Sunday school teacher, Amanda was her name—a name that rightly meant "worthy of love"—confided in me when I was ten or eleven, "Your dad is too good to go to hell, and too useful to the Lord's work here to go to heaven." I think that was one of the few times in my life I felt sorry for him, a wingless angel with eternal chewing gum on the soles of his shoes that allowed him a future in neither some balmy paradise nor a roasting inferno. Since I didn't believe in hell or heaven, though, my sorrow quickly dissipated, was replaced by a mute chuckle, and soon enough I was back to wondering what gently curvy, sweet-spirited Amanda, in her late teens, looked like when she changed out of her clothes for bed.

And yet for all I looked down my freckled nose at my reverend father's zealous and traditionalist beliefs, I missed him at the dinner table, saying the same dull prayer before every meal, passing me and my brother the meat, vegetable, and starch dishes my mother cooked every night. I missed him carefully reading our school papers and suggesting areas for improvement. I missed his attempts at being a regular-Joe father who took his sons to college football games and sat during our annual excursion to the Jersey shore under a beach umbrella while Andrew and I screeched and splashed around in the water, wrestling in the frothy green breakers. Above all, I missed his warm fatherly presence, like a fastgrowing, scraggly rose vine might miss its fallen trellis, despite the fact I had gone out of my way, especially in recent years, to be a thorn in his side.

At the funeral, a hundred mourners converged, and I couldn't help but overhear the rumors about what might have caused him to fall down the set of hardwood stairs that led from the church chancellery to the basement after giving a powerful sermon, by their lights anyway, about the iniquity of avarice and the blessed nature of giving. I knew the message of this sermon well, to the point of nausea honestly, as he and my mother discussed it after dinner for a solid two weeks before he stepped into the pulpit and delivered it on that doomed day. Living in the household of a church father means, for better or worse, having certain insights into the mechanical workings, the practical racks and pinions, of what transpires behind the ethereal parts of any ministry. See, being a clergyman isn't all riding around on puffy clouds and giving godly advice and just generally being a beacon of hope and inspiration. It is about keeping the tithes and offerings flowing, like mother's milk—oh, Amanda—so staff wages can be paid, the church roof doesn't leak, the stained glass window that some local punks saw fit to riddle with thrown rocks can be repaired. The church is a nonprofit, so the tax man never came knocking, but the insurance man did, as well as many others whose services were necessary to keep the ark afloat and the fog machine running—at least, that's how I viewed things from my corner perch in the peanut gallery, knowing leather-winged Lucifer waited for me with open arms in the bowels of Hades.

Simply and seriously put, my father was in desperate need of money. Utility bills were overdue. Last year's steeple restoration remained largely unpaid. The organ was in serious need of an overhaul, and while it had sat idle for a year or so, the piano that replaced it had steadily gone out of tune. Even his own stipend was at risk. I am sure that for every single problem I knew about, watching my folks wringing their hands on a nightly basis and sharing dire worries, there were ten more deviltries utterly unknown to me. One night, when I wandered in on them, deliberately, I must admit, although pretending I only just then heard about these money issues, I offered to pick up a job after school to help out.

"That's good of you, Liam," my father said. "But I don't think you understood what we were talking about. No need for worry, everything's perfectly fine. You just stick to your schoolwork and our lord savior will take care of the rest."

Yes, he often spoke in such ecclesiastical terms. If it weren't so innocently offered, his dimples flexing from nervousness and earnest blue eyes searching for the confidence their owner so badly wanted to convey to his eldest son, I would have snorted, "Please, spare me!" Or, worse, I would simply have laughed. I did neither but left the room knowing that I had tried to intercede and was rejected. Like a latterday Pontius Pius, if a lot more reluctantly, I washed my hands of the matter.

No one at the funeral said that my father was pushed down the stairs, not in so many words. Nobody whispered that he had borrowed himself into debt, very deep debt, on behalf of the church, not in so many words. And not one soul suggested in so many words that in order to get these loans, the church's minister found himself dealing with less than savory elements in the community, churchgoing, god-fearing folks, maybe, but people for whom the less-than-flattering term "elements" was intended nonetheless. The rumormongers were vaguer than all that. It was from their overheard tones of voice that I cobbled together what I knew, or thought I knew, they were huddling about. One can say the phrase "He's such a good boy" so that it means *the boy is good* or *the boy is bad* just by intoning it differently. That much I understood, as I wandered around, shadowed by my brother, for whom our abrupt fatherlessness hadn't yet sunk in fully, accepting people's condolences, not trusting a single one of them, looking into their eyes for a confession of some kind. I wasn't any more in my right mind than Drew, though I felt I needed to put a brave face on my stunned confusion. The way I figured it was that my father was in the peak of health, athletic in his way, cautious of diet, regular of habits, head on his pillow at ten, up with the cock's crow at six. In church business he might have been stumbling, but when walking down that flight of stairs after his sermon that Sunday he did not trip, that much I felt was irrefutable.

The coroner wasn't so sure. While there was no evidence of a heart attack or anything else in the autopsy to suggest that he had collapsed or fainted, the theory was floated that my father had simply slipped. To me that made no sense, as he had descended those well-lit stairs thousands of times, and while some structural elements in the rest of the church might have needed repair, the hardwood treads on that staircase didn't even creak, let alone give. For me, it wasn't his health, wasn't those stairs, and don't even hint at suicide. Christ was far more suicidal than my dad. No, I knew in my heart that my father was shoved to his death. The sole problem with my theory was that no one else had been seen back in the stairwell at the time, no one witnessed his tumble or heard him cry out. The unimaginable sound of his skull cracking open, maybe like the cantaloupe he distractedly dropped on the kitchen floor that morning as he carried it from the refrigerator to the counter, was one I did my level best to self-censor. I kept reminding myself about the tree that falls in the forest with no one there to listen, and how it makes no sound. Pathetic, but I found myself in a completely foreign emotional terrain and was forced to improvise the best I could. Lying awake at night, my game console lost on me, my small television muted although I left the picture on for company, I sleuthed my way through every person I had seen with my father during the last months, trying without luck to identify a possible culprit.

A detective had dropped over the Sunday afternoon of my father's death to ask my mom, who was numb with heartache and barely able to process his queries about whether her husband had any disagreements, arguments, altercations with anybody. When he stopped by again, not a week later, I knew something was afoot.

"I'm very sorry about your loss," he said, repeating his words from that prior visit.

"Thank you," my mother said, repeating hers.

"I wonder if you wouldn't mind going over a few things with me, now that a little time has passed—"

"We only just buried him," she countered, then immediately apologized. "Anything you need. Liam, you should go upstairs."

"No, that's all right," said the detective. "Nothing to hide here. Plus, maybe he'll know something, right? Liam, is it?"

"Yes, sir," I said, all military and respectful for some reason. Badge was unshaven and wearing a pale gray hoodie, a countercultural cop as I saw it, which made me like the man, gave me confidence that a regular blue uniform wouldn't have. There was something familiar and comfortable about him, too. I was no more fond of police than I was of clergymen, my father excepted, but this one with his frayed jeans was copacetic, in my book.

He did ask many of the same questions as he had before when I listened in from the adjacent room. Had my father counseled any domestic violence couples or individuals prone to aggressive behavior and happened to mention that he had been threatened as a result? Had she or the deceased—I hated hearing my father called that—seen anybody unusual lurking around the church premises, anybody who wasn't part of the regular community of worshippers? Had there been any peculiar phone calls, or calls at odd hours? Any menacing letters at home or the church?

My mother gave him the same answers as the first time, but when he got around to asking again if any of the church employees had been fired or cut back on their paid working hours, she interrupted, "Well, wait. You know, we were getting some calls late at night this fall, around Halloween."

"What kind of calls?"

"I couldn't say, really. The reverend always took them, given the hour, and when I asked him who was it, he told me it wasn't anybody and just to go back to sleep."

My mother always referred to my father as the reverend. Others thought it somewhat peculiar, but I was used to it from as far back as I could begin to understand language itself, so to my ear it was second nature, even first nature.

"And what did you do then?" My mother looked confused by the question.

"I went back to sleep."

"Did you ask about it in the morning?"

"No, there was breakfast to make, the boys to get off to school, and all the rest. Since he made no big deal about it, neither did I."

The detective pressed, gently. "How many times would you say these middle-of-the-night anonymous calls happened?"

"Maybe half a dozen or so. And I never said they were anonymous, just that the reverend never told me who it was."

Out of the blue, the detective turned to me and asked, "How are you holding up, son?"

"I'm good, I guess."

"You helping your mother out, I imagine?"

"I'm trying," I said, wondering why he would ask me such lame questions. "You know he was murdered, my dad, right?"

His turn to be taken aback a little. "We don't have any solid evidence to suggest that he was. Chances are, this was a tragic accident. He took a misstep and fell. Sad to say it does happen. Accidents are far more common than murders."

"He was murdered," I said, looking at him coolly in the eyes. "I know it."

"Liam," my weary mother admonished me. "No, that's okay," said the detective. "Since we're not sure what happened yet, he has every right to his opinion. We'll see about looking into those late night calls, if there's any record of them. Meantime, if you think of anything, you already have my cell number, so call me any time," he finished, rising to go. I saw him to the door and walked him out to his unmarked dark blue Chevy. On the sidewalk, he asked me, "Between you and me, Liam, why is it you think your dad was murdered? A hunch or what?"

I weighed whether to tell him about all the people to whom my father owed money, all those who were waiting patiently for the church to raise enough to clear its debts, and all those who were less than patient. But I assumed he and the rest of the authorities were already aware about this darker side of my father's goings-on and were looking into it even as we stood there.

"You know," I said, unhelpfully, "sometimes you just know."

Looking back, I know he knew that I knew nothing.

~

The famous old biblical phrase, *An eye for an eye, a tooth for a tooth*, circulated in my mind like an endless loop in the days that followed the detective's visit to our house. For reasons I could not then explain to myself, it lodged in my dreamy head with such sticky vengeance that even my fantasy thoughts about Amanda—who visited us several times in the wake of the reverend's death, a demure young woman behind whose shy gaze I swore lay an unawakened erotic soul—were pushed to one side of my streaming consciousness. This new obsession, a vehement, dry mania rather than an amorous, damp one, was upsetting on many counts. I far preferred Amanda to Leviticus, but the latter had me in its Old Testament clutches. So much so that I decided to put one of my father's Bibles to use, research where that line came from and exactly what it meant, though I suspect my father wouldn't have approved of his eldest son's deepening desire for justice in the form of revenge if and when the perp was found.

Even though it would have thrilled my mother to see me sitting with a King James, leafing through its chapters and verses in search of this charming retribution adage, I had my pride and independence to uphold, and so waited for the lights in our house to go off and my family, all two of them, to fall asleep. As I thought before, when I first inherited these big fat tomes, one Bible was the same as the next, and so I pulled down the first that came to hand. It was on the medium-sized side, a pebbly, limp leather binding sheltering the holy words, but when I looked at the title page and saw it was printed in some language I didn't know, German I think, I shut it without looking further and reshelved the thing. Why would my otherwise rational, bow-tied, lawn-mowing dad bequeath me a damn Bible in German, or whatever foreign language that was? Maybe he had gone a little more mental in these last years than I'd thought.

Next I chose one of the larger volumes, since it read Holy Bible on the spine in good old-fashioned English. Settling it on my lap as I sat on the edge of my bed, I opened it up to the table of contents for the Hebrew scriptures—I was a methodical fellow, being Methodist, see—and ran my finger past Genesis and Exodus to Leviticus where, after reading around for a while, I found my phrase. Commentary at the bottom of the page confirmed that the maxim meant exactly what it sounded like. Whoever has inflicted an injury must suffer the same injury in order for justice to be served. Leviticus 24:20 cross-referenced me back to Exodus 21:24 which cross-referenced me to Deuteronomy 19:21—these Old Testament types, I thought as I shook my head, were all on the same page when it came to punishment. Then I was referred forward to Matthew 5:21, where, as I knew from my father's frequent references to the verse, stern Old Testament practicality was replaced by the gentler love-your-enemies philosophy of the New Testament. Since I believed in none of this nonsense, I suppose it didn't matter that I sided with the fire-and-brimstone crowd, especially in the wake of my father's abrupt, inexplicable death and maybe fueled by some of the fiercer among my Xbox games. So I decided to see what argument gospeler Matthew might make to convince me otherwise, and opened the Bible about halfway through.

What I encountered made my jaw drop. Right in the middle of the Bible somebody had carefully carved out a secret compartment that couldn't be seen when the book was closed. Hundreds of pages were vandalized, if that was the word for it, in order to hollow out the block of paper just enough to fit inside its dry bowels yet another book. Having no idea what I was doing or what I had stumbled upon, I lifted out the volume that was nestled like an unholy fetus inside the Bible. I set the Bible aside and held this smaller book, as careful as if it were a new alien species and I happened to be the scientist who discovered it, up to my astonished eyes.

The book was in Latin, which was better than German, since I had spent a grueling year in junior high school trying to learn it, for no meaningful reason I could see until now. Using my rickety knowledge of that defunct tongue, I made out that this pretty pocket-sized book was printed in 1502, by one Aldo Manuzio, in Venice. I was fascinated by the image of a dolphin wrapped around an anchor on the last page, but only got truly excited—so excited I started wheezing and had to use my inhaler—when I Googled around and learned that what I had found inside my father's Bible was the first Aldine edition, as it was called, of Dante's *The Divine Comedy*. That, in and of itself, wasn't the source of my shortness of breath and whistling windpipes, though. As my eyes scrolled down the backlit screen of my tablet, I learned that this was one of the most important books in the history of printing, the first of Aldo Manuzio's literary titles available to the regular public, groundbreaking because its revolutionary format made it as portable as one of my risqué paperbacks. And it didn't hurt my opinion of the thing that, five hundred years later, it was worth over twenty thousand dollars.

Mind-blown, rattlebrained, heart pounding in my ears, my first thought was where I should hide this treasure, before realizing that the best place to stow it out of sight was right where I found it. After tucking it away again, a golden Jonah safely back in its whale belly, and sliding it onto the shelf, I slipped the tablet under my pillow and turned off the bedside light. Out my dormer window was a crescent moon that looked like a cockeyed smile, probably like the smile on my face as I lay there mulling over my miraculous find. My dear Amanda, light of my life, fire of my loins—yes, to be sure, I had tried and failed to read *Lolita*—lost out to Dante Alighieri as the center of my focus that night while I drifted off toward sleep, my thoughts bubbling and stewing in a cauldron of questions desperate for answers.

Next morning, fearing the whole thing had been a dream, I checked to see if Jonah was still there inside his squarish whale. That he was came both as a relief and a worry. The relief was obvious. Twenty-thousand reasons why and then some. But the worry was, what now? How was it that my father possessed such a valuable book, secreted away like that?

My mother commented when I staggered into the kitchen, "Liam, your eyes are all bloodshot. You feeling sick?"

"Not so great, Mom," I said without a moment's thought, slumping down in my chair at the breakfast table.

"Maybe you better stay home from school today. It's cold out and I don't want you catching a flu bug."

If I had written the script, I wouldn't have changed a word.

"I want to stay home, too," my brother tried, a bit over-eager.

"Why in heaven's name should you stay home?" our mother asked with a mild scowl, as she forked some toaster waffles onto our plates. "You're not sick."

"Yes, I am," he said, offering his audience what was easily the most fake cough anybody ever made in the entire recorded history of humankind.

Laughter hadn't been heard much in our household those days, so the sound of it, loud and infectious cackles and snorts, was jarring at first. When Drew, knowing his gambit had flamed, broke down laughing, too, I felt as if things were eventually going to be okay for us and that life would hobble on.

Among the very first things my mother told me, after she gave me the calamitous news about Dad, was, "Now you're going to have to be the head of the family and take your father's place in whatever ways you can. He would want you to be responsible and mature enough to do that, Liam." At the time, while I nodded and said I would do her as proud as I could, my fantasy was that Amanda would move in with us as my wife, and Drew and Mom would be like our children. Something along those lines. The implausible reverie didn't linger longer than an August icicle.

Now, though, as our laughter died down, I did sense I might be on the right path to assuming the role she described, wearing the pater's pants, despite the fact that I was faking illness to ditch school like some punk third grader. It was a necessary ploy, though. I wanted time to think. Time to ponder what to do.

Needless to say, I couldn't wait for my family to leave so I could have the house to myself. I traipsed upstairs, my glass of grape juice in hand—the reverend bought bottles of this by the case; we were all addicted to the stuff—and pretended to go back to sleep. When my mother checked on me, I offered her the comfort of finding her sick son safely dozing in bed. I even managed to twitch a little as if I were dreaming, just to add to the effect. She said nothing, although I felt I could plainly hear her thoughts, Poor child's been through the wringer, immune system's off-kilter, good for him to have a day off to rest. After I heard her walk back downstairs, open and close the front door, and drive off in the station wagon with Drew, I swung my legs out of bed and in my pajamas dashed to my parents' bedroom where I easily found a sock stuffed with the keys to the locked volumes in the top drawer of my father's dresser. Not the most canny hiding place any-body ever came up with, but that was him all over again. I wasted no time chasing back to my room and unlocking the first Bible that came to hand.

The hidden book this time was from the fifteenth century, Boethius's *De consolatione philosophiae*, in chestnut colored leather, very plain Jane. It was so rare, or so it seemed, that I couldn't even find a copy offered for sale by any book dealer online and, not knowing as yet how to locate auction records, had to conclude the thing was basically priceless. I marveled at its text, not a line of which I could read, and at its agelessness, these words written in 524 AD or thereabouts, according to my research, while this Boethius, about whom I knew nothing before that morning, was in jail for treason, brought to his knees by yellow-belly treachery. In other words, an outlaw I could get behind. His book seemed to make a bunch of nods to god, but really was a chat with the beautiful Lady Philosophy—Amanda's face floated into view—about how fame and fortune melt away, about how all of us are good inside even though we do wrong things, about how prisoners should be treated with kindness by their captors, about how god doesn't finally run things but men of free will do. Awesomeness incarnate, I thought. I could have spent the whole rest of the term in school twenty-four-seven and not learned as much as I did that morning, sitting with what I began to wonder wasn't just maybe a stolen Boethius and chewing over what my father was doing with it in his possession, not to mention the other concealed rarities I found.

With the exception of one, which I guessed the reverend used to read from, not a single solitary Bible I inherited wasn't hollowed out with a rare book secreted inside. I found out they were called smuggler's Bibles, and were used in the old days for a purpose that wasn't much different than what my dad seemed to be using them for. It was pretty smart of the old man, smarter than I suppose I'd have given him credit for knowing, that if you wanted to hide something in a place nobody would bother looking, a good old Bible was perfectly suited to the task. I started making a list of titles and a tally of market values, aware that my phony cold would have to worsen over the next couple of days so I would have time to finish the job. Since I rarely got sick and had a real excuse for coming down with something—exhaustion from the shock of losing my dad—my mother was lenient about letting me continue to stay home from school that week. My poor brother, who saw right through my hoax, writhed with jealousy. But there wasn't a thing he could do, especially after that bogus cough of his became a running joke at mealtimes. So I tucked the aspirin and cold medication pills in my cheek, just as I had seen in the movies, drank water from the glass my mom handed me, swallowed mightily, then spat out the pills onto my palm the minute she turned her back. I managed to drink hot tea on the sly before she put the thermometer in my mouth to take my temperature, and the results were impressive. Part of me wished I had played this game of charades earlier, but I knew my father would have called me out in a heartbeat, laid a choice line of scripture on me about lying, and that would have been curtains, no encore.

But what about him and lying? Or, if not lying, keeping a secret from his family to the tune of half a million plus for starters—these books added up fast, reaching into six figures even before I was a quarter of the way through the trove. Just for example, the first edition in English, 1640, of Niccolò Machiavelli's *The Prince*, which I learned was the greatest textbook of all time for political leaders interested in wielding power with an iron fist, brought in the neighborhood of sixty grand or more. Little brat of a book, too, a duodecimo they called it. Or what about Voltaire's *Candide*, one of a dozen or so copies of what was known as the quote-unquote true first edition, published in Geneva in 1759? A sheaf of fussy notes about its "points" that verified it as legitimate was tucked into the smuggler's part of the Bible underneath *Candide* itself. Online, a British book dealer—I wondered if they ought to call themselves bookies?—had one of these for £60,000, which the conversion chart made out to be about a hundred thousand dollars just by itself. It went on like that. Mary Shelley's *Frankenstein* in three small volumes hidden in three different Bibles, the 1818 first edition? Worth a hundred and a half, easy.

But what on earth was my dad, the good reverend, doing with *Frankenstein* when he wouldn't even let me and Drew see the movie because he didn't want our snow-pure souls corrupted by the spectacle of a half-man, half-monster roaming around terrorizing people and drowning little girls? Though he never found out, we did see the James Whale original on a friend's computer, harmless enough moth-bait relic that it was, but the more I thought about *Frankenstein*, Boethius, Machiavelli, and the rest, the more I realized that my father and I couldn't be the only ones who knew about the pearls inside these oysters. Couldn't be blind to the fact that his murder probably had to do with all this. Problem was, if I talked to the detective about it, I worried that the authorities might take my books away from me. But if I didn't, then whoever pushed my dad down the stairs might never get caught.

Late morning on the third day of my convalescence—where was Amanda Nightingale when her fallen soldier needed succor?—the telephone rang. This threw me way off, since the house had been quiet as a toothache during the first two days. I debated whether to answer. If I did and it was my mother checking up on me, she might say if I'm well enough to talk on the phone I'm well enough to go to school. Ixnay to that, since I needed at least one more day to finish going through the Bibles. On the other hand, what if it was that detective who maybe had a lead or something? Damned if I did, damned if I didn't, so damn it I did.

"Everett residence," I half-croaked, in case it was the mater.

"Who's this?" was what the man on the other end asked.

I'm not the epitome of etiquette, not by a muddy mile, but that struck me as rude.

"Who is this?" as breezy as I could muster now that I knew it wasn't my mother.

"Is Reverend Everett there, please?"

"This is his son. And who, may I ask, is calling?"

Bread on the water, see.

"I need to speak with the reverend himself, I'm afraid, on a private matter. Would you mind letting him know there's a party on the phone who wishes to speak with him?"

Just as the decision whether or not to pick up this call was a kind of crossroads, I found myself at another crossroads here. Do I tell him about my dad's demise, or play out the line a little more, see what this was about?

"He's not here right now. If you give me a name and number—"

And he hung up. Needless to say, as I continued to work on cataloguing, and roughly, very roughly, appraising the books inside the books as best I could, recognizing my limitations and at the same time continuing to marvel at the literary gems I unearthed, the dark cloud of that call hung over me. Seldom the nervous type, except in the presence of Amanda, whose mild voice raised sweat on my palms and soft scent made my heart race, every lousy sound I heard downstairs, when the furnace boiler went on or the hall clock struck the hour, caused me to jump. I didn't like that man on the horn. I didn't like that my father had left me with such a weird legacy. I didn't like it that my earlier little-boy judgment about my dad's death being a murder had now transformed into my not-so-little-anymore son's conviction that I had been dead-on right. I looked at the confounding array of books, as many of them as worthless as the others were valuable, and shook my head in wonder and despair. If the reverend were here, as I very much wished he were, he would no doubt have had some catchy proverb to impart, some elegant verse from the Bible that would bring this mess into focus and help my suddenly incomprehensible world make sense.

"Where are you, man? What's all this mean?"

I asked and, ashamed as I am to admit it, began crying.

Toggle life back to summer. Hot as skeet, sky the color of a tin can, the air murky as math. My father and I together in the wagon with its fake wood panels and shocks so spongy every pothole made us heave and bounce like a rowboat on rolling waves. We were headed over to the church with some hymnals another ministry was kind enough to donate, or re-donate, to the First Methodist church. Brotherly-love sort of gesture in the "Give and it shall be given unto you" tradition. It was pretty nice of them, since our church, whose lower middle-class congregation was strong in faith but feeble when the collection plate was passed around, had nearly run out of hymnals. Guess some people wanted to take them home so they could sing all the verses of "The Old Rugged Cross" in the comfort of their bathrooms.

I helped the reverend, who was in an off mood that late August day, take the boxes of chunky hymnaries out of the car and into the church, where he had me unpack and tuck them into the book racks behind each pew while he went downstairs to his office. Off, too, was that he palmed me two dollars and told me to head over to the bodega a few blocks away and get myself a soda or candy or whatever I wanted. Hang on, I thought. Wasn't he always on my case, telling me not to drink soda or eat candy? I didn't really want soda or candy anyway, but dutifully tramped off into the sweltering heat, wondering why he wanted me to amscray like that, for no real rhyme or reason. Besides, it was a lot cooler in the sanctuary than it was outside under a sun hotter than the Eye of Sauron.

When I returned, I noticed there were two other cars parked in front of and behind our shabby vehicle, cars with far finer pedigrees than ours. One was a Benz, black as venal sin, and the other a most excellent vintage white bathtub Porsche. For whatever reason, I was alarmed by them, girdling our jalopy the way they did. There was plenty of room to park up and down the street, so why make it impossible for us to squeeze out of our spot? Just seemed sinister to me.

Inside the church all was hushed other than men's voices coming from the basement office, softly distant as if they were murmuring in a mine shaft. Following my instincts, I sat on one of the wooden pews far off to the side and continued to work on my half-melted chocolate bar while waiting to see what there was to see.

I didn't have to wait long. A fellow in a tailored suit soon emerged from the doorway that led to the stairs down at the end of the nave, thickish leather briefcase in hand, and strode with presidential purpose along the far aisle toward the front door. I didn't stir or say a peep, and he didn't notice me as he passed by, his face an unreadable blank, just a man walking along minding his own. When he exited, a shaft of brutal silver daylight invaded the dark interior of the church long enough for the large oak door to open and close. Right after that, my father and another man I no more recognized than the suit that had just come up from the catacombs, in part because he averted his face, were talking about things that, try as hard as I could to understand, I couldn't make hide nor hair about. I do remember the man saying "Milton." But that was only because there was a skinny kid at school with that name, Miltie Milquetoast was his uninspired nickname, and he was always catching flak because of it. And as they walked down the aisle toward the door, their footsteps on the stone floor echoing more audibly than their voices, I swore I heard my father say, ". . . generous margins." Generous margins? Clueless as to what they were talking about and feeling a little weird that they were so close to me but thought they were all by themselves, I cleared my throat.

"Hi there, Liam," the reverend said in a very different, louder, more carefree tone of voice. "Give me a minute here, son," and with that he and his companion, who decidedly looked away so I could no longer see his face, went outside together, not saying a further word in front of me.

I smelled something was up. And if a smell could be deafening, that's the smell I heard. For one, it wasn't like him not to introduce me. He brought me up to be more polite than that, and even if I didn't always measure up, not by a long shot, wasn't it somewhere in the Bible that it was the parent's job to teach by example? Maybe not, but damned if this whole episode didn't made me nervous as a turkey on Pilgrim's day. It didn't help that when my father came back inside, he acted as if nothing out of the ordinary had even happened. Well, I figured, I had my secrets—ah, Amanda, I wonder if you knew how devoted I was to you back then—and I guess he had his. Just that those men didn't look like contractors here to discuss church repairs or even local businessmen offering loans or help or what have you. They and their cars were not, I believed, from our particular backwaters. Crocs from a different swamp, or I'm an alligator's uncle.

Back home, I wondered if the men at the church had anything to do with my parents' after-dinner wringing of hands. Beyond offering to look for a job and assuming they'd let me in on what was happening when it suited them, there was nothing I could do. So what I did was nothing, and put the matter out of my mind. My little brother Drew would ask me what was up, but I'm sorry to admit that I kept him as much in the dark as the progenitors kept me. I reassured him, my arm over his bony shoulder, which he disgustedly shook off, that just as they had persuaded me—not even slightly—that all was well, he should be persuaded, too.

"Kemosabe," I said, to his annoyance, "Life's tough. Chill, my man."

He ran upstairs to his bedroom and I didn't blame him. I knew more than he did, but because of that fact, I was even more confused than he. As I recall, I went up to my room, too, shut and bolted my door, and played on my Xbox all night. I hesitate to provide the name of the game, as it's not one I am proud of, but for partial disclosure, let it be said that pixilated blood was lost, virtual limbs were separated from their host bodies, and mayhem and madness blanketed the screen. In a healthy way, for sure. Getting my angst out, I suppose one could assert. Getting some balance back in my life. Sort of.

Rewind now back to present. My dad is dead. My brother and I are fatherless. My mom's a widow. The First Methodist church has no minister. Winter's coming. None of these are even slightly good things. I liked it better when the reverend was around and I could be a friendly pain in his neck and my mom could feed him his meat, vegetable, and starch every evening, and our little corner of the world thrived on its trivial routines. At the same time, hard as it was to wrap my tired and meager brain around it, thanks to my father's bequest and the literary nougats I discovered inside those dusty Bibles, I was worth well over a million dinero. If there was ever such a thing as a silver lining on a cloud, this was it. Not even silver, a gold lining. I kept everything to myself but wondered why my dad, looking as haggard as our threadbare sofa, wasted so many evenings worrying about church finances when he had to have known that any one of these books would have bought him a new organ or paid for his steeple repairs. I wanted to shout "We're rich" to my mom and brother at the top of my lungs, but I knew I needed to stay calm, remain as stupid as I looked until I got a better handle on how my pater acquired these rare books and why he had been so worried about money during the last months of his life.

Whether from concern or lenience or distractedness or all three, my mother allowed me one last day home from school. I had told her I was feeling a little better, cough cough, but as it happened, a soaker of a rainstorm had settled in, driving the last leaves out of their trees and hammering against the window panes. If it had been nicer outside, she probably would have made me go. But since the weather was rotten and it was a Friday, anyway, she gave me a pass. "Monday means you're back at it, though," she warned while stirring the hot oatmeal she was cooking us for breakfast. "No problem," I said, sitting in my robe at the table, trying to appear chipper and under the weather at the same time. "And I'll get my makeup work going as soon as I can."

Oh, I was a regular valedictorian.

As it turned out, it was a good thing I stayed home that day since I had almost as many visitors as Amahl. Not three friendly kings but two men showed up unexpectedly, one in the morning, the other midafternoon.

I was upstairs documenting books when I heard the doorbell ring. Quickly replacing a slim volume by Samuel Taylor Coleridge back in its biblical hiding place, I cinched my robe, slid into my slippers, went downstairs, and opened the door. The detective, Reynolds was his name, stood there looking every bit the street thug once again, if this time showered and smelling of fresh talc. And, as before, I took his casual appearance to be a sign that he was good people, somebody I could maybe trust. Not that I was in a trusting mood.

"Hey, Liam," he said, as the chilly outside air blew around him and right through me.

"Hello, sir."

"Your mom in?"

"Not right now," I said with an unfeigned sneeze.

"Well, as it happens, I wanted to talk to you, too," he went on. "I see you're home sick, though. I can come back another day if that's better."

I should have said yes, but the words, "No, that's okay, come on in," flew out of my mouth instead.

We sat down in the living room. I knew the polite thing to do would be to offer him some of my mother's leftover coffee, given what a cruddy day it was outside, but kept my mouth shut. Sure, I kind of trusted him, but there was no need for me to roll out too big of a welcome mat. Besides, I didn't want him or anybody else messing with my inheritance. Money aside, I had gotten very possessive of my books just as, or so I'd started to believe, my father had.

Reynolds was speaking about how he was still on the case regarding my dad's death. "I seem to be the only one in the department who isn't convinced it was a hundred percent accidental. Coroner ruled it accidental. Prosecutor's office sees nothing in it for them to pursue a trip-and-fall. I got no leads, just a nagging hunch. Looks like it's only you and me thinking there might have been foul play," as he summed it up, an awkward smile very briefly complicating his face. Smile gone, he asked, "You still thinking, like the last time I saw you, that your father was the victim of a crime?"

"Maybe," I said, less sure now if the reverend wasn't the perpetrator of one, too, since I knew he hadn't enough dough on the up and up to acquire even one of the rarities hidden inside those Bibles upstairs, sharing shelf space with my innocent smut.

"You sounded a lot more sure the last time I dropped by."

I shrugged, feeling almost as guilty as if I had killed him myself.

"Well, since I'm here, let me ask what I asked your mom the other day. Have you had any visitors or phone calls that are out of the ordinary?"

Black sheep atheist though I styled myself, I thought the better of lying to a cop, even one who, like Reynolds, was nonchalantly dressed like a homeless man in fifty cent's worth of threads from Goodwill. Somewhere behind his rumpled sweater and ripped jeans there was a badge lurking, and my personal brand of anarchism only went so far.

"A guy did call looking for my dad. Didn't know he was dead, I guess."

"Did he say what he wanted?"

"Nope. And when I asked him his name and number, he hung up on me."

"You didn't tell him your father was deceased?"

"Not my job."

This made Reynolds smirk a little. "Figured he might give you a clue if you played dumb, eh? Smooth thinking, Liam. One of these days you might want to consider going into my line of work. Better watch out for my job."

I didn't want to insult him by saying that I'd rather be a blind garbage man with brain cancer and no legs than a police officer, so I said instead, "Well, the fish wasn't biting."

"You know what reverse dialing is? You try that?"

"I tried, but it was blocked."

"I have a question for you, Liam," Reynolds said, shifting subjects as he shifted on the sofa, and his voice also shifted to a more buddybuddy tone. "After your dad died, we looked through some of his records at the church just to see if anything was suspicious. You know, to see if he'd gotten any hate mail or stuff like that."

"No way," I said.

"You're right. We didn't find a thing. Your father was very well liked."

All this hollow pitter-patter was now making me antsy. It was my last day with the house all to myself and I still had a dozen Bibles left to open and catalogue, and though I didn't dislike Reynolds, he was getting on my nerves. I waited for him to finish whatever was on his mind.

"Well, since there really is no criminal investigation still going on—like you, I've got the day off—I don't have any legal right to ask you this and doubt if I could even get a judge to issue a search warrant, but I'm wondering if your dad had an office in the house here, as well as in the church basement?"

"Not really," I said, relieved. That was a pretty long windup to a slow pitch, and I was bracing myself against the possibility he was going to ask about my Bibles.

"I was just thinking that since you and I are the only ones who think there might have been wrongdoing involved, that if I could go through his desk at home—"

"Well, my mom's the one who did all the bookkeeping and I guess you could have a look at her stuff if you thought it was important. I doubt she'd care."

"If it's not a lot of trouble," he said. "I don't want to impose."

"No problem," I told the detective, grateful to accompany him to the downstairs family room, a corner of which doubled as my mom's study, because it led him to a part of the house that was in the opposite direction of my trove. Besides, even though he didn't really have any right to riffle through her papers, as he himself conceded, my mother, of all people, had nothing to hide. As I led the way down, I heard him breathing a little heavily behind me, and thought to myself he needn't be so excited about all this since I knew there was nothing to be found that would assist in his investigation. And yet, while I stood there shifting weight from one foot to the other while I watched him go through her files, I found myself feeling a bit annoyed that I'd allowed him access. What if he did find a misplaced piece of paper that might betray the existence of the rare books hidden upstairs? On top of that, long minutes were ticking by that might better have been spent doing my internet research.

I was right, however. He discovered not one thing worthy of pursuing further.

"I knew it was a long shot," he said, clapping his palms down on his knees where he sat on my mother's swivel chair, and rising to go. "I really appreciate your time and trust, Liam." As we headed back upstairs, he added, "We probably should keep this to ourselves, if that's all right by you."

"No reason not to," I said, having no intention of telling my mom anyway.

At the door he thanked me again, requesting that I get in touch if anything developed that I thought he might need to know.

"I'll keep an eye out," I assured him, then hacked out a cough that was almost as fake as my brother's had been a couple of days before. "You take care of that cold, you hear?" he winked, handing me his card before sliding on his raincoat and leaving. I watched through the front door window as he lit a cigarette while ambling down our walk, then neatly tucked the match back into his pocket rather than toss it on the long wet grass that could have used one more mowing before the snow started.

That's one sharp hombre, I recall thinking. Don't want to find myself on the wrong side of his good graces. Bad for health. The fact was, since the reverend didn't keep a separate office at home and they found nothing among his papers at church, I'd figured there were no papers to be found, period. That this assumption would prove to be way wrong was probably what got me started, in my tender middle teens—Amanda, how I missed having all my spare time to think of you and you only—on my first ulcer. Why wrong? Because less than an hour later, having discovered a 1843 first edition, first issue of Dickens's *A Christmas Carol* with hand-colored illustrations by John Leech, and another early sixteenth-century Aldine title by Lucretius that needed more research but looked promising, I opened one of the last of my smuggler's Bibles to find not a rare book but a sizeable stash of cash, about thirty grand, and a bunch of handwritten notes. The tidy wad of barely-circulated hundreds, held together with rubber bands, I put back where I found it, my fingers gone a tad numb. The notes, however, I spread out on my bed with utmost care. I knew what I had stumbled on even before I started combing through the receipts to sort out which ones went with which books.

Hurrying, I glanced at the treasures inside the remaining Bibles, jotted down my own notes about their authors, titles, dates, and so forth, then moved the trove of Holy Books into some boxes where I used to store my childhood comics before I sold most of them for enough to cover my Xbox acquisition. I cleared out the back of my disorganized warehouse of a closet, carefully stacked the boxes there, and proceeded to hide them under layers of wrinkled clothes, sports equipment I never used, a sleeping bag, piles of stuff it would take a team of archaeologists to dig out. The only Bible I kept out, besides the one my preacher father actually used to read when he wasn't busy hoarding high spots of Western culture, was the one with the cash and paper trail in it.

Now, I always thought it strange that my father, who had a booming ser-monizer's voice on Sundays, possessed such dainty old lady's handwriting. Just never made sense to me. Be that as it may, while his lion's roar may have been gone, his little kitty claw marks remained on many of them.

Like some born-again bean counter, I started going through the slips of paper. At first I was frustrated to see some of the notes about prices were coded. What, for example, did $RLTAS and $VEASS possibly mean? My heart sank. I saw reassuring names like Milton, Dryden, Swift, Poe, scattered here and there in the thicket of scrawl. Some of them were in my closet and others listed were not. When I happened to uncover a scrap that had been wadded up like some spitball with the word "$Revlations" penciled on it, I understood after a bewildered moment it was, eureka, the reverend's price code. An ironic one, too, if you stopped to think that it was not meant to reveal a thing. Seemed he had chosen a book of the Bible in which, when he dropped one "e," each letter could stand for a number, one through ten, and who'd be the wiser? Well done, pop, I thought proudly as a wave of missing him spread through me like the fast fever of a real cold, not my pretend act. It made me shiver to think of him somehow managing to assemble these books, to keep his doings so tight to the vest, or vestments I should say, and then the doorbell rang for the second time that day. Sensing this hoard of notes was almost as valuable as the books themselves, I stuffed them back in the hollow with the money and hid the Bible under my pillow. I had to figure that even if my room was searched by an alien strain of vampire stormtroopers they wouldn't deprive a sick, mourning boy of his bedtime copy of the Word of God.

Leery by now of unexpected visitors, I peered out an upstairs window and saw, to my astonishment, the same black Mercedes I'd seen that freakish hot August day, parked right in front of our house. Was there any way this could be good? No, I didn't think there was any way this could be good. But I couldn't hide inside the house like a book in a Bible for the rest of my life hoping my father's rare book contacts—and I was sure, Amanda, that's who this was, wishing like crazy I could disappear in your warm, dreamy embrace—hoping they would leave me alone now and forever, Amen.

The doorbell rang a second time. Nothing ventured, nothing gained, and all that. I slunk downstairs and opened the door. Middle-aged man wearing the most dapper raincoat I ever laid eyes on with its collars turned up. He had a salt-and-pepper moustache, steel-blue eyes, a learned face. City-looking, natty urban.

When he asked if my father was home, very polite and well-spoken, I recognized his as the voice on the phone from before. I also knew, seeing him there, beads of water trickling off the brim of his chic brown fedora, that he really and truly didn't know that the person he was asking after was no longer with us. Which meant, of course, that this wasn't the murderer.

"I'm afraid my father passed away two weeks ago." I didn't need to use any of my pathetic acting skills for it to be clear what I said was true, and that it upset me.

The quick look of shock that swept across his face was more proof that this guy was out of the loop on my dad's status and troubled by the news. "I hadn't heard, been overseas on business. I'm terribly sorry for your loss. He and I had arrangements, you see, to meet and—I don't know what to say."

"It's wet out there. You want to come in?"

"Well, just for a moment."

We stood in the hallway, him dripping, me shivering.

"I think we met once before, in the church some months ago," he said. "May I ask how your father passed away? It must have been a sudden illness. He seemed healthy when I saw him last."

"We weren't introduced," I said, to clarify. "But yeah, we saw each other once. My dad died of a concussion. He fell down the stairs at church. They say it was an accident."

Took me long enough, but only then did I notice he had his leather briefcase with him.

"You don't seem too sure it was. An accident, I mean."

With that, he suddenly sounded concerned. My first impression that he was clean as a fresh-washed window might have been wrong, I thought. "Me, I'm just a kid, so what do I know." Bread on the water, again.

"You seem like a pretty smart kid to me. None of my business, but I assume you've spoken with the police about your suspicions."

"Oh, sure. The detective who's looking into it stopped by this morning to go over a few things with me."

"Did he. Well, let's hope he gets to the bottom of it. I admired your father very much and we shared some of the same interests. In fact, I'd brought him something he and I had discussed before I went abroad," he said, lifting the brief case slightly. "But I suppose it doesn't matter now."

That statement obviously left me in a quandary because I both knew and didn't know what was in the briefcase. Had my father's books so taken hold of me, so seduced me like they had him, and probably this gentleman whose name I still hadn't asked for, fool that I was, that I was dying to know what he had brought? I couldn't recall ever being in such a helpless bind. If I had even the slightest hint of a moustache, not the convincing sculpture of whiskers that crowned this man's upper lip, I might have had a fighting chance to say, Hey, I know about the books. What've you got there? Something in vellum? A duodecimo or, like, a royal quarto? More Boethius, more Lucretius? But I sensed I hadn't a fighting chance.

I did go ahead and venture, "If it's a present or something, I could pass it along to my mom for you," hoping to coax some information out of him.

The wheels in his mind were turning. If he were a cartoon character, the illustrators would make it so you could see inside his head, pistons cranking, smoke billowing in the air like the gray ghost of a cauliflower.

He floored me when he finally said, after, I swear to every angel fluttering around on butterfly wings in heaven and every devil who ever poked a pitchfork in a sinner's behind, what had to have been a full minute, "It's not a present. Your dad wanted it for a—friend of his who was going to buy it. It's a little complicated."

The brief hesitation that ballooned before the word "friend" meant it wasn't a friend. I was young, yes, but I wasn't born yesterday. Curious before, now I was riveted.

He continued, the wheels in his mind still turning, "I'd give it to you but the problem is, you wouldn't really know what to do with it."

"How complicated could it be?" I asked. I mean, I loved my dad but doubted what he had been up to here wasn't beyond my own modest abilities.

"Your name is Liam, isn't it?" he said.

"Yes."

"Well, mine's John Harrison. I'm wondering if you'd mind if I took this coat off for a minute?"

"Oh, sure," I said, feeling that things might be drifting my way.

We sat, as if some movie director told us to and we were obedient actors, just where Reynolds and I had earlier. Harrison settled his briefcase between his polished black wingtip shoes.

"Did your father ever share with you his passion for books?"

Unbelievable, I thought. Was this guy really going to tell me what was what?

"For the Bible, sure. After that, not so much."

"He liked other books, too. You like books, Liam?"

"They have become of real interest to me recently," I said, mangling my English in an effort to sound sophisticated.

"I happen to think that would make your father extremely proud."

"What sort of work do you do, Mr. Harrison?" I asked, hoping to turn the spotlight away from me. I tried to make my question sound chatty, not pushy, but even before he answered, a raft of other questions flooded my mind. How did you know my father? Why all the secrecy around these books? Who was that other guy with the white Porsche? If my dad was pushed down those stairs, why was he pushed? What the hell was going on here?

"You can call me John if you like, Liam. What I am is a librarian," he said. "Like you, I've loved books ever since I was a kid, and when I grew up I figured the best way to be near what I loved was to work in a building filled with books."

"Makes sense," I said, ignoring his patronizing tone, waiting for more.

"It can be a little boring at times, but the job has its benefits."

"That's probably true of all jobs, no?" I could tell he was weighing something most important to him, so didn't stress over it myself but did have to wonder when he would get to the blasted point.

"Listen, Liam," said Harrison, or, that is, John, after another of his pauses, this one briefer than the others. "How good are you at keeping secrets?"

I thought of the more than sixty Bibles buried in my bedroom closet, thought of my beloved Amanda, thought of the often daydreamy life I led behind my locked bedroom door, and answered, "The best."

"Good. I kind of thought so," he said. "Your father, being a man of the cloth, probably taught you what the phrase 'to take a leap of faith' means?"

"Sure, I know what that means."

"All right, I'm going to take a leap of faith in you, okay?"

"I'm chill with that," I said, wishing immediately I had expressed myself less like some wannabe hip-hopster and more like a responsible grownup.

"Good," he continued. "Have you ever heard the word 'deacquisition'?"

"No, sir, I haven't."

"What about 'deaccession?'"

I didn't know that one, either, so he explained what they meant and went from there to tell me a lot of other interesting things. The more I spoke with John Harrison, the cooler, or rather more estimable, he seemed. I could see why my father enjoyed his friendship, or working with him, or whatever they did together. We conversed for an hour, him treating me more like an adult than anybody had in a long time, actually ever, telling me a little about a world I might never have imagined existed before I inherited my trove. Once I got the gist of what he was saying, and hearing the clock strike four, I told him my mother and brother would be coming home pretty soon, and he left after shaking my palm-damp hand, taking that book with him for safekeeping just for a few days, never knowing that it probably would have been just as safe if not safer in my tenderloin clutches. Unless what he let me in on was a pack of lies, which it wasn't, I just felt it in my bones, the reverend had quite an interesting double life going on here for the past several years. On the one hand, it fried my circuits to think of him, my bike-riding, sermon-preaching dad, as an under-the-radar outlaw. On the other, I found myself weirdly proud that he'd led a whole clandestine life nobody might have guessed. That he was so squeaky clean made it possible for him to take a walk on the wild side. Yes, my mind was blown but, at the same time, I was deeply inspired. Looking back, I see that day as the one when I became, for better or worse, a man.

True to my word, veritable poster boy of godless integrity that I was, I didn't let on to my family about my second visitor that Friday, although I did tell my mother that the detective had dropped over.

"He have anything concrete to tell us?" she asked, filling the kitchen cabinets with cans of soup and vegetables after finding a place for a carton of milk in our fridge, which was already overstuffed with casseroles and pot pies that neighbors and congregants had dropped off after the funeral. To her credit, mater had kept up the same dinner regimen that kept pater so hearty during their years of marital solidarity. If meatloaf, mashed potatoes, and canned peas were good enough for a man who ministered to hundreds of unwashed souls over the years, and secretly collected and fenced rare books—I hadn't known, until Harrison told me, that the word "fence" had another meaning beyond chainlink and pickets—then loaf, spuds, and mushy peas were good enough for me.

"Not really," I said, neutral as a glass of water. "He told me that the rest of them he works with say it was an accident. Guess they don't have any clues." I was about to add that maybe we should consider suing the church since there was a little lip on the third step down on which he might have caught the tip of his shoe. But then I realized we would pretty much only be suing ourselves. Besides, who knows whether the insurance was all paid up. Just seemed like a dead end in every sense.

"Well, then, I wish he'd stop coming around and stirring up bad memories."

"I hear you, Mom. But his intentions are good," remembering that line about how the road to perdition is paved with good intentions. She was right. Especially now that I knew what I knew. It was going to be best if Reynolds did back off. If I stuck to that old bit about *An eye for an eye, a tooth for a tooth*, it could wind up being my eye and my tooth that might go missing. I didn't know whether or not my poor father tripped and plunged down the stairs all on his lonesome. Point was, either way he was gone and there was no getting him back. And, like it or not, the less the police looked into his death, the less the chance they would uncover his curious secrets. He was beloved by his tightfisted flock, I thought. Let him stay beloved.

"I think Liam did it," my little brother, who will never get a blue ribbon for sanity, offered up to no one in particular. Three years my junior, he might as well have been a decade younger the way he acted sometimes.

"Hush your mouth," said my mother, a nice little flash of anger stoking her words.

"Yeah, zip it, Kemosabe," I concurred.

"Stop calling me that," he countered.

"Calling you what, Kemosabe?"

"Both of you. Stop it right now."

The soundtrack for dinner that night was all forks and knives against plates, glasses of juice being gulped and set back down on the table, high-lighted by an occasional sniffle from my stuffy nose. Looked like I was finally coming down with the cold I had been faking all week, comeup-pance from a wrathful deity no doubt. I went to bed early, no Xbox, no tube, no *De rerum natura*, and slept in a pool of sweat until late morning the next day.

"You okay in there?" my worried mom asked, knocking lightly on my door.

"Be down in a minute," I said, then lay there for another half an hour thinking about how much I missed Amanda, since the church was closed until a replacement minister was found, but also about Harrison, who'd given me his cell number. I don't think he could believe it any more than I did, that he basically offered to let me consider picking up where the reverend had let off. Obviously my dad had been a fence for the ages, since it didn't look like Harrison was taking his business elsewhere. Although, I had to wonder, maybe there weren't any available elsewheres. Or, at least, elsewheres that could be so covert and trusted.

"You're young to be doing this sort of thing," Harrison had said toward the end of our meeting, or whatever it was, almost as if he was thinking out loud. "But there's a matter of some urgency involved here with finishing up the prearranged transactions—"

I felt proud that I was suddenly asked to be part of a transaction. Transactions were never kid stuff. The word was just too big and stately to have anything to do with playing marbles or touch football or comparable baloney.

"—that were already in process before your father passed. Claude ought to be in touch in a matter of days, and there's quite a lot of money at stake for all three of us."

Again, I loved feeling I was a part of a sophisticated gang or ring where each of us depended on the other and the lucre was flowing like spring melt.

"So if I could trust you to help complete the deal, I'm sure your father would've been grateful. And it'll be some decent walking-around money for you. Just that you can't let anyone notice, or ever tell anybody, ever, is all."

"You can trust me," I said, and meant it. Whether or not the reverend would have been grateful, it didn't seem to me to be very hard work, and its shadier side attracted the anarchist in me. Harrison would give me a book to transfer to another man, this Claude guy, who would give me an agreed-upon amount of money, which I'd pass along to Harrison after taking for myself what he called "the courier's percentage," and everybody was happy as proverbial clams. Since Harrison couldn't safely get directly in touch with Claude and finish things up on his own—they didn't want to meet or talk or know each other at all—it was up to me to bridge them.

"Why not?" I had asked, in all innocence.

"It's better for you that you don't know why not, Liam," Harrison explained, or rather didn't explain. "'Why' is a word best stayed away from."

Never liked that word, anyway, so it was easy enough for me not to ask.

"How do I reach this Claude person?"

"You don't," said Harrison. "He reaches you."

"Well, how will he know if I have something for him?"

"He won't, not exactly. You either will or you won't have what he wants," Harrison said. "Thing is, it all runs along more smoothly than you can imagine. Your father always told me that Claude is a pleasant fellow, and I think you'll agree that your father was a good judge of character."

Fair enough, I thought, not sure whether my dad was a good judge of character or not. Steering clear of the word "why," I tried to push the river a little more. "Does Claude own a white Porsche, like one out of a sixties movie?"

"You know, Liam, I admire your curiosity. I admire your pluck. It's impressive in someone your age. The answer to the question is not necessarily. And the answer to your next question, if I'm guessing it right, is that it's best you don't know at this point. You okay with that?"

"All good," I said, more and more liking the craziness of what I was hearing here.

The warm smile that dawned on Harrison's face made me feel ten stories tall. How I wanted to know what book it was he had in his briefcase. What century, who the writer was, what the binding looked like, all that interesting stuff. No doubt it was worth some righteous dough, but strange as it sounds, that came in kind of second for me. We—my family and my dad's old church—needed money, for sure. But the book itself, the physical object, and my response to it, had a quality that couldn't be put into words, even if I had a thousand years to try. The closest I could come, then or now, was love. I'm not the sentimental kind, not much anyway. But love was what I felt, both pure and simple, and impure and not so simple. No, it wasn't the same love I had for Amanda—I felt no deeper love for anyone or anything—but still, it was a rich, growing love for these old leather-bound antiquarian Xboxes, vellum-covered TVs with programming by Boethius and his excellent crew of fellow scribes caught immortal on the page. How I wanted to tell Harrison right then and there I was all in. Instead, I kept my cool. He would find out soon enough. Smart son of a gun probably already knew he had a partner in me.

Besides, the words my mother told me not long after my father's death came back verbatim, sharp as the razor I'd just started using on the feathery whiskers on my chin, firm as the smooth cement floor on which my dad cracked his skull. "Now you're going to have to be the head of the family," she had told me, "and take your father's place in whatever ways you can." I had no idea what that might require of me when she said it. But times had changed, quick as a slip on a step, and life was upside down and inside out. I couldn't afford to sit around wishing things were like before. I knew what I had to do in order to measure up. Knew what kind of man I had to be.

With that decision, my course was essentially set for many years of my young life. To cut away the fat and the gristle and carve straight to the meat of the matter, I went for it. Harrison met me briefly, furtively, near an elementary school playground, to pass along the book he'd brought for my father—this time in a nondescript brown paper bag—after phoning to find out if I was up to the task after giving it a little thought.

"Yes, sir," I told him. "Proud to have the opportunity."

I fulfilled my obligations well enough that I continued as go-between, wearing my father's sometime mantle with pride, caution aplenty, and in the growing knowledge that any college degree I might have pursued was trumped by the symbiotic education I was getting by handling, researching, and reading these books. Fatuous or gushy as it might sound, they inspired me to learn more than I ever might have learned in academia.

What astounds me, looking back at those callow days, those yearning-to-learn days of methodical madness, those good boy-bad boy days, me watchfully passing back and forth the rarest of rare books and the coldest of cold cash, is that the Harrisons and Claudes of this world would take a chance on an underage, unproven cadet. See, the way I figure it, if my saintly father had been selected as the perfect recruit to be a part of this operation of liberation, as they saw it, or, more like it, pretended to in order to maintain their dignity, their integrity, and all that, then I, his eldest, but an innocent youth, was an even better go-between and minor partner in the scheme.

Wisely, I never spoke with Harrison about the genesis, as it were, of my involvement in my father's onetime sub rosa business. All we discussed was books, payables, receivables, and a number—there were many more than just that one Claude—of code-named collectors and dealers. Claude? As it turned out, all of our buyers were named Claude. Because transactions were cut in cash, I never saw a personal check, never saw a driver's license or any other form of identification. I didn't know and I didn't want to know the real names of these fellow addicts. Claude was a perfect moniker, I thought, since, I mean, please, was anybody in the history of the world ever really named Claude?

And in my father's gone but not forgotten footsteps, I wound up keeping some of the books I should have passed along for my commission but could not part with. All more or less on the up and up, for the record, since I paid Harrison for what I kept, cash out of my savings from the middleman fee, and just told potential buyers that the book wasn't available after all, instead offering them one of my father's books I didn't care to keep any longer. Sure, I ran into disappointment now and then, but, knock wood, not suspicion. Between the reverend's sterling reputation among the various parties and my own winning youthful earnestness—weird that the less innocent I was, the easier it became to make myself look innocent—all moved forward without a hitch. At the same time, I didn't let my immediate family, or anyone else, know about my trove. It was a challenge, but though I didn't increase the number of volumes in my little collection, I systematically increased its value. By the time I was in my early twenties, still living at home after Andrew himself had headed off to college, or, well, community college, my smuggler's Bibles housed rare books that were worth upwards of two and a quarter million dollars in retail value. That family acquaintances thought I was an underachiever who sadly lost his footing after his father's death was flat-out wrong but worked sweet as punch for me. I bagged groceries at the local store and eventually worked my way up to manager, just for show, but was making clandestine gelt hand over fist, or maybe hand under fist would be the more apt metaphor. Either way, an illness, an obsession, a passion—forgive me, my Amanda—for which there was no clear cure had taken me over.

I did figure out ways to funnel money to my mother for household expenses over the years, sometimes considerable amounts that surprised her, covering my tracks by lying that I had hit lottery jackpots, a grand here, a few thousand there. She bought it since she didn't have much choice, and was grateful in her poker-faced way. I also clenched my teeth and tithed to the church, whose new pastor delivered sermons that moved me not one bit more than my father's had. But I attended services anyway, partly to accompany my mom, partly to make Harrison happy, since he wanted me to maintain as virtuous an image as possible. But mostly because Amanda, who worked as a bank teller during the week and, having moved on from her Sunday school teaching, sang in the choir on Sundays, even taking over conducting whenever the regular director—Mrs. Thoth, a nice lady with a pear-shaped face, who had worked with my father for many years—was absent. She, Amanda I mean, had grown more and more fine as the years went by. Age became her, at least to my Amanda-consecrated eye. In all truth, she was a beautiful young woman with a warm smile and ready laugh, a prize many would consider worthy of far better than the lanky likes of me. But that wasn't a roadblock that could stop my heaven-ordained pursuit.

If I was Dante, Amanda was my Beatrice. After some initial hesitation on her part, we began taking walks after services. Walks that were, for many months, opportunities to get to know one another. I think she began to see me less as the minister's son and more as a real person, well-meaning if quirky, devoted if shy—shy at least around her. As for me, my adolescent longings were eclipsed by her simple presence, the presence of a truly decent human being. We spoke of our love of music, hers, and books, mine. She started reading some of the masterworks of literature and philosophy that interested me most—some of which I secretly owned as first editions—as well as a few novels by Lawrence and Henry Miller that

I considered classics. And I went over to her house to listen to recordings with her of her favorite music. I might never have guessed that, along with Bach, Mozart, and Beethoven, her most cherished composers were Maurice Ravel and, yes, Claude Debussy. That she also liked Prince made me fall for her all over again.

Somewhere in one of my smuggler's Bible books, there must be written a theory that would explain the things that came together all at once during that misty May of my twenty-first year. Well, not the things themselves. But how those things were connected by taut invisible strings which that gnarly puppet master known as god had decided in his great wisdom to pull. I can try to explain, since god certainly would never bother and even my beloved Boethius might not have been equal to doing.

Amanda had floored me when, the year before, she allowed me to kiss her during one of our walks. A long, tender kiss beneath a secluded tree, a kiss I had never believed in my heart of hearts would ever translate from fantasy to flesh. Who knows, maybe rubbing elbows with my learned librarian friend Harrison—who I suppose had become a bit of a father figure for me—gave me an air of sufficient sophistication that Amanda, over half a dozen years my senior, considered attractive. Perhaps having more money stashed under a scrap heap of laundry in my closet than all my neighbors had, added up times two, afforded me an adult confidence. Maybe it was because I actually finally succeeded in reading Nabokov and even tried my hand at understanding paperback translations of the works I owned in Greek and Latin, French and German. Who knows. Why ask why?

What happened was that our Sunday walks developed into shared evenings, dinners and movies, a train ride now and again into Manhattan to go to Carnegie Hall and hit some museums, and it wasn't long before she and I were spending lots of time together, more than I had ever hoped for back in my lusting tenderfoot years. In all seriousness, I was astonished to find that my daydreams, my wet dreams, my longing boyhood dreams were not wasted on some kind of delusion, and that the girl I thought I loved back in my youth turned out to be the woman I truly loved later. Cynical and defensive as I had been when I was younger, I always figured what I was experiencing was pure fiction, not the real deal like my father's death, my mother's decline. Such joy was, I knew, dangerous since it was fragile and rare. As fragile and rare as any of my hidden rarities.

Because the reverend had always adored Amanda, never privy to my filthy thoughts, of course, it was easy for my mother to embrace her current presence in my life. Deep down, I think my mom would have given up a dozen of me and my brother to have had just one daughter, not that I could blame her, for all the minor scuffling trouble Drew and I brought into her life over the years. A daughter would have made her time with my starchy pater a little more gently rumpled, and I mean that in a good way. Well, to some degree, Amanda filled that daughterly role for her, helping her make a pot roast after church some Sundays, advising her about hair colors when the old lady wanted to get a dye job, stuff like that. And it couldn't have made me happier for both of them, since it turned out Amanda's mother was no picnic, another story for another day. My courtship, a term my mom actually pulled out of the mothballs of her mind to describe my dating Amanda, was going better than I might ever have imagined possible. Not only did we say we loved each other, but Amanda claimed she liked me more than anyone she'd ever met.

She one day said it like this. "I've always had a secret crush on you, the handsome son of the handsome preacher. I guess you could say I've always loved you from afar. But I really like you, too. Silly as it sounds, I'm in like with you."

I don't think I could honestly claim that anybody I'd ever known, Harrison included, my family included, might be able to make the same statement. Oh, that Liam fellow? Now there's someone I truly and sincerely like. Forget about it.

During one of our Sunday afternoon suppers, I think it was lamb chops and new potatoes on the table, the doorbell rang unexpectedly and I went to answer.

"Hello, Liam," Reynolds said. "How's all and everything?"

Acting unsurprised as I could manage, though he probably wouldn't have been surprised to see me surprised since he hadn't stopped by in years, I told him all and everything was fine, thanks.

"I was just driving by the house and thought I'd check in on you and your family."

No choice but to let him in. "That's really nice of you."

"Who is it, Liam?" my mother called from the dining room.

"Detective Reynolds is here," I answered, praying she wouldn't ask him to join us.

"Ask him on in to join us if he'd like."

"No, tell her that's okay, Liam. I don't want to bust in on Sunday dinner, especially unannounced like this."

Not wanting to shout back and forth, I said to him, "That's all right, come on in why don't you. I'm sure she'd love to say hello. My girlfriend's here, too."

"You have a girlfriend now, do you? That's great," he said, but didn't budge an inch farther into the house. "I hate to be rude, but it was you I wanted to talk to if you had just a moment." He looked at his watch, a fakey-fake gesture that sent up, as my father used to put it, all the red flags in China.

"Hang on," I told him, then went to the dining room to say the detective wanted to have a word with me privately and I'd be back right away.

"Something about your dad?" my mother asked, setting her fork down on her place, voice fluttering like a buckshot bird falling out of the sky.

"No idea," I said, and looked at Amanda, who had picked up on my mom's nerves and clearly shared her concern. "Don't worry. Just go on eating and I'll see what he has to say."

Back in the foyer, Reynolds tipped his head to suggest we step outside. I grabbed my slicker off the coat rack and walked with him into a mist so fine that it looked like it was raining upwards instead of down. Parked at the end of the walkway was that same dark blue unmarked Chevy he was driving when I first met him.

"Guess you like that car," I said, breaking the ice, if ice it was between us that caused the silence.

"You got a good memory, Liam," he said with a light laugh. "I'm still wondering why you didn't become a detective like I thought you might. You have all the smarts it takes to solve mysteries. God knows, you probably have more smarts than the job requires."

I thought it best not to thank him.

"Plus, it might beat working in a grocery store."

"Maybe, maybe not," was all I could think to say. It annoyed and worried me that he knew where I worked, since I had never once seen him in our aisles.

"So, it's been quite a while since we talked about your father, how he passed."

"Yeah," I said, as we turned onto the sidewalk and ambled down the street away from the house.

"I hope you don't mind me bringing it up again, hope I'm not opening old wounds."

"I guess not," I said, looking away from him toward the window of our neighbor's house next door. Why was it their curtains were always drawn, no matter what the weather?

"Well, I didn't want to get your mom's hopes up but I think we may have a possible break in his case. After all this time, it doesn't happen that often. I mean, for a cold case to suddenly get warm again."

That same strange feeling of guilt, like I had killed him myself, came over me then. It wasn't a feeling I liked one bit, a ridiculous sensation since I was sitting right there with my little brother and mom when the accident happened. But I felt it anyway. I just hoped that Reynolds, who was sharp as ever and curiously intimidating, couldn't feel it, too.

"How so? What happened?"

"There's a man, his name doesn't matter, who passed away a few months ago, died of natural causes. Lived with his wife on the Upper East Side of New York. An advertising exec, did well in his career, made good money."

"Doesn't sound like the kind of guy who would push a minister down some stairs."

Reynolds paused, took in a deep breath, exhaled. "Well, you're right. At least partly right. You see, this man was a collector. Collected all sorts of things from coins and stamps to paintings and books. He had great taste, to say the least, and as it's beginning to come clear to those who were tasked with probating his estate, it looks like his taste went way beyond his income, which was already pretty hefty."

I naturally had already made the possible connection, but said, doorknob dumb, or trying to be, "I'm not seeing what this has to do with my dad yet."

"Well, I'll get to that now. You see, it looks like he was working with some dealers, suppliers of fine art stuff, not all of them totally legit. For instance, turns out one of his best paintings, a portrait of some girl by Degas—"

Reynolds mispronounced the name so it rhymed with Vegas, but I kept my tongue glued to the roof of my mouth. I didn't like the direction any of this was going.

"—was stolen from a museum in Austria. And there were other items, not by any means all of them, by the way, that seem to have come from institutions here and there. So, here's the bit that bothers me regarding your father. His address and phone number, both at the church and your house, were in a little book this collector kept in a wall safe."

"That's nuts," I said.

"It is nuts, you're right. Especially since, so far as the authorities working on all this have been able to determine, a number of the other names and contact info listed in his book could be traced to dealers in coins, stamps, art, and various collectibles like that. Now some of them have checked out, but others are under investigation. And as you can imagine, all the assets of the estate are frozen until his collections can be gone through with a fine-toothed comb to see what's what."

I made my first mistake ever with Reynolds when I said, "I'm lost here."

"Well, I have to doubt that, Liam," glancing over at me as the heavy mist turned to light drizzle. "I can imagine you wouldn't want to think your father, being a preacher and all, could be caught up in anything even slightly illegal. But there are some questions about why he was in this man's address book that will have to be answered at some point. Whether your dad found himself involved in any of this, which I seriously doubt, by the way, isn't really my ballywick. But his death was and is."

I said nothing, not wanting to say something wrong. Tongue glued, tongue glued.

"Did you ever know your father to be interested in collectibles at all?"

"No, sir," now finally lying.

"People used to like stamp collecting a lot. My grandfather had a humongous collection of stamps and when he passed away, we had them appraised, since he had always talked about how valuable they were and that we could all retire on it. Well, turned out his stamps were basically worthless, moneywise. The whole value was in his enjoyment cutting them off of envelopes and buying them out of catalogues for nickels and dimes."

"I never saw my father collect anything"—no, I didn't slip up and say, except for Bibles—"and that even included collecting enough during services to keep his church fixed. He and my mom sat around all the time worrying about money. Collecting would have been about the last thing on his mind."

"Well," Reynolds said, taking me subtly by the elbow and turning me around with him to head back toward my house. "If anything comes to mind, anything at all, that might explain what your dad's info was doing in this man's possession, would you let me know?"

"I doubt I'll come up with anything, but you can count on me to call if I do."

"You still have my card?"

"I'm sure I do."

"Look there. You have the instincts of a collector as well as a detective," he said, the wiseass. "Let me give you another one, just in case."

"Thanks," I said. "You sure you wouldn't like to come in for dessert? Amanda, that's my girlfriend, makes a mean pecan pie."

"I'll raincheck that, but next time for sure, okay?"

"You got it," I said, and shook his hand with the best smile I could summon from my slim arsenal of smiles. I turned to head back up the walk as he opened his car door. "Am I supposed to keep all this stuff to myself? Should I ask my brother anything?"

How I hoped he would say yes even as he said, "No. Just keep it to yourself for now."

"What am I supposed to tell my mom when I go back in?"

That did seem to throw him off a little. Hadn't thought that part through, I guess. "I don't know, just say I wanted to check in, catch up a little for old time's sake. I'm sure you'll come up with something."

My thoughts chasing in circles, I used Reynolds' excuse on Amanda and my mom, having no better bright idea.

That night, in bed, having driven Amanda home, my worries only darkened. I wanted to call Harrison but feared that my phone might be tapped. I wanted to get my Bibles and their precious charges to a safer place than my closet, but where in the world could I stow them until any danger passed? Above all, I desperately wanted not to believe my father had been pushed down those stairs to his death because of some sort of book deal gone sour. This last desire was the toughest of the three because it never seemed more plausible that this was exactly what had happened. I went through the faces of all the Claudes I had met over the years, wondering which Claude might have been this attorney who was fishier than sushi, but had no way of sorting out one from the next. That was how it was meant to be, of course. Just for occasions like this. If nobody was connected with anybody else, then nobody would take a fall simply because somebody else did. No game of dominoes here. And no one was ever supposed to have written anything down, which is why the reverend had his cost code and the Claudes were all blank slates. I never asked Harrison where he had deaccessioned all these books from, what library's rarely visited shelves were a little emptier than they had been, their once-upon-a-time presence having been erased forever, like some calculus equation a stupid schoolboy solved incorrectly on the chalkboard. The only common link was, like my father before, me.

What I did early the next morning, dawn failing to slice through the dense overcast, was—Amanda, my saving grace—I drove over to my girl-friend's and asked her if she could take the morning off work.

"You seem serious today, Liam. Are you all right?"

"I am serious, and I am all right. Better than all right, better than I've ever been."

We strolled to a pretty little park, one we liked a lot, not far from Amanda's apartment building. The sun hovered above us, white as a flag of surrender, trying like anything to break through the clouds. The bench we found was, like the rest of the park, empty and wet from last night's rain. I took off my jacket and wiped dry a spot where we could sit, holding hands. Damned if Amanda didn't look lovelier than ever, the shadows on her face softened in the pearl-gray light. Rotten as my juvenile thoughts about her over the years had been, I realized they'd brought me to this place, me sit-ting with her, not with some lewd made-up story about her but Amanda herself. When I asked her, "Manda, I love you so much, always have, and I wonder if you would marry me?" and she answered without hesitation, as if she'd pondered the possibility for a long time, "Nothing would make me happier, Liam," I felt the sun break through and even though it didn't it may as well have, given how full of warmth and light I felt. We kissed each other, held each other close, and as I walked her back so she could get ready for work, we agreed that we would tell my mom that evening and afterwards go out to dinner somewhere special and celebrate. Caviar and champagne, the works.

Back home, I got busy. The Bibles were already in a half a dozen weary boxes that had come from the church way back in the dark ages. A couple had maybe housed quart bottles of grape juice for all I knew, but their labels had all peeled off so the boxes were nondescript, old, and, I hoped, untraceable. I slipped contractors bags around them, to keep any rainwater off and to make them all the more anonymous. Like some criminal, which I suppose I was in fact, I made myself more anonymous too, by putting on my father's very unhip clothes, including a plaid sports jacket that was so hideous even he had never worn it. Up and down our street there were, as almost always, zero signs of life, but I made quick work of it anyhow. My heart heavy as a cobblestone, my eyes welling and blurred, I loaded the boxes into the trunk of my car—my mother still used the old wagon to ship herself to and from her lousy job, so I used our other one, another junker I had bought with my so-called lottery winnings that was good for getting from here to nearby there and nothing more. Our pathetic village library was too close to my neighborhood for comfort—I had considered the town dump, but terrified as I was about getting caught I couldn't bring myself to desert my precious trove there—so I drove a few hamlets over to a larger town, traveling through rolling terrain highlighted by ruined farmhouses and sad swayback horses standing in mucky fields.

At one point, seeing I was driving erratic as hell, I had to pull over to catch my breath and try to calm down. I sat there, muttering an apology to my father, and gazed out at one lone red horse that stood nearby, chewing away, his jaw zagging sideways, his big chocolate eyes trained warily on me. He looked like a mythic sage who had lost his train of thought. When I found myself starting to apologize to him, too, I snapped to, thinking, You have no choice here, Liam, no free will. Get this done already.

The library might as well have been a mortuary. Lights seemed to be on but there were no other signs of life. I parked in back of the building, a yellowish brick structure which, like my father's old church, had seen better days. Underneath a rusting metal eave at the top of a short flight of cement steps, I stacked the boxes against the rear door, which looked to be a delivery entrance. Let me confess that I fought back tears as I looked at the black plastic-wrapped boxes piled there, feeling like a bereft parent who was deserting a newborn on the doorstep of a church or police station, abandoning the child, one whose care and upbringing were beyond the realm of possibility, to the mercies of strangers and fate.

Head downcast and hands in pockets, I walked away from my trove with more grief than could ever be written down and printed in some damned book. As I climbed into my car and turned on the ignition, I leaned my forehead against the steering wheel and felt a breach had opened in my heart that I knew would never mend, a wound that meant I was losing my father all over again. But I was a man now, soon to be a husband, maybe even a real father one day, a father who would never abandon his kids, and to be a man meant sometimes you had to leave certain things behind with the hope that better things lie ahead. That's what I was telling myself, like some fool idiot saying a prayer, until I heard a knock on the car window that caused me to jolt upright in the car seat with the violent abruptness one experiences when waking from a nightmare.

I turned to see my father peering in at me, his face so very familiar with a look both furious and—how could this be?—friendly. My dead father viewed through the shimmering and unsteady lens of my tears, my father who I then recognized was in fact Reynolds staring in at me, his hoodie cowling his visage like a demonic monk. Stunned, speechless, I saw him flick his fingers toward his chest, that vintage gesture used by cops to indicate, Would you mind stepping out of your car, sir?

Defiant, or so I hastily tried to be, knowing my eyes must be ringed pink and wet, I rolled down the driver's side window, saying nothing. "So, Liam," he said, after glancing to his left and right before he rested his forearm on the door. "What's the word?" The playful frown on his unparted lips and the way he tilted his head with the cocky confidence of one in full

Machiavellian control boded nothing but trouble. Once my friend, or so I had naïvely believed,

Reynolds had developed a knack for asking questions that left me speechless.

I had no word for him, I realized. "I'm not sure what you mean," I ventured.

"Well, let me try to help you out. What I mean to say is, I was wondering what's in those boxes over there?" he asked, snapping his head back in the direction of the library while continuing to level his unblinking gaze at me.

Any joy or sadness I had experienced that day, from proposing to Amanda to the necessary decision to abandon my trove, came to a quick terminus. I swear I could literally feel the blood drain from my face.

Reynolds was still speaking. "Don't you want to get a receipt from the librarian if you're going to make a contribution of books? It's tax deductible, you know."

With one last pathetic grab at saving the situation, I said, "I don't make enough money to need a tax deduction. Was just thinking they could use some Bibles."

"Well, that's interesting, Liam. You know why?"

"No, why?"

"Because I was just thinking that I myself could do with reading the Bible more often. Working in my field, I encounter so many bad guys that sometimes I feel they have a negative influence on me. I worry now and then that I might turn into a bad guy myself if I don't watch it. Some Bibles might be just the thing. Some remedial reading, isn't that what it's called?"

I waited. His frown rose into a half-smile now.

"Let me ask you a question, you mind?"

My engine was still idling. I thought if I just dropped into gear I could end this puzzling discussion here and now. But did I really want to go to jail on the same day that the love of my life had accepted my proposal of marriage?

"My strong impression, watching you from afar—or, well, maybe not from so afar as you might think—is that you like those Bibles, even need those Bibles, as much as I do. I also suspect that you know far better than I do about how to mine them, if I can make a little pun, for their true value. Being the son of a preacher, and all, I mean. You agree with that, in principle?"

I squinted and nodded.

"Which is not to say I haven't been given alms now and then to keep prying eyes, so to speak, at bay. And I was happy to oblige, you know, even way back when, until I began to realize, not long before your father passed, what a pittance was being tossed my way."

Was I hearing right? I wondered. Was I just witness to a confession?

"I don't know about any of that," I said.

"Well, that's all right, you don't really need to know more. But look here, meantime. What do you say we get those boxes out of the wet weather, throw half of them in the back of my car"—and he gestured across the street behind me toward the vintage white bathtub Porsche parked there; I suppose I should have been more horrified than I was—"and the other half in yours, and get out of here before whoever is supposed to be running this silly library comes back and claims your donation. We can work out any details about our Bible studies later. What say?"

"Do I have any choice?"

Reynolds paused just a fleeting moment before answering, "None that I can think of, offhand."

Back home, after disposing of my pater's eccentric clothes and burying my remaining half of the trove in the back of my helter-skelter closet, not even bothering to see if I ended up with the Voltaire or the Shelley, the Donne or the Pindar, I opened an account at Amanda's bank with my so-called lottery winnings. Time had come for me to confess to my fiancée I'd been lucky scratching tickets over the years. She forgave me in the car, driving over to tell my mother the happy news of our betrothal, but also was practical enough to realize the money represented a nice nest egg with which to start our fledgling marriage. I swore—not on a stack of Bibles, no, but I meant it anyhow—that I would never gamble again. Both god and the devil, gamblers themselves, could verify I haven't, if only they existed.

For a handful of months after that encounter with Reynolds, a blessed oasis of time, nobody named Claude called me, or Harrison, either. The Claudes I didn't much miss, but one day, feeling a nostalgic longing to hear Harrison's voice, see if he was all right, see if any more books might be coming my way—*our* way, if one counted Reynolds—I called him from the anonymity of a pay phone downtown. It rang a few times before a recorded message came on and a monotone disembodied voice told me this number was no longer in service. My fellow congregants in the religious order of literary rarities had disappeared as if they had never been more than a crazy figment of my imagination. This hiatus soon enough came to an end. One day, a colleague of Harrison contacted me to say he had something either I or Harvey—Claudes were now known as Harveys, to me an equally preposterous moniker—might find of interest. Were it up to me and me alone, I would have respectfully announced my retirement and bowed out. But I had other mouths to feed than my own and, in all honesty, my bibliophilic malady might have been driven by fear into remission, but I could not fairly claim to be cured of it.

Reynolds showed up periodically, asking me if I had read any good books lately and, out of habit or lunacy or simply to remind me he held the dangerous upper hand, inquired if I'd had any contact from anyone suspicious, anyone who might have been involved in the reverend's death. Some days I told him I hadn't and that seemed good enough for him. On other days, I let him know that indeed I'd had a visitor, a fellow book lover, and handed him an attaché case containing either money or, if he liked, a new acquisition—or should I say, rather, deacquistion. Amanda, who knew nothing about any of these activities, of course, thought it was kind of Reynolds to take time away from his demanding job to stay in touch with me, and even come to our wedding, which took place on a sunny Saturday afternoon in my father's beloved old church. It was not her problem that I had become his minion, as it were, one who secretly chafed at the bit and bided his time.

And speaking of time, I had to wonder how many months or even years might pass before the good detective, my objectionable colleague, might make a fatal misstep on a staircase somewhere and plunge, a look of malign astonishment frozen on his face, to the unforgiving floor at the bottom. If and when it happens, will he even have time to curse my name, or my father's? No, I think he will not. His end is foretold in the Bible, after all, in Leviticus and elsewhere, and just because I remain at heart an unbeliever, I recognize that it is a book that holds many valuable truths and worthy mandates.

The Sequel

R.L. Stine

~⟋

Stine's books are read all over the world. He has sold over 350 million books, making him one of the best-selling authors in history. Born in Columbus, Ohio, in 1943, he began writing at the age of nine on an old typewriter found in his attic. After graduating from Ohio State University in 1965, Stine headed to New York City to begin a writing career. He started out writing joke books and humor books for kids under the name Jovial Bob Stine. He is the author of the young adult Fear Street series and the Goosebumps series, which was turned into a popular children's TV show, as well as several other novels. He lives in New York City with his wife, Jane, and their dog, Minnie. Their son, Matthew, is a composer, musician, and sound designer.

1

Witness one Zachary Gold, 33. Youthful, tanned, long and lean, tensed over his laptop in the back corner of the coffee shop, one hand motionless over the keyboard.

Casual in a white Polo shirt to emphasize his tan, khaki cargo shorts, white Converse All-Stars. He grips the empty cardboard latte cup, starts to raise it, then sets it down. Should he order a third, maybe a grande this time?

Zachary Gold, an author in search of a plot, begs the gods of caffeine to bring him inspiration. He is an author in the hold of that boring cliché, the Sophomore Slump. And his days of no progress on the second novel have taught him only that clichés are always true.

Not a superstitious man, not a fanciful man. Practical. A realist.

But today he will welcome any magic that will start him writing. An angel, a muse, a shaman, a voice from beyond the grave, enchanted beads, an amulet, a scrawled message on a crinkled-up paper napkin.

Today . . . perhaps today that magic will arrive.

No, Zachary Gold does not live in *The Twilight Zone*. He lives in a brownstone in the West 70s of Manhattan, a building he bought with the abundant royalties from his first novel.

He tells interviewers that he never reads reviews. But he did read the piece in the *New York Times* that declared him the "once-and-future king of the new American popular literature."

Does the once-and-future king have a future?

Zachary succumbs to a third latte, skim milk with a shot of espresso, and resumes his throne in front of the glaringly blank screen.

The first book wrote itself, he recalls. *I practically wrote it as fast as I could type it. And then I barely had to revise.*

A sigh escapes his throat. The hot cup trembles in his hand. If the first book hadn't crowned him king, he wouldn't be under so much pressure for the second one.

A lot of kings have been beheaded.

And then he scolds himself: Don't be so grim. A lot of authors have had this problem before you.

Zachary has a sense of humor. His wife Kristen says it kept him alive several times when she felt like battering him over the head with a hot frying pan. Kristen is a redhead and—another cliché—has the stormy temperament that is supposed to come with the fiery hair.

Two teenage girls at a table against the wall catch Zachary's attention. They have their green canvas backpacks on the floor and their phones in front of them on the table.

"Mrs. Abrams says we don't have to read *War and Peace.* We can read the Spark Notes instead."

"Mrs. Abrams is awesome."

At the table behind them, a woman with white scraggly hair, round red face, a long blue overcoat buttoned to her throat, two shopping bags at her feet, slumps in her chair as if in defeat, jabbering to herself. Or is she on the phone?

Zachary tells himself he needs the noise, the chatter and movement, the distraction of new faces, to help him concentrate. He wrote most of the first novel in this very coffee shop. He can't stay at home. Not with the baby crying. And the nanny on the phone, speaking torrents of heated Spanish to her boyfriend.

He tried an app that a friend told him about. It offered background coffee shop noise to play through your home stereo. Like those sound machines that play ocean waves to help you sleep. The app had an endless loop with the clatter of dishes and low chatter of voices. But the sounds weren't stimulating enough to force Zachary to beam his attention to the keyboard. He had to get out.

And now he sits gazing from table to table. Studying the faces of those chatting and those caught in the glow of laptop screens. And he thinks how carefree everyone looks. *Because they don't have to write a book.* Most people leave school and never have to turn in another paper. And they are so happy about it.

Why did he choose to be a writer? Was it because he couldn't think of anything else? Was it because his parents begged him to start a real career, to find something he could "fall back on?"

Was it because the Howard Striver character came to him as if in a dream? *Howard Striver, please don't haunt me. I like you, Howard. No. I love you. I'll always be grateful, old buddy. But I need to leave you behind.*

Zachary sips the latte, already on its way to lukewarm. A flash of an idea. *What if an author's character won't leave him alone? Pursues him in real life?*

It's been done. But it's the start of something.

Zachary leans forward. Shuts his eyes to allow his thoughts to flow. Prepares to type. A shock of pain as a hand squeezes his shoulder.

He turns and gazes up at a big, broad man, fifties, maybe sixty, salt-and-pepper stubble of a beard on a jowly, hazel-eyed face. Sandy hair in disarray. The whole face is blurred, Zachary thinks. Like the man is somehow out of focus.

A homeless man looking for a handout? No. He's too well dressed. Pale blue sport shirt open at the neck, dark suit pants well pressed, polished brown wingtips.

The hand loosens on Zachary's shoulder. "We need to talk," the man says through his teeth. The lips don't move.

The harsh tone makes Zachary lean away. "Do I know you?"

"I'm Cardoza," the man says.

"S-sorry." Zachary has always had a stammer when he's surprised.

"Cardoza," the man repeats. The hazel eyes lock on Zachary. "Cardoza. You know me."

"No. Sorry." Zachary turns away and returns his hands to the keyboard. "Please. I'm working. I don't have time—"

The man named Cardoza lunges forward. He reaches for the lid of the laptop and slams it down hard on Zachary's hands.

Zachary hears a *crack*. Then he feels the pain rage over his hands and shoot up both arms.

His scream cuts through the coffee house chatter. People turn to stare.

"You broke my fingers! I think you broke my fingers."

Cardoza hovers over Zachary. Zachary frees his hands from the laptop. He tries to rub the pain off his fingers. "What do you want? Tell me—what do you want?"

2

"What do I want? Just what's coming to me."

Cardoza pulls out the chair opposite Zachary and, with a groan, lowers his big body into it. His smile is unpleasant. Not a smile but a cold warning. He spreads his hands over the table, as if claiming it. Large hands, dark hair on the knuckles, a round, sparkly pinky ring on his right hand.

Zachary rubs his aching hands, tests his fingers. They seem to be working properly. If this man intended to frighten him, he has succeeded. Zachary glances around for a store manager, a security guy, maybe. Of course, there is none.

Why can't he get the man's face in focus? It seems to deflect the light.

He slides the latte cup aside. "I really am working here. I don't know you and I really think—"

Cardoza raises a big hand to silence Zachary. His smile fades. "I don't really care what you think."

Zachary glances around again, this time for an escape route. The narrow aisles are clogged with people. Two women have blocked the aisle with enormous baby strollers.

Two of his fingers have started to swell. Zachary rubs them tenderly. "You've attacked me for no reason. I have to ask you to leave me alone now."

The smile again. "Ask all you like."

Zachary doesn't know how to respond to this. Is Cardoza crazy? If he is crazy and wants to fight, Zachary is at a disadvantage. He's never been in a fight in his life, not even on the playground as a kid in Port Washington.

He eyes the man without speaking. He knows he's never seen him before. A tense silence between them. Zachary's laptop case is between his feet on the floor. Can he slide the computer into the case and get ready to make his escape?

Cardoza breaks the silence. He leans over the small, square coffee-stained table. "Having a productive day, Mr. Gold?" He doesn't wait for an answer. He spins the laptop around, opens it, and gazes at the screen. "Blank? A blank screen? Again?"

Zachary grabs the computer and spins it back around. "What do you mean *again*? What are you talking about?"

The hazel eyes lock on Zachary, now with cold menace. "Isn't that why you stole your book from me?"

"Hah!" Zachary can't help a scornful laugh from escaping. "Is that why you're here, Cardoza? You're crazy. You're messed up. You need to leave now." Zachary jumps to his feet as if to chase the man away.

Cardoza doesn't move. He clasps his hands together on the tabletop. "Word for word, Mr. Gold. Line by line. You stole my book. But I'm not a vindictive man. I just want a little payback."

Zachary's mind spins. Once again, his eyes search the small room for someone who could rescue him. "Cardoza, you need help," he murmurs. "You're deluded." *This man is insane,* Zachary thinks.

But is he dangerous?

And then: *Do other authors have to put up with this kind of harassment?*

And then: *Does he really think I'm going to give him money?*

"Please—leave me alone," Zachary says softly. "I'm asking you nicely."

"I can't, Mr. Gold. "I can't leave you alone. I don't know how you uncovered my manuscript. But you know I'm the one who created the Howard Striver character. He is based on my older brother, after all." Zachary is still standing, hands on the back of his chair. "I'm begging you—" he starts.

Cardoza shakes his head. "I'm not going anywhere." He motions for Zachary to return to his seat. "I think you and I are going to develop a very close friendship." That cold smile again. "Unless you want the world to know you are a thief and a fraud."

Zachary sees the women push out the front door with their strollers. This is his chance. He ignores his suddenly racing heartbeats, grabs the laptop in one hand, leaves the case on the floor, spins to the front and runs.

"Look out!" A young long-haired young man carrying a muffin and a tall coffee cup leaps back as Zachary bolts past him.

Zachary is out the door. Nearly collides with the two strollers. The women have stopped to adjust the babies in the seats. They glare at him as he stumbles and skids to a stop, turns, and runs up Amsterdam Avenue.

A mild, hazy day of early spring. The air feels cool on his blazing hot face. He dodges two men with handcarts, making a flower delivery to the store next-door. Runs past a man setting up his shawarma cart on the corner, a brief whiff of grilled meat as he passes.

Zachary has to stop at the corner as a large Budweiser truck rumbles through the red light, horn wailing like a siren.

Which way? Which way?

He glimpses a dark blur behind him.

Is Cardoza following him?

Zachary shields his eyes with one hand and squints into the sunlight. Yes. The big man is chasing him. Head down like a bull stampeding a toreador. A glint of silver, a flash of light in his hand.

Is he carrying a gun?

3

Maybe it's a phone.

Zachary darts behind the beer truck, crosses the street.

I can outrun him, but it would be better to hide. Especially if that's a gun in his hand.

The branch library stands in the middle of the block. The front window appears dark. Is it open? With the budget cuts, it's closed a lot of days. Zachary trots to the door, tugs the handle. Yes. Open. He swings the door just wide enough to slip inside.

Shouts outside. Is it Cardoza? The sound cuts off as the glass door closes behind him.

The librarian, a young woman, black bangs cropped across her forehead, redframed glasses glinting in the light over the front desk, perched on a tall wooden stool, almost lost inside a loose camisole dress, very lilac, clashinges with the red eyeglasses. She sees Zachary enter, breathing hard, almost wheezing, probably sweat visible on his forehead and cheeks.

He struggles to look calm and collected, as if he intended to visit the library. Flashes her a smile, but she continues to stare warily. He's holding the caseless laptop in one hand. Awkward. *I didn't steal it. Honest.*

She's a librarian. She should recognize him. He was on the *Times* list for forty-two weeks in a row last year.

Tucking the laptop under one armpit, Zachary makes his way to the reading room behind the front desk. It's a big room, deep and wide, lots of dark wood, worn armchairs along one wall, interrupted by a nonworking fireplace. Eight or nine rows of long tables across the middle of the room.

Nearly empty in this late-morning hour. Two bearded Asian men in armchairs reading Chinese newspapers. A middle-aged woman with frizzy, blondstreaked hair, leaning over a table in the front row, seemingly enthralled by an old copy of *People* magazine.

Zachary hurries to the back. Listening hard for the front door to open, for a big man with a gun (or maybe a phone) to burst in, alert to every sound. He drops into the last chair in the back row and hunches low, waiting for his breathing to return to normal, waiting for his eyes to adjust to the pale light from the old coneshaped fixtures high in the rafters.

A good hiding place. Cardoza must not have seen him slip into the library. He would be here by now.

Do I have to be afraid to leave my apartment?

He opens the laptop. Wipes sweat off his forehead with the sleeve of his Polo shirt. His phone rings. His ringtone is an old-fashioned classic phone ring. It's supposed to be ironic but now everyone has it.

Startled, he tugs the phone from his shorts pocket. The Asian men don't look out from behind their newspapers. The woman in the front ignores it, too.

He takes the call. "Eleanor?" His agent.

"Zachary, how are you?"

"Well . . . I'm having an interesting morning." He turns his head and talks in a loud whisper. Obviously, phone conversations in the reading room are not encouraged.

"Well, you know my main job. I'm the nudge. How is the sequel coming, Mr. Z?"

He can't hold back an exasperated groan. "I told you, Eleanor. I'm not writing a sequel. Do I have to tattoo it on my chest before you'll believe me?"

"Zachary, should I call back later?

Sounds like you're having a bad day."

"A bad day? I'm hiding in the library from a guy who chased me down the street because he says I stole my book from him."

"We all have our problems, Z. Know what my problem is? Getting you to write the sequel."

"Eleanor, please—"

"Why do you think you're having so much trouble getting started on the new book? Because you know your readers want another Howard Striver book. Zachary, why are you fighting it?"

"Been there, done that. Ever hear that phrase?" He sighed. "I don't want to be known as the guy who writes the Howard Striver books. I want to be known as an author. Period."

"Stubborn, stubborn. Let's look at it one other way, okay?"

"If we have to."

"Z, let's talk money. You like money, don't you? I know you and Kristen just got back from the Ocean Club on Paradise Island. That's not-too-shabby a resort. You enjoyed it, right?"

"Well, yes. But we had the baby and—"

"Zachary, do the Striver book, and I can get you a million dollars for any book you want to do next. Seriously. Do the sequel. The next book is an instant check for a million dollars. Can you picture that?"

"Of course. Don't talk to me like I'm an infant."

The *People* Magazine woman turns her head and squints at him. He turns his back and hunches lower behind the laptop screen.

"How am I supposed to talk to you when you're acting like a stubborn baby? Hey, think of your baby. Think of all the strained peas a million dollars will buy." She laughs. "Organic artisanal local strained peas, right?"

He didn't reply.

"One last thing, Z., then I'll go. Think of all the new mind powers you can give Howard. Think of all the brain powers you haven't touched upon yet. There has to be a hundred story possibilities."

"Well . . ."

"Think of the story possibilities. And then picture that million-dollar check. Okay?"

Zachary hears his reply as if it's coming from some other body: "Okay, Eleanor. I'll think about it."

4

Zachary thinks about his first novel. *The Cerebellum Syndrome* is a science thriller. Part Michael Crichton, part *Bourne Identity*, with a hint of the sci-fi novels Zachary devoured as a teenager.

Howard Striver is a brilliant brain surgeon and neurological explorer. Fascinated by the fact that seventy-five percent of the human brain is dormant, he sets about finding a way to stimulate the unused parts of the cerebellum.

Unable to find volunteers, Dr. Striver experiments on his own brain—and succeeds in giving himself extraordinary mind powers. His expanded memory, his newly found kinetic abilities, his ability to retain encyclopedic amounts of knowledge make him a powerful superhero of the mind.

Three different governments, including our own, send agents to kidnap Striver. They are desperate to analyze his brain and learn how to use his newly discovered mind powers for military purposes. He escapes again and again, a thrilling chase scenario.

But even while he flees his pursuers, Howard Striver continues his experiments. He knows he is going too far, expanding his abilities too rapidly to analyze what he has accomplished.

To thwart his pursuers, he escapes into his own mind. He begins living entirely in the unexplored spaces of his brain. He transforms reality into an internal reality of his own making.

That's the basis of the first book. Is it ripe for a sequel?

At home, thinking hard, Zachary paces back and forth in his study, holding Emily, the baby, in his arms. Emily's expression is serious, attentive, as if she can read the turmoil in his mind. She makes a gurgling sound. Zachary imagines she is trying to comfort him.

He raises her head to his face and gives it a long sniff. Nothing smells as good as baby skin. He runs a finger gently under her chin, a soft tickle.

"Emily, you are so precious to me," he tells her. "Should I give up writing something new? Write the sequel? For you?" Her pink mouth crinkles up. She starts to cry, thrashing her arms out stiffly.

He hands her back to the nanny.

I have to get out of here. I have to start writing. I have to think.

He picks up his laptop and carries it outside, down the front steps of the brownstone. He decides to return to the reading room of the little library on Amsterdam. Quiet and nearly empty. He can sit in the back and start to outline a plot. But before he can go half a block, he sees the heavyset man leaning on the blue mailbox on the corner. Cardoza. He steps up beside Zachary, matches his quick strides. "You have to acknowledge me, Mr. Gold," he says. He keeps his eyes straight ahead. His big hands swing gently at his sides as he dodges a boy on a silver scooter to keep up with Zachary.

"You can't just walk away. You stole my book."

Zachary tries to sound casual. But his voice is shrill, suddenly breathless. "You have mental problems, Cardoza. Please don't make me call the police."

"That would be a very bad plan," Cardoza replies, still facing forward, keeping pace with Zachary step for step. "You don't want to be exposed. You have only one reputation to keep."

"As I explained, I've never seen you before. My work ... . It's my own."

Zachary stops as the Don't Walk sign locks on red. A yellow cab swerves to the curb to let off a passenger. Zachary steps back and finally turns to face his accuser.

But Cardoza has vanished.

Zachary gazes behind him, then up and down the side street. No sign of the man. Zachary realizes he is sweating. Not because he feels any guilt. He knows he didn't steal anyone's work.

It's the casual menace on Cardoza's face. The certainty of an insane person.

He knows where I live. He was waiting for me.

The reading room is more crowded than the day before. People occupy the tables and the armchairs. One man has spread his papers over a table, taking up at least six places.

Zachary glances behind him. Despite its size, the room suddenly seems more vulnerable. If Cardoza rumbles in, there's no place to hide. Nowhere to run.

Laptop tucked under his arm, Zachary walks along the aisle to the back. He recognizes the same two bearded Asian men, Chinese newspapers spread out in front of them. A broad stairway leads down. The steps are painted bright yellow, red, and blue. A hand-painted monkey on a poster points down. A dialogue balloon above his head: THIS WAY, KIDS.

Zachary finds himself in the children's room. Shelves on three walls jammed with books. Picture books are scattered on a low, round table surrounded by tiny wooden chairs. Tall cardboard cutouts of book characters stand watch. A bright blue Dr. Seuss creature. Tinkerbell dressed as a Disney princess. A Star Wars droid.

Behind them, Zachary spots a long, dark wood table. Grownup height. Chairs on both sides. He positions himself behind the cardboard characters. Sets his laptop down. There is no one here, not even a librarian. The kids are all in school.

Quiet. The air a little warm, a little stuffy and dry. But the perfect place to work, hidden from the world.

He takes a moment to catch his breath. Glances at the framed book cover posters on the wall. All fairy tales. *Rapunzel . . . Snow White and Rose Red . . . Hansel and Gretel . . .*

Dark, nasty stories, he thinks.

He opens the laptop and brings up his *Word* program. He likes to start a book by making random notes. Plot ideas. Characters to populate the story. Story twists. Stream-of-consciousness thoughts. The research will come later.

To write the first book, he had to learn almost as much about the brain and its functions as Striver. He types the name: Howard Striver. He types: Book Two?

Am I really going to write a sequel?

He left Dr. Striver living entirely inside his own brain. Striver had expanded his consciousness enough that his inner world was big enough and interesting enough to inhabit without any outside stimulation.

But a sequel could not take place inside Striver's mind. Too constricting for even the cleverest, most brilliant writer.

How do I bring Striver back? How do I pull him from living inside his own mind, into the world where he can interact with people once again?

And once he is back, what will his mission be?

Zachary knows he has already done all he can do in the government-agents-out-to-capture-Striver's-Brain department. To pursue that plot would be writing the exact same book again.

What new brain powers can I give him?

Time travel?

Can the secret to time travel be locked away somewhere in the human brain, waiting to be discovered?

"Too outlandish," Zachary murmurs. "Too science-fictiony. Bor-ring."

He types: Do I really want to write a sequel? Am I fighting it because I know it won't compare to the first book?

He hears voices upstairs. A woman laughs. Chairs scrape the floor. The light shifts from the narrow, high windows up at street level. A gray shadow slants over the table.

Zachary checks the time on his phone. It is two hours later. He has been sitting here for two hours with nothing to show for it. Nothing on the screen. No idea in his head.

Maybe I'll become like Jack Nicholson in The Shining. *Go crazy. Type the same phrase over and over. Even that is better than a blank screen."*

Suddenly weary, he shuts his eyes and rubs them.

He opens them to find a beautiful young woman seated across from him.

Round blue eyes, almost too blue to be real. Full red lips, wavy black hair flowing down past the shoulders of her pale blue top.

She reaches across the table and touches the back of his hand. "Can I help you?"

5

They're making better-looking librarians these days, he thinks.

"I'm sorry if I don't belong here," he says. "I just needed a quiet place to write."

She smiles. "I'm not a librarian." The voice is velvety, just above a whisper.

He gazes back at her. She is radiant. The high cheekbones of a model. He even notices her creamy skin, like baby skin. She isn't wearing any makeup.

She doesn't blink. "Sometimes I help writers," she says.

"Help? What do you mean?"

The cheeks darken to pink. The red lips part. "I . . . do things for them."

She's teasing me. Coming on to me?

She taps the back of his hand again. "I recognized you, Zachary. I loved your book."

"Thank you. I—"

"I can't wait for the sequel." She tosses her hair back with a shake of her head.

Zachary shrugs. "I'm not sure there's going to be a sequel."

She makes a pouty face.

He's tempted to laugh. The expression is so childlike. "Look, I've been sitting here for two hours thinking about a sequel, and . . . well, I haven't exactly been inspired."

"I can help you," she says. "Seriously. I like helping writers."

"You want to write it for me?" he jokes.

She doesn't smile. "Maybe." She tugs his hand and starts to stand up. "Come on. Let's go talk about it."

He closes the laptop. "Where are we going?"

"To talk about your book." She has a clear, childlike laugh from deep in her throat. "You look so tense. Come on. Follow me. I can help you."

Outside, the afternoon sun is high in the sky. Two cherry trees across the street have opened their pink-white blossoms. The air smells sweet like springtime.

She is more petite than he imagined. She can't be more than five-five. Her slimlegged jeans emphasize her boyish figure. He wishes he was better at guessing a woman's age, but he hasn't a clue. She could be eighteen or thirty.

He likes the way she takes long strides, almost strutting, her hair swinging behind her.

She leads him to the Beer Keg Tap on the corner. A broken neon sign over the front promises steaks and chops. But the place hasn't served food in thirty years.

Sunlight disappears as he steps into the long, dark bar, and the aroma of spring is replaced by beer fumes. Two men in blue work overalls are perched at the bar, bottles of Bud in front of them, arguing, their hands slashing the air as they both talk at once. A small TV on the wall above them shows a soccer game with the sound off.

The bartender is a pouchy, middleaged woman with a red bandana tied around henna-colored hair, red cheeks, a long white apron over a yellow *I (heart) Beer* t-shirt. She leans with her back against the bar, eyes raised to the soccer game.

Zachary and his new friend slide into a red vinyl booth at the back. He sets the laptop on the seat beside him. He gazes at the vintage Miller Hi-Life sign on the wall above her head.

"Maybe I'll just have coffee," he tells her. "It's a little early . . ."

"You're a lot of fun," she says. It takes him a few seconds to realize she's being sarcastic. "Guess what I had for breakfast. Vodka and scrambled eggs. Breakfast of the czars."

"You're serious?"

The bartender appears before she can answer. "What are you drinking?"

She asks for a vodka tonic. Zachary, a little stung by her sarcasm, orders a Heineken. He suddenly remembers: "I haven't had lunch."

She smiles. "Then this is lunch."

At the front, the two men walk out, still arguing.

She pretends to shiver, shaking her slender shoulders. "This is exciting, Zachary. We're the only ones here."

She's a groupie? An author groupie?

"Tell me about your new book."

"I told you. There's no book. There isn't a shred of an idea yet. I'm not blocked or anything. At least, I don't think so. I am just so ambivalent about writing a sequel. I think I'm setting up roadblocks for myself."

The bartender sets the drinks on the table. "Need any nuts or anything?"

"That's okay," he says. She walks back to the bar, the floorboards creaking under her shoes.

They clink bottle against glass.

Then what do they talk about?

Here's where the time warp occurs. Zachary can't remember. Yes, he remembers another beer. No. Another after that.

He never was much of a drinker.

He remembers her red-lipped smile and the way those eyes penetrated his brain, like lasers, like he was the only one on the planet and she was determined not to lose him.

But what did they talk about?

And how did they end up in this pink and frilly studio apartment on the East Side? Such a girly apartment with pink throw rugs, and cornball paintings on the wall of children with huge eyes, and shelves of little unicorn figurines, and a pile of stuffed animals, mostly teddy bears and leopards.

Zachary doesn't remember a cab ride here, or a walk through the park. He feels okay, not drunk, not queasy the way he usually does after three or four beers.

He's sitting on the edge of her pink-and-white bedspread. She leans across the bed and starts to pull his Polo shirt over his head.

When did she get undressed?

She's wearing only blue thong underwear. Her skin so creamy. Small perfect breasts tilt toward him as she works the shirt off.

And now she's kissing his chest. Those full red lips moving down his skin, setting off electric charges. She's kissing him. Licking him. Lowering her face as her lips slide down his body.

Is this really happening? Oh, my God—it is!

6

Afterwards, Zachary pulls on his clothes. Glances at his phone. He's late. Kristen is at a conference out of town. He has to get home to relieve the nanny. He feels light-headed. The girlish room tilts and spins. He feels as if he's inside a pink-and-white frosted cake.

I've never been unfaithful before.

She watches him from bed, quilted bedspread pulled up to her chin. Her black hair is spread over the pillow. Is that an *amused* expression on her face?

I held that face between my hands as we made love.

"Zachary, my dear, I'm your muse now. No. I'm more than a muse. I'll write that book for you. You can trust me."

The words rattle in his brain like dice clicking together. He can't line them up to make sense of them. Can he be so wasted from three beers? Maybe it was four.

Why is she talking about his nonexistent book? She can't possibly think she can ghostwrite a sequel for him.

"Of course, there will be a price, Zachary," she is saying. "Everything has a price, right?"

He nods in agreement. "Okay," he says. "You write it."

Later, he realizes he wasn't as delirious as he acted. He just didn't want to admit to the reality of what he had just done.

And he didn't want to face the truth of what he was giving her permission to do.

"Yes. Okay, okay. Write the book for me. I don't want to write it. You write it."

"You understand it isn't for free?"

"Yes. You write it."

He tells himself there will be time to let her down easy when her manuscript is unacceptable. Meanwhile, the project will keep her close to him. Yes, he wants to see her again.

I've never been unfaithful before.

He sits on the edge of the bed to tie his sneakers. The room suddenly feels steamy, swampy. His skin prickles.

He stands up to leave. He feels unsteady, but not as unsteady as he'd like. If only he could blame his bad decisions on his dizziness. The little unicorns gaze up at him.

She's so beautiful. She didn't hypnotize him but she could have. He knows he's fallen under some kind of spell, just being near a creature so perfect.

She doesn't lift her head from the pillow. Just lies there watching him, her hair fanned out beneath her head. "Give me a kiss," she says, pleading, teasing.

He bends down to kiss her. She wraps her hands around his neck and holds him down for a long, thrilling kiss. "I'll see you at the library," she says when she finally lets him go.

He starts to feel more like himself as soon as he is out of her apartment. The late afternoon air feels cool on his hot face. Long blue shadows slant across the sidewalk as the sun slowly lowers itself behind the tall apartment buildings across the street.

Where is he? Zachary doesn't recognize the neighborhood. He walks a few blocks, past a Gristedes supermarket, past a Duane-Reade, past a shoe repair store, until he finds a street sign. Surprised to find himself on Second Avenue. Second and 83rd Street?

How did I get way over here?

He steps off the curb to hail a cab. Several pass with Off-Duty lights on their roofs. It's change-over time. Most daytime drivers are heading to their garage. It might be hard to find a cab.

Zachary suddenly becomes aware of a figure standing in the deep shadow of a building at the next corner. He doesn't have to focus to know it's Cardoza.

A shudder of fear snaps Zachary from any remaining cloudiness of his mind. All is clear now. The sight of this frightening pursuer makes Zachary alert, every muscle tensed for action.

He is stalking me. He is determined to frighten me.

He sees Cardoza begin to lumber toward him. The big man's fists pump at his sides, as if he's warming for a fight.

Zachary turns, considers running. He doesn't need to. A taxi pulls to the curb.

Zachary darts to it, pulls open the door, and dives inside.

He breathlessly tells the driver his address. The taxi begins to bump down Second Avenue. Zachary turns and peers out the back window. Cardoza stands with his meaty hands on his waist, still as a statue, watching . . . watching Zachary escape.

Zachary slumps in the seat, struggling to catch his breath, to slow his hummingbird heartbeats. Someone has left a water bottle on the floor of the taxi. It bumps Zachary's foot. He makes no attempt to set it aside.

Stalking me.

How did he attract these two new people in his life? One accuses him of stealing his book. The other wants to write the next book *for* him.

185

Zachary turns and stares out the back window again. He has to make sure he has left Cardoza behind. When he is satisfied that he has escaped, Zachary turns back, settles into the seat—and utters a gasp.

He slaps the seat with his palm. He twists his body and looks behind him on the seat.

No. No. His laptop.

No. It isn't here.

He left it in her apartment.

7

"Hello?"

"Mr. Z, how's it coming along?"

"And how are *you*, Eleanor? How was your day?"

"I'm hoping you will improve my day, Zachary. I need a yes from you."

"Eleanor, do you ever take a break to be a human? Do you ever stop working?" Zachary balances the baby in one arm, the phone in his other hand. Emily is just the right nestling size. He loves her lightness, the way her round bald head feels on his shoulder.

"Stop working? I don't think that would be fair to my clients."

Zachary laughs. "Just saying. The way you always cut right to business. Sometimes I wonder if you have a life."

"*You* are my life, Z. Enough about me. Now let's talk about the Howard Striver sequel. I need a yes from you today. I wasn't kidding about that million dollars."

"Yes," Zachary says.

"Yes? Did you just say yes?"

"Yes, I'll do the sequel."

Silence at the other end. She's speechless for once. He can *see* the surprise on her face.

"Well, good," she says finally. "I'll let them know. We can have a lunch and discuss delivery date, etcetera."

Emily starts to cry, soft gulps at first, then full-out blasts. He sits down and shifts her to his knee. "Got to run, Eleanor. Baby's crying. I think she's hungry."

"I know the book will be a winner, Mr. Z. And maybe a sequel will help get the movie out of development hell. You never know."

Did she ever congratulate him or compliment him on the baby? He can't remember her ever acknowledging this new addition to his life.

She really isn't *human.*

He clicks off the phone and tosses it onto the couch. He carries Emily to the changing table. Maybe that's why she's crying.

I wish Kristen would get home.

He feels a flash of guilt.

And then more than guilt. He's just promised a new book, and he doesn't even have his laptop. And in a moment of sheer insanity, he told a woman, a total stranger, she could write the book for him.

How crazy was that?

If he could undo the day . . . Maybe he still can.

When the nanny arrives the next morning, he hails a taxi and returns to 83rd and Second. It shouldn't be difficult to find her building. He passes the shoe repair store, the supermarket, the drugstore. He stops at the corner, shielding his eyes from the low morning sun.

Was it the redbrick building across the street? It doesn't look familiar. He turns and gazes at a tall white apartment building on the east side of Second Avenue. Cars are parked in a short, circular driveway that leads to the entrance.

He doesn't remember a driveway in front of her building. But the other buildings don't look familiar, either.

He can't ask for her, he realizes. He doesn't know her name.

I never even asked her name.

He doesn't know her name and he doesn't know where she lives. And, of course, he was too dazed and besotted to get her phone number.

Classic stupidity. But then the word *library* flashes into his head.

"Whoa. Yes," he murmurs. "The library."

She will return to the library and bring his laptop. Why did he go into such panic mode? Well, can you blame him? Writers don't like to lose their laptops (or leave them with total strangers).

Zachary feels a stab of fear as a large man in a pale blue business suit rapidly crosses 82nd Street. Cardoza? No. Another broad-shouldered, sandy-haired man taking elephant strides.

You're going to have to confront Cardoza. You can't be afraid every time you leave the apartment.

He studies the apartment buildings again. It's useless. He takes a taxi back across town to the library on Amsterdam. The reading room is empty. He nods to the librarian at the front desk, who doesn't look up, and makes his way downstairs to the children's room.

Zachary glances around. No sign of the young woman. The room is empty, as before. A very slender man with tall spiked blond hair over a frog-shaped face, and square, black-framed glasses approaches him. "I'm the children's activity director. Can I help you?"

"Well . . ." Zachary hesitates. He plans to stay down here and wait for the young woman with his laptop. But it might be awkward sitting by himself in the children's room. "I'm doing research on fairy tales," he says. "Can you direct me to the right shelves?"

He doesn't realize this is only the beginning of a very long week.

8

For five days, he waits at the table in the children's room, a stack of fairy tale books in front of him. He reads every collection, fairy tales from a dozen countries. He becomes an expert on witches and elves and princesses, evil spells, cauldrons of poisoned soups, power-mad queens, orphans lost in the forest, dragons and angels and talking owls. He spends the week in this terrifying otherworld, and the young woman doesn't show up.

Should he forget about her? Chalk the whole thing up to a crazy, weird experience? Buy a new laptop and get back to his life?

He admits to himself that he really wants to see her. He wants to see her beautiful, almost perfect face and hear her whisper-smooth voice. Yes, he has sexual fantasies about her all the time. But he just wants to see the blue eyes, the red lips, the angel angel-white skin . . .

When she shows up at his apartment on a Monday afternoon, he freezes at the door, tongue-tied. He can feel his cheeks go hot and knows he's blushing.

"You're here," he utters redundantly.

She laughs. "Can I come in?" He's blocking the door.

She slides into the apartment. She's wearing layers of t-shirts, pale blue and pink, and a short, pleated plaid skirt. Her legs are bare down to her white sneakers. She brushes her dark hair back with a shake of her head. Then she hands him the laptop. "Did you miss me, honey?" She draws a finger down his cheek.

"Well, yes. I waited for you. At the library. I mean—"

She gazes around the living room, then dives to the baby in the porta-crib on the couch. "Ooh, she's so cute." She rubs Emily's head tenderly. "And she's so bald."

"She had hair when she was born," Zachary says. "But it fell out. Now she's sprouting her real hair." And then a question forces its way to his mind: "How did you know she's a girl?"

She gives the baby head a last rub, then turns to him. "Zachary, I know everything about you." A strange smile, not warm, maybe ironic. "Today we'll find out what you know about *me*."

He blinks. "Excuse me?"

She points to the laptop. "I wrote the sequel for you, dear. I hope you like it."

He crosses the room to her. He has an impulse to toss down the laptop and throw his arms around her tiny waist. Instead, he squints at her. "You wrote the whole book in one week?"

She giggles. "I'm very fast."

"But—"

"And very good. It didn't take long to pick up your style." She pushes him to the couch. "Go ahead. Read it. I can't wait. Read the first chapter. I want to see the look on your face."

He sits down beside the baby and opens the laptop on his lap. She gets down on her knees in front of the porta-crib and makes cooing sounds, petting the baby's head as if she was a puppy.

Zachary opens the file and starts to read. His mind whirs. He's thinking of how he can tell her the work is not right, not acceptable, without making her angry and driving her away.

He wants to kiss her. He wants to hold her. He's aroused to the point of not being able to concentrate on the words. But he reads. Squinting into the glare of the screen, he reads the first chapter.

When he finishes it, he taps the screen with his fingers. "This is good. This is really good."

She smiles. "I thought you'd approve."

"Seriously. It's excellent," Zachary insists. He stares at her as if he's never really seen her. *This young woman is no-kiddingaround talented.*

He taps the screen again. "Where is the rest? I need to see more. I'm excited. I think . . . I think you've really got it."

She climbs to her feet. Then she reaches down and carefully lifts the baby from the small basket. Emily makes no sound as she lowers her to her shoulder.

"I will show you how to read the rest of the book, Zachary. But, remember, I said you'd have to pay?"

He nods. "That's no problem. We can talk about terms."

She rocks the baby gently on her shoulder. "Don't worry about terms, honey."

"Then . . . what do you want?"

The blue eyes lock on his. "You just have to tell me my name."

A laugh escapes his throat. "I . . . what?"

"You don't know my name, do you?"

"Well, I'm embarrassed. But . . ."

"So go ahead. Guess my name. You want the rest of the book, right? Okay. Guess my name, and the book is yours. That's the deal. Tell me my name. You have three chances."

He closes the computer but leaves it on his lap. "Seriously?"

She doesn't blink. She taps one foot.

Zachary realizes he has to play her game. Okay. No big deal.

He guesses. "Uh . . . Sarah?"

She shakes her head. He sees a flash of merriment in those cold blue eyes. "Two more guesses."

"Jessica?"

"No. Think hard, honey. You're down to your last guess. Make it a good one."

He squints hard at her, studies her as if trying to read her thoughts. *What name does she look like? Well . . .*

"Ashley?"

She lowers her head, hair falling over her face. "Oh, wow. Sorry, Zachary. That's not my name. And that was your last chance." She walks past him toward the door.

"So, tell me," he cries. "What is it? What is your name?"

She sighs. "Zachary, didn't we meet among the fairy tales?"

"Yes."

"So you should have guessed. You really should have guessed. My name is Rumpelstiltskin."

He gasps. "Huh?"

"My name is Rumpelstiltskin. You didn't guess it. So now the baby is mine." Zachary shoves the laptop to the couch and struggles to his feet. But before he can stand up, she and the baby are out the door.

9

He tugs open the door and bolts into the hall. He listens for her footsteps on the stairs. But all he can hear are his pounding heartbeats.

She's crazy, and she has my baby.

He takes off, flying down the stairs two at a time. Out onto the stoop. He gazes up and down the sidewalk. No. No. Not here. Breathing so hard, it feels as if his chest might burst.

Don't give yourself a heart attack.

Did she have a car waiting? How did she disappear so quickly?

He pulls himself back up to the living room. He grabs his phone off the couch.

I've got to call the police. She kidnapped my baby.

But what will the police say when he tells them her name is Rumpelstiltskin? He can already hear the derisive laughter when he describes how he's been living in a fairy tale.

"Oh, you lost your baby to Rumpelstiltskin? Why don't you ask Goldilocks to help you find her?" Followed by: "Hawhawhawhawhaw."

Zachary vows to find her on his own. He knows he isn't thinking clearly. He can't really think at all. He only knows he has to run. He has to run across the city, run to the places she might be, run to *anywhere* he might find her.

He's too frightened, too horrified to stay in one place. If he does, the horror of what he has done will catch up to him and swallow him whole.

He runs to the library. No one has seen her there. He runs to the East Side, back to her block. Which building? Which building? No. No sign of her.

Where to look now? He can't give up. He's walking up Second Avenue almost, to 86th Street, when he sees her seated at a table in a coffee shop window. She has Emily on her shoulder. A plate of scrambled eggs in front of her. And sitting in the opposite chair—Cardoza.

Were they working together?

Of course, they were. Cardoza's job was to get him frightened, off-balance, vulnerable, ready for her to step in and do her thing.

Rage overtakes him. He pounds on the window with both fists.

They turn, surprise then alarm on their faces. Before they can jump up, Zachary is through the door, past the group of people at the cash register waiting for a table.

His fists cut the air as he strides up to their table. His head feels ready to explode. He can feel the blood pulsing at his temples. He glares at them, his eyes moving from Cardoza, to the baby, to the woman. He opens his mouth to speak—and stops. He suddenly feels like a balloon deflating. He can feel the air whoosh from his lungs, feel his whole body sinking . . . shrinking.

He lowers his fists. His breathing slows. Finally, Zachary finds his voice. "I made you up, didn't I," he says softly.

They both nod, faces blank.

"I made you both up. You're not real," Zachary repeats.

"Yes," she answers in a whisper. "You imagined us."

"You're in my mind. You're a fairy tale. You're not really here." Zachary murmurs.

They watch him expectantly. She holds the baby against her shoulder, her eyes, unblinking, on Zachary.

"I imagined you," he says. "And if I shut my eyes . . ."

He doesn't wait for them to respond.

He shuts his eyes.

And when he opens them, he sees faces—unfamiliar faces—staring down at him. Faces hovering over him, features tensed, as if they've been waiting for him to do or say something.

He's lying on his back. He raises his head. "Where am I?" he asks.

10

"We put you in this room, Dr. Striver," a chocolate-skinned woman in a pale green uniform replies. Her curly white hair pokes out from her nurse's cap. "We thought you'd be comfortable here."

He nods and settles his head back on the pillow where it had been resting. Cardoza and Rumpelstiltskin linger in his mind.

A woman bumps the nurse out of her way. Her face hovers above his, her eyes disapproving, cheeks wet with tears. "You did it again, Howard," Debra, his wife, says. "I . . . don't understand. Can you explain it to me? Is living inside your own mind so much better than being with me?"

"No," he replies quickly. He reaches for her but she eludes his arms. The tears glisten on her cheeks. She makes no attempt to rub them away.

"How long have I been out?" he asks.

"Two days," Debra says. "But we had no way of knowing how long you would be away this time." Before he can reply, she continues. "Why do you keep doing this, Howard? Retreating into your own mind. You're trying to escape from me. Just admit it."

"No," he says again. "No. Really." He pulls himself up to a sitting position. He gazes at the doctors and nurses who have retreated to the walls so that Debra can confront him. "The baby," he says to her. "Is the baby okay?"

She narrows her dark eyes at him. "Howard, we don't have a baby. What's *wrong* with you?"

He's trying to get clear. He has to sort things out before he can assure Debra, before he can win her back. "What about my book?" he asks.

She shakes her head. "You keep threatening to write a book about your discoveries. But you'll never have time to write if you keep disappearing into your own mind."

He nods. He's starting to feel stronger. He takes her hand and squeezes it tenderly. "I'm ready to make a new start, Debra. I'll try not to escape again. I promise. Let's make this a new beginning. Part two of our lives. The sequel. Yes, let's start the sequel today."

She eyes him doubtfully, but she doesn't let go of his hand.

"Dr. Striver," the white-haired nurse interrupts. "Those men from the Pentagon have been waiting for two days."

He scratches his head. "What do they want?"

"Remember? They want to talk to you about how the military can make use of your brain powers? Dr. Striver? Dr. Striver?"

Debra drops his hand. She shakes him by the shoulders. "I don't believe it. Howard? Howard? Is he *gone* again? Howard—don't do this. *Howard*?

Mystery, Inc.

Joyce Carol Oates

~~~~

Joyce Carol Oates began writing in 1963 and has since published dozens upon dozens of books, including novels, short story collections, young adult fiction, plays, poetry, and essays. She graduated as valedictorian from Syracuse University in 1960 and went on to earn a master's from the University of Wisconsin in 1961. She has taught at the University of Detroit, the University of Windsor in Canada, and Princeton University. Together with her husband, Raymond J. Smith, Oates founded *The Ontario Review* and later Ontario Review Press in 1974. Oates has been the recipient of many awards, including the Prix Femina Étranger, the Pushcart Prize, and the National Book Award for *Them* (1969) and again for *We Were the Mulvaneys* (1996). She has been on the *New York Times* bestsellers list multiple times. She also has written under the pseudonyms Rosamond Smith and Lauren Kelly.

I am very excited! For at last, after several false starts, I have chosen the perfect setting for my bibliomystery.

It is Mystery, Inc., a beautiful old bookstore in Seabrook, New Hampshire, a town of less than two thousand year-round residents overlooking the Atlantic Ocean between New Castle and Portsmouth.

For those of you who have never visited this legendary bookstore, one of the gems of New England, it is located in the historic High Street district of Seabrook, above the harbor, in a block of elegantly renovated brownstones originally built in 1888. Here are the offices of an architect, an attorney-at-law, a dental surgeon; here are shops and boutiques—leather goods, handcrafted silver jewelry, the Tartan Shop, Ralph Lauren, Esquire Bootery. At 19 High Street a weathered old sign in black and gilt creaks in the wind above the sidewalk:

MYSTERY, INC. BOOKSELLERS
New & Antiquarian Books,
Maps, Globes, Art
Since 1912

The front door, a dark-lacquered red, is not flush with the sidewalk but several steps above it; there is a broad stone stoop, and a black wrought iron railing. So that, as you stand on the sidewalk gazing at the display window, you must gaze *upward*.

Mystery, Inc. consists of four floors with bay windows on each floor that are dramatically illuminated when the store is open in the evening. On the first floor, books are displayed in the bay window with an (evident) eye for the attractiveness of their bindings: leather-bound editions of such 19th-century classics as Wilkie Collins's *The Moonstone* and *The Woman in White*, Charles Dickens's *Bleak House* and *The Mystery of Edwin Drood*, A. Conan

Doyle's *The Adventures of Sherlock Holmes*, as well as classic 20th-century mystery-crime fiction by Raymond Chandler, Dashiell Hammett, Cornell Woolrich, Ross Macdonald, and Patricia Highsmith and a scattering of popular American, British, and Scandinavian contemporaries. There is even a title of which I have never heard—*The Case of the Unknown Woman: The Story of One of the Most Intriguing Murder Mysteries of the 19th Century*, in what appears to be a decades old binding.

As I step inside Mystery, Inc. I feel a pang of envy. But in the next instant this is supplanted by admiration—for envy is for small-minded persons.

The interior of Mystery, Inc. is even more beautiful than I had imagined. Walls are paneled in mahogany with built-in bookshelves floor to ceiling; the higher shelves are accessible by ladders on brass rollers, and the ladders are made of polished wood. The ceiling is comprised of squares of elegantly hammered tin; the floor is parquet, covered in small carpets. As I am a book collector myself—and a bookseller—I note how attractively books are displayed without seeming to overwhelm the customer; I see how cleverly books are positioned upright to intrigue the eye; the customer is made to feel welcome as in an old-fashioned library with leather chairs and sofas scattered casually about. Here and there against the walls are glass-fronted cabinets containing rare and first-edition books, no doubt under lock and key. I do feel a stab of envy, for of the mystery bookstores I own, in what I think of as my modest mystery-bookstore empire in New England, not one is of the class of Mystery, Inc., or anywhere near.

In addition, it is Mystery, Inc.'s online sales that present the gravest competition to a bookseller like myself, who so depends upon such sales . . .

Shrewdly I have timed my arrival at Mystery, Inc. for a half-hour before closing time, which is 7 P.M. on Thursdays, and hardly likely to be crowded. (I think there are only a few other customers—at least on the first floor, within my view.) In this wintry season dusk has begun as early as 5:30 P.M.. The air is wetly cold, so that the lenses of my glasses are covered with a fine film of steam; I am vigorously polishing them when a young woman salesclerk with tawny gold, shoulder-length hair approaches me to ask if I am looking for anything in particular, and I tell her that I am just browsing, thank you—"Though I would like to meet the proprietor of this beautiful store, if he's on the premises."

The courteous young woman tells me that her employer, Mr. Neuhaus, is in the store, but upstairs in his office; if I am interested in some of the special collections or antiquarian holdings, she can call him . . .

"Thank you! I am interested indeed but just for now, I think I will look around."

What a peculiar custom it is, the *openness of a store*. Mystery, Inc. might contain hundreds of thousands of dollars of precious merchandise; yet the door is unlocked, and anyone can step inside from the street into the virtually deserted store, carrying a leather attaché case in hand, and smiling pleasantly.

It helps of course that I am obviously a gentleman. And one might guess, a book collector and book lover.

As the trusting young woman returns to her computer at the check-out counter, I am free to wander about the premises. Of course, I will avoid the other customers.

I am impressed to see that the floors are connected by spiral staircases, and not ordinary utilitarian stairs; there is a small elevator at the rear which doesn't tempt me as I suffer from mild claustrophobia. (Being locked in a dusty closet as a child by a sadistic older brother surely is the root of this phobia, which I have managed to disguise from most people who know me, including my bookstore employees who revere me, I believe, for being a frank, forthright, commonsensical sort of man free of any sort of neurotic compulsion!) The first floor of Mystery, Inc. is American books; the second floor is British and foreign language books, and Sherlock Holmesiana (an entire rear wall); the third floor is first editions, rare editions, and leather-bound sets; the fourth floor is maps, globes, and antiquarian art-works associated with mayhem, murder, and death.

It is here on the fourth floor, I'm sure, that Aaron Neuhaus has his office. I can imagine that his windows overlook a view of the Atlantic, at a short distance, and that the office is beautifully paneled and furnished.

I am feeling nostalgic for my old habit of *book theft*—when I'd been a penniless student decades ago, with a yearning for books. The thrill of thievery—and the particular reward, a *book*! In fact for years my most prized possessions were books stolen from Manhattan bookstores along Fourth Avenue that had no great monetary value—only just the satisfaction of being *stolen*. Ah, those days before security cameras!

Of course, there are security cameras on each floor of Mystery, Inc. If my plan is successfully executed, I will remove the tape and destroy it; if not, it will not matter that my likeness will be preserved on the tape for a few weeks, then destroyed. In fact I am *lightly disguised*—these whiskers are not mine, and the black-plastic-framed tinted glasses I am wearing are very different than my usual eyeglasses.

Just before closing time at Mystery, Inc. there are only a few customers, whom I intend to outstay. One or two on the first floor; a solitary individual on the second floor perusing shelves of Agatha Christie; a middle-aged couple on the third floor looking for a birthday present for a relative; an older man on the fourth floor perusing the art on the walls—reproductions of fifteenth-century German woodcuts titled "Death and the Maiden," "The Dance of Death," and "The Triumph of Death"—macabre lithographs of Picasso, Munch, Schiele, Francis Bacon—reproductions of Goya's "Saturn Devouring His Children," "Witches' Sabbath," and "The Dog." (Too bad it would be imprudent of me to strike up a conversation with this gentleman, whose taste in macabre art-work is very similar to my own, judging by his absorption in Goya's Black Paintings!) I am indeed admiring—it is remarkable that Aaron Neuhaus can sell such expensive works of art in this out-of-the-way place in Seabrook, New Hampshire, in the off-season.

By the time I descend to the first floor, most of these customers have departed; the final customer is making a purchase at the check-out counter. To bide my time, I take a seat in one of the worn old leather chairs that seems almost to be fitted to my buttocks; so comfortable a chair, I could swear it was my own, and not the property of Aaron Neuhaus. Close by is a glass-fronted cabinet containing first editions of novels by Raymond Chandler—quite a treasure trove! There is a virtual *itch* to my fingers in proximity to such books.

I am trying not to feel embittered. I am trying simply to feel *competitive*—this is the American way!

But it's painfully true—not one of my half-dozen mystery bookstores is so well-stocked as Mystery, Inc., or so welcoming to visitors; at least two of the more recently acquired stores are outfitted with ugly utilitarian fluorescent lights which give me a headache, and fill me with despair. Virtually none of my customers are so affluent-appearing as the customers here in Mystery, Inc., and their taste in mystery fiction is limited primarily to predictable, formulaic bestsellers—you would not see shelves devoted to Ellery Queen in a store of mine, or an entire glass-fronted case of Raymond Chandler's first editions, or a wall of Holmesiana. My better stores carry only a few first editions and antiquarian books—certainly, no art-works! Nor do I seem able to hire attractive, courteous, intelligent employees like this young woman—perhaps because I can't afford to pay them much more than the minimum wage, and so they have no compunction about quitting abruptly.

In my comfortable chair it is gratifying to overhear the friendly conversation between this customer and the young woman clerk, whose name is Laura—for, if I acquire Mystery, Inc., I will certainly want to keep attractive young Laura on the staff as my employee; if necessary, I will pay her just slightly more than her current salary, to insure that she doesn't quit.

When Laura is free, I ask her if I might examine a first-edition copy of Raymond Chandler's *Farewell My Lovely*. Carefully she unlocks the cabinet, and removes the book for me—its publication date is 1940, its dust jacket in good, if not perfect, condition, and the price is $1,200. My heart gives a little leap—I already have one copy of this Chandler novel, for which, years ago, I paid much less; at the present time, in one of my better stores, or online, I could possibly resell it for $1,500 . . .

"This is very attractive! Thank you! But I have a few questions, I wonder if I might speak with . . ."

"I will get Mr. Neuhaus. He will want to meet *you*."

Invariably, at independently owned bookstores, proprietors are apt to want to meet customers like *me*.

Rapidly I am calculating—how much would Aaron Neuhaus's widow ask for this property? Indeed, how much is this property worth, in Seabrook? New Hampshire has suffered from the current, long-term recession through New England, but Seabrook is an affluent coastal community whose population more than quadruples in the summer, and so the bookstore may be worth as much as $800,000 . . . Having done some research, I happen to know that Aaron Neuhaus owns the property outright, without a mortgage. He has been married, and childless, for more than three decades; presumably, his widow will inherit his estate. As I've learned from past experiences widows are notoriously vulnerable to quick sales of property; exhausted by the legal and financial responsibilities that follow a husband's death, they are eager to be free of encumbrances, especially if they know little about finances and business. Unless she has children and friends to advise her, a particularly distraught widow is capable of making some very unwise decisions.

Dreamily, I have been holding the Raymond Chandler first edition in my hands without quite seeing it. The thought has come to me—*I must have Mystery, Inc. It will be the jewel of my empire.*

"Hello?"—here is Aaron Neuhaus, standing before me.

Quickly I rise to my feet and thrust out my hand to be shaken—"Hello! I'm very happy to meet you. My name is—" As I proffer Neuhaus my invented name I feel a wave of heat lifting into my face. Almost, I fear that Neuhaus has been observing me at a little distance, reading my most secret thoughts while I'd been unaware of him.

He knows me. But—he cannot know me.

As Aaron Neuhaus greets me warmly it seems clear that the proprietor of Mystery, Inc. is not at all suspicious of this stranger who has introduced himself as "Charles Brockden." Why would he be? There are no recent photographs of me, and no suspicious reputation has accrued to my invented name; indeed, no suspicious reputation has accrued about my actual name as the owner of a number of small mystery bookstores in New England.

Of course, I have studied photographs of Aaron Neuhaus. I am surprised that Neuhaus is so youthful, and his face so unlined, at sixty-three.

Like any enthusiastic bookseller, Neuhaus is happy to answer my questions about the Chandler first edition and his extensive Chandler holdings; from this, our conversation naturally spreads to other, related holdings in his bookstore—first editions of classic mystery-crime novels by Hammett, Woolrich, James M. Cain, John D. MacDonald, and Ross Macdonald, among others. Not boastfully but matter-of-factly Neuhaus tells me that he owns one of the two or three most complete collections of published work by the pseudonymous "Ellery Queen"—including novels published under other pseudonyms and magazines in which Ellery Queen stories first appeared. With a pretense of naïveté I ask how much such a collection would be worth—and Aaron Neuhaus frowns and answers evasively that the worth of a collection depends upon the market and he is hesitant to state a fixed sum.

This is a reasonable answer. The fact is, any collectors' items are worth what a collector will pay for them. The market may be inflated, or the market may be deflated. All prices of all things—at least, useless beautiful things like rare books—are inherently absurd, rooted in the human imagination and in the all-too-human predilection to desperately want what others value highly, and to scorn what others fail to value. Unlike most booksellers in our financially distressed era, Aaron Neuhaus has had so profitable a business he doesn't need to sell in a deflated market but can hold onto his valuable collections—indefinitely, it may be!

These, too, the wife will inherit. So I am thinking.

The questions I put to Aaron Neuhaus are not duplicitous but sincere—if somewhat naïve-sounding—for I am very interested in the treasures of Aaron Neuhaus's bookstore, and I am always eager to extend my bibliographical knowledge.

Soon, Neuhaus is putting into my hands such titles as *A Bibliography of Crime & Mystery Fiction 1749-1990*; *Malice Domestic: Selected Works of William Roughead, 1889-1949*; *My Life in Crime: A Memoir of a London Antiquarian Bookseller (1957)*; *The Mammoth Encyclopedia of Modern Crime Fiction*, and an anthology edited by Aaron Neuhaus, *One Hundred and One Best American Noir Stories of the 20th Century*. All of these are known to me, though I have not read one of them in its entirety; Neuhaus's *One Hundred and One Best American Noir Stories* is one of the backlist best-sellers in most of my stores. To flatter Neuhaus I tell him that I want to buy his anthology, along with the Chandler first edition—"And maybe something else, beside. For I have to confess, I seem to have fallen in love with your store."

At these words a faint flush rises into Neuhaus's face. The irony is, they are quite sincere words even as they are coolly intended to manipulate the bookseller.

Neuhaus glances at his watch—not because he's hoping that it's nearing 7 P.M., and time to close his store, but rather because he hopes he has more time to spend with this very promising customer.

Soon, as booksellers invariably do, Aaron Neuhaus will ask his highly promising customer if he can stay a while, past closing-time; we might adjourn to his office, to speak more comfortably, and possibly have a drink.

Each time, it has worked this way. Though there have been variants, and my first attempt at each store wasn't always successful, necessitating a second visit, this has been the pattern.

Bait, bait taken.

Prey taken.

Neuhaus will send his attractive sales clerk home. The last glimpse Laura will have of her (beloved?) employer will be a pleasant one, and her recollection of last customer of the day—(the last customer of Neuhaus's life)—will be vivid perhaps, but misleading. *A man with ginger-colored whiskers, black plastic-framed glasses, maybe forty years old—or fifty . . . Not tall, but not short . . . Very friendly.*

Not that anyone will suspect *me*. Even the brass initials on my attaché case—*CB*—have been selected to mislead.

Sometime this evening Aaron Neuhaus will be found dead in his bookstore, very likely his office, of natural causes, presumably of a heart attack—if there is an autopsy. (He will be late to arrive home: his distraught wife will call. She will drive to Mystery, Inc. to see what has happened to him and/or she will call 911 to report an emergency long after the "emergency" has expired.) There could be no reason to think that an ordinary-seeming customer who'd arrived and departed hours earlier could have had anything to do with such a death.

Though I am a wholly rational person, I count myself one of those who believe that some individuals are so personally vile, so disagreeable, and make the world so much less pleasant a place, it is almost our duty to eradicate them. (However, I have not acted upon this impulse, yet—my eradications are solely in the service of business, as I am a practical-minded person.)

Unfortunately for me, however, Aaron Neuhaus is a very congenial person, exactly the sort of person I would enjoy as a friend—if I could afford the luxury of friends. He is soft-spoken yet ardent; he knows everything about mystery-detective fiction, but isn't overbearing; he listens closely, and never interrupts; he laughs often. He is of moderate height, about five feet nine or ten, just slightly taller than I am, and not quite so heavy as I am. His clothes are of excellent quality but slightly shabby, and mismatched: a dark brown Harris tweed sport coat, a red cashmere vest over a pale beige shirt, russet-brown corduroy trousers. On his feet, loafers. On his left hand, a plain gold wedding band. He has a sweetly disarming smile that offsets, to a degree, something chilly and Nordic in his gray-green gaze, which most people (I think) would not notice. His hair is a steely gray, thinning at the crown and curly at the sides, and his face is agreeably youthful. He is rather straight-backed, a little stiff, like one who has injured his back and moves cautiously to avoid pain. (Probably no one would notice this except one like myself who is by nature sharp-eyed, and has had bouts of back pain himself.)

Of course, before embarking up the coast to Seabrook, New Hampshire, in my (ordinary-seeming, unostentatious) vehicle, attaché case on the seat beside me, and plan for the elimination of a major rival memorized in every detail, I did some minimal research into my subject who has the reputation, in book-selling and antiquarian circles, of being a person who is both friendly and social and yet values his privacy highly; it is held to be somewhat perverse that many of Neuhaus's male friends have never met his wife, who has been a public school teacher in Glastonberry, N.H. for many years. (Dinner invitations to Neuhaus and his wife, from residents in Seabrook, are invariably declined "with regret.") Neuhaus's wife is said to be his high school sweetheart whom he first met in 1965 and married in 1977, in Clarksburg, N.C. So many years—faithful to one woman! It may be laudable in many men, or it may bespeak a failure of imagination and courage, but in Aaron Neuhaus it strikes me as exasperating, like Neuhaus's success with his bookstore, as if the man has set out to make the rest of us appear callow.

What I particularly resent is the fact that Aaron Neuhaus was born to a well-to-do North Carolina family, in 1951; having inherited large property holdings in Clarksburg County, N.C., as well as money held for him in trust until the age of twenty-one, he has been able to finance his bookstore(s) without the fear of bankruptcy that haunts the rest of us.

Nor was Neuhaus obliged to attend a large, sprawling, land-grant university as I did, in dreary, flat Ohio, but went instead to the prestigious,

white-column'd University of Virginia, where he majored in such dilet-
tantish subjects as classics and philosophy. After graduation Neuhaus
remained at Virginia, earning a master's degree in English with a thesis
titled *The Aesthetics of Deception: Ratiocination, Madness, and the Genius
of Edgar Allan Poe*, which was eventually published by the University of
Virginia Press. The young Neuhaus might have gone on to become a
university professor, or a writer, but chose instead to apprentice himself
to an uncle who was a (renowned, much-respected) antiquarian bookseller in Washington, D.C. Eventually, in 1980, having learned a good
deal from his uncle, Neuhaus purchased a bookstore on Bleecker Street
in New York City, which he managed to revitalize; in 1982, with the
sale of this bookstore he purchased a shop in Seabrook, N.H., which he
renovated and refashioned as a chic, upscale, yet "historic" bookstore in
the affluent seaside community. All that I have learned about Neuhaus
as a businessman is that he is both"pragmatic" and "visionary"—an
annoying contradiction. What I resent is that Neuhaus seems to have
weathered financial crises that have sent other booksellers into despair
and bankruptcy, whether as a result of shrewd business dealings or—more
likely—the unfair advantage an independently wellto-do bookseller has
over booksellers like myself with a thin profit margin and a fear of the
future. *Though I do not hate Aaron Neuhaus, I do not approve of such an
unfair advantage—it is contrary to Nature.* By now, Neuhaus might have
been out of business, forced to scramble to earn a living in the aftermath
of, for instance, those hurricanes of recent years that have devastated the
Atlantic coastline and ruined many small businesses.

But if Mystery, Inc. suffers storm damage, or its proprietor loses money,
it does not matter—there is the *unfair advantage* of the well-to-do over the
rest of us.

I want to accuse Aaron Neuhaus: "How do you think you would do if
our 'playing field' were level—if you couldn't bankroll your bookstore in
hard times, as most of us can't? Do you think you would be selling Picasso
lithographs upstairs, or first editions of Raymond Chandler; do you think
you would have such beautiful floor-to-ceiling shelves, leather chairs and
sofas? Do you think you would be such a naïve, gracious host, opening your
store to a ginger-whiskered predator?"

It is difficult to feel indignation over Aaron Neuhaus, however, for the man is so damned *congenial*. Other rival booksellers haven't been nearly so pleasant, or, if not pleasant, not nearly so well-informed and intelligent about their trade, which has made my task less of a challenge in the past.

The thought comes to me—*Maybe we could be friends? Partners? If . . .*

It is just 7 P.M. In the near distance a church bell tolls—unless it is the dull crashing surf of the Atlantic a quarter-mile away.

Aaron Neuhaus excuses himself, and goes to speak with his young woman clerk. Without seeming to be listening I hear him tell her that she can go home now, he will close up the store himself tonight.

Exactly as I have planned. But then, such *bait* has been dangled before.

Like any predator I am feeling excited—there is a pleasurable surge of adrenaline at the prospect of what will come next, very likely within the hour.

Timing is of the essence! All predators/hunters know this.

But I feel, too, a stab of regret. Seeing how the young blond woman smiles at Aaron Neuhaus, it is clear that she reveres her employer—perhaps loves him? Laura is in her mid-twenties, possibly a college student working part-time. Though it seems clear that there is no (sexual, romantic) intimacy between them, she might admire Neuhaus as an older man, a fatherly presence in her life; it will be terribly upsetting to her if something happens to him . . . When I acquire Mystery, Inc., I will certainly want to spend time in this store. It is not far-fetched to imagine that I might take Aaron Neuhaus's place in the young woman's life.

As the new owner of Mystery, Inc., I will not be wearing these gingery-bristling whiskers. Nor these cumbersome black plastic-framed glasses. I will look younger, and more attractive. I have been told that I resemble the great film actor James Mason . . . Perhaps I will wear Harris tweeds, and red cashmere sweater vests. Perhaps I will go on a strenuous diet, jogging along the ocean each morning, and will lose fifteen pounds. I will commiserate with Laura—*I did not know your late employer but 'Aaron Neuhaus' was the most highly regarded of booksellers—and gentlemen. I am so very sorry for your loss, Laura!*

Certainly I will want to rent living quarters in Seabrook, or even purchase property in this beautiful spot. At the present time, I move from place to place—like a hermit crab that occupies the empty shells of other sea creatures with no fixed home of its own. After acquiring an old, quasi-legendary mystery bookstore in Providence, R.I., a few years ago, I lived in Providence for a while overseeing the store, until I could entrust a manager to oversee it; after acquiring a similar store in Westport, C.T., I lived there for a time; most recently I've been living in Boston, trying to revive a formerly prestigious mystery bookstore on Beacon Street. One would think that Beacon Street would be an excellent location for a quality mystery bookstore, and so it is—in theory; in reality, there is too much competition from other bookstores in the area. And of course there is too much competition from online sales, as from the damned, unspeakable Amazon.

I would like to ask Aaron Neuhaus how he deals with book theft, the plague of my urbanarea stores, but I know the answer would be dismaying—Neuhaus's affluent customers hardly need to steal.

When Aaron Neuhaus returns, having sent the young woman home, he graciously asks if I would like to see his office upstairs. And would I like a cup of cappuccino?

"As you see, we don't have a café here. People have suggested that a café would help book sales but I've resisted—I'm afraid I am just too old-fashioned. But for special customers, we do have coffee and cappuccino—and it's very good, I can guarantee."

Of course, I am delighted. My pleasurable surprise at my host's invitation is not feigned.

In life, there are predators, and prey. A predator may require *bait*, and prey may mistake *bait* for sustenance.

In my leather attaché case is an arsenal of subtle weaponry. It is a truism that the most skillful murder is one that isn't detected as *murder* but simply *natural death*.

To this end, I have cultivated toxins as the least cumbersome and showy of murder weapons, as they are, properly used, the most reliable. I am too fastidious for bloodshed, or for any sort of violence; it has always been my feeling that violence is *vulgar*. I abhor loud noises, and witnessing the death throes of an innocent person would be traumatic for me. Ideally, I am nowhere near my prey when he (or she) is stricken by death, but miles away, and hours or even days later. There is never any apparent connection between the subject of my campaign and me—of course, I am far too shrewd to leave "clues" behind. In quasi-public places like bookstores, fingerprints are general and could never be identified or traced; but if necessary, I take time to wipe my prints with a cloth soaked in alcohol. I am certainly not obsessive or compulsive, but I am *thorough*. Since I began my (secret, surreptitious) campaign of eliminating rival booksellers in the New England area nine years ago, I have utilized poisoned hypodermic needles; poisoned candles; poisoned (Cuban) cigars; poisoned sherry, liqueur, and whiskey; poisoned macaroons; and poisoned chocolates—all with varying degrees of success.

That is, in each case my campaign was successful. But several campaigns required more than one attempt and exacted a strain on nerves already strained by economic anxieties. In one unfortunate instance, after I'd managed to dispose of the bookseller, the man's heirs refused to sell the property though I'd made them excellent offers. . . . It is a sickening thing to think that one has expended so much energy in a futile project and that a wholly innocent party has died in vain; nor did I have the heart to return to that damned bookstore in Montclair, N.J., and take on the arrogant heirs as they deserved.

The method I have selected to dispatch the proprietor of Mystery, Inc. is one that has worked well for me in the past: chocolate truffles injected with a rare poison extracted from a Central American flowering plant bearing small red fruits like cranberries. The juice of these berries is so highly toxic, you dare not touch the outside of the berries; if the juice gets onto your skin it will burn savagely, and if it gets into your eyes—the very iris is horribly burnt away, and total blindness follows. In preparing the chocolates, which I carefully injected with a hypodermic needle, I wore not one but two pairs of surgical gloves; the operation was executed in a deep sink in a basement that could then be flooded with disinfectant and hot water. About three-quarters of the luxury chocolates have been injected with poison and the others remain untouched in their original Lindt box, in case the bearer of the luxury chocolates is obliged to sample some portion of his gift.

This particular toxin, though very potent, is said to have virtually no taste, and it has no color discernible to the naked eye. As soon as it enters the blood stream and is taken to the brain, it begins a virulent and irrevocable assault upon the central nervous system: within minutes the subject will begin to experience tremors and mild paralysis; consciousness will fade to a comatose state; by degrees, over a period of several hours, the body's organs cease to function; at first slowly, then rapidly, the lungs collapse and the heart ceases to beat; finally, the brain is struck blank and is annihilated. If there is an observer it will appear to him—or her—as though the afflicted one has had a heart attack or stroke; the skin is slightly clammy, not fevered; and there is no expression of pain or even discomfort, for the toxin is a paralytic, and thus merciful. There are no wrenching stomach pains, hideous vomiting as in the case of cyanide or poisons that affect the gastric-intestinal organs; stomach contents, if autopsied, will yield no information. The predator can observe his prey ingesting the toxin and can escape well in time to avoid witnessing even mild discomfort; it is advised that the predator take away with him his poisoned gift, so that there will be no detection. (Though this particular poison is all but undetectable by coroners and pathologists. Only a chemist who knew exactly what he was testing for could discover and identify this rare poison.) The aromatic lavender poisoned candles I'd left with my single female victim, a gratingly flirtatious bookseller in New Hope, P.A., had to work their dark magic in my absence and may have sickened, or even killed, more victims than were required. . . . No extra poisoned cigars should be left behind, of course; and poisoned alcoholic drinks should be borne prudently away. Though it isn't likely that the poison would be discovered, there is no point in being careless.

My gracious host Aaron Neuhaus takes me to the fourth floor of Mystery, Inc. in a small elevator at the rear of the store that moves with the antique slowness of a European elevator; by breathing deeply, and trying not to think of the terrible darkness of that long-ago closet in which my cruel brother locked me, I am able to withstand a mild onslaught of claustrophobia. Only a thin film of perspiration on my forehead might betray my physical distress, if Aaron Neuhaus were to take particular notice; but, in his affably entertaining way, he is telling me about the history of

Mystery, Inc.—"Quite a fascinating history, in fact. Someday, I must write a memoir along the lines of the classic *My Life in Crime*."

On the fourth floor Aaron Neuhaus asks me if I can guess where his office door is—and I am baffled at first, staring from one wall to another, for there is no obvious sign of a door. Only by calculating where an extra room must be, in architectural terms, can I guess correctly: between reproductions of Goya's Black Paintings, unobtrusively set in the wall, is a panel that exactly mimics the room's white walls that Aaron Neuhaus pushes inward with a boyish smile.

"Welcome to my *sanctum sanctorum*! There is another, purely utilitarian office downstairs, where the staff works. Very few visitors are invited *here*."

I feel a frisson of something like dread, and the deliciousness of dread, passing so close to Goya's icons of Hell.

But Aaron Neuhaus's office is warmly lighted and beautifully furnished, like the drawing room of an English country gentleman; there is even a small fire blazing in a fireplace. Hardwood floor, partly covered in an old, well-worn yet still elegant Chinese carpet. One wall is solid books, but very special, well-preserved antiquarian books; other walls are covered in framed art-works including an oil painting by Albert Pinkham Ryder that must have been a study for the artist's famous "The Race Track" ("Death on a Pale Horse")—that dark-hued, ominous and yet beautiful oil painting by the most eccentric of nineteenthcentury artists. A single high window overlooks, at a little distance, the rough waters of the Atlantic that appear in moonlight like shaken foil—the very view of the ocean I'd imagined Aaron Neuhaus might have.

Neuhaus's desk is made of dark, durable mahogany, with many drawers and pigeonholes; his chair is an old-fashioned swivel chair, with a well-worn crimson cushion. The desk top is comfortably cluttered with papers, letters, galleys, books; on it are a Tiffany lamp of exquisite colored glass and a life-sized carved ebony raven—no doubt a replica of Poe's Raven. (On the wall above the desk is a daguerreotype of Edgar Allan Poe looking pale-skinned and dissolute, with melancholy eyes and drooping mustache; the caption is *Edgar Allan Poe Creator of C. Auguste Dupin 1841*.)

Unsurprisingly, Neuhaus uses fountain pens, not ballpoint; he has an array of colored pencils, and an old-fashioned eraser. There is even a brass letter-opener in the shape of a dagger. On such a desk, Neuhaus's state-ofthe-art console computer appears out of place as a sleek, synthetic monument in an historic graveyard.

"Please sit, Charles! I will start the cappuccino machine and hope the damned thing will work. It is very Italian—*temperamental*."

I take a seat in a comfortable, well-worn leather chair facing Neuhaus's desk and with a view of the fireplace. I have brought my attaché case with the brass initials *CB*, to rest on my knees. Neuhaus fusses with his cappuccino machine, which is on a table behind his desk; he prefers cappuccino made with Bolivian coffee and skim milk, he says. "I have to confess to a mild addiction. There's a Starbucks in town but their cappuccino is nothing like mine."

Am I nervous? Pleasurably nervous? At the moment, I would prefer a glass of sherry to cappuccino!

My smile feels strained, though I am sure Aaron Neuhaus finds it affable, innocent. It is one of my stratagems to ply a subject with questions, to deflect any possible suspicion away from me, and Neuhaus enjoys answering my questions which are intelligent and well-informed, yet not overly intelligent and well-informed. The bookseller has not the slightest suspicion that he is dealing with an ambitious rival.

He is ruefully telling me that everyone who knew him, including an antiquarian bookseller uncle in Washington, D.C., thought it was a very naïve notion to try to sell works of art in a bookstore in New Hampshire— "But I thought I would give myself three or four years, as an experiment. And it has turned out surprisingly well, especially my online sales."

Online sales. These are the sales that particularly cut into my own. Politely, I ask Neuhaus how much of his business is now online?

Neuhaus seems surprised by my question. Is it too personal? Too—*professional?* I am hoping he will attribute such a question to the naïveté of Charles Brockden.

His reply is curious—"In useless, beautiful art-works, as in books, values wax and wane according to some unknown and unpredictable algorithm."

This is a striking if evasive remark. It is somehow familiar to me, and yet—I can't recall why. I must be smiling inanely at Aaron Neuhaus, not knowing how to reply. *Useless, beautiful . . . Algorithm . . .*

Waiting for the cappuccino to brew, Neuhaus adds another log to the fire and prods it with a poker. What a bizarre gargoyle, the handle of the poker! In tarnished brass, a peevish grinning imp. Neuhaus shows it to me with a smile—"I picked this up at an estate sale in Blue Hill, Maine, a few summers ago. Curious, isn't it?"

"Indeed, yes."

I am wondering why Aaron Neuhaus has shown this demonic little face to *me*.

Such envy I've been feeling in this cozy yet so beautifully furnished *sanctum santorum*! It is painful to recall my own business offices, such as they are, utilitarian and drab, with nothing sacred about them. Outdated computers, ubiquitous fluorescent lights, charmless furniture inherited from bygone tenants. Often in a bookstore of mine the business office is also a storage room crammed with filing cabinets, packing crates, even brooms and mops, plastic buckets and step-ladders, and a lavatory in a corner. Everywhere, stacks of books rising from the floor like stalagmites. How ashamed I would be if Aaron Neuhaus were to see one of those!

I am thinking—*I will change nothing in this beautiful place. The very fountain pens on his desk will be mine. I will simply move in.*

Seeing that he has a very admiring and very curious visitor, Aaron Neuhaus is happy to chat about his possessions. The bookseller's pride in the privileged circumstances of his life is almost without ego—as one might take pleasure in any natural setting, like the ocean outside his window. Beside the large, stark daguerreotype of Poe are smaller photographs by the surrealist photographer Man Ray, of nude female figures in odd, awkward poses. Some of them are nude torsos lacking heads—very pale, marmoreal as sculpted forms. The viewer wonders uneasily: are these human beings, or mannequins? Are they human female *corpses*? Neuhaus tells me that the Man Ray photographs are taken from the photographer's *Tresor interdite* series of the 1930s—"Most of the work is inaccessible, in private collections, and never lent to museums." Beside the elegantly sinister Man Ray photographs, and very different from them, are crudely sensational crime photographs by the American photographer Weegee, taken in the 1930s and 1940s: stark portraits of men and women in the crises of their lives, beaten, bleeding, arrested and handcuffed, shot down in the street to lie sprawled, like one welldressed mobster, face down in their own blood.

"Weegee is the crudest of artists, but he is an artist. What is notable in such'journalistic' art is the absence of the photographer from his work. You can't comprehend what, if anything, the photographer is thinking about these doomed people . . ."

Man Ray, yes. Weegee, no. I detest crudeness, in art as in life; but of course I don't indicate this to Aaron Neuhaus, whom I don't want to offend. The man is so boyishly enthusiastic, showing off his treasures to a potential customer.

Prominent in one of Neuhaus's glass-fronted cabinets is a complete set of the many volumes of the famous British criminologist William Roughead—"Each volume signed by Roughead"; also bound copies of the American detective pulps *Dime Detective, Black Mask,* and a copy of *The Black Lizard Big Book of Pulps.* These were magazines in which such greats as Dashiell Hammett and Raymond Chandler published stories, Neuhaus tells me, as if I didn't know.

In fact, I am more interested in Neuhaus's collection of great works of the "Golden Era of Mystery"—signed first editions by John Dickson Carr, Agatha Christie, and S.S. Van Dine, among others. (Some of these must be worth more than five thousand dollars apiece, I would think.) Neuhaus confesses that he would be very reluctant to sell his 1888 first edition of *A Study in Scarlet* in its original paper covers (priced at $100,000), or a signed first edition of *The Return of Sherlock Holmes* (priced at $35,000); more reluctantly, his first edition of *The Hound of the Baskervilles,* inscribed and signed, with handsome illustrations of Holmes and Watson (priced at $65,000). He shows me one of his "priceless" possessions—a bound copy of the February 1827 issue of *Blackwood's Magazine* containing Thomas de Quincy's infamous essay, "On Murder Considered as One of the Fine Arts." Yet more impressively, he has the complete four volumes of the first edition (1794) of *Mysteries of Udolpho* (priced at $10,000). But the jewel of his collection, which he will never sell, he says, unless he is absolutely desperate for money, is the 1853 first edition, in original cloth with "sepia cabinet photograph of author" of Charles Dickens's *Bleak House* (priced at $75,000), signed by Dickens in his strong, assured hand, in ink that has scarcely faded!

"But this is something that would particularly interest you, 'Charles Brockden'"—Neuhaus chuckles, carefully taking from a shelf a very old book, encased in plastic, with a loose, faded binding and badly yellowed pages—Charles Brockden Brown's *Wieland; or The Transformation: An American Tale*, 1798.

This is extraordinary! One would expect to see such a rare book under lock and key in the special collections of a great university library, like Harvard.

For a moment I can't think how to reply. Neuhaus seems almost to be teasing me. It was a careless choice of a name, I suppose—"Charles Brockden." If I'd thought about it, of course I would have realized that a bookseller would be reminded of Charles Brockden Brown.

To disguise my confusion, I ask Aaron Neuhaus how much he is asking for this rare book, and Neuhaus says, "'Asking'—? I am not 'asking' any sum at all. It is not for sale."

Again, I'm not sure how to reply. Is Neuhaus laughing at me? Has he seen through my fictitious name, as through my disguise? I don't think that this is so, for his demeanor is good-natured; but the way in which he smiles at me, as if we are sharing a joke, makes me uneasy.

It's a relief when Neuhaus returns the book to its shelf, and locks up the glass-fronted cabinets. At last, the cappuccino is ready!

All this while, the fire has been making me warm—over-warm.

The ginger-colored whiskers that cover my jaws have begun to itch.

The heavy black plastic glasses, so much more cumbersome than my preferred wirerim glasses, are leaving red marks on the bridge of my nose. Ah, I am looking forward to tearing both whiskers and glasses from my face with a cry of relief and victory in an hour—or ninety minutes—when I am departing Seabrook in my vehicle, south along the ocean road . . .

"Charles! Take care, it's very hot."

Not in a small cappuccino cup but in a hearty coffee mug, Aaron Neuhaus serves me the pungent brewed coffee, with its delightful frothed milk. The liquid is rich, very dark, scalding-hot as he has warned. I am wondering if I should take out of my attaché case the box of Lindt chocolates to share with my host, or whether it is just slightly too soon—I don't want to arouse his suspicion. If—when—Aaron Neuhaus eats one of these potent chocolates I will want to depart soon after, and our ebullient hour together will come to an abrupt conclusion. It is foolish of me perhaps, but I am almost thinking—well, it is not very realistic, but indeed, I am thinking—*Why could we not be partners? If I introduce myself as a serious book collector, one with unerring taste (if not unlimited resources, as he seems to have)—would not Aaron Neuhaus be impressed with me? Does he not, already, like me—and trust me?*

At the same time, my brain is pragmatically pursuing the more probable course of events: if I wait until Aaron Neuhaus lapses into a coma, I could take away with me a select few of his treasures, instead of having to wait until I can purchase Mystery, Inc. Though I am not a *common thief*, it has been exciting to see such rare items on display; almost, in a sense, dangled before me, by my clueless prey. Several of the less-rare items would be all that I could dare, for it would be a needless risk to take away, for instance, the Dickens first edition valued at $79,000—just the sort of greedy error that could entrap me.

"Are you often in these parts, Charles? I don't think that I have seen you in my store before."

"No, not often. In the summer, sometimes . . ." My voice trails off uncertainly. Is it likely that a bookstore proprietor would see, and take note, of every customer who comes into his store? Or am I interpreting Aaron Neuhaus too literally?

"My former wife and I sometimes drove to Boothbay, Maine. I believe we passed through this beautiful town, but did not stop." My voice is somewhat halting, but certainly sincere. Blindly I continue, "I am not married now—unfortunately. My wife had been my high school sweetheart but she did not share my predilection for precious old books, I'm afraid."

Is any of this true? I am hoping only that such words have the ring of plausibility.

"I've long been a lover of mysteries—in books and in life. It's wonderful to discover a fellow enthusiast, and in such a beautiful store . . ."

"It is! Always a wonderful discovery. I, too, am a lover of mysteries, of course—in life as in books."

Aaron Neuhaus laughs expansively. He has been blowing on his mug of cappuccino, for it is still steaming. I am intrigued by the subtle distinction of his remark, but would require some time to ponder it—if indeed it is a significant remark, and not just casual banter.

Thoughtfully, Neuhaus continues: "It is out of the profound mystery of life that 'mystery books' arise. And, in turn, 'mystery books' allow us to see the mystery of life more clearly, from perspectives not our own."

On a shelf behind the affable bookseller's desk are photographs that I have been trying to see more clearly. One, in an antique oval frame, is of an extraordinarily beautiful, young, black-haired woman—could this be Mrs. Neuhaus? I think it must be, for in another photograph she and a youthful Aaron Neuhaus are together, in wedding finery—a most attractive couple.

There is something profoundly demoralizing about this sight—such a beautiful woman, married to this man not so very different from myself! Of course—(I am rapidly calculating, cantilevering to a new, objective perspective)—the young bride is no longer young, and would be, like her husband, in her early sixties. No doubt Mrs. Neuhaus is still quite beautiful. It is not impossible to think that, in the devastated aftermath of losing her husband, the widow might not be adverse, in time, to remarriage with an individual who shares so much of her late husband's interests, and has taken over Mystery, Inc. . . . Other photographs, surely family photos, are less interesting, though suggesting that Neuhaus is a "family man" to some degree. (If we had more time, I would ask about these personal photos; but I suppose I will find out eventually who Neuhaus's relatives are.)

Also on the shelf behind Neuhaus's desk is what appears to be a home-made art-work—a bonsai-sized tree (fashioned from a coat hanger?)—upon which small items have been hung: a man's signet ring, a man's wristwatch, a brass belt buckle, a pocket watch with a gold chain. If I didn't know that Neuhaus had no children, I would presume that this amateurish "art" has found a place amid the man's treasures which its artistry doesn't seem to merit.

At last, the cappuccino is not so scalding. It is still hot, but very delicious. Now I am wishing badly that I'd prepared a box of macaroons, more appropriate here than chocolate truffles.

As if I have only just now recalled it, I remove the Lindt box from my attaché case. An unopened box, I suggest to Aaron Neuhaus—freshly purchased and not a chocolate missing.

(It is true, I am reluctant to hurry our fascinating conversation, but—there is a duty here that must be done.)

In a display of playful horror Neuhaus half-hides his eyes—"Chocolate truffles—my favorite chocolates—and my favorite truffles! Thank you, Charles, but—I should not. My dear wife will expect me to be reasonably hungry for dinner." The bookseller's voice wavers, as if he is hoping to be encouraged.

"Just one chocolate won't make any difference, Aaron. And your dear wife will never know, if you don't tell her."

Neuhaus is very amusing as he takes one of the chocolate truffles—(from the first, poisoned row)—with an expression both boyishly greedy and guilty. He sniffs it with delight and seems about to bite into it—then lays it on his desk top as if temporarily, in a show of virtue. He winks at me as at a fellow conspirator—"You are quite right, my dear wife needn't know. There is much in marriage that might be kept from a spouse, for her own good. Though possibly, I should bring my wife one of these also—if you could spare another, Charles?"

"Why of course—but—take more than one . . . Please help yourself—of course."

This is disconcerting. But there is no way for me to avoid offering Neuhaus the box again, this time somewhat awkwardly, turning it so that he is led to choose a chocolate truffle out of a row of non-poisoned truffles. And I will eat one with much appetite, so that Neuhaus is tempted to eat his.

How warm I am! And these damned whiskers itching!

As if he has only just thought of it, Aaron Neuhaus excuses himself to call his wife—on an old-fashioned black dial phone, talisman of another era. He lowers his voice out of courtesy, not because he doesn't want his visitor to overhear. "Darling? Just to alert you, I will be a little late tonight. A most fascinating customer has dropped by—whom I don't want to short-change." *Most fascinating*. I am flattered by this, though saddened.

So tenderly does Neuhaus speak to his wife, I feel an almost overwhelming wave of pity for him, and for her; yet, more powerfully, a wave of envy, and anger. *Why does this man deserve that beautiful woman and her love, while I have no one—no love—at all?*

It is unjust, and it is unfair. It is intolerable.

Neuhaus tells his wife he will be home, he believes, by at least 8:30 P.M. Again it is flattering to me, that Neuhaus thinks so well of me; he doesn't plan to send me away for another hour. Another wife might be annoyed by such a call, but the beautiful (and mysterious) Mrs. Neuhaus does not object. "Yes! Soon. I love you too, darling." Neuhaus unabashedly murmurs these intimate words, like one who isn't afraid to acknowledge emotion.

The chocolate truffle, like the cappuccino, is indeed delicious. My mouth waters even as I eat it. I am hoping that Neuhaus will devour his, as he clearly wants to; but he has left both truffles untouched for the moment, while he sips the cappuccino. There is something touchingly childlike in this procrastination—putting off a treat, if but for a moment. I will not allow myself to think of the awful possibility that Neuhaus will eat the unpoisoned truffle and bring the poisoned truffle home to his wife.

To avoid this, I may offer Neuhaus the entire box to take home to his wife. In that way, both the owner of Mystery, Inc. and the individual who would inherit it upon his death will depart this earth. Purchasing the store from another, less personally involved heir might be, in fact, an easier stratagem.

I have asked Aaron Neuhaus who his customers are in this out-of-the-way place, and he tells me that he has a number of "surprisingly faithful, stubbornly loyal" customers who come to his store from as far away as Boston, even New York City, in good weather at least. There are local regulars, and there are the summertime customers—"Mystery, Inc. is one of the most popular shops in town, second only to Starbucks." Still, most of his sales in the past twenty-five years have been mailorder and online; the online orders are more or less continuous, emails that come in through the night from his "considerable overseas clientele."

This is a cruel blow! I'm sure that I have *no overseas clientele* at all.

Yet it isn't possible to take offense, for Aaron Neuhaus is not boasting so much as speaking matter-of-factly. Ruefully I am thinking—*The man can't help being superior. It is ironic, he must be punished for something that is not his fault.*

Like my brother, I suppose. Who had to be punished for something that wasn't his fault: a mean-spirited soul, envious and malicious regarding *me*. Though I will regret Aaron Neuhaus's fate, I will never regret my brother's fate.

Still, Aaron Neuhaus has put off eating his chocolate truffle with admirable restraint! By this time I have had a second, and Neuhaus is preparing two more cups of cappuccino. The caffeine is having a bracing effect upon my blood. Like an admiring interviewer I am asking my host where his interest in mystery derives, and Neuhaus replies that he fell under the spell of mystery as a young child, if not an infant—"I think it had to do with my astonishment at peering out of my crib and seeing faces peering at me. Who were they? My mother whom I did not yet know was my mother—my father whom I did not yet know was my father? These individuals must have seemed like giants to me—mythic figures—as in the *Odyssey*." He pauses, with a look of nostalgia. "Our lives are odysseys, obviously—continuous, ever-unexpected adventures. Except we are not journeying home, like Odysseus, but journeying away from home inexorably, like the Hubble universe."

What is this?—"Hubble universe"? I'm not sure that I fully understand what Aaron Neuhaus is saying, but there is no doubt that my companion is speaking from the heart.

As a boy he fell under the spell of mystery fiction—boys' adventure, Sherlock Holmes, Ellery Queen, Mark Twain's *Pudd'head Wilson*—and by the age of thirteen he'd begun reading true crime writers (like the esteemed Roughead) of the kind most readers don't discover until adulthood. Though he has a deep and enduring love for American hard-boiled fiction, his long-abiding love is for Wilkie Collins and Charles Dickens—"Writers not afraid of the role coincidence plays in our lives, and not afraid of over-the-top melodrama."

This is true. Coincidence plays far more of a role in our lives than we (who believe in free will) wish to concede. And lurid, over-the-top melodrama, perhaps a rarity in most lives, but inescapable at one time or another.

Next, I ask Aaron Neuhaus how he came to purchase his bookstore, and he tells me with a nostalgic smile that indeed it was an accident—a "marvelous coincidence"—that one day when he was driving along the coast to visit relatives in Maine, he happened to stop in Seabrook—"And there was this gem of a bookstore, right on High Street, in a row of beautiful old brownstones. The store wasn't quite as it is now, slightly rundown, and neglected, yet with an intriguing sign out front—*Mystery, Inc.: M. Rackham Books*. Within minutes I saw the potential of the store and the location, and I fell in love with something indefinable in the very air of Seabrook, New Hampshire."

At this time, in 1982, Aaron Neuhaus owned a small bookstore that specialized in mystery, detective, and crime fiction in the West Village, on Bleecker Street; though he worked in the store as many as one hundred hours a week, with two assistants, he was chafing under the burden of circumscribed space, high rent and high taxes, relentless book-theft, and a clientele that included homeless derelicts and junkies who wandered into the store looking for public lavatories or for a place to sleep. His wife yearned to move out of New York City and into the country—she had an education degree and was qualified to teach school, but did not want to teach in the New York City public school system, nor did Neuhaus want her to. And so Neuhaus made a decision almost immediately to acquire the Seabrook bookstore—"If it were humanly possible."

It was an utterly impulsive decision, Neuhaus said. He had not even consulted with his dear wife. Yet, it was unmistakable—"Like falling in love at first sight."

The row of brownstones on High Street was impressive, but *Mystery, Inc: M. Rackham Books* was not so impressive. In the first-floor bay window were displayed the predictable bestsellers one would see in any bookstore window of the time, but here amid a scattering of dead flies; inside, most of the books were trade paperbacks with lurid covers and little literary distinction. The beautiful floor-to-ceiling mahogany bookshelves—carpentry which would cost a fortune in 1982—were in place, the hammered-tin ceiling, hardwood floors. But so far as the young bookseller could see the store offered no first editions, rare or unusual books, or art-works; the second floor was used for storage, and the upper two floors were rented out. Still, the store was ideally situated on Seabrook's main street overlooking the harbor, and it seemed likely that the residents of Seabrook were generally affluent, well-educated and discerning.

Not so exciting, perhaps, as a store on Bleecker Street in the West Village—yet, it may be that excitement is an overrated experience if you are a serious bookseller.

"After I'd been in the store for a few minutes, however, I could feel—something. . . . An atmosphere of tension like the air preceding a storm. The place was virtually deserted on a balmy spring day. There were loud voices at the rear. There came then—in a hurry—the proprietor to speak eagerly with me, like a man who is dying of loneliness. When I introduced myself as a fellow bookseller, from New York City, Milton Rackham all but seized my hand. He was a large, softbodied, melancholic older gentleman whose adult son worked with him, or for him. At first Rackham talked enthusiastically of books—his favorites, which included, not surprisingly, the great works of Wilkie Collins, Dickens, and Conan Doyle. Then he began to speak with more emotion of how he'd been a young professor of classics at Harvard who, with his young wife who'd shared his love for books and bookstores, decided to quit the 'sterile, self-absorbed' academic world to fulfill a life's dream of buying a bookstore in a small town and making it into a 'very special place.' Unfortunately his beloved wife had died after only a few years, and his unmarried son worked with him now in the store; in recent years, the son had become "inward, troubled, unpredictable, strange—a *brooding personality*."

It was surprising to Neuhaus, and somewhat embarrassing, that the older bookseller should speak so openly to a stranger of these personal and painful matters. And the poor man spoke disjointedly, unhappily, lowering his voice so that his heavyset, pony-tailed son (whom Neuhaus glimpsed shelving books at the rear of the store with a particular sort of vehemence, as if he were throwing livestock into vats of steaming scalding water) might not hear. In a hoarse whisper Rackham indicated to Neuhaus that the store would soon be for sale—"To the proper buyer."

"Now, I was truly shocked. But also . . . excited. For I'd already fallen in love with the beautiful old brownstone, and here was its proprietor, declaring that it was for sale."

Neuhaus smiles with a look of bittersweet nostalgia. It is enviable that a man can glance back over his life, and present the crucial episodes in his life, not with pain or regret but with—nostalgia!

Next, the young visitor invited Milton Rackham to speak in private with him, in his office—"Not here: Rackham's office was on the first floor, a cubbyhole of a room containing one large, solid piece of furniture, this very mahogany desk, amid a chaos of books, galleys, boxes, unpaid bills and invoices, dust balls, and desperation"—, about the bookstore, what it might cost with or without a mortgage; when it would be placed on the market, and how soon the new owner could take possession. Rackham brandished a bottle of whiskey, and poured drinks for them in "clouded" glasses; he searched for, and eventually found, a cellophane package of stale sourballs, which he offered to his guest. It was painful to see how Rackham's hands shook. And alarming to see how the older man's mood swerved from embittered to elated, from anxious to exhilarated, as he spoke excitedly to his young visitor, often interrupting himself with laughter, like one who has not spoken with anyone in a long time. He confided in Neuhaus that he didn't trust his son—"Not with our finances, not with book orders, not with maintaining the store, and not with my life." He'd once been very close to the boy, as he called him, but their relationship had altered significantly since his son's fortieth birthday, for no clear reason. Unfortunately, he had no other recourse than to keep his son on at the store as he couldn't afford to pay an employee a competitive wage, and the boy, who'd dropped out of Williams College midway through his freshman year, for "mental" reasons, would have no other employment—"It is a tragic trap, fatherhood! And my wife and I had been so happy in our innocence, long ago." Neuhaus shudders, recalling.

"As Rackham spoke in his lowered voice I had a sudden fantasy of the son rushing into the office swinging a hand ax at us . . . I felt absolutely chilled—terrified . . . I swear, I could see that ax. . . . It was as if the bookstore were haunted by something that had not yet happened."

Haunted by something that had not yet happened. Despite the heat from the fireplace, I am feeling chilled too. I glance over my shoulder to see that the door, or rather the moving panel, is shut. No one will rush in upon us here in Aaron Neuhaus's *santum sanctorum*, wielding an ax . . .

Nervously, I have been sipping my cappuccino, which has cooled somewhat. I am finding it just slightly hard to swallow—my mouth is oddly dry, perhaps because of nerves. The taste of the cappuccino is extraordinary: rich, dark, delicious. It is the frothy milk that makes the coffee so special, Neuhaus remarks that it isn't ordinary milk but goat's milk, for a sharper flavor.

Neuhaus continues—"It was from Milton Rackham that I acquired the complete set of William Roughead which, for some eccentric reason, he'd been keeping in a cabinet at the back of the store under lock and key. I asked him why this wonderful set of books was hidden away, why it wasn't prominently displayed and for sale, and Rackham said coldly, with an air of reproach, 'Not all things in a bookseller's life are for sale, sir.' Suddenly, with no warning, the old gentleman seemed to be hostile to me. I was shocked by his tone."

Neuhaus pauses, as if he is still shocked, to a degree.

"Eventually, Rackham would reveal to me that he was hoarding other valuable first editions—some of these I have shown you, the 'Golden Age' items, which I acquired as part of the store's stock. And the first-edition *Mysteries of Udolpho*—which in his desperation to sell he practically gave away to me. And a collection of antique maps and globes, in an uncatalogued jumble on the second floor—a collection he'd inherited, he said, from the previous bookseller. Why on earth would anyone hoard these valuable items—I couldn't resist asking—and Rackham told me, again in a hostile voice, 'We gentlemen don't wear our hearts on our sleeves, do we? Do *you*?'"

It is uncanny, when Neuhaus mimics his predecessor's voice, I seem—almost—to be hearing the voice of another.

"Such a strange man! And yet, in a way—a way I have never quite articulated to anyone, before now—Milton Rackham has come to seem to me a kind of *paternal figure* in my life. He'd looked upon me as a kind of son, or rescuer—seeing that his own son had turned against him."

Neuhaus is looking pensive, as if remembering something unpleasant. And I am feeling anxious, wishing that my companion would devour the damned chocolate truffle as he clearly wishes to do.

"Charles, it's a poor storyteller who leaps ahead of his story—but—I have to tell you, before going on, that my vision of Rackham's 'brooding' son murdering him with an ax turned out to be prophetic—that is, true. It would happen exactly three weeks to the day after I'd first stepped into the bookstore—at a time when Rackham and I were negotiating the sale of the property, mostly by phone. I was nowhere near Seabrook, and received an astounding call . . ." Neuhaus passes his hand over his eyes, shaking his head.

This is a surprising revelation! For some reason, I am quite taken aback. That a bookseller was murdered in this building, even if not in this very room, and by his own son—this is a bit of a shock.

"And so—in some way—Mystery, Inc. is haunted?"—my question is uncertain.

Neuhaus laughs, somewhat scornfully—"Haunted—now? Of course not. Mystery, Inc. is a very successful, even legendary bookstore of its kind in New England. *You* would not know that, Charles, since you are not in the trade."

These words aren't so harsh as they might seem, for Neuhaus is smiling at me as one might smile at a foolish or uninformed individual for whom one feels some affection, and is quick to forgive. And I am eager to agree—I am not in *the trade*.

"The story is even more awful, for the murderer—the deranged 'boy'—managed to kill himself also, in the cellar of the store—a very dark, dank, dungeon-like space even today, which I try to avoid as much as possible. (Talk of 'haunted'! That is the likely place, not the bookstore itself.) The hand ax was too dull for the task, it seems, so the 'boy' cut his throat with a box cutter—one of those razor-sharp objects no bookstore is without." Casually Neuhaus reaches out to pick up a box cutter, that has been hidden from my view by a stack of bound galleys on his desk; as if, for one not in the "trade," a box cutter would need to be identified. (Though I am quite familiar with box cutters it is somewhat disconcerting to see one in this elegantly furnished office—lying on Aaron Neuhaus's desk!) "Following this double tragedy the property fell into the possession of a mortgage company, for it had been heavily mortgaged. I was able to complete the sale within a few weeks, for a quite reasonable price since no one else seemed to want it." Neuhaus chuckles grimly.

"As I'd said, I have leapt ahead of my story, a bit. There is more to tell about poor Milton Rackham that is of interest. I asked him how he'd happened to learn of the bookstore here in Seabrook and he told me of how 'purely by chance' he'd discovered the store in the fall of 1957—he'd been driving along the coast on his way to Maine and stopped in Seabrook, on High Street, and happened to see the bookstore—Slater's Mystery Books & Stationers it was called—'It was such a vision!—the bay windows gleaming in the sun, and the entire block of brownstones so attractive.' A good part of Slater's merchandise was stationery, quite high-quality stationery, and other supplies of that sort, but there was an excellent collection of books as well, hardcover and paperback; not just the usual popular books but somewhat esoteric titles as well, by Robert W. Chambers, Bram Stoker, M.R. James, Edgar Wallace, Oscar Wilde (*Salome*), H.P. Lovecraft. Slater seemed to have been a particular admirer of Erle Stanley Gardner, Rex Stout, Josephine Tey, and Dorothy L. Sayers, writers whom Milton Rackham admired also. The floor-to-ceiling mahogany bookshelves were in place—cabinetry that would cost a fortune at the time, as Rackham remarked again. And there were odd, interesting things stocked in the store like antique maps, globes—'A kind of treasure trove, as in an older relative's attic in which you might spend long rainy afternoons under a spell.' Rackham told me that he wandered through the store with 'mounting excitement'—feeling that it was already known to him, in a way; through a window, he looked out toward the Atlantic Ocean, and felt the 'thrill of its great beauty.' Indeed, Milton Rackham would tell me that it had been 'love at first sight'—as soon as he'd glimpsed the bookstore.

"As it turned out, Amos Slater had been contemplating selling the store, which had been a family inheritance; though, as he said, he continued to 'love books and book-selling' it was no longer with the passion of youth, and so he hoped to soon retire. Young Milton Rackham was stunned by this good fortune. Three weeks later, with his wife's enthusiastic support, he made an offer to Amos Slater for the property, and the offer was accepted almost immediately."

Neuhaus speaks wonderingly, like a man who is recounting a somewhat fantastical tale he hopes his listeners will believe, for it is important for them to believe it.

"'My wife had a faint premonition'—this is Milton Rackham speaking—'that something might be wrong, but I paid no attention. I was heedless then, in love with my sweet young wife, and excited by the prospect of walking away from pious Harvard—(where it didn't look promising that I would get tenure)—and taking up a purer life, as I thought it, in the booksellers' trade. And so, Mildred and I arranged for a thirty-year mortgage, and made our initial payment through the Realtor, and on our first visit to the store as the new owners—when Amos Slater presented us with the keys to the building—it happened that my wife innocently asked Amos Slater how he'd come to own the store, and Amos told her a most disturbing tale, like one eager to get something off his chest . . .

"'Slater's Books'—this is Amos Slater speaking, as reported by Milton Rackham to me—'had been established by his grandfather Barnabas in 1912. Slater's grandfather was a 'lover of books, rather than human-kind'—though one of his literary friends was Ambrose Bierce who'd allegedly encouraged Barnabas's writing of fiction. Slater told Rackham a bizarre tale that at the age of eleven he'd had a 'powerful vision'—drop-ping by his grandfather's bookstore one day after school, he'd found the store empty—'No customers, no sales clerks, and no Grandfather, or so I thought. But then, looking for Grandfather, I went into the cellar—I turned on a light and—there was Grandfather hanging from a beam, his body strangely straight, and very still; and his face turned mercifully from me, though there was no doubt who it was. For a long moment I stood paralyzed—I could not believe what I was seeing. I could not even scream, I was so frightened. . . . My grandfather Barnabas and I had not been close. Grandfather had hardly seemed to take notice of me except sneeringly—'Is it a little boy, or a little girl? *What is it?*' Grandfather Slater was a strange man, as people said—short-tempered yet also rather cold and detached—passionate about some things, but indifferent about most things—determined to make his book and stationery store a success but contemptuous with most customers, and very cynical about human nature. It appeared that he had dragged a step-ladder beneath the beam in the cellar, tied a hemp noose around his neck, climbed up the ladder and kicked the ladder away beneath him—he must have died a horrible, strangulated death, gasping for breath and kicking and writhing for many minutes. . . . Seeing the hanged body of my grandfather was one of the terrible shocks of my life. I don't know quite what happened . . . I fainted, I think—then forced myself to crawl to the steps, and made my way upstairs—ran for help . . . I remember screaming on High Street. . . . People hurried to help me, I brought them back into the store and down into the cellar, but there was no one there—no rope hanging from the beam, and no overturned step-ladder. Again, it was one of the shocks of my life—I was only eleven, and could not comprehend what was happening. . . . Eventually, Grandfather was discovered a few doors away at the Bell, Book & Candle Pub, calmly drinking port and eating a late lunch of pigs' knuckles and sauerkraut. He'd spent most of the day doing inventory, he said, on the second floor of the store, and hadn't heard any commotion.'"

"Poor Amos Slater never entirely recovered from the trauma of seeing his grandfather's hanged body in the cellar of the bookstore, or rather the vision of the hanged body—so everyone who knew him believed. . . ."

"As Milton Rackham reported to me, he'd learned from Amos Slater that the grandfather Barnabas had been a 'devious' person who defrauded business partners, seduced and betrayed naïve, virginal Seabrook women, and, it was charged more than once, 'pilfered' their savings; he'd amassed a collection of first editions and rare books, including a copy of Charles Brockden Brown's *Wieland*—such treasures he claimed to have bought at estate auctions and sales, but some observers believed he had taken advantage of distraught widows and grief-stricken heirs, or possibly he'd stolen outright. Barnabas had married a well-to-do local woman several years his senior to whom he was cruel and coercive, who'd died at the age of fifty-two of 'suspicious' causes. Nothing was *proven*—so Amos Slater had been told. 'Growing up, I had to see how my father was intimidated by my grandfather Barnabas, who mocked him as 'less than a man' for not standing up to him. 'Where is the son and heir whom I deserve? Who are these weaklings who surround me?'—the old man would rage. Grandfather Barnabas was one to play practical jokes on friends and enemies alike; he had a particularly nasty trick of giving people sweet treats laced with laxatives. . . . Once, our minister at the Episcopal church here in Seabrook was stricken with terrible diarrhea during Sunday services, as a consequence of plum tarts Barnabas had given him and his family; another time, my mother, who was Grandfather's daughter-in-law, became deathly sick after drinking apple cider laced with insecticide my grandfather had put in the cider—or so it was suspected. (Eventually, Grandfather admitted to putting 'just a few drops' of DDT into the cider his daughter-in-law would be drinking; he hadn't known it was DDT, he claimed, but had thought it was a liquid laxative. 'In any case, I didn't mean it to be *fatal*.' And he spread his fingers, and laughed—it was blood-chilling to hear him.) Yet, Barnabas Slater had an 'obsessive love' of books—mystery-detective books, crime books—and had actually tried to write fiction himself, in the mode of Edgar Allan Poe, it was said.

"Amos Slater told Rackham that he'd wanted to flee Seabrook and the ghastly legacy of Barnabas Slater but—somehow—he'd had no choice about taking over his grandfather's bookstore—'When Grandfather died, I was designated his heir in his will. My father was ill by that time, and would not long survive. I felt resigned, and accepted my inheritance, though I knew at the time such an inheritance was like a tombstone—if the tombstone toppled over, and you were not able to climb out of the grave in which you'd been prematurely buried, like one of those victims in Poe. . . . Another cruel thing my grandfather boasted of doing—(who knows if the wicked old man was telling the truth, or merely hoping to upset his listeners)—was experimentation with exotic toxins: extracting venom from poisonous frogs that was a colorless, tasteless, odorless milky liquid that could be added to liquids like hot chocolate and hot coffee without being detected. . . . The frogs are known as Poison Dart Frogs, found in the United States in the Florida Everglades, it is said . . .

"'The Poison Dart Frog's venom is so rare, no coroner or pathologist could identify it even if there were any suspicion of foul play—which there wasn't likely to be. A victim's symptoms did not arouse suspicion. Within minutes (as Grandfather boasted) the venom begins to attack the central nervous system—the afflicted one shivers, and shudders, and can't seem to swallow, for his mouth is very dry; soon, hallucinations begin; and paralysis and coma; within eight to ten hours, the body's organs begin to break down, slowly at first and then rapidly, by which time the victim is unconscious and unaware of what is happening to him. Liver, kidneys, lungs, heart, brain—all collapse from within. If observed, the victim seems to be suffering some sort of attack—heart attack, stroke—'fainting'—there are no gastric-intestinal symptoms, no horrible attacks of vomiting. If the stomach is pumped, there is nothing—no 'food poisoning.' The victim simply fades away . . . it is a merciful death, as deaths go.'" Aaron Neuhaus pauses as if the words he is recounting, with seeming precision, from memories of long ago, are almost too much for him to absorb.

"Then, Milton Rackham continued—'The irony is, as Slater told it, after a long and surprisingly successful life as a small town bookseller of quality books, Barnabas Slater did hang himself, it was surmised out of boredom and self-disgust at the age of seventy-two—in the cellar of Slater's Books exactly as his grandson Amos had envisioned. Scattered below his hanging body were carefully typed, heavily edited manuscript pages of what appeared to be several mystery-detective novels—no one ever made the effort of collating the pages and reading them. It was a family decision to inter the unpublished manuscripts with Grandfather.'"

"Isn't this tale amazing? Have you ever heard anything so bizarre, Charles? I mean—in actual life? In utter solemnity poor Milton Rackham recounted it to me, as he'd heard it from Amos Slater. I could sympathize that Rackham was a nervous wreck—he was concerned that his son might do violence against him, and he had to contend with being the proprietor of a store in which a previous proprietor had hanged himself! He went on to say, as Slater had told him, that it had been the consensus in Seabrook that no one knew if Barnabas had actually poisoned anyone fatally—he'd played his little pranks with laxatives and insecticide—but the 'Poison Dart Frog venom' was less evident. Though people did die of somewhat mysterious 'natural causes,' in the Slater family, from time to time. Several persons who knew Barnabas well said that the old man had often said that there are some human beings so vile, they don't deserve to live; but he'd also said, with a puckish wink, that he 'eradicated' people for no particular reason, at times. 'Good, not-so-good, evil'—the classic murderer does not discriminate. Barnabas particularly admired the de Quincy essay 'On Murder Considered One of the Fine Arts' that makes the point that no reason is required for murder, in fact to have a reason is to be rather vulgar—so Barnabas believed also. Excuse me, Charles? Is something wrong?"

"Why, I—I am—utterly confused . . ."

"Have you lost your way? My predecessor was Milton Rackham, from whom I bought this property; his predecessor was Amos Slater, from whom he, Rackham, bought the property; and *his predecessor* was a gentleman named Barnabas Slater who seems to have hanged himself in the cellar here—for which reason, as I'd mentioned a few minutes ago, I try to avoid the damned place, as much as possible. (I send my employees down, instead! They don't mind.) I think you were reacting to Barnabas Slater's philosophy, that no reason is required for murder, especially for murder as an 'art form.'"

"But—why would anyone kill for no reason?"

"Why would anyone kill *for a reason*?" Neuhaus smiles, eloquently. "It seems to me, Slater's grandfather Barnabas may have extracted the essence of 'mystery' from life, as he was said to have extracted venom from the venomous frog. The act of killing is complete in itself, and requires no reason—like any work of art. Yet, if one is looking for a reason, one is likely to kill to protect oneself—one's territory. Our ancestors were fearful and distrustful of enemies, strangers—they were 'xenophobic'—'paranoid.' If a stranger comes into your territory, and behaves with sinister intent, or even behaves without sinister intent, you are probably better off dispatching him than trying to comprehend him, and possibly making a fatal mistake. In the distant past, before God was love, such mistakes could lead to the extinction of an entire species—so it is that *Homo sapiens*, the preemptive species, prefers to err by over-caution, not under-caution."

I am utterly confounded by these words, spoken by my affable companion in a matter-of-fact voice. And that smile!—it is so boyish, and magnanimous. Almost, I can't speak, but stutter feebly.

"That is a—a—surprising thing to say, for you . . . Aaron. That is a somewhat cynical thing to say, I think . . ."

Aaron Neuhaus smiles as if, another time, I am a very foolish person whom he must humor. "Not at all 'cynical,' Charles—why would you think so? If you are an aficionado of mystery-detective-crime fiction, you know that someone, in fact many people, and many of them 'innocent,' must die for the sake of the art—for *mystery's sake*. That is the bedrock of our business: Mystery, Inc. Some of us are booksellers, and some of us are consumers, or are consumed. But all of us have our place in the noble trade."

There is a ringing in my ears. My mouth is so very dry, it is virtually impossible to swallow. My teeth are chattering for I am very cold. Except for its frothy remains my second cup of cappuccino is empty—I have set it on Neuhaus's desk, but so shakily that it nearly falls over.

Neuhaus regards me closely with concerned eyes. On his desk, the carved ebony raven is regarding me as well. Eyes very sharp! I am shivering—despite the heat from the fire. I am very cold—except the whiskers on my jaws feel very hot. I am thinking that I must protect myself—the box of Lindt's chocolate truffles is my weapon, but I am not sure how to employ it. Several of the chocolate truffles are gone, but the box is otherwise full; many remain yet to be eaten.

I know that I have been dismissed. I must leave—it is time.

I am on my feet. But I am feeling weak, unreal. The bookseller escorts me out of his office, graciously murmuring, "You are leaving, Charles? Yes, it is getting late. You might come by at another time, and we can see about these purchases of yours. And bring a check—please. Take care on the stairs!—a spiral staircase can be treacherous." My companion has been very kind even in dismissing me, and has put the attaché case into my hands.

How eager I am to leave this hellish, airless place! I am gripping the railing of the spiral staircase, but having difficulty descending. Like a dark rose a vertigo is opening in my brain. My mouth is very dry and also very cold and numb—my tongue feels as if it is swollen, and without sensation. My breath comes ever more quickly, yet without bringing oxygen to my brain. In the semi-darkness my legs seem to buckle and I fall—I am falling, helpless as a rag doll—down the remainder of the metal stairs, wincing with pain.

Above me, two flights up, a man is calling with what sounds like genuine concern—"Charles? Are you all right? Do you need help?"

"No! No thank you—*I do not* . . ."

My voice is hoarse, my words are hardly audible.

Outside, I am temporarily revived by cold, fresh wind from the ocean. There is the smell and taste of the ocean. Thank God! I will be all right now, I think. I am safe now, I will escape . . . I've left the Lindt chocolates behind, so perhaps—(the predator's thoughts come frantically now)—the poison will have its effect, whether I am able to benefit from it or not.

In the freezing air of my vehicle, with numbed fingers I am jamming a misshapen key into the slot of the ignition that appears to be too small for it. How can this be? I don't understand.

Yet, eventually, as in a dream of dogged persistence, the key goes into the slot, and the engine comes reluctantly to life.

Alongside the moonstruck Atlantic I am driving on a two-lane highway. If I am driving, I must be all right. My hands grip the steering wheel that seems to be moving—wonderfully—of its own volition. A strange, fierce, icy-cold paralysis is blooming in my brain, in my spinal chord, in all the nerves of my body, that is so fascinating to me, my eyes begin to close, to savor it.

Am I asleep? Am I sleeping while driving? Have I never left the place in which I dwell and have I dreamt my visit to Mystery, Inc. in Seabrook, New Hampshire? I have plotted my assault upon the legendary Aaron Neuhaus of Mystery, Inc. Books—I have injected the chocolate truffles with the care of a malevolent surgeon—how is it possible that I might fail? *I cannot fail.*

But now I realize—to my horror—I have no idea in which direction I am driving. I should be headed south, I think—the Atlantic should be on my left. But cold moon-glittering waters lap dangerously high on both sides of the highway. Churning waves have begun to rush across the road, into which I have no choice but to drive.

The Book of the Lion
Thomas Perry

Born in Tonawanda, New York, in 1947, Thomas Perry received his undergraduate degree from Cornell University and went on to earn his Ph.D. in English from the University of Rochester. Before becoming an author, he worked as a maintenance worker, factory laborer, fisherman, university faculty member, and prime time–television show producer and writer. Thomas Perry has won several awards for his writing, including the first ever Gumshoe Award for best novel for *Pursuit* (part of the Jane Whitefield series) and an Edgar for *The Butcher's Boy*. He has been included in several distinguished book lists; *Metzger's Dog* was a *New York Times* Notable Book and was also voted one of NPR's "100 Killer Thrillers—Best Thrillers Ever," *Vanishing Act* was included in the Independent Mystery Bookseller's Association's "100 Favorite Mysteries of the 20th Century," and *Nightlife* was a *New York Times* bestseller. He has written almost two dozen books thus far. He lives in Southern California with his wife.

D ominic Hallkyn played back the voicemail on his telephone while he took off his sport coat and hung it up to dry in the laundry room. The smell of rain on tweed was one that he knew some people might say was his smell, the smell of an English professor. The coats—tweed or finer-spun wool in the winter and seersucker or summer-weight fabrics in the late spring and early fall—were his work uniform, no different from a mechanic's coveralls. He wore them to repel the skepticism of the young.

The first couple of calls were routine: a girl in his undergraduate medieval lit course had been sick, so could she please hand her paper in tomorrow? Of course. He had plenty of others to deaden his soul until that one arrived. Meg Stanley, the Department Chair, wanted him to serve on a Ph.D. oral exam committee. Unfortunately, he would. Reading the frantically scribbled preliminary exam and then asking probing questions in the oral would be torment to him and the student, both of them joined in a ritual of distaste and humiliation, all of it designed to punish them both for their love of literature, but it was part of his job.

The last call was not routine. "Professor Hallkyn. I know you are considered one of the two or three best living experts on medieval English literature." In spite of Hallkyn's contempt for academics who fancied themselves the best or the most famous, he was irritated at the "two or three." The two were Hallkyn, and Bethune, who was at Harvard. Who did this man think was the third? So when he heard the next sentence, he was already in a bad humor. "I have *The Book of the Lion*. It's written in a fine court hand on thin vellum, legible in its entirety. I will be in touch."

Hallkyn could feel his heart pounding in his chest, and yet he felt light-headed, as though he were being strangled. He realized after a moment that he had forgotten to breathe, and he placed both palms on the table to hold himself up while he corrected the oversight, taking a few deep breaths while he thought. Of course it was a hoax. Nobody could have *The Book of the Lion*.

The book didn't exist except as a reference in Chaucer's Retraction at the end of *The Parson's Tale*, where he listed all of his greatest works by name: "*The Book of Troilus*; *The Book also of Fame*; *The Book of the Five and Twenty Ladies*; *The Book of the Duchesse*; *The Book of Seint Valentynes Day of the Parlement of Briddes*; *The Tales of Canterbury* (thilke that sownen into synne); *The Book of the Leoun*; and many another book (if they were in my remembrance) and many a song and many a leccherous lay—that Crist for his grete mercy foryeve me the synne."

Those colleagues who took the retraction seriously had always amused Dominic Hallkyn. He couldn't fathom how they could profess to know Chaucer and not notice that he had a wicked sense of irony. The Retraction wasn't a confession. It was an advertisement.

The thought brought him back to the tantalizing nature of what he had just heard. In his Retraction, Chaucer did not list everything he had written. He listed only masterworks. He listed only those poems that six centuries later still made up a fair portion of the reason that anyone cared about Middle English literature. He listed them in an order ascending to his sublime achievement, *The Canterbury Tales*. And then, after that, he listed one more work by name, and only one—*The Book of the Lion*.

Chaucer, first of the big three of English—the one from whom Shakespeare learned his true trade, not plays but deep understanding of human beings, and from whom Milton learned to write poetic narrative—was the one who wrote when the language itself was still in its childhood and could be exercised by one writer to grow into its mature strength. And what if, contrary to what everyone had thought for over half a millennium, a copy of *The Book of the Lion* had survived?

Dominic Hallkyn thought, and like any thinking man, he drank. He sat in his library on the leather couch near the 18th-century writing desk, staring past it at the wall of bookshelves. And because he was in a place that was the physical embodiment of his mind, his eyes knew where to focus. He looked at the fifth shelf, where Geoffrey Chaucer resided. There was the familiar Donaldson edition of 1975; the Blake edition including the corrections from the fragmentary Hengwrt Manuscript; the Fisher, with its generous supporting materials and critical essays. And a special purchase from his own graduate school days, the seven-volume Skeat edition of 1899. And because Hallkyn loved the twenty-three painted pictures, including the one of Chaucer the pilgrim, he kept the facsimile of the Ellesmere Manuscript at the end of the row.

Hallkyn drank a single malt scotch that tasted to him like the breath of the British Isles, its rich peat and wet moss and damp air and time. He considered the slim likelihood that there was going to be a second chapter to this experience, and then he made a telephone call.

The call was to the private number of a man named T.M. Spanner. Spanner's personal number was sought-after, a number that powerful men carried in their wallets on small pieces of paper with no notations written beside it. Spanner's wealth was old and hard to trace—it was reputed to have come originally from one of his ancestors inventing the tool that Americans perversely called a wrench, although its true name in English was spanner. But even when Hallkyn had met T.M. Spanner as an undergraduate at Yale, he was already the sort of man who stimulated curiosity. The imagination was always ready to supply speculation and wild stories.

Hallkyn heard the answer, "T.M. Spanner," and the voice impressed him again. He had an accent that retained a trace of the south, a slower Virginia tidewater cadence that had somehow survived the years of northeastern prep schools and universities. The voice conveyed the conviction that the man had the ownership papers in his back pocket to the ground beneath his feet, the air he breathed, and all the things he could see from where he stood.

"T.M.," said Hallkyn. "It's Dominic."

"Herr Doktor Professor," said Spanner. "It's always a pleasure to hear your voice."

Hallkyn hoped that it was a pleasure. If so, it could only be because, unlike most people who called Spanner, Hallkyn was not in any business, and didn't want Spanner's advice, his help, or his endorsement. What he and Spanner always talked about was what had drawn them together thirty years ago—books. "You too, T.M. I hope I'm not bothering you."

"Not at all. I'm sitting at home looking at a television show. I hesitate to say watching, because that implies that I'm actually following along. I have the sound off and I'm gazing at a pretty moving picture of the Alps. What's new with you, Dom?"

"Until a few minutes ago, not much. I've got to tell you, I got a message on my phone that set off a lot of emotions."

"What? You're not sick or something, are you?" There was genuine concern in Spanner's voice.

"No, nothing like that. This isn't even personal. It's intellectual. Literary and historical. A man who didn't identify himself called and said he has *The Book of the Lion*."

"*The Book of the Lion*," Spanner repeated. "The Retraction."

"Yes," said Hallkyn. "That's right. When Chaucer apologizes for the sin of writing his greatest works, it's the last one in the list."

"Hold on a second, Dom. I think I see my old *Canterbury Tales* on a shelf right now. Hold on. It's not more than fifty feet away."

Hallkyn heard the phone click on a hard surface. He was experiencing again who T.M. Spanner was. He was a man of the financial world, and that meant politics and manufacturing and trade and the shrewd application of power, but he had also studied literature with a sincere appreciation and humility. He was at once a man who could own a library where "only fifty feet away" was nearby, and a man who *would* own a library that size, and know where everything was. Hallkyn heard him pick up the phone again. Hallkyn said, "It's at the end, after *The Parson's Tale*."

"Got it," said Spanner. "Oh, yes. '*The Tales of Canterbury* thilke that sownen into synne; *The Book of the Leoun*, and many another book . . . and many a song and many a leccherous lay.' And *The Book of the Lion* has never been found, right?"

"Right. This person who called me claims to have a copy on thin vellum in a fine court hand, legible throughout."

"Do you think it's possible?" said Spanner.

"I doubt it," he said. Then he added, "But it's happened before. People find things, incredible things."

"What is it that you want me to do?"

"I don't know," said Hallkyn.

"That sounds a little disingenuous," Spanner said. "You called an old friend who is probably also the richest man you know."

"We'd have to see what the object looks like. In 1983, a group of Germans paid nearly twelve million dollars for a Romanesque gospel. It was beautiful. But nobody ever spent twelve million because he was wondering what a Bible was going to say, or six million because he didn't know what was in Shakespeare."

"We need a number."

"I don't know," Hallkyn said. "Or maybe I'm afraid to think it through."

"Try."

"All right," said Hallkyn. "Figure that the physical book is, in today's dollars, worth at least five million. It's probably not going to be as pretty as the Ellesmere, but it's much rarer, because there are other manuscripts of the *Canterbury Tales.* Assume this is the last major missing work of the first great writer in English, like finding the last living dinosaur there is or will ever be. Are you with me?"

"Yes. Go on."

"Also, the contents of *The Book of the Lion* are utterly unknown. The first thing a responsible owner would do is publish three editions of it. First would be a facsimile; second, a popular reader's edition; third, a scholarly edition with footnotes, a historical introduction, and a critical introduction.

"Possibly there would also be articles by major experts. We don't know the length of the book. It could be just 1,300 lines of poetry, like *The Book of the Duchess.* But *Troilus and Criseyde* is over 8,000 lines, in five sections. If *The Book of the Lion* isn't as good as the other works, it will still be of equal importance to scholars."

"I'm starting to see a way of recouping some of the price," Spanner said. "The publishing rights might help."

"It probably wouldn't be a crowd-pleaser," said Hallkyn. "But it would sell to scholars in every English-speaking country. The United States, Canada, England, Australia, New Zealand, South Africa, Ireland—"

"I'm familiar with the English-speaking countries."

"And it would keep selling modestly forever. Every student who studies Chaucer would read it. And not every student of English literature is from an English-speaking country. Two thirds of Germany and Switzerland speak English, eighty-five percent of Sweden and the Netherlands, twenty percent of India."

"All right," said Spanner. "We can estimate that whoever owns the manuscript would be able to defray a tiny part of what he paid for it from sales."

"There might also be grants from foundations or even the government," said Hallkyn. "But that all takes time, and they might not add up to much."

"We still have to come up with an idea of what the manuscript is worth if we want to deal with this man," Spanner said. "Suppose we add the twelve million paid by the German cartel for the old gospel in 1983 and the six million paid for the Shakespeare folio in 2001. That's eighteen. I think eighteen million is our number. At least it's based on something real. And it's a number that shows we're serious."

"I think so," Hallkyn said. "Is it possible to get that much?"

"I'll see what I can do," Spanner said. "We'll need investors. It's going to be tricky. We can't tell anybody what the investment is, or we'll be turning our allies into competitors. They'll have to be willing to put up money without knowing what I want to buy with it."

"Are there people like that?"

"We'll see whether my reputation is good enough to make some. Have another scotch, put your feet up, and remain calm. I'm going to start making some calls tonight. The more money we have lined up before this person calls again the better."

Hallkyn slept fitfully that night. Whenever he woke up, he would go over the whole topic in his mind, separating dream from memory until he had them clear, but then couldn't get back to sleep for a time.

He waited for the second call. A day passed, and Hallkyn could hardly bear it. Then a second night passed, and he began to feel unsure of himself. He played back the voicemail from the caller a dozen times, trying to be sure he hadn't misunderstood or missed any part of it—a phone number, a name. Then he called the phone company to be reassured that the messages could not have been cut short by the company's equipment. Yes, they were sure. The plan that Mr. Hallkyn had been paying for would have allowed a message several minutes long. Everything was digital, and so there was not a question of a tape running out. There was no tape. And the caller's number was blocked.

The day after that Hallkyn had to go to the university and teach his classes—a morning medieval survey that the undergraduates had decided to call "Beowulf to the Bowel Shift." That was quick and simple. His goal was mostly to infect the little cynics with the enthusiasm he felt for the early period, and once again the literature itself was doing the job for him. The graduate seminar had been a tedious business—John Gower's *Confessio Amantis*, a perfectly fine and masterful work, but today he kept thinking that Gower was no Chaucer. Nobody else was Chaucer either. Not even the Pearl poet or the Gawain poet had been capable of the breadth of vision, the fascination with humanity, the sheer ambition of Chaucer.

Hallkyn rushed home, swerving into his driveway too fast and nearly hitting the line of privet hedge beside the pavement and then coming too close to the side of the garage door opening. Then had to squeeze out of the driver's seat with the car door too close to the garage wall to open far enough. He hurried into his house, picked up his phone, and listened to the messages.

Nothing. Well, something, but not the call he had been hoping for. First were just a few more undergraduates who had dire symptoms that made paper-writing impossible. Next, that graduate student wanted his oral exam the Tuesday afternoon after the written. Fine. Why prolong the ordeal? Next, his friend Norman Sammons had called inviting him to contribute an article for a collection on Gawain and the Green Knight. He would say yes to that, of course. It would give him an excuse to rework the article he'd done ten years ago for the *Journal of English and Germanic Philology*. Anybody who remembered the JEGP article would be delighted to see how much he'd learned since then.

Hallkyn hit on a new idea. He would change his phone message. He punched in the code and said in his best professorial tones, "This is Dominic Hallkyn. You may leave a message at the tone, or you may call me on my cell phone. The number is," and then he recited the number and hung up. Then he called himself and listened. Perfect. Now he would not have to live in torment, thinking that he might be missing the crucial call from the possessor of *The Book of the Lion*.

Hallkyn spent four full days and nights enslaved by his cell phone. He tested its ring repeatedly to be sure he would hear it over any of the sorts of noise he might encounter in his mostly quiet life. He kept the vibration on too so if the call came, he would feel it, and then kept checking the messages to see if he had missed the call anyway.

And then, like a fever breaking, his worry passed. The call must have been a silly prank. If someone had a treasure like that, he would hardly neglect to do something with it. And no matter what he wanted to do, he would need to have an expert authoritatively authenticate the manuscript. He would have to get somebody like Hallkyn to say "Yes, this is the real thing." The caller had never even mentioned that.

Hallkyn let himself settle back into a normal frame of mind. Normal was restful. He didn't have any responsibility for this supposed manuscript. There was no crisis. He went on with his life.

He had only one problem, which was that his cell phone number was now too easy to get. Undergraduates were calling him past midnight with their excuses and brown-nosing questions, as though his phone were a twenty-four hour emergency literature help line. The department chair had started using his cell number to invite him to her damned cheese and sherry gatherings, making him invent his alibis on the spot.

Hallkyn recorded a new message, left out his cell number, and substituted, "If your business is urgent, you may leave a message after the tone." He was pleased, because the message signaled a more restrictive policy than before the Chaucer hoax.

Still, he didn't call Spanner immediately. It was one thing to change his message to institute a new regime of sanity in his personal life, and another to say good-bye to a glittering possibility by telling Spanner it was a hoax. For about a week he was able to put it off, but then he called.

Spanner answered, and then said, "I was just thinking of calling you. Is it all right to tie up your phone line?"

"Sure. It won't matter."

"I've done it," said Spanner.

"Done what?"

"I've lined up the financing," Spanner said.

"Eighteen million dollars?" Hallkyn felt sick.

"I used some properties I own in Europe and one in Virginia as collateral for letters of credit. I also spoke with a few friends in hedge funds and banks who were willing to invest a bit of money without knowing what it is I'm buying. They've all agreed to have the money available instantly if we need it."

"I'm so sorry, T.M." said Hallkyn. "I've heard nothing. I should have known the whole thing was too good to be true. I'm almost certain I've been duped."

"*Almost* certain," Spanner simply repeated it.

Hallkyn was quiet for a moment. "I'm pretty sure. And it was so unlikely to begin with. Over six hundred years have passed, without even a rumor that the book still existed."

"I respect your telling me, and I thank you for your apology, Dom. But if you don't mind—and even if you do—I'm going to keep the money available for the moment. No money has actually been borrowed, nobody has had to sell anything. We've only agreed to keep some assets liquid for a while."

"You don't have to," said Hallkyn. "I feel pretty stupid about this, and I don't want you to risk your reputation on a hoax."

"No harm done," he said. "We won't worry about this for now. Just be aware that the money is going to be available."

The call came seventeen hours later. Hallkyn was on his way to the university in his car, and when his cell phone rang and vibrated it startled him. He pulled his car over to the curb and answered. "Yes?"

"Hello, Professor Hallkyn." The voice was unmistakable—a bit nasal, pitched a tiny bit higher than the ear liked to hear, the diction formal. Hallkyn had listened to the message so many times that he recognized every tone, every inflection. "Is this a good time for us to speak?"

"I've pulled over to the side of the road," said Hallkyn.

"I assume you got my message."

"I got a message," said Hallkyn.

"Yes. I only called once. And then I gave you some time to think about it, and then to prepare to talk in specific terms. I have what I believe is the only remaining copy of *The Book of the Leoun*." This time he pronounced it using Middle English vowels. "For all we know, it might be the only one ever made for public use after Chaucer's personal draft."

"What makes you think it's genuine, or that it's *the The Book of the Lion*, by Chaucer? There were plenty of lion images throughout medieval literature, and plenty of people with that nickname—Henry the Lion, Duke of Saxony, for instance."

"It says it's *The Book of the Lion* by Geoffrey Chaucer on the first page. I had a snip of the vellum carbon-dated, and it dates to the mid-1930s. The poetry is, like everything else Chaucer wrote, flawless, earthy, brilliant, spiritual, funny, dirty."

Hallkyn tried to sound less enticed than he was. "When can I see it?"

"Now. I've sent you a précis and some sample pages already."

"How?"

"It's an email attachment. You can look any time you want."

"Are you expecting me to authenticate a manuscript, particularly one of this importance, to risk my reputation and credibility without so much as inspecting it in person?"

"I'm not expecting you to do anything. I'm just giving you the opportunity to look." And then the man hung up.

Dominic Hallkyn sat in his car by the side of the road, watching the windshield wipers sweeping back and forth to clear the water away, *bock-bock, bock-bock*. While he hadn't been paying attention, the rain had picked up. The wipers' speed was now too slow, so every time the wipers passed, the rain gained back all the territory that had been cleared before the blades swept back.

Hallkyn realized that he hated the man with the book. He was arrogant, Hallkyn could tell, and he was enjoying holding the prize and making the world wait and drool like starving dogs—making Dominic Hallyn wait and drool like a starving dog, actually. He'd implied Hallkyn was the only one who knew so far, but there was no way to determine whether even that was true. It took Hallkyn five minutes of sitting in the car, letting every other vehicle speed through the puddle beside him and throw a big splash against the window beside his face, to get through the moment of hatred.

Hallkyn watched his mirrors and found an opening, then pulled out onto the road and drove to the university to his assigned parking space, number 364. He had chosen it himself as an Assistant Professor and waited years for it to become available. It was just a few feet from an arbor, so in the summer it was partially shaded, and in winter it gave him shelter from rain. He got out of his car, snatched his briefcase, ran to the arbor, walked with calm and dignity to the end of the covered sidewalk, then launched himself into a full sprint to the alcove where the door to Bacon Hall waited.

He went directly to his undergraduate lecture and performed brilliantly, acting out the lines his memory presented for recitation, varying tone and pitch to portray each character who spoke, his Middle English pronunciation natural and unhalting. Then he gave a concise and fascinating talk about what the works meant, leaving his listeners in a state far beyond the mere enthusiasm he generally aimed to arouse in them.

Hallkyn had achieved a small victory, and that helped. He had spent an hour resisting the temptation to cancel the class and go look at his email. The loathsome man who had sent the email would undoubtedly have a way of knowing when Dominic Hallkyn opened it. This way he would at least have spent an hour wondering if Hallkyn was even going to bother to look.

And then he was in his office. The room was a sanctuary and a workshop, and after thirty years of use, it felt like it belonged to him and not the university. The dark wood paneling and matching bookcases pre-dated his era by three generations, but all of the books were his. The collection of treasures—small fragments of illuminated manuscripts, a few pages from medieval church registers and government lists, were on loan from the university's collection. But by long tenure here they felt like his.

He closed the shade and locked the door. Then he turned on his computer and scanned the list of emails until he found one that said it was "B of L." As he clicked on it he had an instant to hate the man again, and then he forgot about the man.

He could see a page on the screen and he enlarged the image of the first letter at the top left. It was an inhabited initial in the style that had originated with the St. Petersburg Bede of 746, with a picture of a Lion in gold leaf inside the frame of the letter I. There were demi-vinet borders along the left margin like the ones beside the columns of calligraphy on the Ellesmere Chaucer. He enlarged the picture as much as he could, with a bit of both pages together. He could tell the difference between the first page, made of the inner side of the calfskin, which was slightly lighter and much smoother, and the other page, made of the outer side of the hide. It had pores and a couple of places where he could detect imperfections. He looked more closely at the script. It looked very much like the work of the scribe whom Chaucer referred to as "Adam Scriveyn," identified by most scholars as Adam Pinkhurst. And then he looked again at the letter I, done not by the scribe but by a painter. "In," the poem began.

> In th'olde dayes of the King Richard,
> Ther nas but hevinesse and much rue,
> For the King, that was goode and Trewe
> As fare as any man in Engelond
> Was in the German Henry's honds.

And then he was lost. He had begun to read, and the parts that he could see drew him in. He read the two pages of text that he could enlarge enough to see clearly. He compared each letter to the style of the Ellesmere. He studied the specifications the man had supplied, the descriptions of the sections, the physical measurements and specifications.

When he looked up again, he saw that the narrow margins of light around his window shade had gone dark. He stood up and realized he was stiff in the hips and knees. His spine had been bent forward for hours. A headache announced itself, and he realized it had been building behind his eyes for some time.

Hallkyn saved what he had been reading for the eighth time, then emailed it to his laptop at home, to his second university email address, to Iron Mountain for safekeeping, and then to T.M. Spanner.

Next he dialed the telephone, and heard it ring five times before he heard Spanner say, "Hello, Dominic."

"Spanner," Hallkyn began.

"Glad to hear from you, Dom," said Spanner. "Do you think this can keep for a little while? I'm entertaining a dear friend right now."

Hallkyn heard a woman's laugh, a musical sound that made him feel several unrelated emotions. Of course Spanner, being the well-known T.M. Spanner, would have a woman with a voice like that with him at this hour. He controlled his envy. Everything about T.M. Spanner's life was better than anybody else's. Spanner's good fortune was part of the order of the universe. But what was this hour? Nearly one A.M., damn it. This was humiliating.

"T.M., I'm so sorry. I've been working all this time, and I paid no attention to the clock until this second. I'll call you again tomorrow."

"Just tell me this much now," said Spanner. "Are we going to need the money?"

"Yes, I believe we are."

"Great."

Eight hours later Hallkyn's cell phone rang, and he said, "Hallkyn."

"You sound as though you were waiting by the phone, Dom."

"I was," said Hallkyn.

"It's that big a deal to you?"

"It's that big a deal. Period."

"Tell me what you've learned."

"He sent me a teaser, a sample. There's a photograph of the first two pages of the manuscript, and a set of specifications. The book is six thousand, nine hundred and nineteen lines of verse." His voice fell to just above a whisper. "It's exactly what we were hoping for, T.M. It's the actual *Book of the Lion*, the last major work that Chaucer wrote, begun just before, and finished just after, *The Canterbury Tales*."

"What is it like? I mean the words, not the physical manuscript."

"It's beautiful. I could only read two pages of actual lines in the photograph, just enough to be sure it's Chaucer. The frame tale is the story of Richard Coeur de Lion. It's about him and his awful brothers, primarily John, quarreling over the throne of England and the family possessions in France, and takes place during Richard's captivity by the German Emperor Henry VI. By then he was already Richard the Lionheart, having been in several wars, fought against Saladin in the crusade, and so on. While he's locked in a German dungeon, the ghost of Aesop comes and tells him the story of the Lion and the Mouse—how the weak can free the strong, as ordinary Englishmen eventually did by a tithe to pay his ransom—and then tells him about Androcles and the Lion, the recurring value of good deeds. Then Daniel appears and tells him his story of being thrown into the lions' den. You remember the lions left Daniel alone and ate the bad advisors of the king. It's a treatise on politics, alliances, wise government, rewards and punishments. What's the use? It's about everything."

Spanner said, "What did happen to Richard I, anyway? I always had the impression he never did much governing."

"That's right. He was killed by a crossbow bolt from a young boy during a siege in 1199. That's the tragedy in the work, the grim twist of fortune. His brother, John Lackland, the bad guy in the Robin Hood story, lost wars, faced a revolt of his nobles, and was forced to sign the Magna Carta in 1215. People in the 1390s still thought Richard would have been a great king and made everything better for everyone forever. This book is in that vein. Richard is being taught how to be a good king, first by a classical, then by a Biblical, teacher. He'd had a taste of greatness, and now he was brought low, sitting in a dungeon. But they're preparing him for another rise, if he'll change his ways, stop warring and start governing. He didn't, and fortune's wheel brought him down for good. The wheel of fortune was a classical theme everybody knew, mostly from Boethius. Chaucer translated Boethius's *Consolation of Philosophy*, remember."

"But is this thing real? Are we about to get our hands on the real lost masterpiece?"

"I think so."

"When?"

"He said he'd call me again."

"When he does, call me. I don't care what time it is, or where I am, call me."

"He doesn't strike me as a person who will donate the manuscript to a library. He seems to enjoy holding it over everyone's head too much."

"So we'll negotiate with him."

"Should I make him an offer?"

"Only if he asks for one."

"How much?"

"Say you have five million on hand, and can make the deal right away, no waiting or speculating."

"And if he refuses the offer?"

"Then tell him you have to talk to your backers, and then call me."

"All right."

When the next call came he felt ready.

"Professor Hallkyn," said the voice. Hallkyn once again thought that the speech was foreign, but he couldn't identify it with a region, or even a country. For the first time, he began to think it might be an idiosyncratic accent, which would be a very bad sign. The man might be mentally ill. "Have you examined what I sent you?"

"Yes." There was no longer any point in pretending to be unimpressed or uncaring. "How did you come by it?"

"Are we really going to be reduced to that kind of discussion?" the man said. "I'm sure you could have guessed. Or did you guess and feel reluctant to take the risk of being wrong, and looking foolish?"

"I suspect it was in the library of some ancient noble family, probably in an area other than London. A family seat in the north of England, probably."

"Why not London?"

"Too much change. There hasn't been much London real estate that has sat idle for six hundred years. And there was the blitz in World War II—lots of residences blown up, but this wasn't in any of them. The owner of this manuscript was undoubtedly very rich, and possibly even royal. That would lead me to think it was John of Gaunt. He was Chaucer's patron and close friend, and they were married to a pair of sisters. The manuscript could have been lost in one of John of Gaunt's estates. Maybe in Lancaster."

"Bravo," said the man. "And why do you suppose nobody knew it was there?"

"I don't know. John of Gaunt and Chaucer died in 1399 and 1400, very close to each other. The next generation of the Lancaster family were dispersed all over Europe when John of Gaunt died. One daughter was queen of Portugal, and one was queen of Castile. The son Henry was exiled for life, returned to fight for the throne, and then became King Henry IV. It's possible that when John died, some servant was tidying up and put the manuscript in a cubbyhole with a hundred others. John of Gaunt would have been horrified, but most common people were still illiterate, and wouldn't have known what it was."

"I can see I selected the right expert," said the man. "I had considered Bethune at Harvard, and a few others, of course. But you know medieval people as though you meet them on the street every day."

"Thank you," said Hallkyn. Maybe he had misjudged this man, based on a mistaken impression of his manner. "I assume you brought the manuscript to my attention because you'd like my advice, and I'd be happy to help. Are you planning to donate it to a library or a university?"

"No, I'm not," the man said.

Hallkyn's heart sank. "What, then? Are you putting it up for sale?"

"Not quite," said the man. "I'm holding it for ransom. If I don't get the right price, I'm going to kill it."

"What?" said Hallkyn. "I don't understand."

"Sure you do," the man said. "There are rich men who want to own things—a Rembrandt, Da Vinci's sketches, Lincoln's letters. Ordinary, serious men such as you never expect to be the sole owner of an essential piece of our culture. All you care about or need is that it exists. For scholars like you, the manuscript of a great work is only of value because it bears the clear authoritative text. Once the text is reprinted, you can study the work, no matter who owns it. So regrettably, the people I'm threatening directly are those like you. If I don't get my price within a week, *The Book of the Lion* will go back to not existing. It will die."

"But then you'll have nothing."

"No, you'll have nothing. I've read it," the man said. "I'll call you again soon."

"How soon?"

But the man had hung up.

The next call came two days later, and this time Hallkyn had prepared and rehearsed. As soon as he knew whom he had on the line he said, "I've made some effort to come up with an alternative. I would like to buy the manuscript from you and donate it to Oxford or Cambridge—either one, if you have a preference."

"No."

"I've collected a fund for the purpose—five million dollars. You can have it in cash."

The man laughed. "What does five million dollars in cash even look like? Do you know?"

"I imagine like fifty thousand hundred-dollar bills," Hallkyn said. "It's a ridiculous amount of money. I'm told it will arrive in five large boxes, a million dollars to a box."

"I won't sell anyone the manuscript," the man said. "But I've decided that the ransom will be five million dollars."

"That was an offer to buy."

"You're a genuine expert on this piece of merchandise, and you believe that it would be rational to pay five million dollars to own it. It's actually worth more, but I follow your reasoning. But you've tipped your hand a bit. I believe you will pay five million to keep the work in existence. You won't have it, but it means that there is a possibility that some day it will be published, rather than burned right away."

Hallkyn felt sweat forming on his scalp and his forehead. He had bid too low. "If we could increase the price, would you sell?"

"No. It's not for sale. Five million dollars keeps it in existence for now."

"Please," said Hallkyn. "It's worth so much more than one person's whim."

"I'm glad you think so," the man said. "Get the money together, and have it in the city of Boston, loaded in a black Cadillac Escalade before seven A.M. on the day after tomorrow. Please repeat what I said."

"You want the money in a Cadillac Escalade in Boston at seven the day after tomorrow."

"Don't sound so hang-dog. I'm giving you what you really want."

"What makes you think I want that?"

"It's what you *should* want. You could never own such a priceless object under any circumstances. You have backers, and the work would be under their control, not yours. The important thing is that the world won't lose it. A scholar of medieval literature should be better at taking the long view."

Hallkyn said, "I've spent a lifetime studying these works because I love them and have a great deal of curiosity about them, even the ones I know well. I want to read this one."

"Good answer," said the man. "I'll call on Wednesday to tell you where to bring the Cadillac."

"Me? I wasn't planning—"

"Then all is lost. The driver has to be someone who knows what is at stake—you."

"All right," Hallkyn said.

Hallkyn tensed, waiting for more patronizing patter, but all he heard was absence. The man had said all he wanted to.

When Hallkyn called Spanner, he was both afraid to tell him and afraid not to. He repeated, as well as he could, everything that the man had said.

Spanner was silent for a moment. "All right, Dominic. You've done as well as anyone could. It was always possible that this man would turn out to be a lunatic. You still believe that he has the real manuscript?"

"I do," said Hallkyn. "The work that's summarized in his email is exactly the work that Chaucer would have done just at that time of his life. The style of writing in the passages I could read is right. Even the physical manuscript is right for that period of his life—thin vellum written in a fine court hand. Chaucer was already rich and well-known. It all fits too well to be a fake."

"Then let me take over from here and make a few arrangements. You fly to Boston. Stay at the Lenox, so I'll know where to find you."

"But what are you planning to do?"

"For one thing, get a Cadillac Escalade to Boston with five million dollars in cash inside it. Just get settled in Boston, wait for his next call, and do what he says. Whatever happens, we're going to try."

"But what are you thinking?"

Spanner sighed. "I'm thinking that we've reached the point where we can use some professional help. I know some people who will be useful in this situation." Spanner seemed distracted. "Excuse me for a second." In a moment he was back. "Okay. We've got a flight for you and a reservation at the Lenox. Be at the airport tomorrow morning and take the 11:15 flight to Boston."

"But are you sure that's—"

"Yes, I am," he said. "Extorting money in exchange for not destroying a missing piece of the world's cultural history is undoubtedly illegal. Destroying it would be worse. In any case, we have to fight this and preserve it. Get packed."

The next evening, Hallkyn was in his room at the Lenox Hotel when his cell phone rang. He looked at it as though it contained a poisonous snake, but he reached for it anyway. "I know what you thought," said Spanner. "But it's only me. I'm downstairs in the lobby. Come down."

Hallkyn put on his sport coat and hurried to the elevator. When the shining brass door opened he charged out, turned right past the front desk, and spotted Spanner sitting in an easy chair in the lobby, alone.

He realized that he had almost forgotten the most distinctive part of Spanner's appearance—his ease. His elbows rested on the chair's overstuffed arms, and his legs were extended, crossed at the ankle, and his head rested against the chair's back.

When he saw Hallkyn he jumped up and shook his hand. "Dom!" he said. "So glad you could make it."

And then there was an extraordinary thing. He said, "Let me introduce you." He turned his head and two men on a nearby couch stood. "This is Mr. Hanlon, Mr. Stokes." He turned his head the other way. "Mr. Garner. Miss Turner, and Miss Day."

Hallkyn realized that the entire lobby was, at this moment, occupied by Spanner's operatives. The five all seemed very different at first. Hanlon was at least fifty, with gray hair and the build of an old football coach. Stokes and Garner were shorter, one light-skinned with reddish hair, and the other black. The two women were about thirty and both slim but unremarkable looking. Then the five began to seem alike to Hallkyn. They all had the eyes of police officers—patient and observant, but not optimistic, as though they expected everyone they met to do something disappointing very soon.

Hallkyn made a point of going to each one and shaking hands, not only because he knew it would help him remember their faces, but also because of a sudden urge to prove to them that they were wrong about him. He saw that it didn't change their opinion of him. The eyes were still on him, waiting for the inevitable disappointment, and it occurred to him that everybody probably tried to persuade them of his innocence.

Spanner said, "Come out with us," and headed for the door.

Hallkyn hurried to catch up with him, and in a moment they were through the circular door out on Boylston Street. As they walked, Hallkyn looked over his shoulder, wondering if all of them would be walking along Boylston Street like a parade. He was instead mystified by the fact that the others had already faded into the landscape. The two women were walking along talking animatedly to each other, both now unaccountably equipped with shopping bags from nearby stores. They stopped to look in a shop window. Hanlon was lumbering along by himself twenty feet ahead of them. Garner and Stokes came last, and it was difficult to tell whether they were together, much less that they had anything to do with the others. Garner was talking on a cell phone, and Stokes seemed to be looking for a cab.

Hallkyn asked Spanner, "Are they police?"

"Not at the moment. They all have been, of one sort or another. Now they work for a security corporation. They've all handled kidnappings and ransom exchanges, mostly in other countries. That's one of their specialties."

They walked two blocks before Spanner said, "Up here at number 800 is the Prudential Center parking garage. The Escalade is parked there."

They entered the lobby of the building and took an elevator down to the second level. When they got out, the Escalade was in front of them. "An ungainly, ugly car," Spanner said. "But it's all yours for a day."

As they walked closer, the others of their party arrived. Mr. Hanlon began the tour. He opened the back door. "Here are the boxes. The suspect probably won't keep the Escalade because he'll expect that it's bugged, wired, and packed with transponders so he can be located. He'll dump it. The only thing we can be sure he won't dump is the money."

"Wait," said Hallkyn. "You're planning to follow me?"

Hanlon looked at Spanner.

Spanner said, "Of course."

Hallkyn felt desperate. "But if he sees he's being followed, he'll destroy the manuscript."

Hanlon said, "We're fairly certain that this man is not going to be there himself. He'll have an accomplice drive the car. He'll be someplace safe, far away. But you're right. If his co-conspirator doesn't perform some pre-arranged signal at a certain time, he may very well destroy the property. We'll be sure to stay out of sight, and we have no plan to interfere with the co-conspirator's actions."

"What is the plan, then?"

"To find out where the accomplice takes the money," Hanlon said. "We expect that the money will be moved to a second vehicle, and probably this man is smart enough to leave the boxes in the Cadillac and take the money in some other method of containment. And that is why—" He paused to build suspense. "The money itself holds the transponders."

He reached into his coat pocket and handed Hallkyn a stack of hundred dollar bills with a paper band that said, "$10,000." Hallkyn wasn't accustomed to handling banded cash, but it looked about the way he had imagined, black printing on a white band, with the numerals apparently embossed, slightly raised. He held it out to give it back to Mr. Hanlon, but Hanlon only pointed at the band. "The chip containing the circuitry is in the first of the zeros, the other zeros are power storage batteries, and the dollar sign is a thin wire antenna. There are five hundred of these bands, of course."

The "of course" caught Hallkyn by surprise, but he remembered that five hundred wasn't really a choice, just the number of ten thousand dollar stacks in five million dollars. "Yes, I see."

"No matter how many times they change vehicles, or what the new container is, the money is sure to find its way to this extortion suspect."

"What if the co-conspirator takes the money to a bank?" said Hallkyn.

"If he puts it in a bank's safe, we'll know which bank. If he deposits it in an account, the bank has to report the transaction to the federal government. Even if he deposits it in five hundred banks, they'd all have to file reports."

"The money could be traced," said Spanner. "It's another of their specialties."

Hallkyn spent most of the next day waiting for the call, sitting alone in his hotel room. He had brought nothing with him to read. He barely dared to watch the television, but after he had set the volume so low that he could be sure he would hear his phone ring, he tried. He had not watched television in years, and found that the picture was much better than it used to be, but the programs were still of little interest to him. Late in the afternoon, the phone rang.

"Are you still interested in paying me five million dollars not to destroy my manuscript?"

"Yes," Hallkyn said.

"Then drive the money across the Charles River to Cambridge."

"That's it?"

"Yes. When you're there I'll call you again." Hallkyn practically ran to the Prudential Building garage where the Cadillac was parked. As he approached it, he saw Mr. Stokes and Mr. Garner both sitting in cars in different parts of the garage.

He started the Escalade and drove. He knew that the other security people would be somewhere on the streets, watching for the man. Hallkyn had been told that the man wouldn't see the security team, that they would be following the signals that five hundred paper bands would be transmitting.

When he had crossed the bridge to Cambridge, his cell phone rang again. The man told him to drive west, and when he had driven nearly to Waltham on Route 20, the man called to tell him to go down to the Massachusetts Turnpike and drive east.

As Hallkyn drove, cars passed him on the left and on the right, and sometimes the people inside seemed to be studying him. It occurred to him that maybe the man wasn't just sending him on a crazy drive. Maybe he was one of those men driving along beside him, studying the Cadillac, or looking for signs he was communicating with a security team. Maybe the man had helpers searching the traffic lanes for followers.

He had no choice but to follow the man's orders. None of this mattered, he knew, because Spanner's people were following him electronically. He took the exit the man told him to. He drove up one street and down the next as the man directed, and then the man said, "There's a bus stop a block ahead to your right. Pull to a stop there."

When he did, an older man in a coat sweater and brimmed hat who was sitting on a bench there got up, ran to the driver's side, and flung the door open. He said, "Go around to the passenger side and let me drive."

This was not at all what Hallkyn expected. As the man climbed in he retreated to the other seat, and got out the other door. "You can leave me here," he said.

"No. Get in."

Hallkyn obeyed.

The man pulled the car out and accelerated down the street. He turned abruptly without signaling, sped up, turned around, went up an alley, then across several intersections that had no traffic lights, and then into another alley. Hallkyn was both intimidated by the skill of the maneuvers and frightened by their recklessness. He wanted to tell the man that he was risking their lives for nothing. His allies were following them electronically.

The second alley was long and narrow, and seemed more like a conduit than a possible destination, but the man passed a big garage door, stopped beyond it, and backed into the garage. The garage door hummed and came down in front of Hallkyn's eyes. A man stood beside the door, where Hallkyn noted there was a box with two buttons that controlled it. The driver said, "Stay in the car," and got out.

Three younger men ran to the back of the Escalade and the driver unlocked the tailgate and then joined them in the job of removing the five boxes of money. They worked fast, taking the boxes to the side wall of the building, where there were five business machines and five duffel bags waiting.

The machines looked familiar to Hallkyn. They were gray with a texture to their housings. There was a small digital display near the top, and a small tray-like surface in front. And then the men began to work and he remembered where he'd seen machines like that—at his bank. They were counting machines, like the ones that tellers used.

Each man would pick up a ten-thousand dollar stack of money, slip off the band, and place the stack on the machine. The machine whirred as it counted the bills, and the man took the stack off and dropped it into a duffel bag at his feet.

A man a bit older than the others, with graying hair that was trimmed in a buzz cut, stepped up to the window beside Hallkyn. "You look surprised. Didn't you think I'd count it?" The voice was unmistakable. Hallkyn hated it even more now than he had before. He thought he caught a slight resemblance to the driver. Were they a pair of brothers?

"Of course," Hallkyn lied. "Not like this, maybe. Not right away."

"Did I strike you as a trusting soul?" He stared hard at Hallkyn. Then he turned his head and called to the others. "Find anything wrong yet?"

"Not yet," said one. "Nothing," said another. None of them looked up. They were working at a furious pace.

Hallkyn watched. Five boxes, a hundred stacks each. Slip the band off onto the floor, set the stack on the counting machine, and while the machine whirred through that stack, strip the band off the next stack so the machine never stopped. Each man was getting through his hundred stacks at an incredible speed.

The gray-haired man walked toward the counting machines. He bent over to pick up something.

Hallkyn's breath stopped in mid-inhalation. The man was picking up the bands from the floor and putting them in an old-fashioned galvanized trash can.

Hallkyn was desperate to get him thinking about something else. Even a minute might help. "Can you at least let me see it?"

"See what?"

"You know."

The man shook his head. "It's not here. I don't carry it around with me." The man stopped moving, his eyes on the floor. He looked puzzled for a second, then different—suspicious. He spun his head to look at Hallkyn. He picked up a band, then tore it. He ran to the wall, picked up a push broom that was leaning there and ran with it along the line of men at the counting machines. He swept the bands into a pile, and threw them in double handfuls into the trash can. He shouted, "Stop the counting and strip off the rest of the bands. Put them in this can as quickly as possible."

As the men complied, he moved back to the wall, and picked up a small can that looked as though it held kerosene. He poured the clear liquid contents onto the money bands. He took a pack of matches out of his pocket, struck one, and tossed it.

The fire caught with a *poof*, the flame four feet high instantly. He shouted, "Strip all the bands and put them in the fire. Don't do anything else, and don't miss any."

The men obeyed, burning the bands as quickly as they could. When they were finished, he called out, "All right. Toss the rest of the money into the bags and carry them to the street."

The men each lifted a duffel bag and carried it through a man-size door on the side of the building away from the garage door where Hallkyn's Escalade had entered.

The man with the gray hair stepped close to Hallkyn's window. "We had an agreement, and you cheated," he said. "You stupid, stupid man." Then he turned and ran through the doorway where the younger men had taken the duffel bags.

Hallkyn heard a car start, and then drive off.

The five young men each took a counting machine and carried it out through the man-size doorway. He thought about stopping them, but he had no idea how to stop five men from doing anything. Stopping one would probably get him beaten senseless.

He sat still in the passenger seat of the Cadillac Escalade, watching. The men ignored him, as though they had forgotten he was there, and it was a relief to Hallkyn. A moment later, they were gone. There was another engine sound. They were driving away too.

Hallkyn sat in the passenger seat of the Escalade, watching the fire in the trash can burn down to nothing and go out. The bands had been consumed, and now the igniter was exhausted too.

He took out his cell phone and dialed Spanner's number.

"Where are you?" said Spanner. "The security people said the transmitters went dead."

"They were burned," said Hallkyn. "The man realized they were a trick. He was furious. Now I don't know what he's likely to do."

"Where are you?"

"One of his men drove me up an alley to a place that looks like a warehouse or a garage. He took the keys with him."

"Can you go outside?"

"I think so."

"Then do it, and look for a street sign. I'll hold on."

Hallkyn went out the man-sized door where the others had gone and found himself on an ordinary Boston street. People walked past him on the sidewalk, went into stores and restaurants. It felt like he'd gone through a door to another, calmer, ordered world. At the corner he saw a sign for Beacon Street.

An hour later Hallkyn and Spanner crossed the carpeted floor in the lobby of the Lenox Hotel.

"I need a drink," said Hallkyn.

"So do I," said Spanner. He stepped to the door of the bar and opened it, and they entered the dimly lighted, comforting space.

Hallkyn's phone rang. He pulled it from his pocket and swiped his thumb across the screen to answer it.

There was a picture—a video, he realized after a moment. It was a shot of a thick sheaf of elongated sheets a bit yellowed, with neat lines of black ink in a single column of writing down the center, and a demi-venet border on the left margin. Hallkyn thought he saw a glow of gold leaf at the top left that could be an illuminated letter. "Oh, my God," he said.

Spanner leaned close and looked at it too. "Is that it?"

A pair of hands picked up the stack of sheets. The familiar hated voice came over the picture, filled with contempt. "Your word was worthless. My word is true."

The hands set the stack of pages on a shiny metal tray.

Hallkyn said to the phone, "Please don't do this."

There was no reply, and he realized this moving image wasn't live. This had already happened, and nobody was listening. The right hand poured a can of liquid on the sheets. The hands struck a match and tossed it onto the tray. The bright yellow flames rose, flickered and wavered. There was a blue aura around the top as they fluttered a little. Then the picture went black. The video was disconnected.

The two men looked at each other, speechless. After a thirty second silence, Spanner was the first. "I'm sorry," he said. "I'm so sorry, Dominic."

Hallkyn gave a little start, as though he had been wakened from sleep. "Eh? No, T.M. It wasn't your fault. You did everything you could, so generous and brave, as always. It was my fault."

The bartender materialized in front of them like a specter. "What can I get you gentlemen?"

Spanner said, "Single malt Scotch."

Hallkyn nodded, more at Spanner than the bartender.

The bartender said, "We have several single malts. Do you have a favorite?"

Spanner glanced at the row of bottles on the third shelf above the bar. "That one should do it."

"Laphroaig?"

"Fine. We'd like two glasses and the bottle."

The bartender poured the first round, and Spanner poured the second round less than a minute later. They slowed their pace after that, and drank in silence for a time.

Finally Hallkyn spoke. "I've lost your money. I'm afraid it's much more than I can repay, more than I'll have in my lifetime. I feel terrible."

"I don't want it repaid," said Spanner. "I can cover that much by myself. The backers I had lined up won't lose anything. I'll just send each of them ten percent of what he'd promised to invest, and call it a profit. They'll all be delighted." He looked into Hallkyn's eyes, and his expression changed. "Here's the important part. This has to remain our secret. Forever. If the people I deal with knew I had been so foolish, my reputation would be destroyed. I rely on investors who trust my judgment and bet billions on my being right. I have to ask you to swear to me that you'll never tell."

Hallkyn leaned back and focused his eyes on Spanner. "Do you think I want this known? If you lost your career now, you'd still be pretty much the man you are—a winner. But all I have is my reputation as a medieval scholar. Do you have any idea what the people in my field would think of the man who got some lunatic to burn Chaucer's *Book of the Lion*? I'd rather die than tell anyone this happened. I'll swear gladly."

Behind the garage of a house fifty miles away, the man finished cleaning up the residue of the little fire he had lit a couple of hours ago. He'd had to wait until the tray was cool enough to touch. Now the ashes and burned remnants had been bagged, then double bagged, and put in the garbage can. It had been an expensive fire. He had bought the vellum from a company that printed diplomas, rough cut and trimmed the sheets himself, and used a projector to trace the design of the top page so it would look like the real *Book of the Lion* on a video. He'd been pleased. It really had looked a lot like the real one that Uncle Reg had found in the trunk he'd bought at the farm sale in Lankashire after the war. That one was in the climate-controlled room where it belonged.

He hosed off the tray, wiped the surface dry with paper towels, and then took the tray back into the house and set it on the shelf under the counter in the kitchen. He looked at his watch. It was getting to be just about time.

He went into his study and sat down at the desk. He scanned his list of names and numbers, and then took out one of the pre-paid cell phones from the drawer on his right. He dialed.

He waited through four rings and then heard the voicemail message. When it was time he said, "Professor Bethune, the reason I'm calling is that you are one of the three or four most respected medieval scholars in the world. I have what I believe to be the only remaining copy of *The Book of the Lion*. It's on thin vellum, in a fine court hand, legible throughout. I'll call again."

The Mysterious Disappearance of the Reluctant Book Fairy

Elizabeth George

~~◦

Elizabeth George, born Susan Elizabeth George, is a native of Warren, Ohio. She received her higher education in California, studying undergrad at the University of California in Riverside and graduate school at the California State University at Fullerton, where she earned her master's in counseling and psychology with an honorary doctorate of humane letters. After school, George worked as an English teacher in several different areas of California. Her teaching career had its ups and downs, including being fired from her first position for union activity and being honored as Orange County Teacher of the Year at her last. After over a decade of teaching, George left educational work to focus on writing and sold her first novel, *A Great Delicerance*. George has won many awards for her writing, including the Anthony Award, the Agatha Award, and Le Grand Prix de Literature Policiere in France. She has also been nominated for the Edgar and Macavity Awards. Almost all of her novels have been converted into television shows for BBC and for PBS's *Mystery*.

F or an entire generation, the story that follows could not be told. She who effected the vanishing of Langley, Washington's most famous citizen was still among the living and had the knowledge of exactly what she had done been revealed before this moment, there is little doubt that legions of the broken-hearted, the disenchanted, the disappointed, and the downright enraged would have ended up marching along the quiet street where she lived, bent upon violence. This, of course, would have followed whatever the aforementioned legions had done to a disused potting shed in the arboreal confines of Langley Cemetery, where the shape of a body on a moth-eaten blanket and a rotting first edition of an antique novel marked the spot of a deeply mourned departure. But now, at last, everything can be revealed. For all involved have finally passed, and no danger remains to anyone. Langley, Washington, has long since returned to the sleepy albeit lovely little village that has sat above the gleaming waters of Saratoga Passage for more than one hundred years. And what occurred there to its citizenry and to its gentle, well-meaning, but far too malleable librarian has been consigned to history.

Annapurna didn't start out her life intending to become a librarian. She also didn't start out her life intending to become a book fairy. Indeed, she didn't start out her life intending to become Annapurna. Instead she began her time on earth as Janet Shore in a very ordinary manner which, no matter how close the examination, would never suggest to anyone who was acquainted with her that she possessed powers beyond an average mortal's.

She was born at home in the village of Langley, which at that time was a little enclave of colorful cottages and, alas, perpetually dying businesses sitting high on a bluff on Whidbey Island. Above the strait that it overlooked, bald eagles flew and in this strait orcas and gray whales swam. Gold finches flashed the sunlight of their bodies in the air, swallows coursed joyously from the eaves of old storefronts, hummingbirds hovered before spikes of white quamash, and at just the right moment in just the right season, starlings swooped in great dancing clouds near the terminal where the ferries came and went. Here, hemlocks and firs soared into the heavens, rabbits openly munched unmolested in garden beds, raccoons were known to wander through the open hallways of the middle school in a search for discarded lunches, and deer high-stepped among the various cottages, decimating everything from tulips to topiaries.

In this pleasant place Janet Shore made her first appearance, born into a very ordinary family on a very ordinary day in a very ordinary house as her parents had eschewed hospitals for the birth of all their children and were not about to alter this course when Janet—child number six—came along. Perhaps more observation during her birth would have told her parents of Janet's yet-tobe tested powers, but her parents were not the observant sort, nor were her four brothers and single sister, all of whom spent their mother's labor and subsequent delivery of the sixth bundle of Shore joy in the back yard of the family home where a search for forty dollars in dimes—prepared in advance by their wily father—would end up producing only $39.90, no matter the length of time that they spent searching, which would be, naturally, quite considerable. Indeed, the five youngsters—aged three to ten years—had actually managed to dislodge only $25.70 from the lawn, the vegetable beds, the compost heap, and the flower garden when their father emerged from the house to tell them that the Shore line—he had that kind of sense of humor, alas—had been extended once again.

In very short order, they were introduced to Janet who was not—as you might well imagine—nearly as interesting to them as the dimes that still lay unclaimed in the yard. And it must be admitted that as the years of Janet's childhood progressed, matters didn't alter much when it came to her relationship with her siblings. As for her parents, what can one say? They were back-to-the-landers who'd arrived on Whidbey Island to live a simple life described by hard work growing their own fruits and vegetables, raising goats for milk and cheese, practicing skilled carpentry for a local contractor (Dad) and establishing the village's recycling center, its thrift shop, and its food bank while simultaneously home schooling six children (Mom) and then blissfully producing two more (Mom and Dad together, of course). So in the midst of what was a busy life, if one child had a nature that was rather whimsical, as long as she didn't get underfoot or impede the daily progress of life among the Shores, chances were very good that she would remain largely unnoticed. Such was the case with Janet, who easily could have been lost in the shuffle entirely had she not possessed the weakest constitution of all the children.

Thus put to the question, Janet's parents would have noted only one characteristic about their sixth child that caused her to be modestly different from her brothers and sisters (those last two babies being girls, by the way). She was, unfortunately, a rather sickly sort, easily attacked by various viruses, bacteria, and germs, and in such a way that her childhood might best be described as one spent largely in bed with occasional forays into the real world where she would, in very short order, pick up another bug to fell her again.

Most children find imprisonment in a sick bed both trying and tiresome. Some children—especially if they are one among many—find it comforting as they quickly surmise that the only moments that they will actually have the nurturing attention of their parents are those moments of illness. And a few children see the sickbed as a doorway to another world, brought to them courtesy of the dozens of books that one parent or the other rushes to the library to obtain, in the hope of keeping the invalid occupied.

As you have no doubt surmised, Janet was of this last small group. Influenza? Strep throat? Chicken pox? Measles? Mumps? The common cold? An undiagnosed ailment of one kind or another? These were greeted with such enthusiasm by the child Janet Shore that one might have concluded she was headed for lifelong hypochondria had one not known of her penchant for losing herself in stories. She began with fairy tales: the Brothers Grimm and Hans Christian Anderson being her favorites. She went on to mythology, preferring the Romans over the Greeks. She dipped into Biblical picture books in her younger years, and she quickly moved on to *The Boxcar Children* and the Little House books, graduating from there to Nancy Drew's adventures as well as those of Trixie Belden, the Hardy Boys, and the Bobsey Twins, this last group unearthed from her grandmother's house in New Hampshire and sent along when it became apparent that Janet was sure to read the entire collection of children's books available at the village library before she was ten years old.

One reason for Janet's love of reading was, of course, the escape it provided from her constant illnesses and the additionally constant turmoil of living in a very small house with seven other children and two adults. The other reason for this love, however, had everything to do with Janet's talent, that very special quality in her possession that her busy parents had never had the opportunity to notice.

It is often said that individuals escape into books and what this means, of course, is that individuals escape their humdrum lives by sinking into the pages of a novel. But Janet Shore *escaped* into books to the fullest extent that that word can be used. Given a heart rending scene of emotion (Mary Ingalls going blind!), a thrilling adventure in a frightening cave (Tom, Huck, and Injun Joe!), a battle with pirates (Peter Pan and Captain Hook!), and our Janet was actually able to transport herself *into* the scene itself. And not as a passive observer, mind you, but rather as a full participant in the story. Thus the Mad Hatter and the March Hare served *her* tea along with Alice, and when the Prince presented the glass slipper to Cinderella, Janet was able to shove her aside and try the footwear on herself. That other Prince kissed *her* instead of Snow White and who can blame him since kissing Snow was so akin to smooching a corpse, and when Rapunzel lowered her hair, Janet climbed *down* to her rescuer before he could get a decent grip on the locks that would lead him to his love.

Can there be any doubt, then, why Janet Shore greeted her illnesses with the passion of a long lost love come to claim her hand? How could doubt exist in this situation? And it was all so easy to achieve in a household where one went largely unnoticed. Indeed, the very fact of Janet's near anonymity among her siblings allowed her hours and days in which to practice launching herself into novels when she was engaged in a battle with no illness at all. She learned that this required of her only three elements: a story that provided her with enchantment, excitement, terror, thrills, or any other physical or emotional connection to it; solitude to serve as a launching pad; and a tether that allowed her access back into the real world.

Two of these were easily come by. Becoming lost within and enthralled by a story was second nature to Janet, and using the family dog as a tether did not require a great deal of thought. Solitude was the tricky bit, but she finally managed to locate the perfect spot for this when she discovered that, tucked deep within the village's old and crumbling cemetery and just beyond the looming conifers that lined the far side of the area dedicated to the cremated citizens of Langley, an ancient potting shed had been long forgotten and nearly consumed by blackberry bushes, lichen, and moss. In this shed, carefully repaired as best she could to keep out the rain which was plentiful in this part of the world, Janet supplied herself with an ancient hook rug long ago made by one of her aunts, along with what surely was a third hand blanket purchased from the local thrift store, and a pillow pilfered from the hall closet in her parents' house, only disinterred when a relative came to visit and had to sleep on the couch. Supplied with these items of marginal comfort, Janet could retire to the cemetery and to her hidden spot as often as she liked, in the company of whatever rescue dog her family was currently sheltering. With the dog outside of the potting shed and Janet inside with his leash wrapped round her wrist, she was safely anchored to the real world, the dog dragging her back to it the moment his dinner hour rolled around. It was a foolproof way to experience life in the written world, and thus it served her several years.

Janet would no doubt have rested quietly with her talent had not a very silly argument about a Halloween pageant, Boo Radley, and Bob Ewell developed between her and her best friend Monie Reardon. A misreading of the climactic scene in that novel and its subsequent denouement had given Monie the impression that, just as Heck Tate slyly suggested, Bob Ewell had fallen upon his own knife. Nothing that Janet said to Monie could convince the girl of anything else. Even their seventh grade teacher Mrs. Neff could not convince Monie. For Monie was something of a black-and-white reader, and the subtleties of Heck Tate's suggestions and his references to the townspeople leaving grateful gifts on the Radley doorstep did not convince Monie that she was sadly mistaken about Bob Ewell's demise in the climax of the book. Thus, Janet decided to provide her with an experience to alter her viewpoint.

Janet wasn't certain that she could do this, however: to send someone other than herself into a piece of literature. But she discovered that the concentration she applied to her own literary travels worked just as well on others, if she rested the relevant book upon their chests, opened to the relevant scene. Then it was a matter of hands placed in the appropriate position, breathing slowed to a deep and steady pace, the repetition of *welcome me welcome me welcome home* along with five other words whose revelation here would be far too dangerous to the reader of this tale, and with less than an eye blink the literary traveler would be gone. Which is to say that her soul and her mind and her experience would be gone. Her body would, of course, remain where it was, which in this case was the potting shed in the Langley cemetery near the cremation stones.

Thus did Monie Reardon get cast into the pages of *To Kill a Mockingbird* in order to witness the attack beneath the great oak tree and to take careful note of exactly who was wielding the knife upon whom. And can it otherwise be believed that Monie came back an altered individual? She was wide-eyed and open-mouthed and aside from "That Jem Finch is *adorable*," her only remark upon her return to the potting shed was, "How did you *do* that?" which was quickly followed by, "More! More!"

It would have been lovely had Monie been able to keep this skill of Janet's to herself, but this was an impossibility, for Monie was a talker. In very short order, Janet found herself with a line of schoolmates outside the potting shed, all of them wanting to "do the book thing," as Monie so unromantically called it.

Harry Potter's world was, naturally, the choice of many of the boys. Most of girls wanted Edward and Jacob to be in love with *them* instead of Bella. So tedious, repetitive, and downright pedestrian did the demands for literary travel become that Janet began sending individuals where *she* felt they best belonged which, as you can probably imagine, was not a popular move.

To the boys who wanted to ride a broomstick during a game of quidditch, she gave the voyage to Colchis in the company of Jason to have a look for the Golden Fleece. To the girls who believed their lives could not possibly be complete without a vampire's love, she offered the passion of Mr. Rochester discovering his life's great love in plain Jane Eyre. Greeted with the complaints of the literary travelers she so generously accommodated in her woodland potting shack, Janet's retort would be, "Hey! Try reading a decent book for once," herself not being drawn to the great commercial successes of her day. For her were the Greek and Roman myths, the great masterpieces of Victorian literature, the tales of derring do penned by America's mighty writers. And never one to be dragged along as part of a crowd, Janet was a girl who stuck to her literary guns. Thus over time, her grousing school companions either fell by the wayside or became her devotees. There was, as it developed, no middle ground.

So things went for her: through middle school (providing Gilbert Blythe's proposal to Anne Shirley to the romantically inclined; introducing Natty Bumppo's adventures in a juvenile America to those wanting a bit more action) and through high school (a half hour on the rolling decks of the *Pequod* for the boys, Portia putting the psychological thumbscrews to Shylock for the girls). There was plenty of scope during this latter period once Janet became enamored of Dickens, as well. How about a meet and greet with Magwitch? No problem. Want to see what Bob Sikes was truly like? That could also be arranged.

The conclusion of high school brought the big change: both to Janet Shore and to what she did with her curious talent. For off she went to college where she was drawn to library studies (can there be any surprise in that?) and where, unfortunately, cupid's arrow pierced her heart for the first and last time.

Can there be any doubt that, in the mind of a young woman given to taking literature into her very heart, true love exists? Is there any reader of this tale who would argue *against* the likelihood of Janet Shore's locking eyes with a dark-haired stranger across a crowded room and knowing that love can happen in an instant? A reader of this tale might wish to try, but all the arguing would be in vain. For across the crowded Vegetarian Medley station of her university's student dining room, Janet spied one Chadbourne Hinton-Glover. And while the double barreled surname should have told her much and his startling resemblance to Charlie Sheen should have told her more, all she could see was the blaze in his eyes and all she could assume as that blaze devoured her soul—as she would tell it later—was that they had been struck simultaneously by a thunderbolt of love that was bigger than both of them, as these things generally were.

Although she'd been at the Vegetarian Medley station for reasons having largely to do with corn muffins, she became a vegetarian instantly. A question to Chadbourne Hinton-Glover about quinoa (which she disastrously mispronounced in such a manner as nearly to give away her entire omnivorous history prior to the moment) led to earnest talk about puy lentils, the virtues of sprouted nuts, the value of cracked wheat versus whole wheat, and what *tempeh* (also terribly mispronounced) could be transformed into in the hands of a skilled chef. By the time Chadbourne and Janet had worked their way to the end of the Vegetable Medley station and were presenting their food cards to the attendant, they were a couple.

Unfortunately for Janet, the love that bloomed between them was a fragile thing: a rhododendron blossom best left on the bush and not plucked and put into water where it will quickly fade and die. In her innocence Janet did not see this, for even if things turned out disastrously for them, had not Heathcliff and Cathy shared an eternal love? Had not Gabriel waited faithfully for that silly Bathsheba to come to her senses? Jude had Sue and if it hadn't worked out (when one's children are killed at the hands of their half-sibling, it rarely does), how they had worshipped each other for a time! And that was point: the time, its length, which was supposed to be longer than four months in duration.

Janet gave herself to the relationship whole-heartedly, for she knew from her novel reading that there was no other way. For Dorothea Brooke had finally found bliss in the arms of Will Ladislaw, had she not, even if it had taken a good while—not to mention a hell of a lot pages—for her to arrive at this position? So like the innocent she was, she became Chadbourne's schoolmate, soulmate, and bedmate in very short order, eschewing the company of her immediately erstwhile female friends who could have told her much about Chadbourne's proclivity to allow his hands and lips and other body parts to roam as much as he allowed his eyes to do so.

Discovering him enthusiastically engaged with a bronzed Brazilian swimming goddess drove a stake into Janet's heart. The fact that he was embroiled with the young woman upon the Egyptian cotton sheets that Janet had saved her part-time job money to purchase was a further blow. The additional horror of Chadbourne not actually recognizing Janet as his beloved when she came into the room and found him entwined in the arms and legs of the bronzed Brazilian swimming goddess made matters so devastating that no later claim of being without his contact lenses at the moment of discovery could go any distance toward salving the wounds to Janet's heart and soul. She decamped at once, taking her sheets with her.

When one's first great love is so cruelly revealed to be a rodent, recovery is often difficult, and this was the case for Janet. She left the university forthwith and threw herself into the only thing she could come up with to rescue what little self-esteem she had left: an alternative life style. This involved two years of travel on a converted school bus with a merry band of do-nothings who had been deeply influenced by the film *Priscilla, Queen of the Desert* and who had made the decision to duplicate as much of that adventure as they could, albeit on the west coast of the United States. This duplication was achieved through several very long drives to Burning Man during which the music of ABBA played at a disturbing volume, copious amounts of dope were smoked, and alternative garb was created, dependent heavily upon sequins, beads, bell-bottom trousers, and very tight and very plunging tops. And while the ancient school bus did not, alas, make it to Burning Man for a third go (having broken down repeatedly and finally irreparably in Arcada, California), Janet did ultimately find herself in a welcoming community of earnest back-to-the-landers who reminded her of her own family, who treaded the earth in Birkenstocks and flannel, and who expressed their individuality by changing their names from those chosen by The Birthers, as they referred to their parents, to something more reflective of who they were striving to be.

Hence, Annapurna. It must be admitted that Janet chose this name merely for its mellifluous nature. She found that it gave her a sense of being more than she was and of hiding away that part of her that had been so crushed by Chadbourne Hinton-Glover. So she remained Annapurna and she remained in Arcada, California, for fifteen more years till the amount of rainfall and the long bleak winters and a letter from her old friend Monie Reardon—now Monie Reardon Pillerton—suggested a change was in order.

Monie Reardon Pillerton knew about Chadbourne, of course. She knew of the school bus adventure and its final demise in Arcada. She knew that her old friend Janet Shore was no more and in her place was Annapurna. But she also knew of a job that had become available on Whidbey Island, and it was her earnest belief that Janet-who-had-been and Annapurna-who-now-was would be perfect for this position. It must be said that Monie also had an ulterior motive for enticing Annapurna back to Whidbey Island.

Married for twelve years to the world's most faithful man who was, alas, also the world's biggest dullard, she had produced four children in quick succession thinking they might at least provide conversation in the evening prior to lights out. Unfortunately, Monie soon discovered that the production of offspring alone could not a thrilling marriage make. However, not wanting to divorce the man—for how can one divorce someone whose greatest sin is merely to be boring?—Monie was aching for some kind of excitement and when she saw the position of town librarian advertised in the *South Whidbey Record*, her memory of dazzling hours spent inside the cemetery potting shed in the company of everyone from Nancy Drew to Hester Prynne was sparked. Oh, to have at least that much escape from the well-meaning but terminally dull Dwayne Pillerton! To have a few hours away from laundry, housecleaning, grocery shopping, cooking, dog walking, and the required attendance at youthful athletic events! To Monie Reardon Pillerton, the return of the long gone Janet Shore in the person of Annapurna was the answer to what had gone badly wrong in her life. So she got herself appointed to the search committee for the new librarian, penned the letter to Annapurna, and set about making absolutely certain that Annapurna was the chosen one.

Thus Annapurna returned not only to the island of her birth but also to the town in which she had grown up. She had been gone for years, of course, and while she had stayed in communication with her parents and siblings during the long period of her travels and the longer period of her life in Arcada, California, she had no wish to engage intimately in family matters. She longed to live a life she had become used to: one of isolation, contemplation, and self-recrimination. For she had not, you see, been able to forgive the Janet-Shore-who-had-been for her youthful errors in love. That young person's mindless and utterly naïve devotion to matters literary had led her to heartbreak at the hands of a soulless man, and so grave had her heartbreak been that Annapurna had not once allowed herself to become remotely close to any individual—male or female—since. Indeed, she'd kept those Egyptian cotton sheets as a reminder to trust and give her heart to no one, and if they became softer and softer with repeated washings as promised and if their 500 thread-count allowed for their astounding durability, they also served as testimony to the fact that happily ever after can last six months or less and can end in an excruciating betrayal if one does not keep one's eyes peeled for telltale signs of a fellow human's fallibility from the moment of introduction to the moment of that fallibility's inevitable appearance.

Thus it must be said that she felt no loyalty or kinship to anyone on Whidbey Island despite being the actual kin of at least fifty-two individuals at this point, her siblings having grown up to be a familially ambitious and remarkably fecund group. Her only relationship of any note was with Monie Reardon Pillerton who, over skinny vanilla lattes one late afternoon at the village's trendiest coffee house, worked what had been a desultory conversation about persistent tooth decay in her eldest child into a reminiscence of Annapurna's decades-long dormant ability to propel herself and other people into a literary scene of their desire.

"Oh, I don't do that any longer, Monie," was met with a stare of outright incredulity.

"But . . . but . . . but why not?" followed that stare, for it was inconceivable to Monie Reardon Pillerton that such a talent would not be used on a daily basis, especially if one had small children whose continuous squabbling and frequent demands for maternal attention begged to be met either by a quick trip down the rabbit hole with Alice or a tag-along with the Pied Piper of Hamlin. Monie, however, was not likely to say such a thing about her children to Annapurna. Rather she pointed out to her old friend—in somewhat sonorous tones, it must be admitted—the responsibility one had to use one's God given talents for the good of mankind.

Annapurna, however, was not to be moved on this issue. She had suffered too much at the hands of her own talent, as we know, having prompted within herself a belief in happy endings following hard on the heals of true love (it must be admitted that she'd never been a great fan of *Romeo and Juliet*, from which she should have learned much on this topic), which had led her to abject misery.

For Monie, there was only one recourse. Annapurna had to be exposed to children to enhance her understand of a mother's need for blessed escape. Not just any children would do, of course. Annapurna needed exposure to Monie's own. For surely two or three hours in their company—particularly when they were ravenous with hunger—would be sufficient to encourage within Annapurna a desire to help her old friend—if no one else—through the simple means of a dreamy escape to . . . Monie had been delving a great deal into Monte Carlo lately, having just completed her tenth reading of *Rebecca*. Just the scene in which Maxim proposes to the unnamed narrator, she told Annapurna. Really, that's *all* that she would ask although she was also partial to the thrilling moment of "*I* am Mrs. de Winter now," that so memorably put the evil Mrs. Danvers in her place. Of course, that foul creature ended up setting fire to Manderley as a possible result of this moment of assertion on the narrator's part, but some things, Monie knew, could not be helped.

Can it be otherwise than Annapurna's agreeing to give her old friend a bit of respite from the drudgery of her life? While it took more than an initial two or three hours in the company of Monie's children to effect a form of harmony between the women on the subject of literary escapes, they reached an accord on the afternoon when Monie's youngest had a bout of projectile vomiting so severe that nothing other than *The Exorcist* popped immediately into Annapurna's mind. Annapurna then began to see the problem in terms of taking her friend—even for a brief hour or two—*out* of the horror novel in which she was living instead of depositing her into another.

And so it happened that Annapurna began to investigate where she could—for want of a better term—set up shop. It had to be in the library, naturally. Her days were spent there, and it was only during the day when Monie's children were in school that it was possible for Monie to escape the chains that bound her to hearth and home.

Such a location had few requirements beyond privacy and the space for a small cot on which the literary traveler could recline. There was the necessity of a temporal anchor, of course, that would bind the traveler to the here and now in much the same way in her previous life young Janet Shore had used her canine's leash for her own trips and her hand within the hand of the traveler when she was entertaining her friends. A boat's line—easily had from the town marina—would do for this, she decided. She would fix it to the door knob of a convenient room so that when she opened the door after Monie's excursion, her friend would rise as if from a pleasant and refreshing sleep. This would, admittedly, be effected by means of a preemptory and rather rough jerk on her wrist from the boat line that would be tied around it, but some things could simply not be helped. Had she been able to be at Monie's side throughout her trip to Monte Carlo or Manderley—really, it was up to her, as Annapurna had no thoughts on the matter other than wonder that Maxim de Winter had not disposed of that nasty bit of business Rebecca much sooner into their tormented relationship—nothing more than her hand in Monie's would have been necessary. But she had to see to the needs of the library's patrons and as luck would have it, Monie's choice of traveling day occurred in the middle of the Red Hatted Ladies' Book Club Morning, which generally leaked over into the Red Hatted Ladies' Book Club Afternoon if the edibles were good enough and the literary discussion was fierce.

With all of this in mind, only the library's supply room would offer sufficient space for a cot, privacy from the prying eyes of other library patrons, and a doorknob. Because it contained vast library valuables such as paper stock for the coin operated copier, it also was lockable, a decided plus.

Thus on the very next morning following Annapurna's brief, "All right, I'll do it," which itself followed soon after the Pillerton offspring's impressive show of projectile vomiting, Monie presented herself at the library. She'd dressed for the occasion. She'd chosen a form of thirties' garb that she deemed suitable, considering the time period in which she supposed the book took place: between the two great wars. At the local thrift store, she'd managed to put together an approximation of that period's dress. That she looked rather like a cross between Queen Elizabeth the Queen mother (that would be the hat and the shoes) and Bonnie of Bonnie-and-Clyde fame (that would be the skirt, the belt, and the sweater), did not appear to concern her. She announced herself as ready and excited and "oh how I've longed for this moment since you first came back to Langley," in rather too loud a voice that caused Annapurna to shush her. The last thing she wanted was a repeat of her early years in which she'd discovered the pedestrian predilections of her peers in matters literary. To know that they had grown into adults whose tastes had not altered . . .? Life was hard enough, Annapurna thought.

She stamped three books for a local woman. She answered four questions from a man whose knowledge of how to use the library-provided WiFi began and ended with turning a computer on. When at last she was free, she cast a look round the library to make certain she and Monie Reardon Pillerton were not being observed. Finding the coast clear, she hustled Monie behind the check out counter, through the librarian's office, and into the supply closet, which she had made ready.

A camping cot found on Craig's List would serve as the launching pad. A thin mattress covered it and around this was tucked a quilt purchased at a fund raiser for the town's feral cats, always in want of a decent meal. Mood lighting was provided by a candle carefully sheltered by a hurricane globe. The line of reality—so Annapurna thought of the boat's line that would be used to anchor Monie—lay curled at the foot of the cot.

Monie had brought *Rebecca* with her as her memory told her to do. She confessed herself so excited that she feared she'd "let loose in her pants." Disconcerted, Annapurna offered her friend the lavatory at once. "Just an *expression*," Monie said with a laugh. "I *hope* I still have bladder control, Janet." She winced as soon as she said Annapurna's birth name. She apologized quickly. It was all due to excitement, she said. She could only imagine what it was going to be like to witness Maxim de Winter's proposal of marriage to his youthful, inarticulate but nonetheless soon-to-be blushing bride.

"So you've decided?" Annapurna asked her. "You don't want the Mrs. Danvers scene?"

"Maybe later," Monie told her, which should, of course, have warned Annapurna of things to come. But at the moment the bell on the checkout desk rang peremptorily.

"You'll have to wait a moment," Annapurna told her friend.

"Damn it! But there's so little time," was Monie's reply.

Annapurna wanted to tell her that it wasn't an overlong scene in the book anyway: just the narrator interrupting Maxim in the middle of shaving, followed by her wretched and lovestruck goodbye to him, followed by breakfast on the terrace, followed by an abrupt proposal of marriage made over marmalade which, let's face it, was one of the more forgettable marriage proposals ever made. As Annapurna recalled . . . hadn't the word *ninny* even come into play? Perhaps not. But the word *love* certainly hadn't. For heaven's sake, even the imperious Mr. Darcy had managed to cram *love* among the various insults to Elizabeth Bennett's family. *But* . . . no matter. Monie would get her moment in Monte Carlo in which the narrator's life is turned upside down and in that moment Monie too could dream of what it would have been like to be the wife of the dark, brooding, desperately unhappy but at the same time filthy rich Maxim de Winter.

First, however, she had to see to whoever was ringing the checkout desk bell. And thus she met Mildred Banfry, the woman who would forever alter the existence that Annapurna had grown to find so personally burdensome.

It must be said that Mildred Banfry did not for an instant look like a life changer. She didn't look like any kind of changer at all. She looked precisely the way someone named Mildred Banfry *would* look, although Annapurna did not, of course, know her name in the moment that her gaze fell upon her. What she *did* know was what she saw: gangly, potentially suffering from late onset sexual dysphoria, a horrifying dress sense even for this part of the world which was not known for individuals capable of putting together something that might be deemed "an outfit," hair that looked as if mowing might be the better choice than a mere cutting, and eyebrows that snaked across her forehead in a manner that could only be referred to as threatening.

Her voice boomed. "Here. You. Are!" she announced at a volume so stentorian that Annapurna felt it very likely that the police department next door to the library and housed with the confines of the town's brick city hall might have been well informed of the woman's arrival. The members of the Red-Hatted Ladies' Book Club certainly were. More than one furious glance was shot from the discussion room in the direction of the check-out desk. "I. Want. A. Library. Card. Do. You. Hear. Me?"

Well, obviously, was what Annapurna thought. So does everyone else, my dear woman. And like so many people who feel uneasy with correcting anyone's behavior, she modeled what was a more appropriate volume, for as far as she knew, the poor woman had never entered a library in her life. Her teeth certainly suggested as much although the absence of five or six molars couldn't actually make any kind of *accurate* testimony as to one's literacy or lack thereof. "Certainly," Annapurna murmured. "If you have something to show me that you're a resident?"

"Course. I. Do.," Mildred hollered. "I'm. Not. Stupid. Do. I. Look. Stupid. To. You?"

Annapurna lowered her head in embarrassment. "No, no. Not at all. If you'll just—"

"You're. Going. To. Have. To. Speak. Up," Mildred told her. "Or. I. Can. Read. Lips. But. Not. If. You. Don't. Look. At. Me."

"Yes, yes, of course," Annapurna said quickly, as she raised her head. "Only . . . if there's any way . . .?"

"What?" And when Annapurna looked around the library with a gesture to indicate to Mildred that it *was* a library and not perhaps what she thought it might be, which seemed to be a hog calling contest, Mildred said, "Oh! Ha! Too. Loud. Am. I? Didn't. Wear. My. Hearing. Aids. Batteries. Are. Dead. Sorry. Use. This." And she rooted around in a bag printed with *I've Been To Disneyland!* prominently upon it until she found what she sought, which was a tattered notebook to which a ballpoint pen was attached. "Write. It. Out. Here," she said. "Mildred. Banfry. By. The. Way. And. You. Are?"

Annapurna wrote out her name and everything that followed. Did Mildred Banfry have an ID showing she was appropriately domiciled somewhere in Island County? She certainly did. She'd brought along her electricity bill—rather amazingly low so that Annapurna wondered if the woman owned a refrigerator or even turned on a single light—and she had evidence of her checking account as well. This latter wouldn't do for evidence of her habitation, but it was of no import because the electricity bill did the trick. Annapurna began gathering what was needed to give Mildred her library card.

It was at this most unfortunate moment that Monie Reardon Pillerton came wandering out of the supply room. As she still had the boat line tied to her wrist and her shoes had been removed for comfort's sake and the sake of the cleanliness of the aforementioned quilt, she did present a rather startling sight since the reader must recall that she was also dressed somewhat unusually for Langley, Washington. Well, not all *that* unusually considering the Red-Hatted Ladies in one room and Mildred Banfry in the other, but anachronistic dressing not being what generally went on in the little town, Monie did garner Mildred's attention. As did the boat's line tied round her wrist.

"What. The. Hell . . .?" was Mildred's comment, for she was the first person to see Monie emerge. "What's. Going. On. Around. Here?" She cast a speculative eye upon Annapurna. Then another upon Monie Reardon Pillerton. "You. Two. Messing. Around. Or. Something? Hey! Maybe. You. Should. Find. Some. Place. More. Private."

Annapurna wanted to say that things were not what they looked liked, but she couldn't quite work out what they *did* look like and to her horror, several of the Red Hatted Ladies had at this point risen and looked as if they intended to charge the check out desk for some sort of confrontation. She said hastily to Monie, "I'll be there in a minute."

Monie said, "Please" in a tone that suggested heartfelt longing, which indeed it was. "Annapurna, I've only so much time."

Of course, this was a message that could be read several ways and Mildred Banfry seemed to read it in a way that Monie had not intended. She said, "Aren't. You. The. Dark. Horse," to Annapurna, which Annapurna found frankly unfair since she and Mildred had only just met and how Mildred possibly draw any conclusion at all about her metaphorical equine hue?

Foolishly, she said, "It's not what you think," to which Mildred leered and said, "I. Bet. It's. Not."

Thankfully, however, their conversation ended when Monie announced that she'd wait where she was meant to wait and Mildred followed this with an unasked for declaration that for *her* part, she'd return for some *literary* recommendations from the *librarian* when *things* weren't so *busy*. Annapurna watched her leave, shouldering her *I've Been to Disneyland!* bag after shoveling through its contents to put her notebook back into place. She only hoped that Mildred was someone who didn't share with other people matters about which she'd jumped to entirely inaccurate conclusions. Annapurna, after all, needed her job.

She repaired to the supply cupboard and found Monie supine as required, her tattered copy of *Rebecca* opened upon her chest. She confessed that she truly wished there was a wedding night to witness between Maxim de Winter and his blushing bride, but Annapurna told her she would have to make a choice among the library's few modern romance novels if she wanted to head in that direction. Monie said she hadn't the time to paw through romance novels at the moment, so her choice of Maxim's proposal of marriage was going to have to do. She confessed that she could not even remember at this moment of anticipation whether Maxim actually kissed the object of his marital intentions at the end of the proposal. Annapurna would have told that no, she needed to address herself to Maxim's tormented scene of confession—a bullet right through Rebecca's evil heart—if she wanted to see him clasp the soon-to-be world weary wifely narrator in his arms and press his lips upon hers.

Monie settled herself with a happy squirm and announced that she was ready. Annapurna told her that she hadn't sent anyone—even herself—on a literary journey in a good many years so she wasn't sure if she could still manage it. But Monie had faith. She also had a good memory. She said, "It's *welcome me welcome welcome me home*, and all the rest" and she closed her eyes and folded her hands over *Rebecca*.

Once she had the leash in place—with enough play in it to allow her access to the library and its checkout desk—she placed her hand over Monie's, closed her own eyes, and said the words. She felt the *whoosh* of Monie's nearly immediate departure, and when she opened her eyes she saw by the smile that played upon her unconscious friend's face that her wished for trip to Monte Carlo had been achieved and she was even at this moment bearing witness to—as far as she herself was concerned—literature's least romantic proposal of marriage. At least there was Manderley to consider, she thought. Whatever else, the narrator had *that* to look forward to when Maxim declared his intention to take her if only figuratively to his manly breast.

She glanced at her watch. She worked out that, since Maxim had dipped into his breakfast before his proposal of marriage, what with all the chewing and swallowing and the fact that these were better days in which people had better table manners, it would probably take a good fifteen minutes for Maxim to get around the point. Given that amount of time and given a "Hey! C'n someone help me?" coming from the direction of the check-out desk, Annupurna thought it would be safe for her to leave Monie to her spate of time in Monte Carlo while she saw to whatever was going on in the bowels of the library itself.

It was the internet user. He'd run into difficulty. The computer, he announced, was stalled or dead or confused or whatever computers were when everything "froze up on 'em," he said. He was right in the middle of his research on a vacation to New Guinea—did anyone actually wish to vacation in New Guinea, Annapurna could not help wondering—when "the whole kit 'n caboodle of it just went to hell in a hand wagon." And now he didn't know what to do because his credit card number was apparently floating somewhere in cyberspace and he "damn well needed to get it back 'fore every Tom, Dick, and Harry gets their mitts on it and decides to book themselves on a slow boat to Antarctica." Only, his pronounced it Anartica, which Annapurna decided not to correct. She hastened to his side in order to unfreeze the computer, murmuring all the while on the inadvisability of mixing his credit card information and a public computer. Identity theft and all that, she told him. He promised to "kick the fat posterior of anyone trying that kind of business with *me*, I tell you."

Annapurna was bent over the gentleman's computer, attempting to sort out how he'd managed to make such a hash of merely looking up information when Monie began carrying on in the supply room. It was a little cry at first, which no one who did not know what was going on in that room would have even noticed had not it been followed by a series of yips and then a quite distinct, "But she didn't *mean* to! She didn't know! She was tricked!" that could not be ignored. Something had gone badly wrong with Monie's journey to Monte Carlo, it seemed.

Annapurna made short work of nothing with the ageing computer. She excused herself. To the gentleman's cry of "But what about my credit card?" Annapurna said, "It's a far, far better thing I do . . ." before she caught herself. She had to get to Monie before the Red Hatted Ladies rose as one in protest. They could be an unruly bunch when it came to their book discussion group. They did not like interruptions and when it came to distractions. . . . Most of them were not retired schoolteachers for nothing.

Annapurna snapped open the supply room door without thinking about how abruptly this was likely to rouse Monie from her literary communion with Maxim and his newly beloved. Monie's horrified scream as she was whisked from Monte Carlo to Langley, Washington, in an instant electrified everyone gathered in the library. Matters were not helped when Monie's scream turned to sobs which turned to "It was so awful. It was so humiliating. How did she *survive?*" which was the first clue that Annapurna had that something had gone very wrong.

She tried to shush Monie. Monie was not to be shushed. She tried to console her. Monie was not to be consoled. She tried to lock her in the supply closet until she could get control of herself. But this, too, proved to be impossible, for the Red Hatted Ladies, the computer gentleman, and—God forbid—Mildred Banfry (who had left her electrical bill on the library counter as things happened) all stormed the environs of the supply room door upon which Monie began to bang with great force. "It was Mrs. Danvers' idea for her to dress like Caroline de Winter and *how* could he possibly be so stupid not to know that?" she cried. "Let me out of here, Annapurna. Send me back there. I want to rip her eyes out."

Annapurna understood immediately what had happened but she hardly knew what to do about it. Somehow, her friend had opened to the wrong page in the novel, and instead of finding herself a witness to a marriage proposal, she'd found herself caught up in the nameless heroine's humiliation on the night of the Manderley ball. Of course she hadn't intended to torment her husband by dressing as his former black hearted wife had done in years past. It was the evil Mrs. Danvers who had suggested it. Had Maxim possessed a conscience less guilty and sense more common, he would have known this. But that would have wrecked the scene's drama. As, frankly, sending Monie back there to allow her to sort him out would do.

Not that she could have managed this anyway because there was plenty of explaining to do. And while Annapurna did her best with the idea of her old friend napping her way into a terrible nightmare, she could tell that not everyone was buying that story. But she managed to get the Red Hatted Ladies to return to their discussion and the computer gentleman to return to his perusal of New Guinea. She didn't notice Mildred Banfry, however. That was a game changer for her.

Monie was not to be consoled. Once Annapurna had the supply room door open, Monie's outrage at Mrs. Danvers turned itself on poor Annapurna. *This* was to have been her blessed escape from her life among rambunctious children and a husband who, it had to be said, had all the passion and imagination of a Texan horsefly in the middle of summer. To have arranged her schedule; to have dressed herself in a time-appropriate costume; to have managed what it took when it came to laundry, cleaning toilets, ironing, baking brownies for the church group, and all the rest and *all the rest* . . . only to have her one escape from all that to be turned into a tormented witnessing of such a scene of horror . . . .

Annapurna listened to all of this with patience. What she wanted to say was "You want horror? I'll show you horror" while she plopped a copy of *The Gulag Archipelago* upon Monie Reardon Pillerton's chest. But what she said was, "Oh dear. Monie, it was the page! You were supposed to be sure you had the right page, you know."

To which Monie said, "You've got to make it right. I can't go home feeling like this, knowing what it was like, witnessing first hand her utter and *complete* humiliation and you know he wasn't the least understanding, Annapurna. Did he really *think* she would be so heartless? Didn't he even *know* her?"

Well, considering that all they'd done was drive around Monaco for a few days before he asked her to marry him, no he didn't know her, Annapurna wanted to say. But Monie was in such a state of outrage and umbrage and disappointment that it seemed to Annapurna that only answer was to whisk her back into the supply closet as quickly as possible and send her to that breakfast terrace in Monte Carlo where the marriage proposal had taken place.

She hurried her back in. She went in after her. She got her settled. She made absolutely *certain* that the page was correct ("He was ready, as he had promised, in five minutes. 'Come down to the terrace while I eat my breakfast,' he said.") before she set the book on Monie's chest, folded her hands over, murmured the incantation, and prayed her journey would be sweet and swift. The *whoosh* was instantaneous once more. But this time, Annapurna stayed at Monie's side.

Her friend's pinched features softened out. She gave a little sigh. She squirmed delightedly on the cot. She made a kissy noise. She sighed again. Annapurna glanced at her watch and counted the moments. She tried to remember everything that had gone into that scene but other than Maxim's shaving, breakfast on the terrace and something about tangerines, she couldn't come up with it. So she gave it five minutes and then ten and when Monie cooed, she decided she'd witnessed it all. It wouldn't do to allow the scene to go on because the next one, as she recalled, dealt with the unpleasant comments that Mrs. Van Hopper had made about the whys and wherefores of Maxim's interest in the narrator and God knew she didn't want Monie seeing that.

Gently, then, she gave a tug on the line that would bring Monie back to the supply room. When she'd accomplished this, she even took another few minutes to sit with her so that Monie could tell her about the sights and the smells and Maxim's manliness and the narrator's hair which wasn't mousey at *all* but just in need of a good product to bring out its gloss and oh, Monie wished that she could travel back there and slip her a little John Frieda because, really, that was all it would take.

Monie thanked Annapurna tearfully. She hugged her close and called her the best friend she'd ever had. Then she straightened her clothing and made her exit from the supply room as surreptitiously as a woman curiously costumed could do. Annapurna followed her, breathing deeply to center herself once more after the excitement of Monie's journey.

"What. Was. That. Exactly?"

Oh Lord, Annapurna thought. She'd forgotten about Mildred Banfry.

Mildred was still on the other side of the checkout counter—thank God for small favors—and her previously forgotten electricity bill was clutched in what seemed to be a very self-righteously perturbed fist. "What. Were. You. Two. Up. To. In. There?" was a demand that garnered the attention of the Red Hatted Ladies once again. "Don't. You. Shush. Me," didn't do much to alter their displeasure, either.

Monie was oblivious to all of this: Mildred and her electricity bill, Mildred and her stentorian demands, the Red Hatted Ladies and their unhappiness with yet another interruption to their discussion of what Annapurna knew very well was a wretched piece of vaguely pornographic fan fiction self-published by a wretched non-writer on the wretched and deplorable internet. As if they needed silence to concentrate on their discussion! was what Annapurna thought, but as the librarian she could hardly say this. What she did say was, "Terrible dream plus stomach cramps," although she didn't know where the stomach cramps had come from, merely the inspiration of the moment based on Monie's clutching *Rebecca* to her stomach as if this action alone could transport her back into the novel, which it could not.

Mildred, however, did not buy either bad dreams or stomach cramps, especially once she'd snatched *Rebecca* from Monie's damp grasp and peered at the title. It was then she said what Annapurna had hoped never to hear upon her return to Whidbey Island:

"Hey. I. *Thought.* I. Knew. You. You're. That. Janet. Shore. You. Took. Kids. Into. The. Cemetery. And—"

"I don't know what you're talking about, Ms. Banfry," didn't achieve its intended purpose.

"Don't. Give. Me. That. *Mizz.* Nonsense," established Mildred among the non-believers, which might have given Annapurna an entrée into a brisk discussion of women's equality had Mildred not gone on with, "And. Don't. Deny. It. Because. Your. Sister. Told. Me. All. About. You."

Monie mouthed the word *sorry* at Annapurna and pointed to her watch. She *had* to go, she was saying. Her trips into *Rebecca* had taken up what little free time she had and as there were brownies to remove from the pan and then frost individually before carting them off to an evening meeting of her church's women's group. . . . She had to depart.

This left Annapurna as alone with Mildred Banfry as she could be in a public library with a tittering discussion among elderly women on the subject of a borderline pornographic novel going on in the not-distant-enough distant alcove used for this purpose. As for the elderly gentleman and his computer problems, he was long gone, having either resigned himself to the loss of his credit card information via the internet—and wasn't he a fool to be using his credit card to buy something on a public computer, as far as Annapurna was concerned—or having given up on the entire idea of ever having the librarian's attention which was fixed, at this point, upon Mildred Banfry.

Annapurna said, because she could think of nothing else, "My sister?"

And this it unfolded that Jeannie Shore Heggenes—third eldest of the Shore brood and six years Annapurna's senior—had not only been a classmate of Mildred Banfry at South Whidbey High School but had also in a marijuana induced afternoon of bonhomie in the company of Mildred at Double Bluff Beach where a cleverly constructed driftwood hut hid them from sight actually *told* Mildred of young Janet Shore's supposed talent. This, apparently, Jeannie had learned about from her star-of-the-wrestling team boyfriend who himself had heard it from a fellow wrestler who had learned about it from his little sister. Who, as of course Annapurna had known would be the case, happened to be Monie Reardon Pillerton although at the time, of course, she had only been Monie Reardon.

While the revelation made Annapurna want to do violence somewhere, she had learned long ago that violence solved nothing. After all, she had only herself to blame, along with her perverse need to prove to Monie that Boo Radley and *not* Bob Ewell had been the person to effect the death of that latter man beneath the oak tree on Halloween night, thus saving Jem and Scout Finch from being murdered by the their father's sworn enemy. Had she just let that whole thing go and allowed Monie to believe what she would. . . . But she had not done so and once again she was faced with the result of Monie's wagging tongue, all these years later.

"It's just a hypnotism thing," Annapurna said to Mildred. And to get rid of her and her megaphone voice, she offered to meet the blasted woman for coffee "sometime in the future" to explain how it worked if she was interested. She declared it a hobby. She said she'd given it up long ago and had no intention of taking it up again but as Monie was her dearest friend and as she'd begged for old time's sake. . . . Well, she assumed Mildred knew what she meant.

Her fatal words that late morning were, of course, "sometime in the future," for Mildred Banfry was not a woman who let the future drift into *being* the future without firm plans. There and then at the checkout desk, she unearthed from *I've Been to Disneyland!* a tattered wall calendar from the Humane Society, which she opened at once to the appropriate month. "Let's. Just. See. What. We. Have," was spoken at Mildred's accustomed sans hearing aid volume. "Next. Tuesday. Ten. A.M."

Well, of course, Annapurna could not manage that as the calls upon her duty made her appearance anywhere other than in the public library impossible and she told Mildred this, careful to enunciate in such a way that the maddening woman could read her lips.

"No. Problem." Mildred squinted at her calendar. It appeared that she needed proper spectacles in addition to new batteries for her hearing aid, Annapurna thought. "What. Time. Do. You. Clear. Out. Of. This. Place?

Listen. We. Can. Meet. For. Wine. I. Like. Wine. Do. You? Because. Over. On. First. Street . . ."

"Yes, yes, all right," Annapurna said. What else, at this point, could she do? It was becoming each moment more obvious that the only way she would rid herself of the woman was to consent to wine, coffee, greasy cheeseburgers, milk shakes, to *anything* just to see the her ample posterior exit the library door.

So it was that Annapurna met Mildred Banfry for a glass of wine at the suitably darkened First Street Langley Tasting Room, which overlooked Saratoga Passage where the deep and gleaming waters were—at this season of the year—playing host to the occasional migrating gray whale on its way to Alaska. Good fortune was, for once, with Annapurna. Aside from herself and Mildred Banfry, there was no one inside the wine bar save for the anxious owner, a man eager for custom and who can blame him since at this time of year—gray whales be damned for the little they did to encourage tourism—every owner of every business in town was consumed with the worry of going under.

Thus, he was fully determined to accommodate Mildred Banfry and Annapurna, such determination displayed by a tendency to hover, which would not do. Mildred dismissed him by purchasing an entire bottle of wine for them to consume, by saying yes to a plate of cheese and crackers, and further yes to a dish of olives. Unbeknownst to Annapurna at the moment, Mildred would also say yes to handing over the not insignificant bill to her companion—Mildred having a taste for Tempranillo which was not inexpensive—but that was to come.

"So. . . ." was Mildred's prefatory statement, soon to be accompanied by "Tell all," and the single blessing contained within these three words was attached to their volume. Mildred Banfry on this day of days had danced attendance upon Annapurna with hearing aids in place. So her voice was normal, and Annapurna was comforted by the knowledge that whatever she said could remain between the two of them as long as Mildred swore to secrecy.

Such swearing, as things turned out, meant very little to Mildred Banfry although she made no mention of the fact. She swore quite happily with the words "Naturally, naturally, what do you take me for, for heaven's sake?

I don't go around betraying confidences thank you very much" which certainly seemed to indicate that Annapurna's forthcoming words would be held close to Mildred Banfry's heart. But unbeknownst to Annapurna, there were larger forces at work in Mildred that precluded her actually possessing any true sincerity when it came to oath-making in this particular situation. Nonetheless, she said her piece of reassurance to Annapurna and went on to declare herself merely curious, a woman seeking to slake the thirst of her desire for information. And this part was actually and wholly true. Mildred had no *immediate* intention of doing anything with what she learned.

So Annapurna explained her modest talent, doing everything she could to downplay it. She called it "just a game I used to engage in with my friends from school" and she made very light of the efficacy of those *welcome me* declarations that propelled her associates into a literary world they would only otherwise have experienced in imagination.

"D'you mean to tell me this actually works?" Mildred asked her at the culmination of Annapurna's explanation, which she kept as brief as humanly possible. "D'you mean I could. . . . *Any* scene in any book and you can do this? What about . . . say . . . a play? Something by . . . I don't know . . . Shakespeare maybe . . . What about Tennessee Williams? 'Stella!' and all that. Does your victim—"

"Please!" Annapurna cut in. Never had she come remotely close to considering her literary travelers victims of anything other than their own desires to experience what life could be between the pages of their favorite tomes.

"Sorry," Mildred said hastily. "So your . . . patient . . ."

"I'm not a doctor. They're . . . I suppose we could call them clients. They were clients."

"Did they pay you?"

"Of course not!" Annapurna was aghast. She'd never thought of taking so much as a dime for the pleasures she had in childhood given to her friends. The book itself, the experience of the book, the act of encouraging her compatriots to read more, read often, and for God's sake read something decent: These were Annapurna's motivations although when she explained them to Mildred and received in return a look of what could only be called appalled incredulity it must be said that she *did* question the wisdom of her past generosity.

Mildred said, "You could have made a mint, you know," and then she added the six words that allowed Annapurna to see, like Lady Macbeth, the future in the instant: "You could still make a mint."

Of course, making money from her talent was at that moment still quite far from Annapurna's mind. Indeed, the very thought of it was anathema to her. But she was soon to discover that Mildred Banfry did not mean making money as in becoming wealthy from one's gifts. What she meant was more along the lines of spreading the wealth into areas severely in need of it.

Thus did Annapurna learn that her companion of the wine, cheese, and olives raised funds for seventeen of the three hundred and fifty-two non-profits that existed on the south end of Whidbey Island. Suffice it to say that while Annapurna had been off on the mainland living her life, becoming Annapurna, and doing what she could to forget about Char-bourne Hinton-Glover and the evil he had committed to crush her spirit, Whidbey Island had become the Land of Causes and wherever there was a structure needing to be saved, a forest wanting stewardship, an old growth tree needing protection, a farmer's pasture insisting it be spared from the developer's shovel, a child begging for a math tutor, a band looking for anyone willing to purchase instruments for its players, a brand new mother feeling out to sea with her babe, an after school program keeping teenagers off drugs and middle schoolers off the streets. . . . There was a 501c looking for money to pay for it.

"Think of what you could *do* for South Whidbey," Mildred Banfry intoned. "Why we could easily have an entire *festival* dedicated to your book travels. You could become. . . . My dear Annapurna, you could be the Rick Steves of the imagination!"

Of course, the reader of this tale must not think Annapurna jumped upon the runaway train of Mildred Banfry's monetary intentions as spoken that day in First Street Langley Tasting Room. She did not. The truth was that she required something of a lengthy layover at the train station of her own hesitation. The idea of once again embarking upon what had ultimately so blinded her to the evil that men do—the men in question being, of course, one Chadbourne Hinton-Glover—made her of necessity loath to muddy the waters of *anyone's* ability to judge accurately the less admirable qualities of one's fellows. But Mildred was not to be denied.

"Think of the trees," was her first point, which was quickly attended by the imperative to think of the land, think of the pastures, think of the young new mothers yearning to be free, thing of drug-using teenagers saved from the needle and skateboard riding preadolescents saved from heads broken on the uneven pavements of Second Street's precipitous descent into town from Saratoga Road. "It is within your power to change all this," was Mildred's mighty declaration. "And anyway, you can *always* call a halt to it if things get out of hand. You did that when you were a kid, didn't you?"

Privately, of course, Mildred had no thought that things would come within a mile of getting out of hand as she was nothing if not an organizer nonpareil. For her part, privately Annapurna thought that there was, at the end of it all, very little chance that this was truly a money-making proposition. For in these days of a million-and-one diversions most of which were electronic, how many people actually knew enough about literature even to *want* to experience a scene in a book. Moreover, digital reading devices like ebooks wouldn't work for what she had to offer readers. They had to be willing to dive into an *actual* book and—this was Mildred's instantaneous genius at work—it would have to be something purchased from an independent bookstore—no Amazon.com for this venture, thank you very much—with receipt required as proof.

This last bit was what convinced Annapurna since there was in Langley an independent bookstore operating on a shoestring. It had survived in the town an astonishing fifty years at this point, but every week there were more monetary dangers and internet threats that it had to overcome in order to remain in business. Thus it was that Annapurna agreed to Mildred Banfry's plan. Thus it was that she found herself in very short order having to quit her job at the library in order to accommodate the scores of people who—much to her surprise—wished to be sent out upon "the journey of a lifetime," as Mildred Banfry's advertising named it. For Mildred Banfry, Annapurna discovered, was a marketing genius, and an interview with Monie Reardon Pillerton—accompanied by photos of Monie herself, her only marginally winsome offspring hanging heavily upon her, and her husband looking exceedingly out-to-sea about the presence of a journalist in his back yard—printed in the *South Whidbey Record* and then sent forth to entertain thousands upon the internet was all it took to launch their fund-raising business.

Mildred christened it. She chose one word, *Epic!*, which was painted on the frosted glass door of an extremely costly four room suite directly across from the village's chocolate and gelato shop in an enclave of buildings fashioned around a sweet little garden. This was in Second Street—quite a distance from the aforementioned descending hill—and one of the four rented rooms served as their waiting room while the other three allowed Annapurna to try her luck servicing the literary journeying of more than one individual at a time.

People paid depending upon the length of travel they wished to have or the predetermined length of travel required by the scene of their choice. Obviously, the ballroom scene in which Mr. Elton shows his true character through his rejection of sweet but admittedly simple Harriet Smith took a bit more time than the dramatic revelation to his wife of the Scarlet Pimpernel's true identity. Mildred was the person who determined the charges, mostly by leafing through the pages of the book in question to see how many words were involved in the scene desired. She'd bark, "It's going to be $52.25," or "This is a quickie, so $20 will do it," and in one case from *The Far Pavilions*, "Are you sure? Damn longest battle scene I've ever looked at and it'll cost you $625 to live through it if you're really serious about it," which was accepted with astonishing alacrity by a woman who'd fallen hard for the romance of the book but whose husband—and he was to be the traveler—hated every moment she spent reading instead of tending to his wants, which were plentiful.

Need it even be said that business was brisk? For the first two months it was manageable and although Annapurna raced among clients welcoming them home into everything from *Keep the Aspidistra Flying* to the *Illiad*, she was able to maintain the happiness and satisfaction of her literary travelers.

There were, as one could imagine of a former librarian, certain travelers wishing to journey into books that she firmly refused to accommodate. *Fifty Shades of Grey* topped her list and although Mildred Banfry begged her to reconsider—"We've had two hundred thirty nine phone calls on that one! See here, Anna-p (as she'd taken to calling her), do you really want to look a gift horse?"—Annapurna was immovable. Anything by Danielle Steele was rejected out of hand and *anyone* wishing to look upon the ludicrous albino monk in *The da Vinci Code*—"Do you know what an albino human *actually* looks like?" Annapurna demanded—was given the unceremonious boot.

She was perfectly willing to make recommendations, however. Want a bit of wink-wink-nudge-nudge. Fine. Lady Chatterley and the grounds-keeper would do you. Want to witness a stunning confrontation between hero and villain? Sign up for *The Count of Monte Cristo* and you'll have what you need in the hallowed chambers of Epic! there would be only one vampire and Bram Stoker was his godlike creator. Want to see a wizard at work? Fine and dandy. Off you go to Oz.

"I will not deal in trash," was the line Annapurna drew in the sand. Mildred, knowing when she could step over that line and when she could not, submitted. She grumbled at first till she realized that "We do not deal in trash," had a certain ring to it, an angle—if you will—that promised further marketing possibilities. The statement threw down a delicious gauntlet as far as Mildred was concerned. It invited controversy—isn't one man's trash another man's treasure?—and, as Mildred knew, controversy, when handled correctly, sells.

Soon enough—especially with carefully worded press releases distributed to carefully chosen media outlets—all of the major news networks from Seattle made the trek out to Whidbey Island. The national news, NPR, PBS, and—*mirabile dictu*—Anderson Cooper himself picked up on the story and hastily descended upon little Langley. Within very little time at all, every bed and breakfast in a twenty mile radius of Second Street was taking reservations one year in advance while the Inn at Langley—long ago listed as one of the ten most romantic places in America to kiss one's beloved—had no difficulty at all filling its extremely pricey water-viewing rooms rain or shine. Coffee houses, cafes, the village pub, three wine-tasting venues, and Langley's two restaurants saw their cash registers fill quickly and so often that bank runs had to be made twice daily just to relieve the enterprises of cash. Gift shops, boutiques, and the village antiques store were regularly emptied of goods, and the four art galleries could not even keep up with the demand for what the island artists had found nearly impossible to sell for decades. "Business is booming" did not come remotely close to describing what happened to the village. The Gold Rush had been reborn on Whidbey Island.

Naturally, there were difficulties associated with this level of success, especially as the hoo-ha was related only to the talent, the endeavors, and the willingness to be exploited of a single woman. Additionally, the increase in traffic was not universally celebrated, and the elevation of noise was not embraced. The newly born need for reservations at eateries—even at the pizzeria!—was soon deplored. One could barely move through the aisles of the thrift shop, for heaven's sake, because so many people "just wanted to take a bit of Langley home with me" and after having handed over up to—as we have seen—$625 to experience the great mother of all battle scenes in *The Far Pavilions*, some individuals were not left with the funds to purchase a souvenir more costly than a water glass sold at the thrift store.

Hours at Epic! had to be extended to service the hoards. Interviews had to be granted to massage the egos of important journalists so as to promote positive stories which would, in turn, promote more business. YouTube videos, Twitter feeds, Facebook likes, Instagram selfies—"Here I am ready to set off to Pemberley!"—created a global sensation. Within ten months Annapurna began to feel much like the sorcerer's apprentice, chopping wildly at those bucket carrying brooms that were flooding the floors of his master's workshop.

For her part, Mildred began to have uneasy feelings about this venture she'd hit upon. Admittedly, it was a howling success. Every one of the 501c's of which she was chief fundraiser was swimming in money. But despite the obdurate nature of her personality when she hit upon a surefire money-making idea as she'd done when she'd learned of Annapurna's talents, she was not a heartless woman. She could see that Annapurna was looking rather rough around the edges as the months wore on. The calls upon the gifted woman's time had become such that eating regularly scheduled nutritious meals had morphed into eating peanut M&Ms or not eating at all, while sleeping more than four hours a night was a thing of the past. As to such simple luxuries as moderately regular visits to the salon where her hair had once been cut. . . . This was relegated to fond memory. Her presence was needed at Epic! to speed paying customers on their journeys and that was that. Anything less and a riot could easily ensue. With only two policemen in town to deal with trouble, there was little choice but to keep on keeping on, as they say.

It was Monie Reardon Pillerton who decided things had reached critical mass, this conclusion having been prompted one afternoon by her realization that only a ninety-minute wait would get her into the chocolate and gelato shop because of the hoards lined up outside. In that shop, the purchase of two scoops of coconut gelato in a sugar cone was the price Monie had agreed to pay her youngest two children for submitting themselves to a much needed dental cleaning. The children's subsequent howls of protest—in spite of her apologies and her sworn promise to drive seven miles to the nearest grocery store and purchase each of them a Dove bar—made her firm of purpose. Something had to be done and when the next day she also had a glimpse of poor haggard Annapurna for the first time in three months, she swore she was the person to do it.

She lay in wait the following morning. When she saw Mildred Banfry coming up the street from the direction of the post office, heading toward Epic! and another day of raking in the dough, she set upon her. She quickly and efficiently strong-armed that individual into the women's rest room at Useless Bay Coffee House, and it must be said that Mildred—seeing what was coming and knowing, at heart, the truth of whatever Monie was about to say—didn't raise a voice in protest. There was no "Unhand me, woman!" on her part because Monie Reardon Pillerton's hissed words were, "It's time you took a seriously long *look* at her, you cow."

Mildred took no offence although she didn't embrace being called a cow. She knew that *her* referred to Annapurna and, as we have noted, she had *already* taken a look at Annapurna. Mildred had endured more than one sleepless night worrying about her Epic! partner, and she'd spent the great majority of those slumberless hours trying to work out what could be done to improve the conditions that were dominating Annapurna's present life. She'd not gotten much further than *Could someone else be taught this talent?*, however. So she was more than willing not only to forgive the soubriquet with which she'd been addressed but also to exchange ideas on what could be done to get things back under control and to improve Annapurna's health so that their business could continue to prosper albeit with a slightly scaled back nature.

"*That* ship has sailed," Monie announced tartly. "If you think you can say 'sorry folks but we're only doing eight journeys a day' from now on, you're wackier than you look."

Mildred, determined not to be sidelined by slings and arrows of outrageous anything, took a breath and said, "Perhaps a holiday . . . ? There's that spa at the Tulalip casino over town. I've never been—can you see *me* at a spa? Ha ha—but a few days there, and she'll be right as rain."

"And then what?" Monie Reardon Pillerton demanded. "*I'll* tell you then what: It starts all over again. And do you really expect no one to follow her over there to that casino? Someone shows up in Langley desperate to . . . I don't know . . . hunt the hound of the Baskervilles—"

Not a bad suggestion, Mildred thought. And a *very* good replacement for the occasional elderly woman wishing to experience the sleuthing of those terminal dullards Poirot and Marple. No overt violence in Sherlock Holmes and certainly no sex to offend—

"*Are* you listening to me, Mildred?"

"Of course, of course," Mildred told her. She couldn't, she reassured herself, help it if her mind went commercial so easily. It was how she was wired. "You're saying she'd be followed."

"By smart phone-wielding wannabe travelers eager to post selfies online. Me and Annapurna in Langley. Me and Annapurna in the ferry line. Me and Annapurna on the ferry. Me and Annapurna waiting for our massages at Tulalip Spa. And, oh, while you're waiting to be called for your massage, Annapurna, couldn't you just send me to Venice to watch that little gnome or whatever she was knife the poor narrator who *only* wants his little daughter to come back to life?"

"*Don't Look Now?*" Mildred said. "That could be a fine replacement for that insipid *Pray, Eat, Vomit* or whatever it's called. You know the book I mean, I'll wager. Whatsername traveling to exotic places to mend her broken heart and incidentally meet the next man to break it. Puhleez."

"Stop it! We're talking about Annapurna. We're talking about her having a life. We're talking about *saving* her life, which isn't going to happen if you can't get your head out of the cash register for a minute."

But the sad truth was, with all the very best intentions in the world, Mildred Banfry could not do this. It wasn't long into their abortive conversation—just about the time that a woman in grave need began to bang imperiously upon the rest room's door—that Monie Reardon Pillerton recognized this. She also recognized her own responsibility in what had befallen not only her old friend but also the entire village. Had she not begged, cajoled, inveigled, and whatevered Annapurna into giving her a few minutes with Max de Winter and the eternally unnamed narrator, none of this would have happened. Thus she knew it was up to her to unhappen it in whatever manner she could.

Monie decided that only something like the FBI's witness protection program would do: giving Annapurna with a new identity in a place far, far, away from Whidbey Island. Only if Annapurna vanished into thin air could Langley and all of South Whidbey actually go back to the quiet, rural, lovely little place it once had been. Making this happen wouldn't be easy, but it also wouldn't be impossible. There were a billion and one places into which Annapurna could disappear: from Boseman, Montana, to Bangladesh. All Monie needed was the dark of night and Annapurna's cooperation.

This last, alas, was not to be. While Annapurna was fully on board with Monie's conclusion that the wild success of Epic! was going to do her in, she was not about to begin life all over again, a stranger in a strange land. Her family was here—"You never see them!" did not move her—and her friends were here—"I'm the only friend you have!" did not reassure her of her ability to establish social connections elsewhere—and once Annapurna had made these declarations and accompanied them with a gentle but pointed reminder of "Let's not forget how this all began," Monie knew she had to come up with another plan.

One cannot, as it is said, put the genie back into the bottle, although Monie and Annapurna did try, once Mildred agreed to the plan, of course. But they quickly discovered that a reduction in hours did not soothe the savage breasts of those who wished to experience the still-suits and the sand worms of *Dune,* and closing for a day of rest did *not* please a particularly insistent group of elderly women with great sympathy for Miss Havisham, who were not to be denied since they'd traveled to Whidbey all the way from Fort Lauderdale on what they declared to be an exorbitantly priced excursion. These among others *would* have their way, and if their way was denied . . . well, the owners of Epic! knew all about AARP's history of successful litigation based on false advertising, didn't they?

In short, Monie and Annapurna learned that she couldn't go, she couldn't stay, and she couldn't have a moment to herself. Which meant she would either die with her metaphorical boots on—although Annapurna was given to wearing only sandals due to bad feet in need of surgical correction—or she was going to have to disappear. And since she refused to disappear into regions unknown to her, she was going to have to do it right there on Whidbey Island, if only Monie could figure out a way to make this happen.

It came to her, like a bolt from Zeus, one evening in the First Street Langley Tasting Room, where she and Dwayne Pillerton had gone for the one-date-night-each-month that was supposed to keep them romantically charged, attuned to each other, desirous of each other's tired body, and all the rest. Mostly, at the end of each day and particularly on their date nights, they just wanted to sleep. But they knew the cost of not tending to the garden of their marriage and while each secretly hoped the other would cancel the date night, neither ever did.

First Street Langley Tasting Room was teeming with people. Monie and Dwayne huddled over their table. This was the infuriating size of a bottle cap, one of twenty replacements for the once reasonably sized café tables that had occupied the space prior to the tasting room's wild increase in custom. Dwayne made sad note of how things had radically changed in the little village they loved, and Monie told him then and there that she intended to change things back to what they once had been.

She didn't need to guard her words or the volume at which she spoke them. Customers packed the wine bar cheek to jowl and elbow to elbow, and the noise was such that only a near shout sufficed to make oneself heard. She could tell that Dwayne wasn't attending to her, and she couldn't blame him. Everyone around them was exclaiming over the magical journeys they'd recently taken, and they were hard to ignore. The air was filled with *Make her do Sergeant Havers meets Salvatore Lo Bianco! . . . Try that scene where Mariko sneaks into his room in the dead of night! . . . She'd do Tommy and Tuppence, wouldn't she? . . . When Albert Campion realizes that he loves Amanda, my heart totally swooned!*, all of it underscoring the veritable monster that had been created in the village.

Dwayne knew this was all down to Epic!, of course. What he didn't know was Monie's part in creating the monster. She preferred it this way as she felt guilty enough already without having her husband discover that she'd been inside Max de Winter's hotel room during his morning ablutions, no matter how innocent her intentions. Dwayne was, after all, a man dedicated to all things concrete. Not for him was the world of imagination which, as he'd been taught at the knees of his Baptist mother, was the devil's own workshop and best avoided.

She said to him, "We've got to get Annapurna away from Langley. This whole Epic! enterprise is going to kill her."

"Monroe's a nice town," was his sage advice. "And it's got a Lowe's."

Monie felt her spirits sink. Monroe? What on earth was he thinking? There was no there there, and even if there had been, did he really expect that a suburb within an hour's drive of the ferry to Whidbey Island was going to suffice? And anyway, she wasn't *talking* about Annapurna's leaving Whidbey. Annapurna had said she wouldn't go. Which was what Monie next asserted.

"Oak Harbor then," was Dwayne's next offering, not an unreasonable one as it was some thirty plus miles to the north of Langley with a population among whom one might be able to hide. "Walmart's there. So's Home Depot."

"Stop thinking about box stores," Monie cried. "D'you honestly expect that Annapurna is going to be impressed by the presence of box stores?"

"The naval air station? She might meet some officer and fall in love."

"God. You're . . . you're impossible," she said. "I can't come up with where to disappear her on my own, and if you think she'd ever consent to live in some . . . some completely soulless place, then—"

Wish I could have stayed there forever! was what struck Monie to silence in the middle of her thought. *I mean, why not? Couldn't it happen? And if you'd seen the mansion, not to mention the piles of food and endless bottles of champagne . . . and the swimming pool! I swear to God you'd feel the same.* Monie, hearing this and trying desperately not to judge the astonishing butt size of the woman who uttered it—sat up straight in her chair—the eternal posture of the eavesdropper—and picked up further with *I could make him forget Daisy Buchanan in no time flat,* which led Monie to Jay Gatsby first and the miraculous, obvious solution second.

She was afire to speak to Annapurna without delay. She developed an instantaneous headache requiring Dwayne to whisk her home. There, she took an Aleve to reassure him of her intentions not to have a headache when next they met for the necessary culmination of their night of romance, and with a, "Give me a half hour to recover, sweetie," she shut herself up in their bedroom and got on the phone.

She phoned Annapurna first. She said, "Adventure, mystery, crime, or romance?"

"What about them?"

"Just answer. Don't think. Thinking always complicates a situation. Just say it quickly: adventure, mystery, crime, or romance."

"Who is this, please? My number's unlisted."

"Who the hell do you think it is, Annapurna? I bet you haven't had a chance to talk to your siblings or your parents in months."

"Ah. Monie."

"Ah Monie is right. This is date night. I have thirty minutes before Dwayne expects sex. Let's get down to business. Adventure, mystery, crime, or romance. We're talking books here. Make a choice."

"It's not that easy."

"Why?"

"Because I'd have to say at least two of them."

"All right. Fine. We can work with that. Which two?"

"Probably mystery and romance. They seem to go together, don't they?"

"Main character: married or single?"

"Does it actually matter?"

"For this. Yes. It does. Quite a bit."

"Married then. If not at first, then ultimately. Why not try something new?"

"Present day?"

On her end, Annapurna thought for a moment. "I've always been partial to the period between the two world wars," she said. "There was this heightened sense of fashion, a real burst of energy, celebration of one's survival, that sort of thing."

"Are you sure? The Great Depression and all that."

"Well, it would have to be the 20s, then, wouldn't it? Or possibly the 30s and in the company of someone who hadn't invested in the stock market."

"Country?"

"I do love England."

"Ever been?"

"In books, of course. What else could I ever afford? But not in years. You know I don't travel like that any longer."

"Really? What a shame. But no matter. It's time to start. Meet me at the old place. You know where. Set your alarm and be there at five. We're taking care of Epic! once and for all."

"But Mildred will—"

"I'll take care of Mildred afterwards. She's made a pile and she can close up shop and live on her part of the takings forever. You just meet me at five and have in mind where you want to go."

"I don't think I can really—"

"Hey! You listen to me, Janet Shore. How exhausted are you? How much do you hate having to talk every Tom, Dick, Jemima, and Audrey into trying *Cold Mountain* instead of *Gone with the Wind*? Has anyone ever asked for *Cold Mountain* on his own? Don't even answer."

"One woman did want *The Oldest Living Confederate Widow Tells All*," Annapurna said.

"Fine. Wonderful. I'll send up rockets. See you at five. Do *not* be late."

After this, Monie put a call into Mildred. She went for her cell phone because she didn't want to risk having to talk to the woman and since the hour was late, she felt fairly certain that Mildred would have long gone to bed, working on her own beauty rest as she denied the same to poor Annapurna.

"Keep the shop closed tomorrow," she said into the phone when the message signal chimed. "I'm taking Annapurna off island for the day. She needs a rest. Don't bother to call me with an argument, either. By the time you get this, we'll be gone."

And that was it. The rest of the night Monie devoted to Dwayne, an occupation that was mercifully swift. He'd always been a slam-her-and-sleep sort of lover. Ten minutes or less and she was generally left to her own devices as he rolled away and commenced huffing and snorting like a dying gladiator.

She eased out of bed and in the kitchen she made her children's lunches. She would not be at home to see them on their way to school, nor would she be there to make their breakfasts. She unearthed the instant oatmeal, some pecans, and a jar of honey. She hulled a large basket of strawberries and she poured milk into a jug and put it on ice. She wrote a note to each child with hearts and x's and o's. She would be there when they returned home from school, she told them. She packed her husband's lunch next and she wrote him a note that told him much the same. She had responsibilities after all, no matter how she desired to escape them. She'd made her choices and she had to live with them. She only hoped that Annapurna would finally make a choice as well.

When four-forty-five rolled around, she loaded her car with what she needed, and she drove to the Langley cemetery, easing her way cautiously along the rolling fields of an old in-town farm as she kept her eye out for breakfasting deer. It was still dark but dawn was on its way. She'd seen the apricot light of it beginning to streak the sky across the water above the Cascade Mountains as she'd pulled from her driveway into the street.

She parked as close as she could to the memorial garden for the cremated citizens of Langley. She gathered what she needed and as she was about to set off in the direction of the old potting shed, headlights made the turn from Al Anderson Road and came through the old brick pillar of the cemetery. Within moments, Annapurna had joined her.

Annapurna had, during the long night following Monie's call, figured out what was meant to happen. She wasn't anyone's fool, and the list of Monie's questions had been similar to what she asked people who arrived at Epic! without a clue as to the level of preparation in which they should have engaged prior to making an appointment. So her first comments upon getting out of her car were those of protest. But before she could move from protest, to advise, disagree, or disavow, Monie said, "Really, Janet. It's the only way. And you *are* still Janet Shore, aren't you? Beneath all the trappings of Annapurna? You *know* you are and . . . Look, I pretty much think you have to say it. Else . . . I don't think I can help you like I want to. I don't know why but that's how it is. You have to say it."

"I'm Janet," she said. "But that doesn't mean—"

"Good," Monie cut in. "Now come on. We don't have a lot of time. What did you decide?"

Annapurna was silent for a moment and during that moment, which stretched on an on, Monie Reardon Pillerton began to think that her old friend wasn't as ready as she ought to have been to put aside Epic! and the life that had been thrust upon her by Mildred Banfry. But at last she took a breath and wrestled a hard bound book from the carpet bag that she was carrying. She said, "It's a first edition, by the way. Don't even ask how much it cost."

"And does it fill the bill?"

"It has it all: England, between the wars, mystery, and romance."

"What about money?"

"Second son of a duke."

Monie considered this. She'd seen the TV production of *Pride and Prejudice*. She knew Colonel Fitzwilliam's financial state. "But weren't second sons always impoverished? Didn't they all become soldiers?"

"This one isn't."

"Isn't what? A soldier?"

"Isn't impoverished."

"You're sure about that?"

Newly-returned-to-Janet nodded. "He has a servant and he drives a Daimler. That's a Jaguar. He drinks fine port. And he's in love with a woman who doesn't have a penny, so he's not looking to pick up funds from a wife."

"Oh my God! He's in *love*? Annapurna . . . Janet, that's not going to work."

"They're not married. He's asked her two or three times but she's said no. Eleven years since they first met and she's *still* saying no. She says yes at the end of this one, but see how long the book is? That'll give me time."

Those last words charged their way into Monie's heart and gave her incalculable joy. "So you're willing?" she gasped. "Really? Truly? Finally?"

Janet looked around. "I'm tired," she said. "This can't go on. So, yes. I'm willing and it's time."

So Monie Reardon Pillerton led her old friend Janet Shore into the darkened potting shed where she had spent so many blissful hours in days of her youth. Together they spread out the blanket that Monie had brought with her while Janet lit a candle and placed it—as she'd done so long ago—within the protection of a hurricane lamp. She sat, then, and began to leaf through the pages of her book. She was going to have to enter the story early. And she was, obviously, going to have to develop a taste for fine port as soon as she got there.

Monie waited. She was, it must be said, exceedingly nervous. She wasn't at all certain this had a chance in Hades of working, but since Janet had become completely cooperative, it *seemed* to Monie that the all auguries were fair.

Monie produced a length of yarn. That it was insubstantial was, of course, the point. While Janet brought a down pillow from her carpet bag and a largish woolen scarf to keep herself warm, Monie fashioned from the yarn a slip-knotted loop. When all was ready, Janet lay on the blanket. She made a final check of the book's relevant page, for it would hardly do to end up in the punting scene in which the heroine's naked face tells the hero all he needs to know about her love for him. Quelle disaster, that would be! Something early, on the other hand, something that might stop that woman in her cold, unfeeling, and heartlessly independent tracks. . . . That was just the ticket, Janet thought. Give her that and she would definitely take care of the rest. For this story's hero was no Chadbourne Hinton-Glover. He was a gentleman and over eleven years, he'd not so much as pressed his lips against his lady love's hand. Thus, although he might have been *attracted* to her—for reasons, let us face it, more cerebral than physical—there was no commitment or understanding or promise that existed between the two.

"Ready," she said to Monie Reardon Pillerton. "You'll be able to tell when my breathing changes."

Monie nodded and Janet slowly said those words from her childhood, closing her eyes upon the cobwebbed ceiling of the potting shed and upon her old friend, and instead picturing herself at Shrewsbury College in the city of Oxford, within the New Quad, where the Presentation Clock was to be unveiled. The alumnae and resident professors—all of them in their ceremonial black gowns—were just gathering, exclaiming as they saw each other for the first time in years.

Have you seen Trimmer in that frightful frock like a canary lampshade?

That was Trimmer, was it? What's she doing?

"Welcome me—"

Come and get some sandwiches. They're quite good, strange to say.

"—welcome me—"

I saw the election announced somewhere or other, last Christmas or thereabouts. I expect you saw it in the Shrewsbury Yearbook.

"—welcome me home," Janet Shore murmured. And then she said those extra super magical words. And then she waited. As did Monie. Monie waited and listened and watched her old friend for the moment when her breathing altered.

The smile came first. Then the eyebrows lifted, in a movement that Monie might have missed had she not been concentrating on Janet's face. And finally, the breathing, which began with a breath so deep it seemed to be something that could burst her lungs. Then she let it out in a slow and heartfelt sigh. Thirty seconds went by till she breathed again. Another thirty seconds and Monie was ready.

Gently she pulled the yarn from Janet's wrist. The knot was so deliberately loose that only a very slight tug sufficed. For her part, Janet Shore felt nothing. She was surrounded by chatting black gowned women on the lawn of New Quad where, not too far away, a table laden with tea and sandwiches waited. To her infinite surprise, she overheard something that was not part of the book she'd chosen. It was a quiet exchange between two women whose sharp gazes were directed at a third, tall, angular graduate just coming across the lawn, a woman whose coolness of expression and dark bobbed hair and eyes filled with the desire of escape marked her identity as pellucidly as a placard hanging round her neck would have done. A graduate near Janet Shore was saying in a hushed tone, "My God. She's here! She's come!" as another declared, "I had no idea she would even . . . I mean, after the trial and all that" and a third pointed out, "He asked her to marry him, you know, but she turned him down. And more than once, if you can believe it."

That, thought Janet Shore, as she finally and easily walked into the role of one of the college scouts with her tray at the ready and service her business, had been Harriet Vane's crucial mistake. For as a result, it was open season on Lord Peter Wimsey, and Janet-who-had-been-Annapurna was just the woman who was going to bag him.

310

From the Queen

Carolyn Hart

Carolyn Hart has written nearly sixty full-length novels. She grew up in Oklahoma City and studied journalism at the University of Oklahoma, where she later taught professional writing. Over the years, Hart has been a president of Sisters in Crime and a member of Authors Guild, Mystery Writers of America, the International Crime Writers Association, the International Thrillers Association, and the American Crime Writers League. She has been given numerous awards for her writing, including the Arrell Gibson Lifetime Achievement Award from the Oklahoma Center for the Book, the annual Oklahoma Book Award for best novel, and the Ridley Pearson Award at Murder in the Grove in Boise, Idaho. Hart was named a Grand Master by the Mystery Writers of America at the Edgar Allan Poe Awards in 2014.

Annie Darling shivered as she sloshed through puddles. Usually she stopped to admire boats in the marina, everything from majestic ocean-going yachts to jaunty Sunfish. On this February day, she kept her head ducked under her umbrella and didn't spare a glance at gray water flecked with white caps and a horizon obscured by slanting rain. She reached the covered boardwalk in front of the shops, grateful for a respite. She paused at the door of Death on Demand, shook her umbrella, then inserted the key.

The chill of the morning lessened as she stepped inside her beloved bookstore. In her view, Death on Demand was the literary center of the small South Carolina sea island of Broward's Rock. She tipped the umbrella into a ceramic stand, wiped her boots on the welcome mat, and drew in the scent of books, old and new. She clicked on the lights, taking pleasure from the new book table with its glorious array of the best mysteries, thrillers, and suspense novels of the month.

She hurried down the central aisle, turned up the heat and put on coffee to brew. The island didn't teem with visitors in February so customers would be as precious as a first edition of *The Thirty-Nine Steps*. Ingrid Webb, her faithful clerk, was enjoying a holiday in Hawaii with her husband, Duane, and many regular customers were also off-island sunseekers. If Max were next door at Confidential Commissions, his rather desultory business that offered solutions for any situation, he'd be very likely to pop in for a mug of coffee and suggest a prompt departure for home and afternoon delight, one of his favorite pursuits, but her husband was at Pebble Beach for the PGA tournament with a group of golf buddies. It would be quiet on all fronts.

What would be the perfect book to choose for a moment of leisure? As she poured a mug of French roast, she considered which title to select for her treat. Tasha Alexander's *The Counterfeit Heiress*? J. A. Jance's Beaumont struggled between past and present in *Second Watch*? Perhaps the new Darling Dahlia title by Susan Witttig Albert. Or on this rainy, cold (for a sea island) day, she might reach for an old favorite. Just as a baggy sweater and wellworn house shoes afford comfort, so did books from yesterday, *Drink to Yesterday* by Manning Coles, *Ming Yellow* by John Marquand, *Murder's Little Sister* by Pamela Branch.

A sharp mew sounded. She felt a tiny prick on one ankle.

Agatha, the elegant black feline who ruled the store, gazed at Annie with unwinking green eyes.

Why did her cat's stare make her feel like she was back in school and had received a summons from the principal's office?

Agatha paused for one last meaningful look and marched determinedly toward the coffee bar.

Annie followed. She poured fresh cat food into a steel bowl. She lifted a ceramic bowl, swished it out, added fresh water, and placed it next to the steel bowl. She should now, if she were diligent, hurry to the storeroom, place orders, perhaps unpack books. Instead, she headed to the front of the store to the first bookcase, carrying her coffee mug. She smiled as she picked up *Murder's Little Sister.*

She settled on a shabby sofa in an enclave with a Whitmani fern and slipped into Pamela Branch's mordantly funny world, secure in the certainty that nothing exciting was going to happen today.

∾

The front bell sang. Annie slid a crimson Death on Demand bookmark into her book and came to her feet, ready to smile. It was late afternoon and the store had been as quiet as a cemetery all day. She started up the central aisle.

Ellen Gallagher bolted toward her, shoes thumping as she ran. Her frizzy brown hair was in its usual unbrushed, tangled state, but her long, thin, ordinarily sallow face was flushed a bright pink. Near-sighted eyes behind thick lenses blinked rapidly. She clutched a feather pillow tight to her chest. "Annie." Her voice was a mix between a squeal and a highpitched calliope pipe. She skidded to a stop a few inches from Annie, breathing fast. "It's misty on the boardwalk. That's why I covered it up. Maybe it's worth something. It's really old." Then her face drooped, "But I know her books are everywhere. Anyway, maybe it's worth something. I thought you could tell me." She dropped the pillow to one side, thrust a book at Annie, as she burbled eagerly, ". . . they tracked me down . . . old friend of my Mum . . . both war brides . . . she was ninety-seven . . . no family left . . .all her things in a single box . . ."

Annie took the book. She looked at the cover and felt a curious breathlessness. "Mum always said Millicent was in service at the Palace . . . sounded so grand . . . the nursing home said they'd send her things, a single box, but I had to pay postage . . . sixteen dollars . . . I almost didn't and then I thought of Mum . . . I thought maybe some little trinket from England."

The cover was simple to an extreme.

The title: *Poirot Investigates.*

The author's name: Agatha Christie.

The dusk jacket was white with a rectangular illustration in black and white of Hercule Poirot formally attired in a bow tie, morning suit, and spats, carrying a top hat and gloves in his right hand, cane in his left. His eternally curious, appraising, measuring stare challenged the viewer.

". . . didn't expect much of anything. Such few things in the box . . . a Kodak snapshot of an American sergeant and a pretty girl . . . my dad was a sergeant, too . . . Mum was working in a pharmacy shop . . . he had a toothache . . . Mum kept up with Millicent and then she lost track . . . guess they had an old Christmas card from Mum and that's how they tracked me down . . ."

Gently, Annie opened the cover, turned the first pages. That curious breathlessness expanded and she felt dizzy. There it was.

London: John Lane. The Bodley Head, 1924.

A first edition.

She turned to the title page. An inscription, clear and distinct, wavered in her gaze:

> *To Her Majesty, the Queen*
> *I have the honour to be, Madam, Your Majesty's humble and obedient servant.*
> *Agatha Christie*
> *May 15, 1925*

The signature was equally black and distinct with a large rounded A and a C with a little loop at the top. The inscription was in Christie's unmistakable handwriting with characteristic wide spaces between each word. Signed to The Queen the year after publication.

Annie swallowed, tried to speak, all the while carefully easing the book free of the dust jacket. The cover was yellow cloth with black titles and border to the upper board. No nicks, no scrapes, no discoloration. Straight spine.

". . . know the old lady must have treasured it . . . she kept it in a handmade pink quilt cover . . . the only book except for a Bible . . ."

The cover and the jacket were as fresh as the day the book was printed, a first edition in pristine condition. Very fine is the highest accolade that can be awarded to a rare book.

A first edition inscribed by Agatha Christie to The Queen in 1925. George V was on the throne and Mary was Queen.

Ellen once against clutched the pillow to her chest, arms wrapped tight. "I guess," she was slowing down, eagerness fading, "it isn't worth a whole lot." Faded blue eyes looked at Annie hopefully. She sounded embarrassed. "I hoped it might be even worth fifty dollars or a hundred, but I guess not."

A hundred dollars was a great deal of money to Ellen Gallagher, who eked out a sparse living from the her little second handshop. She wore gently used clothes picked up at thrift shops. She'd scrimped and gone without to help her niece, her only living relative, attend medical school. The last time they'd had coffee, Annie inviting Ellen down for a free cup after work, Ellen's thin face had wrinkled in worry about the staggering debt that Ginny was piling up in school. An extra hundred dollars would mean a better winter coat for Ellen or a pair of shoes.

Annie eased the book back into its dust jacket, held it with her fingertips. "A hundred dollars? This book is worth at least a hundred thousand dollars and I think more than that. A hundred and fifty, maybe a hundred and seventy-five."

Ellen managed to push out thin high words, "A hundred thousand dollars?"

"More." Annie placed the book on the coffee bar, first making sure the surface was absolutely clean. "I'll get a plastic cover for it."

Ellen stared at the book lying on the counter. Her lips trembled. "Oh, my goodness. But I don't know what to do with it."

"I'll see what I can find out." Ellen needed to be careful with a book that was worth a small fortune. "I'll make inquiries. I'll check out some rare book appraisal firms and bring you the information. I think the best approach is to contact an appraiser and get a valuation and then we can find out how it can be put up for auction or offered to a high-level rare bookseller."

The most collectible book ever owned at Death on Demand had been a first edition of S.S. Van Dine's *The Benson Murder Case*, which Emma Clyde bought for nine thousand dollars. Sometimes when Annie and Max went to dinner at Emma's, Annie browsed in Emma's library which had a bookcase full of first editions, including *The Dain Curse* by Dashiell Hammett, *A is for Alibi* by Sue Grafton, and *After Dark* by Wilkie Collins.

"A hundred thousand dollars?" Ellen scarcely breathed the words.

"Absolutely."

Ellen's face looked suddenly young.

Annie was touched by the transformation. This must have been what Ellen looked like before life plucked at her, eroding confidence, piling worries.

"Oh. Oh," Ellen breathed. "That would be . . . That could be . . . oh, how wonderful. I can help Ginny. And I hadn't told you but I went to the doctor and he said I had to get treatment for my eyes or I pretty soon I won't be able to see but that new insurance has a five thousand dollar deductible and I don't have five thousand dollars. Oh, Annie." Sudden tears glistened in her eyes.

Annie blinked back tears of her own. It was wonderful to be in the presence of unexpected happiness. "I'm so glad for you, Ellen. Now you can do what you want to do. I'll help you find someone to buy it. Now, let me get the plastic cover."

When the book was carefully eased into its protective holder, Ellen held the plastic-sheathed edition carefully. "If they hadn't told me she was a war bride, I likely wouldn't have bought the box." Her voice was shaky. "They wanted sixteen dollars for the postage. I didn't really have that much extra. I started a letter to say I couldn't send the money and then I decided

I would do it, I would." She peered at Annie. "Just to think . . . the book in that box of her things . . ."

Annie slipped an arm around thin shoulders, gave a squeeze. "I'll start checking. I'll see what I can find out."

Ellen nodded, started up the aisle, stopped. "If it turns out to be so, I don't have to be afraid any more. I don't have to be afraid . . ."

Annie walked with her to the front door. Ellen had arrived bedraggled, shoulders slumping a little in defeat, obviously tired, hoping for a little extra money. Now her thin face was alight, her faded blue eyes bright with happiness.

~

Annie took a last sip of lukewarm coffee, slipped several sheets into a folder, glanced at her watch. A quarter to five. No reason not to go ahead and close up for the day. She'd had a grand total of two customers since she opened, the rector, who wanted the new Julia Spenser-Fleming book, and Hyla Harrison, an off-duty police officer. Always attuned to her surroundings, Hyla was one of Police Chief Billy Cameron's most careful and thoughtful officers. She was partial to police procedurals and picked up a new issue of *Sadie When She Died* by Ed McBain, observing, as Annie rang up the sale, that the weather was great for Spotted Salamanders and maybe that's why they were the official South Carolina salamander and she'd seen one near the pond by her apartment house.

That being the extent of Annie's contact with customers, she'd relished gathering up information for Ellen, a list of appraisers and auctioneers and rare book dealers. She tucked Murder's Little Sister into her purse to finish tonight in front of a roaring fire and gave the dim store a last survey as she turned off the main lights, humming to herself.

Rain swept at an oblique angle beneath the protective ceiling, spattering the boardwalk. Annie passed three closed shops, their owners choosing the February doldrums to close down and sip Margaritas in the Bahamas. A small light gleamed in the window of Ellen's Keepsakes. The display behind the plate glass was eclectic, eccentric: a rusted waffle iron that was new in the 1930s, a plaid raincoat with a sagging hem draped over a wicker chair, a battered small leather trunk with scuffed sides, a stack of Willow pattern plates, postcards with one-cent stamps, rhinestone-studded black satin heels, an accordion missing several keys, a cane fashioned from drift-wood, a handpainted plaster statuette of the Virgin Mary.

Annie pushed open the door. Ellen's shop was partway up the boardwalk in a much smaller space than Death on Demand. A narrow passageway between Ellen's Keepsakes and a men's clothing store, Dandy Jim's, led to the alley that ran behind the stores.

Annie was already calculating whether it would be quicker when she left the shop to dart down the passageway and slosh through the alley, which always puddled in heavy rains, to reach the parking lot or to retrace her steps on the protected boardwalk. Her car was actually nearer the end of the alley than the end of the boardwalk, but she would avoid a drenching on the boardwalk.

She stepped inside, felt colder than on the boardwalk. "Ellen?"

Small tables jammed the shop, leaving a narrow passage to a counter. She passed tables overflowing with what Ellen fondly called collectibles. Annie recognized them for what they were, small, worn remnants of nameless lives. Jumbled willy nilly on every surface were costume jewelry, old clothing, picture frames, dishes, cooking utensils, assorted art ranging from a unicorn fashioned out of gum wrappers to a tray-sized mosaic of the leaning tower of Pisa, vinyl records, WWII dog tags, yellowed post cards with three-cent stamps, a stack of blue enamel basins, a washboard, feathered hats, even an assortment of swizzle sticks.

A thin gauzy curtain separated the shop from the storeroom. The cloth parted and Ellen hurried to a counter with some prized collectibles at one end and a rectangular gray metal cash box and ledger at the other. Ellen didn't have a cash register or a reader for credit cards. She wrote down each sale in the ledger, provided a handwritten receipt to the purchaser.

In the center of the counter lay a pink quilted rectangle. The initials M and K were on the top.

Ellen saw her glance. She sounded a little defensive. "I put the book back in its quilted cover. It's still in the plastic wrap you gave me, but I thought it was nice to keep it in her cover. I think Millicent must have made the cover. Her name was Millicent Kennedy."

Ellen's face was open and vulnerable as she continued to prattle. Passing thoughts popped out without thought or planning. She put the book in its quilted wrap and recalled dim memories of a long-ago meeting with the woman who skillfully created safe harbor for her most valued possession. "I was just a little kid . . . Mum took me with her . . . a tea shop . . . we met Millicent . . ." She smiled, her voice soft. ". . . Mum was so pleased . . ." Then the smile fled. She gently touched the M. "Don't you suppose," she searched for words, "she probably knew the book could bring some money but she kept it because the Queen gave it to her?" Pink tinged her cheeks. "I don't know why the Queen would but maybe it was a memento when Millicent was going to leave to marry an American. Anyway, I know I'm guessing, but the Queen gave her the book and Millicent never parted with it, not even when she was old and poor and had only a little box full of belongings. Just think, the Queen held that book in her hands."

There was awe in Ellen's high voice.

Annie understood that breathless awe. It was the same feeling she had when she looked at old black-and-white photographs. A young woman in a long-sleeved blouse and long skirt stood on a bluff, face shaded as she gazed out to sea. Perhaps she'd been seventeen or eighteen, the photo made in 1914. That moment in time was forever captured. That moment had been real. She had lived and breathed and cared and now she had long been dust. But for that moment she was here again.

The book held that same magic, a book touched by the Queen, a book touched by a writer with auburn hair and blue eyes who in 1925 was still in love with Archie and whose amazing life had yet to unfold.

Ellen's brows drew down. She asked, the words uneven, "Do you think she minds if I sell it?"

Annie felt an odd shiver. It was as if another woman stood near, worn and stooped but clinging to remembered glory.

The money from the book would transform Ellen's life, push away fears of poverty, save her eyesight, give her freedom to be generous to her niece. But Ellen worried that a long-ago war bride might grieve if her greatest treasure were auctioned off to the highest bidder.

Annie searched for words. "I don't know what heaven is like. No one knows. But," she traced her index finger on the knitted M, "she's there now. I believe she's caught up in magnificence and there's no malice or uncharitableness. She will be happy for you."

Ellen's faded blue eyes looked misty. "Thank you, Annie." She cleared her throat. "You are terribly kind to help me."

Annie held out the folder. "It was fun for me to gather this up."

Ellen took the folder, held it against her chest. Her gentle face glowed with happiness.

～

What a difference a day made, although it was still February chilly. Annie was grateful for a thick navy turtleneck, gray wool slacks, and a quilted jacket, but she stopped at the marina to admire a newly arrived white yacht gleaming in the sunlight. She shaded her eyes as she read the name on the hull: *Hot Mama*. She wondered if the yacht belonged to a wealthy woman on the prowl or signified a male owner's fondest dream. Or best memory.

She was still smiling as she turned on the main lights in Death on Demand and greeted Agatha. "I'm sorry I'm late, sweetie. The breakfast chef is in California." Annie hurried down the central aisle. When Agatha was contentedly munching, Annie turned on the coffee maker. Today she really must unpack that latest shipment . . .

"Annie." The high shrill cry pierced the amiable early morning quiet. Rapid footsteps clattered. Ellen Gallagher, tears streaming down her face, mouth working, stumbled toward her. "Somebody took my book. I came to the shop this morning and when I went inside, the cover was lying on my counter and it was empty. I've looked everywhere but my book is gone. It's gone, gone, gone . . ."

～

Officer Hyla Harrison, crisp in her khaki uniform and a belted jacket that read POLICE on the back, stood on the boardwalk and studied the window in the narrow passageway to the alley. The frame was warped, the sash pushed up. She knelt, poked her head inside, then withdrew from the opening and stood. She looked at Ellen Gallagher. "There's no evidence of forced entry but it appears someone pushed aside a table to be able to climb inside. Is this window kept locked?"

Ellen Gallagher shivered in a thin cotton blouse and black wool skirt. She swallowed convulsively. "It wouldn't lock. I couldn't make it lock."

Annie stared at the partially open window. It couldn't have been easier. Last night when the marina and shops were deserted, someone slipped along the boardwalk. "Hyla, how about the surveillance cameras?"

Hyla's cool green eyes scanned the passageway. She jerked a thumb. "The way they're mounted, at either end, it isn't likely they show this window. I'll see what they show. And I'll check for fingerprints, but perps who plan a crime don't usually leave any."

Annie doubted the thief was barehanded. It had been a good night for gloves. She was quite sure gloved hands patiently jerked and pushed and pulled until the old window was raised high enough to permit entry.

"For now," Hyla's voice was as expressionless as always, "let's go inside and Ms. Gallagher can tell me about the missing property."

It was cold inside the shop, but the window wouldn't be pulled down until Hyla dusted for fingerprints that weren't there. The three of them stood at the counter. As Ellen, wretched and drained, spoke in a dull monotone, Annie looked around the shop. She spotted a tartan plaid shawl in a pile of clothing. She hurried to the stack, picked up the shawl, shook it, then returned and draped the thick wool around Ellen's slumped shoulders.

Hyla listened, making an occasional note as Ellen described the letter from the nursing home and her mum's old friend and how she'd send the money though it was such a lot and when the box came how she'd thought perhaps, Agatha Christie and all, that the book might be worth a little money, and taken it to Annie.

Annie remembered too well. Ellen's blue eyes had been young and excited and now they were stricken and defeated.

Hyla looked at the counter. "So the book was in the pink quilted thing when you left last night. Where did you put it?"

Ellen, moving woodenly, stepped behind the counter, pointed below the rim. "I put it right down there on the shelf. That's where I put my ledger and cashbox every night."

Hyla's thin face remained expressionless.

Annie guessed at her swift thoughts, a book worth anywhere from a hundred to a hundred and seventy-five thousand dollars left on a shelf in a shop with no burglar alarm, no surveillance cameras, no security. Sure, the department patrolled during the night, showing up at unexpected times, flashing Maglites here and there. Petty crime was not much of a problem on a sea island accessible only by ferry. Crime happened, the occasional burglary in rural areas, stolen hubcaps and cell phones when the island teemed with vacationers in the summer, but burglaries on the boardwalk shops were rare.

Hyla tapped her pen on her notebook. "Who knew the book was here?"

Ellen lifted a shaky hand, pressed thin fingers against one cheek. She slid a hesitant, shamefaced look at Annie.

Annie wasn't surprised. Ellen prattled. Ellen was open and guileless and yesterday afternoon no one could have helped observing that she was hugely excited. "Who did you tell?"

Ellen's thin shoulders hunched. "I didn't think it was wrong. I guess," the admission came in a doleful voice, "I didn't think at all. I was here and I was so pleased. I sat right down to write Ginny and when Mrs. Benson came in, why the first thing I knew, I was telling her all about it. Well, not everything. I didn't tell her that I talked to Annie. I mean, I wasn't going to tell anyone how *much* money. I didn't tell any of them . . ."

Hyla interrupted. "Let's take it from the first. You told some visitors to the shop about the book. Their names?"

Ellen clutched the edges of the shawl, pulled it tighter around her shoulders. "Nancy Benson came in about two-thirty. She was looking . . ."

Again Hyla interrupted, though her voice was gentle. "Let me get the names first."

Ellen's faded blue eyes stared at Hyla. "Nancy Benson. Professor Pickett. Walt Wisdom."

Annie knew all three, though not well. They were familiar island names: Nancy Benson, a new arrival on the island who worked at Morris Pharmacy, an enigmatic woman with an oval Mona Lisa face and a disconcerting stare when waiting on customers; debonair Walt Wisdom, a divorced, middle-aged raconteur with a taste for young women; and Calvin Pickett, a retired history professor always eager to share his knowledge (the first and second drafts of the Declaration of Independence were written on hemp paper, John Adams was the first president to live in the White House, German U-boats sank 24 ships in Florida waters during WWII, etc.).

"Did you mention the book to anyone else yesterday afternoon or evening?"

Ellen shook her head.

"In regard to the three persons with whom you spoke . . ."

Ellen's eyelashes fluttered rapidly. She looked surprised, a little shocked, excited. "Do you think one of them came back last night and took my book?"

Hyla was careful in her answer. "There are several possibilities. A random thief entered the shop and went to the counter, possibly looking for small change. It may be common knowledge that you do not use a cash register, which would be locked and difficult to open. Are you missing any money?"

Ellen lifted up the cash box, opened it. Her lips moving, she rapidly counted a small number of bills. "Everything's here."

Hyla nodded. "An intruder might assume anything below the counter to be of value and therefore might have looked at the book and decided to take it. Or it is possible that one of the persons who came to the shop yesterday afternoon realized its value and returned last night."

Ellen gazed at Hyla in awe. "Why, then, you can get the book back, can't you? Oh, that's wonderful. How long do you think it will take?"

Hyla's usually unreadable face revealed surprise, dismay, consternation, pity. She started to speak, stopped, took a breath. "I'm afraid it won't be easy to prove what happened to the book."

Ellen looked eager, fluttered a hand. "But now that we know it has to be one of them—and I think you are so marvelous to have figured that out—why then, can't you get a search warrant and look at their houses and everything? They'll have put the book in a safe place so it won't be damaged and you can tell them—whichever one it is—that you know one of them has it and so it would just be easiest and the nice thing to do to give it back to me."

"Ma'am, the fact that three people came to the shop yesterday and are aware of the book doesn't give us the grounds to seek a search warrant. In fact," Hyla sounded dubious, "there's no reasonable basis to interview those people, much less accuse them of grand theft. Moreover," Hyla held up a hand with fingers curled to the palm. As she spoke, she raised one finger after another, "there's no physical evidence of a burglary, only you and Mrs. Darling . . ."

Annie would have smiled at Hyla's formality but didn't because her use of Annie's married name was simply Officer Hyla Harrison's observance of protocol.

". . . can affirm the existence of the item, an empty quilted book cover is no proof that it contained a valuable volume, and, finally, from what you say about a box from a nursing home, you have no bill of sale, no," Hyla thought for a moment, "no record that this particular book belonged to you."

Hope faded from Ellen's face. She seemed to shrink. She stared at Hyla in despair. "Is there anything you can do?"

Hyla closed her notebook. Her voice was brisk, though there was sadness in her eyes. "I will file a report."

~

Annie opted for a Dr. Pepper from the vending machine in the station break room. As the can slid to the opening, she glanced to her left at a detailed map of the island, the northern end with rural roads, the center with the harbor and small downtown, the southern end with golf courses and winding streets in high end enclaves and the marina and its curve of shops, including Death on Demand and Ellen's Keepsakes. She carried the cold can to a long Formica-topped table, slid into a chair opposite Hyla.

Hyla stirred two teaspoons of sugar into turgid black coffee, shook her head. "Annie, honestly, there's no hope. I caught Billy on a break from that trial in Beaufort. He said it wouldn't hurt to wait a day or so. When he gets back, he thought he would approach the people informally, like, ask if they'd mentioned the book to anyone, that we were looking for leads to someone who might have broken in. He can't go around accusing people just because they came to a shop."

Annie felt a hot flicker of anger. Not at Hyla. She was doing her job as best she could. But at the unknown intruder who struggled to open a warped window and clambered inside and took the book that could have transformed Ellen's life, the book that for a few minutes made her face young again and her faded blue eyes eager and bright. Killing joy was the meanest theft of all.

Hyla was still talking, ". . . kind of breaks your heart, looking at me like I was a genius because I'd figured out the thief was one of her customers. When she said I could tell them—whichever one it was—that we knew one of them had it and so it would just be easiest and the nice thing to do to give it back." Hyla was torn between incredulity and pity. In her ordinary crisp, non-nonsense tone, she was rueful. "She's like a kid, but I know five-year-olds with more street smarts."

Annie was lifting the can of Dr. Pepper. Her arm stopped in mid-motion. . . . *just be easiest . . .*

In the sudden silence, Hyla's gaze locked on Annie. "Oh, come on, Annie."

Annie quickly raised the can, drank, sputtered as the tart love-it-or-hate-it soda hit her throat.

Hyla sat stiff and straight, shoulders braced. "Don't even think about it. For starters, that ploy went out a long time ago."

Annie looked at her in surprise. As she well knew, Hyla was late to come to an appreciation of mysteries, yet she spoke with great certainty about a much-ridiculed means of confounding an adversary.

Hyla's gaze was steady. "At the library detection club last month, the speaker debunked the story that Sir Arthur Conan Doyle sent a note to a highly respected man, saying, 'Flee. All is discovered,' and the man disappeared the next day. Henny said the story had also been ascribed to Mark Twain and that if it ever happened, Twain was the likelier candidate because he had a devilish sense of humor. She said the story had been around for a long time and who knew where it originated. But don't think you can distract me."

Annie wished she excelled at guile. According to her husband and his mother, Annie's face was a road map a near-sighted cotton rat could easily follow. She lifted the can of Dr. Pepper in a salute. "I'll admit the thought crossed my mind."

Hyla continued to stare with suspicious green eyes.

"But you're right." Annie made her tone hearty. Once Hyla fastened on an idea, she clung tighter than a barnacle to a dock piling. "That would never work." She smiled.

Hyla didn't smile in return. "Don't ever back anyone into a corner, Annie. So what could happen? You set up a meeting, maybe with Ellen lurking in the bushes. Your idea is you'll see who takes the bait, maybe get a photo, have something to bring to Billy. But any one of those three has plenty to lose if they're ever caught with stolen property. Plus, people will do a lot for a hundred grand. Plus, maybe one of them's a nut, wants to have this book to get it out and look at Agatha Christie's handwriting and gloat that they have a book no one else in the world has. So, don't even think about it."

⁓

Annie reached down and stroked Agatha's back. "How dumb does Hyla think I am?" Flames danced from the logs in the fireplace. Death on Demand was at its winter best, warm, lights blazing, a wreath of steam rising from a mug of hot chocolate on the coffee bar.

Agatha twisted her head and nipped.

Annie yanked back her hand. "Et tu, my imperious feline?"

Mercurial as always, Agatha purred and pressed against Annie's leg.

Annie leaned against the coffee bar, sipped hot chocolate. Sure, the old all-is-known ploy was trite, but triteness reflected a hard nugget of truth. Anyone with a secret was hypersensitive to exposure. Hyla had warned her off. But Hyla's response underscored the fact that each customer in Ellen's shop yesterday afternoon had a great deal to lose. That was real. That was a lever. Yes, it would be stupid to actually meet a respectable thief. Annie had no interest in arranging an I'll-be-waiting-by-the-mausoleum-at-midnight moment.

Annie was too smart for that. She gave a decisive nod, carried the mug with her to the storeroom, settled behind the computer. She searched several sites, found what she sought, placed the order, delivery guaranteed tomorrow.

She pushed away from the computer. There was much to do between now and tomorrow. She pulled her jacket from the coat tree, turned off lights as she walked toward the front door.

Agatha followed, her gaze curious. This wasn't Annie's customary pattern on a winter afternoon. Annie paused at the main cash desk, picked up a brown catnip mouse from a dish holding Agatha's favorite toys, turned and tossed it down the aisle.

Agatha leapt in pursuit.

Annie stepped outside. She locked the door, strode swiftly on the boardwalk, clattered down the steps. She didn't stop to look at the marina. Vagrant thoughts jostled in her mind all the way to her car. She needed a spot easy to access. But her quarry would be alert to a trap. Where could the thief come and feel comfortable that no one was lying in wait?

Annie slid behind the wheel. "Oh, hey," she spoke aloud, pleased with her cleverness. "I've got it." She pushed the ignition, backed and turned, drove toward the beach.

~

Annie was waiting on the delivery dock behind Death on Demand when the UPS truck pulled up late Thursday afternoon. She took the package, hurried inside, put the ten-by-ten inch cardboard box on the worktable. Slitting the top, she lifted the lid, pulled out the bubble-wrapped contents. In a moment, she looked down at a small battery-powered camera. It took only a minute to set the timer for tomorrow morning. Once turned on, the camera would continue to run.

~

Annie loved the beach at dusk in winter, the sea oats with a last glimmer of gold from pale sunlight. She drew her plaid wool coat tighter as she neared the end of the boardwalk. Not even a solitary dog walker broke the solitude. The gentle waves curled, their foam gray in the fading sunlight. She slogged across the sand to the lifeguard tower. She chose a spot below one of the crossbars, applied a patch of adhesive. She pressed the snail-shaped plastic gray camera hard until it adhered to the sticky surface. When she stepped back, she nodded in satisfaction. Only someone aware of the camera's presence would be likely to note it.

～

Annie felt clever as she drove on the main parkway toward town. It wasn't dark yet. She had an hour before night fell, plenty of time for supper at Parotti's Bar and Grill. Then she would walk to the old-fashioned phone booth, place three calls. But there was also time enough to take a stroll around town before businesses closed at five.

She succumbed to temptation.

Morrison's Pharmacy was tucked in a narrow shop between the Mermaid Hotel, the island's oldest hostelry—simple, inexpensive, and beloved by several generations of guests—and a beach shop closed for the winter. Annie stepped inside the pharmacy, paused to look at the display of chocolates in a cardboard stand. She appeared to take her time in choosing as she waited for a customer—Hazel Carey—to pay for her purchases.

Hazel turned away from the cash desk, yelped, "Annie Darling, I haven't seen you in forever!"

Annie liked Hazel, but usually felt as if she'd survived a typhoon after an encounter. After a loud exchange and promises of lunch and maybe a shopping dash into Savannah, Hazel hefted her bundle and departed.

Carrying three Godiva bars with raspberry filling, Annie stepped to the cash desk. "Nancy, how are you?" She put the chocolate bars on the counter. "I thought I saw you on the boardwalk the other day. You aren't usually down on our end of the island." The marina was on the southern tip of the island. Main Street and the harbor with the ferry dock were on the west coast, midway up the island.

Nancy's cool blue eyes studied her unblinkingly. Her oval face, framed by silvery gold hair, appeared placid. "The boardwalk?"

"I think it was Tuesday."

"Perhaps." Her voice was deep for a woman. Those blue eyes continued to stare. "Will this be all?"

"Yes, thanks."

Nancy rang up the sale, put the candy in a small plastic bag. Her features remained impassive. She handed the bag to Annie.

Annie tried for a chummy smile. "Next time drop in and see me. We have a lot of new books in. Who's your favorite author?"

Nancy looked vaguely surprised, then said slowly. "I like Lee Smith."

"She's one of our bestsellers."

Nancy said nothing.

There was an awkward pause. Annie tried for a smile, then turned away.

~

Calvin Pickett's expression was dreamy, abstracted. He held a fountain pen in one plump hand, gazed toward a corner with a bust of Pocahontas.

"Professor Pickett?"

He looked up from behind a mound of books on a worn wooden table in the middle of the Island Historical Society. Slowly he focused. "Yes, yes, I know you. Darling. Annie Darling. The store on the boardwalk. Love those reprints of the Lily Wu books. Do you know the ones I mean?" He didn't give her time to answer. "Quite striking. The first Chinese-American sleuth, much more than a sidekick to Janice Cameron. Lily was the brains of the outfit. And several of the books have provide a snapshot in time of Hawaii at mid-century. The author was an intriguing woman, rather sad life, but that's so often true of greatly talented people. You have an impressive array of books. Much more interesting that the old tomes here." He patted the stack of books. "Now," he beamed at her, "what brings you to my dusty kingdom?" As if on cue he sneezed, managing to smother the eruption behind the arm of a floppy shirt sleeve. "That's what we find with history. Lots of dust. I've just delved into a fascinating pamphlet about *Queen Anne's Revenge*. Much more is known now that they've found Blackbeard's ship. Edward Teach, of course, as we should call him. Quite a rogue. He and Stede Bonnet terrorized the area. Such a contrast from William Penn, both active in the same era, and Penn a man of great morality and character. But it was ever so in the annals of history." He abruptly popped to his feet, his full stature of five feet and possibly four inches, and beamed. "How can I help you this winter afternoon?"

Annie said the first thing that came to mind. "I wondered if I missed you at the store?"

His faded brown eyes blinked rapidly. "Missed me? Have I been there recently? Dear me, sometimes I forget where I'm going but I don't think I was going there. Though I will visit soon. I like to browse the used book section. You never know when you'll find an old book that a collector might want. Not that I'd expect you to miss a copy of Poe's *Tales*, but it never hurts to look."

A current of cool air eddied. Annie felt a slight chill. Calvin Pickett looked like an academic, distinguished by a thatch of white hair and a trim white mustache, a rumpled tweed jacket, and a generally cherubic expression. Was he toying with her, enjoying dismissive inner laughter?

She gave him a steady look. "Since you like old mysteries," she was scrabbling though titles in her mind, "I wondered if you'd be interested in a first edition of Constance and Gwenyth Little's *The Great Black Kanba*? It's in nice condition. I'll let you have it for twenty dollars."

He pursed his lips, looked judicious. "That's a good price. Very good indeed. Why yes, I'll drop by tomorrow and pick it up."

Wisdom Investments occupied what had once been a stately dining room on the bottom floor of Walt Wisdom's antebellum frame house a block back from Main Street. Walt had inherited the house from his grandmother. Set high on a tabby foundation, steps led to a front door protected from weather by a gallery. The formal living room served as a waiting area for clients. Walt lived in the upper story.

Annie hurried up the steps. It was a quarter to five, rather late for a prospective client to arrive, but Annie had no doubt Walt would welcome her. Although she enjoyed only a modest income from Death on Demand, Walt would be well aware that both Max and his mother, Laurel Roethke, were, as aficionados of wealth liked to say, seriously rich.

She stepped into a lovely hallway with an ormolu mirror over a small Georgian marbletopped side table. The heart pine flooring was original to the house. A graceful stairway led to the upper floor.

Walt loomed in the doorway to her left. Six feet tall with thick chestnut hair, sideburns a la the Tarleton twins, strong features and full lips, he fancied himself as irresistible to women. Annie was aware of the appraisal in his swift gaze and the invitation.

Her smile was restrained. "I have a friend who needs some investment advice and I told her I'd do some checking."

He gave a partial bow. "Of course. Come in," he stood aside for her to enter the room now used as his office. The walls were still the original pale blue of the old house. Red velvet hangings framed ceiling-high windows. An enormous mahogany desk was spread with papers. Flames flickered in a fire beneath an Adam mantel with two Chinese porcelain vases.

Walt seated her ceremoniously, his hand lingering on her arm, in a shield-back chair that faced the desk.

He didn't move to his chair, but remained quite near Annie, leaning against a corner of the desk. "A friend?"

Annie nodded, molded her face in an admiring gaze. "She's never had any money, but it looks as though she may realize perhaps a hundred and fifty thousand dollars from an item she can sell."

Walt nodded, placed his fingertips together. "Does she have other investments?"

Annie shook her head. "Actually, she has nothing." She gave him a steady stare. Was she being foolish? Perhaps. But anger burned deep inside; Ellen thrilled, Ellen thinking she had money to save her sight, Ellen left with nothing.

"Hmm. Perhaps she should consider an annuity. Or a mutual fund with a good record on rate of return." His smile was kindly. "That's not the sort of thing I handle for clients, but," he stood, "you can share that information with her."

Annie rose, too, resisted saying thanks for nothing, and turned toward the door.

A large warm hand touched her shoulder. "Would you care to have a drink before you leave?"

Annie looked up into a suggestive gaze. "Thanks, Walt. But I have some errands to run."

She walked briskly to the door, opened it, was on the porch.

Walt stood in the doorway. "Getting rather dark out now. That's one of the hazards on the island. Poor lighting. Don't take a wrong turn."

The words rang in her mind as she hurried to the curb and slid into her car. His deep voice had been smooth. Had it also carried a note of amusement? And threat?

Walt was right about dusk falling. The street was full of shadows and any faraway figures were indistinct and unrecognizable. She parked in front of Parotti's Bar and Grill, feeling that she had earned a self-indulgent dinner.

~

Night covered the small commercial district like a pall of black velvet. Brilliant stars glittered, providing a faint radiance, but street lamps were few and far between, shedding small pools of light. Annie waited for her eyes to adjust when she stepped out of the warmth of Parotti's, replete after a bowl of chili topped by grated Longhorn cheese and onions and a cheerful welcome from gnome-sized Ben Parotti, who owned the island's oldest eatery combined with a sawdust-floored bait shop.

Ben's farewell lingered in her mind. *You and Max are letting us down. How about scaring up some excitement?* She wished she could share the next few minutes with Ben, lift him out of winter doldrums. She walked briskly toward the end of Main, her goal the old-fashioned telephone booth. The boardwalk was deserted. The brisk breeze off the harbor carried not only the February chill but was heavy with moisture. She shivered, walked faster.

The booth was as she remembered, worn wood, the door partially open. She grabbed the cold moisture-slick handle, pulled. The door jammed midway, but she squeezed inside. The light didn't work. She used a pencil flash from her purse to illuminate the battered pay phone. She stacked change on the metal counter, dropped coins into slots, dialed.

"Hello." Nancy's deep voice evinced neither welcome nor hostility.

Annie took a breath, whispered, "I saw you Tuesday night. I know you have the book. I want the book. Bring it to the lifeguard stand next to the south beach pavilion. Ten o'clock tomorrow morning. Leave the book there, or I'll tell the police." She depressed the hook switch.

Calvin Pickett's voice mail message was ebullient: As Lewis Carroll said, *Who in the world am I? Ah, that's the great puzzle.* If you can top that, leave a message after the tone.

Despite her task, Annie was amused. But quite clever people can also be quite cleverly dishonest. She whispered into the receiver, depressed the switch.

She fed coins, punched the third number. After several rings, an answering machine responded. Walt Wisdom was almost surely home, but likely he ignored calls that registered Unknown in Caller ID. It took only a moment to record her whispered threat.

~

Dorothy L, their ebullient white cat, crouched and watched intently as Annie built a fire. She gave a last puff from the bellows, watched flames dance. She closed the metal mesh screen, settled on a plaid sofa facing the fireplace. As she tucked a cushion behind her, her cell phone rang. Her heart sang. She loved her ring tone for Max, the first few bars of *Anything Goes*.

They both spoke at once. Then Annie breathed in awe, "You saw Rory McIlroy?" Annie practically quivered with envy. She'd adored the Irish golfer ever since his heroics at the Masters.

Max's tenor voice was chiding. "You are only to lift your voice in that tone for your adored spouse."

Her laughter rippled. "All you have to do is win the Masters. Is he playing great?" She snuggled on the sofa in their den, Dorothy L cuddled in her lap.

"Three birdies in a row. If I . . ."

Annie listened, smiling, soaking in Max's voice, glad he was having fun.

". . . enough about me. What's up there?"

"Oh, not much." Her tone was careless. "Grand theft . . ."

"On the island?" He was startled.

Quickly she related Ellen's glorious discovery and heartbreaking loss and the three customers. ". . . so I left each one a message."

"Do you honestly," his voice was amused, "think the thief is going to obligingly arrive at the lifeguard stand at oh ten hundred?"

"Probably not. But if the camera picks up one of the three, we know where to start. Anyway, all it cost me was the camera and shipping fee."

"Right." His tone was kind, an obvious indication he thought she was wasting her time. "When I get back, we'll put together a description of the book and send it off to everyone we can think of. That's more likely to have some results."

"But even if some buyer alerts us, how can we prove the book belonged to Ellen?"

"Someone at the nursing home packed that box. We'll get a statement and you can identify it on this end."

"Spoken like Perry Mason to Della Street. But your plan will probably work better than mine." Annie was feeling generous. "Anyway, I'll let you know if the camera picks up anyone—and tomorrow get a photo of Rory . . . have a great weekend . . . root for Rory . . . love you, too."

As she clicked off the cell, she smiled. "Dorothy L, your favorite human will be home in four days."

By then, if all went well, they might have some idea about the identity of the thief. Her telephoned threat might not work, but if she had stolen a book worth more than a hundred thousand dollars and a whispering voice called to say she had been seen, she would scarcely settle in for a long winter nap. The call would surely elicit a response.

A frightened thief might decide to take the book tonight to the lifeguard stand, make certain no one was near, use gloved hands, wrap the book in newspaper, place the bundle on the seat. The camera would not yet be running. But apprehending the thief wasn't as important as restoring the book to Ellen, once again opening up vistas of happiness for her.

The worst outcome would be if the thief walked down to the harbor tonight, threw the book into the ocean. Or the thief might gamble on denying an accusations, hold on to the book. But nothing ventured, nothing gained, and, she blinked drowsily, if she didn't get the book back, no harm, no foul. The refrain rippled in her mind, no harm, no foul, definitely time to re-read Sarah Caudwell. If she were as clever as Sarah Caudwell, she'd figure out another way to retrieve the book. And Max's idea was very good . . .

Annie felt utterly relaxed in the warmth of the fire. Only nine o'clock. Too early for a solitary bedtime. She turned to the stack of TBR books on the end table, *Predator* by Janice Gable Bashman, *The Skin Collector* by

Jeffrey Deaver, *Queen of Hearts* by Rhys Bowen, *Riders on the Storm* by Ed Gorman. Her hand hovered . . .

Squeak.

She looked toward the hallway to the kitchen.

An eddy of cool air reached her, just as if the back door had opened. A hinge on the door needed a pump of three-in-one oil. She hadn't yet locked up the house for the night. Like most islanders, she never bothered with locked doors when she was home. Was she imagining . . .

Calvin Pickett stood in the doorway, dark cap, dark sweater, dark jacket, dark trousers, dark running shoes, right hand jammed in the bulging pocket of the jacket.

She felt her eyes widen in shock, her face tighten, her breath draw in.

His gaze locked with hers. He stepped into the room.

She had never seen him without that bush of white hair. A navy seaman knit cap hid his hair. His rounded face no longer appeared cherubic. He balanced on his feet, like a wary boxer, faded brown eyes cold and intent. "I was right."

"You were right?" She heard her words and knew she'd made a mistake. She should have come to her feet, asked why he was here, pretended surprise. *I didn't hear you knock.*

"You have quite an expressive face. It was rather interesting to watch. Easy to read." His tone was clinical. "You were afraid. You had no reason to fear me unless you left that message on my answering machine. So Ellen did take the book to you."

Annie struggled to breathe. Calvin was speaking openly about the book, the book he had stolen. Dark clothes . . . Why was he here? "What do you want?"

"Silence. Your silence." He pulled his hand from his pocket. The gun he held with easy familiarity was dark, too, blue black steel. "Ellen told me how she opened a box and her life changed in less than an hour. She'd found an old book, thought it might be worth a few dollars and," his voice went falsetto in an eerily accurate imitation, *"You could have knocked me over with a feather when I found out it's worth thousands."* He moved nearer. "She isn't an expert. She'll never be able to prove I haven't had a similar book for some time. As I reflect," his tone was amused, "I came across my book in a box of books I bought somewhere or other. I've enjoyed having such a precious book, slipping a finger across the page with that inscription to The Queen. But now I'm ready to see the world and that's why I'm selling it." His full lips moved into a mocking smile. "Do you like my musings about a book I've owned for several years?"

Annie stared at the barrel. If he pulled the trigger . . . There was no escape. He was too near. Pain . . .

"As for Ellen, apparently she opened a box a little while before I came and found a book but she didn't know if it was valuable. Yet by the time I came in, she'd learned the book was worth thousands of dollars. What did that reveal? She doesn't have a cash register, much less a computer. She had to ask someone. Who told her?" There was sharp intelligence in his brown eyes. "There was only one person near enough with the knowledge to realize the book's value. So I knew who called a little while ago. Whether you saw me or not doesn't matter. Somehow you knew or guessed I took it. If you alert appraisers and rare book collectors that the book was stolen, it would be hard for me to make a sale. No one will pay any attention to Ellen. But you have expertise."

He gestured with the gun. "Get up."

Annie's lips were dry, her throat tight. Slowly she stood. She couldn't dodge him. He was too near and the gun's barrel never wavered. Maybe if she rushed him. . . . He would shoot and she would feel hot agony and fall. Max would come home to find her lying there, blood congealed into blackness. With Ingrid out of town, there would be no one to notice the store hadn't opened, no one to notice and come and see. Even if someone came, it would be too late for her. She had to do something, figure out a way. Max mustn't find her lying on the heart pine floor stained with blood. He would know the killer was one of Ellen's customers, but it would be forever too late to matter to her. Whatever she had to do, she would do.

"Or maybe," his tone was considering, "you thought I'd leave the book on the beach for you and you'd sell it. Your husband's rich. You're rich. Maybe you're never rich enough. Trips to Paris, a safari in Africa. I read all about the favored ones in *The Gazette*." Dislike and envy curdled his voice. "That's how I knew your husband was at Pebble Beach. *A Broward's Rock golf foursome is enjoying the best of the links with a trip to Pebble Beach.*

I never had enough money to play golf. After I sell the book, I can take trips, too. I'm going to get the money. I'm going to sell the book and you aren't going to get in my way. I've never had anything. I told everybody I was a retired professor. Professor. That's an honored word. You know what I was? An instructor. Adjunct faculty. The lowest of the low. Bastards with tenure never bothered to say hello in the halls. No recognition for adjunct faculty scum. I went from college to college. Then I couldn't get hired anywhere. Do you know how much I get paid to squat in that little hole in the wall with its lousy collection of second-rate historical documents? A thousand dollars a month. Did you ever live on a thousand dollars a month?"

"Calvin, please leave."

His full lips spread in a sardonic smile. "Oh, my, a rich woman speaks. She orders a minion begone. But give your request some thought. Are you in a hurry for me to go? You'll be dead when I walk out of here."

Cool air eddied.

Annie felt the coolness. Or was she chilled by the specter of death?

A slim, athletic figure stepped lightly into the doorway. Hyla Harrison's green eyes stared at her in warning. Hyla, too, was dressed all in black, sweater, slacks, sneakers, her red hair hidden beneath a dark cap.

Annie steeled her face. She would not, must not reveal she saw Hyla.

Hyla carried a rope loose in her right hand.

Annie was suffused with thanksgiving and understanding. During their conference at the station break room, Hyla looked at Annie with suspicion, warned her against trying to set a trap for the thief. Hyla obviously wasn't persuaded Annie would remain quiescent. Probably she had been trailing behind when Annie went to the beach and the lifeguard stand, likely later explored and spotted the camera. She then figured Annie would set up a meeting. Once Hyla set out on a course, she never deviated. She would watch Annie's every move, day or night. She was outside when Calvin Pickett arrived. The instant he entered the back door without knocking, Hyla had been at work, likely summoning other officers as well.

Hyla lifted her left hand, touched her lips with a forefinger, then rapidly fluttered closed fingertips against her thumb.

Talk. Talk. Talk. She had to talk, keep Calvin talking.

A second figure eased into the doorway, stocky, powerfully built Officer Lou Pirelli, he in uniform. Lou was in a slight crouch, both hands holding his pistol, his eyes locked on Calvin. But Calvin Pickett was dangerous. If he realized they were behind him, he could whirl and fire. Possibly Lou might shoot in time. If not, if either Hyla or Lou were hurt, Annie was at fault.

Annie kept her gaze focused on Calvin. "You don't want to take this kind of chance. If you walk out . . ."

Calvin's eyes flickered away from her. His gaze was riveted for an instant beyond her.

What was he seeing?

Too late she knew. On the wall behind her hung a large glass-covered framed print. The glass reflected the room, the shine of the lamp, Annie and Calvin face-to-face, and behind him in the doorway to the hall, Hyla and Lou.

Calvin took three fast steps, grabbed her arm, turned her to face the doorway. He pulled her in front of him, jammed the barrel of the gun against her neck.

Hyla started forward, Lou moved, too, his gun leveled toward them.

"Stop where you are. Drop the gun." Calvin's low, hoarse voice held the darkness of death.

Hyla rocked to a stop, the cord in her hand moving eerily back and forth. Lou stopped too, his eyes measuring the distance between him and Calvin with a rigid Annie as a shield.

Chaotic thoughts seared Annie's mind. Everyone remained frozen in place . . . a tableau . . . Lou still held the gun . . . Calvin could push her ahead of him out into the night . . . Would he decide better to kill all of them now . . . her fault . . . gun looked huge in Lou's hand . . . superb shot . . . had to distract Calvin . . . up to her . . . she'd played roles in island theater . . . Elaine Harper in *Arsenic and Old Lace* . . . Judy Bernly in *Nine to Five* . . .

Annie wavered unsteadily. . . her body relaxed . . . she gave a sighing moan, sagged toward the floor, a terrified woman fainting . . .

The blast from the guns was huge, magnified in the small room, the smell of gunpowder acrid.

A grunt of pain. Calvin fell heavily across her, pushing her down.

Footsteps thudded. Shouts. "Grab him. Get him."

A blow caught her in the ribs. Annie struggled to pull away from the terrible weight that pressed against her as they tangled in a struggle. Calvin pushed Annie out of the way, staggered to his feet. He punched with his left hand, kicked at Hyla as he lurched toward his gun lying a few feet away. Blood streamed from his shattered right hand. Lou moved in, used his gun as a truncheon.

Calvin dropped to the floor, a gash on the side of his head.

∾

Annie waited on the boardwalk. All was well, bright sun, calm sea, seagulls wheeling above the marina, a day full of promise. Annie glanced at her watch. From what she'd learned since yesterday, Calvin Pickett, now in jail and charged with a series of crimes, lived in a small one-bedroom unit in a rundown apartment house on the north end of the island. How long could it possibly take to search that small space? It had been more than two hours since Hyla called, told her they had the warrant, were on their way.

Hyla Harrison strode around the corner of the shops, trim and athletic in her khaki uniform. Though Hyla moved with her head high, shoulders back, her narrow face was somber. She stopped a foot away, slowly shook her head.

Annie blurted, "You looked . . ."

"We looked everywhere. We went over every inch of his place. We even took the seats out of his car." Hyla's nose wrinkled. "Found a dead mouse. Weird."

"The book has to be somewhere."

Hyla's face squeezed in thought. "He didn't expect trouble when he came to your place. So, it makes sense he hadn't hidden the book some place special. We've checked and he hadn't mailed any packages to himself. He didn't have a safety deposit box. Nobody who knows him admits to taking care of anything for him. Plus these folks are people we know and they wouldn't cover up for him when he's accused of attempted murder and kidnaping and resisting arrest and a bunch of stuff. So it figures," Hyla worked it out, "that he left the book that night where he'd been keeping it. But," she turned her thin hands up in expressive defeat, "we can't find it."

Annie didn't ask if Hyla was sure. She knew Hyla. Any search she undertook would be careful, complete, exhaustive.

". . . a locker at the Historical Society. Not much in it. Half empty bottle of bourbon. Thought Jane Corley would surely have a hissy fit . . ."

Annie knew, without pleasure, Jane Jessop Corley, director of the society, tall, thin, iron gray hair in rigid waves, humorless and selfimportant.

". . . and I asked her," there was a wicked gleam in Hyla's green eyes, "if bourbon was the drink of choice at the society. I imagine he sipped along as he worked. She wasn't amused, insisted I take my evidence case and leave. Very grudging about letting me see the locker."

Annie imagined Calvin Pickett found it demeaning to be relegated to a small employee locker, probably enjoyed keeping whisky there. She remembered him sitting behind the old wooden table and the stack of books . . .

~

Jane Corley barred their way, her bony face flushed with anger. "You have no right to intrude here. He was an employee, nothing more. I permitted you access to his locker. I demand you leave . . ."

"Ma'am," Hyla was stolid, "I have a search warrant that gives me the right to search the premises. If you wish to be arrested for impeding an officer in the discharge of her duties, I will escort you to the police station and then return and proceed to fulfil my orders."

Jane drew herself up to her full height, folded her arms. "Very well. But I will have recourse to the law if you damage any society papers."

Annie pointed to the table to the right of the entrance. "Look at the books stacked there."

Jane followed them to the table, head jutting forward, face twisted in anger.

Hyla Harrison placed a fingerprint kit on the edge of the table. She flipped up the lid, pulled out plastic gloves, drew them on. She stepped around the table. She lifted up a book with leather covers that were crumbling, looked at Annie.

Annie came around the table, bent forward, shook her head.

One book, two, three . . .

The fourth book had a garish jacket with a woman's head bent back, long hair falling, gloved hands at her throat.

Not a likely book jacket to be found in a historical society.

"Take off the jacket."

Hyla carefully eased the tattered cover away to reveal a white dusk jacket with a rectangular illustration in black and white of Hercule Poirot, formally attired in a bow tie, morning suit, and spats, carrying top hat and gloves in his right hand, cane in his left.

"That's it." Annie was triumphant. No wonder Calvin had been amused when she came to the society and the book she sought was included in a stack in front of him.

"Everything in here belongs to the society." Jane Corley had no doubt read in *The Gazette* about the missing book and its worth. If she could claim it for the society, there would be money to achieve great historical glory for the island. "No one can prove this is a book that belonged to someone else . . ."

Annie pointed at the book. "Do you see the plastic cover?"

Jane's gaze shifted to the book.

"Hyla, fingerprint that cover. My fingerprints will be on it because I put the book in that cover. Ellen Gallagher's prints will be on it because she took the plastic covered book and placed it in its knit cover. And besides," she felt comfortable stretching the truth a bit, "a statement from the nursing home where the previous owner lived will prove the box belongs to Ellen Gallagher."

⁓

The front door bell at Death on Demand sounded. Ellen Gallagher bolted to the cash desk, eyes wide behind the thick lens of her glasses. "I just heard. Annie, the book sold for," her voice dropped to a shaky whisper, "one hundred and seventy thousand dollars." She reached across the counter, took Annie's hand. "Thanks to you."

The Little Men

Megan Abbott

~ↄ

Megan Abbott is a Michigan native, born in the Detroit area. She graduated from the University of Michigan and received her Ph.D. in English and American literature from New York University. She has written a number of novels, including *Queenspin*, *The Song Is You*, *Die a Little*, *Bury Me Deep*, *The End of Everything*, *Dare Me*, and *The Fever*. She has also written several non-fiction works. *Queenspin* won the 2008 Edgar Award for Best Paperback Original, as well as the 2008 Barry Award for Best Paperback Novel. *The Fever* was named one of the Best Books of the Summer by the *New York Times*, *People Magazine*, and *Entertainment Weekly*, and was also named one of the Best Books of the Year by Amazon, National Public Radio, the *Boston Globe*, and the *Los Angeles Times*. Abbott has taught at NYU, the State University of New York, and the New School University. In 2013–14 she served as the John Grisham Writer in Residence at the University of Mississippi. Abbott has been nominated for many awards, including three Edgar Awards, the Hammett Prize, the Shirley Jackson Prize, the *Los Angeles Times* Book Prize, and the Folio Prize.

At night, the sounds from the canyon shifted and changed. The bungalow seemed to lift itself with every echo and the walls were breathing. Panting.

Just after two, she'd wake, her eyes stinging, as if someone had waved a flashlight across them.

And then, she'd hear the noise. Every night.

The tapping noise, like a small animal trapped behind the wall.

That was what it reminded her of. Like when she was a girl, and that possum got caught in the crawlspace. For weeks, they just heard scratching. They only found it when the walls started to smell.

It's not the little men, she told herself. *It's not.*

And then she'd hear a whimper and startle herself. Because it was her whimper and she was so frightened.

I'm not afraid I'm not I'm not.

It had begun four months ago, the day Penny first set foot in the Canyon Arms. The chocolate and pink bungalows, the high arched windows and French doors, the tiled courtyard, cosseted on all sides by eucalyptus, pepper, and olive trees, miniature date palms—it was like a dream of a place, not a place itself.

This is what it was supposed to be, she thought.

The Hollywood she'd always imagined, the Hollywood of her childhood imagination, assembled from newsreels: Kay Francis in silver lamé and Clark Gable driving down Sunset in his Duesenberg, everyone beautiful and everything possible.

That world, if it ever really existed, was long gone by the time she'd arrived on that Greyhound a half-dozen years ago. It had been swallowed up by the clatter and color of 1953 Hollywood, with its swooping motel roofs and shiny glare of its hamburger stands and drive-ins, and its descending smog, which made her throat burn at night. Sometimes she could barely breathe.

But here in this tucked away courtyard, deep in Beachwood Canyon, it was as if that Old Hollywood still lingered, even bloomed. The smell of apricot hovered, the hush and echoes of the canyons soothed. You couldn't hear a horn honk, a brake squeal. Only the distant *ting-ting* of window chimes, somewhere. One might imagine a peignoired Norma Shearer drifting through the rounded doorway of one of the bungalows, cocktail shaker in hand.

"It's perfect," Penny whispered, her heels tapping on the Mexican tiles. "I'll take it."

"That's fine," said the landlady, Mrs. Stahl, placing Penny's cashier's check in the drooping pocket of her satin housecoat and handing her the keyring, heavy in her palm.

The scent, thick with pollen and dew, was enough to make you dizzy with longing.

And so close to the Hollywood sign, visible from every vantage, which had to mean something.

She had found it almost by accident, tripping out of the Carnival Tavern after three stingers. "We've all been stood up," the waitress had tut-tutted, snapping the bill holder at her hip. "But we still pay up."

"I wasn't stood up," Penny said. After all, Mr. D. had called, the hostess summoning Penny to one of the hot telephone booths. Penny was still tugging her skirt free from its door hinges when he broke it to her.

He wasn't coming tonight and wouldn't be coming again. He had many reasons why, beginning with his busy work schedule, the demands of the studio, plus negotiations with the union were going badly. By the time he got around to the matter of his wife and six children, she wasn't listening, letting the phone drift from her ear.

Gazing through the booth's glass accordion doors, she looked out at the long row of spinning lanterns strung along the bar's windows. They reminded her of the magic lamp she had when she was small, scattering galloping horses across her bedroom walls.

You could see the Carnival Tavern from miles away because of the lanterns. It was funny seeing them up close, the faded circus clowns silhouetted on each. They looked so much less glamorous, sort of shabby. She wondered how long they'd been here, and if anyone even noticed them anymore.

She was thinking all these things while Mr. D. was still talking, his voice hoarse with logic and finality. A faint aggression.

He concluded by saying surely she agreed that all the craziness had to end. *You were a luscious piece of candy*, he said, *but now I gotta spit you out*.

After, she walked down the steep exit ramp from the bar, the lanterns shivering in the canyon breeze.

And she walked and walked and that was how she found the Canyon Arms, tucked off behind hedges so deep you could disappear into them. The smell of the jasmine so strong she wanted to cry.

"You're an actress, of course," Mrs. Stahl said, walking her to Bungalow Number Four.

"Yes," she said. "I mean, no." Shaking her head. She felt like she was drunk. It was the apricot. No, Mrs. Stahl's cigarette. No, it was her lipstick. Tangee, with its sweet orange smell, just like Penny's own mother.

"Well," Mrs. Stahl said. "We're all actresses, I suppose."

"I used to be," Penny finally managed. "But I got practical. I do makeup now. Over at Republic."

Mrs. Stahl's eyebrows, thin as seaweed, lifted. "Maybe you could do me sometime."

It was the beginning of something, she was sure.

No more living with sundry starlets stacked bunk-to-bunk in one of those stucco boxes in West Hollywood. The Sham-Rock. The SunKist Villa. The smell of cold cream and last night's sweat, a brush of talcum powder between the legs.

She hadn't been sure she could afford to live alone, but Mrs. Stahl's rent was low. Surprisingly low. And, if the job at Republic didn't last, she still had her kitty, which was fat these days on account of those six months with Mr. D., a studio man with a sofa in his office that wheezed and puffed. Even if he really meant what he said, that it really was kaput, she still had that last check he'd given her. He must have been planning the brush off, because it was the biggest yet, and made out to cash.

And the Canyon Arms had other advantages. Number Four, like all the bungalows, was already furnished: sun-bleached zebra print sofa and key lime walls, that bright-white kitchen with its cherry-sprigged wallpaper. The first place she'd ever lived that didn't have rust stains in the tub or the smell of moth balls everywhere.

And there were the built-in bookshelves filled with novels in crinkling dustjackets.

She liked books, especially the big ones by Lloyd C. Douglas or Frances Parkinson Keyes, though the books in Number Four were all at least twenty years old with a sleek, high-tone look about them. The kind without any people on the cover.

She vowed to read them all during her time at the Canyon Arms. Even the few tucked in the back, the ones with brown-paper covers.

In fact, she started with those. Reading them late at night, with a pink gin conjured from grapefruit peel and an old bottle of Gilbey's she found in the cupboard. Those books gave her funny dreams.

"She got one."

Penny turned on her heels, one nearly catching on one of the courtyard tiles. But, looking around, she didn't see anyone. Only an open window, smoke rings emanating like a dragon's mouth.

"She finally got one," the voice came again.

"Who's there?" Penny said, squinting toward the window.

An old man leaned forward from his perch just inside Number Three, the bungalow next door. He wore a velvet smoking jacket faded to a deep rose.

"And a pretty one at that," he said, smiling with graying teeth. "How do you like Number Four?"

"I like it very much," she said. She could hear something rustling behind him in his bungalow. "It's perfect for me."

"I believe it is," he said, nodding slowly. "Of that I am sure."

The rustle came again. Was it a roommate? A pet? It was too dark to tell. When it came once more, it was almost like a voice shushing.

"I'm late," she said, taking a step back, her heel caving slightly.

"Oh," he said, taking a puff. "Next time."

That night, she woke, her mouth dry from gin, at two o'clock. She had been dreaming she was on an exam table and a doctor with an enormous head mirror was leaning so close to her she could smell his gum: violet. The ringlight at its center seemed to spin, as if to hypnotize her.

She saw spots even when she closed her eyes again.

The next morning, the man in Number Three was there again, shadowed just inside the window frame, watching the comings and goings on the courtyard.

Head thick from last night's gin and two morning cigarettes, Penny was feeling what her mother used to call "the hickedty ticks."

So, when she saw the man, she stopped and said briskly, "What did you mean yesterday? 'She finally got one'?"

He smiled, laughing without any noise, his shoulders shaking.

"Mrs. Stahl got one, got you," he said. "As in: Will you walk into my parlor? said the spider to the fly."

When he leaned forward, she could see the stripes of his pajama top through the shiny threads of his velvet sleeve. His skin was rosy and wet looking.

"I'm no chump, if that's your idea. It's good rent. I know good rent."

"I bet you do, my girl. I bet you do. Why don't you come inside for a cup? I'll tell you a thing or two about this place. And about your Number Four."

The bungalow behind him was dark, with something shining beside him. A bottle, or something else.

"We all need something," he added cryptically, winking.

She looked at him. "Look, mister—"

"Flant. Mr. Flant. Come inside, miss. Open the front door. I'm harmless." He waved his pale pink hand, gesturing toward his lap mysteriously.

Behind him, she thought she saw something moving in the darkness over his slouching shoulders. And music playing softly. And old song about setting the world on fire, or not.

Mr. Flant was humming with it, his body soft with age and stillness, but his milky eyes insistent and penetrating.

A breeze lifted and the front door creaked open several inches, and the scent of tobacco and bay rum nearly overwhelmed her.

"I don't know," she said, even as she moved forward.

Later, she would wonder why, but in that moment, she felt it was definitely the right thing to do.

The other man in Number Three was not as old as Mr. Flant but still much older than Penny. Wearing only an undershirt and trousers, he had a moustache and big round shoulders that looked gray with old sweat. When he smiled, which was often, she could tell he was once matinee-idol handsome, with the outsized head of all movie stars.

"Call me Benny," he said, handing her a coffee cup that smelled strongly of rum.

Mr. Flant was explaining that Number Four had been empty for years because of something that happened there a long time ago.

"Sometimes she gets a tenant," Benny reminded Mr. Flant. "The young musician with the sweaters."

"That did not last long," Mr. Flant said.

"What happened?"

"The police came. He tore out a piece of the wall with his bare hands." Penny's eyebrows lifted.

Benny nodded. "His fingers were hanging like clothespins."

"But I don't understand. What happened in Number Four?"

"Some people let the story get to them," Benny said, shaking his head.

"What story?"

The two men looked at each other. Mr. Flant rotated his cup in his hand.

"There was a death," he said softly. "A man who lived there, a dear man. Lawrence was his name. Larry. A talented bookseller. He died."

"Oh."

"Boy did he," Benny said. "Gassed himself."

"At the Canyon Arms?" she asked, feeling sweat on her neck despite all the fans blowing everywhere, lifting motes and old skin. That's what dust really is, you know, one of her roommates once told her, blowing it from her fingertips. "Inside my bungalow?" They both nodded gravely.

"They carried him out through the courtyard," Mr. Flant said, staring vaguely out the window. "That great sheaf of blond hair of his. Oh, my."

"So it's a challenge for some people," Benny said. "Once they know."

Penny remembered the neighbor boy who fell from their tree and died from blood poisoning two days later. No one would eat its pears after that.

"Well," she said, eyes drifting to the smudgy window, "some people are superstitious."

Soon, Penny began stopping by Number Three a few mornings a week, before work. Then, the occasional evening, too. They served rye or applejack.

It helped with her sleep. She didn't remember her dreams, but her eyes still stung lightspots most nights.

Sometimes the spots took odd shapes and she would press her fingers against her lids trying to make them stop.

"You could come to my bungalow," she offered once. But they both shook their heads slowly, and in unison.

Mostly, they spoke of Lawrence. Larry. Who seemed like such a sensitive soul, delicately formed and too fine for this town.

"When did it happen?" Penny asked, feeling dizzy, wishing Benny had put more water in the applejack. "When did he die?"

"Just before the war. A dozen years ago."

"He was only thirty-five."

"That's so sad," Penny said, finding her eyes misting, the liquor starting to tell on her.

"His bookstore is still on Cahuenga Boulevard," Benny told her. "He was so proud when it opened."

"Before that, he sold books for Stanley Rose," Mr. Flant added, sliding a handkerchief from under the cuff of his fraying sleeve. "Larry was very popular. Very attractive. An accent soft as a Carolina pine."

"He'd pronounce 'bed' like 'bay-ed.'" Benny grinned, leaning against the window sill and smiling that Gable smile. "And he said 'bay-ed' a lot."

"I met him even before he got the job with Stanley," Mr. Flant said, voice speeding up. "Long before Benny."

Benny shrugged, topping off everyone's drinks.

"He was selling books out of the trunk of his old Ford," Mr. Flant continued. "That's where I first bought *Ulysses*."

Benny grinned again. "He sold me my first Tijuana Bible. *Dagwood Has a Family Party*."

Mr. Flant nodded, laughed. "*Popeye in The Art of Love*. It staggered me. He had an uncanny sense. He knew just what you wanted." They explained that Mr. Rose, whose bookstore once graced Hollywood Boulevard and had attracted great talents, used to send young Larry to the studios with a suitcase full of books. His job was to trap and mount the big shots. Show them the goods, sell them books by the yard, art books they could show off in their offices, dirty books they could hide in their big gold safes.

Penny nodded. She was thinking about the special books Mr. D. kept in his office, behind the false encyclopedia fronts. The books had pictures of girls doing things with long, fuzzy fans and peacock feathers, a leather crop.

She wondered if Larry had sold them to him.

"To get to those guys, he had to climb the satin rope," Benny said. "The studio secretaries, the script girls, the publicity office, even makeup girls like you. Hell, the grips. He loved a sexy grip."

"This town can make a whore out of anyone," Penny found herself blurting.

She covered her mouth, ashamed, but both men just laughed.

Mr. Flant looked out the window into the courtyard, the *flip-flipping* of banana leaves against the shutter. "I think he loved the actresses the most, famous or not."

"He said he liked the feel of a woman's skin in 'bay-ed,'" Benny said, rubbing his left arm, his eyes turning dark, soft. "'Course, he'd slept with his mammy until he was thirteen."

As she walked back to her own bungalow, she always had the strange feeling she might see Larry. That he might emerge behind the rose bushes or around the statue of Venus.

Once she looked down into the fountain basin and thought she could see his face instead of her own.

But she didn't even know what he looked like.

Back in the bungalow, head fuzzy and the canyon so quiet, she thought about him more. The furniture, its fashion at least two decades past, seemed surely the same furniture he'd known. Her hands on the smooth bands of the rattan sofa. Her feet, her toes on the banana silk tassels of the rug. And the old mirror in the bathroom, its tiny black pocks.

In the late hours, lying on the bed, the mattress too soft, with a vague smell of mildew, she found herself waking again and again, each time with a start.

It always began with her eyes stinging, dreaming again of a doctor with the head mirror, or a car careering toward her on the highway, always lights in her face.

One night, she caught the lights moving, her eyes landing on the far wall, the baseboards.

For several moments, she'd see the light spots, fuzzed and floating, as if strung together by the thinnest of threads.

The spots began to look like the darting mice that sometimes snuck inside her childhood home. She never knew mice could be that fast. So fast that if she blinked, she'd miss them, until more came. Was that what it was? If she squinted hard, they even looked like little men. Could it be mice on their hind feet?

The next morning, she set traps.

"I'm sorry, he's unavailable," the receptionist said. Even over the phone, Penny knew which one. The beauty marks and giraffe neck.

"But listen," Penny said, "it's not like he thinks. I'm just calling about the check he gave me. The bank stopped payment on it."

So much for Mr. D.'s parting gift for their time together. She was going to use it to make rent, to buy a new girdle, maybe even a television set.

"I've passed along your messages, Miss Smith. That's really all I can do."

"Well, that's not all I can do," Penny said, her voice trembling. "You tell him that."

Keeping busy was the only balm. At work, it was easy, the crush of people, the noise and personality of the crew.

Nights were when the bad thoughts came, and she knew she shouldn't let them.

In the past, she'd had those greasy-skinned roommates to drown out thinking. They all had rashes from cheap studio makeup and the clap from cheap studio men and beautiful figures like Penny's own. And they never stopped talking, twirling their hair in curlers and licking their fingers to turn the magazine pages. But their chatter-chatter-chatter muffled all Penny's thoughts. And the whole atmosphere—the thick muzz of Wool-worth's face powder and nylon nighties when they even shared a bed—made everything seem cheap and lively and dumb and easy and light.

Here, in the bungalow, after leaving Mr. Flant and Benny to drift off into their apple-jack dreams, Penny had only herself. And the books.

Late into the night, waiting for the lightspots to come, she found her eyes wouldn't shut. They started twitching all the time, and maybe it was the night jasmine, or the beachburr.

But she had the books. All those books, these beautiful, brittling books, books that made her feel things, made her long to go places and see things—the River Liffey and Paris, France.

And then there were those in the wrappers, the brown paper soft at the creases, the white baker string slightly fraying.

Her favorite was about a detective recovering stolen jewels from an unlikely hiding spot. But there was one that frightened her.

About a farmer's daughter who fell asleep each night on a bed of hay. And in the night, the hay came alive, poking and stabbing at her. It was supposed to be funny, but it gave Penny bad dreams.

"Well, she was in love with Larry," Mr. Flant said. "But she was not Larry's kind."

Penny had been telling them how Mrs. Stahl had shown up at her door the night before, in worn satin pajamas and cold cream, to scold her for moving furniture around.

"I don't even know how she saw," Penny said. "I just pushed the bed away from the wall."

She had lied, telling Mrs. Stahl she could hear the oven damper popping at night. She was afraid to tell her about the shadows and lights and other things that made no sense in daytime. Like the mice moving behind the wall on hindfeet, so agile she'd come to think of them as pixies, dwarves. Little men.

"It's not your place to move things," Mrs. Stahl had said, quite loudly, and for a moment Penny thought the woman might cry.

"That's all his furniture, you know," Benny said. "Larry's. Down to the forks and spoons."

Penny felt her teeth rattle slightly in her mouth.

"He gave her books she liked," Benny added. "Stiff British stuff he teased her about. Charmed himself out of the rent for months."

"When he died she wailed around the courtyard for weeks," Mr. Flant recalled. "She wanted to scatter the ashes into the canyon."

"But his people came instead," Benny said.

"Came on a train all the way from Carolina. A man and woman with cardboard suitcases packed with pimento sandwiches. They took the body home."

"They said Hollywood had killed him." Benny shook his head, smiled that tobacco-toothed smile of his. "They always say that."

"You're awfully pretty for a face-fixer," one of the actors told her, fingers wagging beneath his long makeup bib.

Penny only smiled, and scooted before the pinch came.

It was a Western, so it was mostly men, whiskers, lip bristle, three-day beards filled with dust.

Painting the girl's faces was harder. They all had ideas of how they wanted it. They were hard girls, striving to get to Paramount, to MGM. Or started out there and hit the Republic rung on the long slide down. To Allied, AIP. Then studios no one ever heard of, operating out of some slick guy's house in the Valley.

They had bad teeth and head lice and some had smells on them when they came to the studio, like they hadn't washed properly. The costume assistants always pinched their noses behind their backs.

It was a rough town for pretty girls. The only place it was.

Penny knew she had lost her shine long ago. Many men had rubbed it off, shimmy by shimmy.

But it was just as well, and she'd just as soon be in the warpaint business. When it rubbed off the girls, she could just get out her brushes, her power puffs, and shine them up like new. As she tapped the powder pots, though, her mind would wander. She began thinking about Larry bounding through the backlots. Would he have come to Republic with his wares? Maybe. Would he have soft-soaped her, hoping her bosses might have a taste for T.S. Eliot or a French deck?

By day, she imagined him as a charmer, a cheery, silver-tongued roué.

But at night, back at the Canyon Arms, it was different.

You see, sometimes she thought she could see him moving, room to room, his face pale, his trousers soiled. Drinking and crying over someone, something, whatever he'd lost that he was sure wasn't ever coming back.

There were sounds now. Sounds to go with the two A.M. lights, or the mice or whatever they were.

Tap-tap-tap.

At first, she thought she was only hearing the banana trees, brushing against the side of the bungalow. Peering out the window, the moon-filled courtyard, she couldn't tell. The air looked very still.

Maybe, she thought, it's the fan palms outside the kitchen window, so much lush foliage everywhere, just the thing she'd loved, but now it seemed to be touching her constantly, closing in.

And she didn't like to go into the kitchen at night. The white tile glowed eerily, reminded her of something. The wide expanse of Mr. D.'s belly, his shirt pushed up, his watch chain hanging. The coaster of milk she left for the cat the morning she ran away from home. For Hollywood.

The mouse traps never caught anything. Every morning, after the rumpled sleep and all the flits and flickers along the wall, she moved them to different places. She looked for signs.

She never saw any.

One night, three A.M., she knelt down on the floor, running her fingers along the baseboards. With her ear to the wall, she thought the tapping might be coming from inside. A *tap-tap-tap*. Or was it a *tick-tick-tick?*

"I've never heard anything here," Mr. Flant told her the following day, "but I take sedatives."

Benny wrinkled his brow. "Once, I saw pink elephants," he offered. "You think that might be it?"

Penny shook her head. "It's making it hard to sleep."

"Dear," Mr. Flant said, "would you like a little helper?"

He held out his palm, pale and moist. In the center, a white pill shone.

That night she slept impossibly deeply. So deeply she could barely move, her neck twisted and locked, her body hunched inside itself.

Upon waking, she threw up in the waste basket.

That evening, after work, she waited in the courtyard for Mrs. Stahl.

Smoking cigarette after cigarette, Penny noticed things she hadn't before. Some of the tiles in the courtyard were cracked, some missing. She hadn't noticed that before. Or the chips and gouges on the sculpted lions on the center fountain, their mouths spouting only a trickle of acid green. The drain at the bottom of the fountain, clogged with crushed cigarette packs, a used contraceptive.

Finally, she saw Mrs. Stahl saunter into view, a large picture hat wilting across her tiny head.

"Mrs. Stahl," she said, "have you ever had an exterminator come?"

The woman stopped, her entire body still for a moment, her left hand finally rising to her face, brushing her hair back under her mustard-colored scarf.

"I run a clean residence," she said, voice low in the empty, sunlit courtyard. That courtyard, oleander and wisteria everywhere, bright and poisonous, like everything in this town.

"I can hear something behind the wainscoting," Penny replied. "Maybe mice, or maybe it's baby possums caught in the wall between the bedroom and kitchen."

Mrs. Stahl looked at her. "Is it after you bake? It might be the dampers popping again."

"I'm not much of a cook. I haven't even turned on the oven yet."

"That's not true," Mrs. Stahl said, lifting her chin triumphantly. "You had it on the other night."

"What?" Then Penny remembered. It had rained sheets and she'd used it to dry her dress. But it had been very late and she didn't see how Mrs. Stahl could know. "Are you peeking in my windows?" she asked, voice tightening.

"I saw the light. The oven door was open. You shouldn't do that," Mrs. Stahl said, shaking her head. "It's very dangerous."

"You're not the first landlord I caught peeping. I guess I need to close my curtains," Penny said coolly. "But it's not the oven damper I'm hearing each and every night. I'm telling you: there's something inside my walls. Something in the kitchen."

Mrs. Stahl's mouth seemed to quiver slightly, which emboldened Penny.

"Do I need to get out the ball peen I found under the sink and tear a hole in the kitchen wall, Mrs. Stahl?"

"Don't you dare!" she said, clutching Penny's wrist, her costume rings digging in. "Don't you dare!"

Penny felt the panic on her, the woman's breaths coming in sputters. She insisted they both sit on the fountain edge.

For a moment, they both just breathed, the apricot-perfumed air thick in Penny's lungs.

"Mrs. Stahl, I'm sorry. It's just—I need to sleep."

Mrs. Stahl took a long breath, then her eyes narrowed again. "It's those chinwags next door, isn't it? They've been filling your ear with bile."

"What? Not about this, I—"

"I had the kitchen cleaned thoroughly after it happened. I had it cleaned, the linoleum stripped out. I put up fresh wallpaper over every square inch after it happened. I covered everything with wallpaper."

"Is that where it happened?" Penny asked. "That poor man who died in Number Four? Larry?"

But Mrs. Stahl couldn't speak, or wouldn't, breathing into her handkerchief, lilac silk, the small square over her mouth suctioning open and closed, open and closed.

"He was very beautiful," she finally whispered. "When they pulled him out of the oven, his face was the most exquisite red. Like a ripe, ripe cherry."

Knowing how it happened changed things. Penny had always imagined handsome, melancholy Larry walking around the apartment, turning gas jets on. Settling into that club chair in the living room. Or maybe settling in bed and slowly drifting from earth's fine tethers.

She wondered how she could ever use the oven now, or even look at it.

It had to be the same one. That Magic Chef, which looked like the one from childhood, white porcelain and cast iron. Not like those new slabs, buttercup or mint green.

The last tenant, Mr. Flant told her later, smelled gas all the time.

"She said it gave her headaches," he said. "Then one night she came here, her face white as snow. She said she'd just seen St. Agatha in the kitchen, with her bloody breasts."

"I . . . I don't see anything like that," Penny said.

Back in the bungalow, trying to sleep, she began picturing herself the week before. How she'd left that oven door open, her fine, rain-slicked dress draped over the rack. The truth was, she'd forgotten about it, only returning for it hours later.

Walking to the closet now, she slid the dress from its hanger pressing it to her face. But she couldn't smell anything.

Mr. D. still had not returned her calls. The bank had charged her for the bounced check so she'd have to return the hat she'd bought, and rent was due again in two days.

When all the other crew members were making their way to the commissary for lunch, Penny slipped away and splurged on cab fare to the studio.

As she opened the door to his outer office, the receptionist was already on her feet and walking purposefully toward Penny.

"Miss," she said, nearly blocking Penny, "you're going to have to leave. Mac shouldn't have let you in downstairs."

"Why not? I've been here dozens of—"

"You're not on the appointment list, and that's our system now, Miss."

"Does he have an appointment list now for that squeaking starlet sofa in there?" Penny asked, jerking her arm and pointing at the leather-padded door. A man with a thin moustache and a woman in a feathered hat looked up from their magazines.

The receptionist was already on the phone. "Mac, I need you . . . Yes, that one."

"If he thinks he can just toss me out like street trade," she said, marching over and thumping on Mr. D.'s door, "he'll be very, very sorry."

Her knuckles made no noise in the soft leather. Nor did her fist.

"Miss," someone said. It was the security guard striding toward her.

"I'm allowed to be here," she insisted, her voice tight and high. "I did my time. I earned the right."

But the guard had his hand on her arm.

Desperate, she looked down at the man and the woman waiting. Maybe she thought they would help. But why would they?

The woman pretended to be absorbed in her *Cinestar* magazine.

But the man smiled at her, hair oil gleaming. And winked.

The next morning she woke bleary but determined. She would forget about Mr. D. She didn't need his money. After all, she had a job, a good one.

It was hot on the lot that afternoon, and none of the makeup crew could keep the dust off the faces. There were so many lines and creases on every face—you never think about it until you're trying to make everything smooth.

"Penny," Gordon, the makeup supervisor said. She had the feeling he'd been watching her for several moments as she pressed the powder into the actor's face, holding it still.

"It's so dusty," she said, "so it's taking a while."

He waited until she finished then, as the actor walked away, he leaned forward.

"Everything all right, Pen?"

He was looking at something—her neck, her chest.

"What do you mean?" she said, setting the powder down.

But he just kept looking at her.

"Working on your carburetor, beautiful?" one of the grips said, as he walked by.

"What? I . . . "

Peggy turned to the makeup mirror. That was when she saw the long grease smear on her collarbone. And the line of black soot across her hairline too.

"I don't know," Penny said, her voice sounding slow and sleepy. "I don't have a car."

Then, it came to her: the dream she'd had in the early morning hours. That she was in the kitchen, checking on the oven damper. The squeak of the door on its hinges, and Mrs. Stahl outside the window, her eyes glowing like a wolf's.

"It was a dream," she said, now. Or was it? Had she been sleepwalking the night before? Had she been in the kitchen . . . *at the oven* . . . in her sleep?

"Penny," Gordon said, looking at her squintily. "Penny, maybe you should go home."

It was so early, and Penny didn't want to go back to Canyon Arms. She didn't want to go inside Number Four, or walk past the kitchen, its cherry wallpaper lately giving her the feeling of blood spatters.

Also, lately, she kept thinking she saw Mrs. Stahl peering at her between the wooden blinds as she watered the banana trees.

Instead, she took the bus downtown to the big library on South Fifth. She had an idea.

The librarian, a boy with a bowtie, helped her find the obituaries.

She found three about Larry, but none had photos, which was disappointing.

The one in the *Mirror* was the only with any detail, any texture.

It mentioned that the body had been found by the "handsome proprietress, one Mrs. Herman Stahl," who "fell to wailing" so loud it was heard all through the canyons, up the promontories and likely high into the mossed eaves of the Hollywood sign.

"So what happened to Mrs. Stahl's husband?" Penny asked when she saw Mr. Flant and Benny that night.

"He died just a few months before Larry," Benny said. "Bad heart, they say."

Mr. Flant raised one pale eyebrow. "She never spoke of him. Only of Larry."

"He told me once she watched him, Larry did," Benny said. "She watched him through his bedroom blinds. While he made love."

Instantly, Penny knew this was true.

She thought of herself in that same bed each night, the mattress so soft, its posts sometimes seeming to curl inward.

Mrs. Stahl had insisted Penny move it back against the wall. Penny refused, but the next day she came home to find the woman moving it herself, her short arms spanning the mattress, her face pressed into its applique.

Watching, Penny had felt like the Peeping Tom. It was so intimate.

"Sometimes I wonder," Mr. Flant said now. "There were rumors. Black Widow, or Old Maid."

"You can't make someone put his head in the oven," Benny said. "At least not for long. The gas'd get at you, too."

"True," Mr. Flant said.

"Maybe it didn't happen at the oven," Penny blurted. "She found the body. What if she just turned on the gas while he was sleeping?"

"And dragged him in there, for the cops?" Mr. Flant and Benny looked at each other.

"She's very strong," Penny said.

Back in her bungalow, Penny sat just inside her bedroom window, waiting.

Peering through the blinds, long after midnight, she finally saw her. Mrs. Stahl, walking along the edges of the courtyard.

She was singing softly and her steps were uneven and Penny thought she might be tight, but it was hard to know.

Penny was developing a theory.

Picking up a book, she made herself stay awake until two.

Then, slipping from bed, she tried to follow the flashes of light, the shadows.

Bending down, she put her hand on the baseboards, as if she could touch those funny shapes, like mice on their haunches. Or tiny men, marching.

"Something's there!" she said outloud, her voice surprising her. "It's in the walls."

In the morning, it would all be blurry, but in that moment, clues were coming together in her head, something to do with gas jets and Mrs. Stahl and love gone awry and poison in the walls, and she had figured it out before anything bad had happened.

It made so much sense in the moment, and when the sounds came too, the little *tap-taps* behind the plaster, she nearly cheered.

～

Mr. Flant poured her glass after glass of amaro. Benny waxed his moustache and showed Penny his soft shoe.

They were trying to make her feel better about losing her job.

"I never came in late except two or three times. I always did my job," Penny said, biting her lip so hard it bled. "I think I know who's responsible. He kited me for seven hundred and forty dollars and now he's out to ruin me."

Then she told them how, a few days ago, she had written him a letter.

Mr. D.—

I don't write to cause you any trouble. What's mine is mine and I never knew you for an indian giver.

I bought fine dresses to go to Hollywood Park with you, to be on your arm at Villa Capri. I had to buy three stockings a week, your clumsy hands pawing at them. I had to turn down jobs and do two cycles of penicillin because of you. Also because of you, I got the heave-ho from my roommate Pauline who said you fondled her by the dumbwaiter. So that money is the least a gentleman could offer a lady. The least, Mr. D.

Let me ask you: those books you kept behind the false bottom in your desk drawer on the lot—did you buy those from Mr. Stanley Rose, or his handsome assistant Larry?

I wonder if your wife knows the kinds of books you keep in your office, the girls you keep there and make do shameful things?

I know Larry would agree with me about you. He was a sensitive man and I live where he did and sleep in his bed and all of you ruined him, drove him to drink and to a perilous act.

How dare you try to take my money away. And you with a wife with ermine, mink, lynx dripping from her plump, sunk shoulders.

Your wife at 312 North Faring Road, Holmby Hills.

Let's be adults, sophisticates. After all, we might not know what we might do if backed against the wall.

—yr lucky penny

It had made more sense when she wrote it than it did now, reading it to them.

Benny patted her shoulder. "So he called the cops on ya, huh?"

"The studio cops. Which is bad enough," Penny said.

They had escorted her from the makeup department. Everyone had watched, a few of the girls smiling.

"Sorry, Pen," Gordon had said, taking the powder brush from her hand. "What gives in this business is what takes away."

When he'd hired her two months ago, she'd watched as he wrote on her personnel file: MR. D.

"Your man, he took this as a threat, you see," Mr. Flant said, shaking his head as he looked at the letter. "He is a hard man. Those men are. They are hard men and you are soft. Like Larry was soft."

Penny knew it was true. She'd never been hard enough, at least not in the right way. The smart way.

It was very late when she left the two men.

She paused before Number Four and found herself unable to move, cold fingertips pressed between her breasts, pushing her back.

That was when she spotted Mrs. Stahl inside the bungalow, fluttering past the picture window in her evening coat.

"Stop!" Penny called out. "I see you!"

And Mrs. Stahl froze. Then, slowly, she turned to face Penny, her face warped through the glass, as if she were under water.

"Dear," a voice came from behind Penny. A voice just like Mrs. Stahl's. *Could she throw her voice?*

Swiveling around, she saw the landlady standing in the courtyard, a few feet away.

It was as if she were a witch, a shapeshifter from one of the fairytales she'd read as a child.

"Dear," she said again.

"I thought you were inside," Penny said, trying to catch her breath. "But it was just your reflection."

Mrs. Stahl did not say anything for a moment, her hands cupped in front of herself.

Penny saw she was holding a scarlet-covered book in her palms.

"I often sit out here at night," she said, voice loose and tipsy, "reading under the stars. Larry used to do that, you know."

She invited Penny into her bungalow, the smallest one, in back.

"I'd like us to talk," she said.

Penny did not pause. She wanted to see it.

Wanted to understand.

Walking inside, she realized at last what the strongest smell in the courtyard was. All around were pots of night-blooming jasmine, climbing and vining up the built-in bookshelves, around the window frame, even trained over the arched doorway into the dining room.

They drank jasmine tea, iced. The room was close and Penny had never seen so many books. None of them looked like they'd ever been opened, their spines cool and immaculate.

"I have more," Mrs. Stahl said, waving toward the mint-walled hallway, some space beyond, the air itself so thick with the breath of the jasmine, Penny couldn't see it. "I love books. Larry taught me how. He knew what ones I'd like."

Penny nodded. "At night, I read the books in the bungalow. I never read so much."

"I wanted to keep them there. It only seemed right. And I didn't believe what the other tenants said, about the paper smelling like gas."

At that, Penny had a grim thought. What if everything smelled like gas and she didn't know it? The strong scent of apricot, of eucalyptus, a perpetual perfume suffusing everything. How would one know?

"Dear, do you enjoy living in Larry's bungalow?"

Penny didn't know what to say, so she only nodded, taking a long sip of the tea. Was it rum? Some kind of liqueur? It was very sweet and tingled on her tongue.

"He was my favorite tenant. Even after . . . " she paused, her head shaking, "what he did."

"And you found him," Penny said. "That must have been awful."

She held up the red-covered book she'd been reading in the courtyard.

"This was found on. . . . on his person. He must've been planning on giving it to me. He gave me so many things. See how it's red, like a heart?"

"What kind of book is it?" Penny asked, leaning closer.

Mrs. Stahl looked at her, but didn't seem to be listening, clasping the book with one hand while with the other stroked her neck, long and unlined.

"Every book he gave me showed how much he understood me. He gave me many things and never asked for anything. That was when my mother was dying from Bright's, her face puffed up like a carnival balloon. Nasty woman."

"Mrs. Stahl," Penny started, her fingers tingling unbearably, the smell so strong, Mrs. Stahl's plants, her strong perfume—sandalwood?

"He just liked everyone. You'd think it was just you. The care he took. Once, he brought me a brass rouge pot from Paramount studios. He told me it belonged to Paulette Goddard. I still have it."

"Mrs. Stahl," Penny tried again, bolder now, "were you in love with him?"

The woman looked at her, and Penny felt her focus loosen, like in those old detective movies, right before the screen went black.

"He really only wanted the stars," Mrs. Stahl said, running her fingers across her décolletage, the satin of her dressing robe, a dragon painted up the front. "He said their skin felt different. They smelled different. He was strange about smells. Sounds. Light. He was very sensitive."

"But you loved him, didn't you?" Penny's voice more insistent now.

Her eyes narrowed. "Everyone loved him. Everyone. He said yes to everybody. He gave himself to everybody."

"But why did he do it, Mrs. Stahl?"

"He put his head in the oven and died," she said, straightening her back ever so slightly. "He was mad in a way only Southerners and artistic souls are mad. And he was both. You're too young, too simple, to understand."

"Mrs. Stahl, did you do something to Larry?" This is what Penny was trying to say, but the words weren't coming. And Mrs. Stahl kept growing larger and larger, the dragon on her robe, it seemed, somehow, to be speaking to Penny, whispering things to her.

"What's in this tea?"

"What do you mean, dear?"

But the woman's face had gone strange, stretched out. There was a scurrying sound from somewhere, like little paws, animal claws, the sharp feet of sharp-footed men. A gold watch chain swinging and that neighbor hanging from the pear tree.

She woke to the purple creep of dawn. Slumped in the same rattan chair in Mrs. Stahl's living room. Her finger still crooked in the tea cup handle, her arm hanging to one side.

"Mrs. Stahl," she whispered.

But the woman was no longer on the sofa across from her.

Somehow, Penny was on her feet, inching across the room.

The bedroom door was ajar, Mrs. Stahl sprawled on the mattress, the painted dragon on her robe sprawled on top of her.

On the bed beside her was the book she'd been reading in the courtyard. Scarlet red, with a lurid title.

Gaudy Night, it was called.

Opening it with great care, Penny saw the inscription:

> *To Mrs. Stahl, my dirty murderess.*
> *Love, Lawrence.*

She took the book, and the tea cup.

She slept for a few hours in her living room, curled on the zebra print sofa.

She had stopped going into the kitchen two days ago, tacking an old bath towel over the doorway so she couldn't even see inside. The gleaming porcelain of the oven.

She was sure she smelled gas radiating from it. Spotted blue light flickering behind the towel.

But still she didn't go inside.

And now she was afraid the smell was coming through the walls.

It was all connected, you see, and Mrs. Stahl was behind all of it. The lightspots, the shadows on the baseboard, the noises in the walls and now the hiss of the gas.

~

Mr. Flant looked at the inscription, shaking his head.

"My god, is it possible? He wasn't making much sense those final days. Holed up in Number Four. Maybe he was hiding from her. Because he knew."

"It was found on his body," Penny said, voice trembling. "That's what she told me."

"Then this inscription," he said, reaching out for Penny's wrist, "was meant to be our clue. Like pointing a finger from beyond the grave."

Penny nodded. She knew what she had to do.

"I know how it sounds. But someone needs to do something."

The police detective nodded, drinking from his Coca-Cola, his white shirt bright. He had gray hair at the temples and he said his name was Noble, which seemed impossible.

"Well, Miss, let's see what we can do. That was a long time ago. After you called, I had to get the case file from the crypt. I can't say I even remember it." Licking his index finger, he flicked open the file folder, then beginning turning pages. "A gas job, right? We got a lot of them back then. Those months before the war."

"Yes. In the kitchen. My kitchen now."

Looking through the slim folder, he pursed his lips a moment, then came a grim smile. "Ah, I remember. I remember. The little men."

"The little men?" Penny felt her spine tighten.

"One of our patrolmen had been out there the week before on a noise complaint. Your bookseller was screaming in the courtyard. Claimed there were little men coming out of the walls to kill him."

Penny didn't say anything at all. Something deep inside herself seemed to be screaming and it took all her effort just to sit there and listen.

"DTs. Said he'd been trying to kick the sauce," he said, reading the report. "He was a drunk, miss. Sounds like it was a whole courtyard full of 'em."

"No," Penny said, head shaking back and forth. "That's not it. Larry wasn't like that."

"Well," he said, "I'll tell what Larry was like. In his bedside table we found a half-dozen catcher's mitts." He stopped himself, looked at her. "Pardon. Female contraceptive devices. Each one with the name of a different woman. A few big stars. At least they were big then. I can't remember now."

Penny was still thinking about the wall. The little men. And her mice on their hind feet. Pixies, dancing fairies.

"There you go," the detective said, closing the folder. "Guy's a dipso, one of his high-class affairs turned sour. Suicide. Pretty clear cut."

"No," Penny said.

"No?" Eyebrows raised. "He was in that oven waist deep, Miss. He even had a hunting knife in his hand for good measure."

"A knife?" Penny said, her fingers pressing her forehead. "Of course. Don't you see? He was trying to protect himself. I told you on the phone, detective. It's imperative that you look into Mrs. Stahl."

"The landlady. Your landlady?"

"She was in love with him. And he rejected her, you see."

"A woman scorned, eh?" he said, leaning back. "Once saw a jilted lady over on Cheremoya take a clothes iron to her fellow's face while he slept."

"Look at this," Penny said, pulling Mrs. Stahl's little red book from her purse.

"*Gaudy Night*," he said, pronouncing the first word in a funny way.

"I think it's a dirty book."

He looked at her, squinting. "My wife owns this book."

Penny didn't say anything.

"Have you even read it?" he asked, wearily.

Opening the front to the inscription, she held it in front of him.

"'Dirty murderess.'" He shrugged. "So you're saying this fella knew she was going to kill him and, instead of going to, say, the police, he writes this little inscription, then lets himself get killed?"

Everything sounded so different when he said it aloud, different than the way everything joined in perfect and horrible symmetry in her head.

"I don't know how it happened. Maybe he was going to go to the police and she beat him to it. And I don't know how she did it," Penny said. "But she's dangerous, don't you get it?"

It was clear he did not.

"I'm telling you, I see her out there at night, doing things," Penny said, her breath coming faster and faster. "She's doing something with the natural gas. If you check the gas jets maybe you can figure it out."

She was aware that she was talking very loudly, and her chest felt damp. Lowering her voice, she leaned toward him.

"I think there might be a clue in my oven," she said.

"Do you?" he said, rubbing his chin. "Any little men in there?"

"It's not like that. It's not. I see them, yes." She couldn't look him in the eye or she would lose her nerve. "But I know they're not really little men. It's something she's doing. It always starts at two. Two A.M. She's doing something. She did it to Larry and she's doing it to me."

He was rubbing his face with his hand, and she knew she had lost him.

"I told you on the phone," she said, more desperately now. "I think she drugged me. I brought the cup."

Penny reached into her purse again, this time removing the tea cup, its bottom still brown-ringed.

Detective Noble lifted it, took a sniff, set it down.

"Drugged you with Old Grandad, eh?

"I know there's booze in it. But, detective, there's more than booze going on here." Again, her voice rose high and sharp, and other detectives seemed to be watching now from their desks.

But Noble seemed unfazed. There even seemed to be the flicker of a smile on his clean-shaven face.

"So why does she want to harm you?" he asked. "Is she in love with you, too?"

Penny looked at him, and counted quietly in her head, the dampness on her chest gathering.

She had been dealing with men like this her whole life. Smug men. Men with fine clothes or shabby ones, all with the same slick ideas, the same impatience, big voice, slap-andtickle, fast with a back-handed slug. Nice turned to nasty on a dime.

"Detective," she said, taking it slowly, "Mrs. Stahl must suspect that I know. About what she did to Larry. I don't know if she drugged him and staged it. The hunting knife shows there was a struggle. What I do know is there's more than what's in your little file."

He nodded, leaning back in his chair once more. With his right arm, he reached for another folder in the metal tray on his desk.

"Miss, can we talk for a minute about *your* file?"

"My file?"

"When you called, I checked your name. S.O.P. Do you want to tell me about the letters you've been sending to a certain address in Holmby Hills?"

"What? I . . . There was only one."

"And two years ago, the fellow over at MCA? Said you slashed his tires?"

"I was never charged."

Penny would never speak about that, or what that man had tried to do to her in a back booth at Chasen's.

He set the file down. "Miss, what exactly are you here for? You got a gripe with Mrs. Stahl? Hey, I don't like my landlord either. What, don't wanna pay the rent?"

A wave of exhaustion shuddered through Penny. For a moment, she did not know if she could stand.

But there was Larry to think about. And how much she belonged in Number Four. Because she did, and it had marked the beginning of things. A new day for Penny.

"No," Penny said, rising. "That's not it. You'll see. You'll see. I'll show you."

"Miss," he said, calling after her. "Please don't show me anything. Just behave yourself, okay? Like a good girl."

Back at Number Four, Penny laid down on the rattan sofa, trying to breathe, to think.

Pulling Mrs. Stahl's book from her dress pocket, she began reading.

But it wasn't like she thought.

It wasn't dirty, not like the brown-papered ones. It was a detective novel, and it took place in England. A woman recently exonerated for poisoning her lover attends her school reunion. While there, she finds an anonymous poisoned pen note tucked in the sleeve of her gown: "You Dirty Murderess . . . !"

Penny gasped. But then wondered: Had that inscription just been a wink, Larry to Mrs. Stahl?

He gave her books she liked, Benny had said. *Stiff British stuff that he could tease her about.*

Was that all this was, all the inscription had meant?

No, she assured herself, sliding the book back into her pocket. It's a red herring. To confuse me, to keep me from finding the truth. Larry needs me to find out the truth.

It was shortly after that she heard the click of her mail slot. Looking over, she saw a piece of paper slip through the slit and land on the entry-way floor.

Walking over, she picked it up.

Bungalow Four:
You are past due.
　　—*Mrs. H. Stahl*

"I have to move anyway," she told Benny, showing him the note.

"No, kid, why?" he whispered. Mr. Flant was sleeping in the bedroom, the gentle whistle of his snore.

"I can't prove she's doing it," Penny said. "But it smells like a gas chamber in there."

"Listen, don't let her spook you," Benny said. "I bet the pilot light is out. Want me to take a look? I can come by later."

"Can you come now?"

Looking into the darkened bedroom, Benny smiled, patted her forearm. "I don't mind."

Stripped to his undershirt, Benny ducked under the bath towel Penny had hung over the kitchen door.

"I thought you were inviting me over to keep your bed warm," he said as he kneeled down on the linoleum.

The familiar noise started, the *tick-tick-tick.* "Do you hear it?" Penny said, voice tight. Except the sound was different in the kitchen than the bedroom. It was closer. Not inside the walls but everywhere.

"It's the igniter," Benny said. "Trying to light the gas."

Peering behind the towel, Penny watched him.

"But you smell it, right?" she said.

"Of course I smell it," he said, his voice strangely high. "God, it's awful."

He put his head to the baseboards, the sink, the shuddering refrigerator.

"What's this?" he said, tugging the oven forward, his arms straining.

He was touching the wall behind the oven, but Penny couldn't see.

"What's what?" she asked. "Did you find something?"

"I don't know," he said, his head turned from her. "I . . . Christ, you can't think with it. I feel like I'm back in Argonne."

He had to lean backward, palms resting on the floor.

"What is it you saw, back there?" Penny asked, pointing behind the oven.

But he kept shaking his head, breathing into the front of his undershirt, pulled up.

After a minute, both of them breathing hard, he reached up and turned the knob on the front of the oven door.

"I smell it," Penny said, stepping back. "Don't you?"

"That pilot light," he said, covering his face, breathing raspily. "It's gotta be out."

His knees sliding on the linoleum, he inched back toward the oven, white and glowing.

"Are you . . . are you going to open it?"

He looked at her, his face pale and his mouth stretched like a piece of rubber.

"I'm going to," he said. "We need to light it." But he didn't stir. There was a feeling of something, that door open like a black maw, and neither of them could move.

Penny turned, hearing a knock at the door. When she turned back around, she gasped. Benny's head and shoulders were inside the oven, his voice making the most terrible sound, like a cat, its neck caught in a trap.

"Get out," Penny said, no matter how silly it sounded. "Get out!"

Pitching forward, she leaned down and grabbed for him, tugging at his trousers, yanking him back.

Stumbling, they both rose to their feet, Penny nearly huddling against the kitchen wall, its cherry-sprigged paper.

Turning, he took her arms hard, pressing himself against her, pressing Penny against the wall.

She could smell him, and his skin was clammy and goosequilled.

His mouth pressed against her neck roughly and she could feel his teeth, his hands on her hips. Something had changed, and she'd missed it.

"But this is what you want, isn't it, honey?" the whisper came, his mouth over her ear. "It's all you've ever wanted."

"No, no, no," she said, and found herself crying. "And you don't like girls. You don't like girls."

"I like everybody," he said, his palm on her chest, hand heel hard.

And she lifted her head and looked at him, and he was Larry.

She knew he was Larry.

Larry.

Until he became Benny again, moustache and grin, but fear in that grin still.

"I'm sorry, Penny," he said, stepping back. "I'm flattered, but I don't go that way."

"What?" She said, looking down, seeing her fingers clamped on his trouser waist. "Oh. Oh."

Back at Number Three, they both drank from tall tumblers, breathing hungrily.

"You shouldn't go back in there," Benny said. "We need to call the gas company in the morning."

Mr. Flant said she could stay on their sofa that night, if they could make room under all the old newspapers.

"You shouldn't have looked in there," he said to Benny, shaking his head. "The oven. It's like whistling in a cemetery."

A towel wrapped around his shoulders, Benny was shivering. He was so white.

"I didn't see anything," he kept saying. "I didn't see a goddamned thing."

She was dreaming.

"You took my book!"

In the dream, she'd risen from Mr. Flant's sofa, slicked with sweat, and opened the door. Although nearly midnight, the courtyard was mysteriously bright, all the plants gaudy and pungent.

Wait. Had someone said something?

"Larry gave it to me!"

Penny's body was moving so slowly, like she was caught in molasses.

The door to Number Four was open, and Mrs. Stahl was emerging from it, something red in her hand.

"You took it while I slept, didn't you? Sneak thief! Thieving whore!"

When Mrs. Stahl began charging at her, her robe billowing like great scarlet wings, Penny thought she was still dreaming.

"Stop," Penny said, but the woman was so close.

It had to be a dream, and in dreams you can do anything, so Penny raised her arms high, clamping down on those scarlet wings as they came toward her.

The book slid from her pocket, and both of them grappled for it, but Penny was faster, grabbing it and pushing back, pressing the volume against the old woman's neck until she stumbled, heels tangling.

It had to be a dream because Mrs. Stahl was so weak, weaker than any murderess could possibly be, her body like that of a yarn doll, limp and flailing.

There was a flurry of elbows, clawing hands, the fat golden beetle ring on Mrs. Stahl's gnarled hand against Penny's face.

Then, with one hard jerk, the old woman fell to the ground with such ease, her head clacking against the courtyard tiles.

The ratatattat of blood from her mouth, her ear.

"Penny!" A voice came from behind her. It was Mr. Flant standing in his doorway, hand to his mouth.

"Penny, what did you *do*?"

Her expression when she'd faced Mr. Flant must have been meaningful because he had immediately retreated inside his bungalow, the door locking with a click.

But it was time, anyway. Of that she felt sure.

Walking into Number Four, she almost felt herself smiling.

One by one, she removed all the tacks from her makeshift kitchen door, letting the towel drop onto her forearm.

The kitchen was dark, and smelled as it never had. No apricots, no jasmine, and no gas. Instead, the tinny smell of must, wallpaper paste, rusty water.

Moving slowly, purposefully, she walked directly to the oven, the moonlight striking it. White and monstrous, a glowing smear.

Its door shut. Cold to the touch.

Kneeling down, she crawled behind it, to the spot Benny had been struck by.

What's this? he'd said.

As in a dream, which this had to be, she knew what to do, her palm sliding along the cherry-sprig wallpaper down by the baseboard.

She saw the spot, the wallpaper gaping at its seam, seeming to breathe. Inhale, exhale.

Penny's hand went there, pulling back, the paper glue dried to fine dust under her hand.

She was remembering Mrs. Stahl. *I put up fresh wallpaper over every square inch after it happened. I covered everything with wallpaper*

What did she think she would see, breathing hard, her knees creaking and her forehead pushed against the wall?

The paper did not come off cleanly, came off in pieces, strands, like her hair after the dose Mr. D. passed to her, making her sick for weeks.

A patch of wall exposed, she saw the series of gashes, one after the next, as if someone had jabbed a knife into the plaster. A hunting knife. Though there seemed a pattern, a hieroglyphics.

Squinting, the kitchen so dark, she couldn't see.

Reaching up to the oven, she grabbed for a kitchen match.

Leaning close, the match lit, she could see a faint scrawl etched deep.

> *The little men come out of the walls.*
> *I cut off their heads every night. My mind is gone.*
> *Tonight, I end my life.*
> *I hope you find this.*
> *Goodbye.*

Penny leaned forward, pressed her palm on the words.

This is what mattered most, nothing else. "Oh, Larry," she said, her voice catching with grateful tears. "I see them, too."

The sound that followed was the loudest she'd ever heard, the fire sweeping up her face.

The detective stood in the center of the courtyard, next to a banana tree with its top shorn off, a smoldering slab of wood, the front door to the blackened bungalow, on the ground in front of him.

The firemen were dragging their equipment past him. The gurney with the dead girl long gone.

"Pilot light. Damn near took the roof off," one of the patrolman said. "The kitchen looks like the Blitz. But only one scorched, inside. The girl. Or what's left of her. Could've been much worse."

"That's always true," the detective said, a billow of smoke making them both cover their faces.

Another officer approached him. "Detective Noble, we talked to the pair next door," he said. "They said they warned the girl not to go back inside. But she'd been drinking all day, saying crazy things."

"How's the landlady?"

"Hospital."

Nobble nodded. "We're done."

It was close to two. But he didn't want to go home yet. It was a long drive to Eagle Rock anyway.

And the smell, and what he'd seen in that kitchen—he didn't want to go home yet.

At the top of the road, he saw the bar, its bright lights beckoning.

The Carnival Tavern, the one with the roof shaped like a big top.

Life is a carnival, he said to himself, which is what the detective might say, wryly, in the books his wife loved to read.

He couldn't believe it was still there. He remembered it from before the war. When he used to date that usherette at the Hollywood Bowl.

A quick jerk to the wheel and he was pulling into its small lot, those crazy clown lanterns he remembered from all those years ago.

Inside, everything was warm and inviting, even if the waitress had a sour look.

"Last call," she said, leaving him his rye. "We close in ten minutes."

"I just need to make a quick call," he said.

He stepped into one of the telephone booths in the back, pulling the accordion door shut behind him.

"Yes, I have that one," his wife replied, stifling a yawn. "But it's not a dirty book."

Then she laughed a little in a way that made him bristle.

"So what kind of book is it?" he asked.

"Books mean different things to different people," she said. She was always saying stuff like that, just to show him how smart she was.

"You know what I mean," he said.

She was silent for several seconds. He thought he could hear someone crying, maybe one of the kids.

"It's a mystery," she said, finally. "Not your kind. No one even dies."

"Okay," he said. He wasn't sure what he'd wanted to hear. "I'll be home soon."

"It's a love story, too," she said, almost a whisper, strangely sad. "Not your kind."

After he hung up, he ordered a beer, the night's last tug from the bartender's tap.

Sitting by the picture window, he looked down into the canyon, and up to the Hollywood sign. Everything about the moment felt familiar. He'd worked this precinct for twenty years, minus three to Uncle Sam, so even the surprises were the same.

He thought about the girl, about her at the station. Her nervous legs, that worn dress of hers, the plea in her voice.

Someone should think of her for a minute, shouldn't they?

He looked at his watch. Two A.M. But she won't see her little men tonight.

A busboy with a pencil moustache came over with a long stick. One by one, he turned all the dingy lanterns that hung in the window. The painted clowns faced the canyon now. Closing time.

"Don't miss me too much," he told the sour waitress as he left.

In the parking lot, looking down into the canyon, he noticed he could see the Canyon Arms, the smoke still settling on the bungalow's shell, black as a mussel. Her bedroom window, glass blown out, curtains shuddering in the night breeze.

He was just about to get in his car when he saw them. The little men.

They were dancing across the hood of his car, the canyon beneath him.

Turning, he looked up at the bar, the lanterns in the window, spinning, sending their dancing clowns across the canyon, across the Canyon Arms, everywhere.

He took a breath.

"That happens every night?" he asked the busboy as the young man hustled down the stairs into the parking lot.

Pausing, the busboy followed his gaze, then nodded.

"Every night," he said. "Like a dream."

Citadel

Stephen Hunter

~~~

Born in 1946, Stephen Hunter graduated from Northwestern University in 1968. Following his graduation, he spent two years in the U.S. Army as a ceremonial soldier in the Old Guard in Washington, D.C. He was a journalist for *The Baltimore Sun* from 1971–96, then moved to *The Washington Post* until retiring in 2008. In 1998, Hunter won the ASNE Distinguished Writing Award in the criticism category. He has also been nominated for the Pulitzer Prize on several occasions, and he was a finalist in 1995 and 1996. He was awarded the Pulitzer in 2003 for his authoritative film criticism in *The Washington Post*. Hunter is the author of the popular Bob Lee Swagger series. His novel *Point of Impact* was turned into a successful Hollywood blockbuster, *Shooter*, in 2007, starring Mark Wahlberg. Hunter lives in Baltimore, MD, with his wife.

FIRST DAY

The Lysander took off in the pitch-dark of 0400 British Standard War Time, Pilot Officer Murphy using the prevailing south-southwest wind to gain atmospheric traction, even though the craft had a reputation for short takeoffs. He nudged it airborne, felt it surpass its amazingly low stall speed, held the stick gently back until he reached 150 meters, then commenced a wide left-hand bank to aim himself and his passenger toward Occupied France.

Murphy was a pro and had done many missions for his outfit, No. 138 (Special Duties Squadron), inserting and removing agents in coordination with the Resistance. But that didn't mean he was blasé, or without fear. No matter how many times you flew into Nazi territory, it was a first time. There was no predicting what might happen, and he could just as easily end up in a POW camp or against the executioner's wall as back in his quarters at RAF Newmarket.

The high-winged, single-engine plane hummed along just over the 150-meter notch on the altimeter to stay under both British and, twenty minutes on, German radar. It was a moonless night, as preferred, a bit chilly and damp, with ground temperature at about four degrees centigrade. It was early April 1943; the destination, still two hours ahead, was a meadow outside Sur-la-Gane, a village forty-eight kilometers east of Paris. There, God and the Luftwaffe willing, he would deviate from the track of a railroad, find four lights on the ground, and lay the plane down between them, knowing that they signified enough flatness and tree clearance for the airplane. He'd drop his passenger, the peasants of whichever Maquis group was receiving that night (he never knew) would turn the plane around, and in another forty seconds he'd be airborne, now headed west toward tea and jam. That was the ideal, at any rate.

He checked the compass at the apex of the Lysander's primitive instrument panel and double-checked his heading (148° ENE), his fuel (full), and his airspeed (175 mph), and saw through the Perspex windscreen, as expected, nothing. Nothing was good. He knew it was a rare off-night in the war and that no fleets of Lancasters filled the air and radio waves to and from targets deep in Germany, which meant that the Luftwaffe's night fighters, Me110s, wouldn't be up and about. No 110 had ever shot down a Lysander because they operated at such different altitudes and speeds, but there had to be a first time for everything.

Hunched behind him was an agent named Basil St. Florian, a captain in the army by official designation, commissioned in 1932 into the Horse Guards—not that he'd been on horseback in over a decade. Actually Basil, a ruddy-faced, ginger-haired brute who'd once sported a giant moustache, didn't know or care much about horses. Or the fabulous traditions of the Horse Guards, the cavalry, even the army. He'd only ended up there after a youth notorious for spectacular crack-ups, usually involving trysts with American actresses and fights with Argentine polo players. His father arranged the commission, as he had arranged so much else for Basil, who tended to leave debris wherever he went, but once in khaki Basil veered again toward glamorous self-extinction until a dour little chap from Intelligence invited him for a drink at Boodle's. When Basil learned he could do unusual things and get both paid and praised for it, he signed up. That was 1934, and Basil had never looked back.

As it turned out, he had a gift for languages and spoke French, German, and Spanish without a trace of accent. He could pass for any European nationality except Irish, though the latter was more on principle, because he despised the Irish in general terms. They were so loud.

He liked danger and wasn't particularly nonplussed by fear. He never panicked. He took pride in his considerable wit, and his bons mots were famous in his organization. He didn't mind fighting, with fist or knife, but much preferred shooting, because he was a superb pistol and rifle shot. He'd been on safari at fifteen, again at twenty-two, and a third time at twenty-seven; he was quite used to seeing large mammals die by gunshot, so it didn't particularly perturb him. He knew enough about trophy hunting to hope that he'd never end up on another man's wall.

He'd been in the agent trade a long time and had the nightmares to show for it, plus a drawerful of ribbons that someone must organize sooner or later, plus three bullet holes, a raggedy zigzag of scar tissue from a knife (don't ask, please, don't *ever* ask), as well as piebald burn smears on back and hips from a long session with a torturer. He finally talked, and the lies he told the man were among his finest memories. His other favorite memory: watching his torturer's eyes go eightball as Basil strangled him three days later. Jolly fun!

Basil was cold, shivering under an RAF sheepskin over an RAF aircrew jumpsuit over a black wool suit of shabby prewar French manufacture. He sat uncomfortably squashed on a parachute, which he hadn't bothered to put on. The wind beat against him, because on some adventure or another the Lysander's left window had been shot out and nobody had got around to replacing it. He felt vibrations as the unspectacular Bristol Mercury XII engine beat away against the cold air, its energy shuddering through all the spars, struts, and tightened canvas of the aircraft.

"Over Channel now, sir," came the crackle of a voice from the earphones he wore, since there was entirely too much noise for pilot and passenger to communicate without it. "Ten minutes to France."

"Got it, Murphy, thanks." Inclining toward the intact window to his starboard, Basil could see the black surface of the Channel at high chop, the water seething and shifting under the powerful blast of cold early-spring winds. It somehow caught enough illumination from the stars to gleam a bit, though without romance or beauty. It simply reminded him of unpleasant things and his aversion to large bodies of the stuff, which to him had but three effects: it made you wet, it made you cold, or it made you dead. All three were to be avoided.

In time a dark mass protruded upon the scene, sliding in from beyond to meet the sea.

"I say, Murphy, is that France?"

"It is indeed, sir."

"You know, I didn't have a chance to look at the flight plan. What part of France?"

"Normandy, sir. Jerry's building forts there, to stop an invasion."

"If I recall, there's a peninsula to the west, and the city of Cherbourg at the tip?"

"Yes, sir."

"Tell me, if you veered toward the west, you'd cross the peninsula, correct? With no deviation then, you'd come across coastline?"

"Yes, sir."

"And from that coastline, knowing you were to the western lee of the Cherbourg peninsula, you could easily return home on dead reckoning, that is, without a compass, am I right?"

"Indeed, sir. But I have a compass. So why would—"

Basil leaned forward, holding his Browning

.380 automatic pistol. He fired once, the pistol jumping, the flash filling the cockpit with a flare of illumination, the spent casing flying away, the noise terrific.

"Good Christ!" yelped Murphy. "What the bloody hell! Are you mad?"

"Quite the opposite, old man," said Basil. "Now do as I suggested—veer westerly, cross the peninsula, and find me coastline."

Murphy noted that the bullet had hit the compass bang on, shattered its glass, and blown its dial askew and its needle arm into the vapors.

A FEW DAYS EARLIER

"Basil, how's the drinking?" the general asked.

"Excellent, sir," Basil replied. "I'm up to seven, sometimes eight whiskies a night."

"Splendid, Basil," said the general. "I knew you wouldn't let us down."

"See here," said another general. "I know this man has a reputation for wit, as it's called, but we are engaged in serious business, and the levity, perhaps appropriate to the officers' mess, is most assuredly inappropriate here. There should be no laughing here, gentlemen. This is the War Room." Basil sat in a square, dull space far underground. A few dim bulbs illuminated it but showed little except a map of Europe pinned to the wall. Otherwise it was featureless. The table was large enough for at least a dozen generals, but there were only three of them—well, one was an admiral—and a civilian, all sitting across from Basil. It was rather like orals at Magdalen, had he bothered to attend them.

The room was buried beneath the Treasury in Whitehall, the most secret of secret installations in wartime Britain. Part of a warren of other rooms—some offices for administrative or logistical activities, a communications room, some sleeping or eating quarters—it was the only construction in England that might legitimately be called a lair. It belonged under a volcano, not a large office building. The prime minister would sit in this very place with his staff and make the decisions that would send thousands to their death in order to save tens of thousands. That was the theory, anyway. And that also is why it stank so brazenly of stale cigar.

"My dear sir," said the general with whom Basil had been discussing his drinking habits to the general who disapproved, "when one has been shot at for the benefit of crown and country as many times as Captain St. Florian, one has the right to set the tone of the meeting that will most certainly end up getting him shot at quite a bit more. Unless you survived the first day on the Somme, you cannot compete with him in that regard."

The other general muttered something, but Basil hardly noticed. It really did not matter, and since he believed himself doomed no matter what, he now no longer listened to those who did not matter.

The general who championed him turned to him, his opposition defeated. His name was Sir Colin Gubbins and he was head of the outfit to which Basil belonged, called by the rather dreary title Special Operations Executive. Its mandate was to Set Europe Ablaze, as the prime minister had said when he invented it and appointed General Gubbins as its leader. It was the sort of organization that would have welcomed Jack the Ripper to its ranks, possibly even promoted, certainly decorated him. It existed primarily to destroy—people, places, things, anything that could be destroyed. Whether all this was just mischief for the otherwise unemployable or long-term strategic wisdom was as yet undetermined. It was up for considerable debate among the other intelligence agencies, one of which was represented by the army general and the other by the naval admiral.

As for the civilian, he looked like a question on a quiz: Which one does not belong? He was a good thirty years younger than the two generals and the admiral, and hadn't, as they did, one of those heavy-jowled authoritarian faces. He was rather handsome in a weak sort of way, like the fellow who always plays Freddy in any production of *Pygmalion*, and he didn't radiate, as did the men of power. Yet here he was, a lad among the Neanderthals, and the others seemed in small ways to defer to him. Basil wondered who the devil he could be. But he realized he would find out sooner or later.

"You've all seen Captain St. Florian's record, highly classified as it is. He's one of our most capable men. If this thing can be done, he's the one who can do it. I'm sure before we proceed, the captain would entertain any questions of a general nature."

"I seem to remember your name from the cricket fields, St. Florian," said the admiral. "Were you not a batsman of some renown in the late twenties?"

"I have warm recollections of good innings at both Eton and Magdalen," said Basil.

"Indeed," said the admiral. "I've always said that sportsmen make the best agents. The playing field accustoms them to arduous action, quick, clever thinking, and decisiveness."

"I hope, however," said the general, "you've left your sense of sporting fair play far behind. Jerry will use it against you, any chance he gets."

"I killed a Chinese gangster with a cricket bat, sir. Would that speak to the issue?"

"Eloquently," said the general. "What did your people do, Captain?" asked the admiral.

"He manufactured something," said Basil. "It had to do with automobiles, as I recall."

"A bit hazy, are we?"

"It's all rather vague. I believe that I worked for him for a few months after coming down. My performance was rather disappointing. We parted on bad terms. He died before I righted myself."

"To what do you ascribe your failure to succeed in business and please your poor father?"

"I am too twitchy to sit behind a desk, sir. My bum, pardon the French, gets all buzzy if I am in one spot too long. Then I drink to kill the buzz and end up in the cheap papers."

"I seem to recall," the admiral said. "Something about an actress—'31, '32, was that it?"

"Lovely young lady," Basil said, "A pity I treated her so abominably. I always plucked the melons out of her fruit salad and she could not abide that."

"Hong Kong, Malaysia, Germany before and during Hitler, battle in Spain—shot at a bit there, eh, watching our Communists fight the generalissimo's Germans, eh?" asked the army chap. "Czecho, France again, Dieppe, you were there? So was I."

"Odd I didn't see you, sir," said Basil.

"I suppose you were way out front then. Point taken, Captain. All right, professionally, he seems capable. Let's get on with it, Sir Colin."

"Yes," said Sir Colin. "Where to begin, where to begin? It's rather complex, you see, and someone important has demanded that you be apprised of all the nuances before you decide to go."

"Sir, I could save us all a lot of time. I've decided to go. I hereby officially volunteer."

"See, there's a chap with spirit," said the admiral. "I like that."

"It's merely that his bum is twitchy," said the general.

"Not so fast, Basil. I insist that you hear us out," said Sir Colin, "and so does the young man at the end of the table. Is that not right, Professor?"

"It is," said the young fellow.

"All right, sir," said Basil.

"It's a rather complex, even arduous story. Please ignore the twitchy bum and any need you may have for whisky. Give us your best effort."

"I shall endeavor, sir."

"Excellent. Now, hmm, let me see . . . oh, yes, I think this is how to start. Do you know the path to Jesus?"

THE FIRST DAY (CONT'D.)

Another half hour flew by, lost to the rattle of the plane, the howl of the wind, and the darkness of Occupied France below. At last Murphy said over the intercom, "Sir, the west coast of the Cherbourg Peninsula is just ahead. I can see it now."

"Excellent," said Basil. "Find someplace to put me down."

"Ah . . ."

"Yes, what is it, Pilot Officer?"

"Sir, I can't just land, you see. The plane is too fragile—there may be wires, potholes, tree stumps, ditches, mud, God knows what. All of which could snarl or even wreck the plane. It's not so much me. I'm not that important. It's actually the plane. Jerry's been trying to get hold of a Lysander for some time now, to use against us. I can't give him one."

"Yes, I can see that. All right then, perhaps drop me in a river from a low altitude?"

"Sir, you'd hit the water at over 100 miles per hour and bounce like a billiard ball off the bumper. Every bone would shatter."

"On top of that, I'd lose my shoes. This is annoying. I suppose then it's the parachute for me?"

"Yes, sir. Have you had training?"

"Scheduled several times, but I always managed to come up with an excuse. I could see no sane reason for abandoning a perfectly fine airplane in flight. That was then, however, and now, alas, is now."

Basil shed himself of the RAF fleece, a heavy leather jacket lined with sheep's wool, and felt the coldness of the wind bite him hard. He shivered. He hated the cold. He struggled with the straps of the parachute upon which he was sitting. He found the going rather rough. It seemed he couldn't quite get the left shoulder strap buckled into what appeared to be the strap nexus, a circular lock-like device that was affixed to the right shoulder strap in the center of his chest. He passed on that and went right to the thigh straps, which seemed to click in admirably, but then noticed he had the two straps in the wrong slots, and he couldn't get the left one undone. He applied extra effort and was able to make the correction.

"I say, how long has this parachute been here? It's all rusty and stiff."

"Well, sir, these planes aren't designed for parachuting. Their brilliance is in the short takeoff and landing drills. Perfect for agent inserts and fetches. So, no, I'm afraid nobody has paid much attention to the parachute."

"Damned thing. I'd have thought you RAF buckos would have done better. Battle of Britain, the few, all that sort of thing."

"I'm sure the 'chutes on Spits and Hurricanes were better maintained, sir. Allow me to make a formal apology to the intelligence services on behalf of the Royal Air Force."

"Well, I suppose it'll have to do," sniffed Basil. Somehow, at last, he managed to get the left strap snapped in approximately where it belonged, but he had no idea if the thing was too tight or too loose or even right side up. Oh, well, one did what one must. Up, up, and play the game, that sort of thing.

"Now, I'm not telling you your job, Murphy, but I think you should go lower so I won't have so far to go."

"Quite the opposite, sir. I must go higher. The 'chute won't open fully at 150 meters. It's a 240meter minimum, a thousand far safer. At 150 or lower it's like dropping a pumpkin on a sidewalk. Very unpleasant sound, lots of splash, splatter, puddle, and stain. Wouldn't advise a bit of it, sir."

"This is not turning out at all as I had expected."

"I'll buzz up to a thousand. Sir, the trick here is that when you come out of the plane, you must keep hunched up in a ball. If you open up, your arms and legs and torso will catch wind and stall your fall and the tail wing will cut you in half or at least break your spine."

"Egad," said Basil. "How disturbing."

"I'll bank hard left to add gravity to your speed of descent, which puts you in good shape, at least theoretically, to avoid the tail."

"Not sure I care for 'theoretically.'"

"There's no automatic deployment on that device, also. You must, once free of the plane, pull the ripcord to open the 'chute."

"I shall try to remember," said Basil.

"If you forget, it's the pumpkin phenomenon, without doubt."

"All right, Murphy, you've done a fine job briefing me. I shall have a letter inserted in your file. Now, shall we get this nonsense over with?"

"Yes, sir. You'll feel the plane bank, you should have no difficulty with the door, remember to take off earphones and throat mike, and I'll signal go. Just tumble out. Rip cord, and down you go. Don't brace hard in landing—you could break or sprain something. Try to relax. It's a piece of cake."

"Very well done, Murphy."

"Sir, what should I tell them?"

"Tell them what happened. That's all. I'll happily be the villain. Once I potted the compass, it was either do as I say or head home. On top of that, I outrank you. They'll figure it out, and if they don't, then they're too damned stupid to worry about!"

"Yes, sir."

Basil felt the subtle, then stronger pull of gravity as Murphy pulled the stick back and the plane mounted toward heaven. He had to give more throttle, so the sound of the revs and the consequent vibrations through the plane's skeleton increased. Basil unhitched the door, pushed it out a bit, but then the prop wash caught it and slammed it back. He opened it a bit again, squirmed his way to the opening, scrunched to fit through, brought himself to the last point where he could be said to be inside the airplane, and waited.

Below, the blackness roared by, lit here and there by a light. It really made no difference where he jumped. It would be completely random. He might come down in a town square, a haystack, a cemetery, a barn roof, or an SS firing range. God would decide, not Basil.

Murphy raised his hand, and probably screamed "Tally-ho!"

Basil slipped off the earphones and mike and tumbled into the roaring darkness.

A FEW DAYS EARLIER (CONT'D.)

"Certainly," said Basil, "though I doubt I'll be allowed to make the trip. The path to Jesus would include sobriety, a clean mind, obedience to all commandments, a positive outlook, respect for elders, regular worship, and a high level of hygiene. I am happily guilty of none of those."

"The damned insouciance," said the army general. "Is everything an opportunity for irony, Captain?"

"I shall endeavor to control my ironic impulses, sir," said Basil.

"Actually, he's quite amusing," said the young civilian. "A heroic chap as imagined by Noël Coward."

"Coward's a poof, Professor."

"But a titanic wit."

"Gentlemen, gentlemen," said Sir Colin. "Please, let's stay with the objective here, no matter how Captain St. Florian's insouciance annoys or enchants us."

"Then, sir," said Basil, "the irony-free answer is no, I do not know the path to Jesus."

"I don't mean in general terms. I mean specifically *The Path to Jesus*, a pamphlet published in 1767 by a Scottish ecclesiastic named Thomas MacBurney. Actually he listed twelve steps on the way, and I believe you scored high on your account, Basil. You only left out thrift, daily prayer, cold baths, and regular enemas."

"What about wanking, sir? Is that allowed by the Reverend MacBurney?"

"I doubt he'd heard of it. Anyway, it is not the content of the reverend's pamphlet that here concerns us but the manuscript itself. That is the thing, the paper on which he wrote in ink, the actual physical object." He paused, taking a breath. "The piece began as a sermon, delivered to his congregation in that same year. It was quite successful—people talked much about it and requested that he deliver it over and over. He did, and became, one might say, an ecclesiastical celebrity. Then it occurred to him that he could spread the Word more effectively, and make a quid or two on the side—he was a Scot, after all—if he committed it to print and offered it for a shilling a throw. Thus he made a fair copy, which he delivered to a jobbing printer in Glasgow, and took copies around to all the churches and bookstores. Again, it was quite successful. It grew and grew and in the end he became rather prosperous, so much so that—this is my favorite part of the tale—he gave up the pulpit and retired to the country for a life of debauchery and gout, while continuing to turn out religious tracts when not abed with a local tart or two."

"I commend him," said Basil.

"As do we all," said the admiral.

"The fair copy, in his own hand, somehow came to rest in the rare books collection at the Cambridge Library. That is the one he copied himself from his own notes on the sermon, and which he hand-delivered to Carmichael & Sons, printers, of 14 Middlesex Lane, Glasgow, for careful reproduction on September 1, 1767. Mr. Carmichael's signature in receipt, plus instructions to his son, the actual printer, are inscribed in pencil across the title page. As it is the original, it is of course absurdly rare, which makes it absurdly valuable. Its homilies and simple faith have nothing to do with it, only its rarity, which is why the librarian at Cambridge treasures it so raptly. Are you with me, Basil?"

"With you, sir, but not with you. I cannot begin to fathom why this should interest the intelligence service, much less the tiny cog of it known as Basil St. Florian. Do you think exposure to it would improve my moral character? My character definitely needs moral improvement, but I should think any book of the New Testament would do the job as well as the Reverend MacBurney."

"Well, it happens to be the key to locating a traitor, Basil. Have you ever heard of the book code?"

THE SECOND DAY

There was a fallacy prevalent in England that Occupied France was a morose, death-haunted place. It was gray, gray as the German uniforms, and the conquerors goose-stepped about like Mongols, arbitrarily designating French citizens for execution by firing squad as it occurred to them for no reason save whimsy and boredom and Hun depravity. The screams of the tortured pierced the quiet, howling out of the many Gestapo torture cellars. The Horst Wessel song was piped everywhere; swastikas emblazoned on vast red banners fluttered brazenly everywhere. Meanwhile the peasants shuffled about all hangdog, the bourgeoisie were rigid with terror, the civic institutions were in paralysis, and even the streetwalkers had disappeared.

Basil knew this to be untrue. In fact, Occupied France was quite gay. The French barely noted their own conquest before returning to bustling business as usual, or not as usual, for the Germans were a vast new market. Fruit, vegetables, slabs of beef, and other provisions gleamed in every shop window, the wine was ample, even abundant (if overpriced), and the streetwalkers were quite active. Perhaps it would change later in the war, but for now it was rather a swell time. The Resistance, such as it was—and it wasn't much—was confined to marginal groups: students, Communists, bohemians, professors—people who would have been at odds with society in any event; they just got more credit for it now, all in exchange for blowing up a piddling bridge or dynamiting a rail line which would be repaired in a few hours. Happiness was general all over France.

The source of this gaiety was twofold. The first was the French insistence on being French, no matter how many panzers patrolled the streets and crossroads. Protected by their intensely high self-esteem, they thought naught of the Germans, regarding the *feldgrau* as a new class of tourist, to be fleeced, condescended to ("Red wine as an aperitif! *Mon Dieu!*"), and otherwise ignored. And there weren't nearly as many Nazi swastikas fluttering on silk banners as one might imagine.

The second reason was the immense happiness of the occupiers themselves. The Germans loved the cheese, the meals, the whores, the sights, and all the pleasures of France, it is true, but they enjoyed one thing more: that it was Not Russia.

This sense of Not-Russia made each day a joy. The fact that at any moment they could be sent to Is-Russia haunted them and drove them to new heights of sybaritic release. Each pleasure had a melancholy poignancy in that he who experienced it might shortly be slamming 8.8 cm shells into the breach of an antitank gun as fleets of T-34s poured torrentially out of the snow at them, this drama occurring at minus thirty-one degrees centigrade on the outskirts of a town with an unpronounceable name that they had never heard of and that offered no running water, pretty women, or decent alcohol.

So nobody in all of France in any of the German branches worked very hard, except perhaps the extremists of the SS. But most of the SS was somewhere else, happily murdering farmers in the hundreds of thousands, letting their fury, their rage, their misanthropy, their sense of racial superiority play out in real time.

Thus Basil didn't fear random interception as he walked the streets of downtown Bricquebec, a small city forty kilometers east of Cherbourg in the heart of the Cotentin Peninsula. The occupiers of this obscure spot would not be of the highest quality, and had adapted rather too quickly to the torpor of garrison life. They lounged this way and that, lazy as dogs in the spring sun, in the cafés, at their very occasional roadblocks, around city hall, where civil administrators now gave orders to the French bureaucrats, who had not made a single adjustment to their presence, and at an airfield where a flock of Me110 night fighters were housed, to intercept the nightly RAF bomber stream when it meandered toward targets in southern Germany. Though American bombers filled the sky by day, the two-engine 110s were not nimble enough to close with them and left that dangerous task to younger men in faster planes. The 110 pilots were content to maneuver close to the Lancasters, but not too close, to hosepipe their cannon shells all over the sky, then to return to schnapps and buns, claiming extravagant kill scores which nobody took seriously. So all in all, the atmosphere was one of snooze and snore.

Basil had landed without incident about eight kilometers outside of town. He was lucky, as he usually was, in that he didn't crash into a farmer's henhouse and awaken the rooster or the man but landed in one of the fields, among potato stubs just barely emerging from the ground. He had gathered up his 'chute, stripped off his RAF jumpsuit to reveal himself to be a rather shabby French businessman, and stuffed all that kit into some bushes (he could not bury it, because a] he did not feel like it and b] he had no shovel, but c] if he had had a shovel, he still would not have felt like it). He made it to a main road and walked into town, where he immediately treated himself to a breakfast of eggs and potatoes and tomatoes at a railway station café.

He nodded politely at each German he saw and so far had not excited any attention. His only concession to his trade was his Browning pistol, wedged into the small of his back and so flat it would not print under suit and overcoat. He also had his Riga Minox camera taped to his left ankle. His most profound piece of equipment, however, was his confidence. Going undercover is fraught with tension, but Basil had done it so often that its rigors didn't drive him to the edge of despair, eating his energy with teeth of dread. He'd simply shut down his imagination and considered himself the cock of the walk, presenting a smile, a nod, a wink to all.

But he was not without goal. Paris lay a half day's rail ride ahead; the next train left at four, and he had to be on it. But just as he didn't trust the partisans who still awaited his arrival 320 kilometers to the east, he didn't trust the documents the forgery geniuses at SOE had provided him with. Instead he preferred to pick up his own—that is, actual authentic docs, including travel permissions—and he now searched for a man who, in the terrible imagery of document photography, might be considered to look enough like him.

It was a pleasant day and he wandered this way and that, more or less sightseeing. At last he encountered a fellow who would pass for him, a welldressed burgher in a black homburg and overcoat, dour and official-looking. But the bone structure was similar, given to prominent cheekbones and a nose that looked like a Norman axe. In fact the fellow could have been a long-lost cousin. (Had he cared to, Basil could have traced the St. Florian line back to a castle not 100 kilometers from where he stood now, whence came his Norman forebears in 1044—but of course it meant nothing to him.)

Among Basil's skills was pickpocketing, very useful for a spy or agent. He had mastered its intricacies during his period among Malaysian gun-runners in 1934, when a kindly old rogue with one eye and fast hands named Malong had taken a liking to him and shown him the basics of the trade. Malong could pick the fuzz off a peach, so educated were his fingers, and Basil proved an apt pupil. He'd never graduated to the peach-fuzz class, but the gentleman's wallet and document envelopes should prove easy enough.

He used the classic concealed hand dip and distraction technique, child's play but clearly effective out here in the French hinterlands. Shielding his left hand from view behind a copy of that day's *Le Monde*, he engineered an accidental street-corner bump, apologized, and then said, "I was looking at the air power of *les amis* today." He pointed upward, where a wave of B-17s painted a swath in the blue sky with their fuzzy white contrails as they sped toward Munich or some other Bavarian destination for an afternoon of destruction. "It seems they'll never stop building up their fleet. But when they win, what will they do with all those airplanes?"

The gentleman, unaware that the jostle and rhetoric concealed a deft snatch from inside not merely his overcoat but also his suit coat, followed his interrupter's pointed arm to the aerial array.

"The Americans are so rich, I believe our German visitors are doomed," said the man. "I only hope when it is time for them to leave they don't grow bitter and decide to blow things up."

"That is why it is up to us to ingratiate ourselves with them," said Basil, reading the eyes of an appeaser in his victim, "so that when they do abandon their vacation, they depart with a gentleman's deportment. *Vive la France.*"

"Indeed," said the mark, issuing a dry little smile of approval, then turning away to his far more important business.

Basil headed two blocks in the opposite direction, two more in another, then rotated around to the train station. There, in the men's loo, he examined his trove: 175 francs, identity papers for one Jacques Piens, and a German travel authority "for official business only," both of which wore a smeary black-and-white photo of M. Piens, moustachioed and august and clearly annoyed at the indignity of posing for German photography.

He had a coffee. He waited, smiling at all, and a few minutes before four approached the ticket seller's window and, after establishing his bona fides as M. Piens, paid for and was issued a firstclass ticket on the four P.M. Cherbourg–Paris run.

He went out on the platform, the only Frenchman among a small group of Luftwaffe enlisted personnel clearly headed to Paris for a weekend pass's worth of fun and frolic. The train arrived, as the Germans had been sensible enough not to interfere with the workings of the French railway system, the continent's best. Spewing smoke, the engine lugged its seven cars to the platform and, with great drama of steam, brakes, and steel, reluctantly halted. Basil knew where first class would be and parted company with the privates and corporals of the German air force, who squeezed into the other carriages.

His car half empty and comfortable, he put himself into a seat. The train sat . . . and sat . . . and sat. Finally a German policeman entered the car and examined the papers of all, including Basil, without incident. Yet still the train did not leave.

Hmm, this was troubling.

A lesser man might have fumbled into panic. The mark had noticed his papers missing, called the police, who had called the German police. Quickly enough they had put a hold on the train, fearing that the miscreant would attempt to flee that way, and now it was just a matter of waiting for an SS squad to lock up the last of the Jews before it came for him.

However, Basil had a sound operational principle which now served him well. *Most bad things don't happen.* What happens is that in its banal, boring way, reality bumbles along.

The worst thing one can do is panic. Panic betrays more agents than traitors. Panic is the true enemy.

At last the train began to move.

Ah–ha! Right again.

But at that moment the door flew open and a late-arriving Luftwaffe colonel came in. He looked straight at Basil.

"There he is! There's the spy!" he said.

A FEW DAYS EARLIER (CONT'D)

"A book code," said Basil. "I thought that was for Boy Scouts. Lord Baden-Powell would be so pleased."

"Actually," said Sir Colin, "it's a sturdy and almost impenetrable device, very useful under certain circumstances, if artfully employed. But Professor Turing is our expert on codes. Perhaps, Professor, you'd be able to enlighten Captain St. Florian."

"Indeed," said the young man in the tweeds, revealing himself by name. "Nowadays we think we're all scienced up. We even have machines to do some of the backbreaking mathematics to it, speeding the process. Sometimes it works, sometimes it doesn't. But the book code is ancient, even biblical, and that it has lasted so long is good proof of its applicability in certain instances."

"I understand, Professor. I am not a child."

"Not at all, certainly not given your record. But the basics must be known before we can advance to the sort of sophisticated mischief upon which the war may turn."

"Please proceed, Professor. Pay no attention to Captain St. Florian's abominable manners. We interrupted him at play in a bawdy house for this meeting and he is cranky."

"Yes, then. The book code stems from the presumption that both sender and receiver have access to the same book. It is therefore usually a common volume, shall we say Lamb's *Tales from Shakespeare*. I want to send you a message, say 'Meet me at two P.M. at the square.' I page through the book until I find the word 'meet.' It is on page 17, paragraph 4, line 2, fifth word. So the first line in my code is 17-4-2-5. Unless you know the book, it is meaningless. But you, knowing the book, having the book, quickly find 17-4-2-5 and encounter the word 'meet.' And on and on. Of course variations can be worked—we can agree ahead of time, say, that for the last designation we will always be value minus two, that is, two integers less. So in that case the word 'meet' would actually be found at 17-4-2-3. Moreover, in picking a book as decoder, one would certainly be prone to pick a common book, one that should excite no excitement, that one might normally have about."

"I grasp it, Professor," said Basil. "But what, then, if I take your inference, is the point of choosing as a key book the Right Reverend MacBurney's *The Path to Jesus*, of which only one copy exists, and it is held under lock and key at Cambridge? And since last I heard, we still control Cambridge. Why don't we just go to Cambridge and look at the damned thing? You don't need an action-this-day chap like me for that. You could use a lance corporal."

"Indeed, you have tumbled to it," said Sir Colin. "Yes, we could obtain the book that way. However, in doing so we would inform both the sender and the receiver that we knew they were up to something, that they were control and agent and had an operation under way, when our goal is to break the code without them knowing. That is why, alas, a simple trip to the library by a lance corporal is not feasible."

"I hope I'm smart enough to stay up with all these wrinkles, gentlemen. I already have a headache."

"Welcome to the world of espionage," said Sir Colin. "We all have headaches. Professor, please continue."

"The volume in the library is indeed controlled by only one man," Turing said. "And he is the senior librarian of the institution. Alas, his loyalties are such that they are not, as one might hope and expect, for his own country. He is instead one of those of high caste taken by fascination for another creed, and it is to that creed he pays his deepest allegiance. He has made himself useful to his masters for many years as a 'talent spotter,' that is, a man who looks at promising undergraduates, picks those with keen policy minds and good connections, forecasts their rise, and woos them to his side as secret agents with all kinds of babble of the sort that appeals to the mushy romantic brain of the typical English high-class idiot. He thus plants the seeds of our destruction, sure to bloom a few decades down the line. He does other minor tasks too, running as a cutout, providing a safe house, disbursing a secret fund, and so forth. He is committed maximally and he will die before he betrays his creed, and some here have suggested a bullet in the brain as apposite, but actually, by the tortured rules of the game, a live spy in place is worth more than a dead spy in the ground. Thus he must not be disturbed, bothered, breathed heavily upon—he must be left entirely alone."

"And as a consequence you cannot under any circumstances access the book. You do not even know what it looks like?" Basil asked.

"We have a description from a volume published in 1932, called *Treasures of the Cambridge Library*."

"I can guess who wrote it," said Basil.

"Your guess would be correct," said Sir Colin. "It tells us little other than that it comprises thirty-four pages of foolscap written in tightly controlled nib by an accomplished freehand scrivener. Its eccentricity is that occasionally apostolic bliss came over the author and he decorated the odd margin with constellations of floating crosses, proclaiming his love of all things Christian. The Reverend MacBurney was clearly given to religious swoons."

"And the librarian is given to impenetrable security," said the admiral. "There will come a time when I will quite happily murder him with your cricket bat, Captain."

"Alas, I couldn't get the bloodstains out and left it in Malay. So let me sum up what I think I know so far. For some reason the Germans have a fellow in the Cambridge library controlling access to a certain 1767 volume. Presumably they have sent an agent to London with a coded message he himself does not know the answer to, possibly for security reasons. Once safely here, he will approach the bad-apple librarian and present him with the code. The bad apple will go to the manuscript, decipher it, and give a response to the Nazi spy. I suppose it's operationally sound. It neatly avoids radio, as you say it cannot be breached without giving notice that the ring itself is under high suspicion, and once armed with the message, the operational spy can proceed with his mission. Is that about it?"

"Almost," said Sir Colin. "In principle, yes, you have the gist of it—manfully done. However, you haven't got the players quite right."

"Are we then at war with someone I don't know about?" said Basil.

"Indeed and unfortunately. Yes. The Soviet Union. This whole thing is Russian, not German."

THE SECOND DAY (CONT'D.)

If panic flashed through Basil's mind, he did not yield to it, although his heart hammered against his chest as if a spike of hard German steel had been pounded into it. He thought of his L-pill, but it was buried in his breast pocket. He thought next of his pistol: Could he get it out in time to bring a few of them down before turning it on himself? Could he at least kill this leering German idiot who . . . but then he noted that the characterization had been delivered almost merrily.

"You must be a spy," said the colonel, laughing heartily, sitting next to him. "Why else would you shave your moustache but to go on some glamorous underground mission?"

Basil laughed, perhaps too loudly, but in his chest his heart still ran wild. He hid his blast of fear in the heartiness of the fraudulent laugh and came back with an equally jocular, "Oh, that? It seems in winter my wife's skin turns dry and very sensitive, so I always shave it off for a few months to give the beauty a rest from the bristles."

"It makes you look younger."

"Why, thank you."

"Actually, I'm so glad to have discovered you. At first I thought it was not you, but then I thought, Gunther, Gunther, who would kidnap the owner of the town's only hotel and replace him with a double? The English are not so clever."

"The only thing they're any good at," said Basil, "is weaving tweed. English tweed is the finest in the world."

"I agree, I agree," said the colonel. "Before all this, I traveled there quite frequently. Business, you know."

It developed that the colonel, a Great War aviator, had represented a Berlin-based hair tonic firm whose directors had visions, at least until 1933, of entering the English market. The colonel had made trips to London in hopes of interesting some of the big department stores in carrying a line of lanolin-based hair creams for men, but was horrified to learn that the market was controlled by the British company that manufactured Brylcreem and would use its considerable clout to keep the Germans out.

"Can you imagine," said the colonel, "that in the twenties there was a great battle between Germany and Great Britain for the market advantage of lubricating the hair of the British gentleman? I believe our product was much finer than that English goop, as it had no alcohol and alcohol dries the hair stalk, robbing it of luster, but I have to say that the British packaging carried the day, no matter. We could never find the packaging to catch the imagination of the British gentleman, to say nothing of a slogan. German as a language does not lend itself to slogans. Our attempts at slogans were ludicrous. We are too serious, and our language is like potatoes in gravy. It has no lightness in it at all. The best we could come up with was, 'Our tonic is very good.' Thus we give the world Nietzsche and not Wodehouse. In any event, when Hitler came to power and the air forces were reinvigorated, it was out of the hair oil business and back to the cockpit."

It turned out that the colonel was a born talker. He was on his way to Paris on a three-day leave to meet his wife for a "well-deserved, if I do say so myself" holiday. He had reservations at the Ritz and at several four-star restaurants.

Basil put it together quickly: the man he'd stolen his papers from was some sort of collaborationist big shot and had made it his business to suck up to all the higher German officers, presumably seeing the financial opportunities of being in league with the occupiers. It turned out further that this German fool was soft and supple when it came to sycophancy and he'd mistaken the Frenchman's oleaginous demeanor with actual affection, and he thought it quite keen to have made a real friend among the wellborn French. So Basil committed himself to six hours of chitchat with the idiot, telling himself to keep autobiographical details at a minimum in case the real chap had already spilled some and he should contradict something previously established.

That turned out to be no difficulty at all, for the German colonel revealed himself to have an awesomely enlarged ego, which he expressed through an autobiographical impulse, so he virtually told his life story to Basil over the long drag, gossiping about the greed of Göring and the reluctance of the night fighters to close with the Lancasters, Hitler's insanity in attacking Russia, how much he, the colonel, missed his wife, how he worried about his son, a Stuka pilot, and how sad he was that it had come to pass that civilized Europeans were at each other's throats again, and on and on and on and on, but at least the Jews would be dealt with once and for all, no matter who won in the end. He titillated Basil with inside information on his base and the wing he commanded, Nachtjagdgeschwader-9, and the constant levies for Russia that had stripped it of logistics, communications, and security people, until nothing was left but a skeleton staff of air crew and mechanics, yet still they were under pressure from Luftwaffe command to bring down yet more Tommies to relieve the night bombing of Berlin. Damn the Tommies and their brutal methods of war! The man considered himself fascinating, and his presence seemed to ward off the attention of the other German officers who came and went on the trip to the Great City. It seemed so damned civilized that you almost forgot there was a war on.

It turned out that one of the few buildings in Paris with an actual Nazi banner hanging in front of it was a former insurance company's headquarters at 14 rue Guy de Maupassant in the sixth arrondissement. However, the banner wasn't much, really just an elongated flag that hung limply off a pole on the fifth floor. None of the new occupants of the building paid much attention to it. It was the official headquarters of the Paris district of the Abwehr, German military intelligence, ably run from Berlin by Admiral Canaris and beginning to acquire a reputation for not being all that crazy about Herr Hitler.

They were mostly just cops. And they brought cop attributes to their new headquarters: dyspepsia, too much smoking, cheap suits, fallen arches, and a deep cynicism about everything, but particularly about human nature and even more particularly about notions of honor, justice, and duty. They did believe passionately in one cause, however: staying out of Russia.

"Now let us see if we have anything," said Hauptmann Dieter Macht, chief of Section III-B (counterintelligence), Paris office, at his daily staff meeting at three P.M., as he gently spread butter on a croissant. He loved croissants. There was something so exquisite about the balance of elements—the delicacy of the crust, which gave way to a kind of chewy substrata as you peeled it away, the flakiness, the sweetness of the inner bread, the whole thing a majestic creation that no German baker, ham-thumbed and frosting-crazed, could ever match.

"Hmmm," he said, sifting through the various reports that had come in from across the country. About fifteen men, all ex-detectives like himself, all in droopy plain clothes like himself, all with uncleaned Walthers holstered sloppily on their hips, awaited his verdict. He'd been a Great War aviator, an actual ace in fact, then the star of Hamburg Homicide before this war, and had a reputation for sharpness when it came to seeing patterns in seemingly unrelated events. Most of III-B's arrests came from clever deductions made by Hauptmann Macht.

"Now this is interesting. What do you fellows make of this one? It seems in Sur-la-Gane, about forty kilometers east of here, a certain man known to be connected to inner circles of the Maquis was spotted returning home early in the morning by himself. Yet there has been no Maquis activity in that area since we arrested Pierre Doumaine last fall and sent him off to Dachau."

"Perhaps," said Leutnant Abel, his second-in-command, "he was at a meeting and they are becoming active again. Netting a big fish only tears them down for a bit of time, you know."

"They'd hold such a meeting earlier. The French like their sleep. They almost slept through 1940, after all. What one mission gets a Maquis up at night? Anyone?"

No one. "British agent insertion. They love to cooperate with the Brits because the Brits give them so much equipment, which can either be sold on the black market or be used against their domestic enemies after the war. So they will always jump lively for the SOE, because the loot is too good to turn down. And such insertions will be late-night or early-morning jobs."

"But," said Leutnant Abel, "I have gone through the reports too, and there are no accounts of aviation activities in that area that night. When the British land men in Lysanders, some farmer always calls the nearby police station to complain about low-flying aviators in the dark of night, frightening the cows. You never want to frighten a peasant's cows; he'll be your enemy for life. Believe me, Hauptmann Macht, had a Lysander landed, we'd know from the complaints."

"Exactly," said Macht. "So perhaps our British visitor didn't arrive for some reason or other and disappointed the Sur-la-Gane Resistance cell, who got no loot that night. But if I'm not mistaken, that same night complaints did come in from peasants near Bricquebec, outside Cherbourg."

"We have a night fighter base there," said Abel. "Airplanes come and go all night—it's meaningless."

"There were no raids that night," said Macht. "The bomber stream went north, to Prussia, not to Bavaria."

"What do you see as significant about that?"

"Suppose for some reason our fellow didn't trust the Sur-la-Gane bunch, or the Resistance either. It's pretty well penetrated, after all. So he directs his pilot to put him somewhere else."

"They can't put Lysanders down just anywhere," said another man. "It has to be set up, planned, torches lit. That's why it's so vulnerable to our investigations. So many people—someone always talks, maybe not to us, but to someone, and it always gets to us."

"The Bricquebec incident described a roar, not a put-put or a dying fart. The roar would be a Lysander climbing to parachute altitude. They normally fly at 500, and any agent who made an exit that low would surely scramble his brains and his bones. So the plane climbs, this fellow bails out, and now he's here."

"Why would he take the chance on a night drop into enemy territory? He could come down in the Gestapo's front yard. Hauptsturmführer Boch would enjoy that very much."

Actually the Abwehr detectives hated Boch more than the French and English combined. He could send them to Russia.

"I throw it back to you, Walter. Stretch that brain of yours beyond the lazy parameters it now sleepily occupies and come up with a theory."

"All right, sir, I'll pretend to be insane, like you. I'll postulate that this phantom Brit agent is very crafty, very old school, clever as they come. He doesn't trust the Maquis, nor should he. He knows we eventually hear everything. Thus he improvises. It's just his bad luck that his airplane awakened some cows near Bricquebec, the peasants complained, and so exactly what he did not want us to know is exactly what we do know. Is that insane enough for you, sir?"

Macht and Abel were continually taking shots at each other, and in fact they didn't like each other very much. Macht was always worried about Is Russia as opposed to Not-Russia, while the younger Abel had family connections that would keep him far from Stalin's millions of tanks and Mongols and all that horrible snow.

"Very good," said Macht. "That's how I read it. You know when these boys arrive they stir up a lot of trouble. If we don't stop them, maybe we end up on an antitank gun in Russia. Is anyone here interested in that sort of a job change?"

That certainly shut everyone up fast. It frightened Macht even to say such a thing.

"I will make some phone calls," Abel said. "See if there's anything unusual going on."

It didn't take him long. At the Bricquebec prefecture, a policeman read him the day's incident report, from which he learned that a prominent collaborationist businessman had claimed that his papers were stolen from him. He had been arrested selling black-market petrol and couldn't identify himself. He was roughly treated until his identity was proven, and he swore he would complain to Berlin, as he was a supporter of the Reich and demanded more respect from the occupiers.

His name, Abel learned, was Piens.

"Hmmm," said Macht, a logical sort. "If the agent was originally going to Sur-la-Gane, it seems clear that his ultimate destination would be Paris. There's really not much for him to do in Bricquebec or Sur-la-Gane, for that matter. Now, how would he get here?"

"Clearly, the railway is the only way."

"Exactly," said Hauptmann Macht. "What time does the train from Cherbourg get in? We should meet it and see if anyone is traveling under papers belonging to M. Piens. I'm sure he'd want them returned."

A FEW DAYS EARLIER (CONT'D.)

"Have I been misinformed?" asked Basil. "Are we at war with the Russians? I thought they were our friends."

"I wish it were as easy as that," said Sir Colin. "But it never is. Yes, in one sense we are at war with Germany and at peace with Russia. On the other hand, this fellow Stalin is a cunning old brute, stinking of bloody murder to high heaven, and thus he presumes that all are replicas of himself, equally cynical and vicious. So while we are friends with him at a certain level, he still spies on us at another level. And because we know him to be a monster, we still spy on him. It's all different compartments. Sometimes it's damned hard to keep straight, but there's one thing all the people in this room agree on: the moment the rope snaps hard about Herr Hitler's chicken neck, the next war begins, and it is between we of the West and they of the East."

"Rather dispiriting," said Basil. "One would have thought one had accomplished something other than clearing the stage for the next war."

"So it goes, alas and alack, in our sad world. But Basil, I think you will be satisfied to know that the end game of this little adventure we are preparing for you is actually to help the Russians, not to hurt them. It benefits ourselves, of course, no doubt about it. But we need to help them see a certain truth that they are reluctant, based on Stalin's various neuroses and paranoias, to believe."

"You see," said the general, "he would trust us a great deal more if we opened a second front. He doesn't think much of our business in North Africa, where our losses are about one-fiftieth of his. He wants our boys slaughtered on the French beaches in numbers that approach the slaughter of his boys. Then he'll know we're serious about this Allies business. But a second front in Europe is a long way off, perhaps two years. A lot of American men and matériel have to land here before then. In the meantime we grope and shuffle and misunderstand and misinterpret. That's where you'll fit in, we hope. Your job, as you will learn at the conclusion of this dreadful meeting about two days from now, is to shine light and dismiss groping and shuffling and misinterpretation."

"I hope I can be of help," said Basil. "However, my specialty is blowing things up."

"You have nothing to blow up this time out," said Sir Colin. "You are merely helping us explain something."

"But I must ask, since you're permitting me unlimited questions, how do you know all this?" said Basil. "You say Stalin is so paranoid and unstable he does not trust us and even spies upon us, you know this spy exists and is well placed, and that his identity, I presume, has been sent by this absurd book-code method, yet that is exactly where your knowledge stops. I am baffled beyond any telling of it. You know so much, and then it stops cold. It seems to me that you would be more likely to know all or nothing. My head aches profoundly. This business is damned confounding."

"All right, then, we'll tell you. I think you have a right to know, since you are the one we are proposing to send out. Admiral, as it was your service triumph, I leave it to you."

"Thank you, Sir Colin," said the admiral. "In your very busy year of 1940, you probably did not even notice one of the world's lesser wars. I mean there was our war with the Germans in Europe and all that blitz-krieg business, the Japanese war with the Chinese, Mussolini in Ethiopia, and I am probably leaving several out. 1940 was a very good year for war. However, if you check the back pages of the *Times*, you'll discover that in November of 1939, the Soviet Union invaded Finland. The border between them has been in dispute since 1917. The Russians expected an easy time of it, mustering ten times the number of soldiers as did the Finns, but the Finns taught them some extremely hard lessons about winter warfare, and by early 1940 the piles of frozen dead had gotten immense. The war raged for four long months, killing thousands over a few miles of frozen tundra, and ultimately, because lives mean nothing to Communists, the Russians prevailed, at least to the extent of forcing a peace on favorable terms."

"I believe I heard a bit of it."

"Excellent. What you did not hear, as nobody did, was that in a Red Army bunker taken at high cost by the Finns, a half-burned codebook was found. Now since we in the West abandoned the Finns, they were spon-sored and supplied in the war by the Third Reich. If you see any photos from the war, you'll think they came out of Stalingrad, because the Finns bought their helmets from the Germans. Thus one would expect that such a highvalue intelligence treasure as a codebook, even half burned, would shortly end up in German hands.

"However, we had a very good man in Finland, and he managed somehow to take possession of it. The Russians thought it was burned. The Germans never knew it existed. Half a code is actually not merely better than nothing, it is *far* better than nothing, and is in fact almost a whole codebook, because a clever boots like young Professor Turing here can tease most messages into comprehension."

"I had nothing to do with it," said the professor. "There were very able men at Bletchley Park before I came aboard."

What, wondered Basil, *would Bletchley Park be?*

"Thus we have been able to read and mostly understand Soviet low to mid-level codes since 1940. That's how we knew about the librarian at Cambridge and several other sticky lads who, though they speak high Anglican and know where their pinkie goes on the teacup, want to see our Blighty go all red and men like us stood up to the wall and shot for crimes against the working class."

"That would certainly ruin my crease. Anyhow, before we go much further, may I sum up?" said Basil.

"If you can."

"By breaking the Russian crypto, you know that a highly secure, carefully guarded book code has been given to a forthcoming Russian spy. It contains the name of a highly important British traitor somewhere in government service. When he gets here, he will take the code to the Cambridge librarian, present his bona fides, and the librarian will retrieve the Reverend Thomas MacBurney's *Path to Jesus*—wait. How would the Russians themselves have. . . . Oh, now I see, it all hangs together. It would be easy for the librarian, not like us, to make a photographed copy of the book and have it sent to the Russian service."

"NKVD, it is called."

"I think I knew that. Thus the librarian quickly unbuttons the name and gives it to the new agent, and the agent contacts him at perhaps this mysterious Bletchley Park that the professor wasn't supposed to let slip—"

"That was a mistake, Professor," said Sir Colin. "No milk and cookies for you tonight."

"So somehow I'm supposed to, I don't know what, do something somewhere, a nasty surprise indeed, but it will enable you to identify the spy at Bletchley Park."

"Indeed, you have the gist of it."

"And you will then arrest him."

"No, of course not. In fact, we shall promote him."

THE SECOND DAY/THE THIRD DAY

It was a pity the trip to Paris lasted only six hours with all the local stops, as the colonel had just reached the year 1914 in his life. It was incredibly fascinating. Mutter did not want him to attend flying school, but he was transfixed by the image of those tiny machines in their looping and spinning and diving that he had seen—and described in detail to Basil—in Mühlenberg in 1912, and he was insistent upon becoming an aviator.

This was more torture than Basil could have imagined in the cellars of the Gestapo, but at last the conductor came through, shouting, "Paris, Montparnasse station, five minutes, end of the line."

"Oh, this has been such a delight," said the colonel. "Monsieur Piens, you are a fascinating conversationalist—" Basil had said perhaps five words in six hours. "—and it makes me happy to have a Frenchman as an actual friend, beyond all this messy stuff of politics and invasions and war and all that. If only more Germans and French could meet as we did, as friends, just think how much better off the world would be."

Basil came up with words six and seven: "Yes, indeed."

"But, as they say, all good things must come to an end."

"They must. Do you mind, Colonel, if I excuse myself for a bit? I need to use the loo and prefer the first class here to the *pissoirs* of the station."

"Understandable. In fact, I shall accompany you, *monsieur*, and—oh, perhaps not. I'll check my documents to make sure all is in order."

Thus, besides a blast of blessed silence, Basil earned himself some freedom to operate. During the colonel's recitation—it had come around to the years 1911 and 1912, vacation to Cap d'Antibes—it had occurred to him that the authentic M. Piens, being a clear collaborationist and seeking not to offend the Germans, might well have reported his documents lost and that word might, given the German expertise at counterintelligence, have reached Paris. Thus the Piens documents were suddenly explosive and would land him either in Dachau or before the wall.

He wobbled wretchedly up the length of the car—thank God here in first class the seats were not contained as in the cramped little compartments of second class!—and made his way to the loo. As he went he examined the prospective marks: mostly German officers off for a weekend of debauchery far from their garrison posts, but at least three French businessmen of proper decorum sat among them, stiff, frightened of the Germans and yet obligated by something or other to be there. Only one was anywhere near Basil's age, but he had to deal with things as they were.

He reached the loo, locked himself inside, and quickly removed his M. Piens documents and buried them in the wastebasket among repugnant wads of tissue. A more cautious course would have been to tear them up and dispose of them via the toilet, but he didn't have time for caution. Then he wet his face, ran his fingers through his hair, wiped his face off, and left the loo.

Fourth on the right. Man in suit, rather blasé face, impatient. Otherwise, the car was stirring to activity as the occupants set about readying for whatever security ordeal lay ahead. The war—it was such an inconvenience.

As he worked his way down the aisle, Basil pretended to find the footing awkward against the sway of the train on the tracks, twice almost stumbling. Then he reached the fourth seat on the right, willed his knees to buckle, and, with a squeal of panic, let himself tumble awkwardly, catching himself with his left hand upon the shoulder of the man beneath, yet still tumbling further, awkwardly, the whole thing seemingly an accident as one out-of-control body crashed into the other, in-control body.

"Oh, excuse me," he said, "excuse, excuse, I am so sorry!"

The other man was so annoyed that he didn't notice the deft stab by which Basil penetrated his jacket and plucked his documents free, especially since the pressure on his left shoulder was so aggressive that it precluded notice of the far subtler stratagem of the pick reaching the brain.

Basil righted himself. "So sorry, so sorry!"

"Bah, you should be more careful," said the mark.

"I will try, sir," said Basil, turning to see the colonel three feet from him in the aisle, having witnessed the whole drama from an advantageous position.

Macht requested a squad of *feldpolizei* as backup, set up a choke point at the gate from the platform into the station's vast, domed central space, and waited for the train to rumble into sight. Instead, alas, what rumbled into sight was his nemesis, SS Hauptsturmführer Boch, a toadlike Nazi true believer of preening ambition who went everywhere in his black dress uniform.

"Dammit again, Macht," he exploded, spewing his excited saliva everywhere. "You know by protocol you must inform me of any arrest activities."

"Herr Hauptsturmführer, if you check your orderly's message basket, you will learn that at ten thirty P.M. I called and left notification of possible arrest. I cannot be responsible for your orderly's efficiency in relaying that information to you."

"Calculated to miss me, because of course I was doing my duty supervising an *aktion* against Jews and not sitting around my office drinking coffee and smoking."

"Again, I cannot be responsible for your schedule, Herr Hauptsturmführer." Of course Macht had an informer in Boch's office, so he knew exactly where the SS man was at all times. He knew that Boch was on one of his Jew-hunting trips; his only miscalculation was that Boch, who was generally unsuccessful at such enterprises, had gotten back earlier than anticipated. And of course Boch was always unsuccessful because Macht always informed the Jews of the coming raid.

"Whatever, it is of no consequence," said Boch. Though both men were technically of the same rank, captains, the SS clearly enjoyed Der Führer's confidence while the Abwehr did not, and so its members presumed authority in any encounter. "Brief me, please, and I will take charge of the situation."

"My men are in place, and disturbing my setup would not be efficient. If an arrest is made, I will certainly give the SS credit for its participation."

"What are we doing here?"

"There was aviation activity near Bricquebec, outside Cherbourg. Single-engine monoplane suddenly veering to parachute altitude. It suggested a British agent visit. Then the documents of a man in Bricquebec, including travel authorization, were stolen. If a British agent were in Bricquebec, his obvious goal would be Paris, and the most direct method would be by rail, so we are intercepting the Cherbourg–Paris night train in hopes of arresting a man bearing the papers of one Auguste M. Piens, restaurateur, hotel owner, and well-known ally of the Reich, here in Paris."

"An English agent!" Boch's eyes lit up. This was treasure. This was a medal. This was a promotion. He saw himself now as Obersturmbann-nführer Boch. The little fatty all the muscular boys had called Gretel and whose underdrawers they tied in knots, an Obersturmbannführer! That would show them!

"If an apprehension is made, the prisoner is to be turned over to the SS for interrogation. I will go to Berlin if I have to on this one, Macht. If you stand in the way of SS imperatives, you know the consequences."

The consequence: *"Russian tanks at 300! Load shells. Prepare to fire." "Sir, I can't see them. The snow is blinding, my fingers are numb from the cold, and the sight is frozen!"*

Even though he had witnessed the brazen theft, the colonel said nothing and responded in no way. His mind was evidently so locked in the beautiful year 1912 and the enchantment of his eventual first solo flight that he was incapable of processing new information. The crime he had just seen had nothing whatsoever to do with the wonderful French friend who had been so fascinated by his tale and whose eyes radiated such utter respect, even hero worship; it could not be fitted into any pattern and was thus tempo-rarily disregarded for other pleasures, such as, still ahead, a narration of the colonel's adventures in the Great War, the time he had actually shaken hands with the great Richthofen, and his own flight-ending crash—left arm permanently disabled. Luckily, his tail in tatters, he had made it back to his own lines before going down hard early in '18. It was one of his favorite stories.

He simply nodded politely at the Frenchman, who nodded back as if he hadn't a care in the world. In time the train pulled into the station, issuing groans and hisses of steam, vibrating heavily as it rolled to a stop.

"Ah, Paris," said the colonel. "Between you and me, M. Piens, I so prefer it to Berlin. And so especially does my wife. She is looking forward to this little weekend jaunt."

They disembarked in orderly fashion, Germans and Frenchmen com-bined, but discovered on the platform that some kind of security problem lay ahead, at the gate into the station, as soldiers and SS men with machine pistols stood along the platform, smoking but eyeing the passengers carefully. Then the security people screamed out that Germans would go to the left, French to the right, and on the right a few dour-looking men in fedoras and lumpy raincoats examined identification papers and travel authorizations. The Germans merely had to flash leave papers, so that line moved much more quickly.

"Well, M. Piens, I leave you here. Good luck with your sister's health in Paris. I hope she recovers."

"I'm sure she will, Colonel."

"Adieu."

He sped ahead and disappeared through the doors into the vast space. Basil's line inched its way ahead, and though the line was shorter, each arrival at the security point was treated with thorough Germanic ceremony, the papers examined carefully, the comparisons to the photographs made slowly, any bags or luggage searched. It seemed to take forever.

What could he do? At this point it would be impossible to slip away, disappear down the tracks, and get to the city over a fence; the Germans had thrown too many security troops around for that. Nor could he hope to roll under the train; the platform was too close to it, and there was no room to squeeze through.

Basil saw an evil finish: they'd see by the document that his face did not resemble the photograph, ask him a question or two, and learn that he had not even seen the document and had no idea whose papers he carried. The body search would come next, the pistol and the camera would give him away, and it was off to the torture cellar. The L-pill was his only alternative, but could he get to it fast enough?

At the same time, the narrowing of prospects was in some way a relief. No decisions needed to be made. All he had to do was brazen it out with a haughty attitude, beaming confidence, and it would be all right.

Macht watched the line while Abel examined papers and checked faces. Boch meanwhile provided theatrical atmosphere by posing heroically in his black leather trench coat, the SS skull on his black cap catching the light and reflecting impulses of power and control from above his chubby little face.

Eight. Seven. Six. Five.

Finally before them was a well-built chap of light complexion who seemed like some sort of athlete. He could not be a secret agent because he was too charismatic. All eyes would always turn to him, and he seemed accustomed to attention. He could be English, indeed, because he was a sort called "ginger." But the French had a considerable amount of genetic material for the hue as well, so the hair and the piercing eyes communicated less than the Aryan stereotypes seemed to proclaim.

"Good evening, M. Vercois," said Abel in French as he looked at the papers and then at the face, "and what brings you to Paris?"

"A woman, Herr Leutnant. An old story. No surprises."

"May I ask why you are not in a prisoner-of-war camp? You seem military."

"Sir, I am a contractor. My firm, M. Vercois et Fils—I am the son, by the way—has contracted to do much cement work on the coastline. We are building an impregnable wall for the Reich."

"Yes, yes," said Abel in a policeman's tired voice, indicating that he had heard all the French collaborationist sucking-up he needed to for the day. "Now do you mind, please, turning to the left so that I can get a good profile view. I must say, this is a terrible photograph of you."

"I take a bad photograph, sir. I have this trouble frequently, but if you hold the light above the photo, it will resolve itself. The photographer made too much of my nose."

Abel checked.

It still did not quite make sense. He turned to Macht.

"See if this photo matches, Herr Hauptmann. Maybe it's the light, but—"

At that moment, from the line two places behind M. Vercois, a man suddenly broke and ran crazily down the platform.

"That's him!" screamed Boch. "Stop that man, goddammit, stop that man!"

The drama played out quickly. The man ran and the Germans were disciplined enough not to shoot him, but instead, like football athletes, moved to block him. He tried to break this way, then that, but soon a younger, stronger, faster Untersharführer had him, another reached the melee and tangled him up from behind, and then two more, and the whole scrum went down in a blizzard of arms and legs.

"Someone stole my papers!" the man cried. "My papers are missing, I am innocent. Heil Hitler. I am innocent. Someone stole my papers."

"Got him," screamed Boch. "Got him!" and ran quickly to the melee to take command of the British agent.

"Go on," said Abel to M. Vercois as he and Macht went themselves to the incident.

His face blank, Basil entered the main station as whistles sounded and security troops from everywhere ran to Gate No. 4, from which he had just emerged. No one paid him any attention as he turned sideways to let the heavily armed Germans swarm past him. In the distance German sirens sounded, that strange two-note *caw-CAW* that sounded like a crippled crow, as yet more troops poured to the site.

Basil knew he didn't have much time. Someone smart among the Germans would understand quickly enough what had happened and would order a quick search of the train, where the M. Piens documents would be found in the first-class loo, and they'd know what had transpired. Then they'd throw a cordon around the station, call in more troops, and do a very careful examination of the horde, person by person, looking for a man with the papers of poor M. Vercois, currently undergoing interrogation by SS boot.

He walked swiftly to the front door, though the going was tough. Too late. Already the *feldpolizei* had commanded the cabs to leave and had halted buses. More German troops poured from trucks to seal off the area; more German staff cars arrived. The stairs to the Métro were all blocked by armed men.

He turned as if to walk back, meanwhile hunting for other ways out.

"Monsieur Piens, Monsieur Piens," came a call. He turned and saw the Luftwaffe colonel waving at him.

"Come along, I'll drop you. No need to get hung up in this unfortunate incident."

He ran to and entered the cab, knowing full well that his price of survival would be a trip back to the years 1912 through 1918. It almost wasn't worth it.

A FEW DAYS EARLIER (CONT'D.)

"Promote him!" said Basil. "The games you play. I swear I cannot keep up with them. The man's a traitor. He should be arrested and shot."

But his anguish moved no one on the panel that sat before him in the prime minister's murky staff room.

"Basil, so it should be with men of action, but you posit a world where things are clear and simple," said Sir Colin. "Such a planet does not exist. On this one, the real one, direct action is almost always impossible. Thus one must move on the oblique, making concessions and allowances all the way, never giving up too much for too little, tracking reverberations and rebounds, keeping the upper lip as stiff as if embalmed in concrete. Thus we leave small creatures such as our wretch of a Cambridge librarian alone in hopes of influencing someone vastly more powerful. Professor, perhaps you could put Basil in the picture so he understands what it is we are trying to do, and why it is so bloody important."

"It's called Operation Citadel," said Professor Turing. "The German staff has been working on it for some time now. Even though we would like to think that the mess they engineered on themselves at Stalingrad ended it for them, that is mere wishful dreaming. They are wounded but still immensely powerful."

"Professor, you speak as if you had a seat in the OKW general officers' mess."

"In a sense he does. The professor mentioned the little machines he builds, how they are able to try millions of possibilities and come up with solutions to the German code combinations and produce reasonable decryptions. Thus we have indeed been able to read Jerry's mail. Frankly, I know far more about German plans than about what is happening two doors down in my own agency, what the Americans are doing, or who the Russians have sent to Cambridge. But it's a gift that must be used sagely. If it's used sloppily, it will give up the game and Jerry will change everything. So we just use a bit of it now and then. This is one of those nows or thens. Go on, Professor."

"I defer to a strategic authority."

"General Cavendish?"

Cavendish, the army general, had a face that showed emotions from A all the way to A–. It was a mask of meat shaped in an oval and built bluntly around two ball bearings, empty of light, wisdom, empathy, or kindness, registering only force. He had about a pound of nose in the center of it and a pound of medals on his tunic.

"Operation Citadel," he delivered as rote fact, not interpretation, "is envisioned as the Götterdämmarung of the war in the East, the last titanic breakthrough that will destroy the Russian warmaking effort and bring the Soviets to the German table, hats in hand. At the very least, if it's successful, as most think it will be, it'll prolong the war by another year or two. We had hoped to see the fighting stop in 1945; now it may last well into 1947, and many more millions of men may die, and I should point out that a good number of those additional millions will be German. So we are trying to win—yes, indeed—but we are trying to do so swiftly, so that the dying can stop. That is what is at stake, you see."

"And that is why you cannot crush this little Cambridge rat's ass under a lorry. All right, I see that, I suppose, annoyed at it though I remain."

"Citadel, slated for May, probably cannot happen until July or August, given the logistics. It is to take place in southwest Russia, several hundred miles to the west of Stalingrad. At that point, around a city called Kursk, the Russians find themselves with a bulge in their lines—a salient, if you will. Secretly the Germans have begun massing matériel both above and beneath the bulge. When they believe they have overwhelming superiority, they will strike. They will drive north from below and south from above, behind walls of Tigers, flocks of Stukas, and thousands of artillery pieces. The infantry will advance behind the tanks. When the encirclement is complete, they will turn and kill the 300,000 men in the center and destroy the 50,000 tanks. The morale of the Red Army will be shattered, the losses so overwhelming that all the American aid in the world cannot keep up with it, and the Russians will fall back, back, back to the Urals. Leningrad will fall, then Moscow. The war will go on and on and on."

"I'm no genius," said Basil, "but even I can figure it out. You must tell Stalin. Tell him to fortify and resupply that bulge. Then when the Germans attack, they will fail, and it is they who will be on the run, the war will end in 1945, and those millions of lives will have been saved. Plus I can then drink myself to death uninterrupted, as I desire."

"Again, sir," said the admiral, who was turning out to be Basil's most ardent admirer, "he has seen the gist of it straight through."

"There is only one thing, Basil," said Sir Colin. "We have told Stalin. He doesn't believe us."

THE THIRD DAY

"Jasta 3 at Vraignes. Late 1916," said Macht. "Albatros, a barge to fly."

"He was an ace," said Abel. "Drop a hat and he'll tell you about it."

"Old comrade," said Oberst Gunther Scholl, "yes. I was Jasta 7 at Roulers. That was in 1917. God, so long ago."

"Old chaps," said Abel, "now the nostalgia is finished, so perhaps we can get on with our real task, which is staying out of Russia."

"Walter will never go to Russia," said Macht. "Family connections. He'll stay in Paris, and when the Americans come, he'll join up with them. He'll finish the war a lieutenant-colonel in the American army. But he does have a point."

"Didi, that's the first compliment you ever gave me. If only you meant it, but one can't have everything."

"So let's go through this again, Herr Oberst," said Macht to Colonel Scholl. "Walter reminds us that there's a very annoyed SS officer stomping around out there and he would like to send you to the Russian front. He would also like to send all of us to the Russian front, except Walter. So it is now imperative that we catch the fellow you sat next to for six hours, and you must do better at remembering."

The hour was late, or early, depending. Oberst Scholl had imagined himself dancing the night away at Maxim's with Hilda, then retiring to a dawn of love at the Ritz. Instead he was in a dingy room on the rue Guy de Maupassant, being grilled by gumshoes from the slums of Germany in an atmosphere seething with desperation, sour smoke, and cold coffee.

"Hauptmann Macht, believe me, I wish to avoid the Russian front at all costs. Bricquebec is no prize, and command of a night fighter squadron does not suggest, I realize, that I am expected to do big things in the Luftwaffe. But I am happy to fight my war there and surrender when the Americans arrive. I have told you everything."

"This I do not understand," said Leutnant Abel. "You had previously met Monsieur Piens and you thought this fellow was he. Yet the photography shows a face quite different from the one I saw at the Montparnasse station."

"Still, they are close," explained the colonel somewhat testily. "I had met Piens at a reception put together by the Vichy mayor of Bricquebec, between senior German officers and prominent, sympathetic businessmen. This fellow owned two restaurants and a hotel, was a power behind the throne, so to speak, and we had a brief but pleasant conversation. I cannot say I memorized his face, as why would I? When I got to the station, I glanced at the registration of French travelers and saw Piens's name and thus looked for him. I suppose I could say it was my duty to amuse our French sympathizers, but the truth is, I thought I could charm my way into a significant discount at his restaurants or pick up a bottle of wine as a gift. That is why I looked for him. He did seem different, but I ascribed that to the fact that he now had no moustache. I teased him about it and he gave me a story about his wife's dry skin."

The two policemen waited for more, but there wasn't any "more."

"I tell you, he spoke French perfectly, no trace of an accent, and was utterly calm and collected. In fact, that probably was a giveaway I missed. Most French are nervous in German presence, but this fellow was quite wonderful."

"What did you talk about for six hours?"

"I run on about myself, I know. And so, with a captive audience, that is what I did. My wife kicks me when I do so inappropriately, but unfortunately she was not there."

"So he knows all about you but we know nothing about him."

"That is so," said the Oberst. "Unfortunately."

"I hope you speak Russian as well as French," said Abel. "Because I have to write a report, and I'm certainly not going to put the blame on myself."

"All right," said Scholl. "Here is one little present. Small, I know, but perhaps just enough to keep me out of a Stuka cockpit."

"We're all ears."

"As I have told you, many times, he rode in the cab to the Ritz, and when we arrived I left and he stayed in the cab. I don't know where he took it. But I do remember the cabbie's name. They must display their licenses on the dashboard. It was Philippe Armoire. Does that help?"

It did.

That afternoon Macht stood before a squad room filled with about fifty men, a third his own, a third from Feldpolizei Battalion 11, and a third from Boch's SS detachment, all in plain clothes. Along with Abel, the *feldpolizei* sergeant, and Hauptsturmführer Boch, he sat at the front of the room. Behind was a large map of Paris. Even Boch had dressed down for the occasion, though to him "down" was a bespoke pin-striped, double-breasted black suit.

"All right," he said. "Long night ahead, boys, best get used to it now. We think we have a British agent hiding somewhere here," and he pointed at the fifth arrondissement, the Left Bank, the absolute heart of cultural and intellectual Paris. "That is the area where a cabdriver left him early this morning, and I believe Hauptsturmführer Boch's interrogators can speak to the truthfulness of the cabdriver."

Boch nodded, knowing that his interrogation techniques were not widely approved of.

"The Louvre and Notre Dame are right across the river, the Institut de France dominates the skyline on this side, and on the hundreds of streets are small hotels and restaurants, cafés, various retail outlets, apartment buildings, and so forth and so on. It is a catacomb of possibilities, entirely too immense for a dragnet or a mass cordon and search effort.

"Instead, each of you will patrol a block or so. You are on the lookout for a man of medium height, reddish to brownish hair, squarish face. More recognizably, he is a man of what one might call charisma. Not beauty per se, but a kind of inner glow that attracts people to him, allowing him to manipulate them. He speaks French perfectly, possibly German as well. He may be in any wardrobe, from shabby French clerk to priest, even to a woman's dress. If confronted he will offer well-thought-out words, be charming, agreeable, and slippery. His papers don't mean much. He seems to have a sneak thief's skills at picking pockets, so he may have traded off several identities by the time you get to him. The best tip I can give you is, if you see a man and think what a great friend he'd be, he's probably the spy. His charm is his armor and his principle weapon. He is very clever, very dedicated, very intent on his mission. Probably armed and dangerous as well, but please be forewarned. Taken alive, he will be a treasure trove. Dead, he's just another Brit body."

"Sir, are we to check hotels for new registrations?"

"No. Uniformed officers have that task. This fellow, however, is way too clever for that. He'll go to ground in some anonymous way, and we'll never find him by knocking on hotel room doors. Our best chance is when he is out on the street. Tomorrow will be better, as a courier is bringing the real Monsieur Piens's photo up from Bricquebec and our artist will remove the moustache and thin the face, so we should have a fair likeness. At the same time, I and all my detectives will work our phone contacts and listen for any gossip, rumors, and reports of minor incidents that might reveal the fellow's presence. We will have radio cars stationed every few blocks, so you can run to them and reach us if necessary and thus we can get reinforcements to you quickly if that need develops. We can do no more. We are the cat, he is the mouse. He must come out for his cheese."

"If I may speak," said Hauptsturmführer Boch. Who could stop him?

And thus he delivered a thirty-minute tirade that seemed modeled after Hitler's speech at Nuremberg, full of threats and exotic metaphors and fueled by pulsing anger at the world for its injustices, perhaps mainly in not recognizing the genius of Boch, all of it well punctuated by the regrettable fact that those who gave him evidence of shirking or laziness could easily end up on that cold antitank gun in Russia, facing the Mongol hordes.

It was not well received.

Of course Basil was too foxy to bumble into a hotel. Instead, his first act on being deposited on the Left Bank well after midnight was to retreat to the alleyways of more prosperous blocks and look for padlocked doors to the garages. It was his belief that if a garage was padlocked, it meant the owners of the house had fled for more hospitable climes and he could safely use such a place for his hideout. He did this rather easily, picking the padlock and slipping into a large vault of a room occupied by a Rolls-Royce Phantom on blocks, clear evidence that its wealthy owners were now rusticating safely in Beverly Hills in the United States. His first order of the day was rest: he had, after all, been going full steam for forty-eight hours now, including his parachute arrival in France, his exhausting ordeal by Luftwaffe Oberst on the long train ride, and his miraculous escape from Montparnasse station, also courtesy of the Luftwaffe Oberst, whose name he did not even know.

The limousine was open; he crawled into a back seat that had once sustained the arsses of a prominent industrialist, a department store magnate, the owner of a chain of jewelry stores, a famous whore, whatever, and quickly went to sleep.

He awoke at three in the afternoon and had a moment of confusion. Where was he? In a car? Why? Oh, yes, on a mission. What was that mission? Funny, it seemed so important at one time; now he could not remember it. Oh, yes, *The Path to Jesus*.

There seemed no point in going out by day, so he examined the house from the garage, determined that it was deserted, and slipped into it, entering easily enough. It was a ghostly museum of the aristocratic du Clercs, who'd left their furniture under sheets and their larder empty, and by now dust had accumulated everywhere. He amused himself with a little prowl, not bothering to go through drawers, for he was a thief only in the name of duty. He did borrow a book from the library and spent the evening in the cellar, reading it by candlelight. It was Tolstoy's great *War and Peace*, and he got more than three hundred pages into it.

He awakened before dawn. He tried his best to make himself presentable and slipped out, locking the padlock behind himself. The early-morning streets were surprisingly well populated, as workingmen hastened to a first meal and then a day at the job. He melded easily, another anonymous French clerk with a day-old scrub of beard and a somewhat dowdy dark suit under a dark overcoat. He found a café and had a *café au lait* and a large piece of buttered toast, sitting in the rear as the place filled up.

He listened to the gossip and quickly picked up that *les boches* were everywhere today; no one had seen them out in such force before. It seemed that most were plainclothesmen, simply standing around or walking a small patrol beat. They preformed no services other than looking at people, so it was clear that they were on some sort of stakeout duty. Perhaps a prominent Resistance figure—this brought a laugh always, as most regarded the Resistance as a joke—had come in for a meet-up with Sartre at Les Deux Magots, or a British agent was here to assassinate Dietrich von Choltitz, the garrison commander of Paris and a man as objectionable as a summer moth. But everyone knew the British weren't big on killing, as it was the Czechs who'd bumped off Heydrich.

After a few hours Basil went for his reconnaissance. He saw them almost immediately, chalkfaced men wearing either the tight faces of hunters or the slack faces of time-servers. Of the two, he chose the latter, since a loafer was less apt to pay attention and wouldn't notice things and further-more would go off duty exactly when his shift was over.

The man stood, shifting weight from one foot to the other, blowing into his hands to keep them warm, occasionally rubbing the small of his back, where strain accumulated when he who does not stand or move much suddenly has to stand and move.

It was time to hunt the hunters.

A FEW DAYS AGO (CONT'D.)

"It's the trust issue again," said General Cavendish, in a tone suggesting he was addressing the scullery mice. "In his rat-infested brain, the fellow still believes the war might be a trap, meant to destroy Russia and Communism. He thinks that we may be feeding him information on Operation Citadel, about this attack on the Kursk salient, as a way of manipulating him into overcommitting to defending against that attack. He wastes men, equipment, and treasure building up the Kursk bulge on our say-so, then, come July, Hitler's panzer troops make a feint in that direction but drive en masse into some area of the line that has been weakened because all the troops have been moved down to the Kursk bulge. Hitler breaks through, envelops, takes, and razes Moscow, then pivots, heavy with triumph, to deal with the moribund Kursk salient. Why, he needn't even attack. He can do to those men what was done to Paulus's Sixth Army at Stalingrad, simply shell and starve them into submission. At that point the war in the East is over and Communism is destroyed."

"I see what where you're going with this, gentlemen," said Basil. "We must convince Stalin that we are telling the truth. We must verify the authenticity of Operation Citadel, so that he believes in it and acts accordingly. If he doesn't, Operation Citadel will succeed, those 300,000 men will die, and the war will continue for another year or two. The soldiers now say 'Home alive in '45,' but the bloody reality will be 'Dead in heaven in '47.' Yet more millions will die. We cannot allow that to happen."

"Do you see it yet, Basil?" asked Sir Colin. "It would be so helpful if you saw it for yourself, if you realized what has to be done, that no matter how long the shot, we have to play it. Because yours is the part that depends on faith. Only faith will get you through the ordeal that lies ahead."

"Yes, I do see it," said Basil. "The only way of verifying the Operation Citadel intercepts is to have them discovered and transmitted quite innocent of any other influence by Stalin's most secret and trusted spy. That fellow has to come across them and get them to Moscow. And the route by which he encounters them must be unimpeachable, as it will be vigorously counterchecked by the NKVD. That is why the traitorous librarian at Cambridge cannot be arrested, and that is why no tricky subterfuge of cracking into the Cambridge rare books vault can be employed. The sanctity of the Cambridge copy of *The Path to Jesus* must be protected at all costs."

"Exactly, Basil. Very good."

"You have to get these intercepts to this spy. However—here's the rub—you have no idea who or where he is."

"We know where he is," said the admiral. "The trouble is, it's not a small place. It's a good-sized village, in fact, or an industrial complex."

"This Bletchley, whose name I was not supposed to hear—is that it?"

"Professor, perhaps you could explain it to Captain St. Florian."

"Of course. Captain, as I spilled the beans before, I'll now spill some more. We have Jerry solved to a remarkable degree, via higher mathematical concepts as guidelines for the construction of electronic 'thinking machines,' if you will . . ."

"Turing engines, they're called," said Sir Colin. "Basil, you are honored by hearing this from the prime mover himself. It's like a chat with God."

"Please continue, your Supreme Beingness," said Basil.

Embarrassed, the professor seemed to lose his place, then came back to it. ". . . thinking machines that are able to function at high speed, test possibilities, and locate patterns which cut down on the possible combinations. I'll spare you details, but it's quite remarkable. However, one result of this breakthrough is that our location—Bletchley Park, about fifty kilometers out of London, an old Victorian estate in perfectly abominable taste—has grown from a small team operation into a huge bureaucracy. It now employs over eight hundred people, gathered from all over the empire for their specific skills in extremely arcane subject matters.

"As a consequence, we have many streams of communication, many units, many subunits, many sub-subunits, many huts, temporary quarters, recreational facilities, kitchens, bathrooms, a complex social life complete with gossip, romance, scandal, treachery, and remorse, our own slang, our own customs. Of course the inhabitants are all very smart, and when they're not working they get bored and to amuse themselves conspire, plot, criticize, repeat, twist, engineer coups and countercoups, all of which further muddies the water and makes any sort of objective 'truth' impossible to verify. One of the people in this monstrous human beehive, we know for sure from the Finland code, reports to Joseph Stalin. We have no idea who it is—it could be an Oxbridge genius, a lance corporal with Enfield standing guard, a lady mathematician from Australia, a telegraph operator, a translator from the old country, an American liaison, a Polish consultant, and on and on. I suppose it could even be me. All, of course, were vetted beforehand by our intelligence service, but he or she slipped by.

"So now it is important that we find him. It is in fact mandatory that we find him. A big security shakeout is no answer at all. Time-consuming, clumsy, prone to error, gossip, and resentment, as well as colossally interruptive and destructive to our actual task, but worst of all a clear indicator to the NKVD that we know they've placed a bug in our rug. If that is the conclusion they reach, then Stalin will not trust us, will not fortify Kursk, et cetera, et cetera."

"So breaking the book code is the key."

"It is. I will leave it to historians to ponder the irony that in the most successful and sophisticated cryptoanalytic operation in history, a simple book code stands between us and a desperately important goal. We are too busy for irony."

Basil responded, "The problem then refines itself more acutely: it is that you have no practical access to the book upon which the code that contains the name for this chap's new handler is based."

"That is it, in a nutshell," said Professor Turing. "A sticky wicket, I must say. But where on earth do I fit in? I don't see that there's any room for a boy of my most peculiar expertise. Am I supposed to—well, I cannot even conjure an end to that sentence. You have me . . ." He paused.

"I think he's got it," said the admiral.

"Of course I have," said Basil. "There has to be another book."

THE FOURTH DAY

It had to happen sooner or later, and it happened sooner. The first man caught up in the Abwehr observe-and-apprehend operation was Maurice Chevalier.

The French star was in transit between mistresses on the Left Bank, and who could possibly blame Unterscharführer Ganz for blowing the whistle on him? He was tall and gloriously handsome, he was exquisitely dressed, and he radiated such warmth, grace, confidence, and glamour that to see him was to love him. The sergeant was merely acting on the guidance given the squad by Macht: if you want him to be your best friend, that's probably the spy. The sergeant had no idea who Chevalier was; he thought he was doing his duty.

Naturally, the star was not amused. He threatened to call his good friend Herr General von Choltitz and have them *all* sent to the Russian front, and it's a good thing Macht still had some diplomatic skills left, for he managed to talk the elegant man out of that course of action by supplying endless amounts of unction and flattery. His dignity ruffled, the star left huffily and went on his way, at least secure in the knowledge that in twenty minutes he would be making love to a beautiful woman and these German peasants would still be standing around out in the cold, waiting for something to happen. By eight P.M. he had forgotten entirely about it, and on his account no German boy serving in Paris would find himself on that frozen antitank gun.

As for SS Hauptsturmführer Otto Boch, that was another story. He was a man of action. He was not one for the patience, the persistence, the professionalism of police work. He preferred more direct approaches, such as hanging around the Left Bank hotel where Macht had set up his headquarters and threatening in a loud voice to send them all to Russia if they didn't produce the enemy agent quickly. Thus the Abwehr men took to calling him the Black Pigeon behind his back, for the name took into account his pigeonlike strut, breast puffed, dignity formidable, self-importance manifest, while accomplishing nothing tangible whatsoever except to leave small piles of shit wherever he went.

His SS staff got with the drill, as they were, fanatics or not, at least security professionals, and it seemed that even after a bit they were calling him the Black Pigeon as well. But on the whole, they, the Abwehr fellows, and the 11th Battalion *feldpolizei* people meshed well and produced such results as could be produced. The possibles they netted were not so spectacular as a regal movie star, but the theory behind each apprehension was sound. There were a number of handsome men, some gangsters, some actors, one poet, and a homosexual hairdresser. Macht and Abel raised their eyebrows at the homosexual hairdresser, for it occurred to them that the officer who had whistled him down had perhaps revealed more about himself than he meant to.

Eventually the first shift went off and the second came on. These actually were the sharper fellows, as Macht assumed that the British agent would be more likely to conduct his business during the evening, whatever that business might be. And indeed the results were, if not better, more responsible. In fact one man brought in revealed himself to be not who he claimed he was, and that he was a wanted jewel thief who still plied his trade, Occupation or no. It took a shrewd eye to detect the vitality and fearlessness this fellow wore behind shoddy clothes and darkened teeth and an old man's hobble, but the SS man who made the catch turned out to be highly regarded in his own unit. Macht made a note to get him close to any potential arrest situations, as he wanted his best people near the action. He also threatened to turn the jewel thief over to the French police but instead recruited him as an informant for future use. He was not one for wasting much.

Another arrestee was clearly a Jew, even if his papers said otherwise, even if he had no possible connection to British Intelligence. Macht examined the papers carefully, showed them to a bunco expert on the team, and confirmed that they were fraudulent. He took the fellow aside and said, "Look, friend, if I were you I'd get myself and my family out of Paris as quickly as possible. If I can see through your charade in five seconds, sooner or later the SS will too, and it's off to the East for all of you. These bastards have the upper hand for now, so my best advice to you is, no matter what it costs, get the hell out of Paris. Get out of France. No matter what you think, you cannot wait them out, because the one thing they absolutely will do before they're either chased out of town or put against a wall and shot is get all the Jews. That's what they live for. That's what they'll die for, if it comes to that. Consider this fair warning and probably the only one you'll get."

Maybe the man would believe him, maybe not. There was nothing he could do about it. He got back to the telephone, as, along with his other detectives, he spent most of the time monitoring his various snitches, informants, sympathizers, and sycophants, of course turning up nothing. If the agent was on the Left Bank, he hadn't moved an inch.

And he hadn't. Basil sat on the park bench the entire day, obliquely watching the German across the street. He got so he knew the man well: his gait (bad left hip, Great War wound?); his policeman's patience at standing in one place for an hour, then moving two meters and standing in that place for an hour; his stubbornness at never, ever abandoning his post, except once, at three P.M., for a brief trip to the pissoir, during which he kept his eyes open and examined each passerby through the gap at the pissoir's eye level. He didn't miss a thing—that is, except for the dowdy Frenchman observing him from ninety meters away, over an array of daily newspapers.

Twice, unmarked Citroëns came by and the officer gave a report to two other men, also in civilian clothes, on the previous few hours. They nodded, took careful records, and then hastened off. It was a long day until seven P.M., a twelve-hour shift, when his replacement moseyed up.

There was no ceremony of changing the guard, just a cursory nod between them, and then the first policeman began to wander off.

Basil stayed with him, maintaining the same ninety-meter interval, noting that he stopped in a café for a cup of coffee and a sandwich, read the papers, and smoked, unaware that Basil had followed him in, placed himself at the bar, and also had a sandwich and a coffee.

Eventually the German got up, walked another six blocks down Boulevard Saint-Germain, turned down a narrower street called rue de Valor, and disappeared halfway down the first block into a rummy-looking hotel called Le Duval. Basil looked about, found a café, had a second coffee, smoked a Gauloise to blend in, joked with the bartender, was examined by a uniformed German policeman on a random check, showed papers identifying himself as Robert Fortier (picked freshly that morning), was checked off against a list (he was not on it, as perhaps M. Fortier had not yet noted his missing papers), and was then abandoned by the policeman for other possibilities.

At last he left and went back to rue de Valor, slipped down it, and very carefully approached the Hotel Duval. From outside it revealed nothing—a typical Baedeker two-star for commercial travelers, with no pretensions of gentility or class. It would be stark, clean, well run, and banal. Such places housed half the population every night in Europe, except for the past few years, when that half-the population had slept in bunkers, foxholes, or ruins. Nothing marked this place, which was exactly why whoever was running this show had chosen it. Another pro like himself, he guessed. It takes a professional to catch a professional, the saying goes.

He meekly entered as if confused, noting a few sour-looking individuals sitting in the lobby reading *Deutsche Allgemeine Zeitung* and smoking, and went to the desk, where he asked for directions to a hotel called Les Deux Gentilhommes and got them. It wasn't much, but it enabled him to make a quick check on the place, and he learned what he needed to know.

Behind the desk was a hallway, and down it Basil could see a larger room, a banquet hall or something, full of drowsy-looking men sitting around listlessly, while a few further back slept on sofas pushed in for just that purpose. It looked police.

That settled it. This was the German headquarters.

He moseyed out and knew he had one more stop before tomorrow. He had to examine his objective.

A FEW DAYS PREVIOUSLY (CONT'D.)

"Another book? Exactly yes and exactly no," said Sir Colin.

"How could there be a second original? By definition there can be only one original, or so it was taught when I was at university."

"It does seem like a conundrum, does it not?" said Sir Colin. "But indeed, we are dealing with a very rare case of a second original. Well, of sorts."

"Not sure I like the sound of that," said Basil. "Nor should you. It takes us to a certain awkwardness that, again, an ironist would find heartily amusing."

"You see," said Basil, "I am fond of irony, but only when applied to other chaps."

"Yes, it can sting, can it not?" said General Cavendish. "And I must say, this one stings quite exhaustively. It will cause historians many a chuckle when they write the secret history of the war in the twenty-first century after all the files are finally opened."

"But we get ahead of ourselves," said Sir Colin. "There's more tale to tell. And the sooner we tell it, the sooner the cocktail hour."

"Tell on, then, Sir Colin."

"It all turns on the fulcrum of folly and vanity known as the human heart, especially when basted in ambition, guilt, remorse, and greed. What a marvelous stew, all of it simmering within the head of the Reverend Mac-Burney. When last we left him, our God-fearing MacBurney had become a millionaire because his pamphlet *The Path to Jesus* had sold endlessly, bringing him a shilling a tot. As I said, he retired to a country estate and spent some years happily wenching and drinking in happy debauchery."

"As who would not?" asked Basil, though he doubted this lot would.

"Of course. But then in the year 1789, twenty-two years later, he was approached by a representative of the bishop of Gladney and asked to make a presentation to the Church. To commemorate his achievement, the thousands of souls he had shepherded safely upon the aforenamed path, the bishop wanted him appointed deacon at St. Blazefield's in Glasgow, the highest church rank a fellow like him could achieve. And Thomas wanted it badly. But the bishop wanted him to donate the original manuscript to the church, for eternal display in its ambulatory. Except Thomas had no idea where the original was and hadn't thought about it in years. So he sat down, practical Scot that he was, and from the pamphlet itself he back-engineered, so to speak, another 'original' manuscript in his own hand, a perfect facsimile, or as perfect as he could make it, even, one must assume, to the little crucifix doodles that so amused the Cambridge librarian. That was shipped to Glasgow, and that is why to this day Thomas MacBurney lounges in heaven, surrounded by seraphim and cherubim who sing his praises and throw petals where he walks."

"It was kind of God to provide us with the second copy," said Basil.

"Proof," said the admiral, "that He is on our side."

"Yes. The provenance of the first manuscript is well established; as I say, it has pencil marks to guide the printer in the print shop owner's hand. That is why it is so prized at Cambridge. The second was displayed for a century in Glasgow, but then the original St. Blazefield's was torn down for a newer, more imposing one in 1857, and the manuscript somehow disappeared. However, it was discovered in 1913 in Paris. Who knows by what mischief it ended up there? But to prevent action by the French police, the owner anonymously donated it to a cultural institution, in whose vaults it to this day resides."

"So I am to go and fetch it. Under the Nazis' noses?"

"Well, not exactly," said Sir Colin. "The manuscript itself must not be removed, as someone might notice and word might reach the Russians. What you must do is photograph certain pages using a Riga Minox. Those are what must be fetched."

"And when I fetch them, they can be relied upon to provide the key for the code and thus give up the name of the Russian spy at Bletchley Park, and thus you will be able to slip into his hands the German plans for Operation Citadel, and thus Stalin will fortify the Kursk salient, and thus the massive German summer offensive will have its back broken, and thus the boys will be home alive in '45 instead of dead in heaven in '47. Our boys, their boys, all boys."

"In theory," said Sir Colin Gubbins.

"Hmm, not sure I like 'in theory,'" said Basil.

"You will be flown in by Lysander, dispatched in the care of Resistance Group Philippe, which will handle logistics. They have not been alerted to the nature of the mission as yet, as the fewer who know, of course, the better. You will explain it to them, they will get you to Paris for recon and supply equipment, manpower, distraction, and other kinds of support, then get you back out for Lysander pickup, if everything goes well."

"And if it does not?"

"That is where your expertise will come in handy. In that case, it will be a maximum huggermugger sort of effort. I am sure you will prevail."

"I am not," said Basil. "It sounds awfully dodgy."

"And you know, of course, that you will be given an L-pill so that headful of secrets of yours will never fall in German hands."

"I will be certain to throw it away at the first chance," said Basil.

"There's the spirit, old man," said Sir Colin.

"And where am I headed?"

"Ah, yes. An address on the Quai de Conti, the Left Bank, near the Seine."

"Excellent," said Basil. "Only the Institut de France, the most profound and colossal assemblage of French cultural icons in the world, and the most heavily guarded."

"Known for its excellent library," said Sir Colin.

"It sounds like quite a pickle," said Basil.

"And you haven't even heard the bad part."

THE FOURTH DAY, NEAR MIDNIGHT

In the old days, and perhaps again after the war if von Choltitz didn't blow the place up, the Institut de France was one of the glories of the nation, emblazoned in the night under a rippling tricolor to express the high moral purpose of French culture. But in the war it, too, had to fall into line.

Thus the blazing lights no longer blazed and the cupola ruling over the many stately branches of the singularly complex building overlooking the Seine on the Quai de Conti, right at the toe of the Île de la Cité and directly across from the Louvre, in the sixth arrondissement, no longer ruled. One had to squint, as did Basil, to make it out, though helpfully a searchlight from some far-distant German antiaircraft battery would backlight it and at least accentuate its bulk and shape. The Germans had not painted it *feldgrau*, thank God, and so its white stone seemed to gleam in the night, at least in contrast to other French buildings in the environs. A slight rain fell; the cobblestones glistened; the whole thing had a cinematic look that Basil paid no attention to, as it did him no good at all and he was by no means a romantic.

Instead he saw the architectural tropes of the place, the brilliant façade of colonnades, the precision of the intersecting angles, the dramatically arrayed approaches to the broad steps of the grand entrance under the cupola, from which nexus one proceeded to its many divisions, housed each in a separate wing. The whole expressed the complexity, the difficulty, the arrogance, the insolence, the ego, the whole *je ne sais quoi* of the French: their smug, prosperous country, their easy treachery, their utter lack of conscience, their powerful sense of entitlement.

From his briefing, he knew that his particular goal was the Bibliothèque Mazarine, housed in the great marble edifice but a few hundred meters from the center. He slid that way, while close at hand the Seine lapped against its stone banks, the odd taxi or bicycle taxi hurtled down Quai de Conti, the searchlights crisscrossed the sky. Soon midnight, and curfew. But he had to see.

On its own the Mazarine was an imposing building, though without the columns. Instead it affected the French country palace look, with a cobblestone yard which in an earlier age had allowed for carriages but now was merely a car park. Two giant oak doors, guarding French propriety, kept interlopers out. At this moment it was locked up like a vault; tomorrow the doors would open and he would somehow make his penetration.

But how?

With Resistance help he could have mounted an elaborate ruse, spring himself to the upper floors while the guards tried to deal with the unruliness beneath. But he had chosen not to go that way. In the networks somebody always talked, somebody always whispered, and nothing was really a secret. The Resistance could get him close, but it could also earn him an appetizer of strychnine L-pill.

The other, safer possibility was to develop contacts in the French underworld and hire a professional thief to come in from below or above, via a back entrance, and somehow steal the booklet, then replace it the next day. But that took time, and there was no time.

In the end, he only confirmed what he already knew: there was but one way. It was as fragile as a Fabergé egg, at any time given to yield its counterfeit nature to anyone paying the slightest attention. Particularly with the Germans knowing something was up and at high alert, ready to flood the place with cops and thugs at any second. It would take nerve, a talent for the dramatic, and, most important, the right credentials.

A FEW DAYS PREVIOUSLY (FINI)

"Are you willing?" said Sir Colin. "Knowing all this, are you willing?"

"Sir, you send men to their death every day with less fastidiousness. You consign battalions to their slaughter without blinking an eye. The stricken gray ships turn to coffins and slide beneath the ocean with their hundreds; *c'est la guerre.* The airplanes explode into falling pyres and nobody sheds a tear. Everyone must do his bit, you say. And yet now, for me, on this, you're suddenly squeamish to an odd degree, telling me every danger and improbability and how low the odds of success are. I have to know why. It has a doomed feel to it. If I must die, so be it, but somebody wants nothing on his conscience."

"That is very true."

"Is this a secret you will not divulge?"

"I will divulge, and what's more, now is the time to divulge, before we all die of starvation or alcohol withdrawal symptoms."

"How very interesting."

"A man on this panel has the ear of the prime minister. He holds great power. It is he who insisted on this highly unusual approach, it is he who forces us to overbrief you and send you off with far too much classified information. Let him speak, then."

"General Sir Colin means me," said the professor. "Because of my code-breaking success, I find myself uniquely powerful. Mr. Churchill likes me, and wants me to have my way. That is why I sit on a panel with the barons of war, myself a humble professor, not even at Oxford or Cambridge but at Manchester."

"Professor, is this a moral quest? Do you seek forgiveness beforehand, should I die? It's really not necessary. I owe God a death, and he will take it when he sees fit. Many times over the years he has seen fit not to do so. Perhaps he's bored with me and wants me off the board. Perhaps he tires of my completely overblown legendary wit and sangfroid and realizes I'm just as scared as the next fellow, am a bully to boot, and that it ended on a rather beastly note with my father, a regret I shall always carry. So, Professor, you who have saved millions, if I go, it's on the chap upstairs, not you."

"Well spoken, Captain St. Florian, like the hero I already knew you to be. But that's not quite it. Another horror lies ahead and I must burden you with it, so I will be let alone enough by all those noisy screamers between my ears to do my work if the time comes."

"Please enlighten."

"You see, everyone thinks I'm a genius. Of course I am really a frail man of many weaknesses. I needn't elucidate. But I am terrified of one possibility. You should know it's there before you undertake."

"Go ahead."

"Let us say you prevail. At great cost, by great ordeal, blood, psychic energy, morale, whatever it takes from you. And perhaps other people die as well—a pilot, a Resistance worker, someone caught by a stray bullet, any of the routine whimsies of war."

"Yes."

"Suppose all that is true, you bring it back, you sit before me exhausted, spent, having been burned in the fire, you put it to me, the product of your hard labors, and *I cannot decode the damned thing.*"

"Sir, I—"

"*They* think I can, these barons of war. Put the tag 'genius' on a fellow and it solves all problems. However, there are no, and I do mean no, assurances that the pages you bring back will accord closely enough with the original to yield a meaningful answer."

"We've been through this a thousand times, Professor Turing," said the general. "You will be able, we believe, to handle this. We are quite confident in your ability and attribute your reluctance to a high-strung personality and a bit of stage fright, that's all. The variations cannot be that great, and your Turing engine or one of those things you call a bombe ought to be able to run down other possible solutions quickly and we will get what we need."

"I'm so happy the men who know nothing of this sort of work are so confident. But I had to face you, Captain St. Florian, with this truth. It may be for naught. It may be undoable, even by the great Turing. If that is the case, then I humbly request your forgiveness."

"Oh, bosh," said Basil. "If it turns out that the smartest man in England can't do it, it wasn't meant to be done. Don't give it a thought, Professor. I'll simply go off and have an inning, as best I know how, and if I get back, then you have your inning. What happens, then that's what happens. Now, please, gentleman, can we hasten? My arse feels as if Queen Victoria used it for needlepoint!"

ACTION THIS DAY

Of course one normally never went about in anything but bespoke. Just wasn't done. Basil's tailor was Steed-Aspell, of Davies & Son, 15 Jermyn Street, and Steed-Aspell ("Steedy" to his clients) was a student of Frederick Scholte, the Duke of Windsor's genius tailor, which meant he was a master of the English drape. His clothes hung with an almost scary brilliance, perfect. They never just crumpled. As gravity took them, they formed extraordinary shapes, presented new faces to the world, gave the sun a canvas for compositions playing light against dark, with gray working an uneasy region between, rather like the Sudetenland. Basil had at least three jackets for which he had been offered immense sums (Steed-Aspell was taking no new clients, though the war might eventually open up some room on his waiting list, if it hadn't already), and of course Basil merely smiled drily at the evocations of want, issued a brief but sincere look of commiseration, and moved onward, a lord in tweed, perhaps *the* lord of the tweeds.

Thus the suit he now wore was a severe disappointment. He had bought it in a secondhand shop, and *monsieur* had expressed great confidence that it was of premium quality, and yet its drape was all wrong, because of course the wool was all wrong. One didn't simply use *any* wool, as its provincial tailor believed. Thus it got itself into twists and rumples and couldn't get out, its creases blunted themselves in moments, and it had already popped a button. Its rise bagged, sagged, and gave up. It rather glowed in the sunlight. Buttoned, its two breasts encased him like a girdle; unbuttoned, it looked like he wore several flags of blue pinstripe about himself, ready to unfurl in the wind. He was certain his clubman would not let him enter if he tried.

And he wanted very much to look his best this morning. He was, after all, going to blow up something big with Germans inside.

"I tell you, we should be more severe," argued SS Hauptsturmführer Otto Boch. "These Paris bastards, they take us too lightly. In Poland we enacted laws and enforced them with blood and steel and incidents quickly trickled away to nothing. Every Pole knew that disobedience meant a polka at the end of a rope in the main square."

"Perhaps they were too enervated on lack of food to rebel," said Macht. "You see, you have a different objective. You are interested in public order and the thrill of public obedience. These seem to you necessary goals, which must be enforced for our quest to succeed. My goal is far more limited. I merely want to catch the British agent. To do so, I must isolate him against a calm background, almost a still life, and that way locate him. It's the system that will catch him, not a single guns-blazing raid. If you stir things up, Herr Hauptsturmführer, I guarantee you it will come to nothing. Please trust me on this. I have run manhunts, many times successfully."

Boch had no remonstrance, of course. He was not a professional like Macht and in fact before the war had been a salesman of vacuums, and not a very good one.

"We have observers everywhere," Macht continued. "We have a photograph of M. Piens, delicately altered so that it closely resembles the man that idiot Scholl sat next to, which should help our people enormously. We have good weather. The sun is shining, so our watchers won't hide themselves under shades or awnings to get out of the rain and thus cut down their visibility. The lack of rain also means our roving autos won't be searching through the slosh and squeal of wiper blades, again reducing what they see. We continue to monitor sources we have carefully been nurturing since we arrived. Our system will work. We will get a break today, I guarantee it."

The two sat at a table in the banquet room of the Hotel Duval, amid a batch of snoozing agents who were off shift. The stench of cigarette butts, squashed cigars, and tapped-out pipe tobacco shreds hung heavy in the room, as did the smell of cold coffee and unwashed bodies. But that was what happened on manhunts, as Macht knew and Boch did not. Now nothing could be done except wait for a break, then play that break carefully and . . .

"Hauptmann Macht?" It was his assistant, Abel.

"Yes?"

"Paris headquarters. Von Choltitz's people.

They want a briefing. They've sent a car."

"Oh, Christ," said Macht. But he knew this was what happened. Big politicos got involved, got worried, wanted credit, wanted to escape blame. No one anywhere in the world understood the principle that sometimes it was better not to be energetic and to leave things alone instead of wasting energy in a lot of showy ceremonial nonsense.

"I'll go," said Boch, who would never miss a chance to preen before superiors.

"Sorry, sir. They specified Hauptmann Macht."

"Christ," said Macht again, trying to remember where he'd left his trench coat.

A street up from the Hotel Duval, Basil found the exact thing he was looking for. It was a Citroën Traction Avant, black, and it had a large aerial projecting from it. It was clearly a radio car, one of those that the German man-hunter had placed strategically around the sixth arrondissement so that no watcher was far from being able to notify headquarters and get the troops out.

Helpfully, a café was available across the street, and so he sat at a table and ordered a coffee. He watched as, quite regularly, a new German watcher ambled by, leaned in, and reported that he had seen nothing. Well organized. They arrived every thirty minutes. Each man came once every two hours, so the walk over was a break from standing around. It enabled the commander to get new information to the troops in an orderly fashion, and it changed the vantage point of the watchers. At the same time, at the end of four hours, the car itself fired up and its two occupants made a quick tour of their men on the street corners. The point was to keep communications clear, keep the men engaged so they didn't go logy on duty, yet sacrifice nothing in the way of observation. Whoever was running this had done it before.

He also noted a new element. Somehow they had what appeared to be a photograph. They would look it over, pass it around, consult it frequently in all meetings. It couldn't be of him, so possibly it was a drawing. It meant he had to act today. As the photo or drawing circulated, more and more would learn his features and the chance of his being spotted would become greater by degrees. Today the image was a novelty and would not stick in the mind without constant refreshment, but by tomorrow all who had to know it would know it. The time was now. Action this day.

When he felt he had mastered the schedule and saw a clear break coming up in which nobody would report to the car for at least thirty minutes, he decided it was time to move. It was about three P.M. on a sunny, if chilly, Paris spring afternoon. The ancient city's so-familiar features were everywhere as he meandered across Boulevard Saint Germain under blue sky. There was a music in the traffic and in the rhythm of the pedestrians, the window shoppers, the pastry munchers, the café sitters, the endless parade of bicyclists, some pulling passengers in carts, some simply solo. The great city went about its business, Occupation or no, action this day or no.

He walked into an alley and reached over to fetch a wine bottle that he had placed there early this morning, while it was dark. It was, however, filled with kerosene drained from a ten-liter tin jug in the garage. Instead of a cork it had a plug of wadded cotton jammed into its throat, and fifteen centimeters of strip hung from the plug. It was a gasoline bomb, constructed exactly to SOE specification. He had never done it before, since he usually worked with Explosive 808, but there was no 808 to be found, so the kerosene, however many years old it was, would have to do. He wrapped the bottle in newspaper, tilted it to soak the wad with the fuel, and then set off jauntily.

This was the delicate part. It all turned on how observant the Germans were at close quarters, whether or not Parisians on the street noticed him, and if so, if they took some kind of action. He guessed they wouldn't; actually, he gambled that they wouldn't. The Parisians are a prudent species. Fortunately the Citroën was parked in an isolated space, open at both ends. He made no eye contact with its bored occupants, his last glance telling him that one leaned back, stretching, to keep from dozing, while the other was talking on a telephone unit wired into the radio console that occupied the small back seat. He felt that if he looked at them they might feel the pressure of his eyes, as those of predatory nature sometimes do, being weirdly sensitive to signs of aggression.

He approached on the oblique, keeping out of view of the rear window of the low-slung sedan, all the rage in 1935 but now ubiquitous in Paris. Its fuel tank was in the rear, which again made things convenient. In the last moment as he approached, he ducked down, wedged the bottle under the rear tire, pulled the paper away, lit his lighter, and lit the end of the strip of cloth. The whole thing took one second, and he moved away as if he'd done nothing.

It didn't explode. Instead, with a kind of airsucking gush, the bottle erupted and shattered, smearing a billow of orange-black flame into the atmosphere from beneath the car, and in the next second the gasoline tank also went, again without explosion as much as flare of incandescence a hundred meters high, bleaching the color from the beautiful old town and sending a cascade of heat radiating outward.

Neither German policeman was injured, except by means of stolen dignity, but each spilled crazily from his door, driven by the primal fear of flame encoded in the human race, one tripping, going to hands and knees and locomoting desperately from the conflagration on all fours like some sort of beast. Civilians panicked as well, and screaming became general as they scrambled away from the bonfire that had been an automobile several seconds earlier.

Basil never looked back, and walked swiftly down the street until he reached rue de Valor and headed down it.

Boch was lecturing Abel on the necessity of severity in dealing with these French cream puffs when a man roared into the banquet room, screaming, "They've blown up one of our radio cars. It's an attack! The Resistance is here!"

Instantly men leaped to action. Three ran to a gun rack in a closet where the MP 40s were stored and grabbed those powerful weapons up. Abel raced to the telephone and called Paris command with a report and a request for immediate troop dispatch. Still others pulled Walthers, Lugers, and P38s from holsters, grabbed overcoats, and readied themselves to move to the scene and take command.

Hauptsturmführer Boch did nothing. He sat rooted in terror. He was not a coward, but he also, for all his worship of severity and aggressive interrogation methods, was particularly inept at confronting the unexpected, which generally caused his mind to dump its contents in a steaming pile on the floor while he sat in stupefaction, waiting for it to refill.

In this case, when he found himself alone in the room, he reached a refill level, stood up, and ran after his more agile colleagues.

He stepped on the sidewalk, which was full of fleeing Parisians, and fought against the tide, being bumped and jostled in the process by those who had no idea who he was. A particularly hard thump from a hurtling heavyweight all but knocked him flat, and the fellow had to grab him to keep him upright before hurrying along. Thus, making little progress, the Hauptsturmführer pulled out his Luger, trying to remember if there was a shell in the chamber, and started to shout in his bad French, "Make way! German officer, make way!" waving the Luger about as if it were some kind of magic wand that would dissipate the crowd.

It did not, so taken in panic were the French, so he diverted to the street itself and found the going easier. He made it to Boulevard Saint-Germain, turned right, and there beheld the atrocity. Radio Car Five still blazed brightly. German plainclothesmen had set up a cordon around it, menacing the citizens with their MP 40s, but of course no citizens were that interested in a German car, and so the street had largely emptied. Traffic on the busy thoroughfare had stopped, making the approach of the fire truck more laggard—the sound of klaxons arrived from far away, and it was clear that by the time the firemen arrived the car would be largely burned to a charred hulk. Two plainclothesmen, Esterlitz, from his SS unit, and an Abwehr agent, sat on the curb looking completely unglued while Abel tried to talk to them.

Boch ran to them. "Report," he snapped as he arrived, but nobody paid any attention to him. "Report!" he screamed. Abel looked over at him.

"I'm trying to get a description from these two fellows, so we know who we're looking for."

"We should arrest hostages at once and execute them if no information is forthcoming."

"Sir, he has to be in the area still. We have to put people out in all directions with a solid description."

"Esterlitz, what did you see?"

Esterlitz looked at him with empty eyes. The nearness of his escape, the heat of the flames, the suddenness of it all, had disassembled his brain completely. Thus it was the Abwehr agent who answered.

"As I've been telling the lieutenant, it happened so quickly. My last impression in the split second before the bomb exploded was of a man walking north on Saint-Germain in a blue pinstripe that was not well cut at all, a surprise to see in a city so fashion-conscious, and then *whoosh*, a wall of flame behind us."

"The bastards," said Boch. "Attempting murder in broad daylight."

"Sir," said Abel, "with all due respect, this was not an assassination operation. Had he wanted them dead, he would have hurled the Molotov through the open window, soaking them with burning gasoline, burning them to death. Instead he merely ignited the petrol tank, which enabled them to escape. He didn't care about them. That wasn't the point, don't you see?"

Boch looked at him, embarrassed to be contradicted by an underling in front of the troops. It was not the SS way! But he controlled his temper, as it made no sense to vent at an ignorant police rube.

"What are you saying?"

"This was some sort of distraction. He wanted to get us all out here, concentrating on this essentially meaningless event, because it somehow advanced his higher purpose."

"I—I—" stuttered Boch.

"Let me finish the interview, then get the description out to all other cars, ordering them to stay in place. Having our men here, tied up in this jam, watching the car burn to embers, accomplishes nothing."

"Do it! Do it!" screamed Boch, as if he had thought of it himself.

Basil reached the Bibliothèque Mazarine within ten minutes and could still hear fire klaxons sounding in the distance. The disturbance would clog up the sixth arrondissement for hours before it was finally untangled, and it would mess up the German response for those same hours. He knew he had a window of time—not much, but perhaps enough.

He walked through the cobbled yard and approached the doors, where two French policemen stood guard.

"Official business only, *monsieur*. German orders," said one.

He took out his identification papers and said frostily, "I do not care to chat with French policemen in the sunlight. I am here on business."

"Yes, sir."

He entered a vast, sacred space. It was composed of an indefinite number of hexagonal galleries, with vast air shafts between, surrounded by very low railings. From any of the hexagons one could see, interminably, the upper and lower floors. The distribution of the galleries was invariable. Twenty shelves, five long shelves per side, covered all the sides except two; their height, which was the distance from floor to ceiling, scarcely exceeded that of a normal bookcase. The books seemed to absorb and calm all extraneous sounds, so that as his heels clicked on the marble of the floor on the approach to a central desk, a woman behind it hardly seemed to notice him. However, his papers got her attention and her courtesy right away.

"I am here on important business. I need to speak to *le directeur* immediately."

She left. She returned. She bade him follow. They went to an elevator where a decrepit Great War veteran, shoulders stooped, medals tarnished, eyes vacant, opened the gate to a cage-like car. They were hoisted mechanically up two flights, followed another path through corridors of books, and reached a door.

She knocked, then entered. He followed, to discover an old Frenchie in some kind of frock coat and goatee, standing nervously.

"I am Claude De Marque, the director," he said in French. "How may I help you?"

"Do you speak German?"

"Yes, but I am more fluent in my own tongue."

"French, then."

"Please sit down." Basil took a chair.

"Now—"

"First, understand the courtesy I have paid you. Had I so chosen, I could have come with a contingent of armed troops. We could have shaken down your institution, examined the papers of all your employees, made impolite inquiries as we looked for leverage and threw books every which way. That is the German technique. Perhaps you shield a Jew, as is the wont of your kind of prissy French intellectual. Too bad for those Jews, too bad for those who shield him. Are you getting my meaning?"

"Yes, sir, I—"

"Instead I come on my own. As men of letters, I think it more appropriate that our relationship be based on trust and respect. I am a professor of literature at Leipzig, and I hope to return to that after the war. I cherish the library, this library, any library. Libraries are the font of civilization, do you not agree?"

"I do."

"Therefore, one of my goals is to protect the integrity of the library. You must know that first of all."

"I am pleased."

"Then let us proceed. I represent a very high science office of the Third Reich. This office has an interest in certain kinds of rare books. I have been assigned by its commanding officer to assemble a catalog of such volumes in the great libraries of Europe. I expect you to help me."

"What kinds of books?"

"Ah, this is delicate. I expect discretion on your part."

"Of course."

"This office has an interest in volumes that deal with erotic connections between human beings. Our interest is not limited to those merely between male and female but extends to other combinations as well. The names de Sade and Ovid have been mentioned. There are more, I am sure. There is also artistic representation. The ancients were more forthright in their descriptions of such activities. Perhaps you have photos of paintings, sculptures, friezes?"

"Sir, this is a respectable—"

"It is not a matter of respect. It is a matter of science, which must go where it leads. We are undertaking a study of human sexuality, and it must be done forthrightly, professionally, and quickly. We are interested in harnessing the power of eugenics and seek to find ways to improve the fertility of our finest minds. Clearly the answer lies in sexual behaviors. Thus we must fearlessly master such matters as we chart our way to the future. We must ensure the future."

"But we have no salacious materials."

"And do you believe, knowing of the Germans' attributes of thoroughness, fairness, calm and deliberate examination, that a single assurance alone would suffice?"

"I invite you to—"

"Exactly. This is what I expect. An hour, certainly no more, undisturbed in your rare book vault. I will wear white gloves if you prefer. I must be free to make a precise search and assure my commander that either you do not have such materials, as you claim, or you do, and these are the ones you have. Do you understand?"

"I confess a first edition of Sade's *Justine*, dated 1791, is among our treasures."

"Are the books arranged by year?"

"They are."

"Then that is where I shall begin."

"Please, you can't—"

"Nothing will be disturbed, only examined. When I am finished, have a document prepared for me in which I testify to other German officers that you have cooperated to the maximum degree. I will sign it, and believe me, it will save you much trouble in the future."

"That would be very kind, sir."

At last he and the Reverend MacBurney were alone. *I have come a long way to meet you, you Scots bastard*, he thought. *Let's see what secrets I can tease out of you.*

MacBurney was signified by a manuscript on foolscap, beribboned in a decaying folder upon which *The Path to Jesus* had been scrawled in an ornate hand. It had been easy to find, in a drawer marked *1789*; he had delicately moved it to the tabletop, where, opened, it yielded its treasure, page after page in the round hand of the man of God himself, laden with swoops and curls of faded brown ink. In the fashion of the eighteenth century, he had made each letter a construction of grace and agility, each line a part of the composition, by turning the feather quill to get the fat or the thin, these arranged in an artistic cascade. His punctuation was precise, deft, studied, just this much twist and pressure for a comma, that much for a (more plentiful) semicolon. It was if the penmanship itself communicated the glory of his love for God. All the nouns were capitalized, and the *S*'s and the *F*'s were so close it would take an expert to tell which was which; superscript showed up everywhere, as the man tried to shrink his burden of labor; frequently the word "the" appeared as "ye," as the penultimate letter often stood in for *the* in that era. It seemed the words on the page wore powdered periwigs and silk stockings and buckled, heeled shoes as they danced and pirouetted across the page.

Yet there was a creepy quality to it, too. Splats or droplets marked the creamy luster of the page—some of wine perhaps, some of tea, some of whatever else one might have at the board in the eighteenth century. Some of the lines were crooked, and the page itself felt off-kilter, as though a taint of madness had attended, or perhaps drunkenness, for in his dotage old MacBurney was no teetotaler, it was said.

More psychotic still were the drawings. As the librarian had noticed in his published account of the volume in *Treasures of the Cambridge Library*, the reverend occasionally yielded to artistic impulse. No, they weren't vulvas or naked boys or fornicators in pushed-up petticoats or farmers too in love with their cows. MacBurney's lusts weren't so visible or so nakedly expressed. But the fellow was a doodler after Jesus. He could not compel himself to be still, and so each page wore a garland of crosses scattered across its bottom, a Milky Way of holiness setting off the page number, or in the margins, and at the top silhouetted crucifixions, sketches of angels, clumsy reiterations of God's hand touching Adam's as the great Italian had captured upon that ceiling in Rome. Sometimes the devil himself appeared, horned and ambivalent, just a few angry lines not so much depicting as suggesting Lucifer's cunning and malice. It seemed the reverend was in anguish as he tried desperately to finish this last devotion to the Lord.

Basil got to work quickly. Here of all places was no place to tarry. He untaped the Riga Minox from his left shin, checked that the overhead light seemed adequate. He didn't need flash, as Technical Branch had come up with extremely fast 21.5 mm film, but it was at the same time completely necessary to hold still. The lens had been prefocused for 15 cm, so Basil did not need to play with it or any other knobs, buttons, controls. He took on faith that he had been given the best equipment in the world with which to do the job.

He had seven pages to photograph—2, 5, 6, 9, 10, 13, and 15—for the codebreaker had assured him that those would be the pages on which the index words would have to be located, based on the intercepted code.

In fact, Sade's *Justine* proved very helpful, along with a first edition of Voltaire's *Pensées* and an extra-illustrated edition of *Le Decameron de Jean Boccace*, published in five volumes in Paris in 1757. Ah, the uses of literature! Stacked, they gave him a brace against which he could sustain the long fuselage of the Minox. Beneath it he displayed the page. Click, wind, click again, on to the next one. It took so little time. It was too sodding easy. He thought he might find an SS firing squad just waiting for him, enjoying the little trick they'd played on him.

But when he replaced all the documents in their proper spots, retaped the camera to his leg, and emerged close to an hour later, there was no firing squad, just the nervous Marque, *le directeur*, waiting with the tremulous smile of the recently violated.

"I am finished, *monsieur le directeur*. Please examine, make certain all is appropriate to the condition it was in when I first entered an hour ago. Nothing missing, nothing misfiled, nothing where it should not be. I will not take offense."

The director entered the vault and emerged in a few minutes.

"Perfect," he said.

"I noted the Sade. Nothing else seemed necessary to our study. I am sure copies of it in not so rare an edition are commonly available if one knows where to look."

"I could recommend a bookseller," said *le directeur*. "He specializes in, er, the kind of thing you're looking for."

"Not necessary now, but possible in the future."

"I had my secretary prepare a document, in both German and French."

Basil looked at it, saw that it was exactly as he had ordered, and signed his false name with a flourish.

"You see how easy it is if you cooperate, *monsieur*? I wish I could teach all your countrymen the same."

By the time Macht returned at four, having had to walk the last three blocks because of the traffic snarl, things were more or less functioning correctly at his banquet hall headquarters.

"We now believe him to be in a pinstripe suit. I have put all our watchers back in place in a state of high alert. I have placed cars outside this tangled-up area so that we can, if need be, get to the site of an incident quickly," Abel briefed him.

"Excellent, excellent," he replied. "What's happening with the idiot?"

That meant Boch, of course.

"He wanted to take hostages and shoot one every hour until the man is found. I told him that was probably not a wise move, since this fellow is clearly operating entirely on his own and is thus immune to social pressures such as that. He's now in private communication with SS headquarters in Paris, no doubt telling them what a wonderful job he has been doing. His men are all right, he's just a buffoon. But a dangerous one. He could have us all sent to Russia. Well, not me, ha-ha, but the rest of you."

"I'm sure your honor would compel you to accompany us, Walter."

"Don't bet on it, Didi."

"I agree with you that this is a diversion, that our quarry is completing his mission somewhere very near. I agree also that it is not a murder, a sabotage, a theft, or anything spectacular. In fact, I have no idea what it could be. I would advise that all train stations be double-covered and that the next few hours are our best for catching him."

"I will see to it."

In time Boch appeared. He beckoned to Macht, and the two stepped into the hallway for privacy.

"Herr Hauptmann, I want this considered as fair warning. This agent must be captured, no matter what. It is on record that you chose to disregard my advice and instead go about your duties at a more sedate pace. SS is not satisfied and has filed a formal protest with Abwehr and others in the government. SS Reichsführer Himmler himself is paying close attention. If this does not come to the appropriate conclusion, all counterintelligence activities in Paris may well come under SS auspices, and you yourself may find your next duty station rather more frosty and rather more hectic than this one. I tell you this to clarify your thinking. It's not a threat, Herr Hauptmann, it's simply a clarification of the situation."

"Thank you for the update, Herr Hauptsturmführer. I will take it under advisement and—"

But at that moment Abel appeared, concern on his usually slack, doughy face. "Hate to interrupt, Herr Hauptmann, but something interesting."

"Yes?"

"One of Unterscharführer Ganz's sources is a French policeman on duty at the Bibliothèque Mazarine, on Quai de Conti, not far from here. An easy walk, in fact."

"Yes, the large complex overlooking the river. The cupola—no, that is the main building, the Institut de France, I believe."

"Yes, sir. At any rate, the report is that at about three P.M., less than twenty minutes after the bomb blast—"

"Flare is more like it, I hear," said Macht.

"Yes, Captain. In any event, a German official strode into the library and demanded to see the director. He demanded access to the rare book vault and was in there alone for an hour. Everybody over there is buzzing because he was such a commanding gentleman, so sure and smooth and charismatic."

"Did he steal anything?"

"No, but he was alone in the vault. In the end, it makes very little sense. It's just that the timing works out correctly, the description is accurate, and the personality seems to match. What British intelligence could—"

"Let's get over there, fast," said Macht.

This was far more than *monsieur le directeur* had ever encountered. He now found himself alone in his office with three German policemen, and none were in a good mood.

"So, if you will, please explain to me the nature of this man's request."

"It's highly confidential, Captain Macht. I had the impression that discretion was one of the aspects of the visit. I feel I betray a trust if I—"

"*Monsieur le directeur,*" said Macht evenly, "I assure you that while I appreciate your intentions, I nevertheless must insist on an answer. There is some evidence that this man may not be who you think he was."

"His credentials were perfect," said the director. "I examined them very carefully. They were entirely authentic. I am not easy to fool."

"I accuse you of nothing," said Macht. "I merely want the story."

And *le directeur* laid it out, rather embarrassed. "Dirty pictures," said Macht at the conclusion. "You say a German officer came in and demanded to check your vault for dirty pictures, dirty stories, dirty jokes, dirty limericks, and so forth in books of antiquarian value?"

"I told you the reason he gave me." The two dumpy policemen exchanged glances; the third, clearly from another department, fixed him with beady, furious eyes behind pince-nez glasses and somehow seemed to project both aggression and fury at him without saying a word. "Why would I make up such a story?" inquired *le directeur*. "It's too absurd."

"I'll tell you what we'll do," said the third officer, a plumper man with pomaded if thinning hair showing much pate between its few strands and a little blot of moustache clearly modeled on either Himmler's or Hitler's. "We'll take ten of your employees to the street. If we are not satisfied with your answers, we'll shoot one of them. Then we'll ask again and see if—"

"Please," the Frenchman implored, "I tell the truth. I am unaccustomed to such treatment. My heart is about to explode. I tell the truth, it is not in me to lie, it is not my character."

"Description, please," said Macht. "Try hard. Try very hard."

"Mid-forties, well-built, though in a terrible-fitting suit. I must say I thought the suit far beneath him, for his carriage and confidence were of a higher order. Reddish-blond hair, blue eyes, rather a beautiful chin—rather a beautiful man, completely at home with himself and—"

"Look, please," said the assistant to the less ominous of the policemen. He handed over a photograph.

"Ahhhh—well, no, this is not him. Still, a close likeness. Same square shape. His eyes are not as strong as my visitor's, and his posture is something rather less. I must say, the suit fits much better."

Macht sat back. Yes, a British agent had been here. What on Earth could it have been for? What in the Mazarine Library was of such interest to the British that they had sent a man on such a dangerous mission, so fragile, so easily discovered? They must have been quite desperate.

"And what name did he give you?" Abel asked. "He said his name was . . . Here, look, here's the document he signed. It was exactly the name on his papers, I checked very closely so there would be no mistake. I was trying my hardest to cooperate. I know there is no future in rebellion."

He opened his drawer, with trembling fingers took out a piece of paper, typed and signed.

"I should have shown it to you earlier. I was nonplussed, I apologize, it's not often that I have three policemen in my office."

He yammered on, but they paid no attention, as all bent forward to examine the signature at the bottom of the page.

It said, "Otto Boch, SS Hauptsturmführer, SSRHSA, 13 rue Madeleine, Paris."

ACTION THIS DAY (CONT'D.)

The train left Montparnasse at exactly five minutes after five P.M. As SS Hauptsturmführer Boch, Gestapo, 13 rue Madeleine, Paris, Basil did not require anything save his identification papers, since Gestapo membership conferred on him an elite status that no rail clerk in the Wehrmacht monitoring the trains would dare challenge. Thus he flew by the ticket process and the security checkpoints and the flash inspection at the first-class carriage steps.

The train eased into motion and picked up speed as it left the marshaling yards resolving themselves toward blur as the darkness increased. He sat alone amid a smattering of German officers returning to duty after a few stolen nights in Paris. Outside, in the twilight, the little toy train depots of France fled by, and inside, the vibration rattled and the grumpy men tried to squeeze in a last bit of relaxation before once again taking up their vexing duties, which largely consisted of waiting until the Allied armies came to blow them up. Some of them thought of glorious death and sacrifice for the fatherland; some remembered the whores in whose embraces they had passed the time; some thought of ways to surrender to the Americans without getting themselves killed, but also of not being reported, for one never knew who was keeping records and who would see them.

But most seemed to realize that Basil was an undercover SS officer, and no one wanted to brook any trouble at all with the SS. Again, a wrong word, a misinterpreted joke, a comment too politically frank, and it was off to that dreaded 8.8 cm antitank gun facing the T-34s and the Russians. All of them preferred their luck with the Americans and the British than with the goddamn Bolsheviks.

So Basil sat alone, ramrod straight, looking neither forward nor back. His stern carriage conveyed seriousness of purpose, relentless attention to detail, and a devotion to duty so hard and true it positively radiated heat. He permitted no mirth to show, no human weakness. Most of all, and hardest for him, he allowed himself to show no irony, for irony was the one attribute that would never be found in the SS or in any Hitlerite true believer. In fact, in one sense the Third Reich and its adventure in mass death was a conspiracy against irony. Perhaps that is why Basil hated it so much and fought it so hard.

Boch said nothing. There was nothing to say. Instead it was Macht who did all the talking. They leaned on the hood of a Citroën radio car in the courtyard of the Bibliothèque Mazarine.

"Whatever it was he wanted, he got it. Now he has to get out of town and fast. He knows that sooner or later we may tumble to his acquisition of Herr Boch's identity papers, and at that point their usefulness comes to an abrupt end and they become absolutely a danger. So he will use them now, as soon as possible, and get as far away as possible."

"But he has purposefully refused any Resistance aid on this trip," said Abel.

"True."

"That would mean that he has no radio contact. That would mean that he has no way to set up a Lysander pickup."

"Excellent point, Walter. Yes, and that narrows his options considerably. One way out would be to head to the Spanish border. However, that's days away, involves much travel and the danger of constant security checks, and he would worry that his Boch identity would have been penetrated."

They spoke of Boch as if he were not there. In a sense, he wasn't. *"Sir, the breech is frozen." "Kick it! They're almost on us!" "I can't, sir. My foot fell off because of frostbite."*

"He could, I suppose, get to Calais and swim to Dover. It's only thirty-two kilometers. It's been done before."

"Even by a woman."

"Still, although he's a gifted professional, I doubt they have anyone quite that gifted. And even if it's spring, the water is four or five degrees centigrade."

"Yes," said Macht. "But he will definitely go by water. He will head to the most accessible seaport. Given his talents for subversion, he will find some sly fisherman who knows our patrol boat patterns and pay the fellow to haul him across. He can make it in a few hours, swim the last hundred yards to a British beach, and be home with his treasure, whatever that is."

"If he escapes, we should shoot the entire staff of the Bibliothèque Mazarine," said Boch suddenly. "This is on them. He stole my papers, yes, he pickpocketed me, but he could have stolen anyone's papers, so to single me out is rather senseless. I will make that point in my report."

"An excellent point," said Macht. "Alas, I will have to add that while he *could* have stolen anyone's papers, he *did* steal yours. And they were immensely valuable to him. He is now sitting happily on the train, thinking of the jam and buns he will enjoy tomorrow morning with his tea and whether it will be a DSC or a DSO that follows his name from now on.

I would assume that as an honorable German officer you will take full responsibility. I really don't think we need to go shooting up any library staffs at this point. Why don't we concentrate on catching him, and that will be that."

Boch meant to argue but saw that it was useless. He settled back into his bleakness and said nothing.

"The first thing: which train?" Macht inquired of the air. The air had no answer and so he answered it himself. "Assuming that he left, as *le directeur* said, at exactly three forty-five P.M. by cab, he got to the Montparnasse station by four-fifteen. Using his SS papers, he would not need to stand in line for tickets or checkpoints, so he could leave almost immediately. My question thus has to be, what trains leaving for coastal destinations were available between four-fifteen and four forty-five? He will be on one of those trains. Walter, please call the detectives."

Abel spoke into the microphone by radio to his headquarters and waited. A minute later an answer came. He conveyed it to the two officers.

"A train for Cherbourg left at four-thirty, due to arrive in that city at eleven-thirty P.M. Then another at—"

"That's fine. He'd take the first. He doesn't want to be standing around, not knowing where we are in our investigations and thus assuming the worst. Now, Walter, please call Abwehr headquarters and get our people at Montparnasse to check the gate of that train for late-arriving German officers. I believe they have to sign a travel manifest. At least, I always do. See if Hauptsturmführer—ah, what's the first name, Boch?"

"Otto."

"SS Hauptsturmführer *Otto* Boch, Gestapo, came aboard at the last moment."

"Yes, sir."

Macht looked over at Boch. "Well, Hauptsturmführer, if this pans out, we may save you from your 8.8 in Russia."

"I serve where I help the Führer best. My life is of no consequence," said Boch darkly.

"You may feel somewhat differently when you see the tanks on the horizon," said Macht.

"It hardly matters. We can never catch him. He has too much head start. We can order the train met at Cherbourg, I suppose, and perhaps they will catch him."

"Unlikely. This eel is too slippery."

"Please tell me you have a plan."

"Of course I have a plan," said Macht.

"All right, yes," said Abel, turning from the phone. "Hauptsturmführer Boch did indeed come aboard at the last moment."

He sat, he sat, he sat. The train shook, rattled, and clacked. Twilight passed into lightless night. The vibrations played across everything. Men smoked, men drank from flasks, men tried to write letters home or read. It was not an express, so every half hour or so the train would lurch to a stop and one or two officers would leave, one or two would join. The lights flickered, cool air blasted into the compartment, the French conductor yelled the meaningless name of the town, and on and on they went, into the night.

At last the conductor yelled, "Bricquebec, twenty minutes," first in French, then in German. He stood up, leaving his overcoat, and went to the loo. In it, he looked at his face in the mirror, sallow in the light. He soaked a towel, rubbed his face, meaning to find energy somehow. Action this day. Much of it. A last trick, a last wiggle.

The fleeing agent's enemy is paranoia. Basil had no immunity from it, merely discipline against it. He was also not particularly immune to fear. He felt both of these emotions strongly now, knowing that this nothingness of waiting for the train to get him where it had to was absolutely the worst.

But then he got his war face back on, forcing the armor of his charm and charisma to the surface, willing his eyes to sparkle, his smile to flash, his brow to furl romantically. He was back in character. He was Basil again.

"Excellent," said Macht. "Now, Boch, your turn to contribute. Use that SS power of yours we all so fear and call von Choltitz's adjutant. It is important that I be given temporary command authority over a unit called

Nachtjagdgeschwader-9. Luftwaffe, of course. It's a wing headquartered at a small airfield near the town of Bricquebec, less than an hour outside Cherbourg. Perhaps you remember our chat with its commandant, Oberst Gunther Scholl, a few days ago. Well, you had better hope that Oberst Scholl is on his game, because he is the one who will nab Johnny England for us." Quite expectedly, Boch didn't understand. Puzzlement flashed in his eyes and fuddled his face.

He began to stutter, but Abel cut him off.

"Please, Herr Hauptsturmführer. Time is fleeing."

Boch did what he was told, telling his UberHauptsturmführer that Hauptmann Dieter Macht, of Abwehr III-B, needed to give orders to Oberst Scholl of NJG-9 at Bricquebec. Then the three got into the Citroën and drove the six blocks back to the Hotel Duval, where they went quickly to the phone operator at the board. Though the Abwehr men were sloppy by SS standards, they were efficient by German standards.

The operator handed a phone to Macht, who didn't bother to shed his trench coat and fedora.

"Hullo, hullo," he said, "Hauptmann Macht here, call for Oberst Scholl. Yes, I'll wait."

A few seconds later Scholl came on the phone. "Scholl here."

"Yes, Oberst Scholl, it's Hauptmann Macht, Paris Abwehr. Have things been explained to you?"

"Hello, Macht. I know only that by emergency directive from Luftwaffe Command I am to obey your orders."

"Do you have planes up tonight?"

"No, the bomber streams are heading north tonight. We have the night off."

"Sorry to make the boys work, Herr Oberst. It seems your seatmate is returning to your area. I need manpower. I need you to meet and cordon off the Cherbourg train at the Bricquebec stop. It's due in at eleven-thirty P.M. Maximum effort. Get your pilots out of bed or out of the bars or brothels, and your mechanics, your ground crews, your fuelers. Leave only a skeleton crew in the tower. I'll tell you why in a bit."

"I must say, Macht, this is unprecedented."

"Oberst, I'm trying to keep you from the Russian front. Please comply enthusiastically so that you can go back to your three mistresses and your wine cellar."

"How did—"

"We have records, Herr Oberst. Anyhow, I would conceal the men in the bushes and inside the depot house until the train has all but arrived. Then, on command, they are to take up positions surrounding the train, making certain that no one leaves. At that point I want you to lead a search party from one end to the other, though of course start in first class. You know who you are looking for. He is now, however, in a dark blue pin-striped suit, double-breasted. He has a dark overcoat. He may look older, more abused, harder, somehow different from when last you saw him. You must be alert, do you understand?"

"Is he armed?"

"We don't know. Assume he is. Listen here, there's a tricky part. When you see him, you must not react immediately. Do you understand? Don't make eye contact, don't move fast or do anything stupid. He has an L-pill. It will probably be in his mouth. If he sees you coming for him, he will bite it. Strychnine—instant. It would mean so much more if we could take him alive. He may have many secrets, do you understand?"

"I do."

"When you take him, order your officers to go first for his mouth. They have to get fingers or a plug or something deep into his throat to keep him from biting or swallowing, then turn him facedown and pound hard on his back. He has to cough out that pill."

"My people will be advised. I will obviously be there to supervise."

"Oberst, this chap is very efficient, very practiced. He's an old dog with miles of travel on him. For years he's lasted in a profession where most perish in a week. Be very careful, be very astute, be very sure. I know you can do this."

"I will catch your spy for you, Macht."

"Excellent. One more thing. I will arrive within two hours in my own Storch, with my assistant, Abel."

"That's right, you fly."

"I do, yes. I have over a thousand hours, and you know how forgiving a Storch is."

"I do."

"So alert your tower people. I'll buzz them so they can light a runway for the thirty seconds it takes me to land, then go back to blackout. And leave a car and driver to take me to the station."

"I will."

"Good hunting."

"Good flying."

He put the phone down, turned to Abel, and said, "Call the airport, get the plane flight-checked and fueled so that we can take off upon arrival."

"Yes, sir."

"One moment," said Boch.

"Yes, Herr Hauptsturmführer?"

"As this is a joint SS-Abwehr operation, I demand to be a part of it. I will go along with you."

"The plane holds only two. It loses its agility when a third is added. It's not a fighter, it's a kite with a tiny motor."

"Then I will go instead of Abel. Macht, do not fight me on this. I will go to SS and higher if I need to. SS must be represented all through this operation."

"You trust my flying?"

"Of course."

"Good, because Abel does not. Now, let's go."

"Not quite yet. I have to change into my uniform."

Refreshed, Basil left the loo. But instead of turning back into the carriage and returning to his seat, he turned the other way, as if it were the natural thing to do, opened the door at the end of the carriage, and stepped out onto the rattling, trembling running board over the coupling between carriages. He waited for the door behind him to seal, tested for speed. Was the train slowing? He felt it was, as maybe the vibrations were further apart, signifying that the wheels churned slightly less aggressively, against an incline, on the downhill, perhaps negotiating a turn. Then, without a thought, he leaped sideways into the darkness.

Will I be lucky? Will the famous St. Florian charm continue? Will I float to a soft landing and roll through the dirt, only my dignity and my hair mussed? Or will this be the night it all runs out and I hit a bridge abutment, a tree trunk, a barbed-wire fence, and kill myself?

He felt himself elongate as he flew through the air, and as his leap carried him out of the gap between the two cars the slipstream hit him hard, sending his arms and legs flying wildly.

He seemed to hang in the darkness for an eternity, feeling the air beat him, hearing the roar of both the wind and the train, seeing nothing.

Then he hit. Stars exploded, suns collapsed, the universe split atomically, releasing a tidal wave of energy. He tasted dust, felt pain and a searing jab in his back, then high-speed abrasion of his whole body, a piercing blow to his left hand, had the illusion of rolling, sliding, falling, hurting all at once, and then he lay quiet.

Am I dead?

He seemed not to be.

The train was gone now. He was alone in the track bed, amid a miasma of dust and blood. At that point the pain clamped him like a vise and he felt himself wounded, though how badly was yet unknown. Could he move? Was he paralyzed? Had he broken any bones?

He sucked in oxygen, hoping for restoration. It came, marginally.

He checked his hip pocket to see if his Browning .380 was still there, and there indeed it was. He reached next for his shin, hoping and praying that the Minox had survived the descent and landfall. It wasn't there! The prospect of losing it was so tragically immense that he could not face it and exiled the possibility from his brain as he found the tape, still tight, followed it around, and in one second touched the aluminum skin of the instrument. Somehow the impact of the fall had moved it around his leg but had not sundered, only loosened, the tape. He pried it out, slipped it into his hip pocket. He slipped the Browning into his belt in the small of his back, then counted to three and stood.

His clothes were badly tattered, and his left arm so severely ripped he could not straighten it. His right knee had punched through the cheap pinstriped serge, and it too had been shredded by abrasions. But the real damage was done to his back, where he'd evidently encountered a rock or a branch as he decelerated in the dust, and it hurt immensely. He could almost feel it bruising, and he knew it would pain him for weeks. When he twisted he felt shards of glass in his side and assumed he'd broken or cracked several ribs. All in all, he was a mess.

But he was not dead, and he was more or less ambulatory.

He recalled the idiot Luftwaffe colonel on the ride down.

"Yes, our squadron is about a mile east of the tracks, just out of town. It's amazing how the boys have dressed it up. You should come and visit us soon, *monsieur*. I'll take you on a tour. Why, they've turned a rude military installation in the middle of nothing into a comfortable small German town, with sewers and sidewalks and streets, even a gazebo for summertime concerts. My boys are the best, and our wing does more than its share against the Tommy bombers."

That put the airfield a mile or so ahead, given that the tracks had to run north–south. He walked, sliding between trees and gentle undergrowth, through a rather civilized little forest, actually, and his night vision soon arrived through his headache and the pain in his back, which turned his walk into Frankenstein's lumber, but he was confident he was headed in the right direction. And very shortly he heard the approaching buzz of a small plane and knew absolutely that he was on track.

The Storch glided through the air, its tiny engine buzzing away smoothly like a hummingbird's heart. Spindly from its overengineered landing gear and graceless on the ground, it was a princess in the air. Macht held it at 450 meters, compass heading almost due south. He'd already landed at the big Luftwaffe base at Caen for a refueling, just in case Bricquebec proved outside the Storch's 300kilometer range. He'd follow the same route back, taking the same fuel precautions. He knew: in the air, take nothing for granted. The western heading would bring him to the home of NJG-9 very soon, as he was flying throttle open, close to 175 km per hour. It was a beautiful little thing, light and reliable; you could feel that it wanted to fly, unlike the planes of the Great War, which had mostly been underpowered and overengineered, so close to the maximum they seemed to want to crash. You had to fight them to keep them in the air, while the Storch would fly all night if it could.

A little cool air rushed in, as the Perspex window was cranked half down. It kept the men cool; it also kept them from chatting, which was fine with Macht. It let him concentrate and enjoy, and he still loved the joy of being airborne.

Below, rural France slipped by, far from absolutely dark but too dark to make out details.

That was fine. Macht, a good flier, trusted his compass and his watch and knew that neither would let him down, and when he checked the time, he saw that he was entering NJG-9's airspace. He picked up his radio phone, clicked it a few times, and said, "Anton, Anton, this is Bertha 9-9, do you read?"

The headset crackled and snapped, and he thought perhaps he was on the wrong frequency, but then he heard, "Bertha 9-9, this is Anton—I have you; I can hear you. You're bearing a little to the southwest. I'd bear a few degrees to the north."

"Excellent, and thanks, Anton."

"When I have you overhead, I'll light a runway."

"Excellent, excellent. Thanks again, Anton." Macht made the slight correction and was rewarded a minute later with the sudden flash to illumination of a long horizontal *V*. It took seconds to find the line into the darkness between the arms of the *V* which signified the landing strip. He eased back on the throttle, hearing the engine rpm's drop, watched his airspeed indicator fall to seventy-five, then sixty-five, eased the stick forward into a gentle incline, came into the cone of lights, and saw grass on either side of a wide tarmac built for the much larger twin-engine Me110 night fighters, throttled down some more, and alit with just the slightest of bumps.

When the plane's weight overcame its decreasing power, it almost came to a halt, but he revved back to taxi speed, saw the curved roofs of hangers ahead, and taxied toward them. A broad staging area before the four arched buildings, where the fighters paused and made a last check before deploying, was before him. He took the plane to it, pivoted it to face outward-bound down the same runway, and hit the kill switch. He could hear the vibrations stop, and the plane went silent.

Basil watched the little plane taxi to the hangers, pause, then helpfully turn itself back to the runway. Perfect. Whoever was flying was counting on a quick trip back and didn't want to waste time on the ground.

He crouched well inside the wire, about 300 meters from the airplane, which put him 350 meters from the four hangars. He knew, because Oberst Scholl had told him, that recent manpower levies had stripped the place of guards and security people, all of whom were now in transit to Russia, where their bodies were needed urgently to feed into the fire. As for the patrol dogs, one had died of food poisoning and the other was so old he could hardly move, again information provided by Scholl. The security of NJG-9's night fighter base was purely an illusion; all nonessential personnel had been stripped away for something big in Russia.

In each hangar Basil could see the prominent outlines of the big night fighters, each cockpit slid open, resting at the nose-up, tail-down, fifteen-degree angle on the buttress of the two sturdy landing gears that descended from the huge bulge of engine on the broad wings. They were not small airplanes, and these birds wore complex nests of prongs on the nose, radar antennae meant to guide them to the bomber stream 7,600 meters above. The planes were all marked by the stark black Luftwaffe cross insignia, and their metallic snouts gleamed slightly in the lights, until the tower turned them off when the Storch had come to a safe stop.

He watched carefully. Two men. One wore a pilot's leather helmet but not a uniform, just a tent of a trench coat that hadn't seen cleaning or pressing in years. He was the pilot, and he tossed the helmet into the plane, along with an unplugged set of headphones. At the same time he pulled out a battered fedora, which looked like it had been crushed in the pocket of the coat for all the years it hadn't been pressed or cleaned.

No. 2 was more interesting. He was SS, totally, completely, avatar of dark style and darker menace. The uniform—jodhpurs and boots under a smart tunic, tight at the neck, black cap with death's head rampant in silver above the bill at a rakish angle—was more dramatic than the man, who appeared porky and graceless. He was shakier than the pilot, taking a few awkward steps to get his land legs back and drive the dizziness from his mind.

In time a Mercedes staff car emerged from somewhere in the darkness, driven by a Luftwaffer, who leaped out and offered a snappy salute. He did not shake hands with either, signifying his enlisted status as against their commissions, but obsequiously retreated to the car, where he opened the rear door.

The two officers slid in. The driver resumed his place behind the wheel, and the car sped away into the night.

"Yes, that's very good, Sergeant," said Macht as the car drove in darkness between the tower and administration complex on the left and the officers' mess on the right. The gate was a few hundred meters ahead. "Now, very quickly, let us out and continue on your way, outside the gate, along the road, and back to the station at Bricquebec, where your commanding officer waits."

"Ah, sir, my instructions are—"

"Do as I say, Sergeant, unless you care to join the other bad boys of the Wehrmacht on an infantry salient on some frozen hill of dog shit in Russia."

"Obviously, sir, I will obey."

"I thought you might."

The car slipped between two buildings, slowed, and Macht eased out, followed by Boch. Then the car rolled away, speeded up, and loudly issued the pretense that it was headed to town with two important passengers.

"Macht," hissed Boch, "what in the devil's name are you up to?"

"Use your head, Herr Hauptsturmführer. Our friend is not going to be caught like a fish in a bucket. He's too clever. He presumes the shortest possible time between his escape from Paris and our ability to figure it out and know what name he travels under. He knows he cannot make it all the way to Cherbourg and steal or hire a boat. No indeed, and since that idiot Scholl has conveniently plied him with information about the layout and operational protocols of NJG-9, as well as, I'm certain, a precise location, he has identified it as his best opportunity for an escape. He means, I suppose, to fly to England in a 110 like the madman Hess, but we have provided him with a much more tempting conveyance—the low, slow, gentle Storch. He cannot turn it down, do you see? It is absolutely his best—his only—chance to bring off his crazed mission, whatever it is. But we will stop him. Is that pistol loaded?"

Boch slapped the Luger under the flap of his holster on his ceremonial belt.

"Of course. One never knows."

"Well, then, we shall get as close as possible and wait for him to make his move. I doubt he's a quarter kilometer from us now. He'll wait until he's certain the car is gone and the lazy Luftwaffe tower personnel are paying no attention, and then he'll dash to the airplane, and off he goes."

"We will be there," said Boch, pulling his Luger. "Put that thing away, please, Herr Hauptsturmführer. It makes me nervous."

Basil began his crawl. The grass wasn't high enough to cover him, but without lights, no tower observer could possibly pick him out flat against the ground. His plan was to approach on the oblique, locating himself on such a line that the plane was between himself and the watchers in the tower. It wouldn't obscure him, but it would be more data in a crowded binocular view into an already dark zone, and he hoped that the lazy officer up there was not really paying that much attention, instead simply nodding off on a meaningless night of duty far from any war zone and happy that he wasn't out in the godforsaken French night on some kind of insane catch-the-spy mission two kilometers away at the train station.

It hurt, of course. His back throbbed, a bruise on his hip ached, a pain between his eyes would not go away, and the burns on knee and arm from his abrasions seemed to mount in intensity. He pulled himself through the grass like a swimmer, his fear giving him energy that he should not have had, the roughness of his breath drowning out the night noise. He seemed to crawl for a century, but he didn't look up, because, as if he were swimming the English Channel, if he saw how far he had to go, the blow to his morale would be stunning.

Odd filaments of his life came up from nowhere, viewed from strange angles so that they made only a bit of sense and maybe not even that. He hardly knew his mother, he had hated his father, his brothers were all older than he was and had formed their friendships and allegiances already. Women that he had been intimate with arrived to mind, but they did not bring pride and triumph, only memories of human fallibility and disappointment, theirs and his; and his congenital inability to remain faithful to any of them, love or not, always revealed its ugliness. Really, he had had a useless life until he signed with the crown and went on his adventures—it was a perfect match for his adventurer's temperament, his casual cruelty, his cleverness, his ruthlessness. He had no problem with any of it: the deceit, the swindles, the extortion, the cruel manipulation of the innocent, even the murder. He had killed his first man, a corrupt Malaysian police inspector, in 1935, and he remembered the jump of the big Webley, the smell of cordite, the man's odd deflation as he surrendered to gravity. He thought it would have been so much more; it was, really, nothing, nothing at all, and he supposed that his own death, in a few minutes, a few hours, a few days, a few weeks, or next year or the year after, would mean as little to the man who killed him, probably some Hanoverian conscript with a machine pistol firing blindly into the trees that held him.

So it would go. That is the way of the wickedness called war. It eats us all. In the end, it and it alone is the victor, no matter what the lie called history says. The god of war, Mars the Magnificent and Tragic, always wins.

And then he was there.

He was out of grass. He had come to the hardpacked earth of the runway. He allowed himself to look up. The little plane was less than fifty meters away, tilted skyward on its absurdly high landinggear struts. He had but to jump to the cockpit, turn it on, let the rpm's mount, then take off the brakes, and it would pull itself forward and up, due north, straight on till morning.

Fifty meters, he thought. *All that's between myself and Blighty.*

He gathered himself for the crouched run to it. He checked: *Pistol still with me, camera in my pocket, all nice and tidy.* He had one last thing to do. He reached into his breast pocket and shoved his fingers down, probing, touching, searching. Then he had it. He pulled the L-pill out, fifty ccs of pure strychnine under a candy shell, and slid it into his mouth, back behind his teeth, far in the crevice between lip and jawbone. One crunch and he got to Neverland instantly.

"There," whispered Boch. "It's him, there, do you see, crouching just off the runway." They knelt in the darkness of the hangar closest to the Storch.

Macht saw him. The Englishman seemed to be gathering himself. *The poor bastard is probably exhausted. He's been on the run in occupied territory over four days, bluffed or brazened his way out of a dozen near misses.* Macht could see a dark double-breasted suit that even from this distance looked disheveled.

"Let him get to the plane," said Macht. "He will be consumed by it, and under that frenzy we approach, keeping the tail and fuselage between ourselves and him."

"Yes, I see."

"You stand off and hold him with the Luger. I will jump him and get this"—he reached into his pocket and retrieved a pipe—"into his mouth, to keep him from swallowing his suicide capsule. Then I will handcuff him and we'll be done."

They watched as the man broke from the edge of the grass, running like an athlete, with surprising power to his strides, bent double as if to evade tacklers, and in a very little time got himself to the door of the Storch's cockpit, pulled it open, and hoisted himself into the seat.

"Now," said Macht, and the two of them emerged from their hiding place and walked swiftly to the airplane.

His Luger out, Boch circled to the left to face the cockpit squarely from the left side while Macht slid along the right side of the tail boom, reached the landing struts, and slipped under them.

"*Halt!*" yelled Boch, and at precisely that moment Macht rose, grabbed the astonished Englishman by the lapels of his suit, and yanked him free of the plane. They crashed together, Macht pivoting cleverly so that his quarry bounced off his hip and went into space. He landed hard, far harder than Macht, who simply rode him down, got a knee on his chest, bent, and stuffed his pipe in the man's throat. The agent coughed and heaved, searching for leverage, but Macht had wrestled many a criminal into captivity and knew exactly how to apply leverage.

"Spit it out!" he cried in English. "Damn you, spit it out!" He rolled the man as he shook him, then slapped him with a hard palm between the shoulder blades, and in a second the pill was ejected like a piece of half-chewed, throat-obstructing meat, riding a propulsive if involuntary spurt of breath, and arched to earth, where Macht quickly put a heavy shoe on it, crushing it.

"Hands up, Englishman, goddamn you," he yelled as Boch neared, pointing the Luger directly into the face of the captive to make the argument more persuasively.

There was no fight left in him, or so it seemed.

He put up his hands.

"Search him, Macht," said Boch.

Macht swooped back onto the man, ran his hands around his waist, under his armpits, down his legs.

"Only this," he said, holding aloft a small camera. "This'll tell us some things."

"I think you'll be disappointed, old man," said the Englishman. "I am thinking of spiritual enlightenment, and my photographs merely propose a path."

"Shut up," bellowed Boch.

"Now," said Macht, "we'll—"

"Not so fast," said Boch.

The pistol covered both of them.

It happened so fast. He knew it would happen fast, but not this fast. *Halt!* came the cry, utterly stunning him with its loudness and closeness, and then this demon rose from nowhere, pulled him—the strength was enormous—from the plane, and slammed him to the ground. In seconds the L-pill had been beaten from him. Whoever this chap was, he knew a thing or two.

Now Basil stood next to him. Breathing hard, quite fluttery from exhaustion, and trying not to face the enormity of what had just happened, he tried to make sense, even as one thing, his capture, turned into another—some weird German command drama.

The SS officer had the Luger on both of them. "Boch, what do you think you are doing?" said the German in the trench coat.

"Taking care of a certain problem," said the SS man. "Do you think I care to have an Abwehr bastard file a report that will end my career and get me shipped to Russia? Did you think I could permit *that*?"

"My friends," said Basil in German, "can't we sit down over a nice bottle of schnapps and talk it out? I'm sure you two can settle your differences amicably."

The SS officer struck him across the jaw with his Luger, driving him to the ground. He felt blood run down his face as the cheek began to puff grotesquely.

"Shut your mouth, you bastard," the officer said. Then he turned back to the police officer in the trench coat.

"You see how perfectly you have set it up for me, Macht? No witnesses, total privacy, your own master plan to capture this spy. Now I kill the two of you. But the story is, he shot you, I shot him. I'm the hero. Moreover, whatever treasure of intelligence that little camera holds, it comes to me. I will weep pious tears at your funeral, which I'm sure will be held under the highest honors, and I will express my profound regrets to your unit as it ships out to Russia."

"You lunatic," said Macht. "You disgrace."

"Sieg Heil," said the SS officer as he fired. He missed.

This was because his left ventricle was interrupted mid-beat by a .380 bullet fired a split second earlier by Basil's .380 Browning in the Abwehr agent's right hand. Thus Boch jerked and his shot plunged off into the darkness.

The SS officer seemed to melt. His knees hit first—not that it mattered, because he was already quite dead, and he toppled to the left, smashing his nose, teeth, and pince-nez.

"Excellent shot, old man," said Basil. "I didn't even feel you remove my pistol."

"I knew he would be up to something. He was too cooperative. Now, sir, tell me what I should do with you. Should I arrest you and earn the Iron Cross, or should I give you back your pistol and camera and watch you fly away?"

"Even as a philosophic exercise, I doubt I could argue the first proposition with much force," said Basil.

"Give me an argument, then. You saved my life, or rather your pistol did, and you saved the lives of the men in my unit. But I need a justification. I'm German, you know, with that heavy, irony-free, ploddingly logical mind."

"All right, then. I did not come here to kill Germans. I have killed no Germans. Actually the only one who has killed Germans, may I point out, sir, is *you*. Germans will die, more and more, and Englishmen and Russians and even the odd Frog or two. Possibly an American. That can't be stopped. But I am told that the message on the film, which is completely without military value, by the way, has a possibility of ending the war by as much as two years sooner than expected. I don't know about you, sir, but I am sick to death of war."

"Fair enough. I am, too. Here, take this, and your camera, and get out of here. There's the plane."

"Ah, one question, if I may?"

"Yes?"

"How do you turn it on?"

"You don't fly, do you?"

"Not really, no. At least, not *technically*. I mean I've watched it, I've flown in them, I know from the cinema that one pulls the stick up to climb, down to descend, right and left, with pedals—"

"God, you are something, I must say."

And so the German told him where the ignition was, where the brakes were, what groundspeed he had to achieve to go airborne, and where the compass was for his due north heading.

"Don't go over 150 meters. Don't go over 150 kilometers per hour. Don't try anything fancy. When you get to England, find a nice soft meadow, put her down, and just before you touch down, switch off the magnetos and let the plane land itself."

"I will."

"And remember one thing, Englishman. You were good—you were the best I ever went after. But in the end I caught you."

THE WAR ROOM

"Gentlemen," said Sir Colin Gubbins, "I do hope you'll forgive Captain St. Florian his appearance. He is just back from abroad, and he parked his airplane in a tree."

"Sir, I am assured the tree will survive," said Basil. "I cannot have *that* on my conscience, along with so many other items."

Basil's right arm was encased in plaster of Paris; it had been broken by his fall from the tree. His torso, under his shirt, was encased in strong elastic tape, several miles of it, in fact, to help his four broken ribs mend. The swelling on his face, from the blow delivered by the late SS Hauptsturm-führer Boch, had gone down somewhat, but it was still yellowish, corpulent, and quite repulsive, as was the blue-purple wreath that surrounded his bloodshot eye. He needed a cane to walk, and of all his nicks, it was the abraded knee that turned out to hurt the most, other than the headache, constant and throbbing, from the concussion. In the manly British officer way, however, he still managed to wear his uniform, even if his jacket was thrown about his shoulders over his shirt and tie.

"It looks like you had a jolly trip," said the admiral.

"It had its ups and downs, sir," said Basil.

"I think we know why we are here," said General Cavendish, ever irony-free, "and I would like to see us get on with it."

It was the same as it always was: the darkish War Room under the Treasury, the prime minister's lair. That great man's cigar odor filled the air, and too bad if you couldn't abide it. A few posters, a few maps, a few cheery exhortations to duty, and that was it. There were still four men across from Basil, a general, an admiral, Gubbins, and the man of tweed, Professor Turing.

"Professor," said Sir Colin, "as you're just in from the country and new to the information, I think it best for you to acquire the particulars of Captain St. Florian's adventures from his report. But you know his results. He succeeded, though he got quite a thrashing in the process. I understand it was a close-run thing. Now you have had the results of his mission on hand at Bletchley for over a week, and it is time to see whether or not St. Florian's blood, sweat, and tears were worth it."

"Of course," said Turing. He opened his briefcase, took out the seven Minox photos of the pages from *The Path to Jesus*, reached in again, and pulled out around three hundred pages of paper, whose leaves he flipped to show the barons of war. Every page was filled with either numerical computation, handwriting on charts, or lengthy analysis in typescript.

"We have not been lazy," he said. "Gentleman, we have tested everything. Using our decryptions from the Soviet diplomatic code as our index, we have reduced the words and letters to numerical values and run them through every electronic bombe we have. We have given them to our best intuitive code breakers—it seems to be a gift, a certain kind of mind that can solve these problems quickly, without much apparent effort. We have analyzed them up, down, sideways, and backwards. We have tested the message against every classical code known to man. We have compared it over and over, word by word, with the printed words of the Reverend MacBurney. We have measured it to the thousandth of an inch, even tried to project it as a geometric problem. Two PhDs from Oxford even tried to find a pattern in the seemingly random arrangement of the odd crosslike formations doodled across all the pages. Their conclusion was that the *seemingly* random pattern was *actually* random."

He went silent.

"Yes?" said Sir Colin.

"There is no secret code within it," the professor finally said. "As any possible key to a book code, it solves nothing. It unlocks nothing. There is no secret code at all within it."

The moment was ghastly. Finally Basil spoke.

"Sir, it's not what I went through to obtain those pages that matters. I've had worse drubbings in football matches. But a brave and decent man has put himself at great risk to get them to you. His identity would surprise you, but it seems there are some of them left on the other side. Thus I find it devastating to write the whole thing off and resign him to his fate for nothing. It weighs heavily."

"I understand," said Professor Turing. "But you must understand as well. Book codes work with books, don't they? Because the book is a closed, locked universe—that is the *point*, after all. What makes the book code work, as simple a device as it is, is, after all, that it's a *book*. It's mass-produced on Linotype machines, carefully knitted up in a bindery, festooned with some amusing imagery for a cover, and whether you read it in Manchester or Paris or Berlin or Kathmandu, the same words will be found on the same places on the same page, and thus everything makes sense. This, however, is not a book but a manuscript, in a human hand. Who knows how age, drinking, debauchery, tricks of memory, lack of stamina, advanced syphilis or gonorrhea may have corrupted the author's effort? It will almost certainly get messier and messier as it goes along, and it may in the end not resemble the original at all. Our whole assumption was that it would be a close enough replica to what MacBurney had produced twenty years earlier for us to locate the right letters and unlock the code. Everything about it is facsimile, after all, even to those frequent religious doodles on the pages. If it were a good facsimile, the growth or shrinkage would be consistent and we could alter our calculations by measurable quantities and unlock it. But it was not to be. Look at the pages, please, Captain. You will see that even among themselves, they vary greatly. Sometimes the letters are large, sometimes small. Sometimes a page contains twelve hundred letters, sometimes six hundred, sometimes twenty-three hundred. In certain of them, it seems clear that he was drunk, pen in hand, and the lines are all atumble, and he is just barely in control. His damnable lack of consistency dooms any effort to use this as a key to a code contained in the original. I told you it was a long shot."

Again a long and ghastly silence.

"Well, then, Professor," said Gubbins, "that being the case, I think we've taken you from your work at Bletchley long enough. And we have been absent from our duties as well. Captain St. Florian needs rest and rehabilitation. Basil, I think all present will enthusiastically endorse you for decoration, if it matters, for an astonishing and insanely courageous effort. Perhaps a nice promotion, Basil. Would you like to be a major? Think of the trouble you could cause. But please don't be bitter. To win a war you throw out a million seeds and hope that some of them produce, in the end, fruit. I'll alert the staff to call—"

"Excuse me," said Professor Turing. "What exactly is going on here?"

"Ah, Professor, there seems to be no reason for us to continue."

"I daresay you chaps have got to learn to listen," he said.

Basil was slightly shocked by the sudden tartness in his voice.

"I am not like Captain St. Florian, a witty ironist, and I am not like you three high mandarins with your protocols and all that elaborate and counterfeit bowing and scraping. I am a scientist. I speak in exact truth. What I say is true and nothing else is."

"I'm rather afraid I don't grasp your meaning, sir," said Gubbins stiffly. It was clear that neither he nor the other two mandarins enjoyed being addressed so dismissively by a forty-year-old professor in baggy tweeds and wire-frame glasses.

"I said listen. *Listen!*" repeated the professor, rather rudely, but with such intensity it became instantly clear that he regarded them as intellectual inferiors and was highly frustrated by their rash conclusion.

"Sir," said General Cavendish, rather icily, "if you have more to add, please add it. As General Sir Colin has said, we have other duties—"

"*Secret* code!" interrupted the professor.

All were stupefied.

"Don't you see? It's rather brilliant!" He laughed, amused by the code maker's wit. "Look here," he said. "I shall try to explain. What is the most impenetrable code of all to unlock? You cannot do it with machines that work a thousand times faster than men's brains."

Nobody could possibly answer.

"It is the code that pretends to be a code but isn't at all."

More consternation, impatience, yet fear of being mocked.

"Put another way," said the professor, "the code is the absence of code."

No one was going to deal with that one. "Whoever dreamed this up, our Cambridge librarian or an NKVD spymaster, he was a smart fellow. Only two people on earth could know the meaning of this communication, though I'm glad to say they've been joined by a third one. Me. It came to me while running. Great for clearing the mind, I must say."

"You have the advantage, Professor," said Sir Colin. "Please, continue."

"A code is a disguise. Suppose something is disguised as itself?"

The silence was thunderous.

"All right, then. Look at the pages. *Look at them!*"

Like chastened schoolboys, the class complied.

"You, St. Florian, you're a man of hard experience in the world. Tell me what you see."

"Ah . . ." said Basil. He was completely out of irony. "Well, ah, a messy scrawl of typical eighteenth-century handwriting, capitalized nouns, that sort of thing. A splotch of something, perhaps wine, perhaps something more dubious."

"Yes?"

"Well, I suppose, all these little religious symbols."

"Look at them carefully."

Basil alone did not need to unlimber reading spectacles. He saw what they were quickly enough.

"They appear to be crosses," he said. "Just crosses?"

"Well, each of them is mounted on a little hill. Like Calvary, one supposes."

"Not like Calvary. There were three on Calvary. This is only one. Singular."

"Yes, well, now that I look harder, I see the hill isn't exactly a hill. It's segmented into round, irregular shapes, very precisely drawn in the finest line his nib would permit. I would say it's a pile of stones."

"At last we are getting somewhere."

"I think I've solved your little game, Professor," said General Cavendish. "That pile of stones, that would be some kind of road marker, eh? Yes, and a cross has been inserted into it. Road marker, that is, marking the path, is that what it is? It would be a representation of the title of the pamphlet, *The Path to Jesus*. It is an expression of the central meaning of his argument."

"Not what it *means*. Didn't you hear me? Are you deaf?"

The general was taken aback by the ferocity with which Professor Turing spoke.

"I am not interested in what it means. If it means something, that meaning is different from the thing itself. I am interested in what it *is*. Is, not means."

"I believe," said the admiral, "a roadside marker is called a cairn. So that is exactly what it is, Professor. Is that what you—"

"Please take it the last step. There's only one more. Look at it and tell me what it is."

"Cairn . . . cross," said Basil. "It can only be called a cairncross. But that means nothing unless . . ."

"Unless what?" commanded Turing. "A name," said Sir Colin.

Hello, hello, said Basil to himself. He saw where the path to Jesus led.

"The Soviet spymaster was telling the Cambridge librarian the name of the agent at Bletchley Park so that he could tell the agent's new handler. The device of communication was a 154-year-old doodle. The book-code indicators were false, part of the disguise."

"So there is a man at Bletchley named Cairncross?" asked Sir Colin.

"John Cairncross, yes," said Professor Turing. "Hut 6. Scotsman. Don't know the chap myself, but I've heard his name mentioned—supposed to be first-class."

"John Cairncross," said Sir Colin.

"He's your Red spy. Gentlemen, if you need to feed information to Stalin on Operation Citadel, you have to do it through Comrade Cairncross. When it comes from him, Stalin and the Red generals will believe it. They will fortify the Kursk salient. The Germans will be smashed. The retreat from the East will begin. The end will begin. What was it again? 'Home alive in '45,' not 'Dead in heaven in '47.'"

"Bravo," said Sir Colin.

"Don't *bravo* me, Sir Colin. I just work at sums, like Bob Cratchit. Save your bravos for that human fragment of the Kipling imagination sitting over there."

"I say," said Basil, "instead of a *bravo*, could I have a nice whisky?"

Every Seven Years

Denise Mina

~∽

Denise Mina had an eclectic childhood, during which she lived in Glasgow, Paris, London, Invergordon, Bergen, and Perth. She left school early and went through a number of menial jobs before returning to finish her education with night classes at The Glasgow University Law School. Mina went on to receive a PhD at Strathclyde Univserity, where her student grant enabled her to write her first novel, *Garnethill* (despite the grant being intended for a completely unrelated purpose). She has written twelve novels, three plays, five graphic novels, and has contributed to television and radio in the UK. Mina has been the recipient of various awards, including the CWA John Creasy Dagger for Best First Crime Novel in 1998 (*Garnethill*), the Sprit of Scotland Award (*Garnethill*), the CWA Best Story in 2000 (*Helena and the Babies*), and the Theakstons Old Peculiar Crime Novel of the Year in 2012 (*The End of Wasp Season*) and 2013 (*Gods and Beasts*). She has also been nominated for several awards, including the Edgar, the CWA Gold Dagger, and the Nibbie. Mina was a Bailey's Prize for Women's Fiction Judge in 2014.

I am standing on a rostrum in my old school library. An audience of thirty or so people is applauding, I am smiling and mouthing "thank you" and I know that they all hate me.

The audience looks like people I used to know seven years ago, but less hopeful and fatter. Actually, they're not fat, they're normal sized, but I'm an actor. We have to stay thin because our bodies are a tool of our trade. A lot of us have eating disorders and that creates an atmosphere of anxiety around food. The applauding audience isn't fat; I'm just London-actress thin, which is almost-too-thin.

I look down. The rostrum is composed of big ply board cubes that fit together. We are standing on five but the corner one is missing; maybe they ran out of cubes, or one is broken. It's like standing on a slide puzzle, where one tile is missing and the picture is jumbled. This seems hugely significant to me while it is happening: we're in a puzzle and a big bit is missing. The whole afternoon feels like a hyper-real dream sequence so far, interspersed with flashes of terror and disbelief. My mum died this morning.

There is no chair on the rostrum, no microphone, no lectern to hide behind. I stand, exposed, on a broken box and justify my career as a minor actress to an audience who doesn't like me.

There are about thirty people in the audience. Not exactly the Albert Hall, but they are appreciative of my time because my mum is ill. She's in the local hospital and that's why I'm back. It has been mentioned several times, in the introductions and during the questioning. So sorry about your mum.

Maybe pity is fueling the applause.

Maybe time is moving strangely because I'm in shock. I smile and mouth "thank you" at them for a third time. I want to cry but I'm professional and I swallow the wave of sadness that engulfs me. Never bitter. My mother's words: never bitter, Else. That's not for us. My mum said life is a

481

race against bitterness. She said if you die before bitterness eats you, then you've won. She won.

A fat child is climbing up the side of the rostrum towards me. He can't be more than four or five. He's so round and wobbly he has to swing his legs sideways to walk properly. He comes up to me and—tada!—he shoves a bunch of supermarket flowers at my belly without looking at me. The price is still on them. He must be someone's kid. He's not the kid you would choose to give a visiting celebrity flowers, even a crap celebrity. He turns away and sort of rolls off the side of the platform and runs back to his mum.

He pumps his chunky little arms at his side, leg-swing-run, leg-swing-run, running all the way down the aisle to a big lady sitting at the back. Her face brims with pride. He looks lovely to her. She's just feeding him what she's eating; she doesn't see him as fat. I'm seeing that. I'm probably the only person in the room who is seeing that. Everyone else is seeing a cute wee boy doing a cute wee thing.

It's me. Bitterness comes in many forms. Malevolent gossip, lack of gratitude, even self-damaging diet regimes. Today bitterness is a tsunami coming straight at me. It's a mile-high wall of regret and recrimination. Broken things are carried in the threatening wave: chair legs and dead people and boats. And it is coming for me.

My mum died. This morning. In a hospital nearby. My mum died.

This is going on, this stupid event in a dreary public library on the island where I grew up. At the same time an alternate universe is unfolding, the one where I am a daughter and my mum is no longer alive. I love cats. On YouTube there's an eight-minute montage of cats crashing into windows and glass doors they thought were open. It went viral; you've probably seen it. Lots of different cats flying gleefully into what they think is empty space, bouncing off glass. It's funny, not because the cats are hurt; they're not hurt. It's funny because of that moment afterward when the cat sits up. They look at the glass, variously astonished or angry or embarrassed. It's funny because it is so recognizably human, that reaction. The WTF reaction.

Hitting the glass is where I am with the fact that my mum has died. I keep forgetting, thinking other things—I need a wee—that woman has got a spot on her neck—I want to sit down—and then BOOM I hit the glass.

But actors are special. We just keep going. If we forget our lines, or the scenery falls, or a colleague has died on stage, we just keep going. So I just keep going.

I'm standing on the rostrum with Karen Little. Karen and I grew up together.

She made my life a misery at school and we haven't seen each other for seven years. I can see her eyes narrow when she looks at me. I can see her shoulders rise, her lips tighten. Maybe she hates me even more now. I don't have a system of quantification for hate. I've forgotten what it is to be the recipient of this, so maybe that's why it feels heightened. Life has been kind to me since I left.

My mum died and, frankly, I'm not really giving too much of a shit. I want to tell her that: hey, Karen, d'you know what? The human body renews itself every seven years. Each individual cell and atom is replaced on a seven-year cycle. It's been seven years since we met and I'm different now. You're different now. All that stuff from before? We could just let that go.

But that's not how we do things on the island. Aggression is unspoken here. We're too dependent on one another to have outright fights.

Karen Little, just to fill you in on the background, was in my class. There were thirteen in our year. Eight girls, five boys. Karen was good at everything. Head girl material from the age of twelve, she was bossy, sporty, and academic. She was like all of the Spice Girls in one person. Except Baby Spice. Karen was never soft. Growing up on a farm will do that to you.

She has gray eyes and blond hair, Viking coloring. She looks like a Viking, too. Big, busty, kind of fertile-looking hips. She stands on both feet at the same time, always looks as if she is standing on the prow of a boat.

I'm a sloucher. An academic nothing. A dark-haired incomer. My mother moved here to teach but gave it up before I was born. After the accident, they made it clear they didn't want her. Even the children shunned her.

Karen's a full head taller than me. So it was odd that she had this thing about me. I never understood why she hated me so much. Everyone hated Mum because of the accident, but Karen hated me. It wasn't reciprocated and it was scary.

No one there liked my mother or me but Karen took it to extremes. I saw her looking at me sometimes, as if she'd like to hit me. She didn't do anything. I should emphasis that. But I often saw her staring at me, at parties, across roads, in class. I was scared of her. I think she had a lot going on at home and I became a focus for her ire.

Now, Karen is the librarian in the school library.

My face hits the glass.

There is no one here I can confide in. My. Mum. Died. Three words. I haven't said them to anyone yet. If I don't say it maybe the universe will realize its mistake. It will get sorted out. The governor will call at the last minute and stop her dying of lung cancer. Maybe, if I don't say it.

Or maybe I'm worried that if I say it I will start crying, I'll cry and cry and maybe I will die of it.

No one in the school library knows yet. They will as soon as they leave. Mum is headline news around here. Everyone knows that she isn't well, in the local hospital with lung cancer. Since I got back several people have told me that she will get better because the treatment is better than it was. People tell me happy stories about other people who had cancer but got better and now they run marathons, climb mountains, have second lives. Mention of cancer prompts happy stories, as if people feel jinxed by the word and need to rebalance the narrative. I've learned that you can't make them stop with the positive anecdotes. They need them. No one here can believe that my mother is going to die anymore than I can. My mother is an unfinished song. It's out of character that she will simply die of an illness. My mother has never done a simple thing.

But they know that's why I'm back on the island, in the small town of my birth, standing on a rostrum with Karen Little, listening to interminable clapping.

I mouth "thank you" again and watch the fat kid's mother pull him onto her knee. He looks forward, flush from his run. Behind him the mother shuts her eyes and kisses his hair with a gesture so tender I have to look away.

Karen cornered me in the chemist's. Do come, Else, please. We would be so glad to hear from you, all your exciting experiences! Karen covers her loathing with smiles. They all do. Anywhere else we would have been excluded, picked on. Maybe they would have burnt crosses on our lawn. The hostility would have affected our day-to-day interactions, but the island is small, we are so dependent on each other for survival, that instead, aggression is a background thrum in a superficially pleasant existence.

Tourists fall in love with the white beaches and palm trees. The seeds are washed up here on the Gulf Stream and palm trees grow all over the island. The landscape looks tropical until you step off the coach or out of the hotel or from your rented car. It is bitterly cold here. The vegetation makes it perpetually unexpected.

The distillery towns are always dotted with startled tourists from Spain or Japan, all looking for a sweater shop. That's what we're famous for: whisky and sweaters.

Karen is tired of watching me being applauded. It's dying out anyway, so she steps in front of me and blocks my sight lines.

Thank you! Her voice is shrill. Thank you to our local celeb, Miss Else Kennedy! She has prompted another round of applause. Oh, god. My right knee buckles, as if it knows this will never end and it's decided to go solo and just get the hell out of here.

Karen turns to address me. Her face is too close to mine. She has lipstick on, it is bleeding into a dry patch of skin at the side of her mouth, and I can smell it; she's close. I feel as if she's going to bite my face and it makes me want to cry.

We have a present for you! She is smiling with her teeth apart looking from me to the audience. Something special is coming, I can see the venom spark in her eye like the flick of a serpent's tail.

Karen's voice continues to trill through my fog of grief and annoyance. Special gift! It will be presented by—Marie! (I wasn't listening to that bit).

——Marie is also a bit scary looking. She has an unusually big face, her hair is greasy. She climbs up onto the platform holding a yellow hardback with both hands. She looks as if she's delivering a sacred pizza.

I know this isn't a surreal dream. It's just work-a-day grim and I'm bristling with shock and sorrow. My mum died. I feel the glass bounce me backwards on the decking.

——Marie takes tiny steps to get to me, the rostrum isn't big enough for three people and I'm making the best of it, a professional smile is nailed to my face.

But then I see what is in her hand. It's the book. My smile drops.

Karen's voice is loud in my ear. A lovely book about the famous painter:

Roy Lik-Tin-Styne! This is, believe it or not! The very last book Else took out of our library! Isn't that fun? And Anne-Marie is going to present it to her as a memento of this lovely visit!

Karen turns and looks straight at me, giving a loud and hearty laugh. HAHAHA! she says, straight into my face HAHAHA! She is so close her gusty laugh moves my hair.

Anne-Marie drops the big book into one of my hands and shakes the other one. She is smiling vacantly over my shoulder. Then she's gone.

What do you think of that, Else?

I can't speak. I look at it. The flyleaf is ripped but it is the same book. Time-yellowed cover, whitened along the spine from sun exposure. I know then. I will kill Karen Little. And I'll kill her tonight.

Back in the house I sit in my mum's living room with a huge glass of straight vodka in my hand.

I haven't had a drink for seven years and surprise myself by pouring straight Smirnoff into a pint glass. This is what I want. Not a glass of full-bodied red or a relaxing beer. What I want is a sour, bitter drink that will wither my tongue and make me half mad. I want a drink that will make me sick and screw me up.

Before this morning, before the final breath went out of her as I held her hand in the hospital, I thought of Totty as "Mum." Now I find I call her "my mum." In the Scots Gaelic language there is no ownership. It isn't *my* cup of tea. The cup of tea is *with* me. Now that Mum is no longer with me she has become *my* mum. I'm claiming ownership of her.

My mum is all around me in this room, I can smell her. I can see the book she was reading before she went into the hospital, open on the arm of the chair. This house is polluted with books. Her phrase. Polluted. They're everywhere. They're not furniture or mementoes. They're not arranged by spine color on bookcases or anything like that. They're functioning things, on the bathroom floor, in the kitchen by the cooker, on the floor in the hall, as if she had to stop reading that one to pull a coat on and go out. And her tastes were very catholic. Romance, classic, Russian literature, crime fiction. She'd read anything. I've known her to read a book halfway through before realizing that she'd read it before. She didn't read to show off at book groups or for discussion. She never made a show of her erudition. She just liked to be lost.

The book from the school is on the table in front of me. Yellow, accusing. Lichtenstein is on the cover, photographed in black and white. He is standing contraposto in the picture, looking a little fey. The height of the white room behind him implies a studio space.

I can't look at that anymore. The couch is facing the window. A sloping lawn leads down to an angry sea. America is over there, obscured from view by the curvature of the earth and nothing more. Away is over there.

I sat here often while she was alive, on the couch, planning my exit from this small place. *I will get away.* The day after my sixteenth birthday, I left the island like a rat on fire. Down to London, sleeping on floors, in beds I didn't particularly want to be in, just to be away. I would have sold my soul. But my mum stayed.

She came to visit me in London once I got a place of my own, when I was doing the TV soap and the money was rolling in. Nothing makes you feel rich as much as having been poor. Totty came down to London "for a visit." Always "for a visit." Coming back was not negotiable. She was always going to come back here, to an island that hated her.

I asked her to stay with me in London. I did it several times. Sobbing, drunk, and begging her to stay. She took my hand and said *I love you* and *you know I can't* and *they'll win then.* Finally she said she wouldn't come and visit anymore if I asked her again. And you should stop drinking, Else. You don't have a problem but you drink for the wrong reasons. Get drunk for fun, she said, and only for fun. Never get drunk to give yourself guts. That's what I'm doing now. Sipping the foul vodka as if it were medicine, trying to swallow it before it touches the sides. I need guts tonight.

I look at the book on the table and I'm back at the event in the small, packed library. Why did they even have a podium, I wonder now. Everyone could see me perfectly well. In hindsight it feels like a freak show tent, with me as the freak everyone wants to peer at. Karen planned it all around the giving of the book. She must have known while she watched me speak about my pathetic career, my reality show appearances, the failed comedy series. She must have known when she cornered me in the chemist's.

I look down at the book.

I'm getting drunk and I try to think of an alternative explanation: is this a custom? Do people give people "the last book they took out of their school library"? No.

I should have asked: did someone else suggest this? But I know in my gut that the answer would be no. No one else suggested this. Karen Little suggested giving you this book. No one else would know which was the last book you took out of the school library. And why would they? Why the hell would they? It means nothing to anyone but Karen and me.

I open it. Tech solutions hadn't reached this little corner of Scotland yet. There were no chips or automatic reminders sent by text to the mobiles of borrowers. They still stamped books out of the library. The book has never been taken out since I had it, seven years ago. Of course it hasn't. Its been sitting in Karen's cupboard.

I start to cry and stroke the torn flyleaf. I realize that I'm glad my mum was already dead when Karen gave me this.

I flick through the book, as if casually, but I know, even before the pages fall open, that the handwritten note will still be there. The pages part like the Red Sea.

A ripped corner of foolscap paper, narrow, faint lines. Even the small hairs at the ripped edge are flattened perfectly after seven years.

It is facing down, but the ink is showing through. I pick it up and turn it over. There in a careful hand to disguise the writing, it says,

She got herself raped by
Paki Harris. That's why.

The stock in the school library has always been old. Most of it was second hand, given to the school by well-meaning locals after post mortem clearouts of family houses. The history books were hangovers from the Empire. Books that referred to "coolies" and other anachronisms. The Lichtenstein book was bang up to date by comparison. It was only fifteen years old and was about a modern painter. I was thrilled when I stumbled across it. I didn't know Lichtenstein's work. I was a pretentious teenager. I imagined myself walking through town with the book in my hand. I imagined myself in New York, in London, discussing Lichtenstein with Londoners. I didn't know until I got there that, one way or another, most Londoners are from small, hateful islands, too.

At the bus stop, on the way home from school, waiting with the book on my knee so anyone passing could see me reading it. *I'd Rather Drown Than Ask Brad For Help.* And then turning the page and finding the note. My whole life story shifting painfully to the side. Who I was. What I was. Looking up. Karen Little standing across the road, doing her death stare. The greatest acting lesson I ever had.

Replace the note in the pages. Shut the book.

Bite your lip.

Smile past Karen and look for the bus. I thought I might be sick. I thought I might cry. I did neither. I sat, apparently calm, imagined what someone who hadn't just been punched in the heart would look like, and I did that. I looked for the bus.

I scratched my face.

I saw a sheep on the sea front and my eyes followed it calmly for a few minutes. Karen kept her eyes on me the whole time, until the bus came and I got on and smiled at the driver and took my seat. Maybe she thought I didn't get the note. Maybe that's why she's giving it to me again. Karen Little made me an actor anyway. I have to give her that.

When I got to the end of our drive I was struck by terror. Totty might find the book. It might be true and she might tell me so. Why didn't I just throw the note away? It seemed inseparable from the book. I wrapped the book in a plastic bag and tucked it under a thick gorse bush. I left it there all night and picked it up in the morning and took it back to the library. I should have taken the note out but I didn't dare look at it again or touch it.

I wondered about the writing at the time. Did Karen disguise her writing because I knew her? Why stand there, watching me find it at the bus stop? Or did she disguise it in case the police became involved?

I never told Totty about the note. Ever. And I'm glad. And I know I'll be glad about that forever.

I remember that she's gone for the fifteenth time in an hour. My thoughts are flying, racing somewhere and then BANG. Shock. Disbelief.

Totty's gone. The world feels poorer. It feels pointless. The next breath feels pointless.

I sit on the couch and watch the waves break on each other as they struggle inland, then are dragged back out by their heels. Striving pointlessly. Then I make an effort. Studiously, I drink the crazy drink and get crazy drunk.

It's the middle of the night and I wake up on the couch. I'm sweaty and I smell unfamiliar to myself, strange and sour. The sea is howling outside, fierce gray. A selfharming sea. I'm going kill Karen Little. I'm so angry I can hardly breathe in.

The first problem is the car. I get into the car and start the engine and back it into a wall. It sounds as if it was probably a bad crash, from the crumple of metal, but I can't be bothered getting out to look at it. It's windy. The sea spray is as thick as a fog over the windscreen.

It's in *reverse*. That's the problem there.

I've solved a problem and feel buoyed.

I change gear. I go for a front-ways one this time and move off. I pass the gorse bush where I hid the Lik-Tin-Stein all those years ago. The engine is groaning and growling, doesn't sound happy, so maybe it's third gear. First gear. That's the one. So I put it in first and it sounds happy now. Am I wearing a coat? Where does Karen even live now? I'll find her. Wherever she lives.

I get all the way up the hill, looking down on the lights of the town and the harbor. Its inky dark up here and the road is disappearing in front of me, swallowed in the blackness. Lights! Of course! My lights are off.

I stop on the top of the hill, over the town. She's down there somewhere. I crank on the hand break and look for the lights. I don't know this car. The switch should be on the wheel but it's not. Not on the dashboard. Why would they hide a thing like that? It's ridiculous, it's not safe. I'm going to write to the company.

A glass-tap and a shout through the sheeting rain—HELLO?

A face. Man-face at the window. Smiling.

I wind the window down. I'm already indignant about the safety flaws in the car and the rain comes in making my leg cold. Now I'm furious.

The hell're you *doing* out here?

Else? He smiles, sweet, as round faced as he ever was. Tam. God, he's handsome.

I heard she died, Else. I was coming to see you.

So there's a dissonant thing going on now: *inside* my head I'm saying "Tam" over and over in different ways, friendly way, surprised, delighted, how-the-hell-are-ye! ways. But outside my head, I'm making a noise, a squeal like a hurt piglet, very high noise. My face is tight so I can't will it to move and I'm holding the steering wheel tight with both hands. And my face is wet.

Auch, darlin', says Tam. He opens the door and all the rain's getting on me and he's carrying me to his car and then I'm in the kitchen.

Tam.

Tam's pouring coffee. I hope it's for me because it looks really nice. He's telling me a lot of things that are surprising but also nice. Tam was my first boyfriend and, honestly, I have never stopped loving that man. We were inseparable before I left so abruptly. He knew why. I never wrote to him or called. I never asked him to visit. But Tam isn't bitter. He's winning his race. Tam's telling me that he's gay and he has a man and he's happy. It makes me feel so pleased, as if a part of me is now gay and has a man and is happy, too.

Now he's telling me very carefully that it wasn't me that turned him gay, you know. Tam? The hell are you on about? He sees that I'm laughing at him. I'm laughing in a loving way because, Tam, you don't need to explain that to me! For godsake! Well, anyway he's laughing too, now, but his laughter is more from relief really.

He explains that he went out with another girl from the other side of the island. Well, she's kind of angry with Tam for being gay. She thinks either she turned him gay by being unattractive or that he tricked her into covering for him. She hasn't settled on one reading of events just yet, but even though it was five years ago, she's still very annoyed about it.

I think about asking how unattractive can she possibly be, but that's a quip and my lips aren't very agile. Nor is my brain. And then the moment for a joke is past. So I just smile and say, Auch, well. People are nuts.

Tam says, Yeah, people are nuts and gives a sad half shrug. Still, he says, not nice to be the cause of hurt, you know?

He means it. However nasty she was to him, he still doesn't want to be the cause of hurt to her. That's what Tam's like. Like my mum. Better people than me. Good people.

I put my hand on Tam's to say that he's a lovely person, that he always was a lovely person, just like my mum. But he looks at my hand on his and he's a bit alarmed, like he's worried I might be coming on to him and he'll have to explain something else about being gay and how gay isn't just a sometimes type of thing. He's afraid of causing me hurt maybe. So I get out of my seat, sticking my tongue right out and sort of jab it at his face while making a hungry sound. Tam gives a girlish scream and pulls away from me and we're both laughing as if it's seven years ago and we're that whole bunch of different atoms again.

But then, as I'm laughing, I catch a fleeting glimpse of him looking at me. He is smiling wide, his uniform shirt unbuttoned at the neck, his tie loose. His hand is resting on the table and he's looking straight at me through laughing, appreciative eyes. I know that look and I feel for the jilted girl from the other side of the island. Tam would be easy to misread. When I'm not drunk I might tell him: you come over as straight, Tam. It's an acting job, being who you are. I am good at acting and Tam isn't. He's sending out all the wrong signals.

I'll tell him later. When my lips are working.

We're different people, I slur, every seven years, d'you know that?

He says no and I try to explain, but it's not going very well. Words elude me. When I look up he's very serious.

He says, Else, you're drunk. It's a change of topic from the seven years and he's not pleased I'm drunk.

I can get drunk if I want. You're not the goddam boss, Tam.

Yes, he says, seriously. I *am* the boss. I'm a police officer. You're drunk and you're driving a car. It's all banged up at the back. I am the boss. Where were you going?

I look at him and I think he knows where I was going but I just say nowhere. I knew when she died you would do something, he says, as if I'm a loose cannon, a crazy person who can't be trusted not to mess everything up unless my mum is there to tick me off. I look up and see the Smirnoff bottle and know that I wouldn't be drinking if she were still alive. The world has been without her for less than twenty-four hours and I'm already drinking and driving and trying to kill people. Being so wrong makes me livid.

I say, So, Tam, you didn't come to see me, you came to *stop* me? I call him a sweary name. What kind of person are you? You don't give a shit about me or my mum.

But Tam's face doesn't even twitch.

Don't even try, he says.

Don't even try what, *Tam*?

Don't try to make me feel guilty, Else. You haven't been in touch, you never even wrote to me. You didn't call me and tell me she was dead. What happened to her is the reason I became a policeman so don't even try that crap with me.

But I'm still angry because I'm so wrong and I say things to him that are just crude and mean. A drunken rant and I'm cringing even as I'm shouting. I start crying with shame and frustration because I'm saying things so unkind and nasty. I'm not homophobic. I don't think policemen even do that. I'm just really drunk and my mum's dead and they were so mean to her and Karen had the book all along and it's not fair.

I'm furious and drunk and ashamed and wrong and it's making me cry so much that I'm blind. I can hear Tam breathing gasps. Confusing. By the time the tears clear I can see him doubled over, holding his stomach. I think he's being sick but then I realize that he is laughing, very much, at the things I said about policemen and what he might do with them.

If you saw them! he says, the other policemen! You couldn't, even for a dare!

My mood swings as wildly as a change in wind direction over the open sea. I hope that coffee is for me.

My eyes are trying to kill me. They're stabbing my brain. I wake up in bed this time, in the morning. I've got all my clothes on. I have to keep my eyes shut as I sit up. I get hold of the bedstead to steady myself and tiptoe carefully towards the bathroom. My mouth floods with seawater and I have to run, even with my assassin eyes.

~

The smell of coffee lingers in the hallway. I'm worried that I've broken something in my olfactory system with all that vodka, unaccustomed as I am, until I get into the kitchen and find Tam making more coffee.

I feel awful.

Good heavens, says Tam, there's a surprise.

It's a nice thing to say, the way he says it. Kind. I slither into a seat and shade my eyes.

He's making scrambled eggs. I won't be able to eat but I'm too comforted by his presence to interrupt him.

You can't drive today, Else, he says. You've still got high alcohol content in your blood and your car lights are all smashed.

I don't answer. I sit with my hand over my eyes and listen to him putting toast on the grill, scraping the eggs in the pan and I think, if this was the fifties we could have been happy in a sexless marriage of convenience, Tam and I.

Who were you going to see last night, Else?

The memory evokes a misery so powerful it almost trumps my hangover. I tell him: I want to kill Karen Little.

He's stopped cooking and is looking at me. I can't look back. Karen?

He puts two plates of scrambled egg down on the table. And takes the toast from the grill and drops a slice on top of each of the yellow mountains.

I pull my plate over to me. Karen gave me the book back.

Tam is very still. Which book?

The Lichtenstein. She gave it to me at the library yesterday. She said it was the last book I ever took out of the library. No one had taken it out since. The note was still in it.

Tam sits down. His hands rest either side of his plate like a concert pianist gathering his thoughts before a recital.

Finally he speaks. I'll kill the bitch myself, he says.

The hospital tells me that nothing can be done about my mum today. They need a pathologist to come over from the mainland and do a post mortem, but the ferries are cancelled because a storm is coming. I can sit at home alone or I can go and confront Karen. Tam says let's go.

I'm in Tam's work car, a big police Range Rover. He isn't working today, he says, so it's no bother to drive me around. He's very angry about the book. He wants to know how she got the book to me. I tell him about the ceremony, in front of everyone, how she turned and HAHAHA'd into my face. He gets so angry he has to stop the car and get out and walk around and smoke a cigarette. I watch him out there, walking in the rising wind, his shoulders slumped, orange sparks from the tip of his cigarette against the backdrop of the grey sea like tiny, hopeless flares.

When he gets back in he takes a hip flask out of the glove box. He has a sip and gives it to me, as if drinking in a car is okay now, because he's so angry. I drink to please him. I feel it slide down into me and pinch the sharp edges off my hangover. It is comforting to have my anger matched. He nods at me to drink more and I do. The alcohol warms me and eases my headache and just everything feels a little easier, suddenly. Being angry feels easy and the future feels unimportant. What matters is stopping Karen.

When he finally speaks Tam's face is quite red. He tells me that we will find Karen and take her somewhere. We will not even ask about the note or the book; that would be a chance for her to talk herself out of trouble. If we asked she'd say she knew nothing about it. She'd blame someone else. She'd plead ignorance. We will simply get her alone and then, immediately, we'll do it: we will stab Karen in the neck. We will get away with it because we'll be together. We will be one another's alibi. We'll decide which of us will do the stabbing when we get there. But I already know.

He drives and he asks me about the book and I tell him it had never been taken out since I recovered it from the gorse bush and took it back to school. He remembers how upset I was back then. He says it was devastating for him, too, because I just left and I was his only friend. She ruined his life, too, because she chased me away. I know this is true. Back then Tam became fixated on me to a degree that wasn't comfortable. It wasn't always benign. *In vino veritas*: if I hadn't had that drink from his hip flask I might not suddenly know that I didn't really leave despite Tam. It was partly because of him. He was too intense back then. His love was overwhelming, and I never realized that before.

Tam parks in a quiet back street in the town. He has finished his cigarettes. He needs more so he goes off to the shops while I go into the school and look for Karen. He says just pretend that you left something in there. I watch him walk away from the car and he is scratching his head and his hand is covering his handsome face.

Karen Little isn't in today. The librarian's position is part time, the school secretary explains. Karen only works Monday, Tuesday, and half day on Wednesday. Then she tries to segue into a rant about government cuts but she can see I'm not listening. Then she stops and seems to realize that I've been drinking. She waits for me to speak, cocking her head like a curious seagull. Then she guesses: did I leave something yesterday? I'm supposed to say I did but, at just that moment, I think of my mum laying in a dark drawer in a mortuary fridge and, to be honest, I just sort of turn and walk away.

Out in the car park Tam is waiting with the engine running. I get in. Karen's not there, I tell him. She's at home. He starts to drive and I realize that he knows where she lives. But he's a cop in a small community. He probably knows where everyone lives. And then I wonder why the engine was running, before he knew she wasn't in.

We drive out of town, onto the flat, wind-blown moor. I steal a glimpse at Tam. He's furious. He's chewing his cheek and for some reason I think of Totty. Not about her dying but what she said about being bitter. Tam looks bitter and I pity him that. I catch a glimpse of myself in the side mirror and I'm frowning and I look bitter. This is not what Totty wanted for me.

I know this road. We're heading for Paki Harris's house and I ask why. Karen lives there now, says Tam. She was his only blood left on the island. Karen was related to Paki Harris. I've always known that. Everyone is related to everyone here except us incomers, but I didn't realize she was so closely related to Paki. Second cousins, Tam tells me somberly, just as we're passing a small farmhouse by the roadside with a "For Sale" outside it. The sign flaps in the wind like a rigid surrender flag.

"For Sale" signs are a sorrow on the island. People are born, live, and die in the same house here. A "For Sale" sign means the house owner had no one to leave it to, or maybe only a mainlander. Mainlanders don't understand the houses here. They sell them for cash or use them as holiday homes for two weeks a year, a long weekend at Easter. You can't do that with these houses. They need fires burning in them all the time to keep the damp out. To keep the rot out. These island houses aren't built for sometimes. They need commitment. Karen Little has taken on the commitment of Paki Harris's house.

It was an accident when my mother killed Paki. She ran him over on the main street on a Sunday afternoon in May, just before I was born. The Fatal Accident inquiry found no fault with her. She didn't try to explain what happened. She just ran him straight over, once, completely. She never mentioned it to me, I heard it from just about everyone else, with various embellishments. But the note, that note in the book, was the first version I ever heard that made sense of it. Paki raped her. She got pregnant with me. She killed him. That's why.

Paki Harris was from here. My mother was not. So the island took his side because loyalty isn't rational and, in the end, loyalty is all there is in a place this small.

In the seven years since I left I have often imagined what it was to be my heavily pregnant mother and see a man who had raped her day after day, standing in church, shopping at the supermarket, strolling on the sea front. I would have driven a car at him. The note, though, the note made me realize how deep the bitterness is here. It had never occurred to me that she had a motive until I saw that note. And afterwards, I realized, if they knew, if they all knew that he had raped her and that's why, could they not have found one shred of compassion for her? They spat at her in the street. She couldn't eat in the café because no one would speak when she was in there. She used the library until they banned her for "bringing food in." She had a packet of crisps in her bag. I'm not leaving, she'd say, because wherever you live, life is a race against bitterness and staying makes me run faster.

I feel so sad remembering it all. I feel like a house without a fire in it. I glance at Tam driving down the small road. He looks as if he's had a good old fire burning for the past seven years in him. His cheeks are pink, his eyes are shining. He's upright, sitting proud of the seat back. He's wired with bitterness and ready. I'm a sloucher. It seems so odd, us being in a car together, driving. Neither of us could drive back then. Tam takes a minor cut-off road and we follow the line of the hill, out towards the furious sea. At the headland, along the coast, the waves are forty feet high, smashing higher than the bare black cliffs. The sea is trying to claw its way onto the land and failing. Each time it retreats to catch its breath it fails. But it keeps trying.

Suddenly we see Paki Harris's house, a stark silhouette against the coming storm. It's one of those Victorian oddities that seem inevitable because they've been there for a hundred and fifty years. It is big, squat, and solid. The roofline is castellated; the windows are big and plentiful. The wind coming straight off the water is perpetual and incessant on this headland. The house is an act of defiance, an elegant onefingered salute to the wind and the ocean.

Very much like Paki himself, from what I've heard.

Before I knew he might be my father, before the note, I listened to stories about Paki without prejudice. I knew they hated my mum and loved Paki but I didn't see him as anything to do with me. Paki was a wild boy. Paki had bar fights and rode ponies into the town on the Sabbath. Paki pushed a minister into a bush. Paki burned a barn down. I heard a lot of stories about him. He was ugly but wild, and wild is good here.

As we draw up to the house the big heavy car is buffeted by the wind. Tam finds a wind-shaded spot by the side. He drives straight into it and pulls on the hand break. He wants to talk to me before we go in. He gets the hip flask out again. I don't want anymore but he makes me take it. And he tells me quietly what will happen: he will knock on the front door. I will go around behind the house to see if the back door is open. If it is open, I will come in and find the kitchen, first door on the right. There is a knife block with carving knives on it. Karen will come to the front door and let Tam in. Tam will bring Karen into the kitchen where I am hiding behind the door with my knife. I will go for the neck.

He looks at me for confirmation and I nod. I shouldn't be scared, he tells me. He will be right there. He smiles and makes me drink more. He doesn't drink anymore because he is driving. He's a cop. He can't afford to lose his license.

We get out of opposite doors and I slip around to the back of the house. Suddenly, the wind pushes and shoves and pulls at me and I have to crouch low and run for the steps up to the door. It is open. I'm in. I find myself breathless from the pummeling wind and the short sharp run up the worn stone steps.

In the dark stone hallway the house is silent. I don't think Karen is in. This is an eventuality that didn't occur to either of us, so deep were we into our consensus. I flatten myself against the wall and listen to the creaking windows and the hiss of the wind outside. At the far end of the hall I can see the cold white light from the front door spilling into the hallway.

Three knocks. Bam. Bam. Bam. Tam's shadow is on the carpet. Karen isn't even in.

I draw a deep breath.

A creak above. Not wind. A creak of weight on floor above. Karen is standing up somewhere. She takes a step, I feel her wondering if she did hear someone knocking. Then Tam knocks again. Bam. Bam. Bam. She is sure now and comes out to the upstairs hall. At the top of the stairs she pauses, she must be able to see the door from up there. She gives a little "oh" and hurries down to Tam standing outside. She seems a little annoyed by him as she flings the door open.

Why are you knocking? she asks.

Tam keeps his eyes on the hall and slips in, shutting the door behind him, taking her by the elbow and pulling her into a room.

Thomas? She's calling him his formal name, his grown-up name. Why did you wait out in that wind? Did the lawyer call you? She's jabbering like a housewife talking over a garden fence but Tam's saying nothing back.

Their voices move from the hall to nowhere to suddenly coming from the first door on the right. They are in the kitchen. They have gone through a different door into the kitchen and I am supposed to be in there right now with a knife from the knife block.

For the first time in my life, I have missed my cue.

I throw myself at the door and fall into the room. Look up. There is Tam, standing behind Karen, holding her by the elbow, sort of, pushing her forward, toward me. There, right in front of me, is a worktop with a large knife block on it. A lot of knives, maybe fifteen knives, all sizes, and the wooden handles are pointing straight towards the front of my hand. I can reach out and be holding one in a second.

Karen's mouth is hanging open. Tam's face is a glowering cloud of bitterness behind her shoulder.

I say, Hello, Karen.

No one knows what to do for a moment. We all stand still.

Hello, Else, says Karen.

If I was at home, in London, and a person I had been at school with seven years ago fell through my kitchen door I might have a lot questions for them. Karen just looks around the floor in front of her and says, Cuppa?

It takes a moment to compute. Cuppa?

Cup of tea? Hot cup of tea for you?

Actually, I say, looking at Tam who is getting more and more red in the face, A cuppa would be lovely, Karen, thanks.

Expertly, as if she is used to doing it, Karen twists her elbow to snake it out of Tam's grasp and steps away. She picks the kettle up off the range. She turns to look at both of us, thinking about something or other, and then she says, Well, I might as well make a pot of tea.

No one answers. It's the action of the elbow that makes me realize my gut was right. Tam has held her by that elbow before. And Karen has freed herself from that grip many times. He knew she wasn't in school today. I remember his look at me last night, the laughing-eyed assessment of me as he sat at the table.

She has her back to us as she fills it from the tap. Tam nods me towards the knife block. There it is, his face says, over there. And my face says, What? What are you saying? Oh! There? The knives! Oh, yes! I forgot about a knife! Okay then! But inside I'm saying something quite different. It's not his fault. It's understandable because I'm in a lot of crap on telly. Tam doesn't know I'm a good actor.

Karen gets some mugs down and a packet of biscuits. She's talking. To me.

Else, she says, I heard that your mum died. And I know that she died before you came to the school yesterday.

We look at each other and I see that she is welling up. I'm so sorry, she says and I wonder if she means about the book. But she doesn't. About the talk, she says. You must have felt that you couldn't cancel. Or you were too shocked, I don't know, but I'm sorry.

And then she puts her hand on my forearm. I can see in her eyes that she is really sorry, for my loss, for my mum, and for the sorrows of all daughters and mothers and I start to cry.

Karen's arms are around me, warm and safe, and I hear her tut into my ear and say Oh no, oh no, oh dear. She whispers to me, I hope you like the book. I'm sobbing too hard to pull away and she adds, Tam remembered you liked it back then.

I don't think Tam can hear her. He thinks we are whispering lady things. We stand in this grief clinch for quite a long time, until the whistle of the kettle calls an end to the round.

She sits me down at the table and I gather myself, wipe my face, and look at Tam. Tam is staring hard at the table, frowning furiously. He has given up making eye contact with me or nodding at knives or anything. He hasn't heard it but he has realized that I'm not going to stab her and never was. He doesn't know what to do now. Karen puts a plate of sugary biscuits in front of me and gives me a cup of tea.

And I've put sugar in that for you. I know you don't take sugar probably, but there's sugar in that because you've probably had a bad shock.

Karen sits down, her knees towards me. She picks up her mug and flicks a finger out at him without looking.

Did he tell you?

I sniff, What?

She smiles, Us, she says, a wry curl twitching at the side of her mouth.

I shake my head, baffled.

She glances at him. He is staring hard at her but she says it anyway: *Married.*

I lift my sugary tea, for the shock, and drink it though it is too hot. When I put the mug down again, empty, I tell her that my mum never said anything about that.

She hums. It was a secret. They married on the mainland, didn't they, Tam. Tam? Didn't they? In secret. Tam gives her nothing back and that makes her sort of snicker. Because of their families, you know. Because she had a lot of money and houses coming to her and he had nothing. Her family didn't trust him. But, you know, it didn't work out and no kids so, no harm done. They're getting divorced now. Aren't we Tam? Tam? Tam, are you not going to speak at all?

Tam is so uncomfortable that he cannot speak. He is eating biscuit after biscuit to keep his face busy. He is doing a strange thing with this head, not nodding or shaking it but sort of jerking it sideways in a noncommittal gesture.

Karen frowns at him. She doesn't understand. She gives up trying and turns her attention to me. So, what is going to happen with your mum's funeral?

I tell her: I'm flying her out of there. I'm taking her to London and I'm going to have her cremated there.

Karen says, Wouldn't it be easier to have her cremated nearby and then take her to London?

Tam came here to kill you, I say.

Karen says do I want another biscuit?

I actually wonder if I said that out loud because she hasn't reacted at all. But then I look at Tam's face and I know I did say it out loud. Karen lifts the plate and offers me another one, her face a perfect question: biscuit? That's how they do things on the island.

Tam stands up then, knocking his chair over behind him. The sharp clatter on the stone floor ricochets around the kitchen. He turns to the door and walks out, through the hall and out of the front door, slamming it behind him. A skirl of wind curls around our ankles.

Apropos of nothing, Karen says to me, This was Paki Harris's house.

I eat a biscuit and when I've finished I say, I know.

Karen nods. I don't know if you ever discussed him with your mum?

No.

She puts a hand on my hand and cringes, tearful again. Do you know who your father is, Else?

We never discussed my father.

Hm. Karen doesn't know what she can and can't say.

It just falls out of my London mouth: You think Paki raped my mum and that's why she ran him over?

Karen sighs. I don't know, she says, I don't know what happened. Not for me to know. But, Else, I think this house might be yours.

I don't want it.

It's worth a bit of money—

I don't want it.

Karen looks at me and I can see she's glad. She likes the house. She belongs here. These are not sometimes houses.

I was so mean to you when we were young. I'm sorry.

And I say, Oh! Forget it! because I'm flustered.

But she can't. She's been thinking about it, a lot, she says. But she is really sorry. She was jealous, because I was an incomer. It seems so free to me back then, she says, to not be part of all of this—

Aren't you worried, Karen? I blurt, Tam invited me here to stab you in the neck! Doesn't that concern you? You've just let him leave. Where's he going?

She looks fondly towards the front door. Gone to get drunk, I think. It's a rough week. Our divorce is final tomorrow.

And I understand finally. He wanted her killed today so he could inherit this house. And if I committed the murder I couldn't inherit from a woman I killed. It would be his outright.

I think he still has a thing about you.

Really?

Yeah.

I don't think so.

Well, you're wrong.

I look at her and realize that she's nice, Karen. She's not bitter. She is tied to this place and always will be. She accepts what it is to be from here and of here. There's no escape for Karen, not from my rapist father's house or from Tam who wanted to kill her. She accepts where she is and who she is and what had happened. She's like my mum. Karen is winning her race.

Let me drive you back to town, Else, as an apology. And as a thank you, for soldiering on yesterday. She pats my hand. Soldiering on is important.

She goes out to the hallway and pulls on a coat and I see past her to the vicious sea. The wind is screeching a ferocious caw. The waves are streaming over the cliffs. The grass on the headland is flattened and salted and Karen looks back at me. She smiles her soft island smile that could mean anything.

I am getting out of here. I am getting away, and this time I'm taking my mum with me.

Condor in the Stacks

James Grady

❧

James Grady graduated from the University of Montana School of Journalism. He worked for U.S. Senator Lee Metcalf, then with pioneering muckraking investigative journalist Jack Anderson. Grady has contributed to *PoliticsDaily.com*, *Slate*, *The Washington Post*, *American Film*, *The New Republic*, *Sport*, *Parade*, and *The Journal of Asian Martial Arts*. His espionage thriller *Six Days of the Condor* was adapted into the film *Three Days of the Condor*, starring Robert Redford and directed by Sydney Pollack. A member of the Writers Guild of America, East, an Edgar nominee and recipient of French, Italian, and Japanese awards for fiction, Grady has written a dozen novels and many short stories, as well as writing for film and television. Grady writes noir, espionage, intrigue, and police procedurals, and has published under the pseudonyms James Dalton and Brit Shelby. A bookish cinephile, he also enjoys the study of T'ai-chi, swimming, and listening to progressive rock.

A re you trouble?" asked the man in a blue pinstripe suit sitting at his D.C. desk on a March Monday morning in the second decade of America's first war in Afghanistan.

"Let's hope not," answered the silver-haired man in the visitor's chair.

They faced each other in the sumptuous office of the Director of Special Projects (DOSP) for the Library of Congress (LOC). Mahogany bookcases filled the walls.

The DOSP fidgeted with a fountain pen.

Watch me stab that pen through your eye, thought his silver-haired visitor.

Such normal thoughts did not worry that silver-haired man in a blue sports jacket, a new maroon shirt and well-worn black jeans.

What worried him was feeling trapped in a gray fog tunnel of numb.

Must be the new pill, the green pill they gave him as they drove him away from CIA headquarters, along the George Washington Parkway and beneath the route flown by 9/11 hijackers who slammed a jetliner into the Pentagon.

The CIA car ferried him over the Potomac. Past the Lincoln Memorial. Up "the Hill" past three marble fortresses for Congress's House of Representatives where in 1975, he'd tracked a spy from U.S. ally South Korea who was working deep cover penetration of America by posing as a mere member of the messianic Korean cult that provided the last cheerleaders for impeached President Nixon.

The ivory U.S. Capitol glistened across the street from where the CIA car delivered Settlement Specialist Emma and silver-haired *him* to the Library of Congress.

Whose DOSP told him: "I don't care how 'classified' you are. Do this job and don't make trouble or you'll answer to me."

The DOSP set the fountain pen on the desk.

Put his hands on his keyboard: "What's your name?"

"Vin," said the silver-haired stranger.

"Last name?"

Vin told him that lie.

The DOSP typed it. A printer hummed out warm paper forms. He used the fountain pen to sign all the correct lines.

"Come on," he told Vin, tossing that writing technology of the previous century onto his desk. "Let's deliver you to your hole."

He marched toward the office's mahogany door.

Didn't see his pen vanish into Vin's hand.

That mahogany door swung open as the twenty-something receptionist yawned, oblivious to the pistol under her outer office visitor Emma's spring jacket. Emma stood as the door opened, confident she wouldn't need to engage her weapon but with a readiness to let it fill her hand she couldn't shake no matter how long it had been *since*.

The DOSP marched these *disruptions* from another agency through two tunnel-connected, city block-sized library castles to a yellow cinderblock walled basement and a green metal door with a keypad lock guarded by a middle-aged brown bird of a woman.

"This is Miss Doyle," the DOSP told Vin. "One of ours. She's been performing your just-assigned functions with optimal results, *plus* excelling in all her other work."

Brown bird woman told Vin: "Call me Fran." Fran held up the plastic laminated library staff I.D. card dangling from a lanyard looped around her neck. "We'll use mine to log you in." She swiped her I.D. card through the lock.

Tapped the keypad screen.

"Now enter your password," said Fran. "*First*," CIA Emma told the *library-only* staffers, "you two: please face me."

The DOSP and Fran turned their backs to the man at the green metal door.

Vin tapped six letters into the keypad. Hit ENTER.

The green metal door clicked. Let him push it open.

Pale light flooded the heavy-aired room. A government-issue standard metal desk from 1984 waited opposite the open door. An almost as ancient computer monitor filled the desk in front of a wheeled chair. Rough pine boxes big enough to hold a sleeping child were stacked against the back wall.

Like coffins.

"Empty crates in," said Fran, "full crates out. Picked up and dropped off in the hall. It's your job to get them to and from there. Use that flatbed dolly."

She computer clicked to a spreadsheet listing crates dropped off, crates filled, crates taken away: perfectly balanced numbers.

"Maintenance Operations handles data entry, except for when you log a pick-up notice. They drop off the Review Inventory outside in the hall." Fran pointed to a heap of cardboard boxes. "From closing military bases. Embassies. Other . . . secure locations.

"Unpack the books," said Fran. "Check them for security breaches. Like if some Air Force officer down in one of our missile silos forgot and stuck some secret plan in a book from the base library. Or wrote secret notes they weren't supposed to."

Vin said: "What difference would it make? You burn the books anyway."

"*Pulp* them," said the DOSP. "We are in compliance with recycling regulations."

CIA Emma said: "Vin, this is one of those eyeballs-needed, *gotta-do* jobs."

"Sure," said Vin. "And you'll know right where I am while I'm doing it."

The DOSP snapped: "Just do it right. The books go into crates, the crates get hauled away, the books get pulped."

Vin said: "Except for the ones we save."

"*Rescuer* is not in your job description," said the DOSP. "You can send no more than one cart of material *per week* to the Preserve stacks. You're only processing fiction."

The DOSP checked his watch. "A new employee folder is on your desk. We printed it out. Your computer isn't printer or Internet enabled."

"Security policy," said CIA Emma. "Not just for you."

"*Really.*" The DOSP's smile curved like a scimitar. "Well, as your Agency insisted, this is the only library computer that accepts his access code. A bit isolating, I would think, but as long as that's '*security policy*' and not *personal.*"

He and brown bird Fran adjourned down the underground yellow hall.

Vin stood by the steel desk.

Emma stood near the door. Scanned her Reinsertion Subject. "Are you OK?"

"That green pill wiped out whatever OK means."

"I'll report that, but *hey*: you've only been out of the Facility in Maine for—"

"The insane asylum," he interrupted. "The CIA's secret insane asylum."

"Give yourself a break. You've only been released for eleven days, and after what happened in New Jersey while they were driving you down here . . ."

"Look," she said, "it's your new job, first day. Late lunch. Let's walk to one of those cafes we saw when we moved you into your house. Remember how to get home?"

"Do you have kids?" Her stare told him *no*.

"This is like dropping your kid off for kindergarten," said Vin. "Go."

Emma said: "You set the door lock to your codename?"

"Yeah," he said. "*Condor.*"

His smile was wistful: "Can't ever get away from that."

"Call you Vin, call you Condor, at least you have a name. Got my number?"

He held up his outdated flip-phone programmed by an Agency tech.

She left him alone in that subterranean cave. Call him Vin. Call him Condor.

Ugly light. The toad of an old computer squatting on a gray steel desk. A heap of sagging cardboard boxes. The wall behind him stacked with wooden crates—*coffins.*

Thick heavy air smelled like . . . basement rot, paper, stones, old insulation, cardboard, tired metal, steam heat. A whiff of the coffins' unvarnished pine.

He rode the office chair in a spin across the room. Rumbled back in front of the desktop computer monitor glowing with the spreadsheet showing nine cases—*pinewood coffins*—nine cases delivered to this Review Center. He clicked the monitor into a dark screen that showed his reflection with seven coffins stacked behind him.

Only dust waited in the drawers on each side of the desk's well. The employee manual urged library staffers to hide in their desk wells during terrorist or psycho attacks. *Like the atom bomb doomsday drills when I was a—*

And *he remembered!* His CIA-prescribed handful of daily pills didn't work perfectly: he could *kind of* remember!

Tell no one.

He slid open the middle desk drawer. Found three paperclips and one penny.

From the side pocket of the blue sports jacket he fetched the stolen fountain pen.

Sometimes you gotta do what you do just to be you.

He stashed the stolen pen in his middle desk drawer.

Noticed the monitor's reflection of seven coffins.

WAIT.

Am I crazy?

YES was the truth but not the answer.

He turned around and counted the coffins stacked against the back wall: *Seven.*

Clicked open the computer's spreadsheet to check the inventory delivery: *Nine.*

Why are two coffins missing?

The CIA's cell phone sat on his desk.

This is your job now. No job, no freedom.

Condor put the cell phone in his shirt pocket over his heart.

Suddenly he didn't want to be there because *there* was where *they* brought him, *transporting* him like a boxcar of doomed books. He counted the coffins: *still seven.* Walked out the door, pulling it shut with a click as he switched out the light.

The wide yellow-bricked hall telescoped away into distant darkness to his left. To his right, the tunnel ran about thirty steps until it T'ed at a brick wall.

He turned left, the longest route that let him look back and see where he'd been. Floated each stepping foot out in front of him empty of weight like Victor'd taught him in the insane asylum: aesthetically correct *T'ai chi* plus a martial arts technique that foiled foot-sweeping ninjas and saved you if the floor beneath your stepping shoe vanished.

Footsteps! Walking down that intersecting tunnel.

He hurried after those sounds of someone to ask for directions.

The footsteps quickened.

Don't scare anybody: cough so they know you're here.

The footsteps ran.

Pulled Condor into running, his heart jack hammering his chest.

Go right—*no left*, twenty steps until the next juncture of tunnels.

Whirr of sliding-open doors.

Dashing around a yellow brick walled corner—

Elevator—doors *closing!* He thrust his left arm into the doors' chomp—they bounced open and tumbled him into the bright metal cage.

FIST!

Without thought, with the awareness of ten thousand practices, his right forearm met the fist's arm, not to block but to blend with that force and divert it from its target.

The fist belonged to a woman.

And in the instant she struggled to recover her *diverted* balance, the palm of Condor's left hand rocketed her up and back so she bounced off the rear wall of the elevator as those metal doors closed behind him.

The cage groaned toward the surface. "Leave me alone!" she yelled.

"You punched me!"

His attacker glared at him through black-framed glasses. Short dark hair. A thin silver loop pierced the right corner of her lower lip. Black coat. Hands clenched at her sides, not up in an on-guard position. She had the guts to fight but not the know-how.

"You chased me in here!" she yelled. "Don't deny it! I finally caught you! Stop it! You keep watching me! Doing things!"

"I don't do things!"

"Always lurking. Hiding. Sneaking. Straightening my reading room desk. KNOCK IT OFF! Weeks you've been at this, not gonna take it next time I'll punch—"

"*Weeks?*" he interrupted. "I've been doing *whatever* for weeks? Here?"

The elevator jerked to a stop. Doors behind Condor slid open.

He loomed between the glaring woman and the only way out of this cage.

The elevator doors whirred shut. The cage rumbled upwards.

He sent his right hand inside his sports jacket and she let it go there, confirming she was no trained killer. Pulled out his Library of Congress I.D. Showed it to her.

"Activation Date is today, my first day here. I can't be the one who's been stalking you."

The elevator jerked to a stop.

The doors behind Condor slid open. "*Oh.*" She nodded to the open elevator doors.

He backed out the cage. She followed him into a smooth walled hall as the elevator doors closed. "*Um*, sorry."

"No. You did what you could to be *not* sorry. Smart."

"Why were you chasing me?"

"I'm trying to find an exit."

"This is a way out," she said and led him through the castle. "I'm Kim."

He told her he was Vin. "You must think I'm nuts."

"We all have our own roads through Crazytown."

She laughed at what she thought was a joke, but couldn't hold on to happy.

"I don't know what to do," said Kim. "Sometimes I think I'm imagining it all. I feel somebody watching me, but when I whirl around, nobody's there."

"Chinese martial arts say eyes have weight," Vin told her.

"I'm from Nebraska," she said. "Not China."

Kim looked at him, *really looked* at him. "You're probably a great father." She sighed. "I miss my dad and back home, though I wouldn't want to live there."

"But why live here?"

"Are you kidding? Here I get to be part of what people can use to make things better, have better lives, be more than who they were stuck being born.

She frowned: "Why do you live here?"

"I'm not ready die," he said. "Here or anywhere."

"You're a funny guy, Vin. Not funny *ha-ha*, but not *uh-oh* funny either."

They walked past a blue-shirted cop at the metal detector arch by the entrance. The cop wore a holstered pistol of a make Vin knew he once knew.

Just past the security line waited a plastic tub beneath an earnest hand-inked sign:

OLD CELLPHONES FOR CHARITY!

Funny guy Vin pictured himself tossing the CIA's flip-phone into that plastic bin. A glance at the dozen cellphones awaiting charitable recycling told him that would be cruel: His flip-phone was so uncool ancient that all the other phones would pick on it.

Condor and *not* his daughter stepped out into March's blue sky chill.

She buttoned her black cloth coat. "Would you do me a favor? You're new, so you can't be *whoever* it is. Come by my desk in the Adams reading room around noon tomorrow. Go with me to my office. See what I'm talking about, even if it's not there."

Standing in that chilly sunshine on a Capital Hill street, Condor heard an echo from the DOSP: "Rescuer is not in your job description."

Sometimes you gotta do what you do just to be you.

"OK," said Condor.

Kim gave him her LOC business card, thanked him and said goodbye, walked away into the D.C. streets full of people headed somewhere they seemed to want to go.

"Remember how to get home?" Emma'd said. An eleven-minute walk past the red brick Eastern Market barn where J. Edgar Hoover worked as a delivery boy a century before. Condor strolled past stalls selling fresh fruit and aged cheese, slabs of fish and red meat, flowers. He found himself in line at the market grill, got a crab cake sandwich and a lemonade, ate at one of the tall tables and watched the flow of midday shoppers, stay-home parents and nannies, twenty-somethings who worked freelance laptop gigs to pay for bananas and butchered chickens.

Where he lived was a blue brick townhouse on Eleventh Street, N.E., a narrow five rooms, one-and-a-half baths rental. No one ambushed him when he stepped into the living room. No one had broken the dental floss he'd strung across the stairs leading up to the bed he surfed in dreams. A flat screen TV reflected him as he plopped on the couch, caught his breath in this new life where nothing, *nothing* was wrong.

At 8:57 the next morning, he snapped on the lights in his work cave.
Counted the coffins: *Seven.*

Checked the computer's spreadsheet: *Nine.* Crazy or not, that's still the count.

Sometimes crazy is the way to go.

Or so he told himself when he'd flushed the green pills down the blue townhouse's toilet at dawn. Emma'd report his adverse reaction, so probably there'd be no Code Two Alert when that medication wasn't seen in Condor's next urine test.

His thirteen other pills lined up on his kitchen counter like soldiers.

Condor held his cooking knife that looked like the legend Jim Bowie carried at the Alamo. Felt himself drop into a deep stance, his arms curving in front of his chest. The Bowie knife twirled until the spine of the blade pressed against the inside of his right forearm and the razor sharp cutting edge leered out like he'd been taught decades before by a Navy SEAL in a lower East Side of Manhattan black site.

Condor exhaled into his here-and-now, used the knife to shave powder off five pills prescribed to protect him from himself, from seeing or feeling or thinking that isn't part of officially approved *sensible* reality. Told himself that a shade of unapproved crazy might be the smart way to go, because standing in his office cave on the second morning of work, it didn't make sense that the approved coffin count was (still) off by two. He muscled a cardboard box full of books onto a waist-high, brown metal cart, rolled the burdened cart over to the seven empty coffins and lost his virginity.

His very first one. The first book he pulled from that box bulging with books recycled from a closed U.S. air base near a city once decimated by Nazi purification squads and then shattered by Allied bombers. The first volume whose fate he decided: *The List of Adrian Messenger* by Philip MacDonald.

Frank Sinatra played a gypsy in the black and white movie.

That had to make it worth saving, *right?* He leafed through the novel. Noted only official stamps on the pages. Put that volume on the cart for the Preserve stacks.

Book number two was even easier to save: a ragged paperback. Blue ink cursive scrawl from a reader on the title page: *"You never know where you really are.*" That didn't seem like a code and wasn't a secret, so no security breach. The book was Kurt Vonnegut's *Slaughterhouse Five.* Sure, gotta save that on the cart.

And so it went. He found a bathroom outside his cave, a trip he would have made more often if he'd also found coffee. Books he pulled out of shipping boxes got shaken, flipped through and skimmed until the Preserve cart could hold no more.

All seven pine wood crates were still empty, coffins waiting for their dead.

Can't meet Kim without dooming—*recycling*—at least one book.

The black plastic bag yielded a hefty novel by an author who'd gone to a famous graduate school MFA program and been swooned over by critics. That book had bored Condor. He plunked it into a blond pine coffin. Told himself he was just doing his job.

Got out of there.

Stood in the yellow cinderblock hall outside his locked office.

If I were a spy, I'd have maps in my cell phone. I'd have a Plan with a Fallback Plan and some Get Out of Dodge *go-to.* If I were a spy, an agent, an operative, somebody's asset, my activation would matter to someone who cared about me, someone besides the *targets* and the *rip-you-ups* and the *oppo*(sition), none of whom should know I'm real and alive and *on them.* If I were still a spy, I'd have a mission.

Feels like forty years since I was just me.

Terrifying.

No wonder I'm crazy.

Outside where it would rain, the three castles of the Library of Congress rose across open streets from Congress's Capitol dome and the pillars of the Supreme Court because knowledge is clearly vital to how we create laws and dispense justice.

And *yes,* the swooping art decco John Adams castle where Condor worked is magnificent with murals and bronze doors and owls as art everywhere.

And *true,* the high-tech concert hall James Madison LOC castle that looms across the street from the oldest fortress of the House of Representatives once barely kept its expensively-customized-for-LOC-use edifice out of the grasp of turf hungry Congressmen who tried to disguise their grab for office space as *fiscally responsible*. But *really*, the gem of the LOC empire with its half-billion dollar global budget and 3,201 employees is the LOC's Thomas Jefferson building: gray marble columns rising hundreds of feet into the air to where its green metal cupola holds the "Torch of Learning" copper statue and cups a mosaic sky over the castle full of grand marble staircases, wondrous murals and paintings, golden gilt and dark wood, chandeliers, a main reading room as glorious as a cathedral, and everywhere, *everywhere*, books, the words of men and women written on the ephemera of dead trees.

Down in the castles' sub-basement of yellow tunnels, Condor walked beneath pipes and electrical conduits and wires, past locked doors and lockers. He rode the first elevator he found up until the steel cage dinged and left him in a cavern of stacks—row after row of shelves stuffed with books, books in boxes in the aisles, books everywhere.

He drifted through the musty stacks, books brushing the backs of both his hands, his eyes blurred by the lines of volumes, each with a number, each with a name, an identity, a purpose. He circled around one set of stacks and saw *him* standing there.

Tom Joad. Battered hat, sun-baked lean Okie face, shirt missing a button, stained pants, scruffy shoes covered with the sweat dust of decades.

"Where you been?" whispered Condor.

"Been looking. How 'bout you?"

"Been trying," said Condor.

A black woman wearing a swirl of color blouse under a blue LOC smock stepped into the aisle where she saw only Condor and said: "Were you talking to me?"

The silver-haired man smiled something away. "Guess I was talking to myself."

"Sugar," she said, "everybody talks to somebody."

He walked off like he knew what he was doing and where he was going, saw a door at the end of another aisle of books, stepped through it—

BAM!

Collision hits Condor's thighs, *heavy* runs over *hurts* his toes—*Cart!*

A metal steel cart loaded with books slams into Condor as it's being pushed by . . .

Brown bird Fran. Pushing a metal cart covered by a blue LOC smock.

"Oh, my Lord, I'm so sorry!" Fran hovered as Condor winced. "I didn't see you there! I didn't expect anybody!"

She blinked back to her balance, sank back to her core. Her eyes drilled his chest.

"*Vin*, isn't it? Why aren't you wearing your I.D.? LOC policy requires visible issued I.D. The DOSP will not be pleased."

She leaned closer: "I won't tell him we saw each other if you won't."

"Sure," he said. *And thus is a conspiracy born.*

"That's better." She straightened the blue smock over the books it covered on her cart. "You should wear it anyway. If you're showing your I.D., you can go anywhere and do darn near anything. For your job, I mean."

He fished his I.D. from inside the *blah* blue sports jacket issued him by a CIA *dust master* who costumed America's spies. Asked her how to get to the reading room.

"Oh, my: you're a floor too high. There's a gallery above that reading room back the direction I came. You can't miss it." She tried to hook him with a smile. "How soon will you out-process the next shipment of inventory?"

"You mean pack books in the coffins to be pulped? It's only my second day."

"Oh, dear. You really must keep on schedule and up to speed. There are needs to be met. The DOSP has expectations."

"Must be nice," said Condor. "Having expectations."

He thanked her and headed the direction she said she'd come.

Went through the door labeled "Gallery."

That door opened to a row of taller-than-him bookshelves he followed to one of six narrow slots for human passage to the guardrail circling above the reading room with its quaint twentieth century card catalog and research desks.

Nice spot for recon. Sneak down any slot. Charlie Sugar (Counter Surveil-lance) won't know which slot you'll use. Good optics. Target needs to crank his or her head to look up. Odds are, you spot that move in time to fade the half-step back to not be there.

Condor moved closer to the balcony guardrail. His view widened with each step.

Kim sat at a research desk taking notes with an iPad as she studied a tan book published before a man in goggles flew at Kitty Hawk. Kim wore a red cardigan sweater. Black glasses. Silver lip loop. A glow of purpose and focus. She raised her head to—

Condor eased back to where he could not see her and thus she did not see him. He walked behind bookshelves, found the top of a spiral steel staircase.

You gotta love a spiral steel staircase.

That steel rail slid through his hand as the world he saw turned around the axis of his spiraling descent. The reading room. Researchers at desks. Kim bent over her work. A street op named Quiller from a novel Condor'd saved loitered by the card catalog with a bespectacled mole hunter named Smiley. The stairs spiraled Condor toward a mural, circled him around, but those two Brits were gone when he stepped off the last stair.

Kim urged him close: "He's here! I just felt him watching me!"

"That was me."

"Are you sure?"

"Two tactical choices," he answered. Her anxious face acquired a new curiosity at this silver-haired man's choice of words. "Maintain status or initiate change."

"Change how?"

Condor felt the cool sun of Kabul envelop him, an outdoor market-place cafe where what was supposed to happen hadn't. Said: "We could move."

Kim led him into the depths of the Adams building and a snack bar nook with vending machines, a service counter, a bowl of apples. They bought coffee in giant paper cups with snapped on lids, sat where they could both watch the open doorway.

"Oh, my God," whispered Kim. "That could be him!"

Walking into the snack bar came a man older and a whiff shorter than her, a stocky man with shaggy brown hair and a mustache, a sports jacket, and shined shoes.

"I don't know his name," whispered Kim. "I think he tried to ask me out once! And maybe he goes out of his way to walk past where I am!

When I feel eyes on me, he's not there, nobody is, but it could be, *it must be* him."

The counterwoman poured hot coffee into a white paper cup for Mustache Man. He sat at an empty table facing the yogurt display case. At the angle he chose, the refrigerated case's glass door reflected blurred images of Condor and Kim.

Life or luck or tradecraft?

Condor told her: "Walk out. Go to your office. Wait for my call."

"What if something happens?"

"Something always happens. Don't look back."

Kim marched out of the snack nook. Mustache Man didn't follow her. Call him Vin. Call him Condor.

He thumb-popped the plastic lid loose on his cup of hot coffee.

Slowed time as he inhaled from his heels. Exhaled a fine line. Unfolded his legs to rise away from the table without a sound, without his chair scooting on the tiled floor.

Condor carried the loose-lid cup of hot coffee out in front of him like a pistol.

Mustache Man was *five, four, three* steps away, his head bent over a book.

Condor "lurched"—jostled the coffee cup he held.

The loose lid popped off the cup. Hot coffee flew out to splash Mustache Man.

He and the stranger who splashed him yelped like startled dogs. Mustache Man jumped to his feet, reached to help *some older gentleman* who'd obviously tripped.

"Are you all right?" said Mustache Man as the silver-haired stranger stood steady with his right hand *lightly* resting on the ribs over Mustache Man's startled heart.

"I'm sorry!" lied Condor.

"*No, no*: it was probably my fault."

Vin blinked: "Just sitting there and it was your fault?"

"I probably moved and threw you off or something."

"Or something." The man's face matched the I.D. card dangling around his neck.

Mustache Man used a napkin to sponge dark splotches on his book. "It's OK. It's mine, not the library's."

"You bring your own book to where you can get any book in the world?"

"I don't want to bother Circulation."

Vin turned the book so he could read the title.

Mustache Man let this total stranger take such control without a blink, said: "Li Po is my absolute favorite Chinese poet."

"I wonder if they read him in Nebraska."

Now came a blink: "Why Nebraska?"

"Why not?" said Condor.

The other man shrugged. "I'm from Missouri."

"There are two kinds of people," said Condor. "Those who want to tell you their story and those who never will."

"Really?"

"No," said Vin. "We're all our own kind. I didn't get your name."

"I'm Rich Bechtel."

Condor told Mustache Man/Rich Bechtel—same name on his I.D.— that he was new, didn't know the way back to his office.

"Let me show you," volunteered Rich, right on cue.

They went outside the snack nook where long corridors ran left and right.

"Either way," Rich told the silver-haired man whose name he still hadn't asked.

"Your choice," said Condor.

"Sorry, I work at CRS." *CRS*: the *C*ongressional *R*esearch *S*ervice that is and does as it's named. "I'm used to finding options, letting someone else decide."

"This is one of those times you're in charge," lied Condor.

He controlled their pace through subterranean tunnels. By the time they reached Condor's office, he knew where Rich *said* he lived, how long he'd been in Washington, that he loved biking. Loved his work, too, though as a supervisor of environmental specialists, "seeing what they deal with can make it hard to keep your good mood."

"Is it rough on your wife and kids?" asked Condor.

"Not married. No family." He shrugged. "She said *no*."

"Does that make you mad?"

"I'm still looking, if that's what you mean. But *mad*: How would that work?"

"You tell me." He stuck out his right hand. Got a return grip with strength Rich didn't try to prove. "My name is Vin. Just in case, could I have one of your cards?"

That card went into Vin's shirt pocket to nestle beside Kim's that Condor fished out as soon as he was inside his soundproof cave. He cell-phoned her office.

Heard the click of *answered call*. No human voice.

Said: "This is—"

"Please!" Kim's voice: "Please, *please* come here, see what—*Help me!*"

Condor snapped the old phone shut.

Grabbed the building map off his desk.

Couldn't help himself: counted the stacked coffins.

Still seven where there should be nine.

Time compressed. Blurred. Rushing through tunnels and hallways. Stairs. An elevator. Her office in a corridor of research lairs. Don't try the doorknob: that'll spook her more. Should be locked anyway. His knock rattled her door's clouded glass.

Kim clacked the locks and opened the door, reached to pull him in but grabbed only air as he slid past, put his back against the wall while he scanned her office.

No ambusher. Window too small for any ninja. Posters on the walls: a National Gallery print of French countryside, a Smithsonian photo of blue globed earth, a full-face wispy color portrait of Marilyn Monroe with a crimson lipped smile and honesty in her eyes. Kim's computer glowed. A framed black & white photo of a Marine patrolling some jungle stood on her desk: *Father? Grandfather? Vietnam?*

"Thought I was safe," babbled Kim. "Everything cool, you out there dealing with it and I unlocked the office door. It was locked—swear it was locked! Looked around and . . . My middle desk drawer was open. Just a smidge."

Kim's white finger aimed like a lance at a now wide-open desk drawer.

Where inside on its flat-bottomed wood, Condor saw:

HARLOT

Red lipstick smeared, gouged-out letters in a scrawl bigger than his hand.

Kim whispered: "How did he get in here? Do that? Weren't you with him?"

"Not before. And you weren't here then either."

A tube of lipstick lay in desk drawer near the graffiti, fake gold metal polished and showing no fingerprints. Condor pointed to the tube: "Yours?"

She looked straight into his eyes. "Who I am sometimes wears lipstick."

"So he didn't bring it and he didn't take it. But that's not what matters."

"Look under the lipstick," he said. "Carved letters. Library rules don't let anybody bring in a knife, so somebody who does is serious about his blade."

"I'm going to throw up." But she didn't.

"Call the cops," said Condor.

"And tell them what? Somebody I don't know, can't be sure it's him, he somehow got into my locked office and . . . and did *that*? They'll think I'm crazy!"

"Could be worse. Call the cops."

"OK, they'll come, they'll care, they'll keep an eye on me until there's no more nothing they'll have the time to see and they'll go and *then what*? Then more of this?"

She shook her head. "I'm an analytic researcher. That's what I do. First we need to find *more* to verify what we say for the cops to show we're not crazy!"

"First call the cops. Then worry about verifying. Crazy doesn't mean wrong."

"What else you got?" Her look scanned his scars.

"Grab what you need," he said. "Work where I found you, the reading room, in public, not alone. I don't know about afterwards when you go home."

"Nothing's ever . . . felt wrong there. Plus I've got a roommate."

"So did the heroine in *Terminator*."

"Life isn't science fiction."

"Really?" Condor rapped his knuckles on her computer monitor.

Made her take cell phone pictures of HARLOT and email them to herself before he shut that desk drawer. "Got a boyfriend or husband or any kind of ex?"

"The last somebody I had was in San Francisco and he dumped me. No husband, ever. Probably won't be. Evidently all I attract are psycho creeps.

Or maybe that's all that's out there. Why can't I find a nice guy who doesn't know that's special?"

"Do you like mustaches?"

"Hey, I wear a lip ring."

"Have you ever mentioned mustaches to anybody?"

She shook her head *no*.

"Then maybe he's had it for a long time." Kim shuddered.

He escorted her back to the same reading room desk.

Left her there where her fellow LOC employees could hear her scream.

Took the spiral steel staircase up and went out the Gallery door, walked back the way he first came, through the stacks, row after row of shelved books. Down one aisle, he spotted a shamus wearing a Dashiell Hammett trenchcoat and looking like Humphrey Bogart before he knew his dream was Lauren Bacall.

Condor called out: "What's my move?"

The shamus gave him the long look. Said: "You got a job, you do a job."

His job.

Back in the sub-basement cave. Alone with the *still only seven* coffins. Alone with the cart piled high with the few books he could save from *the DOSP's expectations.*

Anger gripped him. Frenzy. Cramming books into the coffins. Filling all seven pine crates, plopping them on the dolly, wheeling it out of his office, stacking the coffins against the yellow cinderblock wall, pushing the empty dolly back into his cave, logging PICK UP in the computer, snapping off the lights, locking the door, home before five with a day's job done and the shakes of not knowing what to do.

Shakes that had him walking back to work before dawn. His I.D. got him inside past cops and metal detectors, down the elevator to the subterranean glow around the corner from his office and into the unexpected rumble of rolling wheels.

Condor hurried around the corner . . .

. . . and coming towards him was a dolly of pinewood coffins pushed by a barbell-muscled man with military short blond hair and a narrow shaved face. The blond muscle man wore an I.D. lanyard and had deep blue eyes.

"Wait!" yelled Condor.

The coffin-heavy dolly shuddered to a jerked stop.

"What are you doing?" said Condor. "These are my coffins—crates."

Couldn't stop himself from whispering: "*Nine.*"

Looked down the hall to where yesterday he'd stacked *seven* coffins.

The barbell blond said: "You must be the new guy. I heard you were weird."

"My name is Vin, and you're . . . ?"

The blue-eyed barbell blond said: "*Like*, Jeremy."

"Jeremy, you got it right, I'm new, but I got an idea that, *like*, helps both of us."

Rush the grift so Jeremy doesn't have time to, like, make a wrong reply.

"I screwed up, *sorry*, stuck the wrong book in a crate, so what we need to do, what *I* need to do, is take them all back in my cave, open 'em up, and find the book that belongs on the rescue cart. Then you can take the crates away."

"I'm doing that now. That's my job. And I say *when*."

"That's why this works out for us. Because you're who says *when*. And while I'm fixing the mistake, you go to the snack bar, get us both—I don't know about you, but I need a cup of coffee. I buy, you bring, and by then I'll be done with the crates."

"Snack bar isn't open this early. Only vending machines."

Don't say anything. Wait. Create space for the idea to fall into.

"Needing coffee is weak," said Jeremy.

"When you get to my age, weak comes easy."

Jeremy smiled. "They might have hot chocolate."

"I think they do." Vin fished the last few dollar bills from the release allowance out of his black jeans. "If they got a button for cream, push it for me, would you?"

Jeremy took the money. Disappeared down the yellow cinderblock hall.

Vin rolled the dolly into his cave. Unlatched the first coffin, found a frenzied jumble of books, one with ripped cover so the only words left above the author's name were: ". . . LAY DYING"

Remember that, I remember that.

The second crate contained another jumble that felt familiar, all novels, some with stamps from some island, Paris Island. *Yeah, this is another one I packed, one of the seven.* So was the third crate he opened, and the fourth.

But not number five.

Neatly stacked books filled that pinewood box. Seventy or more books. But only three titles.

Delta of Venus by Anais Nin. *Never read it, maybe a third of this coffin's books.*

The rest of the renegade coffin's books were editions of *The Carpetbaggers* by Harold Robbins, many with the jacket painting of a blond woman in a lush pink gown and the grip of a fur stole draped round her shoulders as some man towered behind her.

I remember it! A *roman à clef* about whacky billionaire Howard Hughes who bought Las Vegas from the Mob, but what Vin remembered most about the book was waiting until his parents were out of the house, then leafing to *those pages.*

Now, that morning in his locked cave in a basement of the Library of Congress in Washington, D.C., Vin rifled through the coffin of discarded volumes of *The Carpetbaggers* and found nothing but those books, stamped properties of public libraries from New Mexico to New Jersey, nothing hidden in them, nothing hidden under them in the pinewood crates, nothing about them that . . .

What smells?

Like a bloodhound, Vin sniffed all through that coffin of doomed novels.

Smells like . . . Almonds.

He skidded a random copy of each book across the concrete floor to under his desk and closed the lid on the coffin from which they came.

The sixth crate contained his chaos of crammed-in books, but crate number seven revealed the same precise packing as crate five, more copies of Anais Nin and *The Carpetbaggers*, plus copies of two other novels: *The Caretakers* that keyed more memories of furtive page turning and three copies of *Call Me Sinner* by Alan Marshall that Vin had never heard of. Plus the scent of almonds. He shut that crate. The last two coffins held books he'd sent to their doom and smelled only of pine.

Roll the dolly piled high with coffins back out to the hall.

This is what you know:

Unlike the books that filled seven of the *there-all-along* coffins, the volumes in *where'd they-come-from* two coffins were precisely packed, alphabetically and thus systematically clustered C and D titles, and all, *well*, erotic.

And smelled like almonds.

Remember, I can't remember what that means.

Jeremy handed Condor a cup of vending machine coffee. "You find what you were looking for?"

"Yeah," said Condor, a truth full of lies.

Jeremy crumpled his chocolate stained paper cup, tossed it on top of the crates.

"I'll come with you." Vin fell in step beside the man pushing the heavy dolly.

"You are weird. Push the button for that elevator."

A metal cage slowly carried the two men and the coffin dolly up, up.

"Do you see many weird people down here?" asked Condor.

"Some people use this way as a shortcut out to get lunch or better coffee."

Rolling wheels made the only sounds for the rest of their journey to the loading dock. Jeremy keyed his code into the dock's doors, rolled the dolly outside onto a loading dock near a parked pickup truck.

An LOC cop with a cyber tablet came over, glanced at the crates, opened one and saw the bodies of books, as specified on the manifest. He looked at Condor.

"The old guy's with me," said Jeremy. The cop nodded, walked away.

The sky pinked. Jeremy lifted nine crates—*nine*, not *seven*—dropped them into the pickup truck's rear end cargo box for the drive to the recycling dump.

"This is as far as you go," Jeremy told the weird older guy.

Condor walked back inside through the loading dock door.

The rattling metal grate lowered its wall of steel.

Luminous hands on his black Navy SEAL watch ticked past seven A.M. Condor stalked back the way he'd come, as if retracing geography would let him remake time, go back to *when* and do it right. When got to the stacks where he'd been lost before, down the gap between two book-packed rows, he spotted a mouse named Stuart driving a tiny motorcar away in search of the north that would lead him to true love.

Condor whispered: "Good luck, man."

Voice behind you! "Are—"

Whirl hands up and out sensing guard stacks spinning—

Woman brown clothes eyes widening—

Fran, sputtering: "I was just going to say *'Are you talking to yourself?'*"

Condor let his arms float down as he faded out of a combat stance.

"Something like that."

"Sorry to have interrupted." She smiled like a woman at a Methodist church social his mother once took him to. Or like the shaved-head, maroon-robed Buddhist nun he'd seen in Saigon after that city changed its name. "But nice to see you."

Condor frowned. "Wherever I go, there you are."

"Oh, my goodness," twittered Fran. "Doesn't that just seem so? And good for you being here now. The early bird gets the worm. Believe you me, there are worms. Worms everywhere."

Flick—a flick of motion, something—*somebody* ducking back behind a shelf in an aisle between those stacks way down where Stuart drove.

"By the way," he heard Fran say: "Good job. The DOSP will be pleased."

"What?"

"Your first clearance transfer."

"How did you know I was sending out a load of coffins?"

Her smile widened. "Must have been Jeremy."

Amidst the canyons of shelves crammed with books, Condor strained to hear creeping feet beyond the twittering brown bird of a woman.

"Just walking by his shop in the basement, door must have been open, I mean, I used to have your job working with him."

Prickling skin: Something—*someone*—hidden from their eyes in the canyons of stacks moved the air.

"Vin, are you feeling OK?"

"Just distracted."

"Ah." Fran marched away, exited through a door alone.

Alone, Condor telepathed to whoever hid in this cavern of canyons made by rows of shelved books. Just you and me now. All alone.

Somewhere waited a knife.

Walk between close walls of bookshelves crammed with volumes of transcribed RAF radio transmissions, 1939-1941. He could hear the call signs, airmen's chatter, planes' throbbing engines, bombs, and the clattering machineguns of yesterday.

Today is what you got. And what's got you.

What got him, he never knew—a sound, a tingling, a corner-of-his-eye motion, *whatever*: he whirled left to that wall of shelved books, slammed his palms against half a dozen volumes so they shot back off their shelf and knocked away the books shelved in the next aisle, a gap blasted in walls of books through which he saw . . .

Mustached and eyes startled wide Rich Bechtel.

"Oops!" yelled Condor. "Guess I stumbled *again*."

He flowed around the shelf, a combat ballet swooped into the aisle where Rich—suit, tie, mustache—stood by a jumble of pushed-to-the-floor books.

Condor smiled: "Surprised to see me here?"

"Surprised, why . . . ?"

"Yes, *why* are you here?"

The mustached man shrugged. "It's a cut-through to go get good coffee."

"Did you cut through past the balcony of the reading room?"

"Well, sure, that's a door you can take."

"So why were you hiding back here?" said Condor.

Rich shrugged. "I was avoiding *call me* Fran."

Confession without challenge: *As if we were friends*, thought Condor.

"A while back," continued Rich, "I was over here in Adams working on a Congressional study of public policy management approaches. One of the books I had on my desk was a rare early translation of the *Dao De Jing*, you know, the . . ."

"The Chinese Machiavelli."

"More than that, but *yes*, a *how power works* manual that Ronald Reagan quoted. Fran mistook it for something like the Koran. She walked by my research desk, spotted the title and went off on me about how dare I foster such thought. Things got out of hand. She might have pushed my books off the desk, could have been an accident, but . . ."

"But what?"

"I walked away. When I see her now, I keep walking. Or try not to be seen."

Condor said: "Nobody could make up that story."

The caught man frowned. "Why would I make up any story?"

"We all make up stories. And sometimes we put real people in the stories in our heads. That can be . . . confusing."

"I'm already confused enough." Rich laughed. "What are you doing?"

"Leaving. Which way are you headed?"

Rich pointed the way Condor'd come, left with a wave and a smile.

The *chug chug chug* of a train.

One aisle over, between walls of books, railroad tracks ran through a lush green somewhere east of Eden, steel rails under a coming this way freight train and sitting huddled on top of one metal car rode troubled James Dean.

Condor left that cavern of stacks, walked to the Gallery where he could see the empty researchers' desks on the floor of the reading room below. Checked his watch. Hoped he wouldn't need to pee. Some surveillances mean no milk cartons.

What does it mean when you smell almonds?

Don't think about that. Fade into the stacks.

Be part of what people never notice.

On schedule, Kim with her silver lip loop and a woman wearing a boring professional suit walked in to the reading room. The roommate left. Kim settled at her desk. He gave the counter-surveillance twenty more minutes, went to his office. No coffins waited outside against the yellow wall from a delivery by Jeremy: *Watch for that.*

So Condor left his office door open. Sank into his desk chair.

Footsteps: outside the open door in the hall, hard shoes on the concrete floor of the yellow underground tunnel. Footsteps clacking louder as they came closer, closer . . .

She glides past his open door in three firm strides, strong legs and a royal blue coat. Silver-lined dyed blond hair floats on her shoulders, lush mouth, high cheekbones. Cosmic gravity pulls his bones and then she's gone, her *click click click* of high heels turning the basement corner, maybe to the elevator and out for mid-morning coffee.

Don't write some random wondrous woman into your story.

Don't be a stalker.

But he wasn't, wouldn't, he only looked, ached to look more, had no time to think about her, about how maybe her name was Lulu, how maybe she wore musk—

Almonds.

Up from behind his desk, out the lock-it door and *gone*, up the stairs two at a time, past the guards on the door to outside, in the street, dialing *that number* with the CIA cell phone. A neutral voice answered, waltzed Condor to the hang-up. He made it into his blue townhouse, stared at his closed turquoise door for nineteen minutes until that soft knock.

Opened his door to three bullet-eyed *jacket men*.

Emma showed up an hour later, dismissed them.

Sat on a chair across from where Condor slumped on the couch.

Said: "What did you do?"

"I called the cops," answered the silver-haired man who was her responsibility.

"Your old CIA Panic Line number. Because you say you found C4 plastic explosives. But you don't know where. You just smelled it, the almond smell."

"In the Library of Congress."

"That's a lot of *where*. And C4's not as popular as it used to be."

"Still works. Big time boom. Hell of a kill zone."

"If you know how to get it or make it and what you're doing."

"You ever hear of this thing called the Internet?"

She threw him a change-up: "Tell me about the dirty books."

"You know everything I know because I told those *jacket men*, they told you. Sounds crazy, right? And since I'm crazy, that's just about right. Or am I wrong?"

Emma watched his face.

"They aren't going to do anything, are they? CIA. Homeland Security."

"Oh, they're going to do something," said Emma. "No more Level Five, they're going to monitor you Level Three. Increase your surprise random home visits. Watch me watching you in case I mess up and go soft and don't recommend a Recommit in time to avoid any embarrassments."

"How did you keep them from taking me away now?"

"I told them you might have imbibed early and contra-indicated with your meds."

"Imbibed?"

"Tomorrow's St. Patrick's day." She shook her head. "I believe *you believe*. But you're trying to be who you were then. And that guy's gone into who you are now."

"Vin," he said. "Not Condor."

"Both, but in the right perspective."

"Ah," said Condor. "Perspective."

"What's yours? You've been free for a while now. How is it out here?"

"Full of answers and afraid of questions." She softened. "How are the hallucinations?"

"They don't interfere with—"

"—with you functioning in the real world?"

"*The real world.*" He smiled. "I'll watch for it.

What about Kim's stalker?"

"If there's a stalker, you're right. She should call the cops."

"Yeah. Just like I did. That'll solve everything."

"This is what we got," said Emma.

"One more thing we got," said Vin. "At work, I can't take it, packing coffins."

"Is it your back?" said Emma. "Do you need—"

"I need more carts to go to Preserve. I need to be able to save more books."

Emma probed. Therapist. Monitor. *Maybe friend.* "Those aren't just books to you. The ones at work. The novels."

Condor shrugged. "Short stories, too."

"They're things going to the end they would go to without you. You act like you're a Nazi working a book-burning bonfire. You're not. Why do you care so much?"

"We sell our souls to the stories we know," said Condor. "The more kinds of stories, the bigger we are. The better or truer or cooler the story . . ."

His shrug played out the logic in her skull. "I'll see what I can do," said Emma. "About the cart."

"Cart*s*," corrected Condor. "Only if we're lucky."

She walked out of his rented house. Left him sitting there.

Alone.

Sometimes you gotta do what you do just to be you.

Next morning, he dressed for war.

Black shoes good for running. Loose black jeans not likely to bind a kick. His Oxford blue shirt might rip if grabbed. He ditched the *dust master's* sports coat for the black leather zip-up jacket he bought back when an ex-CIA cocaine cowboy shot him in Kentucky. The black leather jacket let him move, plus it gave the illusion of protection from a slashing knife or exploding bomb.

Besides, he thought when he saw his rock-and-roll reflection walking in the glass of the Adams building door, *if I'm going down, I'm going down looking like me.*

Seven pine wood crates waited stacked against the yellow wall outside his cave.

Condor caressed the coffins like a vampire. Inhaled their essence. Lifted their lids to reveal their big box of *empty*: smooth walls, carpentered bottoms of reinforcing slats making a bed of rectangular grooves for books to lay on and die. His face hoovered each of those seven empty coffins, but only in one caught a whiff of almonds.

He tore through his office. The computer said nine coffins waited outside against his wall. Desk drawers: still empty, no weapons. The DOSP's fountain pen filled his eyes. *Use what you got.* He stuck the pen in his black leather jacket.

Two women working a table outside the Adams building reading room spotted a silver-haired man coming their way. They wore green sweaters. The younger one's left cheek sported a painted-on green shamrock. She smiled herself into Condor's path.

"Happy St. Patrick's Day! You need some holiday green. Want to donate a dollar to the Library and get a shamrock tattoo? Good luck *and* keeps you from getting pinched. How about one on your hand? Unless you want to go wild. Cheek or—"

The silver-haired stranger pressed his trigger finger to the middle of his forehead.

"Oh, cool! Like a third eye!"

"Or a bullet hole."

Her smile wilted. He stalked into the reading room. Clerks behind the counter. Scholars at research desks.

There, at her usual place, sat Kim.

She kept her cool. Kept her eyes on an old book. Kept her cell phone visible on her desk, an easy grab and a *no contact necessary* signal. He kept a casual distance between where he walked and where she sat, headed to the bottom of a spiral staircase.

Playing the old man let him take his time climbing those silver steel steps, a spiraling ascent that turned him through circles to the sky. His first curve toward the reading room let him surveil the head tops of strangers, any of whom could be the oppo. The stairs curved him toward the rear wall that disappeared into a black and white Alabama night where a six-year-old girl in a small town street turns to look back at her family home as a voice calls *"Scout."* Condor's steel stairs path to the sky curved . . .

Fran.

Standing on the far side of the reading room. Condor felt the crush of her fingers gripping the push handle of a blue smock covered cart. Saw her burning face.

As she raged across the room at silver lip-ringed Kim.

You know crazy when you see it. When crazy keeps being where crazy happened.

Obsession. Call it lust that Fran dared not name. Call it fearful loathing of all that. Call it outrage at Kim's silver lip loop and how Kim represented an effrontery to The Way Things Are Supposed to Be. Call it envy or anger because that damn still young woman with soft curves Fran would never be asked to touch got to do things Fran never did. Or could. Or would. Got to feel things, have things, be things. Lust, envy, hate: complications beyond calculation fused into raging obsession and made Fran not a twittering brown bird, made her a jackal drooling for flesh and blood.

For Kim.

Kim sat at her desk between where Fran seethed and where Condor stood on spiral silver stairs to the sky. Kim turned a page in her book.

Fran's eyes flicked from her obsession—spotted Vin. Saw him see the real her. Snarled, whirled the cart around and drove hard toward the reading room's main doors.

Cut her off! You got nothing! She's got a knife! Condor clattered down the spiral steel stairs, hurried across the reading room. He had no proof. No justifiable right to scream "HALT!" or call the cops—and any cops would trigger *jacket men* to snatch him away to the secret Maine hospital's padded cell or to that suburban Virginia crematorium where no honest soul would see or smell his smoke swirling away into the night sky.

He caught his breath at Kim's desk: "Not a mustache, a her!"

Kim looked to the main door where he'd pointed, but all she saw beyond Vin charging there was the shape of someone pushing a cart into the elevator.

Vin ran to the elevator, saw its glowing arrow:

Over there, race down those stairs, hit the basement level—

He heard *rolling wheels* from around that corner.

Rammed at Condor came the blue smocked cart.

That he caught with both hands—pulled more. Jerked Fran off balance. Pushed the book cart harder than he'd ever pushed the blocking sled in high school football. Slammed her spine against a yellow cinderblock wall. Pinned her there: *Stalker had a knife and a woman like Fran with knife-tipped shoes once almost killed James Bond.*

Condor yelled: "Why Kim?"

"She doesn't get to be her! Me, should be her, have her, stop her!"

The fought-over cart shook between them.

Its covering blue smock slid off.

Books tumbled off the cart. Books summoned from heartland libraries to our biggest cultural repository where they disappeared on *official business.* Condor registered a dozen versions of the same title banned in high schools across America *because.*

"You filled the coffins! Tricked libraries all over the country into sending their copies of certain titles here to the mothership of libraries!

You murdered those books!" Condor twisted the cart to keep Fran rammed against the wall. "You're a purger, too!"

"Books put filth in people's heads! Ideas!"

"Our heads can have any ideas they want!"

"Not in my world!" Fran twisted and leveraged the cart up and out from under Condor's push. The cart crashed on its side. He flopped off his feet, fell over it.

Wild punches hit him and he whirled to his feet, knocked her away.

Yelled: "Where are the coffins?! Where's the C4?!"

"I see you!" She yelled as the book she threw hit his nose.

Pain flash! He sensed her kick, closed his thighs but her shoe still slammed his groin. He staggered, hit the stone wall, hands snapping up to thwart her attack—

That didn't come.

Gone. Jackal Fran was gone, running down the basement tunnel.

Cell phone, pull out your cell phone. "Kim!" he gasped to the woman who answered his call. "Watch out, woman my age Fran and she's not a brown bird, she's the jackal after you!

"Don't talk! Reading room, right? Stay in plain sight but get to the check-out counter. . . . Yes. . . . The library computer. . . . Search employee data base—No, not Fran *anybody*, search for Jeremy *somebody*!"

A ghost of Fran whispered: *"I used to have your job working with him."*

Over the phone came intel: an office/shop door number, some castle hole.

The DOSP's pen tattooed that number on the back of his left hand.

He hung up and staggered through the underground tunnel.

Scan the numbers on the closed doors, looking for numbers with an SB prefix whatever that—*Sub-basement! Like my office!* One more level down.

At a stairwell, he flipped open his ancient phone and dialed another number: "Rich it's Vin, you gotta go help somebody right now! Protect her. Tell her I sent you. In Adams Reading Room, named Kim, silver lip loop . . . I thought you'd noticed her! And that's all right, you just . . . OK, but when you couldn't find the right words you walked on, right? Go now! . . . Don't worry, nobody knows everything. Play it with what you've got."

He jogged through yellow tunnels like he was a rat running a maze, *I'm too old for this,* staggering to a closed brown metal door, its top half fogged glass.

Condor caught his breath outside that door. The door handle wouldn't turn. He saw a doorbell, trigger-fingered its button, heard it buzz.

The click of a magnetic lock. The door swings open.

Come on in.

Jeremy stands ten steps into this underground lair beside a workbench and holding a remote control wand. The door slams shut behind Condor.

"What do you want?" said a caretaker of this government castle.

Caretaker, like in the novel Fran tried to murder, some story about sex and an insane asylum and who was crazy. *Stick to what's sane.* Condor said: "The coffins."

"They're here already?"

Scan the workshop: no sign of the two missing coffins. A refrigerator. Wall sink. Trash tub of empty plastic water bottles. The back of an open laptop faced Condor from the workbench where the tech wizard of this cave stood. Jeremy tossed the remote control beside an iPhone cabled to the laptop.

"Oh," said Jeremy. "You meant the crates for the books."

He took a step closer. "Why do you care?"

"There's something you don't know you know."

"I know enough."

Off to Jeremy's left waited the clear plastic roller tub holding half a dozen cell phones and its color printer sign proclaiming OLD TELEPHONES FOR CHARITY!

One heartbeat. Two.

"I didn't know you were the one collecting charity phones."

"What do you know?" Jeremy eased another step closer.

Sometimes crazy is the way to go.

Jeremy's blue eyes narrowed, his hands were fists.

Feel the vibe. See the movie.

Sunny blue sky behind the white dome of the

U.S. Capitol. Across the street rises a castle with a green metal top and giant gray concrete walls of columns and grand staircases, windows behind which people work, a fountain out front where bronze green statues of Greek gods flirt and pose their indomitable will.

Tremble/rumble! The Library of Congress's Jefferson building shudders sprays out exploded concrete dust like 9/11, like Oklahoma City. Fireballs nova through castle rooms of wood panels, wood shelves, books that no one would see again. Those walls crumble to rubble. The last moment of the castle's cohesion is a cacophony of screams.

You'll never make it to the door. Locked anyway. And he's between you and its remote control on the workbench by the computer umbilical chorded to an ultra phone.

Make it real: "You and Fran."

"She's just a woman," said Jeremy. "More useful than a donkey, not as trainable. Like, deluded. Like all women in this Babylon where they don't know their place."

"Oh, I like all the places they will go," said Condor, quoting the book he'd heard read a million billion times to a frightened child traveling beside his mother on a bus through a dark Texas night. "Where'd Fran take those two coffins—*crates* that you and her use to smuggle in C4?"

"Somewhere for her stupid crusade."

For *her* stupid crusade. Not *our.*

A lot of roads run through Crazytown.

Jeremy took a step closer.

Condor flowed to walk a martial arts *Bagua* circle around him.

Almonds, a strong whiff in the air of what had been stockpiled down here.

"She even bribed you," guessed Condor as Jeremy turned to keep the silver-haired man from circling behind him.

"She funded the will of God."

"Fran thought the only God she was funding was hers. Didn't know about yours."

"My God is the only God."

"That's what all you people say."

Why is there a floppy flat empty red rubber water bottle on the floor?

Condor feinted. Jeremy flinched: he's a puncher, maybe from a shopping mall *dojo* or hours watching YouTubes of Jihad stars showing their wannabe homegrown brothers out there the throat-cutting ways of Holy warriors.

"Slats!" said Condor. "On the inside bottom of the crates. Reinforcing slats, they make a narrow trough. Somewhere outside, after you dump the books, you mold C4 into those slats—cream color, looks like glue on the wood if the guard outside checks. Odds are the guard won't check all the crates every time, you only use two, and even if somebody checks, nobody notices.

"Fran paid you to cut her out a couple crates before you delivered them. That gave you time with the crates in here to peel out what you hid, pass them on to her, she gives them back full of what you don't care about to fold back into the coffin count."

"Way to go, cowboy." Jeremy had that flat accent born in Ohio near the river. "You get to witness the destruction of the Great Satan's temple of heretical thought."

"Wow, did they email you a script?"

"You think I'd be so careless as to let the NSA catch me contacting my true brothers in the Middle East before I proved myself—"

Lunge, Jeremy lunged and Condor whirled left—whirled right—snake-struck in a three-beat *Hsing-i* counter-charge to—

Pepper spray burned Condor's face.

Breathe can't breathe eyes on fire!

The Holy warrior slammed his other fist into the silver-haired man's guts.

Condor was already gasping for air and flooding tears because of pepper spray. The barbell muscled punch buckled and bent him over, knocked him toward the workbench, teetering, stumbling—crashing to the floor.

Get up! Get up! Get to your knees—

The blue-eyed fanatic slapped Vin, a blow more for disrespect than destruction.

Condor saw himself flopping in slow motion. Kneeling gasping on the hard floor. His arms waving at his sides couldn't fly him away or fight his killer.

White cable connects the laptop to iPhone: Jeremy rips that chord free.

Whips its garrote around the kneeling man's neck.

Gurgling clawing at the chord cutting off blood to brain air to lungs, pepper-sprayed eyes blurring, a roar, a whooshing in his ears, can't—

BZZZZ!

That doorbell buzz startles the strangler, loosens his pull.

Blood rush to the brain, air! BZZZZ!

Strangler jerks his garrote tight.

GLASS RATTLES as someone outside bangs on that door.

Can't scream gagging here in here help me in here get in here!

Jeremy spun Condor around and slammed him chest-first into the workbench.

Hands, your hands on the workbench, claw at—

Seven seconds before blackout, he *saw.*

The remote for the door. Wobbling on the workbench. *Flop reach grab—*

The jihad warrior whirled the gurgling apostate away from the high tech gear.

Thumb the remote.

The door buzzes—springs open.

Fran.

Screaming charging rushing *IN!*

Jeremy knees Condor, throws him to the floor and the garrote—

The garrote goes loose around Condor's neck *but won't unwrap itself from the strangler's hands*, holds his arms trapped low.

"Stop it!" Fran screams at the treasonous pawn who's trying to steal her destiny. "He's mine to kill!"

Down from heaven stabs her gray metal spring-blade knife confiscated from a tourist, salvaged from storage by an LOC staffer who could steal any of the castles' keys.

Fran drove her stolen blade into Jeremy's throat.

Gasping grabbing his hands to his neck/what sticks out of there.

Wide eyed, his hands grab GOT HER weakness percolates up from his feet by the prone

Vin, up Jeremy's legs, he's falling holding on to Fran, death grips her blouse that rips open as the force of his pull multiplied by his fall jerks her forward—

Fran trips over sprawled Condor.

Swan dives through the air over the crumpling man she stabbed.

Crashes *cracks* her skull on the workbench's sharp corner.

Spasms falls flat across the man she stabbed whose body pins Condor to the floor.

Silence. Silence.

Crawl out from under the dead.

Hands, elbows and knees pushing on the concrete floor, straining, pulling . . .

Free. Alive. Face down on the floor, gasping scents of cement and dust, sweat and the warm ham and cabbage smell of savaged flesh. A whiff of almonds.

Jackhammer in his chest:

No heart attack, not after all this. Come on: a little justice.

Condor flopped over onto his back. Saw only the castle's flat ceiling.

Propped himself up on his elbows. Sat. Dizzy. Sore from punches, getting kneed, strangled. Pepper-spray, tears, floor dirt, sweat: his face was caked. Must look like hell.

Nobody will let you walk away from this.

Almonds, C4: where's the C4?

The workbench, the laptop, glowing screen full of . . .

A floor plan. The LOC jewel, the main castle Jefferson Building.

A pop-ad flashed over the map, a smiling salesman above a flow of words:

"CONGRATULATIONS ON YOUR NEW CELL PHONE
BASIC BUSINESS PLAN. NOW CONSIDER MOVING BEYOND
MERE NETWORKED TELECONFERENCING TO—"

The white computer chord garrote lay on the floor like a dead snake.

A snake that once connected the laptop computer to an iPhone.

An iPhone capable of activating all cell phones on its conferenced network.

A *for charity* tub that gobbles up donated old cell phones from our better souls.

The iPhone screen glowed with the LOC castle map and its user-entered red dots.

Dizzy: he staggered toward the wall sink, splashed water on his face, empty plastic water bottles in a tub right by that weird red rubber bag that doesn't belong here.

Vision: Jeremy smiling his Ohio smile, walking through the metal detectors with the baggy crotch of his pants hiding a red rubber bottle full of goo that's not water.

Grab the roller tub for donated cell phones. Close the laptop, put it in the tub beside the iPhone. The phone glowed the map of the castle.

The crisscrossed corpses on the floor kept still.

How long before anyone finds you?

Thumb the remote, the door swings open. Push the plastic tub on wheels into the hall. Condor pulled his blue shirt out of his waistband, used it to polish his fingerprints off the remote, then toss it back through the closing door into the basement shop, plastic skidding along the concrete floor to where the dead lay.

Go!

Race the rumbling plastic tub on wheels through the tunnels of the Adams building to the main castle of Jefferson, down into its bowels and follow the map on the iPhone screen to a mammoth water pipe. Gray duct taped on the inflow water pipe's far side: a cellphone wired as a detonator into a tan book-sized gob of goo.

Boom and no water for automatic sprinklers to fight fire.

Boom and water floods an American castle.

Pull the wires out of the gob of C4. Pull them from the phone. Pull the phone's battery. Toss the dead electronics into the tub.

What do you do with a handful of C4?

A shot bullet won't set it off. And C4 burns.

Only electricity makes it go *Boom!*

Squeeze the C4 into a goo ball, shove it into your black jacket's pocket.

Condor charged the plastic tub on wheels to the next map number on the iPhone: bomb against a concrete weight-bearing wall. The iPhone led him to three more bombs. Each time he ripped away the electronics and squeezed the goo into a shape he could hide in his jacket pockets, and when they were full, he stuffed C4 goo inside his underpants.

Boom.

Run, catch that elevator, roll in with the tub. A man and a woman ride with you. He's a gaudy green St. Patrick's Day tie. She looks tired. Neither of them cares about you, about what happens in your crotch if the elevator somehow sparks static electricity.

Next floor plan in the iPhone.

Stacks, row after row of wooden shelves and burnable books and *there*, under a bookshelf, another cell phone wired goo ball. Rubber bands bind this apparatus to a clear plastic water bottle full of a gray gel that a bomb will burst into a fireball.

Lay the bottle of napalm atop the cell phones in the wheeled tub.

Your underpants are full.

Cinch the rubber bands from that bomb around the ankles of your pants. Feed a snake of C4 down alongside your naked leg in the black jeans.

Roll on *oh so slowly*.

Hours, it takes him hours, slowed more by every load of C4 he stuffs in his pants, inside his blue shirt, in the sleeves of his black leather jacket.

Hours, he rolls through the Jefferson building for hours following iPhone maps made by an obsessed fanatic. Rolls past tours of ordinary citizens, past men and women with lanyard I.D. Rumbles down office corridors, through the main reading room with its gilded dome ceiling, until the final red X on the last swooped-to page of the iPhone's uploaded maps represents only another pulled apart bomb.

In an office corridor, a door: mens room.

Cradle all the napalm water bottles in your arms.

The restroom is bright and mirrored, a storm of lemon ammonia.

And empty.

Lay screwed open water bottles in the sink so they *gluck gluck* down that drain.

One bottle won't fit. Shuffle it into the silver metal stall.

Can't stop, exhausted, drained, slide down that stall wall, slump to sitting on the floor, hugging the toilet like some *two beers too many* teenager.

The C4 padding his body makes it hard to move, but he drains the last non-recyclable water bottle into the toilet. That silver handle pushes down with a *whoosh*.

The world does not explode.

He crawled out of the stall. Made sure the water bottles in the sink were empty. Left them there. Left the tub of cellphones and wires in the hall for janitors to puzzle over. Dumped Jeremy's laptop in a litter barrel. Waddled to an elevator, a hall, down corridors and down the tunnel slope to the Adams building toward his own office.

Kept going.

Up, main floor, the blonde went this way, there's the door to the street, you can—

Man's voice behind Condor yells: "You!" The blue pinstripe suit DOSP. Who blinks.

Leans back from the smell of sweat and some kind of nuts, back from the haggard wild-eyed man in the black leather jacket.

"Are you quite all right, Mister . . . *Vin?*"

"Does that matter?" says this pitiful excuse

for a government employee foisted on the DOSP by another agency.

Who then unzips his black leather jacket, fumbles inside it, pulls out—

A fountain pen Vin hands to the DOSP, saying: "Guess I'm a sword guy."

Vin waddled away from his stricken silent LOC boss.

Stepped out into twilight town.

They'll never let you get away with this.

Capital Hill sidewalk. Suit and ties with briefcases and work-stuffed backpacks, kids on scooters. That woman's walking a dog. The cool air promises spring. An umbrella of night cups the marble city. Some guy outside a bar over on Pennsylvania Avenue sings *Danny Boy*. Budding trees along the curb make a canopy against the streetlights' shine and *just keep going, one foot in front of the other.*

Go slow so nothing shakes out of your clothes.

Talking heads blather from an unseen TV, insist *this*, know *that*, sell *whatever.*

Waves of light dance on that three story high townhouse alley wall. Music in the air from the alley courtyard's flowing light. Laughter.

Barbecue and green beer inspired the St. Paddy's Day party thrown by the *not-yet-thirty* men and women in that group house. They did their due diligence, reassured their neighbors, *come on over*, we're getting a couple of kegs, buckets of ice for Cokes and white wine, craft or foreign beers for palates that had become pickier since college. There was a table for munchies. Texted invites blasted out at 4:20 before "everybody" headed out to the holiday bars after work. Zack rigged his laptop and speakers, played DJ so any woman who wanted a song had to talk to him and his wingman who was a whiz at voter precinct analyses but could never read a curl of lipstick.

Bodies packed the alley. Everybody worked their look, the *cool* stance, the way to turn your face to scan the crowd, the right smile. Lots of cheap suits and work ensembles, khakis and sports jackets, jeans that fit better than Condor's bulging pants. Cyber screens glow in the crowd like the stars of a universe centered by whoever holds the cellphone. Hormones and testosterone amidst smoke from the two troughs made from a fifty-gallon drum sliced lengthwise by a long gone tenant of yore. Those two barbecue barrels started out the evening filled by charcoal briquettes and a *Whump!* of lighter fluid. By the time Condor'd eased his way to the center of the churning crowd, a couple guys from a townhouse up the street had tossed firewood onto the coals so flames leapt high and danced shadows on the alley courtyard's walls. The crowd surged as Zack turned up the volume on a headbanger song from the wild daze of their parents.

Who were Condor's age. Or younger.

Hate that song, he thought.

He reached the inner edge of the crowd who amidst the flickering light tried not to see the *getting there* debts pressing down on them or the pollution from the barrel fires trapping tomorrow's sun. They'd made it here to this city, this place, this idea. They worked for the hero who'd brought them to town, for Congress *of course that would matter*, so would the group/ the project/the committee/the caucus/the association/the website they staffed, the Administration circus ring that let them parade lions or tigers or bears, *oh my*, the downtown for dollars firm that pulled levers, the Agency or Department they powered with their sweat and so they could, *they should* sweat here, now, in the flickering fire light of an alley courtyard. Swaying. Looking. Hoping for a connection—heart, mind, flesh, community: get what you can, if nothing else a contact, a move toward more. The music surged. An American beat they all knew pulsed this crowd who were white and black, Hispanic and Asian, men and women and maybe more, who came from purple mountains' majesty and fruited plains to claim the capital city for this dream or that, to punch a ticket for their career, to get something done or get a deal, *to do* or *to be*—that is this city's true question and they, *oh they*, they were the answer *now*.

Near the burning barrels, a dozen couples jumped and jived to their generation's music blaring out of the speakers. Glowing cell phones and green dotted the crowd—bowlers, top hats. Over there was a woman in green foil boa. That woman blew a noisemaker as she shuffled and danced solo—not alone, no, she was not alone, don't anyone dare think that she was alone. She saw him, a guy old enough to be her father, all battered face lost in space, heard herself yell the question you always ask in Washington: *"What do you do?"*

He felt the heat of the flames.

"Hey old guy!" yelled Zack, DJ earphones cupped around his neck like the hands of a strangler. "This one's for you. My dad loves it."

Zack keyboarded a YouTubed live concert, Bruce Springsteen blasting *Badlands*.

Cranked up the volume as elsewhere in this empire city night, silver lip looped Kim shyly thanked a man with a mustache for being the knight by her side, for dinner, for *sure*, coffee at work tomorrow morning, for however much more they might have.

But in that alley, in that pounding drums and crashing guitars night, lovers like that became just part of the intensity of it all, like individual books in the library stacks of stories stretching into our savage forever.

Call him Vin. Call him Condor.

His arms shot toward the heaven in that black smoked night and he shuffled to the music's blare, arms waving, feet sliding into the dancing crowd.

A roar seized the revelers. A roar that pulled other arms toward heaven, a roar that became the whole crowd bopping with the beat, the hard driving invisible anthem.

"Go old guy!" shouts someone.

A silver-haired frenzy in black leather and jeans rocks through the younger crowd to the burning barrels, to the fire itself, reaches inside his jacket, throws something into those flames, something that lands with a shower of sparks and a sizzle and crackles and on, on he dances, pulling more of that magic fuel out of his jacket, out of its sleeves, out his—*Oh My*

God! He's pulling stuff out of his pants and throwing it on the fire! Every throw makes him lighter, wilder, then he's dancing hands free in the air, stomping feet with the crowd bouncing around him. "Old guy! Old guy!" Cop cruisers cut the night with red and blue spinning lights. The crowd throbs.

"Old guy! Old Guy!" Burning almonds and fireplace wood, barbecue and *come hither* perfume, a reckless whiff of rebel herb that will become legal and corporate by the decade's end. "Old guy! Old Guy!" There are bodies in a basement, mysteries to be found, questions clean of his fingerprints, books to be treasured. There are lovers sharing moments, dreamers dancing in the night, madmen in our marble city, and amidst those who are not his children, through the fog of his crazy, the swirl of his ghosts, the weight of his locked-up years, surging in Condor is the certainty that this *oh this,* this is *the real world.*

Ghosts In Our Eyes

I am grateful to be haunted by the authors who swirled through this story: L. Frank Baum, Harlan Ellison, William Faulkner, Ian Fleming, Theodore Seuss Geisel, Adam Hall, Dashiell Hammett, Lao-Tzu, Harper Lee, John le Carre, Philip MacDonald, Anais Nin, Li Po, Harold Robbins, Bruce Springsteen, John Steinbeck, Dariel Telfer, Kurt Vonnegut, Donald E. Westlake (*aka* Alan Marshall), E.B. White.

The Travelling Companion
Ian Rankin

Ian Rankin was born in 1960 in the Kingdom of Fife. After graduating from the University of Edinburgh in 1982, he briefly pursued a PhD in Scottish Literature before devoting himself to writing novels full-time. The first of his Inspector Rebus novels was published in 1987, introducing a bestselling series that would go on to be translated into over thirty languages. Since then, Rankin has won numerous international awards for his fiction, including four Crime Writers' Association awards, the Edgar Award for Best Novel, the French Grand Prix du Roman Noir, and the Deutscher Krimi Preis. In addition to the twenty Inspector Rebus novels, Rankin has published other fiction, short story collections, non-fiction, and a graphic novel. He was a regular contributor to BBC 2's Newsnight Review and has presented multiple other television programs, such as the Ian Rankin's Evil Thoughts miniseries. In 2002, Rankin was named an Officer of the British Empire. He lives in Edinburgh with his wife and two sons.

M y French isn't very good," I told him.

"The seller's English. You'll be fine." Mr. Whitman thrust the postcard towards me again. He had insisted I call him George, but I couldn't do that. He was my employer, sort of. Moreover, if the stories were to be believed, he was a descendant of Walt Whitman, and that mattered to me. I had graduated with First Class Honors from the University of Edinburgh that same summer. My focus had been on Scottish rather than American Literature, but still—Whitman was Whitman. And now my employer (of sorts) was asking me to do him a favor. How could I refuse?

I watched as my fingers plucked the postcard from his grip. It was one of the bookstore's own promotional cards. On one side were drawings of Shakespeare and Rue De La Bucherie, on the other my handwritten destination.

"A five-minute walk," Mr. Whitman assured me. His accent was an American drawl. He was tall, his silver hair swept back from his forehead, his eyes deep-set, cheekbones prominent. The first time we'd met, he had demanded a cigarette. On hearing that I didn't smoke, he had shaken his head as if in general weariness at my generation. This meeting had taken place outside a nearby cous-cous restaurant, where I had been staring at the menu in the window, wondering if I dared go inside. Money wasn't the main issue. I had been rehearsing my few French phrases and considering the possibility that the staff, seeing me for a lone traveler, might mug me for my pocketful of francs before selling the contents of my heavy rucksack at some street market in the vicinity.

"Passing through?" the stranger next to me had inquired, before demanding that I give him one of my "smokes."

A little later, as we shared a table and the menu's cheapest options, he had told me about his bookstore.

"I know it," I'd stammered. "It's rightly famous."

He had offered a tired smile, and, when we'd filled our bellies, had produced an empty thermos flask, into which he poured the leftover food before screwing the lid back on.

"No point wasting it," he had explained. "The store doesn't pay, you know, but there's the offer of a bed. A bed's all you get."

"I was going to look for a hotel."

"You work the till for a few hours, and mop the floor at closing time. Rest of the day's your own, and we do have some interesting books on the shelves . . ."

Which is how I came to work at Shakespeare and Company, 37 Rue De La Bucherie, Paris 5. On the postcard we boasted "the largest stock of antiquarian English books on the continent," and added Henry Miller's comment that we were "a wonderland of books."

It wasn't the original shop, of course—not that we trumpeted the fact. Sylvia Beach's Shakespeare and Company had opened in the year 1919 on Rue Dupuytren, before moving to larger premises on Rue de l'Odeon. This was where Joyce, Pound and Hemingway could be found. Mr. Whitman had called his own bookstore Le Mistral, before renaming it in Beach's honor—her own Shakespeare and Co. having closed for good during the German occupation of Paris. The new Shakespeare and Company had been a magnet for Beat writers in the 1950s, and writers (of a sort) still visited. I would lie on my hard narrow bed in a curtained-off alcove and listen as poems were workshopped by ex-pats whose names meant nothing to me. Contemporary writing was not my period, however, so I tried hard not to judge.

"You're from Scotland, right?" Mr. Whitman had said to me one day. "Edinburgh, specifically."

"Walter Scott and Robbie Burns, eh?"

"And Robert Louis Stevenson."

"Not forgetting that reprobate Trocchi . . ." He had chuckled to himself.

"Stevenson is my passion. I'm starting my PhD on him in the autumn."

"Back into academe so soon?"

"I like it there."

"I can't imagine why." And he had fixed me with one of his looks, before opening the till to examine the evening's scant takings. It was August, and still hot outside. The tourists were sitting at café tables, fanning themselves with menus and ordering cold drinks. Only one or two people my own age were browsing the shelves of our airless shop. There was an original copy of *Ulysses* in the window, a siren to draw them inside. But this night it was proving ineffectual.

"Was Paris always your destination?" he asked, sliding the drawer closed again.

"I wanted to travel. Stevenson visited France several times."

"Is that the subject of your PhD?"

"I'm looking at how his health may have affected his writing."

"Sounds fascinating. But it's hardly living, is it?" I watched him as he turned away and headed for the stairs. Three more hours and I could lock up before heading for bed and the various biting insects who seemed to feast nightly on my ankles and the backs of my knees.

I had sent postcards—Shakespeare and Company postcards—to friends and family, making sure to add a few centimes to the till in payment. I didn't mention the bites, but did make sure that my ongoing adventure sounded as exotic as possible. I had actually sent a first postcard home soon after disembarking from the overnight bus at London's Victoria Coach Station. Another had been purchased and sent from the ferry terminal in Dover. I knew my parents would prefer written communication to an expensive phone call. My father was a Church of Scotland minister, my mother an invaluable member of our local community. I was a rarity of sorts in having stayed at home during the four years of my undergraduate degree. My parents had offered financial assistance towards rent, but my arguments about wasted money had swayed them. Besides, my childhood bedroom suited me, and my mother was the finest cook in the city.

Before leaving, however, I had promised to phone Charlotte every two days, just so she would know I was safe. There was a public phonebox just along the Seine from the store, with a view towards Notre Dame which made up for its general lack of hygiene. With the receiver wrapped in a clean paper serviette from a café, I would spend a few francs telling Charlotte of any new experiences, in-between listening to her tell me that she loved me and missed me and couldn't wait until I found a place of my own in time for the start of term back in Edinburgh.

"Absolutely," I would agree, my mouth suddenly dry.

"Oh, Ronnie," she would sigh, and I would swallow back the inclination to correct her, since my preference (as she well knew) was for Ronald rather than Ronnie.

My name is Ronald Hastie. I was born in 1960, making me twenty-two. Twenty-two and three months as I stood on the banks of the Seine, surrounded by heat and traffic fumes and a sense that there was another world being kept hidden from me. A series of worlds, actually, only one of them represented by Charlotte and her cropped red hair and freckled complexion. Cous-cous and a famous bookshop and morning espressos (consumed standing at the bar—the cheapest option)—these were all wonders to me that summer. And, yes, the original plan had been to drift much further south, but plans could change, as could people.

"The seller's English," my employer said, waking me from my reverie. "You'll be fine, trust me. A five-minute walk . . ."

His name was Benjamin Turk and he lived in a sprawling apartment at the top of five winding flights of stairs. When he opened his door to me, I stood there breathless, staring past him at a long hallway filled with groaning bookshelves. I felt lightheaded, and it seemed in that moment that the shelves were endless, stretching to infinity. Turk slid an arm around my shoulders and guided me into the gloom. "Whitman sent you but he didn't mention the climb. That's the reason he wouldn't drag his own sorry rump over here, you know." Laughter boomed from his chest. He was stocky and bald and probably in his fifties or early sixties, with dark bushy eyebrows above eyes filled with sly humor. His voluminous white shirt and crimson waistcoat could have come from a different century, as could their owner. I'd read enough Dickens to see that Mr. Turk would have slotted right into one of those comedic episodes from *Copperfield* or *Pickwick*.

"A drink's what's needed," he went on, steering me down the hall. Varnished parquet floor stretched its length, and it ended eventually at a wall furnished with a large mirror, in which I glimpsed my sweating face. Doorways to left and right, both open, showing a tidy kitchen and a cluttered living-room. We entered this last and Turk positioned me before an armchair, thumping it so hard dust rose into the air.

"Sit!" he commanded, before pouring red wine from a glass decanter. I noticed for the first time that he had a discernible limp.

"I don't really . . ." I began to apologize.

"Nonsense, lad! This is Paris—you do realize that? Get it down you or I'll have you deported for crimes against the state!" He had poured himself a glass not quite as generous as mine, and raised his hand in a toast before filling his mouth.

I realized I really was thirsty, so took a sip. The stuff was nectar, unlike the cheap, weak compromises of Edinburgh lunches and dinners. Cherries and blackcurrants replaced the bitter memories, and Turk could tell I was in love. He beamed at me, nodding slowly.

"Delicious," I said. "Did you ever doubt it?" And he toasted me again with his glass before settling on the chaise longue opposite. "Do I detect a Scottish accent?"

"Edinburgh."

"That most Presbyterian of cities, explaining your aversion to pleasure."

"I'm not averse to pleasure." As soon as the words were out, I regretted them, hoping they wouldn't be misinterpreted. To cover my embarrassment, I took more sips of wine, causing Turk to spring to his feet in order to refill my glass.

"Mr. Whitman says you're one of his oldest customers," I stammered.

"We've known one another more years than I care to remember."

"So you've lived in Paris a long time?" He smiled, this time a little wistfully.

"How about you?" he asked.

"This is my first visit. I'm taking a break from university."

"Yes, George said as much—too short a break, he seems to think. Your hero Stevenson didn't let college hold him back, did he?" He saw my surprise. "George again," he explained.

"Stevenson completed his studies."

"And passed the law exam," Turk said airily. "But his family expected him to stick to that path, or one very like it, but the bold Louis had other ideas." My host was swirling the wine in his glass. I found the motion hypnotic, and sensed I was not yet fully recovered from the climb. The room was stuffy, too, with the smell of leather-bound books, old curtains and faded rugs. "You should take your jacket off," Turk said. "Who the hell wears a black velvet jacket in Paris in the heat of summer?"

"It's not velvet," I mumbled, shrugging my arms out of the sleeves.

"But the nearest you could find?" Turk smiled to himself and I could tell that he knew—knew that Stevenson's nickname at university had been "Velvet Jacket."

I lay the jacket across my knees and cleared my throat. "Mr. Whitman says you have some books to sell."

"A few boxes—mostly bought from George himself. He says you've memorized the stock so will know if they're worth taking or not."

"He's exaggerating."

"I think so, too. I know only too well how many books are in that shop of his."

"You're a collector." I was looking around the room. Every inch of wall-space was filled with shelving, and those shelves groaned. The books all seemed very old—few had dust jackets. It was impossible to make out any of the titles, but they seemed to be in several languages. "Are you a professor? A writer?"

"I've been many things." He paused, watching me above the rim of his glass. "I'm guessing you'd like to be both some day."

"I've never thought about writing. I mean to say, I would hope to finish my thesis and try to get it published."

"A thesis about Stevenson and his ailments?"

"And how they made him the writer he was. He was trying out an experimental drug called Ergotine when he got the idea for *Jekyll and Hyde*. It gave him hallucinations. And the Edinburgh he grew up in was all science and rationalism and men who *did* things, while he felt sickly, his only real strength his imagination . . ." I broke off, fearing I was beginning to lecture my host.

"Interesting," Turk said, drawing the word out. He rose to fill my glass again, emptying the decanter. My mouth felt furred and sweat was trickling down my forehead. I took out a handkerchief and began to mop at my face. "He had a nursemaid, didn't he?" Turk asked as he poured. "She told him ghost stories. Must have frightened the life out of him."

"He called her 'Cummy'—her real name was Alison Cunningham. She told him about the wardrobe in his room."

"The one made by William Brodie?" And Turk nodded to himself again, because he knew this story too. Brodie, a respectable man by day but a criminal by night, the Deacon of Wrights who led a gang, breaking into houses, thieving and terrorizing, until caught, tried and hanged on a gibbet he had previously crafted by his own hand. The lazy theory was that Stevenson had plundered this story wholesale for *Jekyll and Hyde*, but it comprised only one part of the overall puzzle.

"Maybe we should look at these books," I said, hoping I wasn't slurring my words.

"Of course." Turk rose slowly to his feet, and came over to help me up. I followed him into the kitchen. There was a narrow stairway I hadn't noticed and we climbed into the eaves of the building. It was hotter, gloomier and stuffier up here. Two people, no matter how emaciated, could not have passed one another in the corridor. Several doors led off. One seemed to be a bathroom. I guessed there had to be a bedroom, but the room Turk led me into was the study. Three boxes sat on an antique desk. Piles of books lined the walls, threatening to topple as our weight shifted the bare floorboards beneath. I draped my jacket over the room's only chair.

"Shall I leave you to it, then?" Turk inquired.

I looked in vain for a window to open. The sweat was stinging my eyes now and my handkerchief was drenched. Outside, bells were chiming. The scratching noises could have been pigeons on the roof-tiles immediately overhead or rats somewhere below the floor. My lips felt as if they had been glued together. More dust flew into my face as I peeled open the flaps of the first box.

"You don't look well, my boy." Turk's words seemed to come from far off. Were we still in the attic, or had we somehow moved to that infinite entrance-hall with its books and mirror? I had a sudden vision: a cold drink, something non-alcoholic, in a tall glass filled with ice. I craved it without being able to say the words out loud. There was a book in my hand, but it seemed to weigh far more than its size would suggest, and the title on its spine seemed to be a jumble of letters or hieroglyphs of some kind.

"My boy?"

And then a darkening tunnel. "Wait, let me . . ."

And then sleep.

⁓

I awoke laid out on a bed. My shirt had been unbuttoned and Benjamin Turk was dabbing at my chest with a damp towel. I sat bolt upright, a hangover pulsing behind my eyes.

It was quite obviously *his* bedroom. My jacket had been placed on a hook on the back of the door, but below it I could see a long red satin bath-robe. There was also a wardrobe whose doors wouldn't quite shut and a bedside table bearing a basin half-filled with water. When I angled my feet off the bed on to the floor, I made contact with several hardcover books lying there.

"Careful you don't faint again," Turk cautioned as I started to rebutton my shirt.

"I just need some air," I muttered.

"Of course. Can I help you negotiate the stairs?"

"I'll be fine."

"I'm relieved to hear it—I had the devil's own job bringing you this far . . ."

I wasn't sure what he meant until I grabbed my jacket and pulled open the door. We were just inside the front door of the apartment. I must have missed the bedroom on arrival. I stared at Turk, who shrugged.

"It wasn't easy—those steps from the attic are treacherous." He was holding something out for me to take. I unfolded the piece of paper. "A list of the books," he explained, "so that your employer can be kept in blissful ignorance—if that's what you would like."

"Thank you," I said, pocketing the note. He had unlocked the door. The stairwell was a few degrees cooler, but I could still feel sweat clinging to my hair.

"Safe descent," Benjamin Turk said, giving a little wave of one hand before disappearing behind the closing door. Holding on to the banister, I made my way slowly to the street, pausing outside and filling my lungs with air. A young woman on the pavement opposite seemed to be watching me. She wore a full-length floral-print dress, almost identical to one Charlotte owned. I did a double-take and my jacket slid to the ground. By the time I'd picked it up, she had gone. I began walking back to the shop, aware that my headache was going nowhere. Passing a bar, I headed in and ordered a Perrier with plenty of ice and lemon. Having finished it in two long draughts, I ordered another. I doubted the place would sell painkillers, but then remembered the old saying about the hair of the dog. Kill or cure, I thought to myself, adding a glass of red wine to my order.

And it worked—I could feel the pain easing after just one small measure. It was thin, vinegary stuff, too, the very antithesis of the contents of Turk's decanter, but I felt better for it, and ordered one final glass. While sipping this, I removed the list of books from my pocket and went through it. A solid line had been drawn across the sheet two thirds of the way down. Underneath was a message from Turk:

> *Not for sale, but possibly of interest:*
> *The Travelling Companion*

I blinked a few times and furrowed my brow. I knew that title, but couldn't immediately place it. The books listed above it could probably find buyers. Historical non-fiction and philosophy titles mostly, with Balzac, Zola and Mann thrown in. Turk omitted to say whether they were first editions, or what condition they were in, and I had only the most fleeting memory of opening the first box. I felt I had let Mr. Whitman down somehow—not that he need ever know, unless Turk decided to tell him. But that didn't stop me feeling bad. Preoccupied, I was halfway to the doorway before the barman reminded me I hadn't yet paid. I mumbled an apology and rooted in my pockets for change. Curiously, there seemed a couple of hundred-franc notes there that I thought I'd spent earlier in the week. There would be cous-cous again that evening, rather than a tin of cheap tuna from the supermarket. Heartened, I added a small tip to the bill. An Australian backpacker called Mike was minding the store on my return. He told me, to my relief, that Mr. Whitman would be gone the rest of the day. I resented Mike his broad-shouldered height, perfect teeth and mahogany tan. His hair was blond and curly and he had already made his mark on a couple of female students who liked to hang about the place, reading but never buying. When he ended his shift and I took over, I found that there was a letter for me next to the till. Typical of him not to have mentioned it. It was from my father and I opened it as respectfully as possible. Two small sheets of thin blue airmail. He had news of my mother, my aunt and uncle, my clever cousins—clever in that they both had good jobs in the City of London—and the neighbors on our street. His tone was clipped and precise, much like his sermons, not a word wasted. My mother had added a couple of lines towards the foot of the last page, but seemed to feel that nothing really need be added to my father's update. The return address had been added to the back of the envelope, lest it be lost in transit somehow. As I reread it, I caught a glimpse of someone on the pavement outside, someone wearing the same floral dress as before. I sauntered to the open doorway and looked up and down the street, but she had done her vanishing act again—if it had been her in the first place. What I did see, however, was Australian Mike, stepping briskly in the direction of Notre Dame with an arm draped across the shoulders of a couple of giggling students.

Two hours before closing, Mike and his entourage were back. He had promised the girls a lesson in retail, and informed me with a wink and a salute that I was "relieved of all duties." That was fine by me. I slipped into my black almost-velvet jacket and headed out for a late dinner. The staff in the cous-cous restaurant knew me by now, and there were smiles and bows as I was escorted to one of the quieter tables. I had lifted a book from the shelves at Shakespeare and Company—an American paperback of Conrad's *Heart of Darkness*. There was too much food and I half-wished I had thought to pack an empty flask. Instead of which, I refilled my bowl for a third time. The house wine was thinner than anything I had yet tasted, but I nodded my appreciation of it when invited to do so by my waiter. And at meal's end, this same waiter, who had told me a couple of visits back to call him Harry, signaled that he would meet me at the restaurant's kitchen door in five minutes. Having paid the bill, my curiosity piqued, I wound my way down the alley behind the restaurant and its neighbors. The bins were overflowing and there was a strong smell of urine. I skidded once or twice, not daring to look down at whatever was beneath my feet. Eventually I reached Harry. He stood at the open door of the kitchen while vocal mayhem ensued within, accompanied by the clanging of cooking-pots. He was holding a thin cigarette, which he proceeded to light, sucking deeply on it before offering it to me.

"Dope?" I said. "Very good."

After four years of an arts degree at the University of Edinburgh, I was no stranger to drugs. I had been to several parties where a room—usually an underlit bedroom—had been set aside for use by drug-takers. I'd even watched as joints were rolled, enjoying the ritual while refusing to partake.

"I'm not sure," I told Harry, whose real name was more like Ahmed. "It's been a strange enough day already." When he persisted, however, I lifted the cigarette from him and took a couple of puffs without inhaling. This wasn't good enough for Harry, who used further gestures to instruct me until he was happy that I had sucked the smoke deep into my lungs. Another waiter joined us and it was soon his turn. Then Harry. Then me again. I had expected to feel queasy, but that didn't happen. My cares seemed to melt away, or at least take on a manageable perspective. Once we had finished the joint, Harry produced a small cellophane wrap, inside which was a lump of something brown. He wanted two hundred francs for it, but I shrugged to signal that I didn't have that kind of money about my person. So then he shoved the tiny parcel into my jacket pocket and patted it, gesturing to indicate that I could pay him later.

We then fell silent as two new arrivals entered the alley. They either hadn't noticed that they had an audience, or else they simply weren't bothered. The woman squatted in front of the man and unzipped his trousers. I had seen more than a few prostitutes on my nighttime walks through the city—some of whom had tried tempting me—and here was another, hard at work while the woozy client tipped a bottle of vodka to his mouth.

And suddenly I knew.

The Travelling Companion . . .

I lifted a hand to my forehead with the shock of it, while my companions took a step back towards their kitchen, perhaps fearing I was about to be sick.

"No," I whispered to myself. "That can't be right." Harry was looking at me, and I returned his stare. "It doesn't exist," I told him. "It doesn't exist."

Having said which, I weaved my way back towards the mouth of the alley, almost stumbling into the woman and her client. He swore at me, and I swore back, almost pausing to take a swing at him. It wasn't the alcohol or the dope making my head reel as I sought the relative calm of the darkened Shakespeare and Company.

It was Benjamin Turk's message to me . . .

I was unlocking the doors next morning when Mr. Whitman called down to tell me I had a phone call.

"And by the way, how did you get on with Ben Turk?"

"I have a note of the books he wants to sell," I replied, not meeting his eyes.

"He's an interesting character. Anyway, go talk to your woman friend . . ."

It was Charlotte. She had found work at a theater box office and was using their phone.

"I need to pass the time somehow. It's so *boring* here without you."

I was leaning down to rub at the fresh insect-bites above my ankles. The list from Turk was folded up in the back pocket of my trousers. I knew I had to tear a strip from it before showing it to my employer.

"Are you there?" Charlotte was asking into the silence.

"I'm here."

"Is everything okay? You sound . . ."

"I'm fine. A glass of wine too many last night."

I heard her laugh. "Paris is leading you astray."

"Maybe just a little."

"Well, that can be a good thing." She paused. "You remember our little chat, the night before you left?"

"Yes."

"I meant it, you know. I'm ready to take things a bit further. *More* than ready."

She meant sex. Until now, we had kissed, and gone from fumbling above clothes to rummaging beneath them, but nothing more.

"It's what you want, too, isn't it?" she asked.

"Doesn't everyone?" I was able to answer, my cheeks coloring.

"So when you come back . . . we'll do something about it, yes?"

"If you're sure. I mean, I don't want to push you into anything."

More laughter. "I seem to be the one doing the pushing. I'm thinking of you right now, you know. Thinking of *us* lying together, joined together—tell me you don't think about that, too."

"I have to go, Charlotte. There are customers . . ." I looked around the empty upstairs room.

"Soon, Ronnie, soon. Just remember."

"I will. I'll call you tonight."

I put the phone down and stared at it, then took the note from my pocket and tore across it. Downstairs, my employer was manning the till.

"You look like hell, by the way," he said as I handed him the list. "Did Ben ply you with booze?"

"Do you know much about him?"

"He comes from money. Pitched up here for want of anywhere better—not unlike my good self. Drinks fine wines, buys books he wants to own but not necessarily read." He was scanning the list. "He'd probably give these to us for free, you know. I think he just needs space for more of the same." He paused, fixing me with a look. "What did *you* think of him?"

"Pleasant enough. Maybe a bit eccentric . . ." I suppressed a shiver as I remembered waking on Turk's bed, shirt open, and him dabbing at my chest. "Is he . . ." I tried to think how to phrase the question. "A ladies' man?"

Mr. Whitman hooted. "Listen to you," he said. "Remind me—which century is this?" After his laughter had subsided, he fixed his eyes on mine again. "Ladies, gents, fish and fowl and the beasts of field and wood," he said. "Now off you go and find yourself some breakfast. I'll manage these heaving crowds somehow." He waved his arm in the direction of the deserted shop.

It was warm outside, and noisy with tourists and traffic. I slung my jacket over my shoulder as I walked to my usual café, only four shop-fronts away. Benjamin Turk was seated at an outdoor table, finishing a *cafe au lait* and reading *Le Monde*. A silver-topped walking-stick rested against the rim of the table. He gestured for me to join him, so I dragged out the spare metal chair and sat down, slipping my jacket over the back of my chair.

"It was the local prostitutes who called Stevenson 'Velvet Jacket,' you know," Turk said.

The liveried waiter stood ready. I ordered a coffee of my own.

"And an orange juice," Turk added.

The waiter gave a little bow and headed back inside. Turk folded the newspaper and laid it next to his cup.

"I was coming to check on you," he said. "But the lure of caffeine was too strong."

"I'm fine," I assured him.

"And you've looked at the list, I presume?"

I took the scrap of paper from my pocket and placed it between us. He gave an indulgent smile.

"It's a book Stevenson wrote," I said. "Never quite completed. His publisher liked it well enough but considered the contents too sordid."

"It concerned a prostitute," Turk agreed.

"Set in Italy, I think."

"Some of it." Turk's eyes were gleaming.

"Fanny made Stevenson put it on the fire," I said quietly.

"Ah, the formidable Fanny Osbourne. He met her in France, you know. He was visiting Grez. I suppose he became infatuated." He paused, playing with his cup, moving it in circles around its saucer. "It wasn't the only book of his she persuaded him to sacrifice . . ."

"*Jekyll and Hyde*," I said, as my own coffee arrived, and with it the glass of juice. "The first draft, written in three days."

"Yes."

"Though some commentators say three days is impossible."

"Despite the author's Presbyterian work ethic. But then he was taking drugs, wasn't he?"

"Ergotine, and possibly cocaine."

"Quite the cocktail for a writer whose imagination was already inflamed. You know why he consigned it to the flames?"

"Fanny persuaded him. She thought it would ruin his reputation."

"Because it was too raw, too shocking." He watched me as I finished the orange juice in two long gulps, watched as I poured hot milk into the viscous black coffee.

"Nobody really knows, though," I eventually said. "Because only Stevenson and Fanny saw that first version. Same goes for *The Travelling Companion*."

"Not quite."

"Yes, his publisher read that," I corrected myself.

"Not quite," Turk repeated, almost in a whisper.

"You're not seriously telling me you have that manuscript?"

"Do you really think any author could burn the only copy of a work they considered worthwhile?"

"Didn't Fanny see it burn in the grate?"

"She saw *something* burn. She saw paper. I'm guessing there would have been plenty of paper in the vicinity."

Lifting the coffee towards my mouth, I realized my hand was shaking. He waited until I'd taken a first sip.

"I have *both* manuscripts," he then announced, causing me to splutter. I rubbed the back of my hand across my lips.

"I'm not sure I believe you," I eventually said.

"Why not?"

"Because they'd be worth a small fortune. Besides, the world would know. It's been almost a century—impossible to have kept them a secret."

"Nothing is impossible."

"Then you'll show me them?"

"It can be arranged. But tell me—what would it mean for your doctoral thesis?"

I thought for a moment. "They'd probably move me from student to full professor." I laughed at the absurdity of it. Yet I almost believed . . . almost.

"My understanding," Turk went on airily, "is that he entrusted both to his good friend Henley. They found their way into my family because my grandfather bought many of Henley's possessions on his death—they were friends of a sort. There are notations in what seems to be Henley's handwriting. They add . . . well, you'd need to read them to find out."

That smile again. I wanted to grab him and shake him.

"I'm not very good at keeping secrets," I told him.

"Maybe it's time for the truth to be told," he retorted. "Wouldn't you say you're as good a vessel as any?" He had taken some coins from his pocket and was counting them on to the table-top as payment for the drinks. "I should imagine most Stevenson scholars would be on their knees right now, begging to be shown even a few pages." He paused, reaching into his jacket. "Pages like these."

He held them out towards me. Half a dozen sheets.

"Copies rather than the originals, you understand."

Handwritten on unlined paper.

"The openings to both books," Turk was saying as my head swam and my eyes strained to retain their focus. "You'll notice something from the off . . ."

"Edinburgh," I mouthed, near-silently. "The setting for both," he agreed. "Well, there *are* some French scenes in *The Travelling Companion*, but our harlot heroine hails from your own fair city, Ronald. And since Jekyll is reputed to be a conflation between Deacon Brodie and the Scottish physician John Hunter, I suppose Edinburgh makes sense—too much sense for Fanny to bear, as it transpired."

I glanced up at him, seeking his meaning.

"There's too much of Stevenson himself in both works," he obliged, rising to his feet.

"You could be the victim of a hoax," I blurted out. "I mean to say, forgeries maybe." I held the pages up in front of me, my heart racing.

"Handwriting analysis comes later on in the story," Turk said, adjusting the cuffs of his pale linen jacket and seeming to sniff the mid-morning air. "I expect you'll be paying me a visit later—if only to collect those boxes of books."

"This is insane," I managed to say, holding the pages by both trembling hands.

"Nevertheless, you'll want to read them. I'm out most of the day, but should be home later this evening."

He turned and walked away, leaning lightly on his walking-stick. I watched him. He seemed to belong to a different age or culture. It was something about his gait as well as his clothes. I could imagine him with a top hat propped on his head, horse-drawn carriages passing him as he tip-tapped his way down the boulevard. The waiter said "*merci*" as he scooped up the coins and cleared the table, but I was in no rush to leave. I read and reread the excerpts. They revealed little by way of plot, but it was true that Edinburgh was the setting for both, Stevenson's descriptions of his "precipitous city" as trenchant as ever. It was a place he seemed to have loved and hated in equal measure. I recalled something I'd read about his student years—how he spent his time yoyoing between the strict rationalism of the family home in Heriot Row and the drunken stews of the chaotic Old Town—moving, in other words, between the worlds of Henry Jekyll and Edward Hyde.

When the waiter cleared his throat, alerting me to the fact my premium table was needed by a wealthy American couple, I rolled the sheets of paper into a tube and carried them back to the shop. My employer had ceded his place behind the till to a new arrival, an English woman called Tessa with long brown hair, round glasses, and a prominent nose.

"I'll be upstairs if you need me," I told her. The curtain had been drawn closed across my alcove. Pulling it back revealed Mike and one of his female friends, both naked from the waist up and sharing slugs from a cheap bottle of wine. The young woman apologized in French-accented English and slipped a t-shirt over her head.

"Ronnie doesn't mind a bit of tit," Mike told her with a grin. She punched his arm and snatched the bottle from him, offering it to me. I settled on the corner of the bed and took a mouthful.

"What's that you've got?" Mike asked.

"Nothing important," I lied, stuffing the sheets of paper into my jacket pocket. There was something else in there, and I fished it out. It was the lump of dope.

"That what I think it is?" Mike said, his grin widening. "Well, now we've got us a proper party!" He leapt up, returning a minute or two later with everything he needed. Crosslegged, he began to assemble the joint. "You're a dark horse, mate," he told me. "Never would have thought you indulged."

"Then you don't know me very well." His friend had moved closer, her leg touching mine. I could make out the soft down on her face. When she passed me the lit joint, it was as intimate as any kiss.

"It's not the best I've had," Mike said, when his turn came. "But it'll do, n'est ce pas, cherie?"

"It'll do," his friend echoed.

It was not ergotine, nor yet cocaine, but I found my imagination height-ened. I was with Stevenson and his student allies, touring the taverns of Edinburgh, rubbing shoulders with slatterns and sophisticates. I was adrift in France, and sailing to Samoa, and roughing it in Silverado, having survived yet another near-fatal illness. I was weak in body but strong in spirit, and a woman loved me. I was writing *Jekyll and Hyde* as an exorcism of sorts, my demons vanquished, allowing me the less dangerous pleasures *Kidnapped* of less than a year later. External as well as internal adventures were my mainstay—I had to keep moving, ever further from the Edinburgh of my birth and formation. I had to remake myself, renew myself, heal myself, even as mortality drew close. I had to survive.

"What's that?" Mike asked. He was slumped on the bed with his head against the wall.

"I didn't say anything."

"Something about survival."

"No."

He turned to his friend. She had moved next to him so that only her bare unwashed feet now rested near me. "You heard him," he nudged her.

"Survival," she echoed.

"What it's all about," Mike agreed, nodding slowly, before pulling him-self together, the better to roll another joint.

Though I was stoned, I agreed to take over from Tessa while she headed out for food. Mike and Maryse—she had eventually told me her name—decided to go with her. They had the decency to ask if I wanted anything, but I shook my head. I gulped some water from the tap and took up position. A few customers came and went. One or two regulars got comfortable with books they would never buy. Later, a writing group would hold its weekly meeting upstairs. And there she was again. Not just a glimpse this time, but a solidity in the open doorway, in the same floral dress. A willowy figure topped with long blond hair. Her eyes were on mine, but when I signaled for her to approach, she shook her head, so I walked towards her.

"I've seen you before," I said. "You're Ronald," she stated. "How do you know my name?"

"Ben told me."

"You know Benjamin Turk?"

She nodded slowly. "You mustn't trust him. He likes playing games with people."

"I've only met him twice."

"Yet he's already got beneath your skin—don't try to deny it."

"Who *are* you?"

"I'm Alice."

"How do you know Mr. Turk?"

"Services rendered."

"I'm not sure I follow."

"I run errands for him sometimes. I copied those pages he gave you."

"You know about those?"

"You've already read them, I suppose?"

"Of course."

"And you need to read more, meaning you'll visit him again?"

"I think so."

She had lifted her hand and was running the tips of her fingers down my cheek, as if human contact was something new and strange. I leaned back a little, but she took a step forward and pressed her lips against mine, kissing me, her eyes squeezed shut. When she opened them again, I sensed a vast lake of sadness behind them. Tears were forming as she turned and fled down the street. I stood like a statue, shocked to my very core, wondering if I should go after her, but one of the loiterers had decided to break the habit of a lifetime and pay for the book in his hands, so I shrugged off the incident and headed back to the till, not in the least surprised to find that the book being purchased was the copy of *Heart of Darkness* I'd taken with me to the cous-cous restaurant . . .

It was almost eleven by the time I found myself standing outside Benjamin Turk's building. I stared up towards the top floor. A few lights were burning, but I couldn't be sure which rooms were his. I pushed open the heavy door and began to climb the stairs. I could smell the aftermath of various dinners, and hear conversations—mostly, I guessed, from TV sets. There was a dog behind one door, scratching and complaining softly.

Having reached the top floor, and while pausing to catch my breath, I saw a note pinned to Turk's door.

Still out. Come in.

I tried the door. It was unlocked. The overhead light was on in the hallway, but as with most Parisian lighting it seemed woefully underpowered. I called out but received no reply. There was something lying on the floor a few yards into the apartment—further sheets of manuscript, again photocopied. I lifted them and carried them into the living room, where I settled on the same chair as before. A fresh decanter of wine had been laid out, alongside two crystal glasses.

"In for a centime," I muttered to myself, pouring some. Then, having rolled up my shirt-sleeves, I began to read.

The two extracts did not follow on from their predecessors. They were from deeper into both books. I soon saw why Turk had chosen them, however—both recounted very similar incidents, vicious attacks on women whose bodies were for sale. In *The Travelling Companion*, it was the courtesan of the title who was brutalized by an unnamed stranger while passing down one of the steep inclines off Edinburgh's High Street. In the version of *Jekyll and Hyde*, the victim's attacker was Edward Hyde. But Hyde's name had replaced another, scored through in ink until it was all but obliterated. Penciled marginalia, however, indicated that the name Stevenson had originally chosen for his monster was Edwin Hythe. Indeed, the margins of this particular page were filled with notes and comments in various hands—Stevenson's, I felt sure, but maybe also his friend Henley's—and Fanny's, too? Was it she who had written in blunt capital letters "NOT HYTHE!"?

I poured myself some more wine and began deciphering the scribbles, scrawls and amendments. I was still hard at work when I heard the door at the end of the hallway open and close, footsteps drawing close. Then Benjamin Turk was standing there in the doorway, coat draped over both shoulders. He was dressed to the nines, and had obviously enjoyed his evening, his face filled with color, eyes almost fiery.

"Ah, my dear young friend," he said, shrugging off the coat and resting his walking-stick against a pile of books.

"I hope you don't mind," I replied, indicating the decanter.

He landed heavily in the chair opposite, his girth straining the buttons on his shirt. "Do you still imagine you're in the presence of a cruel hoax?" he asked, exhaling noisily.

"Not so much, perhaps."

This caused him to smile, albeit tiredly. "Do we know who wrote the notes in the margins?"

"The usual suspects." He rose long enough to pour some wine. "Edwin Hythe," he drawled.

"Yes."

"You won't know who he is?" Settling himself, he studied me over the rim of his glass.

"He's Hyde."

But Turk shook his head slowly. "He was a friend of Stevenson's, one of the students he drank with back in the day."

"That was his real name? And Stevenson was going to use it in the book?" I sounded skeptical because I was.

"I know." Turk took a sip, savoring the wine. "Hythe had re-entered Stevenson's life, visiting him in Bournemouth not long before work started on the story you're holding. The two had fallen out at some point and not spoken for several years. There are a couple of portraits of Hythe—I've seen them but don't have copies to hand. I do have this though . . ." He reached into his jacket and drew out a sheet of printed paper. I took it from him, unfolding it carefully. It was the front page of a newspaper of the time, the *Edinburgh Evening Courant*, from a February edition of 1870. The main story recounted the tale of a "young woman known to the city's night-dwellers" who had been found "most grievously slaughtered" in an alley off Cowgate.

"Like Stevenson," Turk was saying, "Edwin Hythe was a member of the university's Speculative Society—though whatever speculation they did was accompanied by copious amounts of drink. And don't forget—this was at a time when Edinburgh was noted for scientific and medical experiments, meaning the students had access to pharmaceuticals of all kinds, most of them untested, a few probably lethal. Hythe had a larger appetite than most—for drink, and narcotics, and lively behavior. He was arrested several times, and charged once for 'lewd and libidinous acts.'"

"Why are you telling me this?"

"You *know* why."

"Hyde was Hythe? And the newspaper . . . ?"

"I think you know that, too."

"Hythe killed her, is that what you're saying? And Stevenson knew?"

"Our dear Louis was probably *there*, Ronald, the guilt gnawing at him until he deals with it by writing *The Travelling Companion*. That particular book gets spiked, but word of it reaches Hythe and he hot-foots it down to Bournemouth to make sure his old pal isn't going to crack. Maybe he leans on him, but my hunch is he finds it a lot easier to enlist Fanny instead. She thinks she's succeeded when Louis shows her the burning pages. He then rewrites the story, shifting location from Edinburgh to London and changing Hythe to Hyde . . ."

"Was he a doctor?"

"I'm sorry?"

I met Turk's look. "Was Edwin Hythe a doctor?"

I watched him shake his head. I had emptied my glass and refilled it without thinking. "How do you know all this?"

"It's a tale passed down through my family."

"Why, though?"

"As a warning maybe."

"You're a Hythe," I stated, maintaining eye contact.

He eventually let out a snort of laughter. "I sincerely hope not." And he raised his own glass in a toast.

"Can I see the whole story?"

"Which one?"

"Both."

"In good time."

"Why not now?"

"Because I'm not sure you're ready."

"I don't understand."

But he just shook his head.

"It's like water torture," I ploughed on. "One page, two pages, three . . ."

"When I said that you weren't ready, I meant me—*I'm* not ready to let go, not just yet."

"And after all these generations, why me?"

He offered a tired shrug. "I'm the last of my line. Maybe that's reason enough. How about you?"

"Me?"

"Brothers . . . ? Sisters . . . ?"

"An only child."

"We have that in common, too, then." He yawned and stretched. "Forgive me, I think I need some sleep."

"I could stay here and read."

He shook his head again. "Perhaps tomorrow." He rose to his feet and gestured for me to do the same. As he accompanied me down the hall, helping me into my jacket, I felt the negative mirror image of his fatigue. I was crackling with energy, a need to be in movement, a need for activity and exertion.

"I saw your friend," I told him. "She was passing the shop."

"Oh?"

"Alice, with the blond hair."

"Alice," he echoed.

"I just thought I'd say."

"Thank you." He pulled open the door and I skipped out, almost dancing down the stone stairs. She was waiting, of course—at the same spot across the street, wearing her floral dress and looking cold. I slipped off my jacket and placed it around her, then led her by the hand.

"Where are we going?" she asked. "The river. I feel like walking."

There were no tourist boats at this hour, just a few silent lovers and noisy drunks.

"Do you live with him?" I asked her. "No."

"So where do you live?"

"Not far."

"Can we go there?"

"No." She sounded almost aghast at the idea.

"My room back at the shop then," I offered.

"Why would I go anywhere with you?"

"Because you kissed me."

"I shouldn't have done that."

"I'm glad you did though." I came to a halt, facing her. "I'd like it to happen again."

She took a few moments to make her mind up, then stroked my face again, this time with both hands, as though checking that I really was flesh and blood. I leaned in and our lips met, mouths opening. But partway through, she started to laugh, easing away from me. I tried for a disappointed look, and she had the good grace to look slightly ashamed.

"I'm sorry," she said. "It's just . . ."

"What?"

"Nothing." She shook her head, but then perked up and grabbed my hand, leading me along the riverfront towards the nearest brightly-lit bridge. "We can cross to the other side."

"Why would we do that?"

"It's quieter there. Do you have any dope?"

"Just this." I showed her the remains of the cannabis. "I don't have any cigarettes or papers though."

"That doesn't matter." She peeled away the cellophane and nibbled at a corner. "You can just eat it. It's almost nice."

"Almost?" I smiled and bit into the gritty cube. "Will it have the same effect?"

"We'll know the answer soon enough. Did Harry sell you this?"

"You know him?"

"If you've not paid, offer him half of whatever he asks."

"What if he doesn't like that?"

She looked me up and down. "You're bigger than him."

"He has friends though."

"So pull a knife." She mimed the action of drawing a blade from its sheath and lunging with it. "Straight into his gut and his friends will run for the hills." She saw the look on my face and burst out laughing, hiding her mouth behind the palm of her hand. I grabbed both her arms and pulled her towards me, waiting until she was ready for our next kiss.

"Keep your eyes open this time," I said in a whisper. "I want to see whatever's in them . . ."

For the next week, whenever I walked out of Shakespeare and Company, she was waiting. In deference to the dress she always wore, I'd stopped changing my own clothes, even though Mike had complained, wrinkling his nose as he made show of sniffing my shoulder.

"Mate, when was the last time you saw the inside of a shower?"

But Alice didn't seem to mind. We would buy a plastic bottle of the cheapest wine and head for the river or the Louvre or the Arc de Triomphe, laughing at the tourists as they posed for their little photos. On one occasion, we indulged in a five-liter cubitainer of red, sharing it with the tramps who congregated near one of the bridges, until a fight broke out and the arrival of the *gendarmes* sent us scurrying. I had stopped shaving, and Alice would run her hands down my cheeks and across my chin, calling me her "bit of rough." There was a folded letter in my pocket from my father. I hadn't opened it, and hadn't troubled to call Charlotte. Theirs was another world entirely. I could feel myself changing, growing. When Harry grabbed me one night outside the restaurant to remind me of the money I owed, I laid him out with a single punch, after which I had to keep my distance from the restaurant. Not that this mattered—Alice never ate a thing, and that seemed to suit both of us. With money from the bookshop till, I bought us a few grams of cocaine from an African dealer, which killed any appetite remaining. And when Mike nagged me for missing a shift which he had been obliged to cover, I gave as good as I got, until he backed away, hands held in front of him, fear in his eyes at my clenched fists and gritted teeth.

Oh, yes, I was changing.

I'd been back to Benjamin Turk's apartment, but its door remained locked and unanswered. Alice had advised a shoulder-charge, which had left me with nothing other than a large bruise and a slight deflation of ego.

"I could scale the front wall, window to window," I'd muttered over more pavement wine, receiving an indulgent smile and a hug.

"He's often gone for a few days," she'd sympathized. "He'll be back soon enough."

And then she'd kissed me.

There hadn't been any sex as yet, which suited both of us. We were happy to wait for the right moment, the most intense moment. Hugs and kisses, the holding of hands, fingers stroking an arm, cheek or the nape of the neck. She seemed to have no other friends, or none she wouldn't give up in order to spend time with me, and I felt the same. I wasn't about to share what we had with Mike or anyone else. Every moment I could, I spent with her.

Until the day I walked downstairs into the shop groggy with sleep and saw Charlotte standing there. She carried a rucksack and a wide-brimmed straw hat and looked hot from walking. Her smile was hesitant.

"Hello, you," she said. "We were getting worried."

"Oh?"

"I phone but you're never here. And your mum and dad . . ." She broke off. "Well, do I get a hug?"

I stepped forward and took her by the shoulders, my lips brushing against her damp red hair.

"Bloody hell, Ronnie, look at the state of you. When did you last eat?"

"I'm fine."

"You're really not. Your friend Mike . . ."

"Mike?"

"He answered the phone yesterday."

"And told you to come running? Probably just wanted to size you up as another notch on his bed-post."

"He was right though; you look ill. Have you seen a doctor?"

"I don't need a doctor. What I need is for everyone to stop bothering me."

She was silent for a moment, glaring at me. Then she turned her eyes away. "A lovely warm welcome for your girlfriend," she muttered, pretending to study one of the shelves.

I ran a hand through my matted hair. "Look, I had a bit to drink last night. And the shock of seeing you here . . ." I broke off. I'd been about to say that I was sorry, but part of me resisted. "What time is it?"

"Nearly one."

"I'll buy you something at the café." I opened the till and lifted out a few notes. "Is that allowed?" Charlotte asked as I stuffed the money into my pocket. "I'll put it back later," I lied.

When we stepped outside there was—for once—no sign of Alice, but Maryse was setting out boxes of cheap paperbacks on the pavement.

"Tell Mike I'll be having a word with him later," I said, my face set like stone. Then I led Charlotte a few meters along the road, entering the café and taking up position by the counter. Charlotte slid the rucksack from her shoulders.

"Thinking of staying?" I inquired.

"I wasn't about to do Paris and back in a day. Since when did you smoke?"

I looked down at the cigarette I was rolling.

"Not sure," I admitted. Which was the truth—I had no memory of buying either the pouch of Drum tobacco or the packet of tissue-thin papers. All I knew was that Alice obviously didn't mind. The look on Charlotte's face was properly smallminded and Presbyterian. I could imagine her sitting primly in my parents' drawing-room, holding cup and saucer and allowing herself "one small slice of cake." Home baking? Naturally. The conversation stilted and bourgeois and safe. Everything so fucking *safe*.

"What are you thinking?" she asked as I lit the slender cigarette.

"I'm thinking you shouldn't have come."

Was she really becoming tearful, or merely putting on a show in the hope of sympathy? My espresso had arrived, along with her Perrier. The barman waved a bottle of red in my direction but I shook my head and he seemed to understand.

Pas devant les enfants . . .

"I wanted to see you," Charlotte persisted. "This is Paris, after all. Everyone says it's a romantic city and I've been missing you, Ronnie. I thought maybe this would be the place for us to . . ."

"What?"

She lowered her eyes and her voice. "Don't make me say it."

"Fuck our brains out?"

Her eyes and mouth widened. She glanced at the barman.

"He doesn't have any English," I reassured her, knowing Francois would actually have understood every word. He was polishing glasses at the far end of the bar. All of a sudden I craved something alcoholic, so ordered a *pression*. When it arrived, I demolished it in two gulps, and nodded for a refill while Charlotte stared at me.

"You need help," she eventually said. "Something's happened to you."

"Well, you're right about that at least—yes, something's happened to me. For the first time in my life, and I'm all the better for it."

"You're not though. Look in the mirror."

As it happened, there was a long narrow mirror running the length of the bar, below the row of optics and shelves of drinks. I hunched down so I could make eye contact with myself and couldn't help grinning.

"Who's that handsome devil?" I chuckled.

"Ronnie . . ."

"My name's Ronald!" I roared. Francois clucked and gestured for me to keep it down. I waved a hand in what could have passed for either apology or dismissal of his complaint.

Charlotte's hand was shaking as she lifted her glass of water. I realized that's what she was: carbonated water, while my life had become so much headier and filled with sensation.

"Will you help me find a hotel?" she was asking without making eye contact.

"Of course," I said quietly.

"I'll change my flight to tomorrow, if I can. I was going to stay a few days, but . . ."

"They'll be missing you at your work."

"Oh, I quit the job. My thinking was to do some travelling with you." Finally she fixed her eyes on mine. "But that was when you were you."

"Who am I now?"

"I've really no idea."

"Well, I'm sorry you had to come all this way to find out." I placed a fifty-franc note on the counter and made to lift Charlotte's rucksack from the floor.

"No," she snapped, hoisting it on to her shoulders. "I can manage perfectly well."

As we exited the café, I caught sight of a dress I recognized. Just the hem of it as its owner dodged around the corner of a building. We headed in the opposite direction, into the narrow maze of streets behind the bookshop. I looked behind me, but Alice didn't seem to be following. There were plenty of small hotels here, most of them doing good business at the height of the summer. It was twenty minutes before we found one with a vacancy. The owner led Charlotte upstairs to inspect the room while I said I'd wait in the street. I was rolling a fresh cigarette when

I heard a scooter come to a stop behind me. I was half-turning in its direction when the passenger launched himself from behind the driver and hit me with what looked like a broken chair-leg. It connected with one of my temples and sent me to my knees. A hand was rummaging in my pockets. It pulled out the notes from the till and rubbed them in my face. Then another smack on the side of the head and Harry climbed back aboard, the driver revving the small engine hard as they fled the scene. Pedestrians had stopped to gawp, but only for a moment. There were no offers of help as I scrabbled to pick up my pouch of tobacco. I got to my feet and felt the world spin. I knew I was grinning, but had no idea why. I lit my cigarette and leaned against the wall, head tilted so I could look at the bluest sky imaginable.

Charlotte came out onto the pavement minus her rucksack, which meant the room had been declared acceptable. When she saw me she let out a screech, covering her mouth with her hand. That was when I noticed the blood dripping down from the cut on my temple. It was staining my already-disreputable shirt and trousers, and adding crimson spots to the street beneath.

"What happened?" Charlotte asked.

I took out my handkerchief and pressed it to the cut, feeling it sting for the first time.

"Somebody hit me." I was still grinning. "Don't worry, I'll get him back."

"We need the police."

"What for?"

"You know who did this?"

"I didn't pay him for the drugs."

Her eyes hardened. "Say that again." And when I didn't, she just nodded slowly, as if a small lump of dope explained everything. She clasped me by one wrist. "Come upstairs. We need to wash that clean."

I resisted long enough to finish the cigarette, then allowed myself to be led up a dark twisting stairwell to her room. It was tiny and stifling, the window open and shutters closed in a vain attempt to keep out the after-noon heat. Charlotte's rucksack lay on the bed. She moved it and made me sit down, there being no chair. Then she knelt in front of me, examining the damage.

"It's deep," she said. There was a thin towel on the end of the bed and she took it with her when she left the room. I could hear water running in the sink of the communal bathroom along the hall. Then she was back, dabbing and wiping.

"Any nausea?" she asked.

"No more than usual."

She smiled as if I'd made a joke. "You're being very brave," she cooed.

"I'm tougher than you think."

"I'm sure you are." She made another trip to the bathroom to rinse the towel. This time she wiped it slowly across all of my face, studying my features as she worked. "You're filthy, Ronald. Really you need a bath."

"Will you scrub my back?"

"I might." Her eyes were locked on mine. I leaned forwards and kissed her on the mouth.

"You're bristly," she said afterwards. "But I sort of like it."

So I kissed her again. Then we were standing, arms wrapped around one another. My hands felt beneath her sweat-dampened blouse, running down her spine. Our mouths opened as our tongues got to work, and she gave a small moan. Her fingers brushed the front of my trousers, then started to work at the zip. My eyes were still open but hers were closed, as she concentrated hard on fulfilling the whole purpose of the trip. So greedy and so intent on her own selfish self. I put my hand on hers, squeezing. She opened her eyes.

"I'm going to take that bath," I said.

"Good idea," she replied, sounding only half-convinced. "There's only the one towel though, and it's already wet."

"I'll be fine." I gave a smile and a wink and managed to escape the airless room. The bath was old and stained but hot water gushed from its tap. I locked the door before stripping. There were bruises on my body I was at a loss to explain. Piled on the floor, my clothes looked like rags. I sank into the water and slid beneath its surface. I had been soaking only a couple of minutes when Charlotte tried the door.

"I won't be long," I called out.

"I thought you wanted someone to scrub your back."

"Another time."

I could sense her lingering. But she moved away eventually, her bedroom door closing. I was debating my next move. Get dressed and slink away?

Would that make me a coward? No, I would talk to her face-to-face and explain everything. I would tell her about Benjamin Turk and Alice and my newly blossoming life. We would part as friends, and I would then pay a visit to Harry and Mike, where both men would learn what happened to people who crossed me.

"Yes," I said to the bathroom walls, nodding slowly to myself.

And then I closed my eyes and slid below the waterline again.

The water had turned tepid by the time I climbed out. I used the towel as best I could, and slid back into my clinging clothes. Blood still trickled from the cut, so I held the towel as a compress as I unlocked the door and padded down the hall. The door to Charlotte's room stood gaping. Charlotte herself lay on the bed, half-undressed and with a scarf knotted tightly around her neck, digging into the flesh. Her eyes and tongue bulged, her face almost purple. I knew she was dead, and knew, too, the identity of the culprit. She had unpacked one dress from her rucksack, the one almost identical to Alice's. Pushing open the shutters, I looked down onto the courtyard and saw a familiar flash of color. Alice was heading for the street.

I studied Charlotte a final time, knowing there was nothing to be done, then ran to the stairs, barging past the hotelier, who was on the way up. I crossed the courtyard, scanning the pavement to left and right. Making a decision, I started running again. I didn't know Alice's address or even her surname. Would she head for the Seine and the derelicts we had shared our wine with? Or to the bookshop, where she could wait for me on my infested alcove bed? Bars and cafes and the usual landmarks. . . . We had criss-crossed the city, making it our own.

But there was only one destination I could think of—Turk's apartment.

She wasn't outside, nor was she seated on the stairs. I climbed to the top floor and tried the door—locked, as before. But this time when I hit it with my fist, there were sounds from inside. Benjamin Turk opened the door and studied me from head to foot.

"It looks to me as though you're finally ready," he said with a thin smile, ushering me in.

"Have you seen Alice?" I demanded.

"Forget about her," he said, his back to me as he hobbled towards the livingroom. "I've laid everything out for you." He was pointing towards the desk. Various documents lay there. "Took me some time and effort, but you'll only begin to comprehend when you examine them."

"What are they?"

"The story of Edwin Hythe. Sit down. Read. I'll fetch you a drink."

"I don't want a drink." But I realized that I did—I wanted the darkest wine in the largest glass imaginable. Turk seemed to understand this, and returned with a glass filled almost to the brim. I gulped it down, exhaling only afterwards.

"Does the wound hurt?" he was asking.

I dabbed at my head. "No," I said.

"Then you should read." He pulled over a chair so he could sit next to me, and while I focused on the various sheets of paper he explained the significance.

"Stevenson and Hythe were close friends as students, belonging to the same clubs and drinking in the same low dives late into the night. Then the murder of a prostitute is recorded in the newspaper and there's a parting. Hythe disappears from Stevenson's life. The murderer is never apprehended. When Stevenson writes a novel about just such a woman, his wife persuades him it is not going to be good for his reputation. But Hythe, too, hears about it, and makes his way to Bournemouth. He comes from money so he stays at the best hotel in town, a hotel that keeps impeccable records." He tapped the photocopied sheet showing Hythe's signature in the guest book, along with the duration of his stay. "It's fairly obvious that Hythe was the killer and that Stevenson was either a witness or else was privy to his friend's confession. The golden young man Stevenson had known in Edinburgh was by now a dissolute figure, in trouble with creditors, disowned by his family, earning a living of sorts from any number of illegal activities." He tapped a series of court reports and newspaper stories. "Pimping, trafficking, receiving stolen goods. . . . And with a temper on him. One arrest talks of the superhuman rage of the man after too much drink had been taken." Turk paused. "And when Hythe left Bournemouth, Stevenson sat down and wrote *Jekyll and Hyde* in three days. Not the version we know, but one set in Edinburgh, where Hythe aka Hyde attacks and kills a harlot rather than trampling a child. Again, he was dissuaded from publishing it. Fanny knew what it would mean—people in Edinburgh would talk. They would remember the killing of the prostitute. They would know the name Hythe and point the finger from him to his close friend Robert Louis Stevenson. That couldn't happen—it would mean prison or even worse. The book had to be destroyed, the story reworked, and Hythe's name changed to Hyde."

"All right," I said quietly. Tears were falling from my eyes on to the desk. I was seeing Charlotte, in that horrific pose on her bed, her life snuffed out. I was about to say as much, but Turk was opening a drawer and pulling out more sheets. They comprised a family tree, along with some drawings—portraits of the same man, showing him in his late teens and then in raddled middle age. He looked so familiar to me. . . .

"Edwin Hythe," Turk was explaining. "The first time I saw you, I was struck by the resemblance. This was some time back, through the window of the shop. I asked George about you and decided it was no mere coincidence. Which is why I asked him to send you on that particular errand."

"I don't understand."

"It's on your mother's side," he said, running a finger back up the family tree from my name. "You are descended from Edwin Hythe. His blood in your blood, and with it, unfortunately, his curse."

"His what?" I was rubbing at my eyes, trying to blink them into some kind of focus.

"Your devil has been long caged, Ronald. He has come out *roaring*!"

There was a mad gleam in his eye as he spoke. I leapt to my feet. "You're crazy," I told him. "*You're* the devil here! You and your damned Alice!"

"There is no Alice."

"She knows you—she runs errands . . ." But he was shaking his head.

"There's only you, Ronald. You and the demon that's been sleeping deep inside you, waiting for the right catalyst. Paris is that catalyst."

"Where are the manuscripts?" I demanded, looking about me. "The two unpublished novels?"

He gave a shrug. "You've seen all there is. Nothing more than fragments."

"You're lying!"

"Believe what you will."

"Alice is *real*!"

He was chuckling as he shook his head again. His silver-topped walking-stick glinted at me from its resting-place by the desk. I grabbed it and raised it over my head. Rather than shrink from me in fear, his smile seemed to widen. I bared my teeth and struck him across the side of the head. He staggered but stayed on his feet, so I hit him again. He wheeled away from me into the long hallway. I stayed a few footsteps behind him as I continued to rain down blows upon his head and back until he fell, just inside the front door. He was still conscious, but his breathing was ragged, blood bubbling from his mouth. A few more blows and he lay still. I hauled him by his feet away from the door so I could open it and make my escape.

Outside, I could hear sirens. Police cars, probably, heading for a hotel not too far away, where passers-by would be able to describe the bloodied figure running from the scene. Alice was standing on the opposite pavement, her eyes full of understanding. We shared a smile before I looked to left and right. There was plenty of traffic, but I started to cross towards her, knowing it would stop for me. When I looked again, however, she had vanished. Pedestrians and drivers were beginning to stare. I noted the fresh spattering of bright red blood on my shirt, so began to rip at it, throwing it from me until I stood half-naked in the middle of the road, the sirens drawing closer. I stretched out both arms, angled my head to the heavens above, and roared.

The Haze

James W. Hall

James W. Hall is the Edgar and Shamus Award-winning author of nineteen mystery novels, fourteen of which feature Key Largo-based loner Thorn and his one friend, a private investigator named Sugarman. In addition to his work as a novelist, Hall has published four books of poetry, as well as a book of personal essays and a nonfiction book on bestseller writing. Several of his novels have been adapted for film, often with screenplays written by Hall himself. Now retired from his post at the Florida International University in Miami, where he helped found the creative writing program, Hall lives with his wife Evelyn, and divides his time between South Florida and the mountains of North Carolina.

H e killed for a living. Killed a lot of people a long way back. How far back he wasn't sure. Not sure of a lot these days. The days of haze.

Who he was now, a professional killer stuck in a nursing home. New Jersey, or maybe Florida. Not sure. But a home, the kind of place she promised she'd never take him. Lied to him. After all he'd done for her. Raised her, protected her, funded her hobbies, defended her against her mother. Her mother was the killer's wife. Where was she, that wife? What was her name? More things he didn't remember.

He went about his morning routine. Ate his two sunnyside eggs and toast and half a grapefruit, got a thrill levering the sections out with the pointy spoon. That's where his thrills came from these days.

He showered, doing it the same as always, start at the top. Shampoo his thick white hair, then his face, after that using his chest hair to lather up, with special attention to his armpits, ending with his ass. He valued a clean ass. Even now, even in his current state of disorder. He wasn't so far gone he'd put up with a dirty butt.

He knew he was confused. What he didn't know was exactly how much. In particular, he didn't know which stories from his past were his own actual personal history, or things he lifted from the stories of others. People he'd talked to or maybe books he'd read.

Books, it was mainly crime writers, that's who he'd been reading since he was a snotty kid growing up in West Virginia, or somewhere deprived like that, maybe Kentucky, Tennessee. He's reading crime novels while his wife, sitting on her side of the cold bed, read whatever it was she read. Women's books, how to fix a dying marriage, how to be happy, like that was in a book, like any of it was.

Crime writers, his specialty, was what his daughter did now. Worked in a store that sold the kind of books he used to read. Did he cause that?

Did he drive his daughter, what was her name, did he drive her into crime? He'd ask her if she ever came back for a visit, built up her courage to face her father again after dumping him in this hellhole.

He had a mission. You had to have a mission. Something you thought about first thing in the morning when you woke up. His was to break out of this damn place. Kill anybody stood in his way. Especially the Puerto Rican who made him swallow the pills.

Force feeding dope pills was an old standby in the stories he read. Was it Chandler with the stocky guys in white uniforms? He thought he remembered a Travis book. Nightmare something. A guy being fed pills or maybe shots in the arm. A guy stuck in a perpetual nightmare. It was in Chandler too, he thought. Marlowe or Sam Spade. Maybe Archer, what was his name? Jake? No, no, it was Lew.

He'd known a Lew. He'd killed a Lew. A job, one of his last. Italian guy was boffing somebody's young wife. He couldn't recall whose. But a wife. He was sure of that. Or maybe a daughter. But he'd shot Lew. Three in the head, one in the heart. His signature. Four rounds. That way the dead stayed dead. He'd made a name for himself, thirty years in the business. Four slugs, three up, one down. His trademark. He remembered that very clearly. Not lost in the haze.

So there, that's what his mission was. Shoot his way out of this place.

First he needed to find his pistol. A .38, snubbie. Not a fancy gun. You get up close enough, you didn't need a top of the line gun to whack somebody. That was his approach, old school. Walk right up to the hit, breathe his air, nose to nose, then three up, one down. He looked in the bureau for his gun. Dug under his socks and his Jockeys, looked in the closet, in the teeny kitchen, behind the dishes, the bowls, the glasses, everything on the shelves. He went in the bathroom, lifted the lid on the toilet. That's where they taped the guns sometime. Movies, books, that's where it was. Place nobody looked. The Godfather, that scene with whoever it was.

But here in the home, there was no gun. No gun anywhere.

Okay, fine. He'd find another way, maybe bribe somebody to unlock a door.

He needed to get on a schedule. He always had a schedule. It was another hallmark. A schedule: first this, then that, bing, bing, bing. In bed by eight, lights out at nine, up by four. Wake in the dark. An hour or two when nobody was up. He'd plan his day. Map out the hours ahead. Print it in a Month-in-a-Glance calendar. He'd never been good with dates and times and days of the week, had to see it written down for it to make sense. Maybe the haze had started early. Or was that some other guy, some guy from a book. Elmore whatever his name was.

So there you go. That was his problem. His big mountain to climb. Not sure if he was remembering shit he actually did or shit he read.

A plan. A sneaky plan, that's what he needed. He walked around the room. Trying to outwalk the haze, get some blood flowing into his skull. The room was tiny. He'd been in bigger jail cells. Spent years in a couple, one down in Florida, Raiford, he thought, counting the days, finding ways to cope.

That was all it was, all any of it was. Ways to cope. Doing things to fill up the hours, make them pass. That was the big secret. You climb a mountain, claw your way to the top, finally you're there at the summit, there's a wise man up there, you ask what's the secret and he says, hey, find something to fill up the hours. That's all there is. You can pay on your way down.

She came, his daughter. She smiled at him. Brought him some books. His weekly ration.

Four hardbacks. His eyes weren't good enough for paperbacks.

"You'll like this one, Pop."

A red cover, the shadow of a man looking down an alley.

"Already read it."

"Just came out this week, Pop. No way you read it."

"I'm on top of things. I read it already. What else you got?"

She showed him the other three. Covers used to have dames on them. You could stare at the women, imagine sinking into them. You could fall in love. Stare for hours before you even started to read. Every time you closed the book, there she was and her cleavage, her legs and hips. All those curves.

Now it was all shadows and shit.

"That all you got? You work in a bookstore, you bring me this crap?"

She left. The books stayed behind.

There was one written by a woman author. A photo of her in the back. Blonde, nice rack, trying to hide them under all those fluffy clothes like she was embarrassed by them. But still you could catch the outline. Just barely. But worth looking at. Better than the other photos, guys trying to be tough, slouching against walls or against the hoods of old cars, wearing leather jackets, mean ass dogs with spiked collars. Big deal. They were writers for christsakes. How tough could they be, sitting in a room all day, writing down the shit in their heads, make-believe shit.

His pills came at six. Right on time. Javier, the Puerto Rican, shiny shaved head. Earrings. Christ, he'd lived too long. Guys wore earrings now. Guys married guys. He'd lived a century too long.

He palmed the pills, faked slinging them into his mouth. Then talking to Javier, showing him the photo of the woman writer.

"How big you think her tits are?"

"I saw what you did with them pills, Mr. Connors. You need to take them. They're good for you."

"Like vitamins?"

"Better than vitamins."

"You live in the haze, Javier?"

"I don't know what you mean."

"The haze, this shit."

He swung his arm around through the air.

"Let's see the pills, Mr. Connors. I help you with them."

He swallowed the pills. The haze hung on. In bed by eight, reading the book by the woman. About a serial killer. Like there weren't enough of those already. But this one was a woman. An old woman. She was about his age. Suffering from the haze like him, only not so dense yet. She goes out every night, finds somebody doing wrong, it could be a little thing, a little mean thing, somebody pursesnatching, shoplifting, whatever, not bad enough to kill somebody over, but she goes ahead and kills. That helps her sleep.

Something he should try.

He could use a good night's sleep.

He reads. Comes to a good part. The old woman bumps into a man her age. A retired killer. They talk, they have dinner, they walk on the city sidewalk, Manhattan maybe, they laugh about something. They look at the moon. They look at the stars. The two of them, they've got things in common. Killing is just one. They like pasta. They like to read. They got problems with their kids who want to stash them away somewhere, force feed them pills.

"I'm going to have to kill my daughter," he tells her.

"Your own daughter? That's extreme."

"Is it?"

"Your own flesh and blood, hell yes, extremely extreme."

"If I'm going to escape the home, be with you, there's only one choice. She's got to go."

"Maybe you could sneak out of the home."

"I tried that. They're always watching."

"I could help you."

"You'd do that?"

"What else I have to do? I'm tired of killing. I'm ready to hang it up. I just been doing it to fill up the hours."

"Giving up killing isn't as easy as you think. Killing becomes a way of life."

They kissed. They went to bed. All of it described the way he liked it in books. None of this timid bullshit like they close the bedroom door and the reader is stuck out in the hallway, can't even hear them moaning. No, this woman writer showed everything. Not flinching at any of it, or being coy like how he hated some writers did it. That was one of his peeves. Not showing the real world. Like nobody ever took a dump in books. Dumps were important. You couldn't live without taking a dump. After the two old farts made love, both of them took dumps.

It was a good book. He fell asleep.

Woke in the haze. Deep gray smog. Javier was there with his sunnysides. "You have a good night, Mr. Connors?"

"You ever screw an old lady, Javi?"

"Not that I recall."

"You having trouble with your memory, boy?"

Javier set the breakfast tray on his table. Little round thing by a window.

"Eat your eggs, Mr. Connors. Drink that coffee while it's hot."

"Who do I have to kill to get out of here?"

"You're being funny again, Mr. Connors."

"A regular Jack Benny," he said. "Know who that was?"

Javier was gone, leaving behind the eggs and coffee and unbuttered toast.

He spent the day with his book. The old lady serial killer and the retired hitman.

They caught a cab together, went downtown, way down to the bookstore where his daughter worked. They walked past the store, looked in the window, kept walking.

"She's pretty."

"Dark-haired like her mother."

"Only girl I saw was a blonde."

"Yeah, that's her."

"What's her name?"

"Like what, this is a test? I got to remember everybody's name?"

"Don't get huffy."

"That was huffy? You haven't seen huffy." Their first big fight.

They walk for a while without talking. She's mad. He's mad too and hurt.

At a corner, it's down near Soho, she hails a cab, gets in, drives away. Doesn't look back. "Shit," he said. "Left me standing in the cold, not sure where I am. Shit."

He threw the book at the door.

Javier is there to check on him. Wondering why there's noise. Why the book's sprawled on the floor.

"I'm fine. It's the book that's screwed up. I'm fine."

"You look pale."

"She left the guy, just walked away. Left him on the sidewalk, it's a part of town I don't know where I am. Way down there, it's cold, it's freezing and she's gone. I don't have my wallet. I can't get a cab. Nobody's stopping for me."

"It's summer, Mr. Connors. There's flowers blooming out your window."

"I'm talking about the book, you idiot. It's freezing on the streets. She dumped me, walked away. We had a little disagreement is all. A spat."

"You're in this book?"

Javier is holding the book he threw.

"I'm telling you, I'm lost, don't know which way is up, and she just walked away. Broke my heart. Broke it in half and pissed on the pieces."

Javier left. His daughter came.

"You keep throwing things, Pops. They don't allow that."

"What're they going to do, toss me out?"

"If you keep acting like a child, yeah, they might."

"It's these goddam books you bring. You're trying to drive me nuts. Breaking my heart. Making me climb up the mountain and I get up there and it's some asshole making fun of me. Pay on your way down he says. Like it's all some kind of joke and I'm not in on it."

"Pops, they won't let you stay, you keep throwing things."

"Don't bring any more of those goddam books. You hear me? I got better things to do with my time. I don't need books breaking my heart all day and night. Okay? We clear?"

It was another day or maybe it was the same one only later. Hazy day.

He picked up the book and found his place. It was easy enough. Let the book fall open, it's the place.

He's out on the freezing ass street and the cab is disappearing and his heart is aching like there's a slug in it. Three in the head, one in the heart. His motto. His calling card. He's out there looking around for a street sign, not sure which way is uptown where he wants to go, his hotel, or his apartment.

A cab pulls up, door comes open.

It's her. The serial killer who cracked his heart in half and drove off and left him.

"You still angry at me?"

"I was never angry. You haven't seen angry."

"You're a gruff old man."

"You going my way or you here to taunt me?"

They drive off. The cabbie is a black guy. He's checking them out in the mirror like they're the first two old fart killers he's ever seen.

"Your place or mine?"

"Do you even have a place?" She smiled like it was a joke.

"Your place," he said. "I bet your sheets are rose petals."

"Poetry all of a sudden. That's supposed to sweep me up?"

"Poetry? You haven't seen from poetry." Javier was back with the pills.

"I've got a mission," he told Javier. "You want in?"

"Depends."

"In or out? Make up your mind and make it quick."

Was that from somewhere? Maybe that guy Higgins. There was a name he remembered. Guys talking, that's the whole story. Guys talking and talking, the back and forth, street shit. Getting it right, hitting the notes pure and simple.

"You want to break out of here, am I right?"

Sometimes it's better not to talk. Sometimes that's wiser.

Javier spoke into the silence. "You want, I could help you."

He let some more silence mount up and Javier said, "Okay, I got a price. Nothing's free in this world, you know that. I could help you. I like you, Mr. Connors, and I can see you're suffocating in this joint. I'll arrange an exit. It won't be easy. They's cameras, security stuff. People on duty around the clock. It's not easy, but I got a way to do it if you're interested."

He was interested, but the silence was working for him so it was hard to stop. Spent his life talking. Spent his life giving shit and taking it, messing with people, making them do what he wanted them to, setting them up with just the right words. Now he was seeing the beauty of stillness, the raw power of it.

"I can see you're not up to talking about it just now. But I'll be back at bedtime, if you want to discuss it, what I got in mind, we can do it then, or whenever you're ready, fine by me."

Javier left.

He climbed into bed and read the book. The story was waiting for him like stories do. Right where he left it. Christ it was hard to keep it all straight. You had a life, a long, complicated life full of a thousand things every day, you heard things, read things, lived things, how could you know which compartment anything was stored in, where it happened originally? Some people could do it, sure. People could say, yeah, that was from here and that was from there. And that meant they could stay in their own houses and not get shipped to the home. But what was that? Knowing where something was from, where it originated. Hey, who gives a shit? It was all knocking around inside him, equal parts this, and equal parts that.

The old lady serial killer was an experienced lover, a woman of the world who knew her business. She was beautiful in bed, perfect and beautiful.

She reminded him of someone he'd made love to a long time ago when he was a young man. A Mexican girl of nineteen or twenty named Linda Vargas, black shining hair, black shining eyes. Or was she a character in a book? It didn't matter. He loved that woman, Linda Vargas, just the same as he loved the lady serial killer, loved her up and down and inside and out, her skin like rose petals and silk, her skin as sleek and soft as summer moonlight filtering through a sweet midnight haze.

And he stopped reading.

You had to stop sometimes. Show a little discipline, leave some in the bottle for tomorrow. He pulled up the sheets. His hand sliding into his underpants. His old friend. Been through the wars together, sleeping now, taking a furlough, on the sidelines. But he gave it a few pulls for old times sake, felt it come to life. Half life anyway. Half was all he could manage. This time of life half was plenty.

He slept.

The important thing about missions is to keep them going. They can change, you had to adjust to circumstances, but you keep going forward, keep the goal in mind, otherwise, what've you got? You got that Greek guy pushing the boulder up the mountain and it sliding down the other side. You got one hazy day after another, the days stacking up without any progress, any hope.

Javier came with his sunnysides. "You have a nice night sleeping?"

"I might've slept, I don't know. The state I'm in, how'm I supposed to tell?"

"You consider my proposal?"

"I need to hear a price."

"I been thinking about that, about money, you know what it's worth to you, what the risk I'm taking is worth to me, and I'm having a hard time putting a number on it. But okay, since you want a number, okay, five thousand, I get you out of here, take you wherever you want to go, drop you off free and clear."

"Five thousand bucks."

"American dollars. You get the first class ride out of here."

"I don't trust you, Javi."

"You think I take your money, don't deliver? What am I, crazy? You think I risk that, knowing who you are, what you did in your life, before you came to the home, the way you made your money. You think I'd cross a man like you?"

"I'm old. Some days I'm confused.

Wouldn't be hard to pull one on me."

"I know you'd come for me. I know you'd track me down wherever I hid. Isn't no running from men like you. Professionals. I know that. So you can trust me, Mr. Connors. I'm not stupid like that, take your money and walk away."

"I'll have the five for you tomorrow." Back to the book by the woman writer.

Things heating up. The old lady serial killer, her name is Varla, nice exotic ring to it, Polish or gypsy or something, she'd decided she wanted to kill a young lady who worked in a bookstore, a young lady who'd done harm to her new manfriend, the retired professional killer, Little Mo Connors.

"That's my daughter, my own flesh and blood. You can't kill her."

"It's the only way you're going to get out of the home. She's the impediment. Once she's gone, you're free."

"Am I?"

"I'm doing you a favor."

They staked out the bookstore. It was summer, tables out on the sidewalk at the Italian place across the street. They took a table, the two old killers, and watched the bookstore. It was close to lunch time, the restaurant getting busy, so they had to order. Fettuccini alfredo for her, tortellini for him.

"Bad for my blood sugar," he said. "But what the hell. Screw my blood sugar."

"There she is, coming out the front door."

"Christ, she's coming this way. She'll see us. She'll know what we're up to. We should move."

Varla put a hand on his leg below the table.

An electric thrill he hadn't felt in years. "Dad, what're you doing here?"

"Reading a book, what does it look like?"

"The woman novelist, I told you you'd like her. She's right up your alley."

"I want out of here," he told her. "That's my goal, to escape this hellhole."

"Dad, this is a beautiful place. The food is good, people love you here. I was just talking to Javier and he was going on and on about what a funny guy you were, all the stories you been telling him."

"He keeps me doped up."

"Those are blood pressure pills, Dad. If you don't take them, you could have a stroke."

"Who do I have to kill to get out of this hellhole?"

"I brought you some more books. Another one by the woman writer. I'm glad you like her so much. I thought you would."

"I met somebody. Her name is Varla."

His daughter smiled at him.

"Javier told me. She sounds wonderful. When can I meet her?"

"Who?"

"Varla, your gal pal."

He'd said too much, given away a secret. The haze did that, it confused him, kept him loopy. He wasn't sure who he was talking to or why. He wasn't sure if he was remembering shit he did or shit he read or some other kind of shit entirely. Shit he made up while he sat at the window and looked out at the snow and the palm trees. He stopped talking. Refused to say another word.

His daughter left. Good riddance.

He searched his room for his pistol. Took out each pair of underwear, every T-shirt, scooted the bureau away from the wall, felt the floorboards for a secret shelf, a hidey hole like he'd used back in his day for all his weapons. Killers threw the guns away off bridges into rivers. But that was in books. That was bullshit. Buying new guns was a hassle. So he avoided it, held on to the ones he'd used. So what if some cop came around and took his gun and ran a ballistics test on the slugs. So what? He'd get sent to prison. Big deal. He was in prison already. Everyone told him how great it was, the food was good, like that mattered. Like it wasn't a box with a single, tiny window.

He didn't find the gun. But he knew it was there. He was tired of looking.

He put on his pajamas and got into bed to read. It was the middle of the afternoon. Big snowflakes coming down, white as the birds standing in the lawn. He opened the book he'd been reading, found his place.

Varla and Little Mo were still in bed together. They'd been making love all afternoon and now they were smoking cigarettes and blowing the smoke up at the ceiling.

"How do you feel?" Varla asked him.

"Got my ashes hauled three times in a row, how'm I supposed to feel? Good, real good."

"I mean about killing your little girl, your own flesh and blood."

"Kind of shitty. But there was no choice, was there?"

"There wasn't."

"I feel shitty anyway."

"How many is that for you?"

"How many what?"

"Notches on your pistola."

"I stopped counting years ago. It's just a number."

"I'm at sixteen," she said. "I'm going to stop soon. It's lost its thrill."

"I never got a thrill. It was just work. A job."

"You didn't enjoy it at all?"

"That's sick," he said. "You're calling me sick?"

"Thrill killing is sick, yeah. Don't take it personally."

"How else am I going to take it?"

Varla got out of bed. Her breasts were sagging, her pubes were half gone. But Little Mo thought she was hot anyway.

"We having another fight?"

"This is turning into a stormy relationship. I'm not sure I want that."

Someone was knocking on the door.

"It's the cops," Little Mo said. "Come to arrest us for all our sex noise."

It wasn't the cops. It was Javier. He kept his eyes down, not looking at Varla's nakedness.

"I'm sorry to bother you, Mr. Connors and Mrs. Hardy. I apologize, but something happened. Something bad happened. I got to tell you some bad news."

Varla said, "His daughter's dead. Little Miss Priss got herself shot. Selling violent books, it came back to bite her in the ass."

"How'd you know that?" Javier said. "Somebody call you?"

"Go on, Little Mo, tell Javier. Confess what you did."

He didn't know what to say. He'd never confessed to anything. His lawyers told him that. Keep your mouth shut, take the fifth, I'll do the talking.

Javier picked up the book that was lying on the floor and brought it over to the bed and set it on the bedside table.

"You were throwing books again, Mr. Connors. Your daughter asked me to tell her if you did that again. And I got to report you to the supervisor."

"Why would you report me?"

"You could be dangerous to yourself or others. These are hardbacks. Somebody could get knocked down."

"Paperbacks, the print is too small."

"Maybe you should find a different kind of book doesn't stir you up so much."

"What? A boring book? That what you're saying? If I read a bunch of boring books you'll let me stay in this hellhole?"

"It's time for your pills, Mr. Connors."

"Of course it is. Keep me stoned, I can't read, I can't do anything but look out the window at the palm trees."

"You're a funny guy, Mr. Connors. Always with the joke."

He took the pills. Walked around the room. He stopped. He pressed his ear to the door.

Nobody in the hallway. He opened the door, looked out. Hallway empty. He slipped out, headed up the hall away from the lobby and the card room and the exercise room and the TV room.

He didn't need his .38. He'd killed before with his hands. He wasn't as strong as before, but the moves were still there, the sharp hand blade to the throat, the eye gouge, bring them down, knees on the chest, snap the windpipe. He'd taken out Uncle Marvin Shuster that way. He'd turned off the lights on Billy Shapely and Shorty Crump with his bare hands. It was coming back to him through the haze, his history, his triumphs, his fearsome power, the respect he'd once commanded. Not like the killers in the books he read, always neat and organized, no, he'd been down in the slime and spit and bloody snot, flailing with the targets, feeling the life wriggle out of some badass mothers. Little Mo, one scary ass bastard. Coming back to him, his steely nerve.

"Mr. Connors, how are you this fine evening?"

It was Varla Hardy. She had on a flannel nightgown printed with flowers. Her hair was in a net. Her glasses were smudged.

"I'm breaking out of here. Care to join me?"

"Where would we go?"

"Anywhere but here."

"It's cold outside this time of night."

"I thought you were adventurous. I thought you were strong like bull and my equal in all things."

"You've been reading again, haven't you?"

"So?"

"It makes you silly. It gives you ideas. It confuses you. TV is better."

"TV is in one ear out the other."

"That's the whole point. It's better that way. Stories from books get caught inside you, they make you different. They're dangerous."

"I'm already dangerous. I was a hired gun. You wanted someone gone, you called Little Mo Connors."

"Oh, Mo. I don't like it when you're like this. You scare me."

She leaned forward and whispered in his ear: "Javier is at the door listening, this is for his benefit."

He nodded at her and tiptoed to Varla's door and yanked it open.

Javier jumped back.

"Mr. Connors, the police are out at the front desk. They want to talk to you. I don't know what it's about."

"It's okay, Javi. I'm ready to talk to them."

He turned to Varla. "Don't worry, honey. I'll keep you out of it."

Two cops, one man, one woman came into Little Mo's room.

"I think you better sit down, Mr. Connors."

"I'm not going to hurt you," he said. "I could, but I won't."

The woman cop was built like a racing yacht. Sleek and curvy and with fast eyes. He could look at her for hours and never blink.

She said, "Mr. Connors, your daughter, Jennifer, was the victim of a brutal assault."

He nodded. This is how cops worked. Hit you in the face with a brick then when you were goofy with the pain they move in for the kill. Sneaky bastards.

"She was killed in a robbery at the store where she works."

"A bookstore," he said. "I know the place. I read those books. She brings me three or four every week. A good daughter. We have books in common. And crime."

"Yes, sir." The man cop was fat and sweaty and had a pencil moustache.

"A bookstore downtown. Two suspects entered the store and tied up the owner and one other worker, then they assaulted your daughter. She struggled heroically. We can tell that from her wounds. You should be proud of her courage. But she succumbed to her injuries and is no longer with us. We're deeply sorry, sir."

He said he wanted to go to bed now if that was okay. He was tired. A long day. A lot had happened. Some of it not so good.

They understood and were about to leave when the man cop said, "Hey, I know you."

"Is that right?"

"You're Little Mo, you worked for Slick Dicky Scarlini, that shitface."

"Yes, I did. So?"

The man cop said to the woman cop, "This old guy, looking at him it's hard to picture, but he was Scarlini's top enforcer."

"I thought that guy, the enforcer, was in jail."

"Yeah, how come you're not in jail, all the shit you pulled?"

"Look around you," he said. "This isn't jail?"

"Got a point," the man cop said.

"Sorry about your daughter," the woman cop said. "Though it is kind of poetic justice, you know what I'm saying? Karma kickback for all the nastiness you pulled."

When they left he got in bed and took the book off his bedside table and found his place again. It was good to have a book he liked, a way to escape the confusion of the day. The pain of his daughter's senseless death. He'd liked that girl. He hoped it wasn't him that killed her. He hoped he didn't have that on his conscience. Even if he didn't remember, it would still be there. Like a tiny bright red mole you can barely see, overnight it can turn into a flesh-eating cancer.

The book was good, told a decent story. He followed along and watched it unfold and all the bullshit that had happened that day and in the days and months before that, they didn't bother him while he was reading, while he was off in another place that made more sense, the haze lifted, the hours filled.

Javi was there with the sunnysides. Two of them and toast and another grapefruit with the slices already sliced, all you had to do was spoon them out. So okay, maybe the food was pretty good here, but he still wanted to escape and now that his daughter was gone, there was nothing stopping him.

Javi put the paper cup with his pills on the tray and said, "Time to swallow them all down."

"I got your five thousand," he said. "Today's the day."

"Let me see the cash and we'll talk about it."

"Half up front, half when I'm out of this hellhole."

"Okay, that's fair."

He pulled the money from his bottom drawer. He spotted a gun in there too under his socks where he'd forgotten to look. His old .38 snubbie wrapped in an oily rag. He gave Javi the two thousand five and Javi counted it. All in fifties, didn't take long. Fifties is how he'd done business all his life. Easy to deal them off a wad. Easy to count when Scarlini called him in for a pay day. Hundreds were ostentatious, twenties made too fat a wad.

"Okay, it's all there," Javi said. "So when you want to leave?"

"After dark tonight. And I'm taking Varla with me."

Javi shook his shaved head.

"Oh, no, Mr. Connors. Varla Hardy will set you back another five K. You think I'm giving it away free? No, sir. I'm not some stupid spic. You shouldn't treat me that way. It's insulting to my heritage and my mama. I may have to rethink helping you at all the way you're acting now."

"Varla's coming or the deal's off."

"Ten K for the two of you. That's the going rate, I won't take a peso less."

"Gimme back the two five then. We're done. I'll find another way."

"I'm keeping the cash."

"How you figure that?"

"You try to get it back I tell the super you're trying to escape. They'll double guard you then on."

Javi left with the money.

Little Mo got dressed in slacks and a shirt. Plaid shirt, brown baggy slacks. Like that mattered, but there you go. He kept the shirttail out to hide the snubbie wedged into the waistband at the small of his back. He walked back to Varla's room.

"I'm shooting my way out of here. Ready to go?" Varla purred.

"Let me get my gun."

"I never saw your gun."

"I don't show it to just anybody."

"Hurry up before I change my mind. There's a break in the haze. I'm remembering things. Not all of them pleasant."

"Sorry about your little girl. She was cute but she had to go."

"Everybody does eventually. It's how it works. You climb the mountain, the guru up there, he tells you the secret, but it's a different secret every day. Depends on whether it's Monday or whatever. He's got a ton of secrets. Fill up your hours, that's on Monday. You go on a Thursday, it's find someone to love. Sunday, it's breathe, breathe, take it deep. Always something different. You're looking for what it's all about, the guy up there, he doesn't know any more than Javier. It's all bullshit. It's haze. Everybody is inside it, not just me. Everybody's got their own haze."

"This is stimulating. Big ideas turn me on." Varla unbuttoned herself. She let him see her naked flesh. No underwear today. They don't make underwear can fix what's happened to her body, or his either. But she's hot anyway. They crawled into bed. Crawled over each other. He crawls on her, she on him. They crawled together. It's good, not great. Not much is great anymore. This age, good is about as great as it gets.

They stayed in bed all morning, all afternoon.

"You want me to read to you? I read good."

"I don't know," he said. "No one's ever read to me before."

"Not even your mommy?"

"Not her, no. Nobody."

"I'll do it."

He went back to his room, got the book by the woman writer, brought it back, found his place and showed her the page.

"My daughter gave me this book."

"The poor girl."

The serial killer and the retired hitman were in a cheap hotel room. Bullet holes in the mattress, blood on the sheets, that kind of place. She was lying in the bed in her mink coat smoking and he was looking out the edge of a curtain at the parking lot.

"How do you know this guy?"

"My business, I know a lot of people. All kinds."

"He is trustworthy?"

"Hell, no. What we want him for, that's better. Guy hasn't told the truth since he was old enough to know the difference."

"You think this is necessary? Running off to Mexico, that place ain't what it once was. All the drugs down there, the cartels, beheadings. It's ugly."

"Until this town cools off it's the safest place to be. You'll like it. Cheap tequila, romantic sunsets."

"If you can see them through the haze."

"Isn't any haze where we're headed."

"This guy we're waiting for, is he a stud?" He looked over at her.

"What kind of question is that?"

"I'm getting a little tired of your sex moves. I seen 'em all by now. Covering the same ground over and over."

"Look, I'm distracted at the moment or I'd come over there and slap your face, that kind of disrespect."

"Do it. It might turn my engines back on."

"Later," he said. "Our friend is here."

The Puerto Rican with the shaved head was at the door.

"Come in, porkchop. Don't be standing out there attracting attention."

The kid came in, looked at Varla, got a gleam.

"Javier, meet Varla. And don't get any ideas."

"She's an old lady, amigo. What kind of ideas she give me? Adult diapers?"

"Watch yourself, gringo."

"You're the gringo, gringo. Don't be insulting me with insults."

"I can't read any more of this trash," Varla said. "It's tedious. It's not going anywhere."

"Where does anything go?" he said. "Like in a big circle, that's all."

He got out of the warm bed. Varla closed the book and set it aside.

"Thought you said she was a good writer."

"Hills and valleys, every story has 'em," he said. "Can't be hills all the time."

"What're they running from anyway?"

"The serial killer murdered his daughter. And the cops are on their trail."

"Like us."

"Nobody's like us. We're snowflakes, Varla." Varla stopped talking. She went in the other room and didn't come back. The room was empty. It was his room, not hers. He looked around. Yeah, his room. The book sprawled on the floor against the door.

Javier knocked on the door and came in. "You threw it again, Mr. Connors. That's the last time we accept that. You are now a danger to yourself and others. Hurling large heavy objects."

"Yeah, what're you going to do, toss me out? Great, make my day."

"We move you to another room on the top floor. Up where we put the people throw things. It's real quiet up there. The drugs, they work better in the altitude."

"We had a deal."

"There isn't any deal, Mr. Connors. We got rules and this is the third time, and that's all the strikes you get."

"I got an excuse. I've been under a lot of pressure since I lost my daughter."

"You didn't lose nobody."

"She was murdered in a robbery yesterday or day before. The cops came."

"Your daughter just left, Mr. Connors. She brought you some new books and she took away the old ones. That's what she told me."

"What?"

"She was in a hurry. I think you upset her, the way you're talking lately."

"She took my book? Varla and the retired hitman."

"I don't know any Varla, but yeah, she took four books with her, left those on the table over there."

"Shit, I wasn't through with that book. It was just getting interesting."

"That's nice. Now it's time for your pills. Let's go now, be a big boy today."

"My daughter's alive?"

"She looked alive to me. That's a pretty woman. Nice shape to her, too."

"Watch it, kid. My daughter's not into that stuff."

"Could have fooled me. She's a looker that one. Everybody stops what they're doing she comes around. Including me. I about dropped a bedpan."

Javi left and Little Mo sat at the small table and looked out at the trees. The books were sitting there, a stack of them. Something different with these. He could smell them. He leaned close. Musty. And they had price stickers on them. Used, two dollars. Discounted hardbacks. His daughter was going cheap on him.

He pushed the stack over, let them tumble onto the tabletop.

Four books. Every one of them with a babe on the cover. Juicy pictures. Fishnet stockings, garter belt, kimonos half open, breasts spilling out.

Old books.

He leaned close and inhaled them. Reminded him of somewhere. It took him a long time, he wasn't sure how long, smelling them and trying to remember until he had it. A library. A half dark library. Not a big city library. Somewhere out in the sticks. An older gentleman behind the desk stamping books for a young girl.

"I like mysteries," the little girl said.

"Oh, so do I," the man said. He stamped her books and passed them to her. "Nothing like a good murder to pass the time, fill up the hours."

"They're scary," the girl said. "I like that. Give me goosebumps."

"Me too. Scary is fun."

"My mom doesn't like me to read. Thinks it's a waste of time. Nobody gets ahead that way, nose in a book."

"Your mommy is an idiot."

The girl took the books into her arms like loaves of bread.

"I'll tell her you said that."

"Please do. Tell her Mo Connors thinks she's an idiot."

"I will. I'll tell her that."

Did he read that somewhere, a character in a story? He wasn't sure.

He opened one of the books, went to the back and there was an envelope pasted to the back cover. Raybun West Virginia Central Library. He looked at the other books. All from the same place, Raybun.

Little Mo went out to the front desk.

"I need to use a phone," he told the nurse.

Black woman named Hazel.

"You don't have a cell phone, Mr. Connors?"

"Would I be asking to use the phone if I did?"

"No reason to get nasty."

"You think that was nasty? You don't know from nasty."

"I'll have to dial for you. No long distance calls allowed."

"Call information, Raybun, West Virginia."

"What you want to do that for?"

"Is my business your business?"

"There you go being nasty again."

Hazel punched in the numbers and handed him the phone.

An operator came on. Her hillbilly voice sounded like the slow moan of a coondog.

He told her he wanted the number for the Raybun Central Library.

"That library done closed ten years ago."

"It did?"

"Yes, sir. I hated to see it shut down. But you know how it is, people don't read books no more with the Internet and all. I used to go there my own self when I was a little girl."

"So you remember the librarian in that library? Maybe she still lives in the area, she can answer some questions."

"Oh, sure, I remember real good. Head librarian, it wasn't no woman."

He waited.

"Librarian was a fine gentleman. I can't recall his name but he was a nice man."

"Was it Connors?"

"Why yes, I do believe you're right. It was Connors, Mr. Mo Connors. A small man with a big smile. We all called him Little Mo. He knew them books inside and out. Read everything in that whole library then started over and read them again. Got me started reading, got a lot of people started. He'd lead you right down all them aisles and pick out a book like he could read your mind and knew just what it was you wanted to read and he'd hand it to you and it was the best damn book you ever did read. He did that for me. Got me started on a lifetime of reading murder stories."

Two sunnysides came the next morning. Javi hung around waiting for him to take his pills. Hello, haze.

Dense as the fog on a West Virginia morning, a white smoke that hung till noon some days, so thick nobody could go to work, everybody stuck at home reading the books Little Mo had suggested for them. In their shanty houses reading. Like the information operator in Raybun. That same little girl he'd been stamping her books.

He opened one of the books his daughter brought from the West Virginia library. Ten pages in, then twenty, it's Varla again and it's the old retired hit man, same characters as the other book, only this one was a few years later on. The hitman had escaped the nursing home and he and Varla were living in a small hotel room in the West Village. An Orange Julius was across the street, Washington Square they could see from their window. They spent their days cleaning their guns and lying beside each other in the old saggy bed.

"We're free," Varla said. "We're out of that two bit home."

"If you can call this free," Mo said. "Living in one room, drinking Orange Julius for breakfast, lunch and dinner."

"I'd like to know what their magic ingredient is. Maybe we can hold the place up, take hostages, extract the secret from an employee."

"The food was better before. I liked how they cut up my grapefruit."

"You're bored with me. I'm old and everything's sagging. You're through with me."

"We need a mission. We just sit around without a mission. It's the secret of life, the way to fill up your days."

"We accomplished our mission," Varla said. "This is how it is afterwards."

"Well, we need a new one."

"Okay, so if we get a new mission, we accomplish that one, then what?"

Javier brought his breakfast. Little Mo was still lying in bed turning the pages of that book. In a hurry to see how it turned out.

"Here's your scrambled eggs," Javi said. "And your fruit cup."

"Where's my grapefruit and sunnysides?"

Javi didn't know what he was talking about.

"You ever read a book, Javi? Start to finish, a novel."

"I gave up on it," Javier said. "I didn't like it, not knowing how things turned out."

"What do you mean?"

"You get to the end of a story, it's over, and the characters just keep on living and you don't know how things are going to turn out for them. Leave you hanging. I didn't like that."

"Everything turns out the same way," he said. "That's stupid, Javi. End of the story, everybody dies. Isn't but one outcome and that's it."

"I know that. But people in books they're not the same as real people."

"You don't like living with uncertainty. That what you're saying?"

"Yeah, that's what I'm saying. I like things to be reliable. But books, the ones they made me read in school, nobody could say for sure what any of it added up to. It was on a test, I usually failed cause whatever I thought, it turned out it wasn't the right thing. So I quit reading."

"Grapefruit is what I have for breakfast. Pre-sliced." Javi left.

He got back to his book. A gangster came into the library one day, real tough guy, smelled like aftershave and gunpowder, walked right over to the librarian and said, "You know how to handle a gun?"

"Sure I do. I been shooting since I was knee high to a caterpillar."

"I'm looking for somebody to do a job for me. It pays five grand."

The librarian came out from behind his desk.

"Why me?"

"Cops take one look at you, little runty geriatric, they keep on walking. You're perfect. It's like a disguise, the old guy look. You look confused, your eyes are hazy."

Later Little Mo met the gangster at his cheap motel on the edge of town. Tiny cabins with a gravel lot out front. The Davy Crockett Inn. A hot sheets joint in Raybun, West Virginia. Little Mo had lost his virginity in the same cabin where he met with the gangster. Jilly Johnson, a little girl, Mo took her to the mountaintop, showed her the sights, a first class orgasm, and she cried afterwards, couldn't stop crying. From the beauty of it, or the sadness, he was never sure.

"I could use the five G's."

"Yeah? Glad to hear it. How you feel about shooting a girl? You sexist or anything?"

"For five thousand I can get over it."

"She works in a store downtown, little shop sells books. The girl knows too much. She's going to testify, send me to jail. I'd do the job myself but they'd see me coming. You, hell no, you could just walk up to her put three in her head, one in her heart. That could be your calling card. Start a new career."

He didn't sleep good that night, worrying about his daughter, what was about to happen to her. She was the target. Working in that store, no protection. He turned and he tossed and in the morning he didn't have any appetite for his sunnysides and grapefruit.

"You keep leaving your food, Mr. Connors, we gonna stop feeding you."

"I need a ride downtown to my daughter's place of business. She's in danger. I need to warn her."

"Your daughter's outside in the lobby talking to the super, you can warn her in a minute."

His daughter came.

"Dad, Javier said you wanted to talk to me. You're very agitated."

Little Mo didn't say anything. He was trying to blink away the haze, get a good look at this girl, see if she seemed familiar.

"Dad, I think you're getting worse. The doctor and I think we should move you upstairs where they can give you better care."

"Upstairs?"

"They have more staff up there. They have pretty views, long distance. You can see across the river all the way to the Empire State Building when the sky's clear."

"Upstairs is where they send the troublemakers."

"It's just that you've been agitated lately, Dad. Throwing things, saying some weird stuff."

"Like what? What weird stuff?"

"Murder, for one thing. Scary stuff."

"I'll stop saying stuff then. I don't want to go upstairs."

"I think it's the books doing it," she said. "I think all that crime and violence isn't good for you. It puts bad ideas in your head. I'm going to have to stop bringing them until you're better."

"I said I'll stop saying stuff."

"We'll take a break from the books. A couple of weeks and see how you're feeling."

"I want my goddam books," he said. "You stop bringing them, I'll die. I'll go cold turkey and die."

"Dad, now don't get worked up. This is exactly what I'm talking about, these outbursts."

She went over to the table and gathered up his books and cradled them in her arms like a small child. She walked to the door.

"You can't do that," he said. "That's torture. I'll go nuts without my books."

"It's just an experiment," she said. "A couple of weeks, maybe a month or two, we'll see how you're feeling and decide then if you should keep reading about so much murder and mayhem. I think you'll start feeling a lot better."

He tried to grab the books but she pushed him away. A frail old man, not the professional hitman he'd once been. Even a girl could push him around.

He sat at his desk and looked out at the hazy yard, the trees, the grass, the snow. Big white tropical birds. He sat and sat and sat.

Then he started to weep. He didn't know how long he cried but it was longer than he'd ever done before. His wife died, he didn't cry as much. A dog he loved got hit by a car, he cried for a few hours. The Raybun Library shut down and his job ended, and he cried. But nothing like this. He cried all afternoon, all evening, all night.

Javier tried to make him take his pills but he couldn't stop crying.

The next morning he stopped. Javier was back with the paper cup of pills.

He looked at the pills and said, "I'm out of the haze. I skipped one round of pills and now I'm feeling fine."

"No, sir. You got to take them. That's the rules. You fight me, you go upstairs today. You already on probation."

He took the pills.

Held them in his cheek, swallowed the water. Javi bought it.

When he was gone, Little Mo spit out the pills, flushed them away.

He looked out his window to check himself. Some patches of snow left, but it looked like it was warming up. No sign of a palm tree, no white birds. He was in Brooklyn, somewhere like that, across the river from Manhattan. Everything was starting to make sense.

He went out into the hallway, wandered up to the lobby. He was allowed to roam. Nobody looked funny at him. People said hello, he said hello back. He went to the little library they had near the aquarium. A woman was sitting in a chair asleep. A book in her lap. The book had a picture of a floozy on the cover. A dame with big red lips and a gun in the holster fixed to her girdle.

Little Mo sneaked the book out of her lap and headed back to his room.

Thank god for libraries. Thank god for free books lying around.

Back in his room he crawled into bed, pulled the covers up so he could hide the book if anybody came in.

He found his place. More than halfway in, things heating up, the pot boiling, action rolling fast down a twisty country road, the kind you'd find in Raybun, West Virginia.

"You gonna take the job or not? I need an answer now."

The five thousand bucks was stacked on the chewed up table by the window.

"It's a girl I got to shoot?"

"That's right. She's a danger to me. A mortal danger."

"Half now, half when I've done the job?"

"That's how it works."

"What'd you do, she's gonna turn you in for?"

"Murder and mayhem. The usual stuff. What's it to you? You some kind of moralizer?"

"Maybe I am."

"So forget it. I made a mistake picking you. Some crazy old bookworm."

Little Mo started to leave but the gangster blocked him.

"You think I'm going to let you walk away, what you know about me? Hell, no. You got to die, old man. You know my face. One phone call from you I get put away. You think I'm nuts?"

His daughter was there.

"Dad, I'm going to have to sign the papers, have you sent upstairs."

"Whoa, whoa. What'd I do?"

"You're threatening people, Pops. A sweet old lady out in the front library, you threatened her. You stole her book."

"Did not."

"I'm sorry, Pops. They're coming in an hour to move you upstairs. You'll like it up there. Everybody says it's very nice. And the food is very good."

"Nobody talks up there. The drugs are stronger. That what you want, send me deeper into the haze?"

"Can you hear me, Pops?"

"Hell yes I can hear you and I don't like what I'm hearing. I don't like it one bit."

Javier said, "He's been like this for a couple of days. All clammed up, acting deaf and dumb. Just looking out that window. Maybe he had another stroke. Doctor needs to check him out."

"I'm not going upstairs and that's all there is to it. I got a say, don't I? You steal my books, you threaten me, it isn't fair. I was a good man. I did good."

"What'd he do for a living?" Javi asked his daughter.

"Librarian," she said. "Spent his life in a library in West Virginia."

"He likes to read. I seen that for sure. He likes his books."

"They only seem to agitate him these days. They make him act out."

"He talks funny sometimes. Like he's playing a part in a play."

He was upstairs.

Big common room, lots of wheelchairs. Everybody ate their meals together. No more sunnysides, no more grapefruit cut up. It was slop. Cold scrambled eggs, some kind of meat, it didn't have a name.

There were magazines but no books. The TV running night and day. Game shows. All the old shitbirds sitting in chairs watching people scream about winning a toaster oven. He stole a magazine, took it back to his room. Tiny room, only one window and it was full of haze.

He lay down on his bed. Lumpy mattress.

Turned the pages of the magazine, came to a story.

And yes, by god, Varla was sneaking up the back stairs. She had her gun, a .38 snubbie. She was coming for him to liberate his ass. Little Mo Connors was trying to do his part, smiling at the nurses, taking his pills, being a good boy. All of it an act. Biding his time while Varla worked her way up the stairs. An old lady, the stairs were tough. She was breathing hard and talking to herself.

"Two more floors, Little Mo. Hang on, baby. I'm coming. I'm coming, fighting my way through the haze."

Little Mo dug through his drawers and found his own snubbie. They'd work together. Him shooting from his end, her from hers. A serial killer and a retired hitman. This place couldn't hold them. These people didn't know from imprisonment. You want to see imprisonment, spend a few years in Raiford. This was a country club compared to that goddam place.

"Almost there, sweet pea, only one more floor. I got to shoot out the locks. And I'm making a lot of noise. They're bound to hear me, someone is bound to. They'll be coming for me, so get ready, honey. Get yourself all set. I'm climbing the mountain and I'm almost at the top and you're up there, the guru with the answers. I'm coming, sweetness, my big virile old man."

He walked down the hall, waited by the locked stairway door. Big red sign on it, No Admittance. He could hear Varla coming up the stairs on the other side of the door. He could hear her breathing hard.

She'd want him to tell her what the secret was, coming all this way up the mountain just to see him. He needed to have something ready for her. The sum total of what he'd learned in these years, the sum total of all he'd learned from books and living and sitting and thinking. If there wasn't something to give her, shit, what was the point?

She was at the door now. He could hear her back there. She was wheezing hard from the climb.

"You there, Little Mo?" she called out. "I'm here, Varla."

"Stand back while I blow open this lock. Stand back."

The lock exploded and she came through the door.

"You made it, Varla. You saved my ass."

They embraced. She smelled musty and wonderful.

"Okay, I'm here. What you got for me?"

"Let's blow this hole first, I can tell you everything later."

"And if there isn't a later? If we get nabbed on our way down. We take some hits, three up, one down. No, you need to tell me now. What is it, I climbed all this way, what's the answer?"

"I don't know, Varla."

"Don't know? I come all this way and you don't have the secret?"

"I think that may be the secret," he said. "The whole enchilada. There's no secret."

"Enchilada? You telling me Mexican food is the secret, I come all this way, work through all this haze and shit and this is what you got? Chimichangas?"

He put the magazine on the little rickety table.

The gong was sounding for dinner.

His heart was beating hard. Varla wanted an answer. He didn't have one for her. He'd come all this way, read a thousand books and a thousand more, had his heart broken and broken again, and the dinner gong was sounding and he didn't have a goddam answer for her. He didn't have an answer to any of it.

He slid the magazine under the mattress. He had to go to dinner or they'd come fetch him and drag him there. But the magazine would still be here when supper was over, and he'd find his place again and he'd finish the story.

He went to dinner. Kept to himself. Piddled with his roast beef. Trying to think of an answer for Varla because she was back there waiting, back in his room. Back there where the magazine was under his mattress.

Maybe that was it.

The story. He had to finish the story, get to the end, see how it turned out. There'd be an answer at the end. He was sure of it. There had to be. Okay, okay. So that was his mission now, the thing he needed so he could hang on a little longer, he had to get to the end of the story. You had to have a mission, a way to fill up the hours.

That was it. That was it.